Chasing the White Bear

More by Brooke Shaffer

The Timekeeper Chronicles

The Chivalrous Welshman
Time to Kill
Tick Tock
Windup
Stopwatch
Free Time
Leap Second
Imminence
Synchronization (Summer 2023)

The Hands of Time
In the Hands of the Enemy
The Hands Pulling the Strings
The Hand Holding the Knife (Winter 2023)

The Lone Wolf
Wolf Pack
Alpha Wolf
Lone Wolf (Spring 2023)

Singles
Of Saints and Sinners
Chasing the White Bear

Chasing the White Bear
a novel of
The Timekeeper Chronicles

Brooke Shaffer

Black Bear Publishing

Published in Michigan by Black Bear Publishing.

ISBN:
    Hardcover: 978-1-953113-25-2
    Softcover: 978-1-953113-26-9
    eBook: 978-1-953113-27-6

For my Mother Bear

Nikita

Avgun Atausiq
One Shot

The sun was finally above the horizon, but it wouldn't be there for long as a chill wind clawed its way through the trees and blasted across the tundra to the hills beyond.

The white bear had led her here, though she couldn't say why. The Russians had given up the chase several days ago, left her to her own devices in the wilderness. She'd managed to grab a small bag of provisions and scrounge up some plants along the way, but both supplies were fast dwindling, something her stomach was happy to remind her of. Otherwise, all she had was a whalebone knife and a bow she barely knew how to use. Even if she did, she had only one arrow.

She left the edge of the trees, retreating into the grove and crawling into her pine bough shelter. What was she supposed to do? Where was she supposed to go? Surely she would not have been led all the way out here just to die alone? She heard the *amakkut* at night, howling endlessly across miles of open land. Would they come to finish her off once she collapsed from hunger and sickness?

Pulling her knees to her chest, Akłaq rocked back and forth a bit. She envied the *amakkut*, honestly, at least at the moment. They had pack. They had family. They had guidance and direction and strength and comfort. She had none of that anymore. Truthfully, she'd had very little of that for a while, but then...

She wiped her eyes and let out a breath as her stomach growled its displeasure. Looking in her pack, she had a few strips of dried seal meat, a handful of mussels, and some forage which was beginning to shrivel up to nothing, kind of like her. The water skin was full; she'd filled it just the previous morning at a small stream. Using the knife, she popped open the mussels and ate of them, then guzzled more water than she probably should have. She wanted to save the meat for later, use it to give her the last burst of energy to go anywhere or do anything to survive.

Not for the first time, she found herself wishing she'd had brothers. Her father had died a couple years ago, and her uncles had fared no better under the Russians. But maybe a brother or two. A brother would know what to do, where to go.

Or it was just as likely that they would have died, laboring for the Russians and their conquests, and she would still be out here alone.

She had to do something, though. Doing nothing was only inviting death to come, and she could have stayed behind—or she could go back —if she wished for that. But she was here now; she had to try.

She had little enthusiasm crawling out of her shelter, and she was nearly knocked to her seat by a sudden gust of wind. Which way? She couldn't go back west, for only death awaited her there. North wasn't much of an option either; there was very little for her at land's end, besides many animals that would happily kill her.

She tried to recall the maps the Russian priests had shown her in school. The world was so very big! And here they occupied only a small, frozen part of it. But the details eluded her now. Was she very far away from Canada? Could she turn south and hope to reach the United States in good time? Surely there had to be people between here and there, people who weren't Russians. And the priest had said that the farther south you go, the warmer it got. That would please her very much indeed.

Turning south, Akłaq started walking. Perhaps her only saving grace so far was that she had already been wearing heavy winter garments when the soldiers came. She'd been slowly repairing them, taking them on and off to find and fix holes or damaged seams. It wasn't so bad when the sun was out, but the days were rapidly shortening, and each night got just a little chillier. Morning frost was no longer a minor inconvenience but a harsh reality, and snow had begun to fall more frequently. She had to find someplace warm.

She trudged southeast for as long as she could manage, trying to stay in the trees even when the wind died down. She barely gave a thought to predators, or the *amakkut* that still howled. Perhaps that would be the only way that she would have a chance at getting more meat, if something came to her.

The sun went down long before she stopped to sleep. Despite staying in the trees, she had less success finding enough boughs to make as good a shelter as she had the night before. The best she was able to manage was a windbreak as she shimmied under the lowest branches of a squat conifer. She wished she knew how to string a snare; she might have been able to catch one of the hares running around. She had caught only a glimpse of one, foolishly chased it a short distance, but there was evidence of many more in the area.

They'd heard stories. Warnings, really, from the Aleut people. Hundreds, even thousands of women and children dead because the Russians had killed their men, leaving the rest to starve. But they didn't listen. How could they? The Russians had brought them trade, hospitals, schools, opened them up to a bigger world with broader possibilities. Maybe the fault was with the Aleut, that they had brought their destruction upon themselves.

Even when things got hard, when the men were sent on longer and more dangerous expeditions, when the barter became more difficult and even ridiculous, when the soldiers started showing up in greater numbers. Even then, they still told themselves that everything would be all right. Things were still good. Things were better because they were no longer so isolated from other people.

Everything was fine.

Until it wasn't.

Akłaq woke up with pine needles in her clothes and sticks in her hair. She again shimmied around under the tree, trying to get unstuck. By the time she accomplished this, the sky had gone from black to gray. She popped open the last of the mussels, gnawed on her shriveled forage, and even ate a strip of meat just to hold herself...until when? She didn't know.

South and east she walked. Sun and moon, sky and cloud, she walked. She never lacked for water, and when her provisions ran out, she filled up on water and meager forage, trying to tell herself that the next day, she would find something.

Reality finally caught up to her about six days after her provisions ran out. She woke to a grumbling stomach and found that she just didn't care. She didn't want to move, didn't want to go anywhere, didn't care about anything. She would just stay there and die.

Her motivation to live trickled into her like water dripping into a dry pool, and she soon found herself at a crossroads. If she acted on the desire to live, she wouldn't get very far before having to bed down again, which was already an exhausting thought. If she didn't act, then she would most certainly die.

Before she could do much more than consider her options, a nearby sound caused her to freeze. It was the sound of something big and heavy. She was tucked into what she had thought was an abandoned den in the base of a large pine; she'd barely had the strength to drag a few boughs to better enclose the entrance. Now she was left with nowhere to run and no good way to observe the animal without giving herself away.

There was some digging and scratching around her den, some heavy breathing. Akłaq slowly moved her hand toward her knife. If it was a small animal, a fox, a wolf, some curious herbivore, she might be able to stab it in the face when it put its head down to sniff around and look inside. Her chest was tight, but her stomach was tighter, and all she could think about was a carcass full of meat.

The claws that crashed through the final layer of dead sticks on the bough were long enough to cause her to flinch and think more about running from this animal than trying to kill it. A second stab put a paw the size of her face uncomfortably close to her chest. Only as the paw withdrew did she realize that the bear in question was white.

Then the paw was gone and, as expected, a nose poked inside the new hole. The bear's muzzle was big, broad, and kind of ugly. The lips parted a little, revealing huge teeth and a massive silver tongue.

The bear huffed hot breath a few times, then backed up and left. Akłaq remained rooted to the ground, hand clenched around her knife. Her thoughts were racing and confused. She could have been eaten. She just let a huge animal—a huge meat carcass—get away. That huge meat carcass had been a bear. That bear had been white.

The white bear!

Akłaq knew she wasn't thinking the most clearly, and she couldn't decide whether she was any more sane for pushing her way out of the den, past the boughs, and following the bear's tracks into the woods, alternating between running and a fast walk. Every so often, she would just glimpse a hind leg or only a tail disappearing around a corner. She was hungry, she was tired, the day was waning fast, but she had to catch that bear.

Deep down, she knew she wouldn't. Not today, maybe not ever. She knew only that she had to follow.

The tracks straightened out, but the bear was nowhere to be seen. Puffing and weak, Akłaq slowed to a walk, then a crawl. Up ahead, the tracks disappeared between two pines growing so close together one might be forgiven for thinking they were a single tree. The snow on the limbs had not been disturbed. A person would have a terrible time trying to fit through at all, never mind leaving the snow undisturbed. For a bear, this might be considered impossible, and this was how she knew it was her bear.

All the same, couldn't the bear have taken her around, a slightly easier path? She was exhausted as it was. She paused only briefly at the two pines, then put her arms out and started weaseling her way through. Needles scored her face and pushed her hood off her head, allowing snow from the branches to tumble down her back. Squeezing her eyes shut, she forced her way forward.

She gasped as her foot hooked a root and she went down on her hands and knees, popping out into the smallest of openings in the middle of four pines packed tightly together. The bear tracks had disappeared, but now her attention was taken by movement ahead of her, mostly hidden by thick branches. Gathering herself into a more comfortable position, Akłaq checked herself over briefly, then shifted her clothes, pack, knife, and bow so they were sitting where she wanted them.

Fingering her knife, she shuffled through the snow toward the slightly less dense branches and peered through.

The smell reached her before she could fully see what it was. *Umiŋmak*, the bearded one. The Russians called it a muskox. Akłaq pushed into the branches, trying to get a better look as it stood perhaps fifty yards past the pines in the open.

It was alone, which was odd enough. Old, then, or sickly, left behind by the herd to be picked off. The hulking beast barely moved as it stood with its head down, lazily sniffing for food under the snow. The shaggy fur looked tattered and greasy, and Akłaq could see it was favoring a hind leg, as if something had already tried to pick it off and been unsuccessful.

One predator's loss was her gain, and Akłaq could just imagine the meat. Old, tough, didn't matter, it was food.

But how to take it down? Muskoxen were prized for their thick skin. Even if this one was as old and injured as she suspected, it clearly still had to strength and will to fight off an attacker.

Akłaq let out a breath. One arrow. She had one arrow. The beast wasn't moving, so she had time to think about her aim.

She pushed forward as far as she dared in the pines, the wind bringing even more of the animal's wretched smell to her nose. Offloading her bow—her father's bow, really—she took the single arrow in hand and looked at it.

The best outcome would be a shot straight through the eye. She would not fool herself into thinking she could pull off such a feat; she was no marksman. She had shot a bow all of half a dozen times in her life, and the targets were always very big and very close. The muskox was a big target to hit, but she had to make it count. If nothing else, she might miss the beast entirely and just have to wait for it to lumber off before attempting to retrieve the arrow.

Letting out a breath, she nocked the arrow, but she did little more than raise the bow. The wind was in her face, and it was coming in gusts. She would have to time her shot with that. And she knew she would have to aim high just so it reached the beast.

She didn't know what she was doing, but she didn't have much of a choice. She also didn't have much strength, but she willed herself to pull the string back as far as she could manage and then some, scraping out a little more will to keep her arms from shaking. Her father could draw the string to his ear with no problem, and send an arrow through the air with the speed of a bullet.

Trying to think of her father rather than her failures, Akłaq took a breath, pulled back just a little more, waited for a gust of wind to pass, and released the arrow.

The good news was that the distance appeared sound. She might have even fantasized that the aim was perfect, that somehow the bear spirit was guiding it straight toward the muskox's eye.

Then the animal, which had been perfectly still thus far, turned.

The arrow struck its wounded leg. The beast bellowed and looked around. Akłaq might have had a chance if she had frozen as she had for the bear, but this time she found herself trying to scoot backwards and hide in the trees. Too late, the muskox already spotted her. With no herd around for it to protect, or protect it, the beast charged.

It was a slower, lopsided charge, true, but no less dangerous to its intended target. The best Akłaq could do was scrabble backwards, again popping out into the small opening in the pines. She frantically tossed her bow aside and grabbed her knife, pressing herself against the boughs to the side but not into them, again seeing only one shot.

The ground shook as the muskox got closer and bulled blindly between the pines. But the opening was smaller than the creature had anticipated. Its shoulders somehow scraped through, but the arrow in its leg got caught, causing the animal just enough pain for it to skid to an almost stop, again bellowing in pain.

Akłaq struck then, jumping forward from her spot and stabbing the beast in the neck. The muskox swung its huge head around. She slipped and went to the ground, losing her grip on the knife which stayed in the muskox's neck.

The opening in the pines was too small for the muskox to do much more than stomp and try to move its mass around on three legs, giving Akłaq time to get a hold of the knife again. She wasted no time in delivering two more quick blows to the animal's neck, finally striking true and sending a massive spray of blood into the snow.

Still the beast fought, swinging its head, stomping, moving, even as its front legs buckled and it went down, blood continuing to pulse from its throat. It made atrocious sounds as it died, but Akłaq was busy ripping her gloves off and cupping her hands to gather blood to drink. Blood was life. It would take her a long time to skin and gut this animal, but the blood would provide the meal she needed now.

She set up camp right there in the small opening. Being only a single person with a single knife, her progress was slow, but she was able to gut the muskox and start a small fire to cook the entrails. She ate the heart, liver, and kidneys, and she opened up the stomach to eat the sour grass inside. The lungs she washed and set aside to make into more carrying packs.

Once that was complete, she started on the proper processing of the skin and muscle.

Suddenly, things didn't seem so bad. Or maybe that was her full stomach talking. As she lay down to sleep, she studied the arrow. The shaft had been broken when the beast forced its way through the pines, but the head still appeared to be good. She might be able to craft another, though it wouldn't be as good as the one her father made.

But she had done it. She had taken down an *umiŋmak* with only an arrow and a knife, and she was going to survive. Coming this far, she couldn't succumb to something as petty as death. She had to keep going; she had to survive. South and east was all she knew. She didn't know what she was going to find, and she wouldn't lie to herself by thinking that it was going to be easy. But she figured that as long as she continued to chase the white bear, things might just be all right.

Avgun Malġuk
Friendly Face

She stayed in her camp for several days, watching the days grow shorter and shorter while she worked hurriedly in the limited light. Her confidence renewed with the slaying of the *umiŋmak*, Akłaq was able to build a crude sled which she used to haul her new tent shelter, made from the muskox's shaggy hide, and the many supplies she had just gained, including some rope, woven from muskox hair; a few new, if crude, bone knives; small bone needles and sinew thread; and other essentials. She was unable to take all of the meat and bone—or even most of it, honestly—and she hated leaving it behind, but she figured it might give her a brief head start, distract the predators before they came after her. The last night in her camp, she heard them getting closer.

Her family would be proud of her. Her clan would be proud of her. If only they could see her. She knew they watched over her now from the stars and the *kiuġuyat*, but she would be lying if she said she didn't want to feel their physical embrace, hear her father's praise for taking down the muskox, hear her mother's praise for processing it well and putting as much as she could to use. She wanted to hear her sisters' envious cries.

She forced herself not to dwell on it, tried to tell herself that all was well. Maybe if she were a boy, she might believe it, that she was just out on the summer expeditions and would return to the village with great bounty. But she was a girl, and this was winter now, and all she had was what she dragged behind her on the sled.

Snow and cold were her constant companions as the darkness closed in. Much of the time her steps were lit only by the *kiuġuyat*.

The meat started to run low. She'd tried to limit herself, tried to find any forage she could, tried—and succeeded a few times—to snare small animals to add to her stores. But she'd occasionally had to leave a bit behind to distract predators, and she feared the day when she might have to dump all of her meat, maybe even her entire sled, in order to stave off the *amakkut* long enough to escape.

The only thing that really mattered anymore was the walking. She did not know her destination, only her direction. With the long night lingering overhead, even day and night barely existed except by the moon overhead.

But she was old enough to understand the long night and about how long it lasted. So it came as a bit of a surprise when she saw a sunrise long before she should have seen a sunrise. It did not last long, and the sun disappeared just as quickly, but it occupied her thoughts for most of the day. There was no way the long night had ended so soon.

The priest had said that the south was warmer. He'd also tried to explain that there were many places that did not experience the long night or the long day. Longer and shorter, yes, throughout the year, in a cycle, but never constant darkness or constant light.

Had she finally reached such a place?

Continuing her travels, she again saw the sun every day, or the implication of one as there was still plenty of snow falling. This revelation cheered her some, but it quickly took second place to, again, considering her food stores. The muskox was just about gone, and she had only a few rabbits and a fox to tide her over.

She walked, dragging the sled behind her. She could not speak to how much warmer it was, but the return of the sun cheered her greatly. She was even more cheered when she finally spotted smoke rising in the distance. Changing course, she charged ahead.

It was a small cabin, such as the Russians built, and that alone gave her pause. Hiding her sled in a pile of brush, she circled the area. A couple horses stood under a shelter attached to a barn maybe twenty yards from the house; their ears pricked up and they looked around as she moved, and she hoped they wouldn't give her away. Some chickens were clucking in a henhouse attached to the other side of the barn. The house itself appeared relatively quiet, and she caught only the faintest hint of movement inside. There was no telling how many people were about, but she guessed not many. She saw no tracks but her own.

She circled back around, grabbed her sled, and crossed the open field toward the house. If nothing else, she had furs to trade, and she did like eggs. She approached the house without incident, dropped her sled at the bottom of the steps, then hiked up to the front door and knocked.

The curtain at the window fluttered, but by the time she looked, whoever was there had gone. A moment later, the door opened.

It was a man, about forty years of age, white, with longish brown hair and a full beard.

"*Nayaaŋŋaq,*" Akłaq managed, throat tight, still trying to sound cheerful. "*Dobri den'.*" (Hello.)(Good day.)

The man blinked. "*Dobri den'.*" (Good day.) He raised a brow. "Who are you? You speak Russian?"

"My name is Akłaq. I am from Qikiqtaġruk."

He shrugged. "Can't say I know where that is, except north I suppose."

"Yes, it is." She faltered, then gestured to her sled. "I have furs to trade."

The man grinned and indicated inside his cabin. "I got no shortage of those, darling. But I do find it strange that a girl your age is out here all alone. How old are you anyway?"

"Fifteen."

He nodded. "Out here all alone. Why are you really here?"

Any enthusiasm she'd been able to muster crumbled. "Please, sir, my food is nearly gone, and I have a long way to go."

"Where you going?"

"I don't know."

"Well, that's a problem, isn't it? Why'd you leave your village, come all the way here? Don't you know it's winter out there?"

She squirmed a little. "Soldiers burned my village to the ground. Most of the men were already dead, but they killed the rest, and the women, too. I managed to escape."

The man frowned and grunted. "Rat bastards. Things like that is why I left them." He sighed and stepped to the side. "Come on in, hon, I got some stew over the fire." When she looked back toward her sled, he waved a hand. "Come on, it won't bother nothing for a few minutes. You're letting in the cold."

She stepped inside the cabin and stayed there while he went around and started rummaging for things. He found a bowl and a spoon and went to the fire to ladle some stew out of a heavy cauldron. He turned back and gestured toward a small table. "Go on, sit down. Take your coat and boots off, hang them by the fire to dry."

She hung up her articles, then sat down. He placed the bowl in front of her, then went to sit in the only other chair in the cabin, not bothering to turn it around as he sat backwards on it and looked at her.

"So, yours is the latest to see the torch, eh?" he said casually.

Akłaq nodded once, but asked, "Please, what is your name?"

"Oh," he scoffed. "I forget my manners. Call me Nikita. And what about yourself?"

"Akłaq."

His expression turned puzzled as he tried to work out the sounds. "Uk..shuk?"

"Akłaq," she corrected, managing a small smile. "I understand if you can't pronounce it."

Nikita let out a breath. "I spent two years over in one of them villages around your people and I never could grasp the language. Learned a few words, sure, but not much more than that."

She did not say anything, just focused on her stew. The change of flavor was most welcome, and he even gave her a second bowl.

"I understand that you're happy to escape with your life," he went on, returning to his chair. "And I understand that yours isn't the first or the last, and none of you are doing too well. But what do you really plan on doing? Where do you expect to go? Do you really expect to survive on whatever small game happens to wander into a trap, hoping to run into a friendly cabin in the woods?"

"I don't know," she admitted. "I just know to go south and east."

He made a sound. "Well, at least it's a direction."

"The priest said that there was warmer weather in the south, places that don't have the long night."

"That priest would be correct, but you've got a long way to go before you find any of that, assuming something or someone doesn't find you first."

"What would you have me do, then? What can I do, where can I go? Do you know where the white bear goes?"

"The white bear doesn't go south, that's for sure, at least not that I've seen. East, maybe." He shifted position, still sitting backwards in his chair, then finally stood. "At any rate, you can't leave tonight. It's too cold, there's a storm coming in, and I think you'd appreciate not having to sleep outside for once, right? That's what I thought. Listen, I'll put your sled in the barn."

He looked like he wanted to say more, but he refrained, grabbed his coat, pulled on his boots, and left the cabin. Akłaq quietly finished off the bowl of stew.

Nikita took a lot longer than she thought it should to simply drag her sled into his barn. She thought about going and making sure he hadn't hurt himself, then she saw him just returning, and a minute later he was back inside. He had a pail of water which he said was for her to use to wash up.

"I'm just going to go and make sure the horses are all right," he said, and again left the cabin.

Akłaq had become quite accustomed to having the bulk of her furs. Stripping down to nothing made her feel all out of sorts, and looking at herself in his tiny, dirty mirror was even stranger. She'd never been especially big, but now she looked terribly skinny. At least washing herself of the sweat and grit made her feel somewhat better.

Nikita allowed her to sleep in the bed while he slept in the chair. She didn't remember anything after pulling the blankets up close, only that she was very, very grateful.

It was still dark when she woke, as was to be expected, and she lay there for a moment staring at the ceiling in the dim firelight. It was like waking from a dream, really. It had all happened. Somehow, stepping into this cabin was like finally stepping into the reality that her family, her clan, her village was gone. She wasn't out on an adventure or an expedition or anything of the sort. She had left home, probably for good. It was all gone. All that remained was forward.

She pushed the blankets back and got out of bed, feeling more rested than she had in a while. The warmth and lack of fear wasn't bad either. The wood box beside the fireplace had been stocked, and she added a few logs, watching flames dance to life.

The door opened and Nikita walked in with a pail of water.

"You sleep like a stone, you know that?" he said, setting the pail on the table and pulling off his outer garments. "Not surprising, I suppose, after sleeping outside for God knows how long."

"It's nice," Akłaq said uncertainly.

"It's what I got. You don't have to pretend."

She looked back at the fire. A moment later, he came up behind her.

"I guess I shouldn't sound so ungrateful. It's nice to have company every now and again." He put his hands on her shoulders. "And maybe you're being sincere when you say it's nice. But know that I am being sincere when I say that you are a nice girl. Pretty girl. And tough, strong. You'd have to be to survive out in this weather for any length of time. But who would I be to send you back out there? What kind of man would I be?"

She turned around and looked up at him.

He went on, "Stay with me for the winter. It's gonna be a long one, I just know it. And if you don't know where you're going, well, I wouldn't feel right if I just let you run off and something happened." He moved his hands down to her hips. "It's not right for anyone to be alone out here."

"Yet here you are," Akłaq said.

He shrugged mildly. "Here I am. A man alone in the woods in the winter. No one would cry for me, either, if something were to happen to me."

She hesitated for only a moment, then reached forward, unlaced his pants, and pushed them and his underlayer to the floor. He let out a breath as his member sprang free, and he pulled her close for a moment, as if to prove to himself that she was a real person standing there.

Akłaq had never known a man before, but she was not ignorant of the practice. When she and others her age, male and female, had reached adolescence, it was not uncommon for them to go to the beach on hot days, strip down to nothing, and explore what was happening to themselves and each other. The Russians, especially the clergy, had condemned the practice for years, but it still happened.

The priest had also preached against the more casual sexual practices of the people, but the people rarely listened. Children were the survival of the people, and a woman could not always wait until her husband returned from an expedition, assuming he returned at all. Nor could a man be restricted to stay with a single woman; it went against his nature.

So it was that Akłaq had little fear of the man who undressed her and laid her on his bed. She may have even said that she was glad to finally know a man. It was part of her life now, that next chapter of her new reality. Her people were gone, but their traditions continued through her, and she wrapped her legs around him as if she could will him to continue forever.

It was a silly thought, true, and afterwards, Nikita sat on the edge of the bed, looking a bit guilty.

"I should not have done that," he said.

"Why not?" she wondered, propped up on one elbow on her side.

"If I remember right, you're supposed to have a tattoo on your chin once you're eligible."

Akłaq frowned. "The practice was banned when I was a child, one of the few they managed to enforce. I watched them cut a woman's lip off because she had done it anyway, and they broke the fingers of the woman who did it to her."

Nikita shook his head. "It's not right."

"Is that why you left?"

He nodded. "I came here to explore, to trade, to spread culture and religion. I didn't come here to enslave women and children." He leaned back and caressed her hip. "I came here to love them."

"Why not return to Russia?"

"And be shot for a deserter?" He shook his head. "No."

"Aren't you afraid they'll find you, though?"

Again he shook his head. "The empire's hold on Alaska is fading fast. That's why they're burning all the villages. If they can't have it, well, they don't want the British to have it either. Or the Americans or the French or the Dutch or anyone else."

For a long moment, they were both silent.

At long last, Akłaq said, "*Nayuqtaullakpiaġipsi naagaqaa ukiiḷuŋa ilipsitñi.* I will stay with you for the winter."

"You don't have to," Nikita told her guiltily.

"I will. You are correct that it's not safe for anyone to be out alone. The white bear brought me here to safety. I will stay until spring."

He nodded. "Well, by then, even if you still don't know where you're going, you'll have an easier time of getting there."

She stretched, got out of bed, and started pulling her clothes on, much to Nikita's dismay. "I will bring in my supplies from the sled."

The warmth of intimacy was ripped away from her the second she stepped outside. It was strange, considering how long she had spent walking, eating, and sleeping in such cold. Still she made her way down the steps to the ground and out to the barn.

The horses looked up from their dozing, and the chickens cackled away, scratching at frozen dirt. A black cat slunk around a corner, green eyes glowing. Half a dozen dog houses sat empty in a heap. In the middle of the barn was her sled, untouched except for another orange cat burrowed into the furry tent. It ran off when it saw her, but she paid it no mind as she rummaged for her supplies. Rope, knives, needles and sinew, most of it had survived the journey fairly well. After thinking about it, she grabbed the tent as well, figuring she could repurpose it as a blanket.

Arms full, she left the barn and halted. There, at the edge of the trees across the way, was a massive white grizzly bear. It did not act hostile in any way, simply studied her with small silver eyes, breath puffing in the cold air. They stared at one another for several long moments.

She took a few cautious steps forward, toward the bear but also toward the cabin. The bear huffed once, turned, and disappeared into the trees.

Akłaq dropped her load and ran to where the bear had been standing. She saw it walking away, southeast.

"Akłaq?"

She jumped and whirled to see Nikita standing on the porch.

"You need help? Something out there?"

She looked back toward the bear, but it was gone, and a light breeze was fast covering the tracks. Again she looked at Nikita, thought of the cabin, the fire, thought of how handsome he'd looked during their lovemaking, and even now. She'd been on her own for far too long, and she couldn't just go out and wait and hope things got better.

"Thought I saw something, but I don't see it now," she answered at last. "But I could use some help bringing things inside."

He nodded once and descended the steps. Together they picked up the things she'd dropped in the snow, then returned to the cabin.

Avgun Piñasrut
Idyllic

Akłaq would have given anything to have her mother and sisters with her for the birth of her first child. As it was, Nika fainted and she was left to do everything herself, with only memories of other women giving birth to guide her. She frequently looked outside, into the darkness, at the *kiuġuyat*, and she felt the presence of her mother, and she knew she would be all right. She was fairly certain that it was from this that the child emerged female. When Nika finally came back to himself, she presented him with a daughter who they named Miiyuk Nikitaevna.

The land had just turned its face toward spring when Akłaq discovered her pregnancy, and any plans she'd had of leaving and heading south and east instantly evaporated. But Nikita was a good man, and he cared well for her over the summer. They had only each other. And now they had Miiyuk.

One night, as the lights flared overhead, Akłaq sat outside on the porch with Miiyuk, both of them bundled tightly against the cold. Nika joined them, bearing hot beverages that cooled quickly so that they had to drink them all at once.

"What are you telling her?" Nika wondered, carefully pushing back the furs to look upon his daughter. She had lighter skin like him, but black hair and facial features that were entirely Akłaq.

"I'm telling her about the *kiuġuyat*, about her grandmother and aunts." At his look, she added, "And grandfather and uncles, too."

"What do you think they would say if they were here?"

"They would be happy, I think."

He nodded. "That's good."

Now she gave him a look. "And what about you? What would your family say if they were here?"

Nika shifted uncomfortably. "Assuming my father and older brother didn't shoot me, they'd probably disown me. My mother and sisters would be greatly disappointed. My younger brother might still talk to me, though."

"Are all Russian families so rigid?"

"Not all of them, and not always so rigid, but it's different when you come from a family of soldiers. My father was a great man, so I'm expected to be one, too. If I'm lucky, all they've heard of me is that I disappeared and I'm likely dead. It will be more honorable to them than having a deserter for a son."

She nodded and looked around at the landscape, dark silhouettes against the glow of the *kiuġuyat*, what the Russians called the northern lights. "You plan on staying here forever then?"

Nika chuckled and shook his head. "Well, that was never my plan. Then you entered my life." He reached over and poked Miiyuk's nose, causing the infant to smile. "And now we have her." He withdrew his hand. "But it's probably still not the best time to leave. The empire is losing ground, but no one else holds much love for either of us."

"What about south to the United States?"

"Even worse. They'd arrest you, steal Miiyuk, and hang me." He shifted position. "No, this really is the safest place for us. The folks in town keep their mouths shut and their prices fair. Besides that, it's winter now."

"Last winter, I intended to leave in the spring, and we ended up making a baby."

He shrugged. "Things happen, what can I say?"

The winter remained uneventful, though by spring, she was pregnant again.

"Seems I might have to put an extra room on the old homestead," Nika mused, standing with Akłaq on the ground looking at the cabin which stood six feet in the air. "I have a feeling these children might start piling up around here if I don't."

"So is the room for the children, or to keep us apart during the winter so we don't make more children?" Akłaq teased, one hand on her stomach that was just starting to bulge.

"Either, if you like," he told her. He let out a breath. "I know men and women back home who try for years, month after month, hoping and praying for a child. With you, it ain't nothing. And I'm not a young man anymore, either."

Nevertheless, that summer he added another room onto the cabin, in addition to all the usual chores that went on. Arguably the most important one was storing up firewood, though storing up foodstuffs was also on the list. Akłaq had never been very good at tending a stationary plot of land and cultivating vegetables, instead preferring to forage, but she learned quickly, with Nika's help. Watching Miiyuk investigate the dirt and the plants and the insects made her think about how she would be teaching all of these things to her daughter in the very near future. And she was glad.

That autumn, just before Miiyuk reached her first year, they welcomed a boy, her new brother Stanislav, affectionately called Stas. He, too, was fair-skinned. In fact, the only thing he appeared to have inherited from his mother was black hair. Otherwise, he was the spitting image of Nika, an opinion that was only held more strongly as he grew over winter.

It was not the life she had imagined as a child, Akłaq thought as winter slowly migrated toward spring, but it was a good life. Oh, she and Nika had arguments over what to teach the children about his people and her people, but on the whole, it was a good life. But when she spotted the first bear tracks of spring, down on the bank by the stream a hundred yards from the cabin, she sometimes wondered what might have happened if she had followed the white bear that one day, if she hadn't decided to stay with Nika. Or perhaps she hadn't been meant to follow the white bear; perhaps it truly had left her here in safety, and the vanishing tracks had simply been a way to communicate this. Otherwise, who knows how far she would have gone, and for how long?

Whatever the case, she was here now, Miiyuk stumbling after her, Stas on her back.

When she returned to the cabin, she found Nika just hitching the horses to the wagon. The nearest town was two days away, where he would trade furs and other goods.

"Now then, you're not going to surprise me this year like you did last year, are you?" he asked, hitching the horses to the rail at the bottom of the cabin supports.

"No," she told him, grinning cheekily. "I'm not pregnant. That I know of yet."

"All right. If you're going to pull something like that, at least wait until after I'm back."

She just shook her head, still smiling. He said his goodbyes to her and the children, then unhitched the horses and climbed on the wagon. With a click of the reins, the load lurched forward, and a minute later they disappeared around a bend in the trail.

"Papa!" Miiyuk cried, toddling after him. She fell in the dirt after several steps and began to cry. Akłaq went to her and scooped her up.

"Papa!" the girl wailed.

"He'll be home in a week," Akłaq told her, turning back to the cabin. "Don't worry."

Of course, there were plenty of reasons to worry, but she couldn't let Miiyuk know that. They had to stay strong and carry on. Besides, if he did well and made good trades, he could be home sooner.

She took her daughter to the garden, trying to engage the child in the art of cultivation. At this point, it was little more than planning what they wanted to plant and where. Akłaq could have done this well enough and fast enough on her own, but now she had to deal with a small child with an already short attention span who was currently distracted by the absence of her father.

It was a less than productive morning, say it that way. Only once lunch came around and food took precedence over father was Akłaq able to really help the child see that everything would be all right. While Miiyuk was picking at her food and putting more of it on her face than in her mouth, Akłaq bared a breast for Stas.

"Maybe we can go with Papa to town next year," Akłaq suggested, unsure just who she was talking to. "Or even this fall, since it doesn't appear that I'll be near to birth again."

She smiled to herself. It was not the life she had imagined, but it was a good life. She and Nika were not technically "married" though she had said that if anyone asked, she would claim that honor and use his family name as hers. She told the children that it was their family name as well. It relaxed him some, though from time to time, he still lost his arousal, citing the fact that she was more than half his age, young enough to be his daughter.

Then there were other times when that same thought seemed to help his arousal and he couldn't get enough of her. Sometimes she didn't know what to do, so she decided to just let him figure it out.

One of the advantages to having him gone, however, was the ability to observe the ways of her people without interruption or argument. She'd fashioned a drum and, once Stas was finished with his meal, brought it out to start teaching her daughter some of the songs of her people. Afterwards, both children were put down for an afternoon nap.

"One day, you will wear the furs of my mother," she told her sleeping daughter. To Stas, "And one day, you will walk the hunting grounds of your father."

She turned away from them and walked to the chest at the end of the bed she shared with Nika. It contained the furs she had worn when she left her village. They were her mother's, really, and truly exquisite now that they'd been cleaned up and repaired. Perhaps it was fate, guidance of the spirits, or some other entity that had made it so these were what she had fled with. And one day, they would pass to Miiyuk, in the same way that Nika would one day hand over his guns to Stas.

She got some food for herself and was actually able to finish it before her children wanted her again.

Overall, the time that Nika was gone was uneventful. Three of the days it rained, so when the outside chores were finished, Akłaq spent a good amount of time drumming, praying, and teaching her children how to do the same. Miiyuk obviously understood more than Stas, and she was greatly pleased when she heard Miiyuk toddler-babbling the songs to herself when she played outside.

Nika might not be overly enthusiastic about it, but, as he'd said on several occasions, he wasn't exactly a committed Orthodox man himself. And there was something interesting, hypnotic even, about the beats and rhythms of the music.

"You'll have to sing for Papa when he gets home," Akłaq told Miiyuk as she put her to bed.

"When Papa home?" Miiyuk mumbled.

"Tomorrow. Go to sleep."

She had no idea when Nika would be back, but it had to be soon; it had been eight days. He always said seven, but promised no more than ten. It had been eight, and Akłaq wasn't sure when she should start getting nervous, or what she would do if he never actually returned. Would anyone know? Would anyone think to tell her?

Well, at least he would have someone to weep for him, she thought, reflecting on the day they met, when she committed herself to him. Except she wasn't ready to weep for him. She wanted Miiyuk to sing for him, Stas to go hunting with him. She wanted to have more children by him and tend a garden with several daughters to help her. No, she was not ready to weep for him.

She got in bed that night, but it was a long time before she fell asleep.

She tried to keep her growing anxiety from influencing her children, and this was made much easier when, the next morning, she heard the telltale squeak and clatter of the wagon rumbling toward the cabin.

"Miiyuk, Papa's home," she said, scooping up her daughter and making for the front porch.

They arrived the same time he broke through the trees. Miiyuk burst into laughter, clapping and squealing, "Papa, papa!"

He grinned at her. "There's my girls! And Stas, too! I'll be up soon."

He said all this as the wagon rolled by them toward the barn. Akłaq set Miiyuk on the ground and took her hand. "Come on, let's get lunch ready for Papa."

They did so, and while Nika ate his lunch, Miiyuk serenaded him with possibly the most awful rendition of any of the traditional songs Akłaq had ever heard, but he smiled and at least pretended to be entertained. When he was finished eating, he cut her off mid-tune and sent her away to play.

"You've been busy," he observed. "Teaching her all sorts of things while I was away. Spending time as mother and daughter."

"Of course," Akłaq said, sitting across from him. "What else do you expect me to do?"

He shook his head and shrugged.

"Nika, what's wrong? Was trading poor?"

He made a sort of dismissive sound, then sighed and stood. Akłaq followed suit. "Trading was fine. Not as great as last year, but decent. No, there were soldiers in town."

"Did they recognize you?"

"Not as such, but they thought it was pretty suspicious that any Russian should be living alone out here, as young and fit as I am." He rolled his eyes at that and left the cabin. Not content to let the conversation die, Akłaq followed.

"What are they doing in town?" she asked.

"On their way to port, leaving the area." He hesitated as they hit the bottom step. "They burned two more villages."

"Survivors?"

"They didn't stick around to check." He made another ambiguous noise, heading toward the barn. "I just hope they forget me entirely, or at least pass me off as an odd, random encounter to be disregarded."

"You really think they would care about you, report you, and come after you?"

"All it takes is one word to the right person." He opened the barn door and ducked inside.

"But would they really come for you?"

"If the empire is in retreat, they can't risk leaving anyone behind, least of all a deserter." He went to the wagon and started rummaging through it, though even Akłaq could see it was just mindless busywork. "I'm a liability. I might tell military secrets to the British or the Americans or whoever."

"Do you think we should leave?"

He paused, thought a moment, then shook his head. "No. Not yet anyway. And the folks in town are good people; I believe they'd come warn us if there was trouble. That would give us a day or two at least."

Akłaq grabbed his shoulder and made him face her. "Nika, we have children. Small children. They don't move quickly or quietly. We need more than one or two days' notice if we're trying to outrun soldiers."

Nika sighed and put his hand over hers. "Akłaq, it's fine. I promise, it's not as bad as it sounds. I'm just being cautious and a little paranoid. Believe me, I understand the risk. It's my head at stake, and I hope not literally."

"So they hang you, but they arrest me and steal my children? Never."

"It's all right. Besides, soldiers aren't a quiet bunch either. We'll know about them long before they get here. And by then, we'll be halfway to anywhere."

She sighed and nodded.

"And Akłaq?"

She looked at him.

He put his arms around her. "It'll be all of us. Together. You won't have to go off on your own again."

She smiled, kissed him, then left him to his work in the barn.

She managed to get a few minutes of peace and quiet, devoid of children and husband, though her thoughts were less than productive. Somehow, she had come to believe that their life here was impervious to misfortune, impenetrable by such evil forces. Somehow, her husband was an indestructible shield between them and the forces that wanted to harm them, that his inner knowledge of those forces would keep them away forever.

But one recognition by one soldier, one word to the right person. Nika could not handle so many soldiers at once, no matter how knowledgeable he might be.

"Mama?"

Akłaq turned and pulled her daughter out of her crib. "Yes, love?"

The little girl rubbed her eyes. "I sing for Papa at dinner? I not finish my song."

Akłaq grinned. "Of course you can. I think he would like that very much."

If the expression on his face later was any indication, this was not necessarily the case, but again he tolerated it, not commenting until he and Akłaq were finally in bed.

"One day, she'll have a voice like an angel," he said evenly. "Right now, though, she sounds more like a dying cat."

"Maybe," Akłaq said, "but she does it for you."

"I know," he admitted grudgingly. "That's why I don't say anything." He added quickly, "As long as she can keep it to a minimum for the time being."

"I might suggest she practices more before serenading you again."

"It would be much appreciated."

She rolled over in bed so she could face him, the sun still bright against the heavy curtains despite the late hour. She scooted closer and put a leg over his hips. "Maybe I should sing you a song now, though."

"Really? I hope you're not teaching this song to Miiyuk."

"No, of course not. It's a song unique to every woman, one she sings only to the man she loves."

"Have I heard this song before?" Now he put his hands on her and pulled her hard against him where she could feel him straining.

She kissed him. "At least a few times. Would you like me to remind you how it goes?"

Avgun Sisamat
Confrontation

By the time Akłaq was twenty years old, she and Nika had been together five years and had four children. It was not the life she had imagined for herself, but it was one she was happy to have.

Miiyuk, now five years old, took after her mother in almost every way and was actually turning into an impressive singer. She was also quite good at quill art, well, for a child. Nika was not as enthusiastic about it after getting a dozen of them stuck in his backside because she hadn't cleaned up after herself very well.

Stas, four years old, turned out to be great help in the garden and on foraging trips. Again, for a child.

Then came Valentin, called Valya, at two years old, often unable to decide who he wanted to toddle after more, but Alexei, called Alyosha, who was just a year old, was more than happy to ride around on Akłaq's back.

When Akłaq had first gotten pregnant with Miiyuk, Nika had agreed to let her decide on a name, perhaps because he was unsure whether she would even stay with him. When she was pregnant with Stas, they'd come to an agreement that she would name the girls and he would name the boys. Well, one girl and three boys later, she was starting to question this arrangement.

With the children growing up and no longer entirely dependent on their parents for basic mobility, breakfast was a rather chaotic affair as Miiyuk and Stas were more interested in playing than sitting and eating. Valya watched them and often attempted to emulate this behavior, though with limited success. On Akłaq's part, corralling the children and getting them to eat, all the while trying to feed a hungry infant, meant that she herself often got very little to eat, at least in the morning.

After breakfast, Stas was eager to follow Nika out to the barn, and Akłaq managed to convince Valya to go with them. This bought her a little time to set Alyosha down to play with Miiyuk and eat whatever happened to be leftover.

"I think Alyosha likes me," Miiyuk stated. The two of them sat on the floor about ten feet from the table, playing with little wooden blocks that Nika had carved for them. Some had Russian letters, others had animal faces

"Of course he likes you, you're his sister," Akłaq told her.

"Well, I like him well enough, I suppose, but I think your next baby should be a girl. I want a sister."

"Oh really?"

Miiyuk nodded decisively and stacked one block on top of another. "Yes. I'm tired of being outnumbered by boys. I only have you." She stood and went to Akłaq, bending slightly and resting her chin on her mother's lap, putting an ear to her stomach. "Am I going to get a sister this year?"

Akłaq raised a brow though her daughter couldn't see. "I don't know. Maybe."

"Is it going to be another skip year, like between Stas and Valya? Does Papa only get two baby seeds at a time to plant, then he has to go back to town for more?"

Akłaq nearly choked on her food. Miiyuk continued, "Are there different baby seeds for girls and boys? Because I really do want a sister."

"No," Akłaq said, trying to keep something like a straight face. "No, there is only one kind of baby seed. We don't get to choose the variety." She coughed a laugh.

"Oh. I guess we don't know until the harvest."

"No, child. No, we don't." Grinning, she said, "Why don't you go outside and play? See what your brothers are up to."

"But I don't want—"

"Puggutchiqiqasriġukpiña?" (Do you want to help me do dishes?)

Miiyuk made a noise and said, *"Aniiqsuaqatigisrukkikpiñ."* (I want to play outside with you.)

"Aquagun. Puggutat naagaqaa aqqaluk." (Later. Dishes or brother.)

Glad to get out of the after breakfast cleaning chores, Miiyuk ran out of the house and bounded down the steps. As soon as the door swung shut, Akłaq burst into laughter. On the floor, still playing with blocks, Alyosha also grinned and burbled a laugh. Akłaq let her laughter die down into a few fitful giggles before rising from the table and going to the wash basin, arranging her cleaning rags just so and pouring water from the pail.

The mind of a child, she mused, picking up the first plate. And why not? Every year, like the planting, Akłaq would announce a pregnancy. And every late fall or early winter, like the harvest, she would have a baby. To Miiyuk, it was just something that happened to her mother. Baby seeds, as she called them.

As for the missed year, well, that had more to do with Nika having injured his knee and, to a lesser extent, his hip and being unable to, ahem, plow the field for a while. They'd spent that winter, rather than making love, talking about their family and what they were really doing together in a cabin in the woods. When she announced her first pregnancy, barely coming into her sixteenth year, he had apologized profusely and promised to do all he could for her and the child. When she announced her second pregnancy, there was a little less guilt, but he renewed his promise to do right by her. Only when he was out with an injured knee did they really decide to consider themselves a family, so that when she announced her third pregnancy, there was no guilt, only joy. The same happened for her fourth pregnancy, only joy. Well, joy and a bit of trepidation in the fact that Nika wasn't exactly a young man anymore.

So while they were not, perhaps, "technically" married, in the presence of God and spirits and any other mortal witnesses, they still lived like it, acted like it, and if anyone asked, Akłaq took his name. She told the children that they also shared Nika's family name because they were family. And that was how things were.

She finished dishes just in time to go out to the garden to gather some early season perennials and begin preparing lunch. This was slightly less chaotic. The children were fed first, then sent out to play while Akłaq and Nika sat on the porch to eat and watch over them. They sat on the north side of the cabin, opposite the front door, facing the woods.

Nika, too, almost choked on his food when she recounted the conversation she'd had with Miiyuk. Then he nearly choked on his water trying to clear the food from his throat. In the end, he could only shake his head, wheeze, and grin.

"So what I think she's trying to say," Akłaq concluded, "is that you need to hurry up and plow the field if we want to have a harvest before the dead of winter."

"Or," he said, his voice still strained, "we can wait a little longer, plant a little later, overwinter the baby vegetable, and harvest in the spring."

"We could do that, too." She leaned back and took a drink of water. "They've also been talking about going with you to town here in the next week or so."

He nodded. "Yes, they were quite adamant about it this morning in the barn."

"I think it would be fun. We can all go together. The kids need to get out and see other people. I need to see other people; it's been a few years since I've gone with you."

"Well, maybe we can." He shrugged. "Stas is getting old enough that he needs to start learning how to trade and do other man things around this place. And, like you said, Miiyuk should get out and see other people. Considering how little contact we have with anyone, we might have to start looking for a husband for her now, so there might be some interest in her in the next ten or fifteen years."

"We don't need to marry her off as young as I was."

"Isn't that part of your customs, though? You weren't exactly hesitant the first time I took you."

"Maybe, but that's when there is a large community and people around to draw support." She took his hand in hers. "I got lucky with you, that you're such a good man."

"And an old one. Maybe she doesn't need to be married at fifteen, but I'd still like to be there."

"You're not that old," Akłaq chided. "You'll be able to see her wedding and her children, I'm sure."

"Papa, papa!"

Miiyuk's voice carried on the breeze while her light footsteps carried her up the stairs and around the house to where Akłaq and Nika were sitting, both with half-eaten lunches.

"Papa, there's people! There's visitors!"

Nika and Akłaq abandoned their food and went around the house. Visitors were extremely rare, even more so in the spring and summer when everyone simply went to town for trade and socializing.

Nika took the lead, around the house and down the steps.

There were four visitors, all white men. They rode horses, though Akłaq thought their saddles looked a bit sparse for any serious travel. As the adults approached, one of the men was kneeling and speaking to Stas who held Valya with one hand and made occasional gestures with the other, looking perfectly at ease.

"Stas!" Nika called, trying to sound amiable. "Come here. Go with your mother to the garden."

"But, Papa, you said it's time for me to learn man things," the four year old protested. "I have to be a good man to welcome the visitors."

"He's got a point," the kneeling man said, giving Nika a look.

"Fine," Nika sighed. "But let's let Valya go with Mama."

He took Valya and guided the toddler over to Akłaq.

Akłaq did not miss the looks the men gave her. As she herded the children into the garden, she took note of where all the tools were and what was within easy reach. It was hardly noteworthy to say that the men were Russian, but there was something about them that made her uneasy. Briefly she considered taking the children in the house where she might at least have quicker access to the guns.

"The men aren't traders, are they?" Miiyuk questioned. "They don't have a wagon or anything."

"No, I don't think they're traders," Akłaq answered wistfully, keeping one eye on the men who hadn't moved.

"Are they soldiers?"

"Why would you say that? They're not wearing uniforms."

"When they first came up, I saw they all had the same pin on their collars. You can't really see it when they're standing up because the coats cover it, but I saw it when they knelt down to say hi to Stas and me." She went on, "Why would soldiers come here?"

"I don't know," Akłaq answered shortly, even as her heart began to beat faster and terrible memories bubbled in her mind. A thousand worst-case scenarios ran through her head, interspersed with every conversation she had ever had with Nika about his desertion and his ever-present fear of being found out.

Again she glanced around at the garden tools, judging distance, judging time. She looked toward the house once, then at the barn, wondering which was the more feasible option. The house had the guns, but if that failed, unless she wanted to try and throw her children and then herself from the six to ten foot porch, the men would no doubt block the stairway and trap them up there. At least the barn had the horses and multiple escape routes.

She closed her eyes as she recalled the flames engulfing her home, her village. She had made a daring choice to run between a couple of burning buildings, the smoke thick enough to mask her escape for a while. She couldn't allow them to be trapped in the house; the barn would be the better option. She, Miiyuk, Valya, and Alyosha would be on one horse; Nika and Stas would be on the other.

More likely, though, Nika would die trying to buy them time to escape.

Akłaq took a calming breath, startling at a tug on her skirt. It was only Stas.

"Papa wants you to get the welcome blanket from the house."

Akłaq's head snapped up toward the men. Nika met her gaze and nodded once.

"Miiyuk," she said, not looking away from her husband. "Stas, Valya, come with me."

"But—" Stas began.

"Come on. You need to know where the welcome blanket is, too."

It was not a blanket at all. It wasn't even a very friendly welcome. It was a way for Nika to tell Akłaq to grab the guns and get the kids to safety. They'd talked about such things, a dozen different scenarios, even as they also talked about how silly it sounded. Why would they come back for one man? He wasn't harming anyone. And this place was so out of the way, it couldn't even be considered a matter of convenience.

Akłaq had never liked talking about the "welcome blanket." It reminded her too much of what could go wrong, what had gone wrong in her village. She didn't want to think about losing Nika, too. She didn't even want to think about the possibility of losing her children.

She herded the kids up the steps, trying to smile, trying to be positive, trying to keep the kids calm though they seemed to be catching on that something wasn't right.

Stas had just opened the door when there was a gunshot behind them. By the time Akłaq turned around, Nika's lifeless body had already hit the ground.

"Papa!" Miiyuk and Stas cried.

Miiyuk ran in the house, but Stas bolted back down the steps before Akłaq could react to grab him. Valya sat down hard on the porch and began to cry along with Alyosha on her back.

The men did not turn away as she might have hoped, leaving them to grieve and perhaps succumb to nature's cruelty. Rather, the four men looked up from Nika's body, their gazes fixed on Akłaq and the children.

Akłaq lunged down the steps after Stas, reaching him on the final landing before he could make the turn to the last five steps. Tears blurred her vision as she scooped him up, swung him around, and began running up the stairs two and three at a time. Stas shrieked as another gunshot fired off and the railing splintered.

When they reached the door, Akłaq tossed Stas in the house like a sack of potatoes, then ducked to pick up Valya, the doorframe splintering above her head.

The so-called welcome blanket was hidden in a narrow, secret compartment beside the door, under the coat hooks. Akłaq ripped on the latch, yanked open the door, and grabbed the gun.

"Miiyuk, Stas, take your brothers," Akłaq said, herding them into the side room Nika had built only a couple years ago. She clumsily slid Alyosha off her back and handed him to Miiyuk. "When the men come inside, climb out the window and run to the barn."

"What about you?!" Miiyuk wailed.

"I'll follow. Go!"

She pushed them forcefully and had just enough time to get the rifle up when the door opened. She didn't think, just fired as soon as she could. The first man's head exploded in a spray of pink and white, worm-like goo. But the second man wasn't far behind, and he already had his pistol ready.

The recoil from the rifle was probably what actually saved her life. As her left shoulder jerked up and back, it intercepted the bullet that was heading straight for her neck. She cried out and doubled over in pain, dropping the rifle.

"Mama!" Miiyuk cried from the door to the next room.

"*Miiyuk, qimaki – !*" Akłaq shouted. (Miiyuk, run!)

Her cry was cut short as one of the soldiers kicked her.

"One bloody thing I always hated about you people," he said. He kicked her again and she went down. "Your words are just too damn long. And that's the least of my complaints."

Akłaq cried out again as another soldier grabbed her under both arms, white-hot pain flaring through her left shoulder. As she was dragged back toward the bed, she saw the other two men advance on her children.

"*Naagaa!*" she shrieked, wrenching against her captor.

"Amiumaa!" (No! Don't you dare!)

She managed to get her good arm free, and she lunged away, trying to rip the other free as well. But between the pain and the strength of the soldier, she only succeeded in dragging him an inch or two. In the other room, she heard her children's cries.

Her captor jerked on her again. In her distraction, she was unprepared for the pain, and she easily succumbed. He got a grip on her other arm and pushed her onto the bed.

In the other room, there came a rapid succession of gunshots, and the children stopped screaming.

The sound that came from Akłaq's throat was something no man should ever brag about witnessing: the primal shock and fear and anger and sorrow and rage that could only come from a mother who has lost her children in the most heinous fashion. The strength that surged through her body along with it managed to push her captor away and get her to the door where she glimpsed the blood in the other room. But the other two soldiers had already turned her way and blocked her at the door.

One man she might have been able to fight, but three was beyond her capabilities. Still she fought, heedless of the pain in her shoulder, trying to get to her children though she knew it was too late.

Something ripped, and she knew a momentary flash of hope, but it was quickly snuffed out as the first man pushed her on the bed again, tearing away her clothes. He and a second soldier held her down while the third fussed with his laces.

She managed to give him one swift kick, though her aim was off. Furious, the man grabbed his gun and put a second bullet in her leg.

It was this pain that she focused on as the three soldiers had their way with her. Two of them went twice. When they started ribbing the third man about being unable, the third man did a number of other acts to her and on her, evidently trying to recover his arousal, but to no avail.

"That's all right," he decided finally, stuffing everything back in his pants. "I guess I'll just have to visit your wives when we get home."

He brandished his pistol one last time. "This one's about wore out anyway." He gave her a look. "You've got a pretty face, dear. I'll leave it in tact so the animals can admire it when they find you."

Then he aimed and fired.

Avgun Tallimat
Five Graves

Akłaq had always envisioned death as being quite a bit colder as she ascended to join her ancestors in the *kiuġuyat*. It sounded logical enough, she supposed, given the landscape and their people. But maybe it was different because it was spring. As the air warmed, so did death.

Sensation was slow in coming, and while she could feel as though she had a body, her eyes were too heavy and tired to open.

She wondered what she would see. Would she see her family, those who had died because of the Russians? Would she see her children? Her heart ached at the thought, with sorrow because of their deaths, with joy because of their reunion. Would she see Nika? Would he be here with her? She sincerely hoped so.

Or perhaps she had made her way to Hell, as the Orthodox priests had explained, and that was why it was so warm. And yet, it only felt warm, hardly like being submerged in a lake of fire.

Perhaps she was somewhere in between.

Then she began to register sound. And wind. And light and dark. And she began to suspect that perhaps she hadn't died at all.

She didn't know how to feel about that, actually. Just five years ago, everything she ever knew had burned down. Now her whole family had been murdered. She'd heard the gunshot that killed her husband. She'd heard her children's screams suddenly cease, silenced by gunfire. And she had lived. For what purpose?

She did not know how long she lay in a bed of sorrow, but eventually she began to consider other things. For one, she was properly laid in bed, with clothes on, and her wounds no longer throbbed. Actually, she didn't really feel them at all.

Maybe she was dead. Maybe she merely had to rise from her place of death and take her place among the spirits.

Taking a breath, she opened her eyes.

She was still in the cabin, still in bed. Yes. She had died here and now needed to rise as one of the spirits. Seemed a bit odd, but then, she'd never been dead before.

Pushing the blanket back, she slowly got out of bed. She stood half a second before she recalled that she'd been shot in the leg. Then she felt silly because she was dead and her leg felt fine. Looking at it, there didn't seem to be even a mark where the wound had been.

She turned around, expecting to see her body lying there in whatever position the soldiers had left her. But the bed was empty. There was no body.

Thinking fast, Akłaq hurried to the other room, expecting to find her children. But that room was empty, too. Only the bloodstains in the floorboards gave any indication of where they had died.

Suddenly panicked, she turned around and made for the door. She reflexively jerked back at a flash of movement of the other side, but she was on the wrong side of the door to grab the rifle. And where had that gone? She didn't know. She'd dropped it, but she didn't see it.

Then the door opened.

Her first wish was for it to be Nika who walked in, but it was not. Nor was it one of her children. Actually, it wasn't even a Russian. It was one of her countrymen, though she could not identify the woman's specific people right offhand.

"You're awake," the woman said, looking as stunned as Akłaq felt. She did not speak Akłaq's tongue, though it appeared close enough that they were able to work out an understanding.

"Am I dead?" Akłaq wondered.

"No, but you would have been, if we had come any later."

"What about my children? Where are they?"

Without waiting for an answer, Akłaq pushed past the woman to the outside, hoping, praying to see her kids running around, just as well as they had been. And Nika, too.

"I'm afraid you're the only one we could save," the woman said behind her. "Your oldest son was still alive when we got here, but his wounds were too great; there wasn't much we could do."

Akłaq shook her head, tears streaming down her cheeks. "I wasn't there. I should have been there with them. For them. I should have."

She went to her knees and wept.

When she was finally able to collect herself, wiping her eyes and nose, she startled at the approach of another person, this one a man. Twenty yards behind him was a third person whose sex she could not readily identify.

"She lives," the man stated, standing a few feet in front of Akłaq. He was an older man, a few years older than Nika.

"Yes," the woman said simply.

The third person, by now she could see it was a young man, caught up to them. Looking around, he asked, "What happened here?"

All eyes were on Akłaq as she stood, still wiping her eyes.

"My husband was a Russian, a deserter from the army. He'd been living here in secret when we met. We never had any problems, but he was always worried that they would find him one day." She took a shuddering breath. "And they did." Another wipe. "Nika tried to warn us, tried to buy us time, but it wasn't enough. Miiyuk ran in the house, but Stas tried to run to Nika. I had to go back for him and I couldn't really get to the gun in time. I shot one of the men, but then…"

Her heart was full of sorrow, but her eyes were empty of tears, and the most she could do was slip into a sullen silence.

"How did you come to be here?" the woman inquired gently. "You speak a northern tongue. Where are you from?"

"Qikiqtaġruk."

The first man grunted. "That was burned down some years ago, not many survivors. How did you end up here?"

"I walked," Akłaq said simply. "I didn't know there were other survivors."

"Well, you made out the best of them."

"I followed the white bear."

The demeanor of the trio changed then.

"Well, that does explain something," the first man said. "For it was a white bear who brought us to you."

Akłaq sighed tiredly. "What does that mean?"

"We'll explain on the way," the woman told her. "At any rate, you can't stay here."

Panic again seized Akłaq. "But my children. And Nika."

"Are gone," the first man told her. He relented. "Matulik, take her to the graves. We'll double-check the horses."

Akłaq did not resist as the woman, Matulik, took her by the arm and led her across the yard and down the slope where five fresh graves sat, crude markers stuck in the dirt.

"They deserve better," Akłaq said, choking. "They deserve more. They deserve life!"

Her descent to her knees was slower this time, and still she did not cry even as she bowed low to the ground, weighed down by pain. She sprang back upright and looked up at Matulik. "How can I just leave them?"

"You can't stay," Matulik told her lamely. "There are more dangers out here than just the Russians."

"Do you know what they did to me?"

"From what we saw of the aftermath, it wasn't hard to guess."

"What animal out there can do worse than that? An animal may kill, but it is only an animal. Only humans are so cruel to each other."

"Staying here won't change that. And it won't bring any of your children or your husband back to life. But you need someone to help you, to look after you. You need a community. We can show you one."

Akłaq brought one knee up and rested her forehead upon it. She laughed humorlessly. "Five years ago, my community was burned to the ground, my family murdered. Now, my family is again murdered and you are asking me to leave everything behind." She looked up. "Is this to be my life?"

Matulik got down beside her. "I don't believe so. You could have died. Easily. We weren't even sure that our efforts would be enough, but they were. Because the white bear brought us in time. You must be alive for a reason, but staying here isn't it."

"When I first came here, I made a choice. I chose not to follow the white bear, not to continue my journey. I chose to stay with Nika, and I chose to lie with him. Am I being punished for that decision?"

Matulik was silent for a long moment. Finally, "I weep with you, sister, for your terrible loss. I also envy you for the joy you must have had. But there's a big world out there, and you clearly need to be there. I don't know why, but the shaman might."

"Your village still has a shaman? Ours were all killed, the boys in training sent to labor."

"Well, he's not so traditional as in the old days, but he's no Orthodox priest."

They sat there in silence for a long moment, staring at the graves. Akłaq knew she could not stay, but she couldn't bear to leave. She wanted to stay and grieve as she had never had a chance to do for her village.

Then what?

If she stayed, she would be cooking for herself tonight. She would sleep alone in the bed where she'd been raped. In the morning she would cook for herself again. She would not have to get her children around and ready, would not have to breastfeed a baby, would not have to make a chore list for the children, would not have any fun banter with Nika. The house would be cold and empty, devoid of all life, including hers. Even looking at the garden, it seemed far too large for a single person.

"All right," she whispered at last. "I'll go with you."

Matulik just nodded and got to her feet.

Akłaq still did not stand. Instead she said, "The last thing we were talking about was going to town next week for spring trading. Normally it was just Nika who went, though I had gone a couple of times, too, early on, before we had many children." She shed a few tears and lazily wiped them away. "This year we were all going to go together. Stas..." She sniffed. "Stas had to learn man things, how to trade and drive the wagon and..." She shook her head. "And we were joking about having to look for a husband for Miiyuk now. Because we were so isolated, it might take a while and...And then they came running up to us. We were on the porch having lunch, and the children were playing. And they came running up to us and they said that there were visitors. And...And Stas said he wanted to talk to the men, too, because it was one of the men things he had to learn."

Akłaq went on before Matulik could speak. "Then Nika sent Stas to me and the children in the garden, told me to bring out the welcome blanket. That was his way of telling us to get to safety. And then...it just...it all collapsed."

She cried again.

When she stood, the men were approaching, about twenty feet away.

"I'm ready," she told them, though she said it to the ground. "But I want to grab something from the house first."

The men looked a bit impatient, but Matulik gently agreed.

Akłaq returned to the cabin. It even felt emptier now, devoid of joy and laughter and everything that made it a home, despite everything being in its proper place.

She grabbed a bag from beside the bed and opened it up. Into it she placed Nika's pipe and whittling knife. Then she went to the children's room, momentarily paralyzed by the sight of the bloodstain. When she got her legs to move, as wobbly as they were, she picked up a small doll that had belonged to Miiyuk, and a carved wooden animal Nika had made for Stas. From Alyosha's things, sparse though they were, she took his blanket. Then she grabbed her mother's furs from the chest.

Her bags were quite full, but it still seemed like so little. With a last look around, she walked out of the cabin, quietly closing the door behind her.

It was the only grief she would be allowed, and it was still more than she had gotten for her village.

At the porch, five horses waited, two of them being the old faithful mounts Nika had hooked up to the wagon twice a year. Akłaq stopped and glanced back at the graves. She hated herself. She hated herself for walking away, for abandoning them, for giving up so soon, as if time might somehow bring them back. But most of all, she hated herself for living. Why should she live, and not them? Was this truly punishment for ignoring the white bear all those years ago? What else could there possibly be for her out there? What did she care about the world, when the world clearly didn't care about the tiny family living in a small part of it?

Her horse was third in line, behind Matulik. The men introduced themselves as Aniqan, the younger man who was leading, and Putu, who brought up the rear along with the pack horse.

And just like that, for the second time in her life, Akłaq walked away from a tragedy that had taken everything from her, riding out into the vast unknown.

There was no conversation to be had. Akłaq had about as much life in her as most of the supplies carried on the horses. She had only a vague inclination of direction, east, away from the town that Nika normally visited for trade. She had virtually no perception of time. When they set out, it had been inclining toward midday. Every so often, when she looked up from staring at a white spot on her horse's neck, she would notice that the sun had changed position.

She startled when Aniqan suddenly spoke, announcing that they were making camp. Looking around, she had no idea where they were, and somehow the sun had moved around to touch the horizon again.

They had only one tent, which the trio agreed Akłaq could privately use. Once it was pitched, a small fire was started, and a bag of cured meat was passed around.

"How long ago did you actually find us?" Akłaq wondered, staring into the fire while she nibbled on a bit of meat.

"What do you mean?" Matulik wondered.

"The soldiers shot me twice, once in the shoulder and once in the leg. Then they took turns raping me. Yet here I am with no apparent wounds, hardly a scar or even a minor ache. So either more time has passed than I realized, or there is some sorcery involved."

Though she did not look, Akłaq knew Matulik and the men exchanged glances.

"You might call it a kind of magic, I suppose," Matulik told her. "It's called Time. Putu and I are Timekeepers. We can bend Time, to make it go faster or slower."

"Can you make it go backwards, that I might go back and save my children and my husband?"

"No. Time moves only forward."

Akłaq looked up, giving the briefest of glances to Aniqan. "Aniqan isn't one of these Timekeepers?"

"He is what's called a Harvester." Again the trio exchanged glances. "When someone is dying, or very soon after death, he...takes Time from them, all the years they might have lived if not for tragedy."

Now she stared at Aniqan, fixing him in a hard glare. "Matulik said my son was alive when you came. Did you kill him?"

"No," Aniqan answered calmly. "I swear to you, I did not. But when he passed, I saved his years, as I saved the years of your husband and other children."

Slowly, he reached for his bag and opened it. He withdrew five strange objects. They were cylinders of some form, with rounded ends and a ring about a third of the way in on each side. Each one was no more than a few inches long, maybe equal in circumference. The ends were solid metal, but the center, between the rings, was a bright, almost glowing green.

"What is that?" Akłaq inquired.

"This is what is called a Time Capsule. This contains the years of life that your husband and children never lived."

"What do you do with it?"

"Some people sell them. These are worth a lot of money to the right people."

"And what do you do with them?"

"We give them back to the people, the lives and memories of our ancestors, carried on from generation to generation."

Akłaq felt her heart sink. "I'm sorry, but I have no money to give you for them. And I...I couldn't..."

Aniqan handed the Time Capsules to Matulik who shifted so she was facing Akłaq. "Some people sell them. When it comes to aiding our own people, there is no charge. Even if there were, I would pay the price for you, for this is not the way things are supposed to be. You should be getting the years of your parents and grandparents, not your children."

Akłaq took the five strange objects, feeling them pulse with life. "Thank you." She let out a breath. "This work you do, is this what the shaman of your village has commanded you to do?"

"It is what has become of us, out of necessity."

"How does one get to be a Timekeeper or a Harvester?"

"If you want, we can discuss it with the shaman when we reach our village," Putu told her. "There are many things to explain about it. For now, simply keep those safe."

"Of course, of course!" Akłaq took her bag and stuffed the Time Capsules inside. The bag bulged and she had to rearrange things several times before she felt confident that she wasn't going to lose anything. "Thank you. I have been poor in expressing my gratitude, but—"

"Don't worry about it," Matulik told her gently. "Why don't you get some sleep? It's a fair distance to our village, and we need to keep moving."

Akłaq nodded and, after another minute or two, crawled into the tent. As she lay down, a terrible tsunami of homesickness, loss, and rage stormed through her, and she silently cried herself to sleep.

Avgun Itchaksrat
Time Capsule

The journey was long, or maybe it only felt that way. Akłaq rode silently along with the others, feeling like a prisoner though her only captor was herself. When they made camp for the evening, she might ask a few questions about the Timekeeping or Harvesting they talked about, or she might just slip into the tent to cry herself to sleep. Overall, her existence was minimal and miserable, until Aniqan announced one night in camp that they were close to the village and should arrive the next day.

"Is it a very large village?" Akłaq wondered, a minor shadow in her mind lifting away.

"Fifty or sixty of us in all," Matulik told her. "Though there may be only twenty or thirty there at any given time."

"And what people are you?"

"We're made up of all kinds," Aniqan answered. "Refugees, like yourself. Inuit, Yu'pik, Tlingit, Haida, even a couple Cree and other southeastern peoples. We are held together by our work in Time."

"Restoring the years of the dead to the bodies of the living."

"Yes."

Akłaq put a hand on her bag, but didn't open it. "And it works on the Russians as well? You saved my husband's years?"

Aniqan nodded once. "Of course. He was your husband."

"Will it work the same, since he was not of our people?"

"Yes, it will. But I would wait until after you've spoken to the shaman."

"You have said this repeatedly, but I don't understand. They are my children, stolen from me and murdered. I thank you for your kindness, now why can I not take it fully?"

"Because if you open those Time Capsules and take their lives into yourself, you will also gain their years," Matulik said. "In doing so, you will lengthen your own life. Perhaps your husband had thirty years left to his life. Now add seventy years times four from your children. You would gain all of those years. Your aging would slow until it nearly stopped. And in doing so, you would gain the ability to Band or Harvest as we do, which, just from sheer use, will also lengthen your years. And there are other side effects to consider."

Akłaq stared at her, as if searching for the punchline to a joke that never came.

"The shaman can explain it to you tomorrow," Putu said, ever serious. "For now, we should all get some rest."

Akłaq did not cry herself to sleep that night. Instead, she lay awake, staring at her bag and the glowing capsules inside. Four of them contained the lives her children might have had if only they had lived. The last contained the rest of the life her husband never lived. The life they had missed out on together.

She wanted to see these lives, to know them, to be able to glimpse what might have been and hold her children and her husband one last time.

And yet, to do so meant that she would have to take in all those years and live them as if they were her own. Three hundred years added onto her life. Another three hundred years without them. Or fifty years of her own life.

But could she stand the wait?

If she had been given the capsules when she'd first woken up, she would have opened them immediately, just to get a glimpse of her children. She wouldn't say she hadn't given it serious, if irrational, thought over the last ten days or so. Now she wasn't so sure.

She fell asleep without touching the Time Capsules and woke the same way.

As promised, they reached the village by early afternoon. A certain sensation washed over Akłaq. Actually there were multiple sensations, all vying to be felt, all trying to be correct. She felt as though she'd been here before, done this before. She felt as though the last five years hadn't happened. She felt the same way she had when she first met Nika and lay with him, that this was simply the next chapter in her life. She felt as though she were coming home, but not quite.

They had come quite a bit south, far enough that there was always a day and always a night, though the former was still significantly longer than the latter. But, in addition to the blending of light and dark, there also appeared to be a blending of cultures. She spied homes covered in furs, others covered in bark, others made solidly of wood, and still a few of a style she did not recognize at all.

The shaman hut was easy to spot, for it was decorated with numerous bones, many with carvings. She spotted a few crosses as well, made of bone or wood.

Matulik, Aniqan, and Putu wasted no time. They handed off their horses to someone they evidently perceived as a friend, then shuffled Akłaq into the shaman's hut.

Akłaq had heard stories of the old shamans, those who had been covered in bones and furs and even feathers, carrying staves of great power and communicating freely with the spirits. By the time she came into the world, the shamans, those who had not been stripped of all finery and sent to labor, had little more than carved walking staves decorated with a few feathers and a bone talisman about their necks.

This shaman had colored his hair and decorated it with many feathers, and he wore many fine furs replete with bone jewelry. He also had a magnificent staff by his side, carved with many shapes. The hut was well furnished with bones and jewelry and other riches. And yet, he somehow still seemed to be a man. Akłaq couldn't help but feel a little disappointed. She did not know what she had been expecting, though anything except the feeling of simply walking into a room would have been preferred. Maybe she'd been hoping to feel more spirit presence, that there might be a chance to speak to her family again, see her husband and children once more before moving on with her life.

"Welcome back," the shaman greeted. "The white bear showed you something, then? Who is this?"

Akłaq glanced at Matulik who nodded. "My name is Akłaq Balabinov."

"Forgive my observation, but that is hardly—"

"I am originally from Qikiqtaġruk, but my village was burned, and I fled. I met Nikita Balabinov and I married him and we had four children. Then more Russians came and murdered them. They would have killed me, except Matulik and the others found me and were able to save me."

She kept her voice low and steady even as her heart threatened to jump out of her chest.

"I see. Then you've already consumed the Time Capsules, or was it too late for them?" He glanced at the trio.

"I have them," Akłaq told him. "They advised me not to consume them until I spoke to you, although I still do not know your name."

The man made a gesture of apology. "Pardon my manners. My name is Ujurak." He nodded. "I assume, then, that they informed you of the decision you face."

"If I take the years of my husband and children, I also gain them and add nearly three centuries to my life."

"Three centuries, possibly more. That is correct. Matulik may have also warned you that with this, it would be very difficult if not impossible for you to have children in the future."

That gave her serious pause.

"I can see that you are tired from your journey," Ujurak stated, not unkindly. "Perhaps you would like to rest a while?"

"What is it that you do here? What is the purpose of Timekeeping or Harvesting?"

"We Harvest so that we may preserve our people," Aniqan answered. "We desire to save their lives within ourselves, within their children and grandchildren if possible. But we also Harvest the Russians, the British, the Americans, anyone who seeks to oppose or subjugate us."

"And what do you do with their years?"

"As I said on the road, Time Capsules are worth a lot of money to the right people."

"Then what?"

"Then we work on buying supplies for the most ravaged peoples," Putu continued. "Supplies, land, anything that may hinder or take away from the people who seek to do us harm."

"And you do this with fifty people?"

It was Ujurak who replied, "Not everyone is suited to our lifestyle. I saw your hesitation just now, when I mentioned the possibility of not having children." He shrugged. "It is not an uncommon reaction, nor unexpected. We force no one to join us, and we try to make sure you understand what you would be doing, what you would be giving up. As for those who do decide to join us, we do what we can."

Akłaq hesitated. Then, "Putu mentioned that the white bear brought them to me. What did he mean? Years ago I was told—by a Russian missionary, even—to follow the white bear. I did, and he led me out of Qikiqtaġruk as it burned, showed me safety with the man who would be my husband. Then I ignored him, abandoned him to pursue a life with my husband."

Ujurak nodded. "About a month ago, I had a vision, a dream of the white bear leading a group of our people to a place filled with blood and lead. Within that place was life, a bear cub covered in ivy. But the cub was in danger, doomed to death unless rescued. So I sent Putu, Aniqan, and Matulik out, to follow the white bear. And it took them to you."

"A bear cub, though? My children are dead."

"Then we can only conclude that the bear cub is you. You have had a hard life, but you are still only just a woman. You are twenty years at most? Still much to see and learn."

"But what? And why?"

"This I have not been able to discern. Now that I have met you, however, this may change. Please, stay a while. Rest and grieve for your loss."

Akłaq nodded. "Thank you."

She turned to leave and Matulik followed, murmuring, "You can stay with me for the time being."

Again the feeling of giving up and abandoning her family. Again the feeling of stepping into a new reality.

"I assume you have no children?" Akłaq asked of her new host as they made their way around the village.

"I do, actually," Matulik answered, "though only one, and he is old enough now that you would believe him my brother instead."

"Then what was Ujurak saying about—?"

"I was taken from my village when I was newly pregnant, forced to live in a large building with many people. We were kept under guard at night, sent out to work during the day. Menial work, for us women. Sewing, crafting, nothing unusual, though food and general conditions were quite poor. I went into labor at a less than ideal time, and the women I was with were hardly more than girls themselves, as I was.

"One of the guards took pity on me. His wife and sister-in-law happened to be visiting at the time, and they came to my aid. They delivered my son but wrote me off as dead. They had me taken out of the building, out of the town entirely to be buried before I was even gone. But the gravedigger was a Timekeeper, and a highly skilled one at that. He'd saved more than one man or woman who had been cast off and left to die, and I was no different."

"You didn't want more children?" Akłaq wondered.

"My husband was dead, and I thought my son was dead as well," Matulik said, pushing aside the furs that constituted a door to her hut. "It wasn't until six months later that I learned he'd survived and was being cared for my the women in the building where I had stayed. I returned just long enough to rescue him."

"He isn't a Timekeeper, I take it?"

Matulik shook her head and poked some coals back to life in the center of the hut. "No. He knew of my power, and I did my best to explain it, but he wanted no part of it."

"Do you still see him?"

"From time to time, yes."

"And what does he think of your work?"

Matulik looked thoughtful for a moment. "He has no problem with the ends, our goal of trying to preserve the people, but he finds the means a bit strange."

She made a gesture and both women sat down. Akłaq studied her. "When your son dies, will you take his years?"

"I expect so, if we can get to him in time."

"What do you mean?"

"For the majority of Harvesters, Harvesting can only be done when a person is near to death, or within a very short time afterwards. Some can Harvest at a touch regardless of a person's health, but no one here has that level of skill."

"That sounds frightening."

Matulik nodded. "It can be a lot to take in."

Akłaq shifted position. "Have the people here always had these sorceries?"

"No, not at all. They were first introduced by the eastern fur traders."

"Oh."

The two women sat in silence, watching the fire. Matulik kept little in her fur-covered hut, and what supplies Akłaq did see were clearly meant for travel.

"Do you go out often to search for the dead and dying?" Akłaq wondered, looking around, her gaze settling on some heavy winter ice trekking gear.

"More often, now that the Russians are pulling out of the region."

"Nika once told me that the Russians were burning the villages in order to spite the British and the Americans."

"It wouldn't surprise me. Once they're completely gone, I expect the Hudson Bay Company would want to try to expand into the area. The Russians may be gone, but the furs aren't."

"Is Hudson Bay very good to their people? I only heard that they employed some peoples or just used them as intermediaries."

"I don't know," Matulik told her. "Every so often, I'll run into someone who does business with them, but outside the land that they've claimed, stories are mixed and unreliable. They abuse these people. They are worshipfully respectful of those people. I suppose it depends on the individual."

They lapsed into silence once more. After a bit, Matulik asked, "Are you hungry? I'm sorry, I've not offered any food or water."

Akłaq didn't want to admit to it, but she was quite hungry. She'd been hungry most of the time on the trail, although her grief had masked most of it. Now, as the light began to break through the clouds of her depression, some things, like hunger, were beginning to return.

"You don't have a lot of food," she answered diplomatically.

"You're right, we don't," Matulik acknowledged, standing. "That's another part of Time. As it slows your aging, you find that you need less and less food. It can be helpful on long journeys, but it ruins your manners when you have guests."

For the first time since waking up, Akłaq found that her face wanted to smile. She could feel the tug in her cheeks and on her lips, but she couldn't quite bring herself to muster up a full grin.

"I'll see if anyone has a carcass they'd be willing to share," Matulik went on, ducking out of the hut.

No need to eat, no children, was it possible that these Timekeepers and Harvesters were actually dead? Had she perhaps stepped into the spirit world without realizing it? Had they realized it yet? Was that why they were able to communicate with the white bear so easily, why it came to them in order to save her? Had they saved her? And what did that mean for her previous interactions with the white bear?

Matulik returned with half a smoked hare and some forage which she gave to Akłaq.

Akłaq instinctively tried to be polite about it, trying to set an example for children who were no longer around to scold for being impolite in their table manners. And yet, when the first taste of hare hit her tongue, she couldn't help but indulge a little, even if that meant being a bit impolite. Matulik offered no comment, just added a few sticks to her fire.

"I'm going to consume the Time Capsules," Akłaq stated once she'd finished her meal.

Matulik gave her a sympathetic look. "You shouldn't make a decision so quickly. It's been hardly a moon and—"

"I failed to follow the white bear years ago, and it is the white bear that brought you to me. I am alive for a reason."

"Yes, but—"

"If I were meant to have a family, whether to carry on or not, then I expect we would still be there, or I would be dead with them. If they were meant to come with me in whatever quest I abandoned years ago, I expect the white bear would have approached me once more. But here I am, alive but without a family, at the will and mercy of the white bear. And he didn't bring just any help, but you, Aniqan, and Putu, who have this incredible power to give me the unrealized lives of my husband and children. That means something." Akłaq shook her head. "I condemned Nika and our unborn children when I turned my back on the white bear. I can't condemn anyone else."

Matulik studied her for a long moment. Finally she said, "Once you do this, it cannot be undone. It is true that you will not become indestructible, as any of us are still susceptible to disease or disaster, but your natural lifespan will increase by an extraordinary number of years."

"I understand."

Matulik gestured toward Akłaq's bag. While Akłaq rummaged for the Time Capsules, trying not to spill anything else out onto the ground, Matulik asked, "Do you know what the white bear wants with you? You say that a missionary spoke of it, and then it led you to safety after your village burned. What does it want?"

"I don't know," Akłaq replied, laying out the Capsules neatly before her. "But I won't know unless I follow him."

Avgun Tallimat Malġuk
Starting Over Again

Akłaq lay abed in Matulik's tent for six days after consuming the Time Capsules, enthralled by the experience but also questioning whether she had made the right decision.

She had not seen moment-by-moment what her children's or husband's lives would have been had they lived, but she had, through some inexplicable means, felt the people they would have been. She knew that Miiyuk would have been bold and confident, much like Akłaq, but also a bit crass, somewhat lacking in tact and sensitivity to others around her. She felt how Stas would have grown into a fine man like his father, though a little shy. Valya had been destined to be bold, stubborn, somewhat arrogant and argumentative. Alyosha would have been quiet, shy, following his mother's background and beliefs more closely than his father's.

For Nika's part, he would have gotten a little crabby in his old age, but otherwise remained the same loving, doting husband she had come to know and love.

And yet, for as much as she had feared what she might have seen and felt, she also found a great deal of closure, and her sorrow was actually lessened. She knew the people her children would become. Maybe not the individual events, but something far deeper, far more personal and intimate. She knew them. And she knew that, even now, they were safe.

So she might live for another three hundred years before seeing them again, but it would be a more peaceful three centuries rather than an anxiety-riddled five decades.

Things would be all right.

"Do Harvesters know everything about the people they Harvest? Does Aniqan know everything that I know about my husband and children?" Akłaq asked, finally emerging from her catatonic state.

"No," Matulik told her gently. "They might glean a passing impression, a sense of familiarity as if they had met them once before, but whatever you felt is yours alone."

Akłaq breathed a sigh of relief. "That's good." She looked around uncomfortably, suddenly feeling very conspicuous, as though she had overstayed her welcome and was now being useless in the community. "What now?"

Matulik got up from her chair. "Well, seeing how you've made your decision, we should start with getting you set up in the village. A place to live, some basic necessities. Once you're all settled in, then we can see about starting your training."

"Training in what?"

"Controlling your Bands, for one. You've been haphazardly Banding while you've been lying down. I imagine your sense of time is a bit distorted, and you're probably hungry and thirsty and need to relieve yourself."

Even as Matulik said all this, the sensations started flowing through Akłaq. The distortion of time was debatable, but her bladder was very unhappy. She went out to relieve herself, then rejoined Matulik in the middle of the small village.

"Why am I not haphazardly Banding now?" Akłaq inquired.

"Because I'm holding you in Base Time," Matulik answered, starting off in a particular direction. Akłaq followed obediently. "It's not difficult and you don't perceive it because you don't quite know what to look for yet. But the basic premise is that in a Fast Band, you will see everything through a lens of red or orange. Slow Bands will show you everything in shades of blue."

"Does everyone here Band? Even Harvesters?"

"Raw Time Capsules only expose you to the workings of Time, give you the ability to manipulate it in some way. By itself it's fairly neutral. Somehow, while you were lying down, you latched onto the concept of manipulating Time, going faster, slower, even forward and back—though, again, Time only moves forward, and at its own rate—and stepped into Timekeeping of your own volition."

"So Aniqan doesn't Band."

"He learned just for curiosity's sake, but it was his choice."

Akłaq nodded. "You said 'raw Time Capsules.' Are there others?"

"Merchants have the ability to purify them, so you gain the years without the intimacy." Matulik went on before Akłaq could speak. "It's not part of our life or business. We don't promote such things, but it's useful to know of their existence. Here we are."

They stopped outside a small hut that looked very much like Matulik's.

"We built this while you were down, that way you would have somewhere to stay when you woke up. Go on inside, see what you think. When you come out, we'll work on helping you control your Bands."

Akłaq nodded and ducked inside. As expected, it was fairly empty save for a bed of furs, an armload of firewood, and a pot and assorted utensils for cooking. As sparse as sparse could be, just waiting for her to add her own touch of home.

The thought was not only daunting, but emotionally overwhelming. This was hers and hers alone. Everything in here would be only hers. Nothing from Nika or any of her children, save for what she had in her bags.

She wiped her eyes as things started to turn blue. The sensation lasted only a moment, and then it was gone, everything popping back into full color. Matulik walked in behind her.

"Was that a Band?" Akłaq wondered.

"Yes, it was," Matulik said guiltily. "I'm sorry, I stepped away for just a minute and let go of my anchor on you, and when I turned around, you were Banding again."

"Everything was blue, which you said was a Slow Band."

"That's right."

"I didn't notice any change other than the color."

"Well, it's a little harder to tell when there is nothing and no one to look at, to judge their movements. Do you want to spend some more time in here, or do you want to get started?"

Akłaq hesitated for just a moment, then set her bags on her bed and followed the Timekeeper out of the hut.

She couldn't have stood there for more than a few moments, yet when she emerged from her hut, it appeared as though half a day had passed. The sun had moved, people had moved, things had moved. Had she done that? Had she slowed time, or herself? What did all of this mean? What about the so-called Fast Band?

"So everyone that you do this for, to rescue the lives and memories of the people and give them, ideally, to their children," Akłaq began, "and because you said that you don't sift out the memories, does that mean that everyone in the area is a Timekeeper or a Harvester?"

"No," Matulik replied simply. She led Akłaq to a clearing about a hundred yards from the main village. "Many such Time Capsules are very insignificant, containing mere moments. They have to reach a certain potency before the one consuming the Time Capsule can perceive Time as we do."

"Oh."

What was she supposed to say to that? It all sounded so far-fetched already, at this point, she had to decide whether it was real or a delusion, and then decide how far she wanted to run with it. If it was real, and so far all evidence suggested it was, then she was obligated by the white bear to continue. If this was somehow a delusion crafted by her own grieving, deluded mind, well...she didn't know what. She didn't know what to do. So she just followed Matulik's lead.

"When I release the anchor on you," the woman said, her shift in tone suggesting that training had begun, "I want you to be fully conscious of the present moment. Everything exactly as it is. Who you are, where you are, your breathing, the movement of the grass and trees, the feel of the air and the earth all around you. Can you focus on that for me?"

Akłaq took a breath and nodded. It shouldn't have sounded or felt like such a chore, but there it was.

She focused on herself. Her breathing. The breeze stirring her hair into her face, the ground beneath her feet and one particular little pebble that was uncomfortably grinding into her arch.

She thought of her garden. Would any of the plants have sprouted? She'd managed to get a few seeds in the ground during an early thaw, and maybe some had accidentally dropped from last year's harvest. It had been a good year, and they'd eaten well. Speaking of food, she was feeling a bit hungry. Actually, a lot hungry. Well, she really hadn't eaten much lately, and if—

Her vision turned orange, and she watched as the world around her began to slow. She saw every wing beat of a bird in flight, every turn of the zigzagging path of a dragonfly. She saw the slow blink of Matulik, only ten feet in front of her.

She marveled at the scene for a long moment. Then, somehow, she willed it back to normal on her own. The look on Matulik's face said she knew what had happened, and Akłaq couldn't decide if the woman was impressed or annoyed.

"You came back on your own, which is good," she stated, "but we're going to have to work on voluntarily going into a Band."

"It was amazing to see," Akłaq said, looking around for the bird and the dragonfly but finding neither.

Matulik nodded, her expression one that Akłaq knew she'd had when seeing her children discover something and be amazed by something she'd always taken for granted and considered ordinary, like how seeds could turn into plants and vegetables.

This time she felt it when Matulik cut into her forming Band to anchor her in what she called Base Time.

"Bands are willful to the skilled, but to an amateur, they are driven more by emotion," Matulik said. "You are wishing yourself out of our Time. I know where and when you want to be, but you have to stay here in the moment. Once you can separate yourself from the past, you can visit it as often as you wish without affecting your standing in the present. Do you understand?"

Akłaq hesitated for a moment, but nodded. "The past is finished. What is happening here and now is still ongoing, and this is where I must be."

"Exactly. It takes a lot of work, a lot of thinking, and it's harder for women than men, but you can do it. I can see it in you, that you have the fortitude."

She had no choice, really, because Matulik also declared that the practice session wasn't going to end until she mastered it, mastered herself. That thought set her back a little as she almost feared giving up on her grief over her family. Would they think she was giving up on them entirely? Or would they be happy that she was moving on with a new part of her life? Neither Nika nor her children ever liked to see her sad, and some of the things they had done to cheer her up had been quite inventive.

But it was, as Matulik said, in the past. It was finished. Thinking about the Time Capsules and the people her children would have been, they would have wanted her to move on and be happy. Whatever it was that the white bear had in store for her, the reason she had been saved, she had to seek it out. And she could only seek it out by going through this training with Matulik.

She focused on her Bands.

"It's not about the strength of your Bands," Matulik told her once. "All we want to accomplish is getting you to stop randomly spawning Bands at all. Once you can voluntarily enter and exit your own Bands, then we'll work on all the extra things."

Considering that there was even more to this manipulation of Time helped lock everything in for her.

She was still grieved by the loss of her family. She didn't know that she ever wouldn't be. She could still call to mind the faces of her husband and children, and she still missed them dearly. She could remember in a heartbeat every event of that fateful day now almost a moon past. And yet, that was all it was. In the past. Finished. Realized. She was no longer in that room, but watching through a window, everything perfectly contained within.

Matulik praised her progress and encouraged her to keep practicing.

"Now what?" Akłaq wondered.

"For now, get settled in your new house," the woman told her. "Get something to eat, arrange your possessions, and do what you think needs to be done to make this place your home. Go out and meet some of the other villagers. We'll continue training tomorrow."

And just like that, Akłaq was left alone in a brand new village full of brand new people.

She returned to her new house, trying to bring to mind everything that needed to be done. Well, she was quite famished by this point, so she would have to eat something. There was a bit of wood and the cooking pot, but nothing in it. That would have to be remedied. But in order to do anything, she would need some kind of trap or snare, as well as a few knives. She would have to try to trade for them, except she didn't have anything. Well, she could borrow for the time being, she supposed, and —

"*Nayaaŋŋaq,*" a new voice said.

Akłaq turned to see a woman ducking inside. She looked about thirty years or so.

"Are you of my people?" Akłaq asked dumbly.

"No, but my people traded with yours, so I know a bit of your tongue. My name's Ilannaq."

"Akłaq Balabinov."

Ilannaq nodded slowly. "Yes, we heard you married a Russian."

Akłaq felt her face burn hot. "We never actually married, but we lived like it. We told the children we were."

Ilannaq made a dismissive gesture. "I'm not here to say you were or weren't. Actually, I came by to welcome you, now that Matulik isn't leading you around everywhere and hiding you away in her house."

"Oh."

"Since you're new, I'm guessing you're probably kind of hungry."

"Starving."

"Why don't I take you out and show you around, show you the

best spots for game and forage? It'll help you get settled in, I think, make this place feel more like home and not some mismatched hoard of freaks with unusual powers."

Akłaq agreed, and soon they were out in the woods.

"Do you not enjoy being part of the village, then?" Akłaq wondered. "Do you not enjoy the Timekeeping?"

"Oh, I'm not a Timekeeper. I Harvest. Matulik and Aniqan are a little weird, since they're the opposite of how it normally goes. But, I mean, they're lovers, so I guess it works out."

Akłaq wasn't sure how to respond.

"Don't let me dissuade you, though. If you broke into Banding and Timekeeping on your own, by all means, learn." She stopped and pointed. "There's a good patch of berries there in the late summer."

And they moved on.

"How long have you been a Harvester?" Akłaq inquired conversationally.

"Eleven years, or thereabouts."

"You must have been a teenager, then."

"No, I was an adult. See, it's not just consuming a Time Capsule that awards you years. For Harvesters, just Harvesting someone will give you some extra time, a sort of bleeding effect. For Timekeepers, the more you Band and whatnot, the more years you get."

"So it's not just the three centuries I absorbed from my family, it's also—"

"—all the Banding and Timekeeping you do, too, yes." Ilannaq stopped again. "This is a good spot for foxes. Just up ahead, the ground slopes down and there are fox dens all over the place."

They went a little farther before kneeling to set a snare, using some small branches to create a funnel through the snare to the bait waiting tantalizingly on the other side.

Then they departed back to the village, Akłaq picking up a good amount of forage along the way.

"Once you start to really get into Timekeeping, your need for food will decrease," Ilannaq told her. "That's kind of why we don't really garden or anything. We'd spend more energy growing the plants only to watch them rot. Not that I want to discourage you, if you want to grow something, but you don't have to worry about feeding everyone."

Akłaq thanked her, then returned home to sort through her forage and try to prepare something.

It was the first meal she'd prepared since having lunch with Nika on the porch, and this realization saw her appetite flee. She distracted herself by remembering her Bands, remembering to stay in the present moment. It was not an easy thing to do, but she managed it, and after about half an hour she returned to her meal. Greens, tubers, flowers, herbs. With any luck, she would be able to add some fox meat to her meals soon. Then she could work on the furs and make herself some new winter clothes.

She thought about this, eating alone in her home. There was a lot of stuff still left in the cabin. Some of it she needed. She wasn't sure that she would be able to return, but maybe she could ask Matulik.

When she was done with her food, Akłaq left her house and sought out Matulik. When she approached the hut, it became apparent that the woman was rather engaged in activity. With Aniqan, if what Ilannaq said was true. Well, she could ask about it later.

This was her life now. And, short of another catastrophe, this would be her life for the next three hundred years, if not more. Although she found this hard to believe. What was she supposed to do here? Train, sure, but what else? Why had the white bear brought them to her? Why had it brought her here? What was she supposed to do next? Where was she supposed to go?

Well, it was only the first day of her new life. Her life with Nika had taken many years to build; no reason to think this wouldn't be similar. All the same, looking around the village which was conspicuously devoid of the energy and laughter of children, she had to wonder what greater destiny there could possibly be, and why only she could fulfill it.

Aniqan

Avgun Tallimat Piñasrut
The Next Step

A year went by. Starting out, Akłaq had made great progress in her Banding, or so it felt like to her, though she knew she was far less skilled than any of the Timekeepers in the village.

In the fall, though, as the weather got cooler and the leaves turned, some kind of dam in her mind burst.

She was supposed to be harvesting the crops with her children.

She was supposed to lie with Nika to make another child.

They were supposed to go into town together for trading and other things.

They were supposed to cuddle up together to watch the snow and wait out the winter.

Her training came to a sudden halt, and there were times where she may as well have not trained at all for as much control as she had over herself and her Bands.

She had convinced Matulik to return to the cabin and fetch some things for her, and she had gathered these things, all of her things, and effectively made a nest, or perhaps a hibernation den, which she crawled into for the winter. Outside, the sun still showed its face during the day for a short period, but inside Akłaq's house there was only darkness and sorrow, and several times she considered killing herself. She may have had more years in her life, but she was still mortal.

As the snows closed in, she thought of the things she had felt when she opened the Time Capsules, the people her children would have grown into. She began to question whether she had really felt such things, or if she had merely wished it so.

Matulik, Ilannaq, and other women had visited frequently. Some just sat quietly, working on furs or other projects. Some had tried to engage her in conversation, of which she was a sorry participant. She wanted company, just not this company. She wanted to be bugged by her children. She wanted Nika to annoy her. She wanted to curl up with all of them and read a story and fall asleep by the fire.

Then the days began to grow long. Then the snows began to melt.

Then Ujurak and the male leaders declared the moon of preparation, time to pack things up and be ready to move.

It was during this time, as Akłaq was now forced to come out of her den or risk being left behind, that she was able to bring herself back to the present moment.

"I was under the impression that this village did not move," she confessed to Ilannaq as the woman helped her to pack up. "Among my people, we had a spring migration and a fall migration, and several smaller moves in between sometimes. We moved for more favorable weather and to keep up with the migrating herds. But if Timekeepers and Harvesters eat but rarely, and we made no move to outrun the weather—"

Ilannaq nodded. "I understand; my people were the same way. But this move is not for the animals or the weather. We move to keep our traditions alive and frustrate those who would try to enslave us."

Akłaq puzzled over her words, suddenly feeling very out of sorts, as though she truly had hibernated and let several months of her life slip by. Had she Banded her way through the time, or just let her mind sink into murky shadows? She looked at the fur blanket in her hands, fairly certain that she had made it, but unsure just when.

"The Russians?" she said, replying to Ilannaq. "Nika said they were on the run, returning to their own land."

"They are, yes," Ilannaq acknowledged, "but you have experienced their wrath as they leave."

"If they can't have our land, no one can."

"Yes. But in the south, the British abuse other peoples, causing some to flee north and west and seek refuge where their abusers have no interest, or where those interests are more invested."

"The Hudson Bay Company."

The women each grabbed a couple baskets and went out to secure them to sleds. Most people still used dogsleds, though there were also a handful of horses and even a few reindeer to pull heavier loads.

"Where are we going?"

"We have a village east of here, at the foot of the mountains. We'll stay there for a year. It's well protected, and we may come across someone from the south who can tell us what is happening there."

"You don't sound overly concerned."

"About the south? The British?" Ilannaq shook her head and made another loop on her strap. "No. My concern is the Russians."

The two women went back inside to grab more stuff.

"I know I am not the best Timekeeper," Akłaq began, "but it would seem to me that Banding would be very advantageous in a fight, to slow down your opponent to counter their attacks, to attack them when they are unaware of you."

Ilannaq nodded. "That is true, and the men—well, the Timekeepers do make use of this advantage when they can."

"But...?"

Ilannaq faced her. "If Time, and Banding especially, have any great weakness, it is fire. I don't understand how it works exactly because I never cared to learn Timekeeping, but Banding does not affect the air, and fire and wind are intertwined. If you try to cut them off from each other, well, it's not good. I saw a man try once, over a cook fire. He's lucky that the worst it did was burn his facial hair. He walked around all summer with no eyebrows, eyelashes, or beard. Even the hair of his head was damaged, as were his clothes."

"Oh."

"So, yes, it is terrible what the British and the Americans are doing to the people in the south and east, but when it comes to the Russians and how they seek to burn our villages, we have as much defense as the villagers being murdered."

Akłaq thought about this as they continued to tear down until there was little left but some old fire pits and a couple of the more permanent houses. Matulik caught her studying them as they moved out.

"They're built like the British and American homes in the south," she explained, guiding Akłaq away from them and onto a trail only the long-time residents knew. "They're not intended for travel."

"Nika and I lived in a cabin like that," Akłaq said. "It was small, but then he added on another room for the children. He made mention once of adding another room, so the girls and boys could sleep separately."

Matulik's gaze was gentle. "How many children did you expect to have?"

Akłaq thought a moment. "I don't know." She blinked rapidly as her eyes misted over, and she wiped tears from her cheeks. "Miiyuk was asking if it was possible for us to plant her a baby sister because she was tired of having so many brothers."

"Oh really? And what did you tell her?"

"I told her that, no, we didn't get to pick what kind of baby came from the baby seeds. We were just as surprised as anyone."

Matulik grinned.

Akłaq wiped away more tears, but her sadness was slowly morphing into something else. "Why did they have to die? Maybe Nika had done terrible things in the past, maybe he hadn't, but why did they have to take my children? Why...why did the white bear have to condemn my children to death?"

Now Matulik's expression turned confused. "What are you saying?"

"Why couldn't the white bear have gotten you to us sooner? Why couldn't it have guided you to us in time to stop them from killing my children? I might still have followed you back to the village. If Aniqan Harvested Nika, I still could have taken his years. I could have joined you."

"Would you have, though?" Matulik questioned. "We can't have children, Akłaq. I know that is what gave you pause, but you had nothing left. If they had lived, and if you had come, you would not be thinking about Timekeeping or Harvesting or any of it. You would have been thinking of your children, how they would have needed a community, needed a father. A father we might have provided, for a while, until you began to age and he did not. And we have no children for them to play with. You would have moved on."

So it still came back to her unwillingness to follow the white bear that fateful day when she met Nika, because she had allowed her immediate needs and desires to overrule her intended path.

"So then what's the next step?" Akłaq inquired intentionally. "Do I simply continue to learn Banding and strengthen my Bands indefinitely? Do I go with you the next time Ujurak has a vision or guidance from his *tuuṅaq*?"

"Actually, the next step is to introduce you to all the other Time Agents from around the world and bring you before the Hands of Time to let them know that you are joining us," Matulik answered simply.

"How are we to accomplish this, being merely on foot?"

"This is not done on foot. Or by horse, or by boat. We simply open a doorway anywhere we need to go."

"What?" Akłaq struggled to envision such a thing.

Matulik nodded.

Akłaq gave her a look. "Then why did it take so long for you to come to us? Why didn't you stop the Russians?"

The women kept her voice level. "It is something that you will understand as you learn how to open Paa, but it is a terribly difficult feat, even if you know where you are going. If you don't know, if can be nearly impossible. We didn't know where we were going when we followed the white bear, so we had to take the long path. And on top of that, the horses aren't the most enthusiastic about it either, for it is taxing even to cross a Paa."

Her explanation fell on mostly deaf ears as Akłaq tried to reconcile everything she was seeing and learning, even by speech alone. How was all of this possible? How was it that they could have such incredible power, and yet fall short on some of the most crucial details?

"And who are the Hands of Time?" Akłaq asked.

"Fifty-one Hands govern the usage of Time across the universe and oversee all Time Agents of all disciplines and ranks," Aniqan said, riding up alongside them. "They reside within the Wheel of Time."

"And where is that?"

"It is its own place, its own location, connected to nothing and everything."

"That makes no sense."

"And it won't, even after you see it. Your best bet is to simply focus on your mission, what you are there to do, and not linger too long."

Akłaq glanced at Matulik, but the woman appeared to support the assessment.

"Who are the Hands?" Akłaq asked again. "Are they elders?"

"Chieftains, of a kind," Aniqan answered. "Once a Time Agent advances so far in his training and discipline, he has a chance to become a leader of that discipline, or a related discipline."

"So there are more kinds of...Time Agents, more than just Timekeepers, Harvesters, and Merchants?"

"There are Scouts as well," Matulik told her, "those who travel far and wide, seeking out new worlds. And secretaries, who keep everything maintained." She went on before Akłaq could speak. "It's easier to show than explain, and even then, we are so few and so isolated, a majority of it doesn't affect us."

Now Putu spoke; somehow he had ridden up to their group without them noticing. "It should also be understood that what we do is frowned upon, even illegal, according to the Laws of Time, and we are called Runners."

"What do you mean?" Akłaq wondered.

"It is expected that every Time Capsule that is Harvested will go to the Merchants to be purified and sold. This is the way of things, or so the Hands proclaim. For us to take Time Capsules and use them on ourselves, give them away to others, especially those who have little or no understanding of our work, it is against their laws." He went on, "The reason that we have not been apprehended is twofold: first, our group is, as Matulik said, small and isolated, difficult to reach and hardly worth pursuing in the grand scheme of things; second, the Timekeepers who are normally dedicated to our apprehension, well, they are right here helping us."

"So the Hands of Time are Russians? Or British? They seem very intent on expanding their influence and making money."

"Neither," Matulik told her. "You will understand when you meet them."

"When am I to do that?"

"Once we reach the village and are settled in. Then I will take you."

Akłaq was still uncertain, but she did not argue. How could she? She was in no position to say one way or the other what was true and what was not. Just two years ago, she would have called it all preposterous, yet here she was.

They reached the village without incident. Like the previous settlement, it was quite small with only a few permanent dwellings. The horses and reindeer were tied out to forage, the dogs loosed from their harnesses, and the people went to work setting up their houses.

Like many instances before, Akłaq felt a sense of calm drape itself over her as she unloaded her things and went to work arranging them in her home. This was her life now. This was how things were now. Nika was gone. Her children were gone. If given half a chance, she would bring them back, but that was no longer at the forefront of her every thought.

She remembered telling Nika about how her youngest sister had been abandoned in the snow as a baby because the clan could not care for her. He'd thought it outlandish and even atrocious. And it wasn't to say that it had been an easy decision or that her mother hadn't wept, but it was life. Sometimes hard decisions had to be made when the people fell on hard times.

This was what she told herself as she arranged the mementos from the cabin. Miiyuk's doll, the carved animals, the blanket, and Nika's pipe. It was how things were. The people had to keep moving.

Once she was satisfied that things were arranged just so, she made herself a small meal. She was not quite feeling the effects of the Banding just yet, but Matulik said that she wouldn't really start feeling it for another year or so, once they really started training and she started to go out with them and actually use her abilities. But to get to that point, she had to go to the Wheel of Time in order to meet the Hands of Time. After eating, she left her home to find Matulik.

"Won't they be upset that we are coming before them as Runners?" Akłaq inquired of her mentor. "What is to stop them from arresting us right there?"

"Because they don't know that we're Runners," Matulik answered simply, grinning. "They don't know unless they're told, and the ones who would tell them are the ones who are breaking their rules. If we don't tell on ourselves, they'll never know." She nodded. "So, are you ready?"

As ready as she would ever be.

The two women went to Ujurak, the only one who was apparently qualified to open a Paa. Akłaq did not know what she expected, but was she saw was not it. He opened a door in thin air. It did not appear to have any physical dimensions, nor any frame on which to rest, yet there before her was a doorway, a Paa, to another place.

And it wasn't just any place. This was like no place Akłaq had ever seen or could even comprehend. Floor and walls of metal, and beasts of all sizes and forms, with multiple heads and legs and indescribable features except that perhaps they were spirits.

Matulik, still grinning, grabbed her hand and stepped through the Paa.

Akłaq was suddenly squeezed from all sides. As a girl, she had once fallen into a river and been swept downstream. The current was strong but her lungs were not. She remembered the tightness, the panic, the darkness closing in. An uncle had rescued her, dragging her back to shore where she spit up at least half the river.

Walking through the Paa was a very similar experience, just

without the water.

"It never really improves," Matulik told her, helping her to her feet. She also appeared a bit pale.

Akłaq opened her mouth to speak, but could find no words.

They stood in a long corridor of Paa, each one leading to a different place. Some looked almost familiar, as field or forest or town, and some were completely foreign. This was not even counting the creatures.

"Is this...this can't be the *kiuġuyat*," she said finally.

"No. This is the Wheel of Time. And these are aliens, creatures from the stars."

"Spirits?"

"No. Other worlds."

Akłaq looked around. She remembered some of the things the Russians had taught, about the stars and the solar system. Never had they said anything about alien creatures living on the other planets.

"Are they animals, then?" she asked, following Matulik down the Paa corridor.

"Not at all," Matulik said. "They are people of their own worlds. And this is where all worlds meet."

The corridor opened up into a larger room where many such creatures waited in line. The two women joined them and eventually came to a machine where Matulik grabbed two small devices and instructed her in how to assemble it on her person. A cloth went around her neck, and a small metal piece went in her ear.

"This will help others understand our speech," Matulik explained. "And we can understand others."

Akłaq took the earpiece and studied it, felt the cloth around her neck. "How is this possible?"

"By means not yet realized on Earth. Come on. Let's get you to the Hands."

"Are they also...like these...people?" Akłaq was struggling to take it all in and again felt as though she were drowning, or maybe going through a Paa.

"They are," Matulik confirmed.

Before she could dwell on this for too long, they stepped through another Paa—this one no different than any common door—into a room that made Akłaq's head spin.

People and creatures walked on walls, on the ceiling, moving this way and that through a multitude of Paa. There were more people in this one place than she had seen in her entire life. She could hardly fathom so many people, never mind that they did not look like people. Her heart jumped into her throat as Matulik took her up a flight of stairs, only for those stairs to somehow change so that they were suddenly walking on a wall which, by her perspective, was now the floor. Something had shifted in her mind, but she didn't know quite what, and she didn't like it.

Fear seized her and she remained rooted to the floor. Matulik was several steps away before noticing her absence. She stopped and turned.

"Well, come on," she said, making a motion.

"I can't," Akłaq squeaked, tears leaking from her eyes for no discernible reason. "I can't."

Matulik sighed and approached, grabbing her hand and getting her away from the stairs where beings of all shapes and sizes were bumping into her, trying to get where they wanted to go. Their mouths made strange sounds and yet Akłaq heard them as if they spoke her own tongue through the metal piece in her ear.

"I can learn and understand a lot of things," Akłaq gasped, her chest tight. "But this...what is this, Matulik? What...?" She wiped her face, feeling light-headed.

"What happened to the isolation you are so used to? When did the world get so big?" Matulik nodded sympathetically. "I understand. I do. And if you don't want to go through with this, there is still time to turn back. You will still keep the years you absorbed from the Time Capsules, but—"

"I can't go back," Akłaq cut in. "But I can't..."

"Listen. We're only talking to the Hands today. It's a formality.

After that, it is very rare that you will have to come back here. This isn't going to be a regular occurrence, not unless you want it to be."

Akłaq swallowed. "The white bear brought me to you for a reason. I have to keep going."

Matulik nodded. "All right. Let's keep moving."

Akłaq remained in a state of fairly perpetual terror throughout their entire trip. Half the time she was staring at the alien beings around her and half the time she was trying to avoid being stared at, feeling as though she were being hunted. Sometimes they had to watch out for larger aliens and avoid being stepped on. Other times they had to watch out and make sure they didn't squish aliens smaller than themselves.

It might not have been so traumatizing, except these appeared to be sentient beings. Through the translating devices, she heard conversations about commerce and economy, laws and government, and various home and family matters. Yes, her people had many stories of animals who spoke and lived as humans, but to see it all laid out before her very eyes was more than she thought she could take.

If she had any saving grace, it was that she didn't have to do any of the talking when going before the Hands of Time, the mysterious governing body that somehow governed millions, billions, even trillions or more throughout the universe. Her mind could barely comprehend such a number, never mind the details behind it. So many stars, so many planets, so many alien species.

She wished to return to a time before. She wished to return to the cabin, to convince Nika to leave before the soldiers found them. She wished to return to her village, convince her family to leave before the Russians burned it. Would things be very different?

What did the white bear intend for her to do, finding these people and training in this sorcery? Had this always been the goal, to bring her here? What was the purpose of all of this? The Hands of Time seemed to think of it as simple commerce and the amassing of wealth and years, but Ujurak and the people had made it so much more. What, then, did that say about the spirits and the white bear itself?

Once the Hands agreed to allow her to train under Matulik, she was too happy to return to the village and the peace and solitude of her home, though she still found herself wishing for the company of her husband and children.

"I will let you think about the things you have seen," Matulik said from the door. "Ujurak is happy to offer guidance and answer questions. Otherwise, we will continue training in the morning."

And she left.

Avgun Qulinnuġutaiḷaq
Mission

As it turned out, simple Bands were the easiest part of Timekeeping. Internal Bands, they were called, where they only affected the user. External Bands were those that involved other people, and it was a surprisingly difficult concept.

"Is it because you're also a Timekeeper?" Akłaq wondered, having tried and failed multiple times to Band both herself and Matulik.

The woman shook her head. "No. That has little, if anything to do with it. But people relate differently to their surroundings, not only the forest and the mountains, but the people and the very air around us. Our lives, our memories, our experiences, even our present dispositions, all tied together to make us who we are."

Akłaq considered this. Then, "So what you're saying is, I need to stop expecting that Banding you is the same as Banding myself, stop trying to impose myself upon you. Instead, I should meet you where you are and draw you to me."

Even as she said it, it was like giving her mentor a hug, but from ten feet away with a Band. Perhaps it was more like enveloping them both in the same blanket. It was not flawless, and the metaphorical blanket had many holes and loose strings, but it wasn't bad for a first attempt.

"I see you, and I understand you," Akłaq said, releasing the Band. "How is this done on strangers whom I have never met, never seen, and who may need saving faster than such time allows?"

Matulik grinned. "This is only your first success, Akłaq, and I know it will not be your last. You are still thinking about it, analyzing it. One day, it will just come to you, as second nature as your Internal Bands are becoming. One day, you will even have Reflexive Banding to aid you."

"I assume this is a Band that happens automatically."

"Of a sort, yes. But it is not something to worry about today."

Matulik made a motion that said training was done for the day. She again congratulated Akłaq on her progress, and the women parted ways, each to her own dwelling.

The days were rapidly shortening, and the chill in the air had long since turned into frost on the ground and overnight snows. Akłaq hurried home in the dying light and added a few logs to her fire. She was far from tired, but there was little she could do in the dark besides menial tasks and minor hobbies.

As she picked up a piece of clothing that needed some repair, she looked around her cozy yet empty home and noted that it was a year and a half since Nika and her children had been murdered. She still knew in her heart that if given the chance she would bring them all back, but now her thoughts were more fixated on the emptiness of her home.

She hadn't fully accepted that she would never again have children. Matulik had promised that her cycles would eventually cease, but so far they hadn't done much more than become a tad bit irregular, nothing she hadn't experienced before. Maybe there was still hope, if she could find the right man.

Their little village of about sixty was comprised primarily of women, numbering about forty or so. The remaining men were all claimed by at least two or three women. Even Aniqan did not belong exclusively to Matulik. And yet, interactions were actually rather infrequent, more of a passing fancy than a true desire to make love and have children. She wasn't sure how she felt about that.

But she wouldn't say that, at least in the last moon or two, she hadn't looked at a few of the men and wondered.

The following morning—using the term loosely as it was still quite dark—Akłaq had just finished up her breakfast when Matulik entered her home and said Ujurak wished to see her.

Curious, Akłaq stood and went at once. The shaman had never summoned her before. Oh, they exchanged greetings and small talk and were generally friendly, but this was a new occasion and she didn't know what to expect.

"Welcome, Akłaq," Ujurak greeted as she ducked inside his small home.

Also inside was Aniqan and a woman by the name of Atuat. They greeted her, and then the three of them waited to hear what the shaman had to say.

"Another vision?" Atuat wondered.

Ujurak dipped his head once. "Indeed. You are to go south, where a woodpecker nests upon the moose, and meet with those who camp there. They have news we may be interested in." He gestured toward Akłaq. "Take her and teach her our ways."

Akłaq couldn't help but feel a little excited, and as she followed Aniqan and Atuat out of the shaman's home, she felt, too, that the air she breathed was somehow new. Maybe it was just her, because her next deep breath only reminded her of how cold it was.

Aniqan and Atuat knew well what was expected of them, and neither said anything when Aniqan departed for his home. Atuat, however, stuck with Akłaq.

"I will help you to prepare," the woman told her, not unkindly. "It would be wise, in the future, to have a bag at least half-prepared so that if Ujurak sends you out, you will have some of your things ready."

"I'm sorry, I didn't know he would call on me," Akłaq said. "I feel so new to all of this still."

"That may be, but he will not knowingly send you into a danger he does not believe you can handle."

They reached Akłaq's home and ducked inside. "Do you know where we're going?"

"I have an idea." Atuat grabbed a bag. "This ought to do."

While she grabbed items as Atuat requested or suggested, Akłaq continued to speak. "What people are we likely to meet?"

Atuat grinned. "There are all kinds of people in this world, Akłaq." At Akłaq's look, she relented just a little. "I can't say for sure. It used to be that we always knew who our neighbors were, and we knew them well. With the Russians in the west and the Canadian British in the east and the Americans in the south, they stir up enough trouble that we are meeting people we never knew existed. It could be a trapper camp that we're approaching, or a gathering of southern peoples who are quite ill-prepared for a northern winter."

"Ujurak said they would have news and information. What do you think is most likely?"

Now Atuat frowned. "Southern people. Trappers are only here for the furs; they don't like to talk about news and politics. That's half the reason they're out here is to get away from all that. I don't blame them."

Akłaq nodded. "We never had any real problems with the trappers and fur traders. You had good men and bad ones, those who would bargain fairly and those who wouldn't. It's when the soldiers came that things started turning ugly."

"That's how it usually is."

By the time they finished packing and returned to the center of the village, Aniqan was ready and waiting for them. Atuat had only to reach inside her house to grab her bag. With all of them ready—Akłaq feeling less confident than the others portrayed—they grabbed a few horses and started out.

"When the snow gets deep, that's when we bring the dogs," Atuat explained. "For now, though, we can still use the horses."

Akłaq just nodded, unsure how to respond. Her people had always used dogs. The Russians understood the concept as well, though they had brought their horses over, too. The great beasts had not been the most suited for the climate, but they had their uses.

Silence was preferred when out on the trail, although Aniqan occasionally asked her to practice her Banding. Seeing how she had only just figured out External Bands—that being on a single person only —her efforts to Band three people and three horses were less than successful. The horses themselves were remarkably tolerant of her efforts, though even they became agitated after half a dozen tries.

"Are the horses exposed to Time?" Akłaq inquired. "Are they able to Band and such?"

Atuat chuckled but Aniqan looked thoughtful. "The animals are exposed to Time during our travels, and I can't say that we've never had a dog or a horse or a reindeer that could Band—not consciously, mind you, it was very much like your first exposure, when you would Band at random. But whenever an animal does show signs of this, we butcher them for meat."

"Why? Animals can be trained to do a lot of things—"

"Yes, and while animals have great spirit, their perception of time is different than ours. We think of time as going forward, wishing for it to go back, making it go faster or slower, conjuring on ourselves or on others. For animals, time simply is. It is the present moment, and all things simply are. All is one. The ability to Band augments our perceptions, but it hinders theirs. It can actually make an animal more dangerous, even the docile ones."

Akłaq considered this, and the three of them rode in silence. It gave her something to think about, anyway, something new to mull over.

Animals with the ability to bend Time made them more dangerous. It seemed somewhat logical. She supposed. And what did it do to people? She looked at Aniqan, then at Atuat, and back ahead between her horse's ears.

Other than having little interest in sexual activity, the people seemed to be fairly normal. They had a purpose in their lives, Harvesting the memories of the dying and saving them within the living for future generations, but otherwise they carried out their daily lives as they always had, or so it appeared to her. Perhaps there were some modifications and allowances, but things did seem rather the same.

The same.

Why, with such tremendous abilities, were things the same? Akłaq was only just starting out in her abilities, but considering even just

Matulik's experience and strength, why wouldn't it be possible to Band something or someone else, be it a prey animal—or a predator for that matter—or an enemy soldier, walk up, and kill him? Akłaq had no experience with trying to Band fire, as everyone agreed that it was a terrible idea, but what about stopping things before it got to that point? Why not Band and kill the man with the torch?

She did not voice her thoughts aloud, for she wanted to think on them more and perhaps ask Ujurak herself. Or maybe even Matulik. Maybe there were more advanced rules that she had not yet learned. Goodness knew she hadn't been in her right mind for most of the first year, and overloading her with rules and abilities and warnings and everything else would have been too much for her to handle.

"Is it possible to Band someone else who isn't a Time Agent?" she inquired instead, hoping she sounded casually curious.

"Of course," Aniqan replied simply. "You can Band anything and anyone you want. The animals aren't overly fond of it, so I would refrain from testing on them."

"We wouldn't appreciate it too much either," Atuat added. "If you want to try something, wait until we ask, or until we get back."

Akłaq nodded once, and they again lapsed into silence.

Band anyone or anything, and this was the best they could do? If Akłaq had had these abilities when her village was burned, she might have killed the soldiers before they could set torch to tinder. If she had had these abilities when her family was murdered, she could have Banded the soldiers and killed them before they could murder her husband and her children.

Why couldn't Aniqan and the others have Banded and gotten to them that much quicker, maybe saved her oldest son, maybe stopped it from happening at all so she and her family could have lived blissfully unaware? Or had they Banded, and that was why she was alive at all?

It was all very frustrating to think about, and having ample time on the road to let her thoughts brew did her no favors.

As it turned out, the place where the woodpecker nests upon the moose was in fact a rock formation through which a tree had grown, and the two together formed the shape of the moose, with a great mass of dead branches forming the moose's "antlers" and providing ample shelter and food for a family of woodpeckers. This place was four days from the village, though they could guess that the people who camped beside the formation had been traveling a lot longer than that.

There were five of them, four men and a woman. While their camp and supplies suggested they were or had been prepared for their journey, their expressions said they were no happier for it.

"Welcome, friends," Aniqan greeted amiably, halting his horse but not dismounting. Akłaq and Atuat followed suit.

"Hello," one of the men replied, struggling to form the basic greeting of a language that was clearly not his own. The man reached for a bag and fished for something inside. Akłaq did not initially understand what he pulled out, but then she was catching something that was tossed her way. It took her a moment to recognize the translator device from the Wheel of Time, the cloth for the neck and the ear piece.

"Now that we may speak comfortably," Aniqan went on, "what brings you our way?"

"News," the first man replied simply, "and trade. Am I correct to assume that Ujurak saw this in a vision and that is why and how you have come to meet with us here?"

"You are correct. Mostly I think he wanted to get our newest member more comfortable with his visions, what he sees and how he sends us out." Aniqan gestured toward Akłaq.

"I see. And what is your name, dear?"

"Akłaq," she answered.

The man dipped his head once. "Well, my name is Yellow Grass. This is Owl, Lion, Swiftly Nocks an Arrow, and Last Light. We are Time Agents from the south."

"Surely there must be a better way to travel and deliver news?"

"If there is, we've not discovered it." Yellow Grass shrugged. "Portal travel is dangerous and fickle, and we do not have anyone skilled in the art of direct travel, at least..." His tone turned grudging. " — none who will help us, or that we would ask anyway."

"Maybe not, but it is not so far to the village now," Aniqan said. "Tie your bags to the horses, and you can tell us your news on the way."

The five travelers did as they were bid, packing up their camp and tying off their bags to the horses. Once everything was secured, the group turned around and headed north.

"We had hoped you would be in this village," Owl mentioned. "We had little desire to journey yet another moon to your other settlement and possibly have to winter here."

His tone was teasing, as was Aniqan's when he responded, "You know Ujurak would send you home, or get you close, anyway."

"All the same, we are glad to have found you here."

"What news from the south, then?" Atuat inquired politely.

"Nothing good," Lion growled. "The United States government has removed as many Native peoples as they can—Cherokee, Choctaw, all of them—and now they're displacing even their own people."

"Where are they supposed to go?"

"West. That's all they care about. Out of colonial lands."

"But there are people in the West, too. Natives, British. Where are they really supposed to go?"

"Quite frankly," Owl cut in, "they're supposed to die." He made a helpless gesture. "That is the real end goal here, just like the first removal. They're supposed to die. If any of them are stubborn enough to live, well, they're not going to have much."

"How does this affect us?" Akłaq wondered. "Surely they're not going to try to come north?"

Owl laughed. "No, of course not. If they truly want to flee, they have only to turn to the Krydik and be whisked away to a fabled, magical land of safety and prosperity." He snorted a laugh at this. "No one wants your frozen wasteland, believe me."

Akłaq just blinked and looked forward, through her horse's ears. She didn't know who the Krydik were, or the Cherokee or Choctaw for that matter. She knew some of the southern peoples, if only from passing mention from the Russian priest, but it seemed as though there were people even farther south than that.

"What other news?" Aniqan prompted.

"Oh, the usual discontent from the whites," Swiftly Nocks an Arrow said, waving a hand dismissively. "The western peoples of the Pacific want to become their own land. The far eastern peoples of 'New England' want to become their own land. Some of the southern United States are trying to become their own land. The land of Canada is experiencing a bit of unhappiness. A new fur trading company is trying to compete with Hudson Bay."

"And where do they expect to go that Hudson Bay does not already claim?" Atuat asked.

Arrow shrugged and gave her a look. "I think they mean to scour the same land and employ the same peoples." He shrugged again. "I don't know the details, but it doesn't sound like things are going to change much."

"And what of your problems with the Russians?" Yellow Grass inquired. "Are they still burning villages?"

"No," Aniqan reported slowly. "They're trying to sell the land to the United States, as if it is theirs to give at all. Considering the Americans are engaged in war against their own brothers, I cannot imagine that they would be much better rulers even if they did 'buy' the land. Our peoples have been decimated, but we are finding new opportunities to rebuild."

He glanced at Akłaq as he said it, and for just a moment, she knew a kind of curiosity about him. Then it was gone, and the conversation resumed.

"I am sorry you continue to have such troubles," Owl was saying. "I fear the troubles of the south will only continue unabated also."

"It is as you said," Atuat said with a hint of malice, "if the southern peoples truly are desperate, they can call on the Krydik."

"Who are the Krydik?" Akłaq blurted.

"A bunch of pompous pricks is what," Lion told her. "An offshoot of the Cherokee, mixed with anyone cowardly enough to run away from a fight rather than face their enemies. Choctaw, Sioux, Anishinaabek. They dine like kings and look like apples, and about once every decade they send a few of their fattened hogs back to the people to offer them refuge. Supposedly they've actually sent fighting men this time, to fight in the American war, but that's just more of their meddling without knowing what they're really doing; they just want to look like they're helping."

" 'Look like apples'?" she echoed, glancing at Aniqan.

"A southern phrase," he explained. "Apple Indian. Red on the outside, but white on the inside."

She nodded once, still unsure.

The conversation moved away from true news and instead dwindled into discontented grumbling, each man echoing and reinforcing the thoughts of the others.

Meanwhile, Akłaq was just trying to wrap her head around everything she'd seen and experienced in the last moon. Conjuring doors out of thin air, walking on walls and ceilings, looking upon a multitude of creatures impossible to imagine if they had not stood all around her, and now hearing news of peoples who had not existed in her mind before now. What was she supposed to do with it all? How was she supposed to react? And who were the Krydik that they lived in safety yet garnered such hostility because of it?

Even when they finally stopped to make camp and rest, she could not find sleep right away. She wanted to know so much more, and yet she was also terribly afraid. Things were not going well for any of the peoples, except, perhaps, her own, now that the Russians were leaving. Everyone else was being made to suffer, taken from their homes, children taken from their parents.

"Do you also do what we do here?" she inquired of the travelers the following morning once they were back on the move. "Do you save the memories of the dead and give them to the living?"

"When we are able to, yes," the woman, Last Light, answered. "But we cannot be everywhere at once. Just as you are only fifty strong for this vast expanse of land, we are only two hundred for an even greater expanse of land. The people are being removed and dying by the thousands, sometimes publicly, sometimes not. We do what we can, but more often than not, it is but a drop in a pitcher of water."

A dam burst in Akłaq's mouth. "Why not make more Time Agents, more Harvesters? Why not get everyone to help? Why not make more Timekeepers who can Band your enemies, freeze them in time so you may kill them? You speak of fighting back, but you don't use the tools you have available."

For a long moment, there was silence. It was Yellow Grass who answered, "We try not to attract attention to ourselves. Doing as you have suggested, it would start out much the same as when any conquerors came to our lands, be they Russian or British or French. They had guns, cannons, other superior weaponry to force us to cooperate. Yes, in using Time, we would have victory. At first. But other Time Agents, those who are not so sympathetic, they would take notice. And they would come. And now both sides have guns and cannons. It would only bring war. And it would be war of a variety that humanity is not ready for."

"Surely there must be a way to use this gift for more than hollow comfort for grieving, dying families. What is the purpose of Harvesting an old man if all his children are dead or dying also? Who carries the traditions of the people then?"

"You are not the first to have such thoughts," Owl told her. "And I will not claim that I have never done as you suggested. But we must choose our battles, choose when to take a life in such a way. It is not so simple as a massacre."

"But if both sides have a deadly weapon, does it not force respect and thoughtful actions on the part of both sides, knowing that the choices they make carry more consequence?"

"Yes, and we have given thoughtful consideration to our actions, knowing that we have the greater tool, the greater weapon. We cannot do to others what they have done to us and not expect some kind of retaliation."

Lion nodded in agreement. "Furthermore, there is something even darker brewing in the Time industry, whispers from across the great eastern ocean. Dark sorceries that reach beyond Time but also into it, even corrupting the Hands themselves."

Aniqan made a sound. "This is the real news you have come to tell us."

"It is."

"Well then we should return as fast as possible."

Atuat got the hint and Banded their entire party, bringing everything around them to a standstill.

Avgun Qulit
Nebulous Darkness

Ujurak welcomed Yellow Grass and his people as if he had been anticipating their arrival for a year. For all anyone knew, he had been. Aniqan, Atuat, and Akłaq were permitted to stay and listen to the news from the southerners.

Most of it had already been discussed on the road, the removal of the Cherokee and other peoples, the discontent of the various regions and the desire for independence among the whites, and assorted minor gossip.

Eventually, however, the news became dull and dry; it was fascinating, but little of it affected the Time Agents so far to the north. The only thing that might affect them was the darkness which Lion had mentioned.

"For the sake of your newest member, I will try to explain how this all started, or how this recently started," he began, turning toward Akłaq. "There is a group that calls themselves the Akarin. They believe in sorceries that give them power over not just Time, but also Matter and Energy, the ability to make the wind blow or turn dust into salt, things of that nature—"

"Can they?" Akłaq interrupted.

"I have never seen it for myself, but there are others whom I trust who claim to have witnessed such things." Lion made a dismissive motion. "On the whole, they are called Akari-bearers. Their primary spirit, their god if you will, is someone they call the Author. This Author, like any god I suppose, has great power and he governs the Akarin faithful, dictating their lives as stories, speaking or writing everything into existence."

"Sounds similar to the Orthodox God the priests taught."

Lion shrugged. "Maybe, maybe not. The more vague the god, the more they sound alike."

"What changed?"

"The Akarin only ever had scraps of writing from their Author deity," Arrow continued. "A short passage, a paragraph, a sentence, all of it they believe came from this Author. But then, about sixty years ago, there appeared what they claim is the first true Authored Book."

Akłaq shrugged and made an odd motion. "So it's a religious text, so what? How is it different from the Bible or anything else?"

"To an outsider, it wouldn't be significant," Lion told her. "But the ramifications of such a thing split the Akarin. For one, the Book is the first 'new' writing of the Author in a very long time. For two, it follows the lives of two men here on Earth. Native men. Cherokee, to be specific, and it describes what we now understand as the founding of the Krydik people."

"What?"

"Some in the Akarin called the Book heresy," Aniqan continued. "Others, primarily alien races, didn't like that it so clearly followed a couple of humans, a nobody race in the larger context of the universe. Still others didn't like that it followed a couple of Native men specifically. The vast majority of Time Agents and so-called Akari-bearers on Earth are of European descent."

Akłaq shook her head. "But that was sixty years ago you said."

"The Book appeared sixty years ago," Owl said. "It took some time for the splitting of the Akarin to really, permanently manifest itself. And even then, once a group breaks off, it takes time to establish itself as self-sustaining and functional."

"What has changed?" Ujurak asked slowly, seriously.

"One of these groups has become more than self-sustaining, they have become ambitious. Some speculated that they somehow influenced the United States government to order the various removals, looking for evidence of Time or Akarin influence among the Native peoples, maybe trying to capture Krydik members themselves seeing how the Book is a bit light on the details concerning their exact location. There was also speculation that they were trying to infiltrate or even subvert the Time industry. Rumors abound, many of them started by the Akarin themselves who would just as soon see this group snuffed out but without drawing too much attention to themselves. Things have been quiet for a while, but there are rumblings that the Zero Hour himself was in on it, and he's since gone missing."

"How does this concern us?" Atuat asked. "We heard of the turmoil of the Missing Zero Hour and took care to avoid it. By the time Akłaq was made a probationary Timekeeper, things were functional again."

"It's because of the Krydik," Arrow said, his expression annoyed. "They keep popping up when and where they are not wanted, like a burrowing animal with many tunnels and many holes. Their presence in the war, combined with the plight of the peoples, some of whom would rather fight and die than be removed from their land...it is fast becoming a toxic brew. The common man would see it erupt as simple war, but there would be terrible ripple effects for Time Agents as well as any of these...Akari-bearers." He nodded. "And that is when trouble may reach even you, even here."

"Because this group is so intent on wiping out the subject of this Book—the Krydik—that they will go after any indigenous Time Agent, just to be sure," Ujurak mused.

"Yes."

The shaman frowned. "This is troubling news."

"Is there anything more about this that you can say for certain?" Aniqan inquired.

"For certain?" Owl gave him a look. "No. I can tell you the most prominent rumors, though."

"Why not?" Atuat sighed, gesturing for him to proceed.

"Some say that this heretical group was led by a former African slave—"

"That makes no sense," Arrow cut in. "If they already don't like the

Book being about Native men, they wouldn't let themselves be led by an African."

Owl put his hands up. "As I said, prominent rumors, but rumors only. Others say it is led by an Englishwoman. Still others say that this is but a militant sect of the Akarin and that is why they won't actually go after them. Another rumor claims that there are more Authored Books to be found, that the Akarin have been suppressing this information for years, and that is why other groups split off."

"But none of this is pertinent to us," Ujurak said. "It matters little who or what their leader is, the fact remains that they seem to have an underlying goal directed against indigeneous peoples. It may start with the Krydik or the Cherokee, but if they cannot find what they are looking for, it will no doubt spread to others, farther and farther until it reaches us. And, as you said, there will be ripple effects within the Time industry, especially if the Zero Hour is part of this in some way."

"We deal so little with the Time industry, though, aside from official training, do you really think it would affect us?" Atuat wondered.

"We must leave nothing to chance," the shaman told her, not unkindly. He turned to the visitors. "Thank you for bringing us these developments. I will seek guidance in this matter. You are welcome to stay as long as you like and take advantage of our hospitality. When you are ready, you may ask me to open a Paa for you so you may return home."

The visitors made motions of thanks and deference.

"Thank you, Ujurak," Yellow Grass said sincerely. "For as difficult as our journey is to get here, your kindness makes it well worth the trip."

The five southerners left the hut, followed by Atuat, Aniqan, and lastly Akłaq.

The day was long since over and snow was falling in fat, wet flakes. Akłaq grabbed her bag and returned to her home, happy to see everything was exactly as she had left it. Not only that, but someone had even started a fire for her to chase away the chill of disuse. She unpacked a few things, but her longing for her own bed saw her retire to an early sleep.

Yellow Grass and the others were still in the village come morning, greeting old friends and trading more minute gossip, handing a translator to whomever they spoke to, taking it back when they were done.

Akłaq had never met a southerner before this group, and even they proclaimed that they were farther north than a majority of the Native peoples. You had the Cherokee and the Choctaw of the southeast, the Apache and Navajo of the southwest. Most of the people of the great south had already been killed or assimilated by the Spanish, though there remained small pockets of Aztec and Mayan people, or their mixed descendants anyway. None of the visitors had ever been quite that far south, but they heard stories.

"Good morning."

Akłaq turned to see Last Light approaching. She walked like a woman unaccustomed to wearing such heavy furs, though she smiled warmly. She offered a translator, which Akłaq took.

"Good morning," Akłaq greeted.

"This must have been your first outing." Last Light was still grinning. "The whole time you looked like a startled hare."

Akłaq felt the blood rush to her cheeks. "Well, yes."

"I know we didn't speak much on the way, and what we did say was less than friendly subject matter, but I promise, we're not all scary."

"I never thought you were."

"Well, maybe not us, but sometimes, when your first impression of someone comes from the news they bring..." She shrugged. "Anyway, if it was your first outing, then you can't have been with Ujurak very long."

"About a year and a half or so."

Last Light raised a brow. "Really? Things must be quiet up here; normally he sends them out just as soon as they have decent control of their Bands or have an idea how to Harvest."

Akłaq shifted uneasily. "Well, for a long time, I was not in my right mind. I was brought into this because my husband and children were murdered. I would have been, too, but Putu, Aniqan, and Matulik found me and were able to save me."

"I'm sorry to hear that. About your husband and children. You took their Time Capsules, then?" Last Light nodded. "Yes, that will do it. Who is your Master?"

"Matulik."

"Oh, you're a Timekeeper? I see." Last Light nodded thoughtfully.

"Listening to the news you bring, I can't help but feel as though I have come in at the middle of a story. Without knowing the beginning of the tale, much of it is lost on me, even with the condensed explanation."

"I understand; believe me, I do. But it has little to do with us yet, and even less to do with you. It's more of a courtesy at this point."

"All the same, it is something new and exciting that I've never seen or heard of before, outside stories of the spirits."

Last Light grinned again. "Yes, that is true."

"So what is this Akari, and who is their Author deity?"

"The Author is just that, an author. You...do know writing, don't you?"

"Of course I do."

"Well, then, that's it. The Author writes and dictates the lives and destinies of all people, and the best that one may hope for is simply a happy ending. If the Author likes you, then you'll have a happy ending. If the Author doesn't like you, well, it may be a little more painful or unfortunate."

"By that logic, then, the Author must have hated my husband and children."

Last Light shrugged. "I suppose so. I don't follow their doctrines, so I won't pretend to speak for those that do. And as I understand it, because the Author is outside the books he writes — or she, I believe I was corrected once — the Akari is a way for her people, her characters, to use her power to manipulate circumstances within the books."

"But if he or she is an all-powerful Author with the ability to dictate everything someone does, what need is there for the Akari?"

"I don't know. Someone once speculated that it is a way for her to make all races equal outside of their biological capabilities."

Akłaq frowned. "Like giving everyone a gun. I may have the greater advantage while hunting, for my prey is unarmed, but if faced with an opponent who also has a gun, we must both consider our words and actions carefully."

"Something like that, yes."

"But...manipulating Time? And...Matter and Energy? What does that mean?"

"I don't know exactly," Last Light admitted. "I know only what I've heard. I have never actually seen it used."

"There must not be very many Akari users then."

"Enough that this split within their organization has been noticed by the Hands of Time, and that this reformation group is considered a potential threat."

"And that the threat may have a direct impact on us, just because we are indigenous peoples."

"Exactly. As I said, I don't follow their doctrine. I don't even know that I've met an Akari-bearer before, so I can only speculate. I just pass on the news."

Akłaq nodded. "It is good information to know, thank you."

She removed the translator and handed it back to Last Light who wished her a fond farewell and moved off to speak to someone else.

"I remember being like that."

Akłaq turned to see Aniqan approaching, grinning lackadaisically.

"Like what?" she wondered. "Did you used to travel far distances to their lands?"

"No, no." He shook his head, still grinning. "I'm talking about being like you." At her look, he clarified, "Everything is so new — the Time industry, Time Agents, Time abilities, the Hands of Time, all the alien species. You want to see just how far it all extends, explore the reaches of this thing that feels like a dream but in your spirit you know it is real. Your eyes have been opened, and you want to make sure they are open all the way, wondering what else there could be that you might be missing out on."

"You don't believe the Akari is real, then," Akłaq stated.

He shrugged. "Another religion of a distant people. Who am I to say? I know what my mother taught me, what her mother taught her, and what her mother taught her. It is the foundation of our people; shall I upend it because new discoveries have been made? Why should new things threaten what already exists?"

"But what if what we have been taught is a lie? Maybe not for malice, but for ignorance? We have physical proof of other beings from other worlds, and yet so many people believe and teach that we are alone."

"You remember the analogy of the gun, and of the responsibilities it carries?"

"Yes."

"You don't put a gun into the hands of a child. For humans, one must be at least thirteen years old before training begins, this way they have developed some sense of maturity. For humanity as a whole, we have not reached even that point. Such power in the hands of an individual is frightening enough, and consider that one man in a faraway land is causing a stir among the Time Agents and so-called Akari-bearers. How would all of humanity react if they saw what we know to be true? How would the United States government react, knowing that they are already responsible for the deaths of thousands of our southern brothers and sisters? How would the Russians react, knowing what they did to our people without this greater power? And how would they react if either one found out that the other had this power? What would they do if they both had it?"

Akłaq huffed a sigh. "When would humanity be ready for such a thing?"

"Maybe once we've learned a bit of respect," Putu said, walking up, his tone suggesting he didn't put much stock in his own words. "Maybe once we've learned to share. Basic concepts that a toddler must learn, sometimes forcefully. But we are toddlers without parents, which means that, at best, we realize our errors and seek solitude while the rest grow up to be savages."

"The Russian priests said God is our Father."

"God?" Putu questioned, giving her a look. "Which god?"

He walked away.

Beside her, Aniqan sighed. "He does that. Make no mistake, he is wise and has many experiences we may learn from, but he really isn't one for social niceties." He shifted position. "I guess conditions in the labor camps made him mistrustful."

"I'm surprised he survived; he looks as old as my father was when he died."

"He's tough, I will credit him that. He stuck it out; I ran away."

"Only death waited for you," Akłaq told him. "Putu is the exception; my father was the rule. Death if you stayed in the camps, and death to those who stayed behind."

Aniqan nodded. "Yes. Perhaps that's what makes it all so frustrating, to stay here, going out only to salvage what may be left instead of preventing it in the first place."

Then he, too, walked away, Akłaq staring after him. She glanced around at the others going about their business. How many of them felt similarly? How many yearned to do more than just, as Aniqan said, salvage remains? How many of them, every time there came a report of another village burned, wondered if they might have been able to prevent it? How many of them wished for the greater weapon to use against their captors, only to be told, once given this weapon, that they could not use it?

But she said none of this aloud. Few were in any real position to challenge Ujurak, for it was by his guidance that they lived as well as they did. She had even less of a position to speak, seeing how she had failed to heed the white bear and so condemned her family to death. She still had to learn her place, learn her way, before she could set a new course. And even then, she was willing to bet that her new course would follow directly in the path of the white bear.

The southern visitors stayed all that day to resupply and continue gossiping with their northern friends, but were on their way the following morning just as soon as it was light enough to see by.

"I'll be glad to get home," Akłaq heard Last Light comment. "There's not so much snow there."

It had been intriguing to listen to the visitors speak of their homes, places where there was always a day and always a night, where the summers lasted for many moons and winter was more of a minor inconvenience.

"Do you think it would be possible to visit some of these places?" she asked of Matulik once they were back to their regular training.

"It would be, yes," Matulik answered simply. "When you become a Journeyman, you have to do some training outside the District—"

"So you've seen these places already."

The woman grinned and shook her head. "No, not exactly. Our peoples—us northerners and our southern kin—we're stubborn. Ever since the first indigenous Time Agent, we have longed to be recognized as our own District, with our own District Captain, our own Lieutenants, our own training and way of doing things. But the British Regional Manager and the American Captains of the other Districts won't allow it. Not officially."

"Before the Hands, you claimed we were from District Nine."

"It does not technically exist, not as far as the Captains, Manager, and Gatekeeper are concerned. According to them, we belong in District One."

Akłaq blinked. "Why do the Hands allow this, then? Or the secretaries, who maintain the records?"

"Because the Gatekeeper and others do not dispute it, because of how we exploit it. When we become Journeymen and have to 'go to another District to train' we simply carry on as we are but claim to have trained in District One. For the others, it means keeping us safely tucked away in a box so we don't have to actually go anywhere."

"Then why not allow us our own Captain and Lieutenants?"

"Districts cannot overlap, for one, and to do so would be granting us a measure of self-governance." Matulik's look was angrily smug. "Can't have that, can we?"

So much to think about, so much to wrestle with. She didn't know where to begin. Every time she thought she found a good starting point, her line of thought would take her to more issues that were beyond her knowledge and experience. She just didn't know where to begin, where to anchor herself. If she didn't have a starting point, she sure wasn't going to know how to get to her destination, assuming she even had one.

After training, she went to visit Ujurak who was out feeding his dogs.

"You look troubled," the shaman observed. "Still thinking about the words and warnings from the visitors?"

"Some, yes," she confessed. "There is so much I don't understand. It seems that some of our petty issues might be resolved because of Time and our expansion into a larger world, a larger universe. But the lines that divide us only seem to cut more sharply."

He made a sort of "mm" sound and nodded. "Yes, they do indeed. But it is not for failure to look out, but in. If we see the world as an extension of ourselves, rather than a reflection, our view can become distorted."

"I don't understand."

"The world is imperfect, corrupted by evil. But if a man does not understand that he is also imperfect and corrupted by evil, he will ignore the weeds in his own self and instead become a weed, spreading rot wherever he goes."

Akłaq shook her head. "Maybe so, but we cannot wait until we are perfect before we act on injustice."

"And if our actions produce more injustice? What then?" He went on before she could speak. "The spirits guide us for a reason, Akłaq. They can see what we cannot. Our deviation from their guidance produces catastrophe. Injustice. Against them, against ourselves." His look had a shadow of accusation. "We must wait upon them for their instruction."

"It was said once among my village that the spirits told the people to be friendly with the Russians when they first arrived, in spite of everything that had happened to the Aleut people. Would it not have been better to drive them away instead?"

"And knowing what you do about the Russians, do you think that would have ended well?" When she remained stubbornly silent, he added, "I think you are arguing just to argue. I think you are trying to justify your own thoughts and actions." His gaze turned kind. "And I think you are trying to figure out how to atone and make things right, that you may again follow the white bear." He nodded. "Do not worry, Akłaq Balabinov. Your path does not end here. Nor will you always be alone."

Akłaq may have thanked him; she wasn't entirely sure. She just knew that, in that moment, she wanted nothing more than to go home to the cabin, hug her children, and fall asleep beside her husband.

Avgun Qulit Atausriq
The First Test

She knew in her head that it wasn't real, but every other sense told her otherwise. She knew this was a mostly empty room, as vast as a meadow and as cold as the tundra.

And yet, she felt the heat from the fire that raged around her, homes and bodies burning, smoke stinging her eyes. She knew in her head that it wasn't real, but still she felt the overwhelming desire to run, flee, hide. These instincts warred with vivid memories of Nika and her children. If she had to do it all over again, knowing what the outcome was going to be, would she still choose to stay with him? At the moment, with everything going on around her, she really couldn't be sure.

Then there was the man standing before her, maybe twenty yards away, her father, weakened by years of labor and starvation, unable to fight back and held fast. The man, the Russian soldier, held a knife to her father's throat while three more soldiers, whose faces she would remember until the day she died as the ones who had raped her, dragged her mother away, no doubt to do the same.

"Are you afraid, little girl?" the soldier hissed, his voice remarkably clear in the chaotic environment. "Go on, try and stop me. I know you want to."

She did not know if she could save her father, for even if she somehow made it to him in time to stop the soldier from slicing his throat, she could not hope to face the man in combat. But if she went after her mother, she would be facing three of them, and she already knew how that scenario played out.

"And after I cut his throat, I am going to Harvest him and take his memories for myself. You will never know him," the soldier taunted.

Except this time, she had another weapon at her disposal. She had the advantage here.

Reining in her wild thoughts and stark fears, she Banded.

She could not Band the soldiers, for the fire raging all around them was too unstable. Even trying to Band herself, pulling everything as tight as she could, nestling it upon her skin and clothes, she could feel it wanting to crumble, to combust. She had to make this quick.

Once she was as satisfied as she could be, with everything almost at a standstill, wavering only because of the fire, she approached the soldier. She did not want to run, did not want to give in to fear, tried to tell herself that it was all an illusion. But as she wiped sweat from her brow and deliberately avoided a pile of burning rubble that used to be someone's home, she couldn't help but wonder, just for a moment, whether she had indeed been transported back in time and given a second chance to right some wrongs.

In the time it took her to close the gap between her and the soldier holding her father, the soldier had done little more than adjust one finger of his grip on the knife. She touched the knife, brought it into the Band with her but kept the soldier out. With the man all but immobilized, it was easier to pry his arms off her father.

She stood there, then, wondering what to do. It wasn't as though she didn't have time to consider this, though the fire pressed harder on her Band than she was really comfortable with.

She could get her father to safety. She could kill the Russian soldier. She probably couldn't do both and still save her mother and still hold her Band against the flames. Even now she was leery of how close her mother and the three soldiers were to a burning house.

Akłaq studied the knife in her hand, looked at the soldier who had held her father, looked back at the knife.

"This cannot be allowed to happen," she said aloud, unsure just who she was speaking to.

With a grunt of effort, she stabbed the Russian soldier in the neck, the same way she had stabbed the muskox. Except men did not have the thick skin that the muskox did, and the blade penetrated easily. There was only minimal blood now, but once she released her Band, it would spray everywhere. She was momentarily distracted by the first droplets flying through the air at less than a snail's pace.

She jerked the blade free and turned to the three men who still had hold of her mother. She knew these soldiers, better than she ever wanted to. She immediately picked out the one who had first grabbed her and threw her on the bed. Then there was the one who had shot her in the leg after she kicked him. Like a tidal wave, she could recall every moment with terrible clarity as they had their way with her, how it felt as they forced their way inside her, sometimes going twice.

But as she got closer, the fire pressed on her Band, trying to force its way in. This sensation combined with her memories put her into a panic and she found herself almost sprinting. Or, she would have sprinted if she could, but it seemed that for as much effort as she put into running, an equal force was pushing her back, squeezing her on all sides. The fire burned hotter, pressed harder, and she opened her mouth to gasp for breath but choked on the smoke.

"Aaka!" she coughed. *"Aaka!"* (Mother! Mother!)

But she couldn't get close and hold her Band at the same time. They were too close to the fire, and if she tried to force her way through, it would consume her. She slowed to a crawl and finally stopped.

She didn't want to let go. She didn't want to give up. She couldn't hope to take on three soldiers by herself, but Banding was useless here. It just wouldn't work. Maybe she was still too unskilled, or maybe it was entirely impossible, she didn't know.

She dropped the Band.

Heat and fire and screaming enveloped her, sweeping away what little good air she had in her lungs. Behind her, the Russian soldier collapsed, blood spraying from his neck. In front of her, the three soldiers were still dragging her mother away.

"Akłaq!" she cried. *"Akłaq!"*

Akłaq wanted to go after her. Wanted to help, wanted to do something. She even managed to take a few steps forward, but fatigue was quickly overpowering everything else.

"*Aaka,*" she said, but couldn't do much more than a quizzical statement.

She stumbled, caught herself, paused. The smoke was getting thicker and she could no longer see where her mother and the soldiers had gone. She thought she might have heard her mother's cries, knew too well what was happening, but felt too slow and powerless to do anything about it.

"*Aaka.*" This time it was little more than a mumble that ended in a small yawn.

Akłaq went to take a step but instead went to her knees. She yawned again. Everything was getting darker with exception of some nebulous firelight, and yet the air tasted clearer, less smoky.

She closed her eyes. When she opened them, she was back in the large empty room, the Seat of the Hands. The village was gone. The fire was gone. Her mother and father and Russian soldiers were gone.

For a long moment, she was the only one that she was aware of. Then there were footsteps, and a hand appeared in front of her. Looking up, she found Matulik.

"You did good," the woman told her gently.

"It doesn't feel like it," Akłaq said.

Then she blacked out. She would not say she slept, for she neither dreamed nor felt rested when she finally opened her eyes again, like peeling hide off an animal.

She lay on the floor in a room that was so white it nearly blinded her, or that was how it felt to her pounding head. There was only the vaguest of difference between floor and walls, and the only real color in the room came from herself and Matulik who sat against the wall near her.

"What was that?" Akłaq whispered.

"That was the psychological part of your Apprentice review," Matulik told her.

They'd talked about the review, the different parts, for a while now. Knowledge, so she could articulate what she was doing, what was supposed to happen, and make sure she understood how the Time industry worked. Skill, to prove that she was learning and could control herself. Psychological, to ensure that she was mature enough in mind and spirit to be trusted with such power.

The first two parts, she'd had little trouble with, although the skills test included a short combat session against a creature called the Bat. Her anxiety had been a greater hindrance than a lack of knowledge or skill, and she feared she failed the combat portion.

It was the psychological review that tormented prospective Apprentices the most, Matulik had told her time and again. Until she actually passed the exam and the review as a whole, she was not permitted to speak of it. It was as much a test of her own mental capabilities as well as a test of her ability to keep a secret. Or so the thinking went.

"Did I pass?"

Matulik shifted position. "The Hands are reviewing your exam now. Actually, I believe they've already rendered a verdict; it's just a matter of waiting until you're strong enough to go before them again."

Akłaq wanted nothing more than to crawl into her own bed and hibernate for a few moons. She could barely conceive of sitting up, never mind standing, walking, listening to the Hands, enduring the chaos of the Wheel, and then having to go back through the Paa to get home.

This time when she went unconscious, she actually fell asleep. She had dreams, though she could not say just what they were. Different parts of the review; short, jumbled memories and moments tossed together into something almost coherent.

Akłaq would not say that she felt ready to test again when she woke, but she was able to sit up and even stand on her own two feet.

"Once we leave here, there's no coming back for a second nap," Matulik told her, the woman's tone almost joking. "We can stay here as long as you need."

Akłaq shook her head, and it felt as though an ice flow sloshed around inside. "No. I want to go home and sleep in my own bed."

"I understand. Come on then."

It was slow going, like trudging through heavy, wet snow, tripping over invisible obstacles, and still feeling worn-out overall.

"How did they do that?" Akłaq asked. "How do they create such an illusion? Is that something that Time can do, an ability known only to Hands?"

Matulik shook her head. "No. I do not understand it fully, but it is a drug that they give you to produce the hallucination. And some great technology of the Seat itself takes that hallucination and makes it visible to everyone else."

Unfortunately, Akłaq was still tired enough that she was unable to walk and think deeply at the same time. Trying to consider such a thing, technology that could augment and even project the mental images of a person, was not something she could accomplish while moving. How could such a thing be? Even some of the simpler aspects of Time and the Wheel were but magic powers known only to the spirits and the shamans, yet were somehow available to even the most common people of the most alien races.

After a moment, Matulik prodded her, and they continued on their way. The larger structure was called the Coliseum. According to Putu, it was modeled after a structure in a place called Italy—or Italy modeled it after the structure in the Wheel—and infused with all the technology that made the Wheel such a headache. It was also about twenty times bigger, or it must have been, in order to accommodate some of the larger races.

It may as well have been a hundred times bigger for as long as it took them to return to the Seat of the Hands. Akłaq still wasn't sure how she was going to manage going back through the Paa. If anything was certain, it was that she was going to sleep good. She would probably sleep for a moon, provided no one disturbed her.

For the knowledge part of the review, each Hand, of which there were fifty, plus the Zero Hour, asked a question. According to them, she answered forty-five of the questions correctly, which was more than enough to pass. Or that was how she understood it. Actually, it was supposed to be a majority of the Hands being satisfied with her performance, not necessarily that she'd gotten the questions correct. Still, forty-five was enough.

The simple skill test, where she just did demonstrations, earned her a forty-nine out of fifty-one. That was surprising enough, but to hear that forty-eight out of fifty-one Hands were satisfied with her combat skill test was unbelievable. She wasn't even happy with it, why should any of them be?

Forty-two out of fifty-one Hands were satisfied with her psychological exam, but it was still enough to pass. Akłaq almost asked them what they had been expecting. If it had been hallucinations conjured by her own mind that she just happened to react to, who were they to say whether it was "satisfactory" or not?

She was given one chance to walk away before committing her life to Timekeeping, but she refused. The white bear had brought her to this place; she couldn't walk away from it now, even if she still didn't understand why she was doing this.

Then she was named an official Timekeeper Apprentice, and she and Matulik were free to leave. It was a long haul through the Wheel. Not a few times, Akłaq was knocked to her seat just from a passing, accidental bump to the shoulder.

"Come on, Akłaq," Matulik said, hauling her to her feet. "We're almost there."

And on they went. Pretty soon, Akłaq wasn't thinking about anything but just getting into bed. She barely registered when they reached the Paa room, and felt only the slightest bit of hope when she spotted the Paa that led to the village.

Somehow, she managed to stay conscious as she went through the Paa, but as soon as she stumbled into her home and felt the warm furs beneath her, she was out.

She slept.

She dreamt.

She slept some more.

She had dreams of her village, memories of the exam mixing with what she knew to be true. She also had nightmares of the three soldiers; sometimes her mother was there, and sometimes she wasn't. And then she had dreams of Nika and her children. Good dreams, bad ones, and for a long time she felt powerless to wake herself from any of it.

Then she woke, and the vast majority of it fled from her mind.

It was Aniqan who first spotted her when she poked her head out into the shortened daylight.

"Well, there she is," he said, grinning as he approached. "You sleep well?"

"I can stand and walk," she offered lamely.

"After two days, I hope so."

"Two days?"

He waved a hand. "It's not uncommon. Every Apprentice no matter the discipline has to go through it. I had to go through it twice because even though I'm a Master Harvester, I am still technically an Apprentice Timekeeper, too. That was not my idea of fun, believe me."

"And you had to go through it again when you reached Master, didn't you?" Akłaq questioned.

He nodded. "That's right. Apprentice, Master, and, for Timekeepers, Gatekeeper, all require psychological exams."

Akłaq couldn't help but sigh audibly.

"You have some time before that, yet, though," Aniqan laughed. "You have a year to make Journeyman, then three years to make Master, and that's just the minimum. You can take as much time as you need. As you can see, we're not exactly pressed for time and talent."

She nodded and looked around. "I'm not sure what to do now, honestly."

Aniqan raised a brow. "You thought something magical was supposed to happen when you became an Apprentice?"

She shrugged. "I don't know. Maybe. What do I do?"

He shrugged in kind. "Continue your training. Continue to go out with us on missions and expeditions." He went on before she could speak. "It's a hard mentality to get into, but understand that we have time. We have long lives. We have the ability to influence the world over centuries. Little by little, piece by piece. I know you want to do something really big right now, but you can't spend three hundred years doing nothing but wage war."

"Why not? Empires have been doing that for thousands of years."

"Yes, because men have short lives and no fear of death."

Akłaq considered this and shook her head. "No. I think they do fear death, and that's why they wage war. They fear death, so they try to make their lives more meaningful in all the wrong ways."

Aniqan nodded slowly. "Be that as it may, we—" He gestured vaguely around the village. "—will not be waging war any time soon. We will not be routing armies and defending cities." He put his hands on her shoulders. "We will, however, preserve the memories of the ancients for the children of the lost. Men will die. Whole generations will pass away. Killing Russian soldiers won't bring your husband and children back from their graves. But they live on within you. Our people are threatened. Keeping the memories and traditions alive for the future is more important than trying to save lost bodies. That's why I chose to become a Harvester rather than a Timekeeper."

For the first time since Nika's death, Akłaq found that her smile toward a man was deeply and truly genuine. She put her hands over top his on her shoulders, squeezed gently, then stepped backwards into her home, Aniqan's hands still in hers. He raised a brow but said nothing as he ducked inside after her.

Akłaq would not say she did not feel guilty, a certain sense of betrayal against Nika, but she also felt a certain sense of relief, and not just sexual tension that had been building up over the last six moons or so. It felt almost like the last piece of a puzzle, the last maneuver of a game that causes one to win or at least be on the clear path to victory. It was another element of moving on from tragedy, finding community, finding love.

And for a little while afterwards, she could almost believe it. This was how things would have been if Qikiqtaġruk had not burned, if she had been able to stay among her people, to grow up and marry. It was how things ought to be.

Then Aniqan kissed her, retrieved his clothes, and left. And with him went the illusion.

She did not despise him for it, though her sense of euphoria drained rapidly.

Their mission was to preserve the future. In order to do that, they had to give up any chance of producing a future of their own. Her children had to be sacrificed so that the children of her people would have the knowledge and traditions they needed to remain Iñupiatun. Otherwise, they were, as Aniqan said, lost bodies. Indistinguishable from those who killed or assimilated them, and unable to learn what their parents could not teach or save. But where weapons and relics could be confiscated, memories could not.

For a while, as she dressed herself and figured out what she wanted to eat, she contemplated doing as Aniqan had done, what almost all of the other women in the village did, becoming a Harvester. It would allow her to save the people, save the memories. She would be able to hand the Time Capsules to the children and tell them what was about to happen, what they were about to experience, and what to do with that experience.

And yet, she didn't know that she would be able to handle it. To have to Harvest so many people, to have to face every single child, whether grown or not, and try to explain things to them. She was still trying to comprehend it herself; there seemed to be no fading of the things she experienced from the Time Capsules of her husband and children. While not at the forefront of her mind, if she wanted to, she could call it up on a whim and still perceive everything with perfect clarity.

With the bleeding effect of Harvesting, even if only a minor thing, could she really go through that over and over again, all the people she would come to know?

And still there was a desire in her heart to not just stand idly by and wait to clean up the mess of a silent war. She did not want to just preserve the memories of the dead, she wanted to preserve the living so they could pass on their knowledge and experiences themselves. That was the task assigned to the Timekeepers: protection, defense. Why should it apply only to the other Timekeepers and Harvesters? Why not to the common people, too? Fine, so they couldn't take on a whole army; what about just helping the people to escape, to live another day?

Well, she wasn't the only one to have had these thoughts, she knew. And she was coming to understand that it might be better for her to experience the world a little before trying to change it. The best way to do that would be to become a Journeyman, when she would be forced to go to other Districts to continue her Timekeeper training. She would not hide behind a technicality and stay safely isolated in the north. If nothing else, she wished to explore the south, this great land of many people, balanced days and nights, and no snow.

But that wouldn't be for at least a year. In that time, she would have to come up with some kind of goal or plan, and right now, all she had was a vague idea and a desire. But if this was at all in line with the spirits and the white bear, she was sure something would come up. The white bear would lead the way, and this time, she intended to follow.

Avgun Qulit Malġuk
Journeyman

It was the first time that Akłaq had ever willingly and intentionally packed up her things to leave. It was an odd sensation, and she found that she almost didn't know how to do such a thing. Oh, she packed her stuff when they moved from village to village, but that was still moving with the people, going with the group. This time, she was striking out on her own, and she had time to gather what she needed.

Her hunger had diminished in the last year or so, such that she ate far less than she did as a normal person, though still more often than the more seasoned Time Agents. She would not have to worry about catching something in a snare every day or every other day in order to ward off starvation, but she would need something. And even if she were eating less, there were still plenty of predators out there to watch out for. Sure, she could Band and kill them easily if she had to, or escape if she felt it necessary, but Banding alone wasn't going to warn her of what lay in wait in the bushes, and she didn't want to rely on sheer reflexes to save her.

She didn't think she'd be able to do it, actually. In the time leading up to her Journeyman review, she'd doubted herself immensely, wondered if she shouldn't bow out and just stay with Ujurak and the villagers, claim the District disparity and continue with what she knew.

But now that she was here, a newly-graduated Journeyman, actually packing her bags and hauling things out to her sled, she found the whole thing rather exciting. She was going somewhere and doing something because she wanted to do it, not because of fate or circumstance. And she was going to explore a much bigger world, far beyond anything she had ever seen or even heard of.

In spite of her reduced needs and increasing talent, Akłaq couldn't help but feel that perhaps she had packed a little too much for her journey. Maybe it was from her latent fears of being left alone in the wilderness with only the clothes on her back, a bow with one arrow, and a whalebone knife. Maybe it came from trying to ensure that her husband and children always had whatever they needed, whether it was for going to town to trade or just teaching chores around the cabin. She didn't want to really need something and not have it.

The four dogs attached to the sled stood to greet her, tongues lolling, hot breath puffing in the air. She had debated whether dogs or horses would be better, then decided on the dogs. A pack of dogs might keep the wolves at bay or attack a bear, where a horse would only entice predators in.

"So, you're really leaving us."

Akłaq turned to see Matulik approaching. The woman's expression was stony, her tone cordial only because she was Akłaq's Master. It was more than she got from most of the others, who apparently despised the thought of her, or anyone, leaving. A few were fine with it, but the coldness from the rest was icier than the winter they were just coming out of.

"You've known this for over a moon," Akłaq told her evenly.

"Everyone feels wanderlust during the winter," Matulik said. "Everyone wishes to be somewhere else when the snow is deep enough that is seems wiser to simply dig tunnels and burrow like the hare."

"True as that may be, I'm still going."

Now Matulik's facade broke. "Why?! You've always been forced out, forced away, abused by the world! Why do you want to leave now?! This is a good thing we have here, a good village, a good people, a good system that lets us stay where we are, where we want to be! I don't understand why you want to leave us!"

"I'm not abandoning the people forever," Akłaq said. "I'm just going to explore, to learn, to train as is required."

"But we have a way to stay here, to stay away from things out there."

"We may leave the world alone, but the world will not leave us alone. I have to go out there and see it. I want to see it...because I want to, not because I have been forced out or forced away. I have to follow the white bear."

Matulik scowled and turned away. After a long moment, she looked back and asked, "Do you know what waits for you out there? I'm not talking about lions and bears. Men will kill you—they will rape you twice and then kill you—just because of who and what you are."

"I can't hide here, Matulik. I understand that I will not be leading armies, and I will not influence governments, but I know that there is more out there for me to do. I can't do it from here."

"What do you expect to do? Our strongest men couldn't keep the Russians out."

"I don't know. I have no idea what I'm going to do or find. Besides, it's not as though I'm leaving forever, just until I complete my required out-of-District Journeyman training."

"Going south or east, you just might be leaving forever. We only have longer lives; we're not indestructible."

"Maybe not, but she won't be defenseless either," a new voice said.

Both women turned to see Aniqan approaching, leading his dogs at a slow walk, his team and sled settling next to Akłaq's.

"What are you doing?" Matulik demanded.

"I'm going with her," he answered.

"What?" both women asked at the same time.

He nodded. "I'm going, too."

"Why?" Again both women spoke at the same time, and now they exchanged the same incredulous look.

"Because it is dangerous to go alone. As a Master Harvester, and even an Apprentice Timekeeper, I can help to keep her safe. And maybe I want to see the world, too."

Matulik looked like she wanted to say or do something, anything, but couldn't figure out what. Finally she shook her head and stormed off in a kind of angry sorrow. Akłaq gave Aniqan a look.

"Are you trying to upset her?" she asked.

He raised a brow. "She's not my wife or my mother. I can make my own choices. I choose to go with you, to protect you and see the world."

There was no point in arguing. He intended to go with her and, short of Ujurak, no one could order him not to. Akłaq wouldn't say she didn't want him to come or that she didn't appreciate the thought, but she had fully prepared and expected to have to do this alone.

"Why not tell me sooner, that you intended to come?" she inquired instead.

He shrugged. "I wasn't sure if you were really intending to go."

She felt the blood rush to her face. "Are you all packed and ready, then?"

"I believe so. If we're going anywhere closer to people, I'm sure they'll have things to trade or buy if we need them." He shifted his stance and folded his arms. "Where did you say we were going, exactly?"

"I don't know. I was going to speak to Ujurak, to see if he had seen anything. If not, then I suppose we should go east and south, where the people are supposed to be."

Aniqan did not say anything, but she could see he was definitely thinking it. She didn't have much of a plan. She knew it. And maybe she was just afflicted by wanderlust from a hard winter.

"I'll see to your sled," Aniqan said, putting his hand over hers as she reached for her things to rearrange them yet again. "You go see Ujurak."

She hesitated, then nodded and headed toward Ujurak's home. The shaman was out scuffing the snow with his foot, apparently planning out his small yearly garden. He grew mostly flowers, but occasionally tended a bit of lettuce that might be used as bait for small herbivores. He looked up and grinned when he saw her.

"Ready to leave, are you?" He knelt down to brush some snow

from a particular spot, scratching at the dirt and thinking.

"Not quite," Akłaq admitted. "I was wondering if you had seen anything."

"Not since the last time you asked." He added quickly, "Though that does not mean there is not something out there to find."

"I am sure there is much out there to find, but how do I know what I am looking for?"

Ujurak gave her a cheeky grin. "What are you looking for, and what you are intended to discover, are sometimes two very different things." He stood using his staff and brushed the snow from his knees. "Go east, Akłaq. Your children need you."

Akłaq's body stiffened, though she mentally tripped over her thoughts and went careening down a hill. For a long moment she was unable to speak, or even think. When she finally came back to herself, Ujurak was already back on his knees, doing this and that in his snowy garden.

"My...children?" she asked, her voice hardly more than a gasp.

Ujurak shrugged and looked up at her. "I know not why I said such a thing, only that you needed to hear it."

"Ujurak, my children are dead, and it is known that Time Agents do not have children."

"I speak not of your past children, nor of Time Agents." He went on before she could speak. "I know nothing, Akłaq. It is the *tuuṅaq* who speaks."

She let out a breath and nodded. "I understand."

He chuckled. "Well, I'm glad you do, for you have been quite a mystery to me." At her look, he said, "Ever since you came here, your path has been very...blurry to me, like a light that I cannot look directly at, but when I try, it vanishes behind a dark wall I cannot penetrate. It is as if your destiny has been denied to me, except in rare instances where you require specific guidance, such as now."

"Specific guidance?" Akłaq folded her arms. "Telling me only to go east isn't what I would consider specific."

"But it is better than nothing. I am afraid I cannot give you more than that. You must follow the white bear now."

There was a subtle change in his voice, a tip of the tone, the intonation, something that told her that his final sentence was not him speaking, but the *tuuṅaq*. Something within her said that the *tuuṅaq* was not happy about the words it spoke. It both frightened and confused her, but she chose not to dwell on it. Instead, she thanked Ujurak and promised to do well on her journey.

When she returned to the sleds, Aniqan had somehow used his own magic from the spirits—or perhaps a bit of his own minor Banding skills—in order to repack the bags and shift the loads so that they were better distributed across both sleds. And they looked a bit nicer, too, more of an intentional trek and less of a hasty escape.

"What did Ujurak have to say?" Aniqan wondered. "Do you know where we're going?"

"East," she answered. "That's all I know. That's all he knows." She elected not to say anything about the children the shaman mentioned.

"Well, it's more than I know."

"You've been south before. Isn't there anything there?"

"Not a lot, really. I know more stories than I have experience. If we stay west of the mountains, we might have some lingering Russians, maybe some Americans, a lot of fur trappers, and the United States once you go far enough. On the other side of the mountains, you've got a lot more fur trappers and traders, forest, plains, greater chance of running into British settlements because they have a harder time crossing the mountains."

Nothing he said sparked anything in Akłaq's imagination, stirred nothing in her soul to say that such and such was the direction to go, the goal to strive for. She let out a breath, hoping to hide her disappointment. "Well, I suppose we should get moving."

"Agreed," Aniqan said, looking at the sky. "The weather is good, for now, and we should cover as much ground as we can while it's still light."

"I can Band us," Akłaq offered, doing a last check of her sled before stepping on and grabbing the anchor.

"For a while, maybe, but don't hurt yourself."

She gave him a look. "What are you talking about? I outrank you now."

"Officially, yes, but I bet I still have a few years of experience over you."

She laughed and prepared to yank the tether that kept the sled secured to a post. Then her gaze happened to dart to a spot a short distance behind Aniqan.

It was Matulik. The woman's posture was rigid, but with a certain, awkward lilt that said she was trying to force herself to relax and failing miserably. Her expression was similar, angry, hurt, but trying to muster up some consolation for herself. Maybe the two of them were just going on an expedition for Ujurak, the same as any other mission. They wouldn't be gone long, certainly not a year or more. If she did happen to get lonely, it wasn't as though there weren't other men in the village.

Their eyes met. And although Matulik was still Akłaq's Master within Time, there was also an undisguised loathing in the woman's gaze. Matulik dropped any pretext of trying to make herself feel better about Aniqan leaving and stalked off back to her own home, grabbing the hand of the first man she walked past.

"Did you forget something?"

Aniqan's voice pulled Akłaq back to the present, and she glanced at him, initially unsure how to respond. Finally she shook her head. "No, I don't think so." She tried to put on a convincing smile. "You? Last chance."

"I've done this plenty of times; I got everything I need. Just waiting on you."

She looked ahead to where her dogs were ready to start running.

She Banded, bringing everything around her to a standstill, and looked around. She was really doing this. They were leaving. As much as she told herself that she was just going out to continue her Journeyman training and advance as a Timekeeper, she also had a gut feeling, beyond Ujurak's words, that there was so much more to be learned and accomplished. It might be that she wouldn't return at all, but not for tragedy.

She looked at Aniqan, still waiting. Was it wise for him to come? Why was he coming at all? True enough, there were many things out there that could kill her, many people who would like to as well. But she had the ability to stop that, to Band and escape or defend herself. What were his real motivations for doing all this? She wasn't complaining, she just wondered whether he was part of this mystery Ujurak claimed he couldn't see.

That thought was enough to make her want to get moving, if only so she didn't have to consider that the shaman was blind to something.

She dropped the Band and snapped a command to her dogs. The pack, already wound up from the prospect of running and going somewhere, leapt into action without question or persuasion. Akłaq gripped her sled tight, shifted her weight, and forced herself to breathe. The first jolt was always the most terrifying and exhilarating. Behind her, she could hear Aniqan shout to his dogs, and the pack took off. A moment later, they were skiing almost side by side.

There was no good way to hold a conversation while snaking through trees and over hills, but that was fine. Akłaq found that she was just glad for the company. Aniqan knew his way through the mountains better than she did, so she let him take the lead.

Any intention she had of Banding the two of them disappeared very quickly. Doing the two of them was fine. Even adding the dogs and sleds wasn't overly difficult. Trying to hold it while they were weaving through trees was a bit more than she could grasp. If they were on a flat stretch or could stay in line of each other, then she could manage it. But when he took a high path and she was left on the lower ground to eat the snow coming off his runners, Banding was not the first thing on her mind.

They continued as long as they could, using the light of the half moon when the sun disappeared. But when clouds started to roll in and the temperature notably dropped, Aniqan steered them to a small cave where they could bed down and stay out of the wind. It was apparently a well-known and well-used cave, for there was already a supply of firewood waiting for them. Akłaq started the fire while Aniqan fed the dogs.

"So why are you here, Aniqan?" Akłaq asked, studying him. He sat to her right at the fire. "And I want the truth. It's not just because you think I need protecting."

He shifted uncomfortably. "Well, no. You're right."

"Then what is it?"

His expression turned a bit guilty. "Matulik is jealous of you."

Akłaq raised a brow and smiled awkwardly. "Jealous? Of me? Whatever for?"

"She's jealous of the life you lived, with your husband and children."

"That makes no sense. She has a son, a living son. My family is dead."

Aniqan shrugged. "She seems to think that you had a perfect life. And now she's got it in her head that you're somehow trying to recreate that life with me."

"Why? We can't have children. Besides, you lie with her, too. And she and I have both been with other men."

He shifted again. "Well, since she's started on her path of envy...I've been avoiding her."

"And now you're leaving with me. That's not going to help her disposition."

"Maybe not, but we're not going to be there, are we?"

Akłaq gave him a look. "Aniqan, you need to go back."

He raised a brow. "Why? She's not my wife." He met her gaze. "And neither are you. I choose to be here. I choose to protect you."

She searched his gaze, his face. After a long moment, she asked, "Do you love me?"

He blinked, his expression suddenly turning uncertain. Finally all he could manage was, "What?"

"Do you love me?" Akłaq repeated. "I have known a man, and loved him. I bore his children. That is something that...Matulik has every reason to be envious of it. I wish for her to be envious of it, even. And if I could have it again, I would. By doing this, coming with me, you are only sharpening that blade on her skin, the life she wishes she could have had. She's afraid she'll never have it. Worse, she's afraid that I will again, and I will have it with you."

Aniqan's expression turned disbelieving. "Isn't that a bit...dramatic? She knows that you and her can't have children."

"Even so, she wishes for a normal life, one of love and stability."

"And she views me as the husband in this fantasy?"

Akłaq shrugged. "Maybe. And maybe as long as everyone in the village is casual, she can keep that fantasy private. Running off into the woods with me...I don't know."

Aniqan made a kind of disappointed noise as he let out a breath. "The life of a Time Agent is not easy. It's even harder when we remain so isolated and the only news we hear is bad news."

She nodded and stared into the fire. "No weddings, no births, no family news from our home villages because they're all burned to the ground..."

"No way to properly grieve for those lost," he added.

Akłaq huffed a sigh. Aniqan scooted closer, then a little closer, until he was close enough to wrap her up with him in the large blanket she'd packed. She didn't know why she'd packed it exactly, but this seemed an appropriate use, she thought.

The next thing she knew, Aniqan was kissing her neck.

"Have I ever shown you," he murmured, "what a Harvester can really do for love?"

"I don't know," Akłaq teased, rubbing his thigh. "Is it as exciting as a Timekeeper being able to keep you harder longer?"

"It might be. You'll have to be the judge."

Truthfully, when it was all over, Akłaq didn't know if she wanted to laugh or cry, do it again or grab the dogs and sled and run. There was a certain terrible euphoria that Aniqan was able to induce as he essentially Harvested her, taking all of her years and bringing her to the point of death without actually taking those years from her and in fact returning them to her when they were done. But given that she had, in fact, been at that point of death, and it had immediately followed her rape at the hands of three men, her mind and heart were in absolute turmoil.

"You hated it," Aniqan sighed, leaning back, looking dejected.

Akłaq took a breath and got up on her elbows. "It's not that. Aniqan, I—"

"I should have known. I should have considered...what you went through...it wasn't right."

She sat up. "Aniqan, it's...it's fine. It was good. I promise, it was. I just...I have to remind myself that you're a friend and this is good."

He still looked uncertain, but as she moved to again lay beside him, he did not say anything more about it and simply accepted her.

"Apparently we started something," he commented instead. He gestured to where one of the dogs was busy mating with another.

"Puppies are something we can trade," Akłaq said.

He nodded. "Agreed." He kissed the top of her head. "So were you just being coy, or do you honestly not know where we're going?"

She shook her head and looked up at him. "I really don't know, other than east. I'm doing as I should have done years ago, following the white bear."

Aniqan grunted. "As long as the white bear doesn't lead us over a cliff. The mountains are not easy to traverse by sled, especially in the spring. Horses would have been a better bet, or just walking."

"If only Paa were a more friendly method of travel."

"Yes, well, we do ourselves no good wishing for something that won't come true. Either one of us has a lot to learn before we can use Paa so whimsically."

Akłaq grinned but said nothing. She just wanted to enjoy the moment. She wanted to pretend, at least for a little while, sitting there by the fire all snuggled up with Aniqan in the blanket, that things were perfectly normal.

Avgun Qulit Piñasrut
Across the Mountains

Horses probably would have been better, Akłaq thought, or even just walking as Aniqan had suggested. The number of times they'd had to divert, go around, or just generally find another path to accommodate the dogs and sleds, it took them twice as long to cross the mountains as it probably should have. It might not have been such a problem, except it was still difficult to Band their entire group—being mindful of exposing the dogs too much and risking having to butcher them because they became aware—and she felt a bit of a rush to get wherever it was they were supposed to go.

The urgency was probably a little silly. With exception of her own rescue and one other instance that she knew of, the spirits never pressed the people for time or deadlines. Even now, even if the white bear were waiting for her at their destination, surely it could appreciate the obstacles they were facing and so allowed for certain delays. One did not hire a mountain guide and expect to cross in a day. Proper planning was essential.

They probably shouldn't have brought the dogs.

But that was neither here nor there. They skied the final downslope that took them into a flat forest where they raced along as far as the momentum would carry them. After the many days of heavy exercise, running up and down hills and navigating uncertain landscapes, the dogs were happy to run hard across flat terrain, but even they could only do so much, being down two and close to being up three to six.

Akłaq's sled carried the bitch with puppies. She hadn't actually given birth yet, but she was far enough along that the constant hard running wasn't good for her. So she laid there, on top of some things, crowded with others, and tucked into the leather cover flap. Most of the time she turned her head back and tucked it into her belly, but every so often she might squint her eyes against the wind and snow and bark at her teammates. Occasionally she looked up at Akłaq, though the dog's thoughts were impossible to read.

Aniqan, meanwhile, also carried a dog, this one recovering from a broken leg. He'd wanted to butcher it after the incident, put it out of its misery and keep a light load. Akłaq talked him out of it. They hadn't been far from the edge of the mountains, and there couldn't be a trading post too far away. So Aniqan set and bandaged the leg, Akłaq used a Pinpoint Band to heal it, but that was still, in effect, time off the leg. The dog wasn't strong enough to keep up with the others. So he, too, lay on top of some things, crowded with others, and tucked under the leather flap.

With their teams each down one dog, they weren't able to make as much progress, and they bedded down early, tucking into a grove of pines, some large boulders providing a windbreak on one side of their camp.

Spring seemed to have been put on hold on this side of the mountains, Akłaq thought as she fed the dogs, but that was all right because it meant they would get more use out of the sleds. Would they have to trade them away at some point? If there was no snow in the south, they would have no need for sleds. And what about the dogs? It was easy to make a new sled. It wasn't all that difficult to breed the dogs for more puppies, but it took time to train a good sled dog. Well, it wasn't as though the village was a terribly busy place with overwhelming responsibilities.

"Do you know where we are?" Akłaq asked as Aniqan returned with firewood.

"I think so," Aniqan answered, arranging the sticks on the fledgling fire. "It's been a long time since I've been this way, and I've never been past the first trading post."

"Where is that?"

He finished arranging the sticks and squatted down to warm his hands. "If I'm right, we just need to head north until we find a river, then east. We'll ride straight into town."

"Town? Is it a very big settlement?"

"I don't know. If it's the one I remember, it wasn't more than a trading post and a couple places for the Hudson men to live in. It could very well be bigger by now. We'll find out tomorrow."

The prospect of seeing people again heartened Akłaq, but this was tempered by the thought of those people being white men. Granted, she'd heard little bad news about them, as it concerned the various peoples, but her experience with whites was mixed at best. Being all the way out here, though, they had to know they were a minority, at the mercy of the land and the people who were part of that land.

It gave her a lot to think about as they lay down to sleep. She was glad that Aniqan had come along, that he hadn't gone back to the village like she had told him to. He was a good guide, a good companion, and perhaps the only thing that had kept her sane at certain parts of the journey, not the least of which being when the dog broke its leg. That dog now was walking around the area, sniffing, marking, and only occasionally favoring the tender limb.

The following morning they were awake and on their way just as soon as it was light enough to see by. They started north, as Aniqan suggested. By late morning, they came to a cliff overlooking a wide, sparkling river about thirty feet below.

"Do you remember this place now?" Akłaq inquired.

Aniqan nodded. "It's grown up some, but the river is as I remember. We turn east, and we should make it to the trading post by evening."

The thought was thrilling and felt almost like an end within itself. They were about to reach the first of likely many destinations along this mysterious path. There was also an element of fear, too, knowing that they were at the outer reaches of useful knowledge. Aniqan was hard-pressed to recall anything about the area other than the general location of the trading post. Once they moved beyond that, they would be at the mercy of land and strangers and whimsical spirits.

Akłaq looked around, hoping to maybe see the white bear, or a glimpse of it. Something, anything to reassure her that they were on the right path. They were heading east as faithfully as they could, but some assurances would be nice.

The path they took started to look more intentional, more like a road than a haphazard footpath. Trees were cut back in a straight line and there was more evidence of use, large human footprints in the snow. As the sun rose high and started to wane, they spotted a couple of men deeper in the woods cutting down more trees and loading the logs onto huge sleds pulled by the biggest horses Akłaq had ever seen. They were probably taller than her just at the shoulder. Even the dogs slowed to watch the beasts and assess whether they were a threat. But the horses stood faithfully where they were as if part of the landscape themselves. On the part of the humans, no words were exchanged, no interactions made whatsoever, and Akłaq and Aniqan continued to ski along the road.

With the shadows now behind them, it was easier to make out the town as they came upon it, smoke rising in the air from chimneys and a certain atmosphere of activity.

Aniqan had described a single trading post and a handful of houses. What they came upon was a full, bustling village. The trading post still stood at the center of town, but there were now about forty or fifty homes as well as a church, the steeple reaching high into the air, the bell silent. Of the two hundred or so people Akłaq saw, the vast majority of them were men, but women and children were not a novelty. There were no indigenous peoples that Akłaq saw, but with the quickly approaching night, they were probably already gone back home.

"Are you sure this is the same place you remember?" Akłaq wondered as they came to a stop outside the trading post.

"It looks like the same post, but I don't know," Aniqan admitted.

It had been several years, but Akłaq would say that she still spoke Russian and Old Slavic as used by the Russian Orthodox. Having to adapt her language to other languages in the village—and them to hers

—she figured she could at least pick out when different languages were used. She would later learn that the languages she heard now in the trading post town were English, English as spoken by Scottish people, the Scottish language itself, and French.

With the apparent growth of the town, the trading post looked to have made a few improvements as well. Sagging walls and ceiling were reinforced by new, strong timbers, and an addition nearly doubled the size of the place, displaying all sorts of merchandise. Akłaq looked around, only half-aware that her mouth was ajar. Some stuff she recognized from the Russian traders, like the dresses and shawls the white women wore, although the styles were vastly different. There were toys and wooden carvings for children, and even items from the southern peoples like Last Light.

She startled as someone snapped something, and she whirled around to see a large white man standing behind a counter in the center of the store, looking directly at her.

"He says not to touch anything unless you have something to trade," Aniqan informed her humbly.

Akłaq felt her ears and cheeks burn, and she silently prayed she wouldn't shed tears for her embarrassment. A few other patrons in the store, all of them white, stared at her as she rejoined her companion.

"You speak their language?" she murmured.

"Not exactly," he replied, his voice low. "But the translator does."

She looked and only just made out the cloth collar around his neck and the piece in his ear, hidden by his furs and hair. Of course, that would have been a sensible thing to do. Seeing how they were only going to be traveling farther and farther from home, the odds of meeting anyone who spoke their language grew longer and longer with every mile.

The man at the counter said something more, his tone and posture a bit irritable, in the way someone got when they wished only to go home, have a hot meal, and a good sleep, but other matters demanded their attention.

"We have dogs," Aniqan said, repeating the last word in what

Akłaq learned to be English. He put his hands awkwardly on his stomach, then on hers. Akłaq jumped. He repeated. "Dogs. One dog with puppies."

When the man spoke, Aniqan repeated what the translator said in his ear.

"Bitch with pups, eh? Well, we got plenty of dogs around here, but your people usually have some pretty good stock." He nodded. "All right, I'll take a look."

He made a motion, and the three of them left the store, returning to the sleds where most of the dogs had laid down. Aniqan showed the man the pregnant dog, still lounging on the sled. The man looked her over, briefly looked over the other dogs, and fiddled with his mustache.

"You do have good dogs, I'll give you that," he said, looking conflicted, as if he had been looking for every reason to refuse but found none. He sighed and put his hands on his hips. "She's a fine bitch. What do you want for her?"

They went back inside. Aniqan did the negotiating, bartering for supplies and necessities. Akłaq saw several items that caught her attention, though she did not point them out. They were fanciful items only, pretty dresses and shiny baubles, nothing that would actually help them. They still didn't know how far they would be going. Once the supplies were settled, Aniqan asked also for bank notes. This gave the post manager pause.

"Bank notes?" His expression was puzzled. "Where do you expect to go?"

In halting, stunted English, Aniqan answered, "We don't know. We're following the white bear." He stole a glance at Akłaq as he said it.

The man made a sort of disapproving sound. "Spiritual thing, eh? Funny journey, then, for a couple of nor'westerners to come this way and—forget it." He waved a hand. "You keep going east, you'll find more posts. Some might even have maps. Turn your compass a little to the south and you'll be heading for Old Fort Providence, though that's decades closed now. Go too far east and you'll hit Canada. I wouldn't recommend going there, though, not good for your kind."

Nevertheless, the manager turned over a few coins and a few bank notes. Aniqan thanked him, and the two of them left the trading post.

"Did any part of that conversation strike you as the direction we should go?" he asked of her as they rearranged the loads on their sleds.

Akłaq sighed. "No, not really."

He grunted.

"Maybe we'll see or find something on the road."

He shrugged. "Maybe."

"You don't think so?"

Aniqan hesitated. "Can I tell you something in confidence, now that we're away from the village and Ujurak?" At her nod, he said, "With everything I've seen and done, everything I know—about Time, the Wheel, the species throughout the universe—it's hard to consider the spirits, assuming they even exist."

"But Ujurak saw the white bear and it led you and the others to me. It couldn't have been coincidence."

"Maybe it was. I don't know. But then why couldn't we be there in time to help your children, or stop it in the first place?"

Akłaq took an even breath. "I don't know. Perhaps as punishment for my not heeding the white bear years earlier."

"So you still think you have some destiny, some calling."

"Maybe. That's why we're out here, isn't it? That's why I'm out here."

Aniqan frowned and paused where he was tightening a strap. "When I was a boy, I was taught that some people had destinies and callings. Usually those people became shamans. And I accepted that I might not be anyone special. Then the Russian priests taught us that God saw and valued everyone, and anyone who was willing to serve could be made mighty and used in powerful ways. I was excited for that, for I wanted to be a powerful man of standing." He went back to his strap. "Then the Russians burned our village. I remembered thinking, 'How can God let this happen, if He sees and values everyone? I was willing to serve, and now I have nothing.' Finally I ended up with Ujurak and, for a short while, fell back into the old beliefs, where not everyone was special. When I was inducted into Time, I started to question whether the spirits — or Anyone or anything — existed at all."

"But what about Ujurak's dreams?" Akłaq wondered. "His *tuunġuq*? How else can he know that things are happening far away and people must be rescued?"

Aniqan's tone turned irritated. "I don't know, but, like you, I wonder why we can't do more. Why must we be reactionary only? Why can we not stop tragedy? If God was all-powerful, why did He not stop the Russians from burning my village? Yet here we are, perhaps with only a fraction of that power or the power of the spirits, and, like God, Ujurak seems to be unwilling to do anything with it. I don't know if I believe in God or the spirits or anything else, but you seem to be the only one willing to step out and search for the answers."

Akłaq studied him. "Does Matulik know you feel this way?"

He sighed. "She tells me to keep my thoughts to myself, and do as Ujurak says. But I just can't anymore. I have to know, and right now, this is the best chance I've got to find out."

She considered this for a moment and nodded. "I would be lying if I said that I didn't feel the same way myself sometimes."

"If you didn't, I don't think you'd be out here."

The day was short, but they decided to keep going as far as they could, still heading east.

After some days, they came upon another trading post, this one with one map left in stock. It came at a steep price, but Akłaq convinced Aniqan to get it in order to aid their travels. They were now well beyond where either of them had ever been, so it seemed a valuable resource.

"We have it now," Aniqan said as they left the post, his tone annoyed. "Now how do we intend to use it?"

"What do you mean?" Akłaq asked.

They reached the sleds where they unfolded the map. His concern quickly became apparent as the labels appears to be entirely English. Of course, had she expected anything less? She took an even breath and said, "Well, it's not entirely useless. See, these are the mountains we crossed and the town there. This is where we are. And I'm guessing that these are more villages and more trading posts."

He didn't look entirely convinced, but there was nothing they could do about it now. Trying to appear confident, Akłaq studied the map to determine their next course of action. She'd learned Russian and Old Slavic from the Russian priests, but the English letters were all so different, she could barely hazard a guess at pronunciation.

Finally she stopped trying to look at the details and instead settled on the bigger picture, looking at the roads and landscape. There were only a couple real roads going east to west, and no matter which one they took, they all seemed to converge on the same spot in the end.

"We'll take this road," she decided, indicating the one she was speaking of. It seemed to be a more true easterly following, until it reached coastline where it arbitrarily turned south.

"One road looks the same as any other," Aniqan said, shrugging. "If you're the one with a destiny, I'll take your word for it."

She gave him a look, but folded the map, tucked it away safely in the sled, then got on the runners and snapped at the dogs to get moving.

They traveled as far as they could and made camp—and love—in a grove of trees. Akłaq still was uncertain about Aniqan using his Harvesting abilities on her, not because she didn't trust him, but because she didn't trust herself. She didn't like the euphoric feeling that accompanied the presence of death. It almost made her think that she'd done it wrong the first time, and that was why death had rejected her, had allowed Matulik and the others to save her. Apparently, death was supposed to be happy and comforting, and she had tried to go into it with too much pain.

Had her husband and children known euphoria when they died?

She tried not to dwell on it, tried not to let her dejection show lest Aniqan blame himself in some way for poor performance.

And anyway, it was years ago.

The euphoria was still a bit unsettling.

They were on their way early the next morning, before the sun was up. Akłaq was noticing that the days were getting longer but almost...slower. Perhaps it was her enhanced perception of time owing to her abilities, but she was fairly certain that the lengthening of days was growing slower. Maybe it was just her.

Trading posts littered the hills, and some had villages growing up around them. The white people spoke varying dialects of English and French, depending on the place and which trading company they were loyal to. Now that they were farther east and south, there were a number of different indigenous peoples to be found as well, all speaking freely in their own languages and getting by in others.

"Do you think it would be wise to learn some of these languages?" Akłaq wondered, looking around as they slowly skated side-by-side through town. Most all of the snow had gone by now and they were riding through mud. The two of them as well as all the dogs were well plastered from the knees down.

"I expect it might," Aniqan replied.

At least Akłaq had learned the markings—in both English and French—for "Trading Post" and as soon as she spotted them over a doorway, she pointed them out to Aniqan and they turned their sleds in the appropriate direction. It was moderately busy—not that she was any judge—and they were not the only indigenous traders in the room. They had to wait a short time to be able to speak to anyone about trading.

Aniqan again did his best to speak, though he still used the translator to interpret everything everyone else was saying.

"Well, couple of northerners," the white man said. "Good, we were worried you'd been swallowed by the snows. Ha! All right, what do you have for us? Whale oil? Walrus tusks? What?"

"We need to trade our dogs and sleds for horses," Aniqan told him as best he could in stunted, accented English.

The man blinked as if he couldn't comprehend him. He folded his arms, shifted his stance. "Well that's all well and good, but what's your haul?"

"I don't understand."

The man said something which, even though Akłaq did not speak English, she knew was something the Russian priests would have called "blasphemy." He sighed. "Things are really that bad, eh? Couldn't even train you to speak basic English."

"I understand well enough. But I don't know what you want. We simply want to trade."

Now the man's expression turned almost accusatory. "Do you even work for the company?"

"We work for no one, sir. We're passing through."

Any interest the man had in their presence suddenly vanished. "Well, I can't help you then."

Aniqan raised a brow. "You're not interested in northern dogs? They're good dogs. And good sleds. You could sell or trade them to the next people going north."

"Mm...I suppose so. But I don't have any horses."

"Does anyone?"

"The stable, I imagine."

"If we sell the dogs and sleds to you, can you give us enough money to buy a couple horses?"

From everything Akłaq understood about how things operated with the Hudson Bay Company and the British and the French, it wasn't so much that they liked the indigenous peoples as much as what they could offer in trade. If the relationship was friendly, it was furs and goods. If it wasn't friendly, it was labor and land.

The man was apparently in a friendly enough mood to give them money for the dogs and sleds which was, indeed, enough to buy a couple horses from the stable on the next street. Once they got their gear secured and their behinds in the saddle, they set out. They might have moved at a trot except there were still too many people around.

"So, where to?" Aniqan asked, leaning over as much as he dared to try and look at the map she held. Or tried to hold. It was difficult to balance, steer the horse, watch out for people, and read a map all at the same time.

"If we follow the road this way, we'll end up in Canada," she said, pointing. She'd managed to work out those letters, too. She let out a breath. "But I think we need to go this way." She pointed south.

"You think?"

"A hunch only."

He craned his neck. "How do you say that?"

Akłaq studied the letters, trying to work out what she knew and add in what she could only guess. "Ss...is — sas...Saska...Saskat..." She shook her head. "I don't know. I mean, I think I know the letters, but they're all jumbled together. I don't understand."

Aniqan was grinning. "It's all right. If you think that's where we need to go, then we'll go there."

Once they were clear of the town, they turned their horses south and started off at a trot.

Avgun Akimiaġutaiḷaq
Sitting Pretty Place

The area was called "Saskatchewan" by the English fur traders, for the Saskatchewan River, which was known to the local Cree people as Kisiskāciwani-sīpiy.

With each trading post and small village they encountered, Akłaq was picking up more and more English and a bit of French. She would not consider herself fluent in any sense of the word, and calling her skills "passable" felt more like undue flattery, but she was getting the hang of it so she didn't need to look at Aniqan every time the men at the trading post opened their mouths.

The horses served them well as hills and forest gave way to sloped prairies. It was almost like the tundra when the vast expanses finally melted, if they ever did.

Beyond the river and the poorly-trodden road that followed it, there was little to remark about the territory, but one man in a particular riverside trading post seemed rather enthusiastic about it all. Curious as to why this one man should be so happy—out of dozens of sullen or drunken company employees—Akłaq left Aniqan to the negotiations and approached the happy man. He had somewhat darker skin, though Akłaq could not say definitively whether he was indigenous or European. He had the look of an indigenous man who wore everything in the European style.

"If I may ask," she began, parroting a phrase she had observed as being very polite, "why are you happy? Are you making money here?" She wished she knew more and prayed his answer would be simple and easy for her to understand. She kept telling herself that she needed to go to the Wheel and get a translator for herself, but then she would reason that she should probably actually learn everything so she didn't need the translator.

The man never stopped smiling as he answered, "I have made enough money that I have built my family a farm, and I am expecting their arrival soon." He sighed and his smile faded, but he continued to exude joyful energy. "Ah, but not today, it seems. Perhaps tomorrow."

She nodded. "Is a town nearby?"

"Not yet, but there will be. Are you looking for a place to settle yourself? I expect several half-breed families from Red River will be heading this way. If you want to stake a claim, now would be the time to do it."

He did not wait for her to answer, but wished her good day, and turned to head outside to his own horse tied up at the hitching post. He paused once, remarked at something on the ground, mounted up, and rode off. Akłaq went out to look after him, still curious. She looked down, wondering what he had seen, and paused.

Bear tracks. Fresh ones. Walking up to the spot where the man's horse had been and vanishing without a trace.

Before she could think twice, Akłaq darted back into the trading post where Aniqan was still talking, though it didn't sound much like negotiating. She grabbed his arm and pulled.

"Hey, what are you doing?!" he demanded, more surprised than angry.

"I know where we have to go, but we have to go now!" she said.

Apparently too bewildered to put up much of a fight, Aniqan just did as he was bade. Once outside, they quickly grabbed their horses and set out. Akłaq led the way, kicking her horse to a trot, spying the happy man just down the road, traveling at a lope.

"What is this, Akłaq?" Aniqan asked finally, bouncing along in his saddle. "What's going on?"

"The white bear," Akłaq told him.

"You saw it?"

"I saw his tracks. We have to follow this man."

Aniqan looked ahead to the man, the gap between them closing rapidly. "Are you sure?"

"As sure as I can be."

He didn't appear too convinced, but it was the best lead they'd had for quite a while, and it was better than a hunch.

The happy man looked a bit surprised by their sudden approach, perhaps a bit anxious as if he expected them to be bandits, but still appeared upbeat.

"Can we travel with you?" Akłaq asked. "Better with more."

He grinned. "You are right about that, my lady. I'm just going to my farm, but you are welcome to accompany me."

"Thank you. What is your name?"

"James Isbister. And yourself?"

"Akłaq, and this is Aniqan."

The man furrowed his brow. "Those aren't Cree names, or names from any of the people I know. Where are you from?"

"Northwest, where the Russians live."

The man, James Isbister, was friendly enough that her guard went down and the words came out. Only after they were out did she consider that maybe it was not the wisest thing to mention that they lived among the Russians, even if they technically didn't. Thankfully, he appeared more thoughtful than offended.

"You're a long ways from home," he commented. "What brings you here?"

"The white bear. We hope to find him."

Isbister nodded slowly. "Well, there are no white bears around here that I am yet aware of. But who knows? Stranger things have happened in my time here in the west. We shall see."

"What strange things?" Akłaq wondered.

The man laughed. "Everything is strange these days. Canada is in some turmoil. There are talks of confederation, annexation, liberation, call it what you will. And I'm afraid that my own people will not be treated so well if that happens."

"Your people?" Aniqan questioned.

"Half-breeds, mixed-bloods, whatever you wish to call us. Most of

139

us get along fine with our indigenous families, but I'm afraid that tension between the groups will force many to choose a side, if there is conflict."

"So what are you doing here if Canada is farther east?"

The man shrugged. "Farm, as I said. There are some families from Red River who are going to come this way and settle with me and mine. We wish only to live peaceably."

"With respect, sir, no one cares what we want. The Russians didn't care in the north, and I don't think the British care in the east. From some news we've heard, the Americans don't care in the south, either. They want what they want, and they'll take it by force if they must."

"Well, there is some truth to that," Isbister acknowledged. "Some men will never possess enough material wealth to make them happy, and some men will never possess a strong enough will to defy those who would exploit them for that purpose."

"So running away to farm is your idea of a strong will to defy exploitation?"

"There are no good answers, I'm afraid. We must do what we think is right, what is best for our families. I have worked long and hard, and now I have a chance at accomplishing my dream of a simple life. I hope others will join me." He laughed. "You have."

Akłaq and Aniqan glanced at each other.

"It's only you out here?" Akłaq asked.

"A few others, too. All men, building homes, tilling soil, waiting for our women."

"Are they all half-breeds like you?"

"Most, yes. A few are the parents that make half-breeds possible." Isbister gave her a cheeky look. "I daresay you will be the first, perhaps the only, northern Inuit people in our settlement."

Again Akłaq and Aniqan glanced at each other.

The white bear had brought them all the way here...to farm? Akłaq began to wonder whether she hadn't been mistaken. She wondered just what they were supposed to accomplish here. Was there someone they were supposed to meet? Well, if nothing else, a rest from traveling and a little community would be a nice change of pace.

The settlement wasn't much. They had encountered trading posts with more established villages. Isbister's settlement was comprised of a handful houses with another under construction, a few small gardens, and half a dozen fields of sprouted grass. Even the common road through the settlement still hadn't been trodden entirely to dirt.

"As I said," Isbister commented, "it's not much now. But just wait until the women get here. And more families, too. We'll have this place lively and expanding in no time."

"Aren't you worried about raids?" Aniqan wondered.

Isbister shrugged. "It's always a possibility. But we are not as much of a target as Red River. We have no trinkets that Red River does not also possess and which would also serve as a political statement—ah, William! I have mail for you!"

One of the men working on the unfinished house peeled away from his work and met the trio where they dismounted and tied off their horses. Isbister handed the man a folded letter which he opened curiously.

"Bad news?" Isbister inquired, noting the man's expression.

"Maria has been advised not to travel in her condition," William reported, "lest the child be born on the road or in the wilderness. She is going to try to make it before the harvest."

"Well, she shouldn't strain herself."

As the two men spoke, a few others migrated their direction. There were maybe thirty in all, the mixed parentage more obvious in some than others.

"Who's your friends?" one man finally asked. "Don't recognize them from Red River."

"No," Isbister said, turning. "Actually, they found me. This is...erm...what were your names again?"

"Aniqan," Aniqan introduced. "And Akłaq." He gestured to her.

"Well, you're not Cree," another man stated.

"Inuit," Isbister cut in before either could respond. "From the frozen north. Come down looking for bears."

"Bears, eh?" a third said, fingering his beard. "Haven't seen many of those around these parts. Wolves a plenty, but not bears."

"We're looking for the white bear," Akłaq blurted.

That didn't go over very well either, as no one had seen any white bears in the area. If such a one were around, the pelt would fetch a fine price for the man who brought it in.

Akłaq Banded herself and Aniqan. "Maybe this was a bad idea."

"We've only just arrived," he told her. "We're new and exciting to them. Give it a few days for some other sign to appear. You dragged me out here because of tracks; there must be something."

"Then it will be tracks only, as these men have just stated that they would kill the white bear and sell its fur," Akłaq said, in some distress.

"If the white bear is truly of the spirits, I don't think the greatest hunter in the world would have a chance at even scratching it."

After a moment, she nodded and dropped the Band. Isbister jumped to their defense in the crowd.

"Please, they've only just arrived," he said gently. "I'm sure there will be time to get to know them and ask questions. For now, I'm sure they'd like to get settled in. And there's still work to be done."

That got the crowd to break up, the men returning to the unfinished house and picking up where they left off. Isbister turned to Akłaq and Aniqan.

"You two can stay with me for the time being. If you want. This sounds like a surprise trip for you, as much as it was a surprise to me, but do you know how long you'll be staying?"

"No, we don't," Aniqan replied.

Isbister nodded. "Well, as I said, you can stay with me if you'd like, figure out what you intend to do. We've lots of strong men here, as you've seen, to help you build a house, get yourselves settled and whatnot."

Neither one of them was sure of the likelihood of that idea at the moment, but they thanked him and followed him inside his house.

It was very much like some of the houses in the village, the ones built as permanent structures, though there was a certain homeliness about it that reminded Akłaq of the cabin she shared with Nika. One day soon, if all went well, Isbister's wife and children would join him here and the whole place would come to life.

They did not linger long in the house, just long enough to claim a place to sleep and drop off their stuff. Then they went back outside to tend to the horses and turn them out to pasture.

When all was said and done, Isbister declared it about time for dinner. When they returned to the house, however, someone was waiting for them.

"Ah, Gerald, what can I do for you?" Isbister asked amiably.

"I was wondering if I might speak with our guests," the man, Gerald, replied, just as pleasantly. "If they understand me well enough."

"We understand," Aniqan cut in.

Isbister made a gesture, then slipped inside his house. Gerald made another motion, for Akłaq and Aniqan to follow him. They did so, walking a fair distance from the hub of activity, through a planted field. Gerald's age was impossible to determine, but he appeared older than Aniqan. Nothing about him looked especially indigenous as he had white skin and sandy brown hair with matching mustache and beard, though looks could be deceiving.

"So, what brings a couple of northerners this far south?" he began, his words friendly, his tone dubious.

"We seek the white bear," Akłaq told him. "He led us to Isbister, and Isbister has brought us here."

The man sighed and put up a Band around the three of them and situated a translator so they could speak freely. "Nice words for normal people. I saw the Band earlier. Why are you here?"

"We do seek the white bear," Aniqan began slowly. "It seems to be part of some destiny Akłaq is a part of. It just happens to coincide with her need to be mentored by others for her Journeyman training."

Gerald did not appear impressed. "And no one told her of the loophole you like to use so you don't have to travel."

"You don't want us to travel."

"I know about it," Akłaq said before tempers could flare. "They told me. I was greatly discouraged from doing this, but the last time I ignored the call of the white bear, people died. I'm not going to do that again."

"And who are you anyway?" Aniqan asked. "Seems to be another great coincidence that the white bear should lead us here, to a settlement of a couple dozen people, and one of them happens to be a Time Agent. More than that, you're a Timekeeper."

"And a Master besides," Gerald added, his tone impossible to judge. "I suppose that means you're going to ask for some training."

"Is there a reason to deny it?"

"I have more of a reason to arrest you and turn you over to the Grandfathers, the way you sneak Time Capsules, hide them, give them to others without actually making new Time Agents. Quite frankly, no one gives a damn about you up in your frozen wasteland, but since you're here..."

"Wouldn't you do the same for your own people?" Akłaq wondered.

"You assume I'm a half-breed. I assure you, I am not. I'm out here as much to ensure that these people assimilate and don't cause trouble, as I am to better survey the region and make more District recommendations, if the population expands as much as I suspect it is going to. With all the troubles in the east, people are going to want to move west. I'm trying to make sure they can safely."

Aniqan muttered something under his breath and took Akłaq by the hand. "Come on. We don't need his training, even if he were offering."

"Maybe I was unclear," Gerald said. "Perhaps my passions made my message ambiguous. If I don't train you, then I'm going to arrest you."

"You call it training, but it's really just forcing yourself on us, just like every other damn invader. We don't want your ways."

"You've already accepted them. Now then, I've given you a choice, a very generous offer. Either you are going to accept my training, or I am going to Suppress you and take you before the Grandfathers. Then, because you've opened this door, I'm going to backtrack your journey to whatever stinking village you've come from and suppress and arrest them, too."

"You can try..." Aniqan growled, fingering his knife.

"All right," Akłaq said. Aniqan looked at her. "All right."

"Akłaq, this is—"

"The way we are intended to proceed." She admitted it, but grudgingly. "The white bear has brought us here for a reason. Even if that reason is manipulative and bad-tempered."

Aniqan lowered his voice. "How do you know this is who the white bear intended for us to find?"

"I just do. I don't know all the details, but this settlement is where we need to be."

Aniqan grumbled something even she couldn't catch. Then, "I hope you're right."

So do I.

He turned back to Gerald who was waiting patiently, his expression smug.

"Fine," Aniqan said. "She'll train with you. I'm a Harvester, so I have nothing to gain from you. I'm here as her protection."

"Lovely sentiment," Gerald said, still smug. "Since you're suddenly going to be here a while, you'll need a place to live, a field for crops, everything we're doing here for Robert." He gestured toward the unfinished home. "I'll give you a day or two to figure out the details, and by then, James' wife and children should be here. We will begin our training then."

He dropped the Band, did an invisible tip of the hat, and walked away.

Aniqan kicked at one of the plants near his feet. "Bastard!" He turned to Akłaq. "There had to be another way. There has to be."

"If there is, the white bear didn't show it to me in that moment. If nothing else, it's bought us a few days to figure out what that alternative might be," Akłaq informed him, feeling no less rotten about the exchange. "Who knows? Maybe one of the incoming settlers is a nicer Timekeeper Master. More importantly, maybe they'll be a more sympathetic half-breed."

"I hope so."

He stalked off without another word. It wasn't much later that Akłaq saw him helping with the new house construction. On her part, she was trying to figure out just what to do next. It seemed as though they had somehow blundered their way into a kind of hostage situation and were now obligated to stay for a time. What to do? And she wasn't referring to the Timekeeper training.

They would need a house. Just from asking questions and listening to conversation, it sounded as though the men here had the construction down to a science and would be able to complete the one they were working on in only a few days, then start on the next one without breaking stride.

They would be expected to farm. The concept was not entirely foreign to Akłaq, though her experience was limited to tending a small garden, coaxing to life whatever would grow over the short, arctic summer. Sure, they'd used the horses to plow up the soil, but growing on the scale that these men were, she'd never even seen it before, never mind done it. Aniqan was just as clueless. The good news was that they did not require so much food, so their inexperience would not be so devastating.

James Isbister, and by extension the rest of the settlers, assumed that Aniqan and Akłaq were man and wife, and the pair did not see a reason to dissuade them from this line of thought. As such, Isbister allowed them to sleep in the room otherwise prepared for his young children.

"I hope the white bear knows what it's doing," Aniqan murmured as they lay down together. "At the very least, if we're not supposed to stay here, I hope the white bear lets us know by mauling that smarmy son of a bitch."

Akłaq giggled. "Well, it would be an fairly obvious sign, I think."

Aniqan just huffed.

"Honestly, Aniqan, it might not be that bad," she said. "At least they're half-breeds, so they have some knowledge of the old ways, whether they're ours or theirs."

"Gerald openly admitted that he's here to make sure they assimilate."

"Then maybe you're here to make sure they don't."

That gave Aniqan some pause, and she could feel him relax. After a moment he said, "It kind of makes you wonder."

"About what?"

"About the southern peoples. It takes a sturdy man and a brave soul to tread where we live. But down here, and farther south, where anyone may walk, I can't imagine what the southern people have gone through, what they're going through now."

"Talking about the removals?"

"And the war."

She shifted uncomfortably. "Well, hopefully we don't have to go quite that far south."

"Given our experiences, it seems we aren't required to go anywhere in order for trouble to find us or our people."

"Is there anything good that we can focus on?" Akłaq asked irritably. "The white bear has brought us here for a reason; surely it wouldn't have brought us so far from home only to abandon us to fate."

He shrugged awkwardly. "I don't know. This is your destiny we're following."

"So you still don't believe in any of it? Spirits, God, nothing?"

"Given some of the things I've seen, I'm inclined to think that something is out there. I just don't know that it likes or cares about us very much."

She huffed. "Well, I think it does, even if we can't see it or understand what we're going through."

"Then you have stronger faith than I do. I envy you for it, honestly." He shifted. "But if we're going to be here for a while, and everything I've seen so far says we are, then we should get some sleep before going out tomorrow and building this new life for ourselves, whatever it is."

That she could agree to. The bed was a comfortable and welcome change from constantly sleeping outside on the hard ground, but she still had a hard time finding sleep. This was mostly due to Aniqan tossing and turning beside her, although her own uncertainty over the situation at large wasn't helping things either.

She was certain that those tracks had been from the white bear. They had to be. Where else would they have come from, and how could they have just disappeared in the middle of the road? What were the odds that there would happen to be a Master Timekeeper at this remote settlement that they just stumbled across based on her whim to follow mystery bear tracks? Yes, the man might be a conniving bastard, but that didn't mean there wasn't more in store for them later by staying here.

Did anyone out there have the answers? Did anyone have a little more insight about what was going on, what was expected of them, of her?

When she at last found sleep, she was suddenly confronted by a feeling of not being alone, and it wasn't a reference to Aniqan beside her. There was a distinct second presence within her sleeping mind, not quite in a dream, but certainly not awake. A spirit, then? Had the white bear come to guide her in a less literal way?

In ways she did not understand, she groped about in her sleeping darkness, looking for the source of the presence. It did not seem to her to be hostile in any fashion, yet there was also a feeling of strength and power, like what a child might feel when held in their father's arms. It was not the same comfort as from a mother, but just as deep and ferocious. It was safety and security, the feeling that everything was going to be all right and the monsters couldn't hurt you.

A sudden homesickness overcame her, a longing for her father, a longing for Nika.

This longing pulled her from her sleep, though she was not yet fully awake. In the darkness, she rolled around, searching for Aniqan.

She found him and pressed close against him. He made some incoherent sounds, sleepily patted her head a few times like a dog, then rolled away.

Akłaq sighed, all feelings of anxiety and homesickness and the mysterious presence receding until all that was left was simple fatigue. She lay back on the bed. Well, as Aniqan said, they had a big day tomorrow. They were building a new life for themselves, its permanence yet to be determined.

Avgun Akimiaq
Master

If Akłaq had ever had any doubts about Gerald Goldsmith, any hope that his gruff personality might give way to something kinder underneath, she was sorely mistaken. In the years that she trained under him, he remained aloof, passive aggressive, Narcissistic, and even outright mean at times.

If she wasn't incompetent because she was Inuit, it was because she was a northerner. If not that, then because she was indigenous. If not that, then because she was a woman. If not that, then obviously she was just wholly inept, just short of needing to be committed for retardation. When she did grasp a concept or make a leap of ability, it was luck only because there was no way his instruction methods were faulty.

Aniqan did not appreciate the man one bit. Not for his training of Akłaq, not for his help in everyday life as more settlers moved into the cluster of homes that had since become a proper village, now called Prince Albert.

As it turned out, very few in the settlement actually liked Gerald. Mostly he was tolerated, accepted more as a helping hand and strong back than a real member of the community. As more people arrived and settled the land, dislike for the man grew until few could find a reason for keeping him around. He was not the only fully white settler, just the most vocal and most annoying in his distaste for the full- and half-indigenous people he lived among.

"I'm only trying to help the people assimilate," he complained once as he and Akłaq trained early in the morning when the sun was barely up. They did everything in a Band so that no one would see them and think their interactions improper.

"Nisbet has done more for the people in the few weeks that he's been here, than you have in all the years that you've been here," Akłaq retorted. "I might have a mind to join them, except I've no children."

"And because I would turn you in to the Grandfathers."

Akłaq relaxed her stance. "So, what, you're not going to pass me on Master rank until I've become sufficiently white? Sufficiently British? Or Canadian?"

Gerald shrugged. "I admit, the proper term does seem to be up in the air these days, but there is something to be said for be mentally and socially mature, in addition to physically skilled. You possess none of these in sufficient quantity. Why would I pass you to Master Timekeeper? Your skills reflect my instruction. None of my students in the past have given me such difficulty."

"Because all of your past students were the same as you. Absolute copies. When you pick up a hammer, you expect it to do the work of a hammer. And I expect that all of your former students did very well. But when you pick up a saw, don't become angry when it does not do the work of a hammer."

He raised a brow. "Interesting analogy, as always. Now then, can we please focus on today's lesson?"

Aniqan swore that the man was going to get his due one day, and sometimes he swore that he would do it himself if he had to.

For his part, Aniqan had settled in rather well. While the first settlers had been interested in farming, the majority of those moving to Prince Albert were half-breeds from Red River who wished to live a more natural lifestyle, largely shunning farming and instead preferring to go on large buffalo hunts. These he participated in with grand enthusiasm, both because he truly enjoyed it as well as to spite Gerald.

By the time Akłaq and Gerald were done training, several hours had passed within the Band, but it was hardly more than a minute or two without. He departed without another word, and she returned to the house she shared with Aniqan, crawling into bed for at least a few minutes of rest before getting on with her day.

"So did you learn anything, or just get another lecture on your inferiority?" Aniqan murmured into her hair.

"He seemed very annoyed that I was using my Bands to alter the time around his speech and change his voice. I thought it was hilarious and an excellent practical use of my skills."

"I feel like he didn't say anything about passing you to Master."

"He didn't."

"You know, we could return to Ujurak. I'm sure Matulik would—"

"No, we're not returning."

"Akłaq, it's obvious that he's not going to pass you, not unless you give up everything. We return to Ujurak, then even if he does scrape together a few Timekeepers, first they'll have to find us and then they'll have to force us. In that time, I'm sure Matulik would pass you. Or someone would. Gerald has done his job and trained you outside the normal District."

"We're not returning."

He sighed. "Akłaq, you've heard the rumors. There's talk about confederation, of Canada becoming its own nation. The expansionists are heading this way. If it's not the Canadians, it's the Americans. Gerald is only the first."

"And you want to run away and hide?"

"I'm saying that we can do some good, fight against the expansionists. But Gerald has the same power, and he could—he will try to stop us. Me and you, we're not much of a match. But if we can get back to the others and force him into our land, force him to come to us, we could take care of him and then come back to help the people here and maybe at Red River and other places, too."

She considered this for a moment. "That might work for one man, but why wouldn't he ask for help from others? District Captains, their Lieutenants, the Regional Manager? We're a quiet exception, Aniqan. They let us live how we do. They let us have our loophole because they don't want us to leave our little bit of land. Even if we got everyone in the village to stand and fight, we're not trained half as well because no one wants to train us up that far. Half don't think we're capable and the other half think we'd turn on them if we did get that kind of power."

"And we have no one to call on? What about the Krydik? They've got their mysterious power."

"They just lost a war fighting against untrained, unaffiliated soldiers with no abilities."

He made a kind of disapproving sound but did not disagree.

"Besides, the Americans want to 'buy' our land from the Russians, as if the land is theirs to give and take as they please. Is going home really going to make us safer?"

Aniqan sighed. "What do you suggest?"

"It was five or six years between when I followed the white bear from my village and when you rescued me, and that was when I was running and unwilling to follow. This time, I am willing. So I can't imagine it's going to be too much longer."

"You think maybe you're putting too many human expectations on the spirits with that line of thinking?"

"It's the only way I can think of to calm my own anxious thoughts. We couldn't have been led here only to be blackmailed by an ill-tempered Narcissist hellbent on turning us into him. There has to be something more. We won't be doing this forever."

Aniqan sat up and slowly got out of bed. "Well, that much is true at least. And I won't say that I wouldn't like this nightmare to end sooner rather than later."

"It's not all bad," Akłaq said, reluctantly conceding defeat and following suit. "You seem to have found your place, or at least something you enjoy."

"Oh, believe me, if I wasn't enjoying myself, I would have left long ago. I just wish for something more. Your vision and need to leave, that was exciting. That was something more than waiting and hoping." He shrugged. "And here we are. Waiting and hoping."

She gave him a look. "Life can't be nonstop action and intrigue, Ani. We'd get worn out, and those of us who survived would probably end up killing each other. Like you said, we can't spend three hundred years only making war."

Not to say she didn't agree with him, to some extent. If Gerald wasn't going to budge on his ridiculous notions and constant berating of her and almost all of the people in Prince Albert, what was the real reason she continued? He'd served his purpose. He didn't have the ultimate say in her becoming a Master Timekeeper. She only needed the approval of three Masters who weren't her mentor, Matulik. There were plenty of Masters in the village who would say she was proficient.

And how did Gerald plan on tracking them down anyway? Would he really want to put so much effort into pursuing and arresting them? They were the people of the north, the keepers of the ice and snow. He would never be able to find them, assuming he survived an arctic winter of endless snow and total darkness.

"It's a bit late now," she said aloud, catching Aniqan before he walked out the door. "Winter is fast-approaching. Let us winter here, and then a summer. If nothing changes, we'll return to the village next autumn. If Gerald wants to arrest us, first he'll have to brave the northern winter to search for us."

Aniqan considered this for a long moment, then nodded. "I like it. We'll see what happens."

Akłaq hoped that the white bear might communicate in some way between now and then. She hoped she didn't sound too demanding. The spirits were understanding, but no one told a grizzly bear what to do.

Summer waned and autumn bloomed. Soon, the first snows began to float to the ground. Twice a week, Akłaq weathered the onslaught of derogatory remarks from Gerald about her abilities, as well as his increasingly Narcissistic remarks about Canada gaining some measure of independence.

"With any luck, then, things will get done a lot faster," he postulated.

"What kind of things?" Akłaq asked innocently.

"Moving west, for one. Expanding. Finding new land for Canadians and establishing new settlements..." He trailed off in a tone of contempt as he vaguely gestured to the town.

"New settlements like this one?" she prodded. "Or is it still too wild and backwards for you?" Normally she might have stopped there with a bit of needling, but this time, she couldn't help herself and the words kept coming. "What's wrong with this place anyway? Is it the religion? Well, Nisbet brought his mission and the church is here. He's even running a school out of it, so it can't be a lack of school. The homes look very much like Canadian homes. Those who farm grow the same crops that you would expect to find. Canadians and Americans enjoy hunting, and they like hunting buffalo; well, Aniqan and other men go out on buffalo hunts. You like furs, we like furs. Is it the language? Some of those from Red River speak English just fine, so maybe it's the French you have a problem with?" She went on, even as Gerald opened his mouth to speak. "What is it, Gerald? What do you have a problem with? What is it that makes everyone who isn't you just so damn inferior? What would it take for us to be equal with you?"

She might have expected him to get angry and launch into a tirade, but he seemed to perceive that that was what she was expecting, maybe even wanted, so, after a huff and a bit of indignant flexing of his muscles, he composed himself and instead answered, "You assume that such a thing is possible. It is not. We are different."

Akłaq gestured to the village as he had done. "They are living just like you!"

"Maybe so, and I commend them for their efforts, but they are not me. They are not my people."

She hoped her look was as incredulous as her feelings. "Then what are you doing here? Why was your own country not good enough? Why do you need ours?"

"Because we are building civilization. You are impeding it."

"And what if we were the aggressors? What if we were able to stave off this 'progress' of your 'civilization'? Then you would call us savage and in need of taming. At least, that's what the Russians believed. No matter what, you see yourselves in the right." Akłaq shook her head. "And I am but a monkey in your circus, an animal you can train."

Gerald shrugged. "I mean, I would say you're wrong, but my mother taught me that lying is also wrong."

Akłaq made a sound that, in her mind sounded like an angry bear, but to her ears was little more than a sound one might make when striking one's thumb with a hammer.

She could tell that Gerald was not holding a very strong grip on the Band that held the two of them out of prying eyes, and she was able to break out of it with minimal effort. Part of her expected him to come after her, part of her knew that he wouldn't. He would be stewing in his self-righteous smugness, watching her leave as though assessing a toddler throwing a tantrum.

Once she was out of sight, walking between a barn and a shed, she Banded, again slowing everything around her until it stopped. She leaned against the wall of the shed she stood beside and made another, less threatening, sound, tearing at her hair, trying to express her frustration.

When she finally looked up, she spotted the shovel, leaning against the side of the barn not fifteen feet away. One door of the shed was open as if someone had intended to put the shovel away but had been distracted by some other errand.

There was no coherent, articulated thought in her mind, only a feeling, a desire, something that she believed would solve her crisis, though she could not readily articulate that, either. She went to the shovel, but before she could reach out and grab it, she heard a distinct noise behind her. Turning, she found the white bear, clear as day and big as life.

"Are you here to tell me I'm right or that I'm wrong?" she asked. She was not snapped out of her malicious trance, but felt instead as if she were seeing everything outside of herself.

The bear did not speak, just puffed hot breath into the crisp air.

"You see what he's doing, don't you? He's part of the problem. He's trying to erase us!"

Still the bear said nothing.

"He's not interested in talking or learning or anything else. Even if we were to become just like him, he wouldn't respect us. Because we're not him. And we're not him! We are our own!"

Now the bear spoke, its voice reminding Akłaq of how her father's voice sounded when she pressed her ear against his chest. The bear simply asked, "Are you?" It swung its huge head around to look at someone, a half-breed, perhaps fifty feet away. "Who are they?"

The bear put the emphasis on "who" in such a way that Akłaq would admit to feeling a little uncomfortable. And yet she replied with, "We are our own people. We shouldn't be made to mimic others like monkeys and hope for a reward!"

She sucked in a breath as her mind and body came back together like a punch in the gut, and she grabbed the shovel even before she felt fully at strength. When she turned around yet again, the bear was gone, and she stumbled out from between the shed and the barn on jellied legs.

Gerald was, as expected, still standing there, just starting to move, but with that look of smug satisfaction she had come to loathe. All his needling and comments, his arrogance and self-righteousness. His racism, sexism, Narcissism, and other words she didn't know but hoped they existed in order to describe every foul thing that was apparent in his rotten personality. She would be doing the town a favor. If any man who had lived in Prince Albert for more than three days didn't fantasize about Gerald's death, at least a little bit, then that man was either a liar or just as wretched. No man had ever asked for this so much. Even the men who had killed her husband and children had been more forthcoming about their intentions. But to deal with this wicked man day after day for years, it was like the entire Russian army had returned in just this one man.

She circled behind the wretched bastard, picked up the shovel — its handle soft pine but head heavy folded iron — and swung it at him, aiming for his brain stem.

One of the less spectacular abilities one developed in Timekeeper training was Reflexive Banding, tying one's sense of danger and self-preservation into Banding so that one had more time to perceive, analyze, and react to potential threats. Already anticipating this reaction, Akłaq was ready to meet it. As every moment ticked by and she saw the shovel get closer and his reflexes started to kick in, she pushed against that Band, digging in Time Tendrils, holding Gerald on his plane of Time while she and the shovel operated on a faster plane.

As the blade of the shovel tore flesh, Gerald's Reflexive Band redoubled itself, and she could feel him begin to react with a conscious Band.

But all the years that he had told her that she wasn't good enough, that she was incompetent and inept, when in fact, she had become stronger than him. It was little trouble for her to keep his Bands at bay. And as the shovel penetrated skin and muscle and hit bone and nerve, his Bands disintegrated and his body began to panic.

Then the shovel stuck. Akłaq was jerked off-balance briefly with a crack of the shovel's handle, but she recovered easily enough. The blade of the shovel had struck true, and Gerald went to the ground. She'd known that she was only likely to get one chance at killing him, but some part of her still hoped that he knew what had happened, that he knew it was her. Some part of her hoped that his smug self-righteousness had broken in that final moment.

She stared at his body for a long moment, then turned and walked away. Two steps in, she realized she was shaking. Five steps, and her legs felt wobbly. She counted herself lucky that she made it back to the shed before she collapsed, tears streaming down her cheeks, body shaking uncontrollably, and yet she did not truly cry. The only word she could think of at the moment was relief. Utter relief. She wouldn't have to listen to any more comments about how stupid she was, nor how bad of a student. Seeing how he'd never intended to give her his recommendation on Master status, she really hadn't lost anything.

After a few minutes, she finally composed herself, wiping her eyes and calming her nerves, and stood. She was still in her Band and stayed there until she was safely back home.

When she dissolved the Band, she made herself something to eat as a kind of reward, then started grabbing bags and packing things up.

It didn't take half an hour for Gerald's body to be discovered. Akłaq went out with everyone else to take a look. While there was plenty of excited chatter and perhaps a little frantic worrying, the overall mood of the crowd seemed to be apathy, even a bit of smug satisfaction.

"Bastard got what was coming to him," someone finally said aloud.

Nisbet, who had come from the church and now knelt beside the body for last rites, looked up. "He was still a child of God."

"Then he was a man only a father could love, because no one else did."

"Poor personality is no excuse for murder. Someone has stolen this man's life, stolen his soul!"

"He did the same here, to the rest of us," a woman said scornfully. "Every day, little by little. I'm surprised it took so long for someone to do him in."

Her words seemed to be some invisible cue, for the crowd began to disperse. As Akłaq was walking away, Aniqan caught up to her. He didn't say anything, but as soon as they were home and the door closed them, he gave her a look.

"We both know no normal person could do that," he stated.

"Then it's a good thing we're not normal," she replied.

His expression turned odd and he shook his head. "What made you do it? What happened to waiting another year and forcing him to come after us?"

She took an even breath. "I don't think he'd do it, honestly. He would get more satisfaction out of knowing that he forced us to run away. We run away, the people here forcibly assimilate or be trampled..." She shook her head. "I'd just had enough. I couldn't stand the thought of another day, another minute, of his stupid smirking face looking down at me while I toiled and trained for nothing." Now she giggled. "Or not for nothing, considering I ended up stronger than him. A Journeyman killed a Master."

"I don't think that's going to earn you a very good recommendation."

She waved a hand. "I'm not worried. I have a few more centuries to make up for it."

Only then did Aniqan seem to realize that she was packing things up, the bags sitting on the floor, numerous household items divided into several piles. "And these are the actions of an innocent woman?"

"The others aren't exactly eager to pursue a murderer," Akłaq defended. "Certainly not his murderer."

"All right, maybe not, but what's all this? If you don't think Gerald would have pursued us, and you just got done killing him, why are we suddenly leaving?"

"Because Gerald was only one man. There is a whole army of Geralds in the east wanting to do exactly what he did."

"And your plan is to go and kill all of them with shovels? How does the white bear feel about that?"

Akłaq hesitated, then repeated her encounter with the white bear. "I think it tried to stop me. But—"

"I seem to remember you once making a comment that the last time you disobeyed the white bear, people died. This time, not only did someone die, but you killed him yourself."

"You can't say he didn't deserve it."

"I absolutely think he did, but why did it fall to you?"

"Like you said, no ordinary person was going to be able to do it."

Aniqan sighed and pinched the bridge of his nose. "All right. Fine. It's not as though I hadn't threatened to do it myself." He glanced at the bags on the floor. "So where are we going, do you know?"

"Red River. Something is driving all these people west, and I want more than just rumors and news of far off places."

He nodded slowly. "All right. And again I ask, what do you plan to do?"

"I won't know until I get there."

"So this has gone from simple curiosity about the world and trying to advance in your Timekeeping, to a crusade against injustice?"

"Isn't that what you wanted, too? You said you were tired of sitting around waiting for Ujurak to have a vision."

"Yes, now I'm living with a woman who also encounters the spirits and decides to ignore them." He put up a hand when she opened her mouth. "Fine. We'll go to Red River. It's not as if we have any great reason to stay. And you're right that I want to actually do something for the people, whether it's our people or someone in a worse position than us, like the Cree and the half-breeds. I just don't want to jeopardize anyone or anything because you obey or disobey the spirits at your whim and leisure. Am I making sense?"

Akłaq took a breath and nodded. "Yes. And maybe I did get a little carried away, but I just...I couldn't take it anymore. I really couldn't. You didn't like him. Nobody liked him. But to have to stand there and have to call him master and listen to him insult me, insult all of us..." She shook her head.

"He wasn't any nicer to the rest of us, believe me." Aniqan took a step forward and gingerly put his hands on her shoulders. "Can I make one suggestion, without you taking a shovel to my head?"

She gave him a look and motioned for him to continue.

"Let's wait until spring before going to Red River. Only a guilty man —or woman—would try to travel in this weather. Now the people here might not care, but we don't need to risk any rumors about it in Red River. If you're right and there are more Geralds in the east, they'll not only try to kill you, but they'll have far more resources at their disposal. Even the Krydik were overwhelmed in the south."

Akłaq hesitated and glanced at the bags on the floor, the haphazard piles on the floor around them. After a long moment, she nodded. "Maybe you're right. I suppose it would look a little suspicious."

"And above all," Aniqan said severely, squeezing her shoulders, "keep your mouth shut. The others might figure it out, they might not. They might be able to feign ignorance for a rumor, but no one likes a braggart."

Avgun Akimiaq Atausriq
Red River

Winter was not the best time to kill someone, and it had little to do with trying to bury a body in the frozen ground. Rather, it had to do with having far too much time for Akłaq to think about what she'd done and why, and the fact that going to Red River meant she probably intended to do it again and on a larger scale.

She would never recant her statement that Gerald absolutely deserved what he got, though she couldn't help but wonder exactly what it was she planned to do in Red River. As Aniqan said, she couldn't just go around killing people with a shovel. And where Gerald was clearly loathed by everyone, that wouldn't always be the case. A monster to one was a hero to another.

Despite her doubts, once spring arrived, she and Aniqan said goodbye to the people of Prince Albert and set off for Red River.

The people who had come from Red River to Prince Albert had tried their best over the winter to dissuade them. The animosity between the French half-breeds and the English half-breeds was only a minor annoyance compared to the disdain the full-blooded Europeans—of all varieties—held for them. Property rights were ignored, sure to be seized when governance was turned over to the Canadians and their expansionist ideals! Be assured, they said, there was nothing for them in Red River.

They went anyway.

It really wasn't a long trip; certainly no trip was longer than the one they'd undertaken to get from their village all the way to Prince Albert. Trotting along on horseback, this felt more like a pleasant outing. And after several years of not going anywhere, it was a breath of fresh air. Even if they were chased out of Red River in the end, the trip was needed.

They spoke little on the road, except for minor observations about the landscape. The road itself was worn enough to see where it twisted and turned over the prairie and through the trees, but it was still sparsely traveled. Any travelers they met were all heading west, some for Prince Albert and some for towns far beyond. All tried to dissuade the two of them from going to Red River. Akłaq and Aniqan thanked them for the warnings, but continued on anyway, through sun and rain, as the days got longer and warmer.

Akłaq had become quite accustomed to shorter winters, as well as winters where the days were very much longer than what she had grown up with. All the same, a part of her yearned for a long winter and the closing in of the night, wrapping everything in its dark embrace. It made the summers feel that much more significant. And as much as she enjoyed having a more constant cycle of day and night, she also missed the part of summer when the sun never went away. Any time she was awake and wanted to do something, the sun was there to show her the way.

"Do you suppose," she began, "since we're doing more to follow the white bear, and seeing how we are discovering more and more about Time and perhaps discovering more purpose, that we'll be able to return to Ujurak and the others soon? Rather than having to wait five, ten, twenty years?"

"It's hard to say," Aniqan mused. "I don't pretend to speak for the spirits, or know what the white bear has in store."

"Yes, but it seems as though we are making progress. Don't you think?"

"It felt that way when you say you saw bear tracks leading us to Isbister, and our initial meeting with Gerald, discovering another Time Agent. Living under his thumb for so long and having to suffer his abuse, that didn't feel like much progress. And who's to say that going to Red River is what we're supposed to do? I can't help but wonder if the white bear tried to stop you, and you ignored it."

Akłaq sighed. "Ani, we've been over this. If it had told me to stop, I would have. But it didn't."

"All right, so, pretending that it was entirely supportive of you killing Gerald, then why didn't it say, 'kill Gerald and go to Red River'? Give a little more direction?"

"I don't think it needed to, not so explicitly. I think I just knew." She went on before he could speak. "We have instincts, too, Ani, just like the animals. If we waited for explicit guidance over every minute issue, nothing would ever get done."

He looked uncertain but did not argue.

And, Akłaq reasoned to herself, the white bear had had all winter to tell them to go or not go. Or even to chastise her for what she'd done, tell her to confess to the murder. It had done neither. Therefore, she could only conclude that it was what she was supposed to do. She had rid Prince Albert of a dreadful person, and now they were going to Red River, perhaps, to do something similar.

The closer they got to Red River, the more well-trodden the road became, and the more people they saw. Smaller clusters of homes had sprung up around the village proper. It somewhat resembled Prince Albert, that some had taken to farming and so had large plots of wheat and other crops, and others preferred to stick to a more traditional lifestyle, their homes surrounded by large racks of meat smoking over large pits.

Red River itself appeared to be more of a conglomeration of people rather than a cohesive settlement. There were whites, there were indigenous, there were English half-breeds and French half-breeds. There were traditionalists, there were Methodists, there were Roman Catholics. And no one seemed able to agree on anything other than how unfair it was that the government was taking so long to send out surveyors for the land and seemed to be governing unilaterally with no regard to the people living there.

"Well, we haven't been run out of town upon entry," Aniqan observed as they halted their horses and looked around. "Where do you propose we start?"

"I don't know," Akłaq admitted. "There are obviously different groups here—" She could feel a number of eyes on her, but every time she glanced at someone, they made a point of looking away. "—but I don't think we need to start any fights by talking to the wrong people."

"Let's see if we can't find a trading post," he suggested. "That seems like it would be the most neutral territory for asking questions."

She agreed, and they nudged their horses forward. They elected not to speak to anyone or ask for directions, instead deciding to search out the post on their own. There was a certain tension in the air that neither felt like rupturing.

Suddenly Akłaq's already nebulous mission felt even more foolish, dangerous, even. Unlike Prince Albert, where it had been one man hated by an entire town, here there were groups and factions and loyalties. Some of these manifested as subtle hints, and others as something just short of outright hostility. And it wasn't always easy to tell who was who, just by looking at them. Only blanket mistreatment by a far away government seemed to cool tempers enough that there wasn't spontaneous violence. The idea that there was an outside evil making their lives miserable was an oddly unifying force among the settlers, though it was a tenuous force at best.

This did not mean that Akłaq feared being shot off her horse, or suddenly seized and dragged away to be raped once she dismounted outside the trading post. But just by riding through town and observing the people, she could see that simply talking to people— even small talk—was going to be a bigger choice with bigger consequences than it had been in Prince Albert.

As Aniqan had suspected, the trading post was viewed as neutral territory. Some people and groups still avoided each other, maybe traded nasty glares, but this was as far as it got.

"Whaddaya got?" the post manager asked at the desk. "Or whaddaya want?"

"We've just arrived in Red River," Aniqan said. "We're looking for somewhere to stay, somewhere to live."

The man raised a brow. "That's interesting. Most people are looking to leave."

"Then there should be plenty of houses."

"Sure, but good luck keeping it. No one can get their land surveyed and all the deed work seems to go missing when it's most convenient for the government." The man waved a hand. "Your better bet is go west. I hear Prince Albert is doing very well."

"We've just come from there. We intend to stay here," Aniqan pressed.

The man shrugged. "I can't help you anyway, even if I wanted to. This is a trading post, not a deeds office or surveyor."

"Where can we find a deeds office or surveyor?"

"There is no surveyor. What do you think we're all waiting for? As for the deeds office, well, they're not the most helpful type. Some of it they can't help you with because of the government. And what they can help you with, they probably won't, for any reason they can think up."

Nevertheless, they got directions to the deeds office. It was a small building, unremarkable, hardly recognizable as anything important except for the small sign near the door that read "Deeds and Titles". Inside, the place smelled of dust, must, old paper, and fresh ink. A man sat behind a desk, a large ledger open before him. He barely glanced up as they approached.

"I'm sorry, we're closed," he grumbled into the paper.

"Your sign says otherwise," Aniqan told him.

"I don't care what the sign says, we're closed."

"We're here anyway. We want to know what it takes to live in one of the houses here. If everyone is moving out, one of them must be empty."

The man still did not look up from his ledger as he scratched away, and he continued to mumble into the paper. "You cannot occupy a residence without a deed or permission from the one who holds the deed. You can't get a deed without a survey of the land. The surveyor is currently tied up in matters back east and won't be out for several months, maybe even next year. That means that all vacant land is property of the government. If you attempt to occupy such a residence, I will have no choice but to have you removed, by force if necessary."

For a long moment, no one spoke. Finally Akłaq asked, "So what do you expect us to do?"

The man with the ledger shrugged, still not looking up. "That's not my problem, is it? I have some surveys and deeds available for land tracts in Prince Albert—"

"We've just come from there. We want to stay here."

He shrugged again. "I'm sorry. I can't help you. Unless you get a deed or permission from someone who has one, there is nothing I can do."

Even Akłaq could see that he was lying, but there was little she or Aniqan could do about it.

They left the office and stood outside, each with a hand on their respective reins but neither mounting their horse.

"What now?" Akłaq wondered, glancing at Aniqan.

"I don't know," he replied, shrugging. "Maybe we should ride around town a little and see if the white bear shows up to tell us what to do."

His look was mildly accusatory as he got on his horse. Akłaq sighed and followed suit.

Their ride around town was not uneventful, and they quickly learned that the different neighborhoods were populated with different peoples. Half-breeds made up a majority of the population, but they seemed to be divided according to which white people they belonged to, and which indigenous people they belonged to. This was broken down even further, it seemed, based on just how much ancestry of one or the other they possessed, their preferred religion, and other factors Akłaq did not understand just based on passing observation.

Akłaq had heard plenty about cities while living in Prince Albert, but she'd never been able to really picture what one looked like, how people just lived together with no room for movement, barely room for a small garden. Now that she was looking at it, she decided she didn't like it. She needed space to move around and get away from people. At least now she was on a horse so she could be above them and look around.

As promised, there were plenty of empty houses—and it was not unreasonable to think that some people were living in houses that the deeds office might consider unoccupied.

"What do you suppose would happen if we just laid claim to one of these outlying homes?" Aniqan wondered. "If we farmed a bit and helped keep the people fed in the city, would they really kick us out?"

"Aniqan, you hate farming," Akłaq reminded him. "And the most I can handle is a small garden."

"Maybe, but I'm sure some people here still go out on buffalo hunts."

"You're in the wrong neighborhood if you're looking to do that," a new voice said.

They turned to see a man approaching them on horseback. If he was a half-breed, he clearly favored his indigenous side. He looked not much older than Aniqan. He tossed something to them, which Akłaq caught. When she opened her hand, she found a couple of translators, as from the Wheel.

"If it makes you more comfortable," the man said.

Akłaq glanced at Aniqan, then handed him one of the devices which they situated appropriately.

"How did you know we were—?" Akłaq began.

"Because you're northerners, for one," the man told her. "Few northerners come so far south, especially here. For two, with certain other clues, I deduced that you're the one who killed Goldsmith."

Aniqan bristled and moved his horse between Akłaq and the man.

But the man just laughed. "I mean no harm. Believe me, no one was sorry to see him go."

"And who are you?" Aniqan wondered.

"Forgive me. You may call me Everett. My mother was Cree, my father the son of a Cree and a Frenchman."

Aniqan and Akłaq introduced themselves in turn.

"I'm sorry to hear how fortune has treated you," Everett went on. "Ujurak was a good man."

Akłaq gave him a look. "What do you mean, was?"

Everett's expression turned puzzled. "You didn't know?" He pursed his lips. "We thought Goldsmith had taken you hostage in some way, using your training and the designation of District Nine as some kind of leverage."

"He did. He said that if we didn't cooperate, he was going to arrest us and our village and take us before the Grandfathers."

"He did that anyway, didn't he?" Aniqan guessed.

Everett nodded. "In the time that he held you, he managed to find Ujurak and the others. He got the Regional Manager, some of the District Captains, and others together. They raided the village. A few were killed, a few escaped. Most were taken before the Grandfathers. My guess is, you weren't far from being arrested yourselves. Actually, I thought perhaps you killed him because he was trying to arrest you."

Akłaq didn't know what to think. Ujurak and Matulik and the others. Just gone. Vanished. Arrested and imprisoned just like that. While she toiled under the very same man who arranged it. Rage and anger and even sorrow bubbled within her, but she didn't know that she could feel it properly seeing how she'd already killed Gerald. Killed him for a crime she wasn't aware he'd committed.

"What does that mean for us now?" Akłaq asked. "Are the Manager and Captains looking for us?"

"It's not impossible," Everett said honestly. "It didn't take me long to put together who you were; it wouldn't take them very long either, if they tried. And there are plenty more whites who are Time Agents than any of us." He nodded. "But District Nine protects our own."

"What do you suggest?" Aniqan inquired. "Clearly we can't return to Ujurak, and we shouldn't return to Prince Albert. Red River seems a bit...obvious. And even so, it appears that we are last on the list to find a home or any land here."

"Red River will suffice for now. As for finding a place to stay, I assume it's because of the deeds and surveys and whatnot?"

"The man at the deeds office told us it could be next year before the surveyor came out," Akłaq said.

Everett's look turned mischievous. "Only for those who don't have certain resources at their disposal."

"What do you mean?"

"Find a house or plot of land you want, then come find me. I'll make that deed and survey appear."

Aniqan glanced at the house they stood in front of. "You said we were in the wrong neighborhood. We've seen the divisions among the people here. Where would you suggest we start?"

An hour and a half later, the three of them stood in the Wheel of Time, waiting on a secretary who was busy duplicating the deed and survey of Everett's home, then forging the details of the home they wanted. By the time it was finished, there was no visual or tactile difference between the two papers, nothing that gave away the one as a copy. Then a second copy was made, just in case.

"Now you take one copy of the documents to the deeds office, give it to that rat-faced son of a bitch, and the house and lands is yours," Everett told them as they retraced their steps through the Wheel, heading for the portal room.

"I thought for sure we would be arrested if we came here," Akłaq said. "All the looks and the stares...even the secretaries didn't seem to like you, Everett."

Everett shrugged. "Well, normally you need an appointment for such forgeries. As for being arrested, there are plenty of people who have minor crimes against them. It's just not worth it to pursue them, usually. Timekeepers on Earth are generally pretty relaxed about small things, compared to some of the Engaged worlds. But Goldsmith and the others had enough of a vendetta that they pushed the issue and made it happen. Besides, even though you killed Goldsmith, that alone is not a crime according to the Laws of Time. They could care less about murder, but don't you dare cut into their profits." He rolled his eyes dramatically.

"What about my training, though? How long will they be imprisoned? Gerald didn't exactly give me a recommendation and I still have other training I need to do, but I still need Matulik."

"I don't know how long they'll be imprisoned." They reached the portal that would take them back to Everett's home. "This political business with District Nine always makes things more complicated. As for your training, I will take over for the time being, if you want."

They stepped through the Paa to Everett's home, Akłaq bracing herself for the terrible constriction that would leave her feeling a bit like wet grass. She accepted an arm as it was offered, though Aniqan was in little better shape. Somehow they made it to a couple of chairs where they, along with Everett in a third chair, simply sat and waited for the worst of the vertigo to pass. When it did, Everett stood and fetched some water for all of them.

"What rank are you?" Aniqan wondered, downing his water in a single gulp.

"I am a Master Timekeeper. I am also a Core Akari-bearer."

"Akari-bearer!" Akłaq blurted, her mind getting more excited than her voice. "But we've heard that it was only a myth."

"Men dismiss what they do not understand, and they demonize what they wish to be rid of," Everett told her.

"Where did you learn?" Aniqan asked.

"From the Krydik, initially, for I was raised in their city of Aktiya Waya after being rescued as a child. I returned to try and help the people here, but, as you may know, success is hard to come by."

"How great can the Akari be if they still lost a war?"

"A tool is only as effective as the hand that wields it, and even a skilled tradesman tires. The greatest warrior on the battlefield will eventually become overwhelmed. I have since begun to train with the Akarin and learn from their many centuries of knowledge, rather than the scattering of accidental discoveries the Krydik have made."

Akłaq glanced at Aniqan. "Wasn't there some news about...something about a militant faction or...?"

"It's a long story, and there is much to learn," Everett cut in. "If you want, I can demonstrate and I will teach you. Or I can simply teach you as a Master Timekeeper. However, I feel obligated to warn you that being an Akari-bearer is not a simple nor easy life, especially after the events of the Missing Zero Hour." He went on before either could speak. "If you want to learn, I will teach you. But you have to want it. I understand how frightening it is to learn about Time and the Hands and an entire universe, when all you may have known is your family, your village, and whatever tragedy befell them. If you decide to pursue the Akari, it will be like that all over again."

Akłaq hesitated for a long moment. Then, "Can the Akari stop fire?"

Everett blinked. "A skilled Akari-bearer may come to understand the nature of fire, and he may gain some measure of control, greater than what Timekeeping alone can produce, but fire is a fickle beast and no one's slave."

"Do you believe in the Author?" Aniqan wondered. "That is the Akarin god, isn't it?"

"I don't know how much I believe in the Author as a god," the Cree man admitted humbly, "but someone wrote the story of the Cherokee and the Krydik, and I have even spoken to Anagalisgi and seen the Whites—"

"The white bear?" Akłaq interrupted.

Everett chuckled. "There is more than just a bear. They are Whites of all varieties, some creatures known only to us through the stories of our ancestors, and even some creatures we have no names for."

Akłaq grinned and looked at Aniqan. "I knew we were getting closer."

Like a tumult of clouds, words started pouring out of her mouth as she related her tale of the white bear, how it helped her escape her burning village, led Matulik and the others to her when she'd been left for dead, took her away from Ujurak and brought her south and introduced her to Isbister. Reluctantly, she also told Everett about the white bear's appearance just before she made the decision to actually kill Gerald.

"Does that mean that the Author approves of what I did?" she asked, finally running out of words. "If he writes what we do and what we say, then if he hadn't wanted Gerald to die, then he wouldn't have directed me to kill him."

"I don't know," Everett said thoughtfully. "I don't know where free will and dictation intersect, whether he would have tried to arrest you, whether we would have met at all under different circumstances. But it does appear that this meeting is more than chance."

"You really believe all this?" Aniqan wondered, glancing back and forth between Akłaq and Everett. "You really want to go along with what he has to say?"

"Why not?" Akłaq asked. "The white bear brought me here. If the white bear is one of the spirits and...I don't know who Anagalisgi is, but he sounds important, and there are others..." She looked at him. "You once said that you didn't know what you believed anymore. Between Time and having everyone else impose their lives and their religions on you, you just didn't know. This might be a chance to find out."

"I'll not demand an answer today," Everett said calmly. "For one, I am too tired from the portal. For two, you need to see about moving in to your new home."

That brought things back to the present moment. Akłaq and Aniqan scraped themselves out of their respective chairs. Aniqan held the forged deed and survey. When they reached the door, he turned back to look at Everett. "You're sure this will work?"

Everett grinned, still looking a bit fatigued. "You're not the first people I've helped to find a home here while the government agents are away."

With a bit of trepidation, Aniqan and Akłaq returned to the deeds office. The same man sat at the same desk, staring into the same ledger. Akłaq couldn't even be sure he wasn't on the same page.

Aniqan did not say anything, just laid the deed and survey on the ledger in front of the man's nose.

This finally got the man to look up, and he did appear rat-faced as

Everett had said, with a narrow forehead, pinched nose, high cheeks that seemed to squeeze his eyes, a skinny jaw and jutting chin.

"The deed and survey of our new house," Aniqan told him.

The man looked down at the papers, briefly skimming the text.

"Where'd you steal these from?" he asked snidely.

"How could we have stolen them? If the house is unoccupied, it's unoccupied. And now it's ours."

The man sighed, picked up the papers, looked over them several times, then looked over them again. He seemed to be looking for anything that might disqualify them, out them as fake. Akłaq's heart thudded loudly in her chest as she waited for him to point out something, anything. Finally he sighed and arranged the papers into the piles on his desk. His look was still a bit suspicious, but finally he said, "The house is yours."

Avgun Akimiaq Malġuk
Akari

Everett was right. It was like waking up to the larger universe all over again. Akłaq was only just a Journeyman Timekeeper, but suddenly she felt even smaller than she had on day one of her probationary training.

She watched him pull the water out of a leaf, and extract iron from a chunk of rock, all using only his hands. Those abilities—of which he considered his demonstrations to be "simple" examples—fell in the realm of Matter.

Then she could only stare in awe as he caused various items and even himself to levitate in the air, manipulating a property of Energy called Gravity.

"So you're saying that you can fly?!" Akłaq blurted once everything was safely back on the ground.

"It's not so simple as that," Everett told her. "An Akari-bearer does not master the forces of the earth, he simply manipulates them, works with them. He takes what is already established and changes it, but he does not establish something new. Gravity as a constant must be overcome—"

"But you just lifted yourself off the ground."

"No, I changed the gravitational constant around me so that I was no longer attracted to the earth so forcefully. Birds overcome this force naturally through the beating of their wings, but they must keep moving their wings or else they will fall, for gravity is all around us. If I wanted to 'fly' as you put it, I would have to continuously alter the gravity around me. Therefore, Gravity is best done along a track, a guide."

As far as Akłaq was concerned, the man flew.

Perhaps his most frightening demonstration involved the use of something he called DNA. According to him, DNA was the foundation of life, and it shaped every living thing, told every single part of the body what to be and what to do, even how to present. An Akari-bearer could not only touch one's DNA, but alter it. And he did so, bringing what he called his "French genes" to the surface and showing off what he might have looked like if he looked more like his French grandfather.

"And you change yourself back?" Akłaq wondered, her mouth agape at the whole display. It was like watching layers of ice melt off the man as he first appeared normal, then became a white man, then went back to normal, each phase lasting only a few seconds.

"Our DNA repairs itself when things go wrong," Everett explained. "My DNA knows when I have changed it, so it works to correct the error. It is possible to hold it for long periods of time and Disguise oneself, but eventually, I will always return to who and what I am."

Akłaq stumbled back to sit on a rock next to Aniqan who looked more annoyed than impressed.

"If you can do all these things, why did the Krydik lose their war in the south?" he asked grumpily. "Why is there still war at all?"

"The invention of the sword did not stop war in ancient times, and the invention of the gun has not stopped it in modern times," Everett pointed out. "Simply adding more power will never solve the problem of war." He went on before Aniqan could speak. "As for the Krydik, their problems arose because they only ever trained for peaceful things, assuming they trained at all, for the use of the Akari is of some dispute. A man may wield a knife with some effectiveness against a single, unskilled opponent, but with no further instruction, his ability to enter combat is sorely diminished. The average Krydik man may be able to use Gravity to lift a log that is blocking his way, but such talent is useless if he is unprepared for the chaos and complexity of battle."

"Maybe so, but even a single man with decent skill could do more than a whole army, and it looks to me that the Akari is far superior to meager Time. We know that there are not many Time Agents on Earth, and I imagine that there are even fewer Akari-bearers. But you seem of decent skill, so why were you unable to save Ujurak and the others?"

"I cannot stop a tragedy I do not know is happening. There may be a fight going on back in town at the pub, but if I don't know about it, I can do nothing. No one knew about Ujurak until after it happened. By then, there was nothing anyone could do. Furthermore, you had already killed Goldsmith, so that aspect was also taken care of."

Aniqan shrugged, though he still seemed unwilling to give up the point. He made a vague gesture back toward town. "And what's going on here in Red River. With Canada becoming more or less independent and the people unhappy with the governance over the land, if it did turn into unrest and even violence, what are you going to do? Are you going to stop it?"

"It is surprisingly difficult to find a saint when you are surrounded by sinners," Everett told him, his tone a bit harsh. "I am not judge, jury, or executioner. I play my role as saving those who would otherwise be victims of circumstance, poor planning, and short tempers."

"That works well for a pub brawl, but what about the men like Gerald? Those who would force subjugation or kill us without a second thought? Saving their victims is good, but it does nothing to actually stop evil from spreading." Aniqan scoffed, shook his head, and stood angrily. "You're all talk. Just like Ujurak. All talk, enough action to make yourself feel good, feel like you might be doing something, but not doing anything to actually help anyone."

Everett did not back down. "And what would you do, then? If you could do everything I just demonstrated, and anything your mind could come up with, what would you do? Tell me."

"I would start by killing those like Gerald. Band, so they couldn't detect me, and kill them."

"Them. Those like Gerald?"

"Mhm."

"And who are they? In town. Name them. Who in town is like Gerald?"

"The man at the deeds office."

Everett nodded. "All right. You've killed him. What do you think happens? Someone from back east sends another one just like him to sit in that same damn chair looking at the same damn book, giving everyone here the same damn answers as to why things aren't getting done."

"Then I'll go east," Aniqan stated. "And kill the politicians who want to take our land."

The Cree man nodded again. "Fair enough. You go east. You kill the politicians. What happens next? War is declared. It might take time to mobilize the army proper, but the average person will rise up also. Now everyone in Red River has to choose a side, and with the number and mix of half-breeds here, those divisions will not only be stark, but painful."

"They won't have to choose sides," Aniqan cut in. "Now they can live in peace because they're not being dictated to by foreign mercenaries hundreds of miles away."

"You still have the problem of the army coming to avenge the deaths of the politicians."

"You're assuming they'll figure out it was me, or anyone from Red River."

Everett made a gesture of deference. "Very true. So let's pretend that they don't know that it was you or anyone from Red River. Let's pretend they think it was some other foreign agent—the French, the Americans, the Russians, anyone else. There will still be war. But because it's a foreign war, those soldiers are going to come to every town looking for conscripts."

"Then I'll kill the soldiers, too."

"And become a tyrant," Everett said coldly. He took an even breath. "I'm not saying that violence never solved anything, because sometimes, it does come to that. But you have to think beyond the present moment; you have to consider the consequences. A man without Time, without the Akari, must work ten times harder to effect change, yes, and sometimes he never really leaves his small sphere of influence. He is but a pebble being dropped into a pond. A man with Time, or a man with the Akari, is capable of incalculable devastation if he is not careful. He is a mountain crumbling into an ocean, capable of causing a tsunami that could wipe out cities an ocean away."

"I can't just sit back and do nothing!" Aniqan hissed. "Too long we've let ourselves be trodden into the dirt, burned to ash and rubble. People like you and Ujurak, you're content with picking up the pieces. I want to stop the building from falling in the first place."

He stormed off, back towards town. Akłaq stood but did not go after him. Finally she looked at Everett.

"He's not the only one who thinks that way," she said.

"I know," Everett sighed. "And I would be lying if I said I didn't understand, or share his feelings from time to time."

"Is there really nothing to be done? What is the point of having such great power if you simply sit on it as Ujurak did?"

Everett gave her a look. "Do you read well?"

She shrugged. "I learned Russian and Old Slavic. I can get by in English and French. Why?"

"Come with me. I want to show you something. Maybe it will help you explain things to Aniqan, as I seem to have done a poor job of it."

Akłaq might have expected to follow him to someplace just outside of town, such as they were at now. What she did not expect was for him to conjure a Paa, but not to the Wheel. He looked no less strained for it, however, and she jumped through as soon as she felt it safe.

The Paa to the Wheel were always difficult to traverse, though their appearance always deceptively suggested otherwise. The Paa to this new location looked no different, and yet somehow the journey felt a thousand times worse. For a brief moment, Akłaq feared that her lungs truly would be crushed, or her limbs torn from her body. It put her in mind of childbirth, but as though she were the one being born and was fully aware of the harrowing experience.

Everett did not look any better when he finally stumbled through, and he passed out just as quickly. The Paa snapped shut behind him. Akłaq went to him, relieved to find he was still alive. She didn't know what she would do if she suddenly became stranded; she didn't even know where she was.

She got about four steps away from Everett when he stirred and slowly got to his hands and knees. She might have expected him to start convulsing and throwing up water, but she knew the thought was foolish as soon as it entered her mind. She helped Everett to stand, though it was a few minutes before he looked lucid enough to walk and talk, and the farthest they made it was about twenty feet before he had to lean against the wall which was plated in metal with tubes running horizontally along it.

"It is no secret that traveling to the Wheel is hardly a joy," he sighed. "Trying to bypass their monopoly on portal travel is even worse. And to come here to the fortress..." He shook his head slowly and sighed again. "This is the fortress, what you might rightly consider the Akarin headquarters."

"Isn't it dangerous to just bring someone here?" Akłaq asked. "The Hands don't seem to like you very much, especially with all that Missing Zero Hour business."

Everett faltered, as if he didn't want to have to admit anything about the Missing Zero Hour. Instead he said, "You're right that they don't like us. But first, they'd have to come here, which is no picnic. Then they would have to be a threat, and you've already seen that the Akari is far superior to Time." Now he nodded and looked at her. "Regardless, you are correct that it can be dangerous to bring just anyone here, but I think you'll understand why I am making an exception for you."

He pushed himself away from the wall and, more confidently, began walking toward a large archway. Akłaq followed.

Once through the archway, the room opened up into a massive stone atrium. The whole of Red River could fit in the room, she thought, with room for more. The most prominent feature was an enormous spiral staircase in the center of the room, a single stone piece carved to perfection. Forward and to her left, another huge archway yawned open to what appeared to be a corridor. Forward and to the right just a bit, at a ninety degree corner from the first corridor, was another of the same size and style. More to her right there was a smaller corridor, this one having a gated entrance though no guards appeared to be posted at the moment.

Like the Wheel, there were all manner of creatures and aliens milling about on their own business. But there was no change in directional gravity, so everyone walked on the same plane, and any flying aliens took special delight in swooping here and there, occasionally darting up the center of the spiral staircase or diving down from above.

Akłaq followed Everett through the atrium to the staircase. The closer they got, the bigger the smooth staircase seemed, until she wasn't sure she could climb it.

"We can't use your Gravity trick to get where we need to go?" she asked meekly as they started up.

"It's a matter of courtesy," he explained. "The flying creatures wouldn't take too kindly to it, and if two Gravity tracks cross paths, well, nothing good happens say it that way. Besides, we're only going to the fifth floor."

That didn't sound too bad, except one floor on these stairs felt like four or five on Earth. By the time they reached the fifth floor, then, Akłaq felt as though she'd climbed at least twenty flights of stairs.

Then Everett took them down one of the corridors—north, if she had to pick any direction to orient herself—to a set of stone doors that were as big as everything else in the fortress. She expected them to be terribly difficult to open, but they swung freely with no more resistance than a normal wooden door.

Inside was a room stuffed with books and papers. Akłaq remembered the Russian priests long ago had a few shelves of books and other liturgical material; Isbister and Nisbet from Prince Albert also had small collections of more modern works. Any of those paled in comparison to the enormity of the library the Akarin possessed.

Toward the center of the room, which had to be at least a mile from end to end, or so it felt, was a glass case. The case itself was large, with room for many books, but there were only two inside at the moment. One was called *Wolf Pack*, and the other *Alpha Wolf*. As Everett opened the case and took them out, they were unlike any books Akłaq had ever seen, with smooth covers containing hyperrealistic images and pages with near-perfect typeset.

"These books must remain in the Archives and always within view of the case and this center desk here," Everett told her severely.

She just nodded and followed him to a table not four feet from the case where they sat down.

"These are the Authored Books," he began simply. "No one knows where they came from exactly, except from the Author. A copy showed up here, and the Krydik also received a copy." He gestured. "Go on; it won't bite."

Akłaq cautiously opened up the book. The first thing she noticed was that the pages initially appeared blank, but once she settled on a page, words began to appear in her own language. Her startled expression prompted a chuckle from Everett.

"That's another way we know it's from the Author," he said.

She flipped haphazardly through the pages, then went back to the beginning. Then she saw the copyright. "It says 2022. That's over a hundred and fifty years from now." She flipped back a page or two. "And there are so many more books listed." She looked around but could not spy anyone else with an Authored Book at any of the tables. "Where are they?"

"Already written," Everett told her. "Not yet in existence." He shrugged. "We're not entirely sure how it works, only that the Author seems to be moving again, and she's got big plans." He tapped on the list of books. "And I think you might be part of them."

Chasing the White Bear.

"Winter 2022, it says." She looked at him. "What does that mean? It doesn't even exist, and yet it does?"

"Honestly, I think we're sitting in the middle of it right now.

Everything going on, I think it's part of your story." He nodded, his expression somewhere between a child getting a piece of candy and a father seeing his child walk for the first time. "I think you do have a great calling and destiny, set forth by the Author, and I think we're are seeing in unfold before our very eyes."

Akłaq blinked. "We're sitting in a library."

"We're sitting in a library reading Authored Books, discussing how your Book which has not yet been written or released may in fact be happening all around us right now. That's a little more significant, I think." He leaned back in his chair. "It's also the reason I was less hesitant about bringing you here so soon, despite any security concerns."

For a long minute, the only thing she could do was stare at that one line. *Chasing the White Bear* (Winter 2022). Was it really possible? Could she really have a calling? Could they be sitting in the middle of it right now? What sorcery was this?

Finally she looked back at Everett, whose expression had settled into something resembling bemused. "Why me, though? Why not anyone else? Who is this...Chivalrous Welshman?"

Everett shrugged. "I don't know. No one does. We'll see when we get there, I suppose, even if it takes another century and a half."

She glanced at the Book before her, then at the one in the case. "These are the only two in existence currently?"

"That's correct."

"And you think we may be in one right now, though we won't know until the story is complete?"

"It's a strong suspicion, but suspicion only."

Akłaq again stared at the Book open before her. "Some years ago, in Ujurak's village, we heard about a split within the Akarin, something to do with a militant sect that infiltrated the Hands and resulted in the Missing Zero Hour." She went on before Everett could speak. "Some suspected that the split had to do with the Books, that people weren't happy that they focused on humans, and humans weren't happy because they focused on indigenous peoples, the Cherokee and the

Krydik. How true is that?"

Everett hesitated for half a second. "I wasn't there when the first Book appeared. As I said, I was raised in Aktiya Waya, which, at that time, was well past the end of *Wolf Pack*. When I was older and understood things better, well, Aktiya Waya had its own problems. Honestly, no one from Aktiya Waya ever traveled to the Wheel or did anything formally; certainly no one really knew of the existence of the Akarin and remained blissfully unaware of such problems.

"I didn't leave Aktiya Waya until about ten, maybe fifteen years ago. By then, the Missing Zero Hour had been resolved—not found, but the issue was resolved—hatred against the Akarin and all Akari-bearers remained fairly constant—and the whole thing was like reading last year's newspaper. Even the Akarin leaders here consider the matter closed. The militant sect, called the Cult of the Akari, has been quiet ever since, assuming they even still exist. I don't have enough first- or second-hand knowledge to say either way, but I don't think it's impossible."

"How did you find the Akarin? Why did you join them? If our peoples are hated here, or rather, on Earth, and Akari-bearers are hated among Time Agents, why not return to Aktiya Waya?"

He shifted in his seat. "I spoke to Anagalisgi, and he told me where to go, who to talk to. I didn't know why I had to join the Akarin, at the time, but now I think I might have an idea."

"Do you think you will one day have a Book as well?"

He chuckled. "As interesting as that would be, I don't think anyone would want to read about me. I don't know that I would want anyone to read about me. Besides, the Books may feature certain people, but I don't think they're actually intended to be about us."

She looked down at the Book once more. "Well, whoever this Chivalrous Welshman is, he seems to be important."

Everett nodded. "Perhaps." He shifted again. "But while we can only speculate about the future, I think it may be good for you to read about the past, too."

Akłaq was uncertain. Her mind was already reeling with all the possibilities and implications. Everett had brought her here to show her something that might help her explain things to Aniqan. How was she supposed to explain this? Books already appeared but not yet, Books already written but not yet appeared. And in the middle of it all, it looked as though she was supposed to have a Book about her that they may or may not be standing in right now but wouldn't know until it was completed? And whoever or whatever the Author was, the timeframe for all of this looked to be at least two hundred years, if not longer?

"Maybe so," she said at last, turning the page to start reading.

Everett stood. "Well then, if you don't mind, I'm going to find some books of my own to occupy my time. When you're ready to leave, just let me know."

Akłaq's interest in the first Book, *Wolf Pack*, was mediocre for the first few pages, mildly piqued by the end of the first chapter, and absolutely enthralled halfway through the second. The white animals! Sure, Anagalisgi followed a white woodpecker, but there had to be some connection, right?

She read through the entire thing, absorbing the history of the Krydik, the rise and fall of the "sorceries" as a weapon of war, and the cost of being careless or hasty. Then she turned her attention to the second book, *Alpha Wolf*, bringing herself up to speed on more recent Krydik history and politics, and discovering how they had indeed lost a war in spite of having such awesome power.

"Did you ever fight in the war?" Akłaq asked of Everett, sitting across from her absorbed in his own reading material.

He looked up. "I was in a different regiment, and the only Akari-bearer. The only Akari-bearer or Time Agent, in fact. I managed to keep myself alive, obviously, and a good number of my fellows, but war is a terrible thing, and only the Author—or God—can hope to maintain control over all the moving pieces."

"Did other Akari-bearers fight in the war? What about the person Anagalisgi told you to talk to about joining the Akarin? What about Time Agents?"

Everett nodded. "I can tell you've not lived long. Most people with our extended lives have a tendency to become apathetic, even hostile, to the goings-on of the world. When you've watched the wheel turn the same way enough times, you begin to resent those who think it will turn any other way. I won't say there were no other Time Agents or Akari-bearers in the war, Krydik notwithstanding, but most wanted no part in it, and too few sympathized with our cause to even be of much help otherwise."

"You were a Confederate, then."

"That's right. It was the only side worth choosing."

"Is that where you got your English name?"

He nodded. "I choose to keep the name for two reasons: first, because it does help when negotiating with Europeans; second, because it's still a cause I believe in, the right to self-determination, without being told what to do or how to live by far-off men in suits."

"Which is what brought you to Red River afterwards."

He nodded again.

Akłaq pushed the Authored Books aside. "I think your life would make a more interesting Book than mine."

He stood and gathered up all the scattered texts. "I think that has yet to be seen. If my suspicions are correct, we are only at the beginning of your story."

She stood and stretched. "What now, then? Am I suddenly a member of the Akarin?"

Everett grinned. "No, not yet. This was simply to boost your confidence and help you to understand. No, we will train together a bit so you can get a better grasp of things, understand the differences between Time and the Akari. If you decide to continue, and I have every confidence you will, then we'll talk about what it means to be truly Akarin."

With that, they replaced the Authored Books in the case and set Everett's reading material on the desk so the librarians could replace them.

"Never try to return a book yourself," Everett cautioned, "or Sofa, the head librarian, will throw an absolute fit."

Akłaq nodded uncertainly and followed him out of the library, more formally called the Akarin Archives. From there it was back to the staircase where it was easier to go down than up. All the while Everett explained the layout of the fortress and what rooms and services could be found on each floor. There were seven aboveground floors and three belowground. The first floor was dedicated to recreation, entertainment, and minor non-essentials. There were a couple floors for barracks, so if she needed a place to hide for a while or just wanted to get away from Earth, she could. There were offices and weapons stores and a food storehouse. No, it wasn't as grand or spectacular as the Wheel, but it suited their purposes.

Returning to Earth was no more pleasant than leaving it, and Akłaq was surprised to find that it was well dark.

"Unlike the Wheel, where time stops while you are away, the fortress remains fixed in time," Everett explained once he was recovered enough to talk. "I probably should have warned you."

"Aniqan is going to wonder what's become of me," Akłaq said, perhaps a little harsher than intended.

Everett waved a hand. "Go on, then. Let him know you're all right and tell him what you've seen and learned. In a day or two, if you want, we'll begin training in the Akari."

"What about Time and my Journeyman training?"

He nodded weakly. "We can do that, too, yes. Go on."

She turned and ran back to Red River.

Avgun Akimiaq Piñasrut
The White Bear

Aniqan's skepticism about the Akari itself warred with what he believed about certain people being special, this compounded by his own comments about Akłaq having some great destiny. It seemed as though he were looking for every reason to not believe in anything and discard everything, but was coming up only with more reasons to believe in something. Maybe it was his frustration that the people who had all the power seemed unwilling to use it.

"It's about consequences," Everett told him. "Consequences and control. If you are unwilling to start with the small things, you will not be able to handle the big things. The temptation is too great."

"And what 'small things' have you done?" Aniqan inquired. He sat and watched as Akłaq tried to learn both Time and Akari skills from Everett, but did not participate himself.

"I saved some of my fellows in the war. While they were half-dazed or even unconscious from the pain and severity of their wounds, I healed them. Some I could fix entirely, others not so well, but it was better than a slow death from gangrene. Did I alter the course of the war? No. But those men live and have children; their mothers and wives did not weep for them, which is more than what the dead soldiers can say."

"Why didn't you just stop time, go over to the other side, and kill the enemy soldiers?"

Everett gave him a look. "They may have been soldiers fighting for the opposing side, but they were not my enemies. They were doing as they were told to do, or perhaps forced. It was no secret that rich men would buy their way out of the war and send poor men to fight in their place. Is a beggar from a city thousands of miles away truly my enemy? Was killing him going to stop the war or sway public opinion?" He put his hand up. "I know he was there to kill me. I will not deny that I did kill other men. That is what war is. But he was not my enemy."

"No, but if you kill enough of them, the rest might think twice about fighting for those who send them."

"And raise up how many against yourself?" Everett shook his head. "There are too many poor and desperate men for that to happen anyway, except in rare circumstances which I do not expect to encounter."

Aniqan looked rather displeased by his answer, and Akłaq thought he was going to leave again.

"The use of any sort of power should be strategic and precise. A well-placed arrow may take down even the most ferocious beast where a man using his fists will almost certainly fail. And with that, a man must practice his skills so that he can be such a swift, precise arrow." He took a few steps back, away from them. "The good news is that we have a way to practice new abilities in a controlled environment, without fear of being discovered by outsiders."

"In the Wheel it's called the Arena," Aniqan quipped nonchalantly.

"Here in the fortress, we just call it the recreation area," Everett said. "And unlike the Arena in the Wheel that remains stagnant, the recreation area is a living area that reacts to the people inside."

Aniqan looked around dramatically. "I haven't seen anything."

As if on cue, land formed beneath them, heaving like an ice flow. Trees sprang from the ground, leaves momentarily flung about like snow in a blizzard. Surprised herself, Akłaq stumbled backwards and tripped over a log that had not previously been there.

"The Akari is a living thing," Everett said, going to offer a hand of Aniqan who had also fallen. "It is not mocked, and some say it bears echoes of the Author's sense of humor."

"Well, if that's the case, I'd say he doesn't have one," Aniqan grumbled, reluctantly taking the offered hand and getting to his feet.

"You can conjure anything here?" Akłaq wondered, touching the leaves on a nearby bush. It looked and felt absolutely real. "Then how do you know if you've actually done anything, or if this place simply is simply reacting to you?"

"This is a place to learn, to try, to make mistakes and build confidence."

That first day of training was basically Everett trying to show Akłaq the difference between Banding as done through the Akari and Banding as the Time industry taught it. Time Bands were colored, visible to those who were also exposed to Time, and, while maneuverable, bulky and awkward. Akłaq might have argued the last point, until he demonstrated Akari Banding. Though basically entirely invisible to those who didn't know how to look, they were also much lighter and far more flexible. Suddenly the differences became as apparent as a bear versus a falcon.

Aniqan remained largely bad-tempered, but Akłaq could see that he was at least intrigued.

"If the Akari Bands are so much better, how did they get to be as they are in Time?" he asked, his stony, disinterested facade not holding up well against genuine curiosity.

"Because Time is consumed with vanity," Everett answered. "It wants to be seen and lauded. But this vanity creates a burden all its own, one which must be shouldered and borne every time it is used. This is similar to Harvesting. In the Akari, it is most likened to Matter and Disguises. But Time is also consumed with greed. It desires to take, to steal and store up for oneself."

"The bleeding we can't control," Aniqan defended. "And we've always used Time Capsules for the good of the people."

"I am not questioning your personal motives or intentions," Everett said, entirely at ease. "But that is what Harvesting is, at its core. Vanity and greed are the core of the Time industry." He looked back at Akłaq, then again at Aniqan. "However, I also believe that because your motives are good, and you did the best you could with the tools you had, that you will do well in transitioning into the Akari."

"What about my Journeyman training?" Akłaq wondered.

Everett looked at her and raised a brow. "You think the white bear brought you out of your village, out of the north—where exists an entirely self-contained method of advancing you to Master—introduced you to the Akari—so you could return to the old way of doing things? Why, then, were you called out?"

She had no answer, and a tinge of guilt pricked at her. She was finally discovering her destiny, and she was concerned about her Journeyman training? Compared to what Everett was showing her now, such a thing felt so insignificant, even laughable. Why would she even have a destiny if that were the case?

"I need to go walk around," Aniqan announced. Akłaq realized that he and Everett had been having some small conversation. Aniqan turned and left the recreation area, the doors a stark contrast to the forest surrounding them.

"I should go after him," Akłaq said.

But Everett put a hand out to stop her. "Practice what you have learned. The Akari and the recreation area will help you—don't worry, you'll get the hang of it. I'll go have a talk with him."

Akłaq hesitated but agreed. Everett turned and left the area, leaving her alone in a fictional forest.

"Is it really fictional, though?" a rumbling, familiar voice asked.

She whirled around to see the white bear pushing its way through the undergrowth. She grinned dumbly, but the bear appeared unimpressed.

"I thought I taught you better than that," it said.

"Taught me what?" Akłaq asked, finally breaking her trance.

"Just because you are in a place does not mean you are intended to stay there."

She shook her head. "I don't understand." She looked around, wondering what part of her spirit was conjuring this part of the illusion. As if responding to her uncertainty, the forest vanished, leaving only her and the bear in a bare, stone room.

"The cabin in the woods," the bear stated.

Akłaq took an even breath and nodded sadly. "I know that now. My husband and children paid the price for my disobedience."

"And killing the man?"

Now her sadness turned to indignation. "You were standing right there! You had to have known what I was thinking. At least had an idea of it. You could have told me to stop, and I would have."

The bear turned its head as if questioning. "Would you? A poor decision may garner less offense than a disobeyed command, but that doesn't mean it wasn't a poor decision."

"What would you have had me do? Listen to him berate me for another decade? Be arrested? Everett already told us about what he did to Ujurak and the others; surely that should have authorized some divine vengeance?"

"The past is dead now, its choices made. All that remains to be seen is at what point you decide to start actually listening. The first consequence was the passive death of your family. The second was the murder of a man at your own hand. Think carefully on what the consequence may be next time."

"It might help if I had some kind of real direction, somewhere to go, something to look forward to," she protested. "Even Ujurak's *tuuṅaq—*"

"Speak not of the Shadows," the white bear interrupted forcefully. "And compare us not to them."

Akłaq huffed a sigh. "Fine. I won't say that I'm a perfect person, but you're not the most helpful either. A little clarity goes a long way."

"So does a little obedience," the bear retorted. "The power of the Author is great, but for men to use it requires Faith. Part of Faith is obedience, and trusting that things will work out in the end." It went on before she could speak. "And also realizing that you do not write your own story. The things you want, and the things that must be, are rarely the same."

That did not improve her mood any, and she began to feel how Aniqan looked.

The bear's expression turned thoughtful, if such could be

interpreted on a bear's face, and it almost seemed to nod once to itself, or no one Akłaq could see.

"Return to your den," the white bear said. "The next path is laid, and your guide will be there shortly."

Akłaq nodded and couldn't help but say sarcastically, "See, something like that. A little direction, a little clarity."

"Go!" the bear ordered, drawing its lips back in a small snarl.

Startled, she turned and walked away, leaving the recreation area without looking back to see if the bear was still there, though she was fairly certain she could still feel its eyes on her.

She met up with Aniqan and Everett in the cafeteria. It didn't take much to convince them to leave, though any argument they'd had appeared to have settled into something resembling a reluctant agreement to disagree.

They headed to the portal room where Everett opened a Paa to a secluded area not far from town. Unless someone was already in that area, the Paa would go unnoticed and they could take a few minutes to recover from the trip.

"Why is such travel so difficult?" Aniqan asked, lying on the ground, barely moving. "If the Akari is so superior, why can't it be a little more comfortable?"

"That aspect of it has more to do with physicality rather than spirituality, but I'm too tired to explain just now," Everett answered, yawning.

Eventually, the three of them scraped themselves off the ground and made their way back to town. By the clock, it was getting late in the afternoon, but the sun was quickly taking its colors below the horizon.

What they did not expect was a small crowd of people to be gathered outside their door when they got back. On being spotted, one of the group broke off, and Akłaq saw that it was one of their neighbors, a man called Peter.

"Is something wrong?" Aniqan wondered.

"Caught a stranger trying to break into your house," Peter

announced. He was a bear himself, probably took down the intruder with one hand tied behind his back. "Got him tied up to the front post so you can deal with him. Says he's a friend of yours."

Now curious, Aniqan and Akłaq pushed past Peter, intent on their home. The rest of the group, armed with a few rifles, a pitchfork or two, and plenty of rope, parted for them.

Akłaq broke into a grin. "Putu!"

The older man sat with his back against one of the porch posts, wrists and body bound snugly. He looked about as enthusiastic as he always had, and his expression was hardly that of a warm welcome. "You've arrived at last. Care to vouch for me?"

Aniqan nodded to one of the men who, reluctantly, untied Putu's bonds.

"Thank you for your concern, and your help," Aniqan told Peter, "but I think we can handle it now."

The crowd dispersed into shadows and excited whispers. Aniqan and Akłaq wished Everett a good night, then they and Putu went inside.

"Putu, how did you get here?" Akłaq asked, still grinning. "More to the point, how did you manage to get yourself caught?"

"I allowed it," Putu answered, stretching limbs and cracking joints. "I decided that finding you was more important than winning the fight —and subsequently being run out of town—but your neighbors seemed to think all that was necessary anyway."

"Sorry," Aniqan said humbly. "Things are a little tense around here since the Dominion of Canada was established."

"Well, as exciting as basic politics are, we have bigger problems."

"Everett told us what happened." Aniqan gestured to Akłaq who slowly admitted to the part she'd played, killing Gerald. Then he asked of Putu, "Are you the only one who escaped?"

"No, but we decided it better to split up. Lusa, Ikiaq, and Suluk elected to head for other villages. I decided to try and find you." He shook his head. "Ujurak was killed in the initial ambush. I saw Kanut and Natsik also fall. Once I realized it was a lost cause, that they were there to kill us or take us before the Grandfathers — but I repeat myself — my only thought was escape."

"Do you know for certain that the Grandfathers killed those who were arrested?" Akłaq inquired, suddenly fearful.

"We are still very near to the events of the Missing Zero Hour. While kept out of public eye, it wouldn't surprise that they are still conducting investigations. If they manage to tie it up into the events of the Akarin and their militant faction, as well as the Krydik, why wouldn't they execute potential conspirators? There is no justice in Time, Akłaq; that's why we do what we do."

Akłaq glanced at Aniqan, but he did not disagree.

"How did you find us?" Aniqan wondered.

Putu shrugged. "Followed the roads, followed the movement of people. I figured that if you had gone to be isolated, you could have done just as well around the village. You were searching for people, and I had my suspicions that you would come to live around the enemy."

Aniqan shook his head. "These people are not the enemy —"

"Not the enemy yet," Putu corrected. "Because currently there is a larger enemy uniting them. Just as soon as that threat is removed, they will turn on each other, on you."

"Good news for us, then, because I don't think this larger enemy is going to be removed."

"Isn't that what you came out here to do? You wanted to do something, now here's your chance."

So Akłaq relayed another tale, this one of meeting Everett and being introduced to the Akari, the Akarin, and the Authored Books. Neither Aniqan nor Putu were wholly impressed with the story, but they were polite enough to listen. It was Putu who spoke first, grumbling a sigh. "I might say something about this being a phenomenal waste of time, a deception intent on keeping your starry-eyed and complacent..." He muttered something under his breath. "But I am no shining example of action. At least here, you have done something. Even if it is only to kill the man who orchestrated our demise." His look was accusatory. "Why would the white bear lead you to something or someone who would destroy everything you knew, everyone who cared about you?"

"I don't know," Akłaq admitted, feeling very small. "Maybe I waited too long to kill him. Maybe it was my error for not seeing what he really intended to do."

She could see Putu was not entirely convinced, but there was nothing to be done about it now. Ujurak was dead, the rest, with exception of a few, either dead or imprisoned.

"Now that you've found us," Aniqan began, changing the subject, "what do you intend to do?"

"I don't know," Putu said. "I didn't know whether I would find you at all, or in what state, so I tried not to make too many plans. I thought about bringing you back, finding Lusa and the others again, reestablishing our village. But without a shaman, what good would it do?" He shrugged. "My first goal has been met; I have found the both of you alive and well. I suppose I should first be grateful and take a few days to learn what I can and think about my next move."

"You could stay here," Akłaq suggested. "It's really not so bad. Everett showed us how to forge the paperwork to get a house. You can plant if you wish, or many people, including Aniqan, still go out on hunts. The vast majority of people have at least some indigenous blood in them, though most are Cree."

"I will stay here for a few days at least. Making the migration from here to there is one thing, but all this endless searching has exhausted me."

"Stay as long as you like," Aniqan told him. "We could use some sane company."

He looked at Akłaq as he said it, and she wasn't sure how to interpret his words. Nevertheless, Putu thanked them and made himself comfortable in the spare room.

While the man might have only intended to stay for a few days, even Akłaq knew that would not be the case, and after a month or two, they helped him move into his own home. Of course, the man was a bit dodgy about the whole affair and simply declared that his migration instinct had been driving him for too long, and now that he was settled, he was obligated to settle for an extended period of time. How extended, he did not know or would not say, for he also proposed no ideas of where he could go.

He did not speak much about the raid that destroyed the village, in the same way he rarely spoke about what happened to his home village or his time in the labor camps. He planted, inasmuch that he would have something to sell and make a bit of money—white economy could be very frustrating at times, he said—and he helped to tan the hides of the animals that the men brought back from their hunts.

"But he still isn't willing to consider the Akari," Akłaq fretted to Everett. They were back in the recreation area in the Akarin fortress. Putu had come once or twice, just out of curiosity, and when he'd declared the idea folly, Aniqan went with him. It was almost as if Aniqan had wanted some kind of backup for when he abandoned the Akari—not that he'd cared to learn much.

"You can't force someone to care about something," Everett told her.

"But it's just so...confusing. Why would he be on this journey with me if he's just going to be the same old Aniqan who left the village? Journeys and quests are about change, but I feel like he hasn't changed, not for the better, anyway."

"We don't know his path. There may be more in store for him in the future that we cannot see but are laying the groundwork for. You just never know."

She knew he was right, but she didn't have to like it.

"Do you really think it will come to violence?" she wondered, working through her Akari Bands, testing them on different objects as she managed to conjure them in the recreation area. They were functionally the same as regular Time Bands, but much lighter, much easier to use.

"What? This mess with the Canadians?" Everett's tone said he was mostly unconcerned, but not entirely passive. He sighed. "Given what I heard of and saw in the south, it wouldn't surprise me. I don't think it will come as soon as you think, though it always comes faster than you expect."

"Do you think Red River stands a chance?"

"Maybe, provided we can keep from killing each other at the same time."

Akłaq erected a Slow Band around a conjured rabbit. "Is there anything that the Akari can help with, before it gets to violence?"

Everett took an even breath. "Free will is a terrible thing. Even God can't force men to like each other."

"Even if not God, what about the Author? She's the one writing this story, isn't she? Why doesn't she do something?"

"Maybe this is her doing something. I don't know, Akłaq. I don't pretend to have such universal knowledge." He shifted his stance. "If you're feeling comfortable with your Bands, maybe we can move on to something else."

She put up a Fast Band around a conjured turtle. "Speaking of training or the conversation?"

"Both, if you like."

She dropped all of her Bands and all of the conjurations vanished, leaving them in an empty room. She looked at him. "If there's more to the Akari than just Time, I admit, I would like to learn something more than what I already know."

Everett nodded. "I understand, but Banding is often the easiest way to introduce a Timekeeper to the Akari."

"What about Harvesters?"

"They are usually taught how to Feel, as I will do with you now."

"Feel?"

"Reaching inside yourself, to know and understand your body and its processes. Feel will help you to identify disease, deformities, and other imperfections. You will also be able to navigate what is proper, such as an undamaged bone, in order to help you heal what is damaged."

Akłaq's eyes felt as big as the moon. "How do you even start with something like that?"

He laughed. "Well, the actual healing and such comes later." His expression turned curious. "Do you know anything about Harvesting, beyond rote knowledge?"

She shrugged. "I've watched the others in the village Harvest, and Aniqan has tried to explain it to me, but I wouldn't know how to do it myself. Aniqan and I are a bit odd. Normally the men are the Timekeepers and the women are the Harvesters."

Everett made a curious sound. "I see."

"Is this not how the Krydik do it?"

He shook his head. "The Krydik didn't do much with Time at all, really. Their interests sided more with Touch, understanding the human body, healing injuries, curing diseases, even analyzing the properties of plants, animals, and stone. They also make some use of Energy, Gravity, Light, Sound. But rarely do they use Time." He sighed. "Their pacifism and abandoning of the old warrior ways is what cost them the war, in my opinion."

"Oh."

He waved a hand. "Don't worry about it. Internal politics is what it comes down to. Nothing you need to concern yourself with. Let's get you started on Touch."

"Is that different than Feel?"

"No, no, just a difference of terms and translations. It's the same basic thing. All you need to do to start is focus on some part of your body. Maybe it's a small cut or a bug bite, some discomfort of the teeth, or just your little finger. Close your eyes if you need to, and just focus on that thing." He paused. "Do you have that thing at the forefront of your mind?" She nodded. "Good. Now focus harder, and, like peeling the layers of Time away from your Bands, pick apart that thing. Separate it into its elements and focus on just one."

Akłaq had chosen a small bug bite on the back of her neck, sustained just that morning. She'd waited to heal it in the event Everett taught her something new that she could practice. Good thing she did.

Mildly focusing on it, she knew it was a bug bite. It was itchy and annoying, but not especially painful. Now she narrowed her focus to the opening of the wound, where the nuisance had penetrated skin. As Everett said, it was like peeling back layers, and she found that she was able to go even further. She pinpointed a tiny section of the inflamed skin. Further, until she discovered the individual pieces of skin and the microscopic nature of how they worked.

Stunned, her focus broke, and her eyes flew open.

"Those are called cells," he said, grinning, as if reading her mind.

"How did I do that?" she asked.

"It is a part of who you are. When you experience an injury, you know it because your body tells you through pain. It sends signals to your brain that something is wrong. But the paths between your brain and body do not close when there is nothing wrong. They remain open, always, you just have to learn how to navigate them. In time, you will learn how to do the same with others."

Akłaq shook her head slowly. "I...I don't know what to say or do."

Everett was still smiling. "For now, we will return home. You have much to think about. Continue to practice this skill, and Feel your body. Learn how it works, the marvelous intricacies of the created being that is you. For now, just Feel, but don't try to change anything."

"You mean like the way you became a white man?"

"Like that."

She wordlessly agreed, and they left the recreation area.

"How did the Akari get its name?" Akłaq wondered as they walked the corridor, heading for the southwest atrium and the portal room. "In the Authored Books, the ones about the Krydik, they're just called the sorceries."

"It's what the Akarin have always called it," Everett replied, shrugging. "There are many theories, some more believable than others, but no one knows for sure." He chuckled. "Even some of the Krydik refuse to acknowledge the twisted origins of their own name."

"That they were too critical of the people of the Old World?"

"Exactly." They reached the portal room. "But that is neither here nor there. Practice what I have taught you, and maybe see if you can't get Aniqan to try it, too. As a Harvester, it may be easier for him to start with Touch rather than Time."

Akłaq nodded. "Maybe."

With that, Everett took a breath and, with tremendous painstaking effort, opened a Paa, right back into the grove, as usual. Dreading the journey, Akłaq took a breath and stepped through.

Avgun Iñuiñaġutaiḷaq
Resistance

Everett's seemingly contradictory statement proved to be unnervingly accurate. Violence came later than Akłaq thought, but soon than she expected. She and Aniqan and Putu and Everett might have had the ability to forge documents and fudge certain details in order to obtain housing and land, but no one else had that luxury. It was early 1869 when word came that surveyors were on their way, and their arrival that August was met with some desperate fanfare. Everyone had a claim, but few had titles, deeds, or any sort of documentation.

Akłaq tried not to get suffocated by the mob that formed outside the deeds office, instead skirting the edges and wishing she had better use of Sound, the ability to increase or decrease certain noises so she could hear what was going on. Her skills in this were somewhat lacking, however, and she caught only pieces of the conversations between the deeds man and the newly-arrived government officials.

"...need to perform a complete audit of all the papers..."

"...not disorganized, but there is conflicting information..."

"...too much useless information, none of it pertinent to the situation at hand."

"We have some records..."

"...resurveying the land and remarking lines...rid of the seigneurial system...everything brand new, a fresh start."

"...houses and land that do have proper paperwork?"

"...everything..."

Only the few men by the door and Akłaq with her abilities heard any of the actual conversation. By the time it got back to Aniqan, Putu, and Everett, everything had gotten twisted around so that the government was going to seize the land outright and give it to another wave of Protestant settlers already on their way.

"Aniqan, they're just surveying lines," Akłaq tried to tell him.

In the house, Aniqan was pacing anxiously, eyeing several weapons within reach. Putu, who was visiting, remained still and silent, brooding in the corner. "Of course they are," Aniqan said. "That's their job. And then they'll take those lines and measurements, and they'll put them on crisp, new documents with other people's names on them. They're taking land, just like they always do!"

"You don't know that! How long have the people been waiting for a surveyor to come out and clear things up? Now that they're here, you think they're going to steal everything."

"Why wouldn't they, with McDougall backing them?" He shook his head. "No, we have to do something."

"What do you propose?" Putu asked slowly, not looking up from his thoughtful pose.

Finally Aniqan stopped pacing. He stood still for a moment, then looked at Akłaq. "What if...what if we waited until they completed their surveys? Let them draw up the official documents. Then, we take those documents and fill in the names of the rightful land owners? We can take them to the Wheel to have them forged if we have to. Then they'll have fresh deeds and titles, and they won't go to any new eastern invaders."

She nodded. "Yes, we can do that. We can tie up the Canadian government in their own paperwork, bind them by their own laws." She glanced at Putu. "That sounds reasonable, right?"

Putu made a grunting sound that was neither affirmative nor negative. "It's a start. It might keep the bureaucrats busy for a while."

"Do you have anything better?"

Now he looked up. "Everett has been talking to Louis Riel over the summer. I think they're trying to put together some sort of formal delegation, a way for us to negotiate directly with the Canadian government, ascertain their intentions and voice our concerns."

"Since when have they cared about us?" Aniqan asked. "Hudson Bay sold the land out from under us once already."

"As Akłaq said, it's binding them by their own laws. And if they choose not to honor their own laws and ways of doing things, we are—by our rights and theirs—obligated to escalate the situation if necessary."

Aniqan's expression was mixed and amusing to look at. It was as if he couldn't figure out that Putu was telling him that violence was not only potentially permitted, but maybe even necessary. Truthfully, Akłaq was a little surprised by it, too. Putu wasn't one to fight, instead preferring to think things through and try to find another way. He blamed his time in the labor camps, but it seemed as though it was aiding them now.

"Go talk to Everett," Putu told him. "I imagine he can help in both fields."

Aniqan nodded and left the house, eager to have a course of action. Akłaq and Putu watched him go.

"I've seen Riel around town a few times," Akłaq said. "What makes him different from any of the other disgruntled men with grievances?"

"He knows how to talk to people, how to work with them," Putu replied. "He's got support among the French and the English mixed-breeds. It's not hard to gather the French, true; it's the fact that he's got the support of the English, too. Mixed or not, the English tend to be very proud and don't like to submit to anything or anyone. It's why they have a hard time organizing, outside their governments anyway. Once they've chosen a leader, they keep him. And it looks as though they're ready to choose Riel."

"Do you really think it'll get bad? Choosing a spokesman for grievances is one thing. If they expect him to lead a battle, do you think he would?"

"I don't know. I can't say that I know the man well; I tend to avoid politics. But I think we're going to find out."

The surveyors jumped into their work, and it was a disaster from the beginning. The way it was done—on orders from the government in Ottawa — cut up the land into squares so that farms were completely cut off from the river and could no longer get water. Even if the people could get titles for the land pieces, they didn't want them. The land was useless to them. Aniqan and Everett managed to forge a few documents for the properties that did maintain river access, but it was far too few for far too many people.

"What about our land?" Akłaq asked of Aniqan. It was mid-October. "Is ours changing, even though we have title and deed?"

"Not if we have anything to say about it," he declared.

"What is that supposed to mean?"

"McDougall is on his way to Red River with more government officials. Riel is going to take Everett and some others to meet him — "

" 'Meet' him?" she echoed.

"They're going to stop them from coming in," he said evasively.

She folded her arms. "That doesn't sound like something you'd want to miss."

He paused for a moment, then continued, "I'm going with another group up to Upper Fort Garry. We're going to take it."

"Whatever for?"

"It's going to be our base of operations, our own seat of government. If we can take the fort, and if Riel can hold off the Canadians, force them to retreat for the winter, we can get ourselves established."

"And do what, exactly?"

"Govern ourselves, for one. Have a say in our own affairs. First we have to get that far. We have to stop McDougall and seize the fort." He noted her expression. "What would you have me do? What do you want us to do? Has Everett said anything to you in your Akari training? Does he have some task for you in all of this?"

She let out a breath. "He hasn't said anything."

He made a motion. "So there you go. We came out here to do something. To stop injustice before it starts. Maybe haven't headed it off completely, but this time, we're making a stand."

"Do you plan on using Time, when you seize the fort? Are you going to Harvest the dead, perhaps use some minor Bands?"

He shrugged. "It's possible. What does that matter, other than it gives us an advantage?"

"An advantage for now, until the Captains and Regional Manager hear about it, hear that we're here, what we're doing." She put up a hand. "I'm not saying don't Harvest or don't Band. But start thinking about what we're going to do if the Timekeepers who murdered Ujurak and wiped out the village come for us here."

The thought sobered him up a little, and he went off to brood on it a bit.

Akłaq brought up the topic to Everett later that week as they trained.

"Is there something you want me to do?" she asked. "Something I can do?"

"You can do a great many things to the universe," he replied, "but you cannot forcibly change the minds of men."

"Everett, we're talking about situations that could turn violent, that are going to turn violent. The people in Upper Fort Garry aren't going to just surrender. You're showing me amazing things; I refuse to believe that it's useless."

He shook his head. "Useless, hardly." He sighed. "I'm not going to tell you what to do. And I believe now as I believed in the war in the south, that you, as a woman, should not have to fight."

"I may not have a choice. Aniqan is right, we left the village because we wanted to do something, to actually help people. Here we are."

Everett nodded. "I know. As I said, I don't think you should have to fight. But McDougall and his men are going to be far less agreeable than the people at Upper Fort Garry. It may be a fort, but it's a provisional fort. It's a trading post with a few guns. If you want to help, go there, keep Aniqan alive, stop him from doing anything too stupid that might get him killed."

Akłaq gave him a look. "If McDougall is going to be less agreeable, why are you going?"

"Because Riel wants those with both fighting experience and level heads. He does want to keep this as peaceful as possible. Having too many hotheaded young men around isn't going to help things."

Just because he was right didn't mean she had to like it.

When they returned to Red River, the sun going down, Akłaq found Aniqan just leaving the house to join a crowd in the center of town. She did not say anything, just followed him quietly. The group was comprised of mostly men, though there were some younger teenage boys and even a handful of women. Aniqan met with one man in particular. They exchanged words. Aniqan turned and spotted Akłaq. He walked up to her even as she approached the group.

"What are you doing here?" he asked, sounding a bit annoyed.

"I'm coming with you," she declared.

"No, you're not." He went on, "We're going to take the fort."

"I know. I'm going to make sure you don't do anything stupid and get yourself killed."

"But—"

"You want the Akari to prove its usefulness, then let me come and prove it."

He faltered, hesitated, finally nodded. "All right, fine. You're not wrong. I guess if I've been complaining about something, I shouldn't balk at a chance to fix what I've been complaining about."

"And you'll give it more consideration afterwards?"

Now Aniqan gave her a look. "Let's wait until we're done tonight."

That she could agree to.

"She's coming?" the leader of the group, a man called Robert, asked, approaching. He gave Akłaq a regard, then looked at Aniqan.

"She's with me," Aniqan said. "She can spot for me."

The man grunted but did not argue. He regarded Akłaq for another moment, then walked away.

"It's just a trading post with a few guns," Aniqan told her softly as they also joined the group. "Most of the people inside should be asleep. I really don't think we're going to have much trouble."

She wished she could share his optimism. It wasn't that she didn't believe him, but her experiences with violence had been less than promising so far. But she said none of this out loud. She was here to support Aniqan of her own free will. He wasn't forcing her to come; he would probably be relieved if she changed her mind and decided to go home instead.

They left town without a word save for a small speech from Robert. It was later in the evening now, and they would arrive long after the fort had closed its gates for the night. The plan was to sit and camp as if they were a small band of indigenous traders simply waiting for the morning. A few scouts would tell them when the fort was pretty well settled in for the night, lulled into slumber.

Riel and the other leaders had given instructions to avoid violence if possible. Take the fort with the fewest number of casualties. This would give them the greatest amount of leverage when the Canadians came to negotiate. It would prove their intentions were nonviolent, and if their hand was pressed, they would have a good number of hostages to choose from.

"Do you think it can be done?" Akłaq wondered as she and Aniqan sat in the camp, watching and waiting for the scouts to return. "Do you think this can be peaceful?"

"Can it?" Aniqan shrugged. "Absolutely. But that would require a lot of people realizing that what they're doing is a terrible crime. They won't realize that as long as their politicians and their gods say otherwise. So, yes, it can be done peacefully, but our presence here, I think, proves that it probably won't be."

"But we, Red River has a government. We have leaders, elected officials. You might even say that we have an army. Isn't that what Europeans want, a society that is similar to their own?"

"Yes, but only when they're in charge. Saying that we need all these things is simply a trap, to get us to play by their rules because they know that this is a game they can win." He shook his head. "And here we are, living right alongside them."

Akłaq stared at him for a long moment. "Do you regret leaving the village? Do you regret coming with me?"

"I don't know," he answered honestly. "On the one hand, I'm finally doing something other than just sitting around waiting for some supernatural sign or vision. On the other hand, I'm not sure that—the scout's back." He stood.

His change of tone and disposition was so sudden, Akłaq mentally stumbled. After another moment, she rose.

Four boys between thirteen and eighteen slipped back into camp, making for Robert's tent. While no one wanted to give the impression that there was great activity in the camp, everyone wanted to hear what they had to say. With a little creative Banding, Akłaq and Aniqan were able to get close enough to peek inside the tent and hear the report.

"As quiet as it's going to get," the leader, an eighteen year old named William, reported. "The company might declare neutrality, but they're not fools; they're prepared for confrontation."

"How big of a confrontation?" Robert demanded. "What are their strengths, their weaknesses, their personnel? Guns may be fearsome, but they're useless without a hand to pull the trigger."

"Four pairs of men on patrol, one pair at each tower, one more pair at each gate. There might be a few moving about on the inside."

Robert patted the boy's shoulder. "Good lad."

"What are their capabilities for reinforcements?" another leader, a man called Reginald, wondered.

"We weren't able to get close enough for specifics, but they don't appear to have such capabilities, beyond sending a rider on horseback. Regardless of what they call this place, it's still primarily a trading post. They're not looking to take land or lives, just keep what they have."

Robert nodded thoughtfully and turned to Reginald. "Esther should have her brew prepared by now. Get it from her and distribute it as we've discussed."

A moment later, Reginald left the tent. Not half an hour after that, Akłaq and Aniqan were moving through the darkness, heading for the trading post.

It was a rectangular structure, built of stone, with a tower at each corner and two more midway on the longer sides. From the scout reports, there was a partial wall between them. All of this to protect the dozen or so buildings inside. From a distance, the main gates looked shut and barricaded, though closer inspection proved this to be false. They were open a crack, enough for a man, presumably a guard, to get in and out.

"You! Stop there!" one of them said, once Akłaq and Aniqan were close enough, about ten yards out.

They did as they were told. Akłaq Banded so she could look around and assess the position of the others who were flanking them, making for the towers or other areas of interest or exploitation. Once she was satisfied that all was in order, she dropped the Band.

"Post is closed for tonight," the guard went on. "So just go back to your camp and wait until morning."

"Doctor inside?" Aniqan asked, speaking in an English more broken than she'd heard from him in years. "Doctor? Please. Woman, Akłaq, she has baby."

It may have been a few years since she'd been pregnant, but Akłaq remembered well the pain and discomfort she'd endured through each one, and she brought it all to bear now. All the gestures, the wincing, and grimacing, looking for any kind of relief.

"Don't look pregnant to me," the second guard mumbled. He grumbled a sigh and made a motion. "Come here. Slowly. No sudden moves."

Akłaq shuffled up there as though in great pain, Aniqan close by her side. They were stopped again about ten feet from the gates. The second guard approached, looking very uncomfortable as he tried to determine the authenticity of Akłaq's suffering as well as pat down Aniqan, looking for any weapons. The trick was, Akłaq was the one carrying the weapons.

"All right, fine," the guard said, stepping back. "I won't condemn a mother and child." He made a motion. "Follow me."

They did so, keeping up the charade until they reached the gate.

The first guard was to Akłaq's left, the second in front of Aniqan. With a little Banding, just enough to get the jump on the men, they took a breath, and Akłaq removed two rags tucked into her shirt. The rags were dipped in a brew that, when pressed over the faces of the guards, would put them into a deep slumber, hopefully without killing them. Esther made no promises.

While Aniqan dragged the bodies away from the gate and dumped them in a nearby haystack, Akłaq continued her woman in distress charade. She found one of the roaming soldiers, but before he could call for assistance, she smothered him, too.

Everett hadn't actually taught her anything yet about Gravity, but she remembered reading about it in the Authored Books and attempted to apply the principles explained therein to the situation at hand. She couldn't lift an unconscious man by herself, and dragging him would take too long. A fumbled attempt at using Gravity to lift him, however, worked for the time being, and she put him in one of the stalls in the stables.

By now, others had gotten in; she saw them slinking through the shadows. More unconscious guards were being dragged to various hiding locations. They would have to remember where they put them all so they could retrieve them to the prisons later.

A cry went up, but there was no one to answer. Akłaq heard a commotion, and a minute or two later, four more guards were shuffled down the stairs to the courtyard under heavy guard. The main gates were opened wide, and Robert and Reginald walked in with no resistance. They regarded the captured soldiers and regarded a few unconscious ones still lying out in the open.

"Is this the last of them?" Robert asked.

"Yes, sir," one of the men replied.

"Any casualties?"

"None that we're aware of."

"Excellent. Louis will be glad to hear it." Robert turned to Reginald. "Ride back to Red River and tell him the good news. I believe the committee will want to move their base of operations here posthaste."

Reginald made a motion that resembled a salute, then turned and headed for the stables.

"Aniqan, Akłaq," Robert went on, butchering both their names. They stepped forward, and he regarded both of them, nodding proudly. "Good work getting us in here; I was sure we were looking at a fight. I'll mention your names to Louis once the committee gets here."

"Thank you," they each said in turn.

Robert turned his attention to the entire company who had finally assembled themselves. "All right, we need to get this place cleaned up. Take all these guards to the prisons—"

"With respect, sir," one of the captured men interrupted, "we're not soldiers. We're just people who live and work here. Company employees, mind you."

Robert gave him a bemused look. "Was your intent this evening to simply take a stroll about the walls, or were you looking for possible threats to your fine establishment?"

"Threats, sir."

"That makes you guards. And was your intent to shoot deer and buffalo and wolves and bears from your vantage points, or my men if given the chance?"

The man hesitated half a second, then answered, "Your men, sir."

"That makes you soldiers, enemies." Robert looked back at those gathered. "To the prisons."

It wasn't difficult, as most of the guards were unconscious, but there was some time spent just trying to remember where they'd stashed them all. When they started to come back around, two had been missed, but their stumbling, drunken carcasses were easily rounded up and taken to the prison with the others. It wasn't much of a prison, really, just a loose collection of four cells, enough to hold a few rabble rousers, but a little cramped for all the guards.

"Hey!" one of them barked.

Akłaq and Aniqan turned before they could leave the prison.

The man struggled to his feet and pushed his way to the door.

"You're that bitch from the main gate." He spat. "Pretending to be pregnant. 'Oh, my baby, my baby.' How could you do something like that? My wife is pregnant, so I know what that might be like, and I had mercy on you!"

"So did we," Aniqan stated simply.

They started walking away again. Before they could reach the exit, another man in the nearest cell spoke. "You're not from these parts, are you?"

Aniqan turned, but Akłaq's attention was taken by the appearance of the white bear. Those in the prisons could not see it, for it was down a short hall just walking around the corner. It stopped and made eye contact, sniffing the air.

Akłaq grabbed Aniqan's hand. She, too, started walking, but Aniqan held fast. She turned around to face him, but he was in a Band with the man in the cell. Suddenly alarmed, Akłaq pushed her way into the Band.

"—and you killed them!" Aniqan was saying.

"Not everyone is intended to wield Time," the man in the cell said, shrugging. "It's not uncommon in the universe for more advanced species to withhold Time from less advanced ones and let them advance in their own time, their own way."

"Except you don't want us to advance," Aniqan hissed. "You want us to be exactly like you, and even then, you scorn us because we're not like you. You just want to keep us down, keep us out of power, and enslave us to your ideals."

The man sighed. "You were more than welcome to stay in the north, stay in your little village, and we would overlook your petty crimes. But then you had to leave your lands and enter ours—"

"Enter the lands of the Cree, you mean. And every other people you've displaced."

The man rolled his eyes. "The idiocy of repetitiveness. I swear, if there is a God, He seems to delight in sending small men with childish arguments to the more learned to try our patience." He shook his head. "But if there is no God—and even if there is, I believe it a moral imperative—then I shall suffer no consequences from doing this."

Only Akłaq's quick reflexes and knowledge of the Akari was able to get between the man and the sudden Band he tried to smother Aniqan with. The sheer intensity of it was difficult to look at, but she could feel the power in it. She used a special form of Time Tendrils called a Time Web to keep it at bay, effectively putting one net around Aniqan to keep him grounded in the base Band, and another around the man's attacking Band, preventing it from reaching Aniqan while also trying to turn it back on the man himself.

"I guess you're the bitch who killed Goldsmith," the man spat, grunting and spitting with effort, straining within the Time Web. "You know, as the Regional Manager, I heard a lot of things about your people from the Russians. Bunch of disgusting, godless animals you are." He redoubled his efforts on the Band, and Akłaq could feel her Web begin to buckle. "When I'm done with him, I'm coming for you."

She didn't have to ask for clarification, but even a renewed sense of horror couldn't give her the strength to keep up her Web. Aniqan lent her what strength he could, but he just wasn't skilled enough in Timekeeping. If she dropped the Web to Band them and try to get away, the man would have them both, but she just couldn't hold it. What was worse, the man had also used Time Tendrils to keep Aniqan in place, tying various parts of his body in different planes of Time so as to create a disparity between what his mind wanted and when and how his body could respond.

Behind her, she heard the white bear make a noise. She glanced over her shoulder, feeling one of the Tendrils in her Web snap.

"Akłaq," Aniqan said.

She looked back at him. He was far too calm for the situation, she thought, and her stomach twisted into knots.

"Go."

Akłaq shook her head, tears streaming down her face. "I can't. I can't leave you."

"You have to." His gaze moved past her, and she knew that he could see the white bear, too. She could feel that the large animal was close to her now, still making noises.

"Every time I ignore the white bear, people die," she whimpered.

"And sometimes, bad things happen when you do obey," the bear rumbled behind her. "And worse things when you don't."

"So no matter what, I'm going to lose everything?" she asked, feeling a bit of indignation, but also feeling another few Tendrils snap. The attacking Band was almost through the Web that held it back, but the force of it snapping through the Tendrils would cause the rest of it to crumble. She glanced at the man in the cell. He, too, looked like he was struggling. "Maybe...if I can just outlast him..."

"Akłaq."

She didn't know who had spoken, whether it was Aniqan, the bear, or something else entirely. With a sob, she released everything. The Web disintegrated and the attacking Band enveloped Aniqan. She didn't want to see but she couldn't look away as he dropped dead. Perhaps the man had aged his heart until death, or done some other terrible thing to his insides. She didn't know, and she didn't want to stick around to find out what he had in store for her.

Terrified, she turned, pulled herself up on the bear's back, and together, they ran away.

Putu

Avgun Iñuiñaq
West

Despite the bouncing, Akłaq managed to fall asleep while riding the white bear. When she woke, the bear had slowed to a walk and finally dropped her off beside a river. On one side of her was open plains and on the other side was new forest. She did not recognize the area, nor was she entirely certain whether the sun was rising or setting.

"Where are we?" she asked, rubbing her eyes even as she knelt beside the water to splash her face.

"A place of safety."

It was not the bear who had spoken. When Akłaq looked up, she saw a man sitting on a rock about fifteen feet away. He was obviously one of the people, with dark skin and long, black hair, maybe twenty-five years old or so, though his choice of clothing was a mix of traditional and white. The white bear went to the river to drink, then returned to stand beside the man who put a hand into its fur.

"Anagalisgi?" Akłaq guessed.

"That's right," the man replied simply.

"But...how can I see you? I thought seeing fruit was required for that?"

"Not when you're dreaming."

"Dreaming? I'm still asleep?"

He nodded. "And when you wake, this is where you will be, though your company may be a little less than agreeable."

Akłaq shook her head. "I don't want company." She wiped her face, telling herself it was just water. "Every good thing that happens to me gets taken away. I'm tired of it! I never should have gotten on the white bear. I should have let the man kill me."

"You know that's not what he would have done, not right away at least."

She just sighed.

They sat there in silence for what felt like a long time. If this was a dream, it was the most realistic one Akłaq had ever experienced. It felt more like the false visions she experienced in the Seat of the Hands.

"I don't know what to do," she said at last. "It seems like every choice I make ends in disaster and death."

Anagalisgi nodded somberly. "I understand, believe me. When I had visions of death, it would sometimes leave me paralyzed with fear. If I didn't tell the people, was it an inevitable thing? If I did tell them—first, would they even believe me? If they did, was there anything that could really be done? Or is fate fixed?"

"And what have you learned in the last hundred years? Is fate fixed?"

"It is as fixed as we decide it is, but we should not simply ignore the role of natural consequences. Cause and effect exist for a reason."

She scoffed. "It took a lot of words for you to say you don't know."

Another stretch of silence overcame them. Looking around, Akłaq saw that all of the animals in the dream were white. A white beaver, white fox, white deer. The white bear had wandered off to go fishing in the river, though she could not tell if the fish were white, too. A white woodpecker and a white hawk circled overhead, perfectly at ease.

"What's going to happen to them?" she asked finally, poking at the gravelly sand. "Louis and Robert and Reginald, Red River, all of them? Will they prevail?"

"In their own goals, no. But the people will live on."

"It's something, I guess. What about Everett and Putu?"

"They'll be fine."

It was the best news she thought she could have heard, and she did not ask anything more about it for fear of ruining it with some caveat, some "but" statement.

"What happens now?" she asked. "What do I do?" She felt the kernel of indignation manifest itself. "Why should I follow the white bear if it only brings death, no matter what I do?"

"Sometimes it's not about getting the best outcome, only the least bad," Anagalisgi told her. "And sometimes the consequences of failure have very far-reaching effects."

"So Aniqan's death could have resulted from my killing Gerald? Or from staying with Nika? I followed the white bear tracks to Isbister's horse; was that wrong, too?" She sighed, rubbed her face, and stared at the ground. "I guess even if you did tell me, there's nothing I can do about it now."

Anagalisgi nodded. "There is truth in your words. But you now have an opportunity to start over and reach the place you should have been in many years ago. This does not mean that you will not have troubles or opposition or an antagonist or two, for the world still is what it is. And you are not expected to change the world. But if you change yourself, it's amazing how much the rest of the world changes, too."

When she looked up at him, he was gone. When she turned her gaze back to the river to search for the white bear, a reflection of the sun off the water blinded her.

Then she was blinking awake. Her dream and her current sensory input struggled to reconcile as she sat up. The world spun and she crashed back to the ground. Someone knelt beside her.

"Akłaq?" It was Putu. "Are you all right? How are you feeling?"

She took several breaths, trying to figure that out herself. Finally, "Fine, I think." She sighed. "My head hurts."

He helped her to a sitting position, the landscape still sloshing like a canoe in tumultuous waters. True to Anagalisgi's word, she was in the same place as in the dream, with the river and the gravelly shore, plains on one side and new forest on the other.

"Where are we?" she wondered. "How did you find me?"

Putu stood and moved off to tend to a small fire, meat roasting over a spit. "Word got back to Red River that taking Upper Fort Garry was a grand success, nearly flawless except for an incident while transporting prisoners to the cells. Seems as though one of the men attacked you and killed Aniqan. Last anyone knew, you were riding away from the fort on the back of a massive white bear." He chuckled. "Robert had the men disciplined for drunkenness.

"As for me, well, I didn't know how true it was that you rode off on a bear, but I knew that if someone killed Aniqan, then the threat was great indeed. I tracked you—yes, following bear tracks—and discovered you here, sound asleep. We're about three days from Red River."

"Three days!" Akłaq got wobbly legs under her and stood. "I've been asleep for three days!"

"No, you woke once. I couldn't be sure you weren't sleepwalking, but you went down to the river, splashed your face, relieved yourself, then came back and went back to sleep."

She turned around in all directions, unsure just what she was doing or what she expected to find. Her head was still a bit flimsy in its orientation, but she no longer felt nauseous from it.

"We're safe now, for the moment," Putu said. "But we won't be if we sit in one spot for very long. McDougall and his men are in the area, and if it's not them, then there are still wild animals about. And if not them, well, winter isn't leaving for another six months or so."

Akłaq sat down again and took the meat as Putu offered it to her.

Three days. Could it be true? She'd never slept so long. Even after wandering in the forest for over a month, even after the trauma of childbirth, she never slept so much. What was different about this time? Could Anagalisgi have had something to do with it? She'd had long dreams, vivid dreams before, but everything still remained in the space of a single night. What sorcery was this dream that it required putting her to sleep for three days?

The sun moved overhead with some speed and soon cast everything in the yellow glow of a perfect sunset. The ground began to glitter with frost as it clutched at grasses, shrubs, and the remaining leaves on the trees across the river. Putu pulled out a couple of coats and a heavy blanket which Akłaq accepted wordlessly.

Her mind had gone blank, and she figured that was the safest thing for it to be at the moment. She didn't want to think, didn't want to consider, didn't want to wonder what might have been. She was already dreading the thought of having to sleep alone—or worse, sleep beside Putu. Once again, a long-time companion of hers had vanished, and there was a good chance it had been her fault. How was she supposed to deal with that? How was she supposed to carry on?

After a bit, when the only light to be seen was the flickering of the fire, Putu ducked inside the tent. He may have said something, Akłaq wasn't sure. She just stayed where she was, staring at the flames until they vanished into coals. She knew she should probably put a few more logs on, just to keep it warm enough overnight that it could be rekindled in the morning.

Reluctantly, she broke the seal on her blanket, grabbed some logs, and did just that. Then she also pushed into the tent.

She could almost convince herself that it was Aniqan beside her, but it didn't help her sleep any better.

When she woke the following morning, Putu was already up and had the fire roaring back to life. He boiled water for tea which she accepted with a small word of thanks.

"I don't think we should go back to Red River," he said. "At least, not to stay."

"Why not?" Akłaq asked, her tone dead. "We have the fort. Louis is going to meet McDougall and his entourage." She briefly wondered at Anagalisgi's words, about the men's personal goals failing but the people living on.

Putu shook his head. "It's not our fight, Akłaq. And even so, we've played our part, helped them take the fort. Don't you think Aniqan's sacrifice was enough?" He poured a cup of tea for himself. "And anyway, I don't even believe you could go back to get your things."

"Why not?"

"Because last time, you had to send Matulik to do it for you. It'll be no different."

His words struck her like an arrow and she took a drink to cover up her sudden shortness of breath.

"Tell me what you want retrieved from your home, and I will bring them," he went on. "I know the mementos you keep for your first husband and children. What else do you want me to grab?"

Her mind went blank as she suddenly forgot everything she owned. Everything Aniqan owned. And when she was able to finally bring everything to mind, she was overwhelmed and unable to pick out just a few things. She didn't know it was possible to feel such anxiety; surely she and Nika had never owned so much?

Putu did not appear to be in any real hurry, but her racing thoughts said otherwise. Her scattered mind said all this should have been considered and decided on yesterday. Or even long before that. What if Gerald had killed Aniqan, years ago? What would she have wanted then? Or any of the times he went out on the hunts; sometimes things happened and Aniqan was only an Apprentice Timekeeper, hardly able to control so many moving pieces. And for as much as Louis and Robert declared that peace should be the first option, it wasn't as though there hadn't been other possible dangers at the fort. Was it just poor luck, then, that they happened to run into the Regional Manager? Who was he, and what was he doing here? Had he been hunting them and gotten lucky himself?

So many questions and she still couldn't decide what she might want as a memento for Aniqan. She didn't even know how to think of him, honestly. They weren't married, although they lived like they did and let people assume so. And yet, it didn't feel like a marriage, not in the way she and Nika had shared. But simply relegating him to a long-time lover felt disrespectful.

"He had a pendant," she said at last. "He said it belonged to his sister."

Putu made a disapproving sound. "If he was wearing it when he died, it'll be buried with him."

Akłaq stood. "Then I'll get it—"

"No, no." He stood, put a hand on her shoulder, and forced her back down. "No, I..." He sighed. "I will get it."

It was midday before he made any move to leave the camp, however.

"If you have trouble and flee the camp, go west," he told her, mounting his horse. "I expect I may be able to Band my way back to Red River, but in the interest of not losing the horse, I may have to return in Base Time."

She looked up at him. "I'm not worried."

Her resolve was weak to begin with, and it only lessened as she watched him ride away across the plains and finally vanish into a Band, the wake lighting up the landscape even in the middle of the day. Even at that strength, it would still be a day or two before he reached Red River.

A minute later she looked around the tiny camp. A tent, a fire, a spit, a few small tools and utensils, just enough for a man who was out tracking a woman riding a bear. If he really was intending to head west, he would have to take time to grab some things from his house, too. He would also have to acquire another horse, both for packing and so she could ride.

He was going to be a few days.

This left camp maintenance up to her, and the idea helped to calm her nerves a little. Simple chores, something normal. Gather firewood, gather water, maybe go out for small game once, and keep an eye out for trouble.

By the third day, she was wandering without really looking, stupidly expecting to find Aniqan just around the next tree, or maybe waiting for her back at camp when she returned with a paltry load of sticks. Only when the snow started to really fall on the fifth day did she manage to break out of the worst of her trance and actually do something. She spent a whole day just gathering firewood, taking the opportunity to better refine her use of Gravity in order to minimize the danger of constantly crossing the river and move more wood per trip.

She did not see the white bear, nor did she have any more dreams concerning Anagalisgi.

By the tenth day she began to worry. Even if Putu had taken two or three days to get to Red River and another three to get back, how long was it really going to take him to find a few mementos, pack up some more supplies, grab a horse, and get moving? Even if he had to wait and be sneaky about getting Aniqan's pendant, that still couldn't take more than a night just because of the work.

Had something happened? Had the Regional Manager found him, too? Had McDougall and his men confronted Riel and shattered the leaders of the resistance? She told herself to be patient, give it a few more days. Maybe Putu was fine, but something had happened to the horse. It wasn't impossible that it might have stepped in a hole or burrow and broken its leg. Putu would have had to abandon it and make the trek on foot, which would add a few more days, regardless of Banding. Then he would have to acquire two horses, not an easy thing to do with things the way they were.

That was what she told herself over the next few days when he still didn't show. It was like waiting for Nika all over again, when he left to go trade in town. Seven days, he promised, but no more than ten.

She sat by the fire, the evening of the fifteenth day, staring at the sunset, wondering what was out there. Some of it she knew. Prince Albert was still out there, and she'd heard of several other settlements scattered here and there. But what else? What was it that drove men just one more mile, hoping for something just a little bit better? Maybe the trees would be a little bit taller, the river just a little bit deeper, the grass just a little bit greener. What was it that made them hope for such things? What was it that drove some to chase these endless dreams while others simply found a suitable spot and declared that they would make it their home?

Akłaq added a few logs to the fire and ducked into the tent as it began snowing. Maybe Putu had been delayed by weather. All the power in the world didn't mean anything if you couldn't see and were slowly freezing.

She wished for Aniqan. She wished for Nika. She wished for her children. She wished for anything at all, but the cold and the stillness, broken only by her little campfire, did not allow for anything resembling comfort. She prayed, but took no comfort in it. The prayer felt hollow, the spirits and God far away, empty, aloof, maybe even nonexistent. For a moment she considered the idea of the Author, then pushed that aside, too. Was it her own lack of skill, or was the Akari just not as powerful as the Akarin claimed it to be? If it was so great, why didn't the Akarin take control of the Wheel? Why couldn't the Krydik pull themselves—and the other indigenous peoples—together and make things right?

She understood now why Aniqan had been so cynical, even antagonistic about the spirits, or any religion. And yet, she couldn't help but think of his expression in those last moments. She knew he had seen the white bear, and something in his face said that his faith had been restored, not only in the spirits, but also in her. He believed in her; he believed she had something to live for, something to accomplish. She just wished she knew what that was and how she was supposed to achieve it.

She wished for sleep.

Akłaq was woken up the next morning by the heavy plodding of horse hooves. Eagerly, she poked her head outside the tent, momentarily blinded by the brilliant blue sky, shining sun, and sparkling snow.

It was Putu. He rode on a different horse than he'd left, this one black instead of brown, and the appaloosa following him was also a new mount. Both had full packs. He rode up to the camp and dismounted. His expression was apologetic, but his disposition said he wasn't in any special hurry to pack up camp and leave.

"Three hours in and the horse broke a leg," he said. "Stepped right in a burrow."

"I wondered if that might have been the case," Akłaq replied diplomatically.

He reached in one of the saddlebags and pulled out a small item. It was a necklace decorated with bear claws and carved bones. "Is this the pendant?"

She snatched it out of his hand as an answer and strung it around her neck.

He nodded. "The rest of your stuff is in those bags." He indicated the packs on the second horse. "I grabbed your other mementos, some clothing, other things I thought might be important."

Akłaq glanced at the horse, its nose already down looking for grass, then back at Putu. "Thank you. How are things in Red River?"

"Robert and Reginald still hold the fort, and Riel and Everett and the rest of them turned back McDougall and his entourage."

"You still think we should head west?"

He nodded. "I do, if for no other reason than the Regional Manager. He was taken for questioning in Aniqan's death and has since escaped."

Reluctantly, she agreed. "Do you want to leave now?"

Putu chuckled and squatted next to the fire. "Not today. Tomorrow maybe."

She sat down beside him.

"What happened down in that prison?" he asked after what felt like a long time.

Akłaq hesitated but recounted the tale as best she could remember. They were helping to deliver the last of the prisoners to the cells. The Regional Manager happened to be in the first cell by the door to the outside. Words were exchanged. He tried to attack Aniqan, she held him off. But even her best efforts weren't enough and she had to flee. Yes, she did ride on the back of the white bear.

Putu's expression was grim. "He must have known that you were going to be attacking the fort, or else he made a split-second decision when he recognized you."

"But I've never seen him before, and I don't know that Aniqan has either; how could he have recognized us?"

"Because we're northerners, for one. We don't belong here. And one little Band from Aniqan or you, something to give yourselves away..." He shrugged. "I'm certain he did his research on those from Ujurak's village before attacking. It may be that Goldsmith is the one who gave your description to him. Maybe it was me he was after but challenged you first. I don't know. And I'm not keen to find out."

Akłaq shifted position. "And there's nothing we can do about it, no higher court to appeal to?"

"As far as the Time industry is concerned, we're fugitives, Runners. We stole Time and then resisted and escaped from those who came to bring us to justice for it. Earth-side, assuming we even could prove that Frederickson killed Aniqan, we have no real recourse. No court will hear our grievances, no matter how severe. We are the only justice there is in matters like these."

"What about Everett? Could there be any trouble for him, helping us and all?"

"He's already a Runner because he's an Akari-bearer. You probably are, too, now, by the way. And whether you put stock in it or not, few deny that Akari-bearers are powerful. Maybe that's why he went after Aniqan first, take out the weaker opponent and try to unbalance you."

Akłaq sighed. "It worked, honestly. If the white bear hadn't been there..." She shook her head. "Where do you expect to go?"

Putu shrugged. "West is all I know. For now, it'll work."

"Did you warn Everett at least?"

"He knows, but he's going to stick with Riel and the others. Our personal problems aside, Frederickson could be trying to make trouble for the Red River people. At least with Everett there, he'll be able to stave off any Time encounters."

Couldn't deny that. "Did he say anything about continuing my Akari training? I won't be able to ride for weeks at a time to come back here, and I still cannot open Paa."

"He didn't say anything about it, no." He shifted position. "But if there is an Author out there, I'm sure he'll come up with something."

Akłaq said nothing to that. If there was an Author out there, then why couldn't she save Aniqan? Had he said something, done something, made some offense that condemned him? Was it punishment for his unbelief? She didn't understand. Right now, she didn't want to.

"Do you expect to go all the way to the west coast, then?" she wondered.

"Maybe. Eventually. I'm not in the biggest hurry to cross the mountains during winter, but settling there for a short period might throw Frederickson off, assuming he is pursuing us."

She stared into the fire for a long moment. "Do you think we'll ever be able to go home?"

Out of the corner of her eye, she saw Putu sigh. "Return to the same geographical location? I think so, one day. But returning home?" He shook his head. "Never. Our families are gone, our villages burned. We will never return to that place."

That didn't make either of them feel too good, and sleep seemed to elude both of them that night. Eventually they gave up and decided to just pack up the camp.

"This is a nice place," Akłaq observed, looking around the landscape, still draped in shadow. "It's too bad we couldn't stay here for a while."

"You've already stayed here for a while," Putu pointed out. "But you are right that it is nice. It's just a little closer to Red River than I'm comfortable with right now."

She cinched down a strap on her pack. "But if you expect Frederickson to pursue us, wouldn't it make more sense to stay and let him wander futilely around the wilderness?"

He grinned. "Now there's a satisfying thought."

"But...?"

"But what?"

She blinked. "You don't think they're going to keep Red River, do you?"

He gave her half a look over the back of his horse. "Of course I don't. They're not looking for independence, Akłaq. They're looking for equality. That will never be obtained."

"What do you mean?"

"Riel's committee...the articles of confederation aren't about declaring themselves independent, they're the terms on which Red

River will become part of Canada." He closed one of the bags and jiggled the saddle a bit. "What's going to happen is that there will be a standoff over winter. Maybe they'll skirmish a little, but I doubt it. In the spring, Canada will send a formal delegation to welcome Red River into the fold. They'll say whatever needs to be said to get the committee to agree." He cinched down the girth and the horse snorted and pawed once at the snow. "There will be some big to-do about it, some celebration. Canada will invite Riel and the other members to Ottawa as a gesture of good will and equality." He finished with the girth and continued looking at her over the seat, only his eyes and forehead visible. "Once they arrive—far from home with no support—they'll be arrested. Soldiers will be sent to seize Red River, drive any sympathizers out of town and usher in all the loyalists from the east. Exactly as they've been trying to do for years."

Akłaq didn't know what to say to that, so she just put one foot in the stirrup and hoisted herself up on her horse.

"They're like rats, Akłaq," Putu said, settling in his own saddle. "Once they've conquered an area and bled it dry, they spread, multiply, and do the same everywhere else, all in the name of progress. And those of us who want to live peacefully are called evil, savage, and regressive." He nudged his horse to a walk, and Akłaq followed, moving beside him.

"What do you think the answer is? Complacency got us here, and simply running away will do nothing if they will only spread everywhere. And you're not exactly prone to violence."

"Honestly, if rats have infested your barn, your best option is to burn down the barn, start over again." He gave her a look. "But who really wants to burn down the world? Because just as you are ridding yourself of the rats, you're also destroying your food and shelter. The rats don't care; the ones who survive will just move on to the next place. And there you are, homeless and starving."

Avgun Iñuiñaq Atausiq
Father and Daughter

If anyone ever asked, they were father and daughter. It was believable enough, the way they looked, and, in an odd sort of way, it was a comforting relationship that neither seemed to have realized they needed until the first time they introduced themselves as such. The first time Akłaq introduced Putu as her father, it was like wrapping herself in a warm blanket. There was a feeling of inherent protection and stability in having a father. She noticed a change in his disposition as well, when he introduced her as his daughter, though she could not speak for the changes he felt, the need that was being fulfilled. Protection, maybe. Service.

Or maybe it was just the fact of having each other and forging their own little family. There was something…nice, about being a daughter again, Akłaq thought.

There really wasn't much west of Prince Albert. Mostly trading posts, some with towns grown up around them. There were indigenous villages and white settlements. The indigenous villages were more accepting of Akłaq and Putu when they came through, though their general demeanor said that they had been through so much that they weren't enthusiastic about any new people no matter who they were.

Nevertheless, Akłaq and Putu rented a room for the night. It was a cozy room with two narrow beds, a dresser, a desk, and a window that looked out toward the stable where their horses were housed. Beyond the stable, the snowy mountains loomed ominously over the village, like a cat's paw ready to come down upon its prey.

"If the people weren't so annoyed by us, I might suggest we winter here," Akłaq commented, staring at the shadowy peaks.

"They're not annoyed by us, they're annoyed by our presence," Putu corrected, sitting on one bed and taking off his boots. "We remind them that there is still a big world out there, and it's a hostile one."

She turned away from the window and went to sit on the other bed, facing him. "What are things like in the United States, do you think?"

One boot popped off. "Bad." The other boot came off. "Worse, maybe. You don't go from trying to kill your own brothers back to normal life in an instant."

"But things can't stay bad forever."

"Oh, I agree. But I'm not going to put my canoe into a stormy sea and wait for the waves to calm. I'm going to wait for the waves to calm and then put my canoe in the water."

"Do you think things might be better at home, now that the United States bought the land and kicked the Russians out?"

Putu gave her a look. "You are unusually optimistic for the circumstances."

"Maybe I got tired of your endless pessimism and didn't want to feed into it anymore. Maybe I realized that, pessimism or optimism, you and I still ended up here in the same place at the same time."

"So you're not being optimistic, just sarcastic."

"Come on, Putu, you can't stay grumpy all the time."

"I prefer to think of myself as a realist. We're far from home, unable to return, surrounded by potential dangers, with limited supplies and no support. But we're still breathing and unharmed, so let's do what we can while we can."

Akłaq shifted position. "Who says we can't return home? All right, so things have changed. My family—all of them—are long gone. But the land is ours. It has always been ours. From the mountains to the forests to the tundra and the frozen sea, all the way to the *kiuġuyat*. If the mixed-breeds of Red River could build their culture and find their heart in the middle of the fight, I don't see why we can't do the same."

Putu sighed resignedly. "I admire your optimism, but I fear that it is short-lived."

"At least I have optimism."

"You are the stormy sea, Akłaq. You have periods of rest and periods of rage. I am the calm river, not much to look at, but I always get where I'm going with no hurry." He lay back on the bed and closed his eyes. "For now, though, I think we need rest."

"Even sailors and canoers wish for a strong breeze to help get them where they're going," Akłaq muttered, moving to lie down herself.

"What was that?" Putu asked, not moving.

"Nothing. Go to sleep."

Akłaq lay back on the bed. It was not the most comfortable bed she had ever slept in, but it would work for the night.

Putu had been correct that she was more sarcastic than optimistic, but she was trying to be better than she had in the past. She hated the lows, the sulking, the brooding. Grief was one thing, but she couldn't allow herself to be bound by her losses. Aniqan had believed in her. In his last moments, he had seen the white bear and believed. She had a calling, and she had to see it through.

She wished for another dream of the white bear or Anagalisgi, some guidance to tell her what she had to do. The last thing she had been told was that she was going to the place she should have been at years ago, presumably if she had continued to follow the white bear and not stayed with Nika. She could only assume that she had not yet reached this place. Depending on what Putu had in mind, Akłaq hoped that she would receive some notice when she did reach this place, or else Putu might pull her right out of it again.

But her sleep was notably devoid of guidance, visions, or dreams of any kind. Akłaq would not say she wasn't disappointed, but she had to remain optimistic. She just hadn't reached the place where she was supposed to be.

Of course, that meant that wherever that place was, it was either in or on the other side of the mountains, which meant crossing said mountains. Staring at them through the window the next morning, she just kept telling herself that if she did have some great calling, then her death was highly unlikely. That did not, however, guarantee any protection for Putu, and she wondered what she would do if he did meet some terrible fate.

Breakfast was half a loaf of bread with butter, and then they were out gathering their horses in the pre-dawn light. They distributed the bags, cinched the girths, and mounted up. Their departure from the village was met with no fanfare or even passing acknowledgment, and the only evidence they left of having been there were the hoof prints in the snow.

It was almost a surreal experience. As the first colors of dawn painted themselves across the sky and reflected upon the snow, Akłaq wondered if they weren't riding in the *kiuġuyat* itself among the spirits. She looked around, wondering if she might see the white bear, or any of the other white animals. She didn't see any, though she was almost certain that they saw her.

Putu was a quiet traveling companion. He didn't make idle talk, didn't complain. Looking at him, Akłaq could see that many thoughts crossed his mind, perhaps minor observations of their surroundings, but if it wasn't pertinent to the immediate situation, he voiced nothing. On the one hand, it was kind of nice, that he didn't badger or complain or, in the worst scenarios, give away their position. On the other hand, did he have no questions? Did he have no observations? Sure, a deer might not be anything especially remarkable, but pointing one out might help to pass the time a little, break up the day, marvel at the beauty of nature.

"How long did it take you to find us?" she asked at last.

"The better part of a year, and that only because I was also trying to keep myself hidden as much as possible," he answered.

"What were you going to do if you couldn't find us, or if we had also been captured or killed?"

"I don't know. I try not to make too many plans; they could be interrupted at any time. Running from the Timekeepers, that sense of caution and danger made that principle more relevant than ever. I apply it here as well. That's why I don't know exactly where we're going, because we could be diverted at any time for many reasons."

"But if you don't know where we're going, how will we know when we arrive?"

He sighed. "Because, quite honestly, I think you're going to tell me."

"You think there is something to the Akari and the white bear."

"What I think doesn't matter. What I know is that it's pointless to try to argue with women, politicians, and religious fanatics. You hit at least two of those three."

Akłaq grinned, unsure what else to do with her face. "You think I'm a fanatic?"

"It does seem to have taken over your every thought and action."

"Ah, so you heard my fervent prayers to know whether I was intended to mount my horse from the left side or the right."

That got a chuckle out of him at least. "All right, maybe not quite that much."

Akłaq sighed. "Aniqan admitted that he had forsaken the spirits and the old ways, and he didn't think too highly of Christians either. Don't tell me you're the same way."

Putu gave her a look. "I still believe in the gods and spirits. That much has never been in question for me. I just don't believe they're as involved in our lives and the rhythm of the earth as we were led to think, and this is why Ujurak's visions were so vague, few and far in between. Our people were dying faster than the spirits were telling him."

She did not respond to this, and their journey again lapsed into silence. She considered a conversation she'd had with the white bear. When she brought up Ujurak's *tuungaq*, the white bear had gotten angry, even a bit hostile, and said not to bring up the shadows. Akłaq knew there were evil spirits as well as good, but why would Ujurak's *tuungaq* have been evil when it helped them so much? Maybe not enough to satisfy Aniqan and Putu, but it had helped. Was it some form of trickery? Had Ujurak known that his *tuungaq* might be evil? Somehow, Akłaq had a hard time considering the possibility that either the *tuuṅaq* was evil, or that Ujurak had known about it if it was and so chose to listen to it anyway.

But then, he had said that he couldn't see her path as clearly as the others, and as far as she knew, she was the only one who had made any mention or contact with the white spirits.

Their journey left plenty of time to think, although her thoughts began to wander to other things eventually. Many people assumed that one mountain or section of mountains was very much like any other. From a distance, this did appear to be true. Looming monstrosities rising out of the ether days or weeks before actually setting foot upon their slopes, just their existence was intimidating. When travel became necessary, any number of obstacles had the potential to delay or even kill. Weather, rock slides, avalanches, wild animals. Danger had a way of dulling the beauty of a place, but it was in the beauty that each mountain or section of mountains became unique.

"I saw on a map once that these are the same mountains that Aniqan and I crossed far to the north," she said conversationally. "And they extend even farther to the south, all through the United States territories to Mexico."

"What's Mexico?" Putu wondered.

"Another country, I think. But they're Spanish."

"What's Spanish?"

"I think they're a country, too, from Europe."

"Another conqueror then." He said it with some resignation. "What do the people from Spanish want?"

"Land and gold. They like gold. And I guess they found a lot of it in South America."

Putu grunted. "Good for them if it keeps the Spanish people away from us."

"There's gold in our land, too, you know," Akłaq pointed out.

"Yes, but as long as no one talks and no outsiders find it, we're safe. And even if someone did find some, who's really going to want to travel so far north for it? A bit of shiny metal isn't worth braving the cold and snow and long night. The Russians got some, yes, but more often we found ground oil which just ruined the whole operation, and they called it off. Furs and whale oil were much easier to find and process."

"Well, if they ever find a use for that ground oil, we'll be in big trouble."

He pursed his lips but shook his head. "I don't think so. It has its uses when it's life and death, but it burns dirty so it's not practical for any widespread heating use. You can't drink it. No, I think it functions very nicely as a defense to keep the prospectors out of our land."

Despite being unfamiliar with the land and having no map to guide them, Akłaq knew they were just crossing the center point of the range and were soon traveling on the downslope. There hadn't been much out on the plains, west of Prince Albert, and the mountains themselves were practically devoid of any human activity—Akłaq was surprised Putu didn't suggest they just stop and live there for a decade or two—so she didn't expect to walk down the last hill to flat land and find a huge city of bustling activity.

Eventually they did find a lookout point that showed them the road out of the mountains. It would be several days yet, but she spied the flat land in the hazy distance and the black smoke from a train.

"What if Frederickson took the train and is waiting for us?" Akłaq wondered.

"That would assume that he knew where we're going," Putu answered. "Trains only run to fixed places, often with great distances between them. Horses can go just about anywhere, which is why we're taking them and not the train. He could already be on the west coast, true, but then he would spend a great deal of time searching, wondering if we had already been there and left, just hadn't made it yet, or weren't going to be there at all." He chuckled. "They're very good at inventing ways to move faster and do bigger, but there is some value to slower and smaller."

Their journey remained largely uneventful. If they suspected any danger, a simple Band took care of it. If they needed to eat, Banding had that handled, too, so they didn't spend too much time stalking through unfamiliar, hostile territory. Their next lookout spot showed a clear road to an obvious flat land whose most striking feature was a near-absence of snow despite it still being winter. Akłaq had to rub her eyes to make sure she wasn't imagining things.

"Have we turned south by accident?"

"The days have remained consistent in their lengthening," Putu said. "And I don't believe we've lost any time. Perhaps there is simply no snow here." He shifted position on his horse. "Maybe we are closer to the coast than I thought. We might be in Tlingit land."

That was a welcome thought. Akłaq would be happy to see northerners again.

By the following evening, she figured it was safe to say that they were out of the mountains. The foothills remained hilly and treacherous with many jagged rocks, but it was manageable. She was more distracted by their apparent descent into springtime. Snow turned to slush and green grass popped up all over the place. Putu called for camp early so they could graze the horses.

"We've made it across the mountains," Akłaq said later as they sat around the fire. She poked the coals with a stick and watched embers leap into the darkening sky. "Where are we going from here?"

"If we head for the coast, it shouldn't be long before we find a settlement," Putu said, sounding more certain than he had their entire trip. "Indigenous or white, we can get our bearings and then go from there."

"You still don't have a destination in mind?"

"If we're in or near Tlingit land, I would prefer to stay with them for a time, honestly. They were usually good to us. Our ways are similar enough." He, too, poked at the fire. "We've lived with the whites for too long; we should get back to our old ways. You especially."

"How do you know the Tlingit still keep the old ways? They suffered persecution just as much as we did."

He did not respond to that.

"And if we're not near Tlingit land?" she inquired instead.

Putu looked thoughtful for a long moment. Finally he answered, "I think for now that should be our goal. We'll head to the coast and figure out where we are. Then we'll hope that Tlingit land—or any friendly land—is within reach."

"We've traveled hundreds of miles across the plains and crossed the mountains during the winter. I don't think we're going to have much trouble getting anywhere."

"We can hope." He stretched and stood. "But before all of that, we should get some sleep. Flat land and trains mean more people. We'll have to keep our guard up."

Akłaq reluctantly agreed, though she did not move right away. The fire was warm and the night was calm. She wanted to enjoy it as much as she could, in the event they weren't able to find friendly lands. And if they couldn't, what would they do then? Travel endlessly, moving from place to place with no real home to call their own? There was so much land out here, so vast and wild. There was plenty enough for everyone, so why couldn't they learn to share and live together?

Eventually she got up and ducked into the tent. Putu wasn't Aniqan, and he certainly wasn't Nika, but it was better than sleeping alone.

The next day, they were on the move again. For the first time, Putu seemed to appear almost happy, with a certain confidence and spring in his step even while riding. If it turned out that they were in Tlingit land, or anywhere close to home, he might even broach into the realm of being genuinely happy. Akłaq wasn't sure the man would be able to handle it.

Soon enough they found themselves on a proper road. Putu was a little annoyed by it, but they needed to find a landmark of some kind, even if it was a white settlement. That settlement might at least have a trading post which might have a map, or someone with directions anyway. It would be a place to start. Besides, they couldn't hide from Frederickson forever.

Once out of the foothills, the snow all but vanished completely. The air grew hot and muggy, and the insects came out in swarms. This chilled everyone's good mood, especially the horses, and it was a fairly miserable ride. Riding in the morning or evening helped to beat the heat, but then the insects only got worse. Nearing the coast didn't help either, and Akłaq was afraid she might be carried off by a swarm of flies or mosquitoes. She could think of no trick to make them go away. Banding was good as long as the user was able to hold it, but that lasted only a few days at most—and only while conscious, anyway, which didn't help their camping situation—and she couldn't come up with any Akari ability that might aid them either. Other travelers on the road had their own remedies, but their success was marginal.

The ocean was a welcome sight, and it was a rare occasion that Putu smiled.

"We're almost home," he said. "I can feel it."

There was a small settlement down on the shore, white, as evidenced by the tall church steeple. Akłaq picked out a mill and a cluster of homes and other businesses. As they drew near, she guessed that either the town was very busy or else there was some celebration going on.

They rode down into the settlement, and Akłaq was struck by the sudden disparity between the atmosphere of the town and the attitude the residents had toward them. In the settlement, cheer and light-hearted fun. Toward them, hostility, resentment, and a certain kind of pity that she had come to loathe from whites. It was a pity that arose when seeing someone who is downtrodden and in truly desperate straits, and yet it ignored the fact that that person, who was doing the pitying, was responsible for that someone being downtrodden and in truly desperate straits. It was like beating up a man and stealing everything he had, then tsking and commenting about how the man was clearly unable to take care of himself and so needed more strict governance over his affairs.

Akłaq spied a building with a sign that clearly once read "Trading Post," but it had been poorly painted over and redecorated to say, "General Store." She suggested they try there.

The disposition of the store manager was little better than the rest of the town, his temper likely more dependent on, and perhaps proportional to, the amount of money they had to spend.

"What's the grand occasion, friend?" Putu inquired in a rare display of near-friendliness. Akłaq told herself it was because he also sensed the hostility and didn't wish to start anything.

"We're celebrating British Columbia's entry into the Dominion of Canada," the manager replied stiffly. "Newfoundland and Nova Scotia, too, back east. Sea to shining sea, just like the United States."

Akłaq did not miss the minute muscle movements in Putu's countenance that said he could not muster up any joy over this revelation. Instead he asked, "And where do we find ourselves?"

"Granville, though some call it Vancouver. It's a bit up in the air, but officially we're called Granville."

"I see. Would you happen to have a map? Is Tlingit land nearby?"

The man shrugged. "Got a map, sure."

Putu sighed. "How much is it?"

"Well, let's see..." He ran his tongue over his teeth. "I think you boys over at the mill make a nickel a day, so why don't we call it three pennies?"

It was an obscene price, but given that Putu had no desire to stay in or near a white settlement where money was so important, he turned it over. The man studied the pennies, tapped them on the counter to make sure they were real, then went and grabbed a map. He laid it out.

"All right, we're here." He pointed. "This is Granville. This is the road east out of town, the railroad. Got some Chilcotin reserves here, here, here, here, and here—"

"Reserves?" Akłaq wondered.

The manager gave her a sarcastic look. "Yeah. Reserves. Where you people belong. Like I said, there's Chilcotin here and here. You said something about Tingit—"

"Tlingit," Putu corrected.

"I don't give a damn." The man was clearly agitated. "Tingit's gonna be up here, in the north part of the province. There's a reserve here, but part of 'their land' extends out of the province and even into Alaska. Now then, take the map, pick a reserve, and bugger off."

Only because Putu didn't want to start something did he accept the abuse, taking the map, sourly wishing the man a good day, and turning to leave.

"And one more thing," the man said.

Putu sighed but paused and look back.

The shop manager grinned wolfishly. "Your daughter there is pretty. I'd recommend getting out of town quick if I were you, before the lads catch sight of her."

Akłaq felt her eyes go wide, but Putu just muttered something under his breath and left the store. Akłaq followed hard on his heels.

"I should have known things were going to be bad," he said, stuffing the map in a saddle bag and mounting up. "There is nowhere they go where rot does not follow." He turned his horse around angrily while Akłaq mounted up. "They claim that the west is a land of freedom and opportunity, but it is only freedom and opportunity for those who invade and kick out the people who had lived here since the beginning of time. You can't evict someone from a house and then claim the house is abandoned and open to anyone who wants to take it."

"Putu, calm down," Akłaq said softly.

He went on as though she had not spoken. "And now they force the people onto reserves. Camps. Filled with squalor and sickness and starvation. They take everything from us and then wonder why we have nothing." Now he looked at her. But rather than anger, she saw only hurt. "They are possessed of demons, Akłaq. The demons possess the white men in order to steal and kill and destroy, and when they leave the bodies of the white men they possess, the white men have no memory of what they have done but they still reap the benefits."

"Then our fight is against the demons, not the white men." She nodded toward a couple children playing in the street. "They are not our enemy."

"Not yet," Putu said sadly. "But they will be taught how to be an enemy, how to hate and welcome the demons into their minds and bodies to do exactly as their forefathers have done."

"Let's go north," Akłaq suggested. "Let's find the Tlingit people, whether it's a reserve or on their own land. That's what you wanted to do, right? We still can. Then we can either stay with them, or keep going all the way back home."

For a long moment, she thought he was going to refuse. And for a brief moment, she thought he might have finally reached a breaking point, where he would decide that he'd had enough running and was going to start fighting, though hardly in a way anyone would consider honorable. As a Timekeeper, he had the power to stop time, kill everyone in the town starting with the store manager, and then ride away like nothing happened. Akłaq hoped he wouldn't, if only because she didn't want to be put in the position of having to choose whether to help him or stop him.

"Let's go north," she repeated. "Let's get out of this...British Columbia."

"Even the name is offensive," Putu agreed, sighing. "They buy and sell and trade in goods and land that is not theirs."

He might have had a grander speech, but suddenly he sounded too tired to do anything more than nudge his horse to follow hers. They endured the stares and the glares as they left town, turning north instead of east. Leaving the center of the hostility helped to bring some life back into Putu, but Akłaq couldn't help but think that he looked around at everything like a man about to die, knowing he may never see it again.

Avgun Iñuiñaq Malġuk
Reserve

Almost every white person they came across on the road north showed some hostility toward them, even if it was only a glare. Farmers chased them away from their land with dogs or guns, even if they were just passing by on the road. Soldiers gave them directions to the nearest reserve, whether they'd asked or not.

From this, they found the Tlingit reserve without much issue. Despite Putu swearing time and again that he wasn't going to be forced into a camp again, they stopped anyway, if only in the hopes of finding some friendly faces.

It wasn't a labor camp, as he had feared, and this eased some of his discomfort. To Akłaq's eyes, it appeared as any ordinary stretch of land. Some hills, a lot of trees, small game, large game. True, the haphazard sections of fence were a bit out of place, and the occasional soldier running around outside the fence was a bit strange, but it didn't appear to be anything truly sinister. There was only the barest of paths leading to the interior of the reserve, and there they found a small village. If she didn't know better, Akłaq might have thought she was returning to Ujurak's village, and she almost expected to see Matulik and Ilannaq and everyone else. But as the people looked up, she knew it wasn't true. And she began to understand some of Putu's fears.

There were people, but there was very little spirit in the place. They weren't starving, although they did not appear the most well-fed either. It was getting to be the height of summer, when there should have been racks upon racks of drying meat, dozens of stretching rings for furs, and baskets full of forage and harvest; she counted only half a dozen racks of meat, a few furs, and two baskets of forage. She saw a couple small gardens, though they were hardly anything of note.

Still, a few people rose to meet them. Putu chose a place to stop and dismount, and Akłaq followed his lead.

"You are not Tlingit," one older man, perhaps the village leader, observed. "Who are you?"

"Putu and Akłaq, of the Iñupiatun," he introduced. "I am from Nuurvik, she from Qikiqtaġruk."

The older man nodded. "I have heard of those places. And I have heard of you. You once followed Ujurak the seer of time, didn't you?"

"That's right."

"You are welcome here. Turn your horses out to graze and come speak with us."

They did so, taking the horses to a large, overgrown pen where half a dozen goats also tore at the grass. Then they returned to the village and followed the older man and several others into a particular house.

The house was built very much like a white house, though the decorations reminded Akłaq well of home.

"Welcome, Putu and Akłaq. I am K'alyaan," the older man said. "These are my brothers, Naakilaan and Yeilgooxhu." It was difficult to say whether they were blood brothers or clan brothers, though Akłaq figured there really wasn't much of a difference. "We, as most of the people here, are Taant'a Kwa'an, though there are a handful of Sanyaa Kwa'an as well."

"And the rest of the people?" Putu inquired.

"Fortunate enough to live north, beyond British Columbia."

Naakilaan spat at the name.

K'alyaan ignored this and went on, "Some here have moved north or are planning to. Others of us will stay on our ancestral lands no matter the cost to ourselves." As if in reaction to a doubt or objection that no one had voiced, he added, "We survived the Russians. We will survive the Canadians also."

"But will you survive the winter?" Putu asked. "You don't seem to have had much luck with hunting and gathering."

"It's true, this small tract of land does not offer as much bounty as our normal territory," Yeilgooxhu said slowly, choosing his words. "But what we show is not always a representation of what we have. If we appear to have too much, we may be accused of stealing."

"But if we don't appear to have enough," Naakilaan cut in, "then we will be visited by either soldiers or churchgoers with handouts. And they don't like to leave."

"Is there nothing you can do?" Putu wondered.

K'alyaan shook his head. "Nothing. We barely exist to them except as animals to be kept in a pen. We may graze within our allotted area, and every so often they will come and check on us, make sure we have food and water. We have no recourse for wrongs done to us, but everything we do to them is a slight at best and a crime at worst."

"Yes, we experienced that quite heavily in the south."

"It's not all bad, though," Yeilgooxhu said, his tone slightly optimistic. "They don't want to take care of us; you can see it when they come through. It's just a duty for them to perform. Otherwise they let us do as we please."

K'alyaan put a hand up before Putu could speak. "We know. It's only temporary. Until they decide that they want this squat of land as well because the rest just isn't good enough."

"It's not that the land isn't good," Putu said sourly. "It's that your very existence offends them. Like a man who kills another man in the next town for the simple fact that he can't imagine sharing existence with the other, despite neither one being harmed."

The elder chuckled grimly. "You speak nothing we have not all thought at one time or another. But we have made our choices. Besides, even if we were to leave now, we have no reason to think the land in the north will not come under the same scrutiny in the future. Piece by piece, this is how the ant eats the moose. If we flee, they will surely take this land. In the future, they will do the same in the north. Then we are back where we started but having less land." K'alyaan sighed. "But I do not think you really came here to discuss these things we already know. We heard that Ujurak was dead, and many of his followers as well. How did you escape and where have you been? What news of things?"

So Putu related the tale, as far as he was concerned. Ujurak and most of the others were dead. He met up with Akłaq and Aniqan in Red River. For a time, Red River was able to gain some semblance of independence, but then, as they had learned more recently, lost it earlier in the spring. Riel and the leaders of the resistance had fled to the United States and Red River was absorbed into the new province of Manitoba. But he and Akłaq were already on their way west. The journey was fine, but they had been treated horribly ever since Granville.

"This is not surprising in the least," K'alyaan said, nodding. "Though I am sorry to hear of Red River's loss. It was a small point of hope for us." He shifted position. "What do you plan to do now, then? Are you going north, back to your own ancestral lands?"

"Is it worth it?" Putu wondered. "Or will we simply be herded into pens and labor camps?"

"From what we hear," Naakilaan said, "your people are not well-liked by the United States. This is nothing that anyone here has not already dealt with. But it is not so bad as it is here. Too few people want to go so far north, and not everyone can handle the long night like you do. The United States has industry up there—mining, logging, and so forth—but they do not have the resources or the desire to try and subjugate your people, not like the Russians. Now the more southern people, like our northern clans, they do have some problems. But the Iñupiatun? From what I understand, you are being left pretty well to yourselves."

"How many are left, then? Just because you stop beating a dog doesn't mean it won't still die."

K'alyaan shrugged helplessly. "That we don't know. Some sheltered with our clans here in Canada, but once the Russians left and the heaviest burdens were lifted, many of them fled as far north as they could go, back to their own lands, or so we heard. Maybe they are surviving, maybe not."

"Regardless, it's a promising start," Akłaq said, trying to sound optimistic. "It's the first good news we've had about home in a long time."

"Oh, of course. Many here are envious. But we have our duties here." K'alyaan nodded. "You are welcome to stay with us for a while if you wish. We are not so destitute as we try to portray."

"You are most kind," Putu told him. "We will stay for at least a few days."

"Yes, being on the road so long has likely only exhausted your migration instinct and agitated your hibernation instinct," Yeilgooxhu laughed. "If you get too comfortable here, you might not leave until spring."

"That wouldn't be a problem either," Naakliaan assured them. "You are our brother and sister. You are welcome here."

Putu and Akłaq thanked them heartily. Naakilaan offered to show them around the village, find them a place to stay, and introduce them to some of the others.

"The white men built these houses before relocating us here," he explained. "They hoped it might inspire in us some sort of 'civilization' that we might become more like them. The fact that they did this only warns us that they do intend to come and take this land at a later time."

"I notice you live in them," Putu observed.

"On the one hand, they are nice houses. But if we don't live in them and they go to rot—"

"You look uncivilized and destitute and the soldiers and churchgoers will come to help and never leave."

"Exactly. But you have seen how we have made them our own." Naakilaan gave them a look. "I won't blame you if you choose to pitch your tent or perhaps build your own kind of shelter, but I would advise doing so not in sight of the village, or else disguise it well. A few nights is one thing, but a prolonged stay..."

"We understand," Putu assured him. "Thank you."

There were about eighty to a hundred people in all in the village, half of them children, most of them scarred.

"A few years ago, smallpox swept through the land," Naakilaan explained. "All over the province, this monster sank its claws into the people. Six whole tribes were wiped out, many more lost entire clans, and a few peoples are in danger of extinction because they are the only clan left and have no way to properly marry. We were not spared, even here in the north, or our peoples on the coast and the islands." He gestured to a group of children who were playing a ball game. "Many children lost their parents and had to be adopted by aunts, cousins, even other clans. But the worst crime was the loss of many of our elders."

"It always is." Putu's voice was stiff.

They pitched their tent there in the village. If any white men happened to see it and ask, they were just visiting from the northern clans.

"You don't intend to stay, then?" Akłaq wondered once they were finally set up.

"You do?" he asked.

"I still don't know where I'm supposed to be, but the white bear said I would finally find it."

"I would say that we're supposed to be in our own ancestral lands, among our own people. Naakilaan's news sounded promising."

She nodded. "It does, and it's very tempting. But the white bear said that I would finally come to the place where I should have been when I started out all those years ago, where I should have been had I not chosen to stay with Nika."

He gave her a look. "And where do you suspect that is? Trapped on a reserve?"

"I don't think it's the reserve that matters so much as, maybe, the Tlingit people. I was heading south and east, which would have taken me directly into their land."

"Well, instead of relying on your gut in this cosmic guessing game, maybe you ought to actually go out and seek the white bear, ask it yourself."

It was an odd vote of confidence, Akłaq thought, if a bit gruff in its delivery. At the same time, it was better advice than anything she'd ever gotten from Aniqan.

"I'll see about the rest of our stuff," he went on. "You go out and find the white bear. I want to know how long we're supposed to stay, too." He glanced toward the house nearest them. "And whether I shouldn't just move everything in there."

Akłaq grinned and started out into the forest. Normally she might have consulted a shaman, but she had a small inkling that the spirits that the shamans spoke to were not of the same company as the white bear and Anagalisgi. If she wanted to talk to the white bear, she would have to go it directly.

She was not entirely certain how to go about it, though. She paused beside a bend in the river, just narrow enough that she could probably jump across if she got a running start. She knew the shamanic rituals, though she'd never performed them, nor would ever presume to; differing spirits or not, it would be sacrilege for her to try. She also knew the Christian rituals, the prayers and ceremonies. Did that apply here? She didn't think communion was appropriate here, but what if she went and submerged herself in the river in a sort of baptism? Would that work?

"You could just ask."

She looked up to see the white bear pushing its way through the brush and finally emerging on the river bank just twenty feet upstream. She went to it and, without thinking, put her hands in its thick fur, as if to remind herself what it felt like when she rode on its back. Unlike a normal bear skin, the white bear's fur was not matted and greasy, nor did it smell atrocious. Rather it was soft and fluffy, like a tanned fur, and extremely thick. And it smelled pleasant, like spring flowers.

"If you don't mind?" the bear asked, swinging its huge head around to look at her.

She jerked her hands away. "Sorry. It's just...I mean...you're so soft."

The bear puffed a hot breath as if in a sigh. "You didn't come out here to compliment me on my fur."

Akłaq felt her face burn hot. "No, I didn't. I just want to know where I'm supposed to be. You said I would find the place when we went west. Well we've come west, and now we're heading north toward home. Is that it? Am I supposed to go home? Am I supposed to stay with the Tlingit people? If it's supposed to be the place where I would have ended up if I hadn't stayed with Nika, the Tlingit would make the most sense."

Now the bear snorted, shook its head, looked away, and made a sort of grumbling sound. She giggled and the bear looked back at her. "What's so funny?"

"You remind me of Putu," she said. "Always gruff and grumbling."

Suddenly the bear stood on its hind legs, towering over her, and snarled, lips peeling back to reveal sharp fangs. Akłaq stared, mouth agape, unsure whether she would run or what chance she had if she did. Then the bear dropped to all fours again and huffed again. "Did that remind you of Putu as well?"

Again her face burned hot and she admitted, "Well, no."

"No."

Before the bear could say anything more, she asked, "So, do you have a name? Anagalisgi clearly does, but what about you? Do any of the white animals have names? In the Authored Books, I don't recall that the woodpecker actually gave a name, other than Ge'gwogv, or, you know, Woodpecker."

"You will know my name when it is time for you to know my name," the bear said. "Now as for the reason you came out here?"

She nodded. "Right. Staying with the Tlingit would make the most sense."

The bear snorted and grumbled just as it had previously. "Sense. Human sense is terrible."

"I have sense enough to ask for help."

Even the bear couldn't deny that. In fact, it almost seemed to have been waiting for such a comment, because it said, "And when asked, you have the sense to fulfill your promise, an opportunity to finish what you once started, what was taken from you."

She shook her head. "I don't understand."

"There are many cubs in the village. They will need protection and guidance. They will need a mother."

Akłaq's breath caught in her chest as her mind was suddenly flooded with memories of her children. Miiyuk, her firstborn, her only daughter. Stas and Valya, and Alyosha, only a baby when he was murdered.

"I thought their deaths were a way of punishing me," she finally managed to squeak out.

"Your faithfulness has rewarded you with another gift of life," the bear told her. "And the power to protect it."

"Will I learn more about the Akari? Should I teach the Tlingit?"

The look on the bear's face was a clear answer.

"What about Putu?" she wondered. "He so wants to return home. I know he humors me because he is also hurting and curious and wants things to go back to the way they were before. What should I tell him?"

"Tell him that his own redemption begins here, and he will do more for the people — the Tlingit and others, even your own — by staying and standing rather than running away."

Akłaq wasn't sure what to make of that, but she agreed to tell him anyway.

"Is there anything else I should know?" She looked around. "What about Anagalisgi?"

"He is seeing to other matters. As for you, what has been said is sufficient for the time being."

"What else is there?" Akłaq wondered.

The bear grumbled and snorted. "Humans. So intent on staying where it is comfortable, yet despising what you call 'the rut.' Just because you are in a place does not mean you will be there for eternity. Even this will pass. Make the most of it while you have it."

And it turned and lumbered off, disappearing into thick undergrowth. Akłaq stared after it for a long time, waiting for it to come back even as she knew it would not. The message had been delivered, the mission given. Everything else was up to her.

Akłaq turned and ran back to the village with sudden joy and energy. For the first time in a very long time, it almost felt like things were going right. Rather than feeling like she was living under a dark thundercloud or a smothering blanket of uncertainty, now she could breathe. Her life was free and moving toward fulfillment. Her past errors were going to be righted and she would have a second chance.

Putu was still hanging around the tent when she returned to the village, and he seemed rather perplexed by her enthusiasm.

"This is an unusual response," he commented. If he had any more to say, it got cut off as she threw her arms around him in a huge, bear-like embrace. After a moment, he asked, "What in the universe did the bear tell you?"

She released him, took a few steps back, and relayed the conversation as best she could.

"We made it, Putu!" she said, finishing up. "We made it where we're supposed to be."

He still looked very confused. "The white bear said I have a part in this?"

"If you choose to. We always have a choice. I made the wrong one a long time ago, and I've made more wrong choices since. But this time, I got it right. I got it right and now I can actually do some real good. And you can, too, if you want. If you want to actually help and don't want to run and hide anymore."

"But this is your destiny. I wasn't part of your life when you first left your village. Why would I have a role?"

"Because you're here now. That's all that matters. You think God or the Author or the spirits or whoever else couldn't make changes to the plans of the universe? It's been decades, Putu. Whatever I failed to do all those years ago, I wouldn't be able to do now. But now that I am here, I can do something different, something else to help the people."

"The Tlingit people."

"And others. And it starts with the children." She took a breath. "My poor decisions cost my children their lives." She gestured toward a few children across the clearing. "Whatever is coming in this village, whether it's sickness or white men or something else, I have a chance to save the lives of these children here. You can help me. If you want." When he hesitated, she pressed further. "I know you want to go home. I won't say that I don't. I want to see Qikiqtaġruk, the long night and the long day. But once we go home, then what? How does going home help the people? Maybe there is a need there, I don't know, but this is where we are called to be right now. This is where we have come. Not any of the dozens of reserves we passed on the way here, none of the villages that we would run into heading north. Here."

Putu still hesitated, but she could see that she was winning him over.

"Did the bear say how I would help?" he asked.

Akłaq shook her head. "No, only that you would do the most good here, rather than running away." She looked around at the village, life carrying on peacefully. "I don't think there will be much violence, and I don't think it is going to happen right away. But when it does, we need to be willing and prepared. Will you help me?"

After a long moment, he sighed. "My wives and children starved to death when I was away in the labor camps. One of my daughters was about your age, or your apparent age. She was only a few years married with babes of her own." He gave her an unreadable look. "The babies died first, and they actually...they ate the children, trying to stay alive themselves, just one more day of empty promises and false hope. But they all died in the end." He wiped away a tear and studied the ground. "There was nothing I could do to help any of them, or any of the people who had died. The one time I did say something, I was beaten severely and left for dead. It was how I became a Timekeeper and worked under Ujurak."

"And all the years since, all the missions he sent you on, you never felt fulfilled," Akłaq said softly. "Because you were just picking up the pieces. But if you made too much trouble, if you were caught and killed, then you wouldn't be able to do even that. That's why you sought out me and Aniqan instead of fleeing to another village."

Putu nodded. "You were doing something, actually trying to help."

"Then Aniqan was murdered, and we had to flee." Akłaq paused. "I don't know what to do about Frederickson, where he might be or if he's still looking for us. But these people here will need our help. I don't know how or when, but they will."

"They will need your help," Putu corrected. "This is your destiny, a chance for you to atone for your mistakes. My atonement is merely a secondary concern." He went on before she could speak. "I will help you, as I could not help my children."

Akłaq put a hand on his shoulder. "Thank you."

Their second embrace was far less traumatic, but far more fulfilling. It felt as though the storm they had been living under for years was finally ebbing, and blue sky could be seen in the distance. Putu broke it off first, and though he returned to his standard grumpy disposition, most of his thorns seemed to have fallen away. He stared at the tent.

"I suppose, then," he sighed, "that we just did all of this work for nothing."

"I suppose so," Akłaq said, unable to suppress a small giggle. "Why don't you go talk to K'alyaan and the others, tell them what we've decided, and I'll start moving our things into a new house?"

That he could agree to. So while he was off speaking to the village leaders, and perhaps doing other things, Akłaq spent her time moving all of their stuff out of the tent and packs and into the nearby vacant house. They didn't have much, only what they put on the horses, and the house still seemed very empty. She found herself thinking about the cabin where she and Nika had lived. It had been so easy to push aside when living with Ujurak and the others, or when living among the white men in Prince Albert or Red River. Suddenly she found all those years were stripped away. When she heard the front door open, she was genuinely disappointed to find it was Putu and not her husband.

"What did they say?" she wondered.

"They are happy to have us," he replied, sounding almost optimistic. "They seem even happier to have someone who speaks to the spirits." He clarified, "Smallpox wiped out most of the Tlingit shamans, and the ones who didn't die of illness were arrested or killed."

"Oh."

"But it's no matter." He went and started looking around the house, the empty rooms. "They are happy to have us all the same."

She followed him around. "How much did you tell them about...our mission?"

He poked his head in an empty bedroom. "Seeing how we don't know the details of this supposed mission, I didn't know what to tell them other than we would help any way we could." He moved on to another room. "Having followed Ujurak the seer of time, we knew a few things about hiding from the white men and keeping to the old ways."

"Are there any Timekeepers or Harvesters here, do you know?"

He glanced at her as they returned to the main room. "If there are, they are saying nothing publicly. And we've made a big enough nuisance of ourselves in the region that I think anyone would notice."

"So it really might be all up to us."

"It might be." He turned to face her. "You're sure this is where we're supposed to be?"

Akłaq nodded. "I am. As sure as I've ever been about anything."

His expression faltered. "Well, that's not the most comforting thing, all things considering, but it'll have to do." At her look, he actually smiled. "Come on. Let's go find you some children."

Avgun Iñuiñaq Piñasrut
Second Chances

It was actually a few years before there were any children in the house. A woman decided to leave the reserve and go to the nearest town to trade, but she was attacked and killed on the road. Her husband had died of smallpox and the rest of her family had gone north to the other Tlingit clans. She left behind five children, ages six, five, three, two, and one. The oldest and youngest were girls, and the middle three were boys. Akłaq scooped them up just as fast as she could.

All of a sudden, there was life in the house. Laughing, playing, screaming, and crying. For as overwhelming as it was, Akłaq found herself sliding into a routine as easily as stepping out of a room for a bit and then stepping right back in. It took a little adjusting, going from zero to five children, plus having to get to know the older children, but she embraced it.

Putu was a little slower to come around. It had been many years since he'd had to deal with children and call them his own—although this relationship now was more of a grandfather and grandchildren—and he was a bit unprepared for the sudden noise, especially being woken up by a crying baby. He was also frustrated by the short attention spans and lack of developed thought.

"I don't remember it being this difficult," he lamented.

Akłaq and Putu sat on the back step, watching the children play. Tula'aan, the youngest, was now three years old, running after her siblings, falling down, and having to be rescued by Latseen, the eldest.

"We've lived without life for a long time," she told him. She elbowed him. "And you were younger back then."

He gave her a look. "I'm not exactly old, you know, at least by appearance."

"No, but you act like it sometimes. Grumpy and cranky and whatnot, complaining about how you can't take your nap."

She giggled as his look persisted.

"Has the white bear shown or told you anything more?" he asked instead.

Akłaq shook her head. "No."

"Do you think it's possible that our presence has warded off whatever troubles might have come?"

Now she gave him a look. "Not at all." She went back to watching the children. Gáx, the second-oldest, had Tula'aan on his shoulders and was running around with his brothers Tlaganis and Nooskw chasing him, but looked like he was struggling a bit. Akłaq went on, "No, it's still coming. We just get a chance to enjoy life a little before it does."

"Well, at least we get that," Putu sighed.

"Nothing lasts forever. The Krydik proved that even if you have everything and everything is perfect, you'll only end up creating your own problems." She grinned. "Nika and I didn't have a perfect life. We had everything we needed, but we still snapped at each other for minor missteps."

She could feel his eyes on her. "You talk a lot about your husband, but not so much about Aniqan. Why is that?"

She kept her gaze fixed on Latseen who was now trying to take Tula'aan from Gáx, though Gáx protested and tried to hide his obvious fatigue from carrying the toddler on his shoulders. "Because this is the kind of life we had, the kind of life that I lost. Aniqan and I never had this, but Nika and I did."

"You barely spoke to anyone for a long time when we first found you. It was almost a year before you could grasp the fundamentals of Banding. Honestly, we were waiting for you to kill yourself." He shook his head slightly. "I never got that same impression from you after Aniqan died."

Akłaq sighed. "For a while, I didn't know how to think of Aniqan. We let others believe we were married, but it was never the same as when I was not-quite-married to Nika. I could really believe that Nika was my husband. Aniqan...he never really felt more than a friend to me. A good friend, and I did love him, but still a friend only."

Putu nodded slowly. "And how will you think of me, if I am to perish at the end of this endeavor, whatever it is?"

She smiled. "You remind me of my father. I know that's how we portrayed ourselves on the road, but it's another thing that I could almost believe." She gestured to the children who had ceased to run around and now looked in the midst of a brewing argument. "Just like you're their grandfather."

"And you're their mother," he said, expression turning sarcastic. "And I think your children might be about to get into trouble amongst themselves."

She gave him a look even as she stood and went to calm the brewing storm, catching Tula'aan just before she could hit Nooskw. The three year old plopped herself on the ground and started screaming. Only Latseen made any attempt to help calm the child, even as Gáx and Tlaganis both erupted with their own versions of some perceived slight and Nooskw started in on the meanness of Tula'aan trying to hit him.

Apparently equally annoyed but having less patience than Akłaq, Latseen turned her attention from calming Tula'aan to telling her brothers to shut up and stop bothering mommy while she was trying to help the baby. This didn't please them one bit and only started a new argument which only fueled Tula'aan's frustrated shrieks.

Eventually it all got sorted out, as it always did.

If Akłaq could wish for anything, she might have wished for a husband. Putu was good and kind and helped in many fatherly and grandfatherly ways—not only for her children, but others as well—but it wasn't the same as standing beside a partner as an equal. With Putu as her father, she came under his wing. She just wished someone were there with her. She wished for Nika. She found herself wondering how

Aniqan might have responded to the situation.

But it did no good to wish for such things. The children were a gift, but eventually they would grow up and she would send them off, at least in a social sense, if not a physical one. They were still Tlingit, and they needed to be among other Tlingit. The village was good, but more and more people were choosing to leave the reserve and head to the northern clans. It wasn't unreasonable to think her children might wish to do the same when they came of age.

Her choice of partner would have to be made more carefully, given her extended youthfulness. No one in the village made comment about it; if they made any connection at all about the years between Ujurak's death and their appearance, they never said anything. Akłaq and Putu did not volunteer anything.

Perhaps the parents didn't matter much when the children could be observed to grow. Tula'aan finally emerged from her temper tantrum toddlerhood, though the sibling she appeared to most idolize was Tlaganis, and it was not unusual to see the now five year old child running after her seven year old brother like an annoying gnat. Gáx and Nooskw, nine and six, were also becoming much closer, with Gáx frequently taking Nooskw out into the forest to show him things. Meanwhile, Latseen took after Akłaq and tried to emulate everything she did, which included peacekeeping duties, though the ten year old still had less patience and could often be provoked into an argument.

Fortunately, once the snow melted, the children could be sent outside to play so Akłaq didn't have to deal with them all cooped up in the house. It was just as well, for Putu arrived home from an elders meeting looking a bit grim.

"What's wrong?" Akłaq asked. "Are soldiers coming through the area again?"

"No, but they could," he replied evasively. He nonchalantly glanced around the house, then spotted the children outside. Appearing relieved, he closed the door and faced her. "What do you know about the religious missions and residential schools? I know there were some back east, but I didn't pay much attention."

She shrugged. "There was one in Prince Albert. Parents sent their children there so they could learn English, French, reading, maths, geography, religion, things of that nature. I know there were some near Red River, primarily used as orphanages, but there were voluntary students as well."

"You say voluntary."

"Yes. The people of Red River were mixed, true, but many were Christian of varying denominations. They sent their children to the schools of their particular denomination. Why?"

Putu shifted his stance. "News from the south. Children are being sent to these schools and not returning. The people who do return are as white as white men, at least in their culture."

"That sounds terrible, but what—?"

"And it sounds like these schools are becoming less voluntary. In the southern reserves, along the border, children are being stolen from their homes and forced to go to these schools."

"How can they do that, though?" Akłaq glanced at the door.

"With guns," Putu answered. "They come through the villages, asking for volunteers first. They tell them the schools will help them, maybe they can leave the reserve once they learn what the schools have to teach. After that, they come back a second time, demanding the children. If any are withheld, they'll come back, days or weeks later, in the middle of the night, raid the homes and take the children and shoot anyone who tries to fight back."

Akłaq didn't know what to say or do or even think. How could anyone do such a thing? Going to war was one thing, but stealing children in the middle of the night was unforgivable. Now she knew the reason she and Putu had been brought to this place and given these children.

"We don't know the details," he went on, "but something's happened in the Canadian government, some permission given, and more of these so-called schools are starting to pop up all over the country. We won't be immune to this."

"Is anything being done? Can anything be done?" she wondered.

"Our people are not permitted to go to court. Anyone who fights back or physically tries to stop them is shot. You tell me."

She nodded slowly. "I understand. What do you suggest?"

He hesitated, and his next words sounded foreign coming from him. "We've been charged with protecting this village and these children. I don't know why, but this is where we are and this is who we'll defend."

"Are there any of these schools in the Yukon?"

"The northern Tlingit say there is one school, but as of right now, it's still a regular, voluntary school. There have been no reports of kidnapping or anything that we're hearing from the south."

"It's something, anyway."

"Whatever the case, we have time to prepare," he stated. "If there is any good news, it's that the churches who run them take their time in selecting the priests they will send, and few of the churches already in the province have anyone to spare. It will take time for the prison wardens to get here."

Akłaq nodded. "All right. So what is the plan? What do the elders expect to do?"

Putu sighed. "Right now, the others expect to simply hide the children. Let the soldiers come through the first time with their polite demands, then hide them so that the next time, we might be able to say that we sent the children voluntarily."

She made a disapproving sound. "They keep records too well to believe that."

"Not necessarily. If the schools claims the children are orphans, they'll have a hard time trying to say that they also came from villages with parents."

"It still feels flimsy."

"Another idea is to send the children north, but there's no guarantee that the school in the Yukon won't try to do the same thing one day."

"No, but it would be easier to hide them up there if necessary. And I think the Tlingit have some land in the United States."

"Akłaq, the Americans are doing the same thing."

She could only sigh.

"These are just the ideas that the elders and leaders know about and can participate in on their end," Putu went on, putting a hand on her shoulder. "You and I can do a lot more, but it's kind of hard to explain the details to them. But just because we're the most capable people doesn't mean we're the only ones who have to be involved to pull off...whatever it is we're going to do."

She nodded. "I know. But...it's frustrating. I mean, you and I have been dealing with this sort of thing our whole lives. It started long before us, and there are some elders who are dying who have known nothing else. Is there any future for us, Putu? Could the Krydik be in the right on this?"

"I don't know. Maybe. But unless you want to go running off to their city, this is where we've been placed. And I'm not going to let you be a coward and run away after you put so much effort into stopping me from running away."

Akłaq couldn't help but grin. She nodded. "All right. You're right." She paused. "How fast is news in coming? How much time is there between something happening in the southern reserves and when we hear about it?"

"The news we got was a couple months old," he reported. "The government has likely been doing this all winter, knowing how difficult it is to travel."

"How difficult it is for us to travel," she corrected. "And you're right. Summer is when they'll build the schools and winter is when they'll steal the children."

"Well, they'll steal them at any time, I think, but your line of thought isn't illogical."

Actually, it proved to be almost prophetic, as they received news over the summer about land being considered or set aside for more "residential schools." A few even started laying foundations.

The people who remained on the reserve were mostly elders and children. The children couldn't do much, true, but something about the loss of Red River had sparked a fire in the adults, fueled by the knowledge that the elders had known nothing but abuse their entire lives. They didn't want the same for their children. Maybe they didn't have guns, but there were other means of destruction, and fire was a popular conspiracy.

"They're going to kill us anyway," Akłaq heard one of the men grumble. She sat on the front step of the house. "They're going to kill us and steal our children. Well I'm not going to go quietly, and if I can take a few of them with me, so much the better. Then even if they do kill me, they still have to contend with the flames."

Akłaq wouldn't say the thought never crossed her mind, but perhaps the only thing that really stopped her was the knowledge that fire was the one thing Time or the Akari couldn't save her from. All her grand abilities, and they were all useless in the face of fire. At best, they just wouldn't work. At worst, it would backfire so tremendously it could kill her or someone else. She'd asked Putu about it on several occasions as he took over her training, and she remembered asking Everett about it a time or two, but no matter how she worded it or how she went about proposing her ideas, the answer remained the same: Even if there were a way to manipulate fire, or make it less dangerous, it was a far more advanced skill than she was presently capable of.

On the other hand, she could just do it the old fashioned way.

She watched her children. Latseen was now eleven and would be showing signs of womanhood in the next year or so, and soon after that, Gáx would begin to mature into a man. It was a bittersweet recognition as Akłaq considered her own children. Then she realized that these were her children, too. Maybe she hadn't carried and birthed them, but she loved them all the same.

Maybe it was time to go set some fires.

"I can see your mind working," Putu observed, sitting next to her on the step. "I hope you're not going to attempt anything too unorthodox, at least not without help."

"I think it would be better to wait until winter," she stated. "It's easy to rebuild in the summer, even now in the fall, but it's a lot harder in the winter."

"Normally, yes, but there isn't as much snow here. The land is warmer, the growing season longer."

"Every little bit helps. We shouldn't proclaim a willingness to die and then balk when a plan of action might cause us a bit of discomfort or inconvenience."

"That much is true at least. Then the question becomes, if we are destined to die, what can we do to ensure we gain the most reward and momentum for those who follow?"

Akłaq sighed. "Well, I can't say that I'm much of a strategist or a politician. I can't think that deviously."

Putu folded his hands. "I'm sure you could, if you had to. It's amazing the things we think up or do when those we love are in danger. Or ourselves, too."

"Seeing how I have a habit of getting those I love killed, I think I need to come up with a new strategy." She watched her children as they played with others a short distance away. "I've been given a second chance and don't want to squander it. Before anything, I think I should probably consult the white bear."

"Seeing how he's the one who brought us here, apparently for this very reason, that might make some sense," Putu agreed. He looked up at something far across the village. "On the other hand, if your comment just now was a prayer, I think our answer may have already arrived."

She didn't see what he was talking about immediately. When he stood, she did as well and followed his gaze. Then she grinned.

"Everett!"

The man was being passively investigated by some villagers and more actively questioned by others, but when Putu and Akłaq identified him in a friendly way, most of the heat came off him and he was permitted free passage to meet them.

Theirs was perhaps the only truly friendly greeting he got, but he didn't seem to mind.

"It's been a few years," Putu observed. "How are you?"

"Myself, I am still alive, but that is about all I can say," Everett admitted.

"Yes, we heard that Red River was absorbed into Manitoba."

Everett nodded. "We fled to the United States, yes. Riel and the others remain there and plan how to retake the settlement, but I decided to leave instead."

"If you thought they had a chance, I suspect you would not be here."

Everett hesitated but nodded. "Their hearts are in the right place, but willpower alone does not win wars. I decided to try and find you, at least, see what had become of you after Upper Fort Garry." He looked around. "It doesn't look all bad."

"It's not," Putu confirmed. "The Tlingit are good people."

"I thought you would have been home by now, honestly."

Putu gestured to Akłaq. "Well, the white bear told her other things, and we've been obliged to stay."

Everett gave her a sly look. "I heard rumors that you fled the fort on the back of a large white bear. You are still practicing your Akari skills, then?"

"It's hard," she admitted. "Without a mentor and without the ability to open Paa so I may go the fortress, I can practice only what I know and what I might discover just from observation and curiosity. Even then, I don't get to practice often with the children around and constantly needing my attention."

He raised a brow. "Children?"

She pointed them out to him. "A second chance, to right my wrongs, and to give meaning to our journey and our time here."

Everett glanced back and forth between her and Putu. "I think there's a story here."

They invited him inside and told him the whole story, everything that had happened at Upper Fort Garry and afterwards, all the way to present day. It was nice to be able to share the true story, to speak in terms of Time and the Akari. They also spoke of the schools and the rumors surrounding them, the stories of kidnapping and forced assimilation, and of the many infant plans they had to ensure the children of their village would not suffer the same fate.

"I am not unfamiliar with these so-called schools," he said, nodding gravely. "There are hundreds of them across the United States doing to the same thing to all Native children. Some families are trying to flee here to Canada where they think they'll be safe, places like what Red River and Prince Albert used to be."

"We're afraid it won't help them," Putu said. "At best, it only buys them time."

"And we of all people can appreciate that time is a precious commodity."

"Do you have some ideas on how to help?" Akłaq wondered. "Without guns and other weapons, many here are thinking in terms of using fire."

Everett made a disapproving sound. "Aside from physical logistics that say we are on the losing end of that fight, there is little that we can do as Timekeepers or Akari-bearers to help them. Fire is a terrible thing to try and control. I know I can't do it, not to the degree that I imagine you're talking about."

"So what can we do? We weren't brought here just so we could languish together in the same trials in the same way."

"That is true. But I don't have all the answers right off-hand. Let me think about it for a few days and see if I can't offer some suggestions."

He stood from the table and Putu followed, asking, "How long do you expect to be in the area?"

Everett chuckled. "My people are back east. I came out here to find you two, though I knew not why. Now I think I have an idea. Assuming your friends here in the village will let me."

"They will, once we assure them you are a friend also."

"Well, I will let you decide whether or not to tell them I was with Riel. The cause was noble, but we still failed."

"You escaped injustice," Akłaq clarified. "You live to fight another day and help protect our children."

Framing it in such a way seemed to lend him some measure of confidence. The Tlingit were a bit wary of having him around, given "how white he acts," but allowed him to stay once Putu explained to them his friendship and leadership with Riel and the others in Red River. He took up residence in a house near theirs, his possessions currently rather sparse. Even so, Akłaq and Putu helped him get settled in.

"Has Akłaq shown you anything in the Akari, then?" Everett inquired of Putu.

"No, not really," Putu replied evasively. "She gets very little time to practice herself."

"I understand. Going from having no kids to suddenly having five running around...I admire you both. But if you want, I could—"

Putu put up a hand. "No. I've little desire to learn."

Everett blinked. "Oh. I'm sorry, it's just that you seemed so...optimistic. I thought she must have explained things to you."

"She convinced me to stop running, at least for the time being. I won't say that I don't enjoy having children and grandchildren again. And I can't deny that something has brought us here. But I'm still not sold on the idea that the white bear belongs to the Author or that any of this holds any real significance."

Everett glanced at Akłaq as if searching for support, but she could offer none. She had tried on several occasions to talk to Putu about the Akari, but even when she could get into a deep conversation and detailed explanations, he simply claimed that he wasn't particularly interested. He was still trying to learn how to not run away when it suited him; he wasn't quite ready to get into combat. Time would help him escape a situation, but it sounded like the Akari had more practical applications that he wasn't sure he was ready for.

"At any rate, while I'm here, I will help," Everett was saying. "If either of you would like, I will continue to train in the Akari also."

"I would like to learn more," Akłaq said quickly. "But I don't know if the kids could stand me being gone for more than an hour."

"Latseen is old enough to watch Tula'aan for an hour or two," Putu told her. "And the boys follow me around anyway."

She gave him a look. "Putu, you surprise me."

"If we're going to keep the children safe and out of those infernal schools, we're going to need all the help we can get."

"Yet you won't learn the Akari."

He made a sound. "I'm not the one called by the white bear. I won't interfere in whatever destiny the spirits have planned for you."

It was a flimsy excuse, but they let it slide.

"We'll let you get yourself situated and accustomed to village life first," Putu told Everett. "It's not so free as Red River, as far as our ability to come and go from the reserve, but our lives are our own. For now."

"K'alyaan explained things to me," Everett said. "And you have helped to enlighten me even more." He looked at Akłaq. "I will meet with you in four days to continue training. We will not go to the fortress. For your sake, we will stay here."

Putu folded his arms. "Is that wise? Even in Red River you insisted on the utmost secrecy."

"The stakes were not so high nor the danger so imminent in Red River. But if something does happen, if the soldiers decide to drop the pretense of simply asking the people to surrender their children, we must be aware of it and ready to act. Going to the fortress not only removes us from the ability to know of a threat, but even if we were told, portal travel would render us useless when we are needed most."

No one could deny his words. Putu and Akłaq wished him will in his new home, then departed for their own.

"I wonder if it wouldn't be a good idea to consider training Latseen," Akłaq commented, "if the danger to us can hold off for another year or two until she becomes a woman."

"Why would you want to?" Putu wondered. "I understand that we are facing danger, but do you think it would be wise to put that power in the hands of a child?"

"I'm only talking about the simplest of things. Simple Banding for instance, teach her how to Fast Band so she has time to run away."

He considered this. "It may not be a bad thing, but would you really want to rob her of her womanhood, her ability to marry and have children of her own?"

"Putu, the life that she is facing, if she gets taken to one of those schools, is no life at all. And once they let her out of the school as a fully reformed white woman, she will be placed into a people that she does not belong to. Who will she marry? What kind of children will she have? White. And we will slowly be erased from history." She went on before he could speak. "Besides, the Krydik use the Akari, and they still have children. I've read about it in the Authored Books. It's not entirely impossible."

Putu hesitated. "And what if she doesn't want to learn? Of what if she starts and then decides she wants to stop?"

"Then at least I tried. But I can't stand the thought of them being helpless. We're supposed to train our children to be adults, to not need us, except even we adults are failing. We have to try something different."

"Well, we've got a couple years to think about it, and that's assuming the danger stays away that long."

It stayed away for another four days at least, long enough for Everett to visit and ask if it was a good time to continue Akari training. Akłaq had sent the boys with Putu on a minor hunting expedition, and Latseen had taken Tula'aan to a woman they regarded as a grandmother. With everyone else occupied, she invited him in.

"It's encouraging to hear that you've not completely abandoned your training," Everett began, "although I can understand that it can be difficult to keep up with five children running around."

"It's not all bad," Akłaq told him. "I actually use Feel quite a bit when the kids come home crying from skinned knees and minor injuries. I also use a little Time, too, to heal the wounds some while they sleep."

"Then I won't put you through the rigors of a complete review, but you may have to remind me whether I've already taught you something or not."

It didn't take long for them to establish what she'd been taught, what she remembered, what she was proficient in and where she was lacking. Had she not had children who frequently accumulated minor wounds, she was sure that she would have forgotten most of her Matter skills.

"Have you thought any more about how to help the people when the soldiers come for the children?" she inquired.

"I've given it a great deal of thought," Everett answered.

"Your tone says you are not so confident."

"I can come up with a thousand ways to sabotage their efforts: burning down cities, destroying the schools, killing the men. But I can't come up with any way to truly stop them, to make them see that what they're doing is wrong. That will be the way to truly end this. Otherwise all we're doing is inviting war, and we don't have the numbers or ability to win."

"But we're here, with Time and the Akari."

"And as soon as Frederickson and others get wind of us—or even if they don't—they'll come in with a vengeance. We only want to stop them. They want to annihilate us."

"We can't surrender."

"I'm not saying we should. Far from it. If it comes right down to it, I will burn down every city and every school to stop them from getting our children. I just don't have any other answers."

She gave him a look. "Maybe there are no other answers. Once we've eliminated the paths that got us here, all we have left are things we haven't tried."

He did not seem pleased with the thought, but he did not deny it. Instead, he changed topic. "Putu mentioned something about you were thinking about training Latseen in a couple years, once she reaches womanhood."

"That's right. Even being able to Band might give her a chance to escape if they come for her and her siblings."

"I'm not disagreeing. Many of the Krydik hold the same philosophy, about training their children once they reach adolescence.

But the Akari is no secret among the Krydik. Is Latseen even mildly aware of what you can do? Are any of your children?"

"They've hinted at certain observations—Feel, as I told you before. But K'alyaan and Putu and the others simply perpetuate the story that I am chosen by the white bear for something and so have minor mystical abilities."

Everett nodded thoughtfully. "If I can recommend anything, start explaining things to Latseen. Let her in on some of these mystical abilities, what they are, what you can do. Try to judge her reaction and see if she is interested in these things. Get a feel for her natural affinity for such things. That way, when the time comes, the shock will already be worn off and you can start her training right away."

It seemed a logical thing to do, and it helped to focus her own efforts. If she was going to show or teach something, she wanted to be proficient in it herself, at least enough to impress a curious eleven year old and not hurt her. Everett tried to assure her that it wasn't going to be as difficult as she was fearing. She didn't have to bend the entire universe, only a small portion of it.

Banding, making Time go faster or slower. Pinpoint Bands, focusing a Band. Double Bands, changing one's perception of a Band. Time Tendrils, locking someone or something into a certain plane of Time. Time Webs, a way to hold Bands and Tendrils. These she knew well enough.

In Matter, she had honed her ability to Feel, and she had a phenomenal understanding of the human body. She knew things that she was willing to bet even the greatest scientists on Earth wouldn't know for another century or more. Tissue and blood, nerves and neurons, immunity, DNA, all of it constantly at work just so they could take a single breath, never mind everything else they did in a day. But thanks to the curiosity and clumsiness of her children, even some of the more serious wounds were now but minor inconveniences as she combined Time and Matter to knit wounded flesh back into proper working order.

She'd tried to get into Energy on several occasions, but she couldn't quite remember how it was explained in the Authored Books. Given that it was considered more advanced, if not unstable and dangerous, her efforts had been minute and fleeting.

"You've done well to keep your skills sharp in the last five years," Everett commended. "I think your children have helped you in this more than you can appreciate."

"Thank you," Akłaq acknowledged. "Now tell me honestly: this thing, whatever it is that we're going to try and do, do you think it will work? Do you think we really can save our children?"

"Given that there is no official plan in the works other than some suggestions and half-heartened threats, I can't speak to actual probabilities and possibilities," he answered evasively. "But if you're wondering whether I think we have an actual fighting chance, then yes, I would say so."

"Do you think Frederickson will show up again?"

Now Everett hesitated. Then, "Yes. Whether it's just to use his abilities to 'quell some unusually resilient agitators' or because he learns of our presence, I do believe he will make an appearance at some point."

Akłaq sighed and folded her arms. "We can't keep running from him."

"I'm inclined to agree. The problem is, the first time it's just him, out here helping local law. Once he sees us, he'll go and grab the rest of the Timekeepers. Keep us busy, kill us maybe, and the soldiers make off with the children. If we're going to take him out, it's going to have to be at first sight. Then we'll have to prepare for the rest of the Timekeepers anyway. Like Goldsmith, it would take a lot for an ordinary person to get the jump on him."

She frowned and sat down at the table. "We can't all try to plan everything. Nothing is getting done."

Everett leaned against the wall. "That much is obvious."

"K'alyaan and his brothers can plan for the peaceful receptions, what the village will say and do when the white men are still asking politely. Putu and I can then work out how to get the children to safety. You can come up with a plan to deal with Frederickson and any other Time Agents that might show up."

"Sounds reasonable enough."

Akłaq tapped a finger on the table. "We'll need faster communication between the reserves. By the time any news reaches us, it could be too late. And we should have lookouts as well, in case they try anything sneaky."

Everett stood up from the wall. "Sounds like you've given this some thought. Why don't you do all of that you just said, except let Putu handle getting the children out. You can stand back and get all the pieces to work together and be the hub of information."

She nodded. "We might have months or years, but we can't be caught unprepared."

"Well then, let's get to work."

Avgun Iñuiñaq Sisamat
Theft

In the three years that followed, Akłaq began to show things to Latseen and, in time, Gáx. The wisdom of Everett's words quickly made itself known. The children, who were just breaking into adolescence, were astonished, and all Akłaq showed them was simple Banding and basic Touch. In a way, it saddened her, because she saw the look in their eyes change when they looked at her. She was no longer just their mother who had some vague mystical abilities granted by the white bear. Now she had demonstrated those abilities, and offered to teach them once they came of age.

But by the time Latseen reached womanhood, the sharp relief of awe had dulled to the point that Akłaq actually felt comfortable about asking if she wanted to learn as well. She described the reasoning behind it, so Latseen could protect herself and her brothers and sister.

"You really think the soldiers are coming?" the fourteen year old asked. She'd shed her baby looks and now stood as a young, figured woman. She was also shorter than Akłaq who wasn't so tall herself and couldn't have weighed as much as some of the dogs that roamed the village.

"There are more schools being built every year," Akłaq told her. "Politeness is waning to the point where if the children are not sent the same day that the soldiers ask, the soldiers return that night to steal them. By the time they get here, there may be no civility left at all."

"Why not send us away now, then, with Grandfather?"

Akłaq sighed. "We can't give the white men the satisfaction of seeing us run. It will look like a surrender. You know how the wolf stalks the rabbit and gives chase when it runs?" The girl nodded. "If we run, they will only give chase."

"You intend to stay and fight."

"I don't know for sure because nothing has happened yet. I don't know what's going to happen. But if it comes down to it, yes, I will stay and fight."

"Why you? It's the men who fight. Grandfather will protect us in the wilderness, until we reach the northern clans."

For a long moment, Akłaq did not answer. Then, quietly, "Because a long time ago, I had children, and they died. They were murdered. And I couldn't defend them." She shook her head. "I couldn't defend my babies. I was left for dead, too, but Grandfather rescued me." She looked Latseen in the eye. "I won't let the same thing happen to you. I will defend you. I will make sure that you can escape, so you can live."

Latseen stared at her, trying to process all the information. "Everett is part of this, too, isn't he? He's the one who taught you."

"Yes. And there are others, not all of them like us."

"He's here to stop those others, in case they come. Because the powers that protect us, they could use them to hurt us."

"That's right."

"There's a lot more to this isn't there?"

Akłaq grinned as she nodded. "There most certainly is. Right now, I just want to show you enough to be able to defend yourself and your siblings and keep yourselves safe. I plan on making this same offer or request to Gáx, now that he's near to manhood."

"We'd be defending Tlaganis and Nooskw and Tula'aan."

"And the other children as well, yes."

Her daughter's expression turned unreadable. "How many in the village know about this? Is this normal to learn?"

She laughed. "No, it's not normal. No, I, your grandfather, and Everett, we're the only ones who really know how far it goes." She put her hand up before Latseen could speak. "It's a difficult thing to comprehend and can be tough to learn. But more than that, those who use it extensively suffer other side effects."

"Like what?"

And that was when Latseen learned Akłaq and Putu's full backgrounds. They were not merely from Red River in the east, but northerners from a time now decades gone, and yet they hadn't aged. They wouldn't age. Putu had come from a labor camp after the death of his family. Akłaq had been married with children and lost everything. The stories sounded impossible, even outrageous, but something about Latseen's expression said it was all starting to making sense.

Somehow, Akłaq made it through the retelling, becoming more emotional than she thought she would. And they sat there, staring at each other, for a long time.

"Teach me," Latseen said finally. "Help me save my brothers and sister. And help me help Gáx when he comes of age, too."

"The choice will be his own," Akłaq told her.

But Latseen was shaking her head. "No. He will learn. As long as we're here and in danger, he's going to help. He's too small to fight well, but he can still learn this and help. And if we have enough time that Tlaganis can learn, he will. And Nooskw—"

"Don't plan too far ahead. First you must learn. And you have to pay close attention; these powers are not something you can use just carelessly."

"I understand."

So it was that the next day, Latseen joined Akłaq and Everett to begin Akari training. Because they had no Time Capsules on hand to force an initiation, it took a little more effort and concentration of will to get the girl started. Fortunately, Everett, having grown up with the Krydik, knew of several different methods to help speed the process along, and by the end of the session, Latseen was discovering the amazing intricacies of the human body through Feel.

"Wait, so you know that we're made up of millions of tiny particles?" Latseen asked Akłaq, long after Everett had departed.

"I've known that for years," Akłaq told her. She was growing a bit weary of the boundless enthusiasm, even as she told herself she ought to be encouraging it.

"But if there are others like us who know this, why doesn't everyone know it? Why don't people know more?"

"Because people aren't ready for it. Believe it or not, but today was the easiest, simplest thing I've done in a very long time. My own introduction to Time was not so smooth, and I don't mean absorbing the years of my husband and children. If we ever go to the Wheel or the fortress, you'll understand why people don't know more."

"When can we do that? Is that where Grandfather is really taking us to be safe?"

Akłaq chuckled. "No, you're going to the northern clans. As for the Wheel or the fortress, we'll go there once all this is over and we can afford to do minor, frivolous activities."

That seemed to calm her down some. Still, she asked, "Do you think the soldiers will come soon?"

"I don't know, and I don't wish for it."

"I do. Gáx does. So do some of the others. We're tired of tiptoeing around the village and the whole reserve. Let's just fight and get it over with."

"Hush, child," Akłaq said crossly. "That might work between two people, but it is not so easy when you're talking groups and whole nations. There is no fight and get it over with. The conflict will always continue as long as someone wants it to. Even if we fought today and won, it wouldn't be over. There would be no victory, only a pause." She gave Latseen a look. "Do well to remember the failures of your ancestors, and see that you don't repeat them."

"The only failure of my ancestors that I hear about is their passivity, their compliance. The only alternative to that, that I see, is violence. Fight and get it over with."

Akłaq sighed. "Child, I don't know whether you are wise beyond your years or foolish beyond reason. It's easy to critique something when you don't understand the effort that goes into it. Remember that you are a woman, and I am teaching you this for your protection, so you can help the younger children. Let the men do the fighting. If nothing else, I suggest you talk to Grandfather when he gets back, see if his tale in his own words changes your mind any."

"You're a woman, and you're going to fight."

"In a different capacity, and I do it because I am called to. Whether it's mine or someone else's, don't try to take someone else's destiny for yourself; you don't know where it may lead."

That finally gave Latseen pause, which gave Akłaq a break. Would Miiyuk have become so headstrong in womanhood? Had she herself been so headstrong? Akłaq thought about it and decided she must have been, to be able to run away and survive like she did. True, the white bear helped, but the spirits did not call those who were too weak to handle the task given to them.

"Think about what you have seen and learned," Akłaq told her daughter. "You may tell Gáx, but don't try to teach him anything and don't tell the others. Now go and fetch them for dinner."

Latseen nodded wordlessly and scampered off.

Less than a year later, Gáx joined them in their training. By this time, Latseen had a fair grasp on Banding, both herself and others, as well as the basics of Touch. But that was about all she knew. Aside from Akłaq not wanting to burden the child too heavily and bring her too deeply into the fight, the teenager had also discovered the existence of boys, the three or four of them who were of an appropriate age to also be looking at her.

Gáx was starting to make this discovery about girls, and Akłaq could only pray she was able to impart some good knowledge into his mind before he abandoned it completely to follow the girls. On the other hand, it might help his chances if he knew how to protect the girls when they went north and be the warrior he tried, badly, to portray himself as.

These attempts would soon be put to the test. Spring came, and so did the soldiers.

They weren't all soldiers, not at first, though they did accompany the men in fine clothes who strode into the village like they owned it. If the white men noticed the glares and hostility the Tlingit sent their way, they gave no indication of it.

"Who do you call your leader?" the head white man asked loudly. He was a large man with a big chest and the beginning of a belly. His beard was just starting to turn gray though his hair remained a very stark blond. Akłaq did not know much about the latest fashion trends, but she guessed that his clothes were considered nice—fine enough to let people know he was in charge, but not so fine that they couldn't be worn onto a reserve. Previous visitors had made comments about picking up fleas and disease on the reserves.

"That would be me," K'alyaan said, emerging from behind a house. He'd aged, as could be expected from a normal person, but his determination to stand and die on his ancestral lands had maintained a strong physique. He looked over the group, three men in fine clothes and half a dozen soldiers. "Normally it's John who comes to talk to us."

"John was indisposed this time," the blond man said smoothly. "You may address me as Mr. Sanders. These are my associates, Mr. Davis and Mr. Prince."

"I am only called K'alyaan, and that is how to may address me."

"Well, K'alyaan, walking through your fine village here, I see a huge problem. Do you know what it is?"

"You standing in it?"

Mr. Sanders went on as though he hadn't spoken. "Poverty. Squalor. Destitution!"

"We have food, sir. We have food, clothing, and our homes are clean and winter-tight. We've never taken any handouts from the church."

"I'm not here on behalf of the church, sir. Although I do admire their goals, I find them to be a little too nice, a little too compliant in matters like these. And why not? They're in hostile territory, don't want to get scalped. Oh, they're happy to be stoned, burned, and crucified, but for some reason, they are unusually adverse to scalping. But they are good people, don't get me wrong. They want to help. No, I'm here on behalf of the government. We want to help make your lives better."

"Our lives were better before the government existed," Naakilaan said, coming to stand beside his brother.

Again Sanders ignored them. "I see a lot of children here. Nice kids, I'm sure. But what kind of a future do they have here? More poverty, more starvation, no hope of improving their lives. But the churches, you see, they want to help. They've built these schools, see, where they can educate your kids. Teach them to read and write, do math, learn geography and religion. They'll even learn helpful home trades like farming and smithing and logging, and cooking and sewing for the girls."

"I already know all that!"

Akłaq jumped as Latseen piped up behind her. Sanders turned and picked her out of the crowd. As he moved toward her, Akłaq moved to intercept him. Sanders regarded her, looked at Latseen, then back to Akłaq. "The school will also teach her to mind her place."

"Her place is here," Akłaq informed him. "Among her people."

Sanders sighed, his disposition completely at ease. "See, the government just doesn't agree with you. And I don't either, quite frankly." He gestured around. "What is this place, really? Where is your life, your culture? Where is your general store and your stables and your church and everything else that makes a town a town?"

"If you don't plan on living here yourself, I don't see what it matters to you."

The man made as if to slap her, but Time allowed Akłaq to perceive each moment as it passed. With Time, she was able to intercept his hand before it reached her face. With Matter, she was able to cut off the signal between his brain and his muscles, and his hand and arm went limp. Finally she met his fear-stricken gaze. Then she let him go. He stumbled back several steps, and his compatriots crowded him, looking at his hand as he held it.

"You're going to pay for that, you bitch," Sanders hissed, flexing his hand to get feeling back into it.

"Now that doesn't sound like something a proper, civilized man should say," Everett commented on his other side.

The people moved in closer around the white men, and the soldiers warily raised their rifles.

"Leave this place," K'alyaan said calmly, trying to smooth things over before it turned into a bloodbath. "Do not return. If you try to take our children, we will kill you and send your scalps back to the government."

There was no good way for Sanders to recover his boisterous personality, and the best he could do was walk out of the village with his head high, if hidden within the group of soldiers that surrounded him and his two friends.

The villagers stood together for a long time after they left, at least until Akłaq's scouts reported that they were no longer in sight of the village at all. Akłaq turned to Latseen who shrank back, her expression saying she knew exactly what she'd done.

"Stupid child!" Akłaq hissed. "K'alyaan had a role to play and you stole it from him! Now the soldiers will almost certainly be back! I wouldn't be surprised if they came back tonight!"

"I'm sorry, I just..." Tears were streaming down Latseen's cheeks.

Everett and Putu approached. It was Putu who said, "We need to start moving the children."

"Agreed," K'alyaan said, walking up. "Akłaq, begin rotating the scouts so we have regular reports on any movement from the soldiers. Putu, gather the men who will accompany you north. Everett, I don't know what exactly you intend to do, but any preparations you've made need to be ready to execute. Latseen, help me round up the children."

They dispersed, each to his own task. Akłaq gathered up the young men. They'd discussed the plan a hundred times, even worked on it off and on over the last few years. Even so, having to put it into practice now felt clumsy and disjointed, like trying to organize a bunch of children with short attention spans.

By the time she was finished with that, Putu had rounded up his men. All that remained was to retrieve the children.

The older children understood that they were going to the northern clans to hide. Even the younger children knew that they were leaving. They just didn't like the thought of being separated from their families, and there were many tears and temper tantrums. A few of the young mothers were also going in order to look after the very youngest, but it still wasn't enough for some children.

"I'm sorry!" Latseen blurted when Akłaq found her. "I didn't mean for this to happen!"

"I know," Akłaq said gently, putting a hand on her cheek. "I know. But it did. And honestly, it was always going to. It's just not what we had in mind." She lifted Latseen's chin to look her in the eye. "Remember what I've taught you, and what you've learned from Everett. You're not helpless, Latseen. You can help protect the children. So can Gáx, but he might need a little help himself. Do you understand?"

Latseen nodded reluctantly. "But what if I forget?"

"You won't. You're smart. Too smart for those schools, obviously." They both grinned nervously. "You'll know what to do. And you'll have Grandfather helping you, too."

"And the white bear?"

Akłaq smiled. "And the white bear, too, I'm sure. You are not alone."

Before anyone could say anything more, one of the scouts returned. At first, anyone might have assumed that he'd just been running or climbing and perhaps taken a fall, and this was the reason for his apparent exhaustion. It was Naakliaan who noticed that the dirt on his clothes was actually blood.

"They're coming!" the scout gasped. "The soldiers, they're on their way!"

"How many? Where are they?" Putu demanded.

"A dozen, two? They're only a few miles out. They have guns and they're starting fires."

"The forest is too green to burn well," Everett said, clearly confused.

"They don't need to burn down the forest," K'alyaan stated, "just use the smoke to herd us into a trap." He made a large gesture. "Take the children! Run!"

The parents, who a moment ago had been trying to reason with young children, now scooped them up arbitrarily and started running. The sudden chaos made it difficult for Putu to coordinate his men and get them in any semblance of formation around the group which was now much more spread out than originally planned. Telling them to stick together did little good.

Akłaq watched as Latseen, Gáx, Tlaganis, Nooskw, and Tula'aan disappeared into the trees. She felt her heart break, but there was also a flicker of hope. Her children would live. This time, her children would live.

"We need to cover their escape as much as possible."

Everett's approach startled her and she whirled around. "What?"

"When the soldiers arrive, they'll likely burn the village, and we won't be able to do much to help as far as Time and the Akari. Our best move will be covering the escape and giving them the best chance possible."

Akłaq nodded. "What did you have in mind?"

"We need to make them believe the children are still here, that they've surprised us and interrupted our plans, more than they already have." Everett motioned over those who remained. "Set out half-packed bags full of children's things, and scatter toys around. Go in your homes and make noise as though you are packing to leave hurriedly. Speak as though you are trying to direct your children."

Some of the women, already catching on, left before he was even finished speaking.

"Remember, this only buys them time!" he went on as the people dispersed. "The soldiers will discover their absence. Be prepared to fight! Always keep a weapon in hand!" He turned to Akłaq still beside him. "I'm going to catch up to the group and help them. Stay here with the people."

"What about the fire?" she asked, catching his arm as he turned.

He sighed. "Do what you can. Just as I will with the group. Your best bet may be to not use Time or the Akari at all. But above all, follow the white bear."

With that, he turned and departed, jogging out of the village, then Banding and vanishing completely.

Akłaq stood in the middle of a harried village preparing for battle, and yet she felt terribly alone and woefully unprepared.

Three more scouts came limping back into the village, all of them wounded to varying degrees, all shouting that the soldiers were upon them. The noise behind them suggested as much, and Akłaq wondered if the soldiers really were going to take time to look for the children or if they'd just start shooting.

There were no men in fine clothes this time, no attempt at polite conversation or reasoning. Two dozens soldiers swarmed into the village like angry wasps. They knocked aside the scouts and anyone in their way. Their ruthless efficiency and lack of hesitation or confusion — or even orders — suggested that they had done this many times before and knew exactly what to expect. The belongings and toys were completely disregarded, and no ear was given to the fake yelling and conversations going on inside the home.

When the first door was kicked in, a startled shriek echoing inside, Akłaq snapped out of her trance. First she Fast Banded herself so she could look around and assess exactly what was going on. There appeared to be two or three soldiers in each group, heading for the different houses. She did not see anything especially significant about any of them. Each one had a rifle plus another small firearm and a knife or two. They did not appear to carry any provisions or supplies, so either their supply wagon was a distance away or else they were fairly local, bets on the former.

Seeing all this, Akłaq managed to calm herself enough that she was able to pull off an inversion of her Band. Like turning socks inside out, she took the Fast Band around herself and turned it into a Slow Band around the soldiers. Having to stretch her Band and divide it off to the various groups was no small feat and caused her no shortage of stress and strain. The Band was not perfect; she was unable to fully encapsulate the soldiers, but she was able to slow them down significantly.

The people had never really been privy to the exact nature of her abilities, if they were aware of them at all. Seeing them in action now gave most of the people pause, all of them donning the same wide-eyed, open-mouthed expression her children had gotten when she showed them.

But her strength was waning, her control slipping. The Band fluctuated, and the soldiers began to slide out of slow motion. A few people picked up on some silent cue and, wielding the weapons Everett had told them to grab, began injuring and even killing the soldiers. Some people, especially the women, were vengeful enough that they stabbed the soldiers multiple times or cut their throats, the blood spraying out in painful slowness, each droplet perfectly visible until it reached the edge of the Band. Other people were not strong enough to go for the kill, or they were uncomfortable at the thought, and the most they did was severely injure the soldier nearest them.

Only when black spots started dancing in her vision did Akłaq release the Band. More than half of the soldiers dropped dead. Those who didn't still went to their knees or their sides, screaming or bawling in pain. Akłaq also went to her knees, but no one noticed over the initial cheering that erupted from the villagers.

"Take them away!" Naakilaan ordered. "Kill those who live, take them away and feed them to the wolves and bears. Erase all trace of what has happened here. Return to your normal lives."

As he was speaking, K'alyaan approached Akłaq and helped her back to her feet. She was still quite dizzy, but her vision had cleared. "Are you all right?"

"I'm fine," Akłaq said wearily.

"I don't know what you did, but it helped tremendously."

She nodded, her brain sloshing around inside her skull. "I have to get to the children. I have to help them escape."

She lurched forward drunkenly and almost went down except for K'alyaan still holding onto her.

"Rest a bit," he coaxed. "Putu and Everett have them well looked after. Besides, we've just killed all the soldiers."

After a moment of consideration, Akłaq agreed. Her head was coming back to her rather quickly, but, she figured, five minutes wouldn't make much of a difference. The men would prod the women and children along as fast as they could, but there was still no true hurrying with an obstinate child.

She returned home and sat on the step, staring into the forest. At some point, she realized she was shaking. The villagers who had taken out the bodies returned in short order, looking deviously upbeat. Had all that just happened? It really couldn't have been more than ten minutes. Maybe twenty. So why did it feel like hours had gone by? And this was coming from someone who perceived time more acutely than most.

There was movement in the forest, and suddenly everyone was again on high alert. Commotion, voices, and a horse without a rider came running back to the village.

Akłaq stood. "What's going on? Are there more soldiers?"

A few minutes later, a dozen of those who had gone north returned, battered and bloody. Two of them carried a man Akłaq soon recognized as Everett. At the tail end of the group was Putu, limping badly and cradling a broken arm. Akłaq leaped from the step and raced toward them. She went to Everett first as those who carried him took him to K'alyaan's house and laid him out on the floor.

"Is he dead?" she asked fearfully, gingerly touching his forehead.

"Not yet," one of the men said, "but if he does die, it will be with great honor."

K'alyaan shoved his way into his house, pushing everyone aside, including Akłaq. He felt Everett all over. Finally the elder man said, "He's in rough shape, but I should be able to help him."

Akłaq got close again. "Let me help."

Without being asked, she touched Everett and Felt him. Multiple broken ribs, some internal bleeding, broken arm, broken leg, broken collarbone, several bullet wounds, a head wound. His pain senses were going off so hard they began to bleed over into her own body and she gasped in shock. K'alyaan moved her hand away from him.

"Let me work, child. You've done enough for today."

Akłaq stood and left K'alyaan's house, making for her own where she found Putu trying to wriggle out of his clothes without having to cut them. A broken arm made this difficult at best.

"What happened?" Akłaq demanded, jumping in and helping Putu out of his clothes, not without a few growls and snaps of pain. "Where are my children?"

"It was an ambush," Putu said, "or close enough to it. We only got so far north when we realized the soldiers had already begun burning in that direction. They knew which way we'd run. We tried to keep everyone together, but between the fear and the smoke, we started getting separated. The soldiers picked off some. I tried to Band, to figure out our position and theirs." He shook his head. "I can only conclude that Frederickson is involved somehow, or else the soldiers got extremely lucky. Time—and the Akari, too, I imagine—was only so useful. But the soldiers stayed near to fire, or else they carried torches that made Banding difficult, if not impossible. I tried to engage directly but...you can see it didn't go so well. I lost track of Everett. I tried to find the children, but by then we'd been scattered to the wind. I could hear the children as they cried and begged not to be taken away, but there was little I could do. Eventually I made the decision to just come back and see what happened here. It looks like you fared better than we did."

"Broken arm," she reported blankly. "Broken ankle. You're bruised pretty badly, but not so damaged as Everett."

"I don't suppose he taught you how to set and bind broken bones with the Akari so it doesn't hurt?"

"Sorry, no."

The whole time, all she could think was, *We failed. We worked on this plan for months, thought ourselves brilliant, but we failed. The children are gone, stolen from us.*

"What about Latseen?" Akłaq asked. "And Gáx? Were they able to

Band? Were they able to help—?"

"Akłaq, I don't know," Putu told her, not unkindly. "Maybe they got away and are simply lost."

"If that's true, then—"

He gritted his teeth as she worked on his ankle. Somehow he managed to sputter out, "Focus on this first. Then go see to Everett. He may be able to shed more light on the situation."

She wanted to go out and search for her children. She had to know they were all right. No doubt a dozen other women were thinking the same thing. But her hands were kept busy with Putu's wounds. She was able to use Feel to know when the bones were correctly set, and then she used Time to condense several moons of healing into only a few minutes. Then she did the same for his arm. After the events of the day, with everyone witnessing the spectacle she'd pulled on the soldiers, she wasn't worried about them noticing that Putu had miraculously healed from his injuries.

Once Putu was fixed up, Akłaq went back to K'alyaan's house and did the same for Everett, at least everything that wasn't his head. K'alyaan had removed any bullets that remained lodged in his flesh, making it much easier to heal the soft tissue.

But the head and brain were a different issue. Even a normal person knew that they were to be dealt with delicately, and she didn't want to get cocky about abilities she barely understood. She was able to Feel his head and understand that his wound was not life-threatening, and the most she did for him was Band him and give him about twelve hours of rest in only a minute or two. Feeling him again, things appeared to be better, more stable, but still he did not wake.

"Leave him be for a while," K'alyaan said gently. "Let him rest in the care of the spirits."

Akłaq nodded and left the house. She left the village entirely, heading deep into the woods, occasionally calling for the white bear, for Anagalisgi, for anyone or anything who might hear her. What happened? How had they been bested? What were they supposed to do now? Why had she been brought here if it only meant leading her to yet another failure and crushing her soul with the loss of yet more children?

But the woods were eerily silent. She might have thought that the spirits were silent as well, except she knew they weren't. The problem was that she wasn't sure it was the white spirits that she was feeling. The presence that surrounded her now was dark, smothering, foreboding, and it laughed at her, spat at her in her shame. These were not friendly spirits here. Carefully, she began backing up. Then she turned and ran, and she could have sworn that something audibly laughed at her.

Nothing had changed in the village except for the weeping of the women for their lost children. Their victory had been turned into a tragic defeat, and no one knew what to do. All their plans, their powerful, spirit-endowed saviors, and still they ended up like every other reserve in the province, maybe the whole country. Maybe the whole continent.

A terrible silence, like a void, settled over the village. No one spoke. No one ate. Akłaq was willing to bet that she wasn't the only one who didn't sleep that night either. She cried. She prayed. She dozed a bit, then came awake again, at first wondering why the house was so quiet, and then remembering.

It was the middle of the next afternoon before Everett woke, and even then he was very groggy and uncoordinated for about the first hour. If there was any good news, it was that once he could articulate his thoughts, he appeared to be the same old Everett. Even better, he remembered what happened. Like Putu's tale, however, it wasn't any good.

"Was it Frederickson?" Putu demanded. "Was he the one who sabotaged us?"

Everett still lay abed, and his movements were as slow as Akłaq's thoughts as he shook his head. "I don't know. It wouldn't surprise me if he were the mastermind, but he himself was not there that I saw." He looked at Akłaq. "Given your success here, it's safe to say he wasn't here either." Back at Putu. "One of his Lieutenants, however, was there. He's the one who hit me."

"I'm shocked he didn't kill you."

"He may have had other things on his mind and I was just in his way. I don't know, but I'm not arguing."

"What now?" Akłaq asked quietly. "Where are the children?"

"On their way to a school, no doubt," Naakilaan said distastefully. He shifted position. "We need to intercept them on the road; we'll never penetrate those fortresses."

"We can and we will," Putu stated. "And it may be to our advantage to wait until they've reached the school. Right now, they're expecting some form of retaliation. We will have no more success on the road than we did here."

Everett nodded. "He's right. There are more soldiers on the road, but few, if any, at the schools. We'll have better luck there."

"But which school?" K'alyaan wondered. "The rumors say that they split up the children so that the villages cannot hope to retaliate in such a way."

"Then we burn them all," Putu said.

Akłaq found herself nodding in agreement. "We may not be able to attack them on the road, but we should follow them at least, to avoid losing too much time. Every day that the children are in school is another day they are removed from their people, their ancestors, their land. We have to rescue them before they become strangers."

"Agreed," Everett said, swinging his legs over the edge of the bed and standing slowly. "This time, I believe it will be more beneficial to have only a small group."

"By this, you mean, yourself, Putu, and Akłaq," Naakilaan stated.

"That's right."

"How do we know, then, that you didn't sabotage the escape yourselves, deliver the children to the soldiers, and are now making your escape?"

"That's absurd!" Putu cried. "You think I broke my own arm, or Everett hit himself in the head? Do you think Akłaq would have helped to slaughter twenty soldiers if that were the case?"

"You are outsiders; who knows what you might do?" He gestured to Everett. "You're a half-breed, so who knows where your loyalties lie at any given moment? You two—" He gestured to Putu and Akłaq. "—are northerners, safely tucked away in your icy land—"

"Safe?!" Putu got in his face. "Let me tell you something about safe."

"Please!" K'alyaan snapped, getting between them. He glared at his brother. "Akłaq lost her children, too. And they have helped us too much to start spouting obscene conjecture!"

Naakilaan snorted but took a step back, then another. "If you really want to prove your loyalty, bring back our children."

He left the room. Everett turned to K'alyaan. "That's exactly what we're going to do."

Avgun Iñuiñaq Tallimat
Missions

The stories about the schools and what they did to the children had been slow to come out, the dam not permitted to burst until the government was confident that there was nothing the people could do about it even if they did know everything.

Depending on the school, the girls and boys might be separated long before they ever reached their destination. When the three of them set out, they had agreed that if the children were separated early, Akłaq and Putu would follow the girls and Everett would follow the boys.

They had little trouble finding the kidnapping convoy, and they stayed as close as possible, Banding to get through any tight spots.

"Why don't we just Band, steal the children back, and go home?" Akłaq grumbled one night as they bedded down.

"The soldiers will only come back," Everett said, not the first time he'd answered the question. "We not only want to take back our children, but free any others we may find and destroy the schools so they can't destroy any more lives."

It didn't make it any easier to follow them, day after day. Akłaq wondered what her children were doing, what they were thinking. Had Latseen tried to Band and run away? Had Gáx? Had they been able to get far? Had they perhaps gotten away and were even now still heading north, looking for the northern clans?

She would fight for her children. This time, she was going to do something about the injustice.

The rumors said that when the children reached the school, they were given a bath and every possession they might have with them was taken away. Every doll and blanket, every piece of clothing. They were given a new uniform to wear, every child the same as every other. The boys would have their hair cut, and all children would have their hair styled in plain, white fashion. Afterwards, they would be assigned a bed in a large dormitory and given a schedule of classes they were expected to attend. Punishment for disobedience was harsh. Punishment for speaking in the indigenous languages or referring to any of the old ways was especially brutal. Beatings, isolation, starvation. And if anyone spoke up in defense of the one being punished, he was subjected to the same punishment.

Akłaq could hardly imagine it. Years ago, she had never beaten her children for speaking Russian, and Nika never so much as gave them dirty looks when they spoke Iñupiatun. They may have had religious disagreements, but they never took it out on the children. Even the concept was unholy.

Every second on the road felt like a year, and the summer quickly grew hot. Still they followed the children. From the northern border of the province to the southern, they followed. As much as Akłaq wanted to run up to them and hug them, or at the very least show her face to give the children hope, she knew she could not. If she did, the children would react and potentially give away their position. There were fewer soldiers now, but their mission went beyond just their children.

For a while, she might have hoped that the children would not be separated, that they would be taken to a school where the boys and girls stayed together, at least on the same land. But, one day they were all traveling together, and the next they were taking different paths on a forked road.

"As we planned it, then," Everett said, moving to break off and follow the boys.

"We'll see you back in the village," Putu told him.

"If you have any trouble, come find me. We still don't know to what extent Frederickson is involved. Don't risk the children."

Akłaq had a sharp reply to that, but before she could speak, Putu butted in with, "Of course. Good luck."

And they parted ways.

It was harder to move around in the south because there were many more towns and settlements. Akłaq remembered a few here and there when they traveled west just a few years ago. Like the schools, however, these towns seemed to pop up out of nowhere, like spring dandelions.

Even before they reached the school, the children were subjected to horrendous personal violations. In one town, the girls were made to get rid of their normal clothes they had worn on the reserve and instead don white clothes provided by the local church. In the next town, they were all taken to a woman who cut and styled their hair exactly the same way. Many of the girls undid the styling once they were back on the road, but the point remained. In a third town, all remaining personal possessions were taken from them, and each girl given a Bible instead. Some of the older ones also got rosaries or crucifixes.

"Do you think," Putu wondered as they observed from afar, safely in a Band, "if we had forced the Russians, or even now the Canadians or Americans, to perform our dances while barefoot over hot coals, that they would have a different view of what they're doing here? Or sing our song under threat of having to eat those hot coals?"

"No," Akłaq said absently. "It's always right when you do it. You always have a reason."

"Well so do they, but that doesn't make it right."

"Yes, but if you didn't believe your reasoning superior, you wouldn't be doing it." She shifted position in her seat, longing to lunge at the kidnappers. "I will give them credit for one teaching, that we're all equal in the sight of God and the spirits. The problem is that they seem to have forgotten that themselves and instead focus on being superior among men."

"One pig in the mud is as clean as any another," Putu agreed. "But the time for philosophy is past, I think."

They retreated to their normal following distance, and Akłaq dropped the Band. She looked at Putu and grinned. "I like this Putu."

He raised a brow. "Which Putu?"

"The one who stands and fights and doesn't run away."

"Those are my granddaughters they have over there, what am I supposed to do? Bad enough I have to leave my grandsons with Everett."

"You don't think he can pull it off?"

He shrugged. "I just know that he's always been very confident, even arrogant, about the Akari and everything he's teaching you and the kids, and then the one chance he has to show off how superior it is, he's knocked out by a Lieutenant Timekeeper."

"Maybe it was the fire," Akłaq suggested. "Or, sometimes, things happen. We can't control everything that goes on."

"Oh, I understand that, I'm just saying that for all his postulating, the Akari doesn't seem to be much more than overglorified Time."

She gave him a look. "It healed your arm and ankle well enough, as well as Everett's wounds."

Putu grumbled something resembling assent, but before he said anything confirming it, he pointed to the group. "Come on, they're moving. We have to be getting close to the school."

They were closer than they thought. The school was about nine or ten miles outside of town — Akłaq forgot the name — on a piece of land which encompassed three large hills. Only because she had heard descriptions of other schools was she not more in awe, though it was still an impressive structure.

There was one main building, visible from the road though not easily accessed. Aside from a somewhat prohibitive landscape, the whole place was surrounded by a large brick wall with a massive iron gate. Other, smaller buildings dotted the landscape: a smaller stone building, a few sheds, and probably a stable somewhere, too, as there were several horses out to pasture on one hillside.

The group was met at the gate by a black-robed priest and a couple of nuns. Words were exchanged, the gate lock undone, and a couple of the soldiers heaved the gate open. The children were herded inside and the gate shut menacingly behind them. One of the nuns stayed behind long enough to reassemble the chain and lock, then turned to catch up to the group once more.

"Pinpoint Band will take care of the lock and chain easily enough," Putu murmured. "Rust them right off."

"Too much time and energy," Akłaq said. "Galo'ondiha ale Agi'a will get us over the wall faster, and they'll never suspect anything."

"You're proposing we fly?"

"In a manner of speaking. Not far, just over the wall."

Putu rolled his eyes and sighed. "Fine. We get inside. Our best bet is going to be the main building. I can Band so you can grab the children."

She shook her head. "I'll Band."

"You're not as strong as I am."

"No, but I can use Akari Bands that are invisible." She went on before Putu could speak. "If Frederickson or any of his men are here, they'll see the wake of your Band. They'll know we're involved. Use an Akari Band, they'll never notice."

"I think they're going to know something's up regardless. One or two children might escape, but not an entire school."

"We need every possible advantage."

He grunted. "Well, whatever the case, we'll have to wait for nightfall."

Simple nightfall proved to be useless, as the soldiers stayed overnight, probably to thwart any initial escape attempts. Akłaq and Putu took watch in shifts, noting any and all movement, whether it was people and animals or just the appearance and disappearance of lanterns. Nothing exciting happened that they were aware of, and morning returned soon enough.

The soldiers did not actually leave until about midday, and Akłaq counted, with some relief, the same number leaving as had entered.

"Tonight," Putu stated.

She did not disagree.

They watched and waited. They did not see any children, though they may have heard them at some point, perhaps playing outside. A nun came to the gate once to meet a man on the road. Papers were handed through the gate, but the lock was never opened. The sun moved overhead and clouds began to roll in later in the evening.

"Rain will give us cover," Putu observed, looking up at the distant sky.

"Should we wait for it?" Akłaq wondered.

"Darkness will be best for us. Rain only helps. We still go in at dark."

Between Putu being a historical coward, and Akłaq unsure how to pull this off anyway, it was actually past dark before either of them actually moved to approach the school. They slid down the hill to the road, trying to be as quiet as possible. But as they stood on the road itself, studying the wall and the gate, noise from the other side grabbed their attention. Akłaq pressed herself hard against the wall and motioned for Putu to do the same.

"Here we go, here we go." There was whispering on the other side. "Come on. Up here. In my arms. And up you go!"

There was the sound of kicking and scrambling, some scraping, a grunt of effort. A moment later, "Well?"

"It's so far down!"

Akłaq knew that voice. She practically jumped away from the wall and whirled to see Tula'aan, now ten years old, standing on top of the wall, absolutely frozen.

"Mama!" Tula'aan cried.

"Shh!" Akłaq said, putting a finger to her lips. "Hush, child."

From the other side of the wall came, "Tula, what's going on?"

Tula'aan turned around. "Latseen, Mama's here!"

"What?"

"Tula," Akłaq said, "come here. Come down off the wall. Mama will help you down."

The small child turned and, with Akłaq and Putu helping, got to the ground. Her new clothes were dirty and her styled hair was messy, but she'd never looked happier. She hugged each adult in turn, then dug around in a small pocket in her skirt and pulled out a key.

"How did you get this?" Akłaq asked, taking the key.

"Latseen used your magic to steal it from the nun," Tula'aan said. "She's so awful!"

"Latseen or the nun?" Putu inquired lightly, taking the key.

He walked over to the gate and unlocked it, heaving it open just enough for Latseen to slip out.

The first thing Latseen did was rush over to Akłaq and throw her arms around her.

"I'm sorry, Mama," Latseen cried into her shoulder. "I didn't mean for this to happen."

Akłaq stroked her daughter's hair. "Oh, child, it's not your fault. I shouldn't have come down so hard on you. They were going to try this anyway, whether you said something or not." She pushed Latseen back enough to look her in the face. "The important thing is that you didn't forget what you were taught, and you got out. Right? And you helped your sister. Right?"

Latseen nodded and wiped her face. "Right."

"Everett has gone to rescue your brothers, too. Soon this will all be behind us, all right?"

She nodded again. "That sounds nice."

"I don't like this place," Tula'aan interjected.

"We know you don't," Putu said, kneeling down to her eye level. "But we need to talk about this place for a minute. You're not the only ones we came for. We're here for everyone. Not just you, not just the children from our village, but all of them."

Latseen shook her head. "It won't work. Not everyone wants to leave."

Akłaq shifted her stance. "But they need to return home, to be with their people."

"Some of them have renounced their people. And they're not just speaking to tell the nuns what they want to hear, they truly have turned their back on the people and the old ways, no matter who or what they are."

"How can you know this after only a day?"

Latseen's expression was one of dead seriousness. "You can tell."

"How many girls are in the school?" Putu asked. "How many do you think can be saved?"

"Including all of us who just got here, there's probably seventy or eighty total. I counted fifteen or twenty of them who were traitors."

"They're not traitors," Akłaq said. "They're just lost, even if they don't realize it yet."

"They're not traitors until they give us away," Putu said, standing. "Could you tell us who they are?"

Latseen faltered. "I mean, I can tell by their face, but I don't know their names or anything. Or, I mean, they might have told me their names but I don't really know anyone yet."

"Would you feel comfortable going back and showing us?" Akłaq wondered.

"I don't want to go back," Tula'aan stated firmly, stomping her foot for emphasis.

"We don't doubt that," Putu said, "but you need to help us rescue the others so we can all go home."

Thankfully, it wasn't too difficult to reason with the ten year old; the biggest thing she wanted was to stay with Latseen which was easily arranged.

"Latseen, you know this place more than we do," Putu said. "You'll have to guide us."

The teenager hesitated.

"They're not going to catch us," Akłaq assured her. "I'll be Banding us, just like I'm sure you did to steal the key." Latseen got an embarrassed expression. "Just take us to the girls, point out the ones from home and the ones you think haven't turned traitor, we'll put them into the Band, and then we'll leave."

"Point out the ones you know aren't traitors," Putu clarified. He gave Akłaq a look. "We bring a traitor with us, then even if we deliver them to their people, they'll go right back to the white men and the soldiers and tell them what we've done. Worse, they'll tell them who we are. It not only jeopardizes the village, but it could get back to

Frederickson or one of his men."

Akłaq sighed but nodded. "Agreed." She looked at Latseen. "Only the girls from our village and the ones you know aren't traitors."

Latseen nodded. "All right."

"If nothing else, at least the girls from our village."

That gave Latseen some measure of confidence. She took Tula'aan by the hand and cautiously walked back through the gate, not really moving until Akłaq had all four of them Banded.

"When we were in the woods, trying to escape," Latseen began sheepishly, "I tried to Band. I wanted to grab the others and run away. But I couldn't. I messed up the Band and it wouldn't hold and then..." She shook her head. "I knew I would forget."

"You didn't forget," Putu told her. "The first important thing is that you did try. But the soldiers used fire, and fire is almost impossible to overcome, even for more experienced people like me or your mother. It's no surprise at all that you couldn't get around it. That's why Everett and I couldn't save you either."

Latseen looked thoughtful. "So there are limits to the magic? There are things you can't do?"

"That's right."

"Can I learn the magic?" Tula'aan wondered.

"Not yet," Putu said, grinning. "You have to become a woman first, just like your sister did, just like your brothers have to become men before they learn." His grin faded. "What about Gáx? How did he fare?"

"I couldn't keep track of him and lost him in the woods," Latseen admitted. "I didn't see him again until the road. He didn't say anything about Banding or trying to escape or any of it." She shrugged. "I guess it really doesn't matter what happened or didn't happen, because we all ended up here anyway."

"We'll worry about it when we get home."

"Are we still going to go to the northern clans?"

"Well, first we're going to stop at the village so everyone else can see the children and know they're all right. Then, yes, we'll probably take you to the northern clans as originally planned."

"How long will we have to stay there?"

"I don't know," Putu confessed. "At least until you're too old to be brought to these so-called schools. A few years for you, a few more years for Tula'aan. Maybe a couple more years just to be sure."

"I don't like it," Latseen said. "It feels so...restrictive. Like a rabbit in a cage with a wolf prowling around it."

"We know," Putu assured her. "We know that very well."

They rounded the last tree and crested the last rise before reaching the school. It was an enormous building, the foundation built of large stones and the rest with wood. It didn't even look complete as there was still scaffolding on one end, like dead, twisted branches against the dim clouds.

"The classrooms are all downstairs," Latseen explained. "The dorms are upstairs. They say it's so we can run from class straight outside to play, but really it's so we have a harder time escaping at night. The priest and the nuns all sleep on the first floor here near the doors."

Not only did they sleep near the doors, but they kept their bed near the doors to their rooms which were open. Akłaq only had to take a passing glance into the rooms to see the large shapes of the priest and nuns sleeping soundly.

All four of them froze and cringed at the squeak of a floorboard. It was only Tula'aan stepping on a board just inside the front door.

"Brand new building shouldn't have creaky floors," Putu said disapprovingly. "It's done that way on purpose."

"The back door is the same way," Latseen mentioned casually. "Come on."

From the outside, the building seemed to be able to house whole armies. Standing next to it, it appeared to block out the sky and run forever in either direction. The inside, while large, felt rather cozy. The hallways were narrow, as were the stairs (also purposely creaky). The wood was finely polished and there was still a lingering odor of fresh varnish. The white walls also held a scent of new paint, and everywhere she looked, Akłaq saw crucifixes, icons, and other religious art. The classrooms they passed were the same way, and she only glimpsed all the small desks and chairs laid out in neat rows, all facing the blackboard that took up almost an entire wall.

Finally they arrived at the fourth floor where Latseen pushed open a set of (creaky) double doors. This room was three times the size of any other room she had seen and might have taken up half the space of the floor. It was divided in half, but two more sets of double doors were wide open between them. Both rooms also had varnished floors and white walls adorned with religious paraphernalia, but they were furnished with at least fifty beds each, thin mattresses on shaky metal frames.

"We should move quickly," Putu murmured.

Akłaq agreed, if only because she didn't want her Band to falter at the last minute. She was holding out all right for the moment, but once they started pulling more girls in and she had to encompass them all, it was going to put a strain on her, much the same as it had when she Banded the soldiers in the village. Hopefully the girls would stay close by so she didn't have to stretch it too thin.

Without being asked, Latseen and Tula'aan started going bed to bed, waking up the girls, telling them to be quiet and be prepared to leave. A few protested the futility of an escape attempt, up until they saw Akłaq and Putu standing there with them.

"We still have to be quiet," Latseen warned. "And stay close to Putu."

Suddenly Putu took on the likeness of a mother hen gathering chicks. Meanwhile, Akłaq was starting to feel the pressure on her Band. They got all the girls from their own village, but Latseen and Tula'aan were still waking up others and asking if they wanted to go home. Some girls they intentionally skipped, and Akłaq assumed that these were the traitors.

"I'll go ahead of us," Putu said once all the girls were gathered. "Latseen, you bring up the rear and help keep everyone moving. Akłaq, stay in the middle and keep the Band around us."

She had no other plans, but she could feel the sweat at her hairline.

Then they started moving, and Akłaq almost lost the Band. This was far more than just suspending soldiers long enough to kill them; this was trying to herd children. A lot of children. There were probably sixty total in the group. And how, exactly, had they planned to get them all away from the schools and delivered back to their appropriate reserves? Akłaq was going to count herself lucky to be able to get them out to the road, never mind hundreds of miles in all directions.

Maybe they should have stuck to their own village. Maybe she should have stuck to her own children.

She felt ashamed for even thinking it and pushed the thought from her mind. She was not the only hurting mother, and she should not be the only one to rejoice at her child's return, not when she had the ability to help others.

All the same, it was a trying task. She didn't know whether it helped or hindered her when the entire group froze every time someone stepped on a squeaky board. It was probably just fear—the girls really didn't understand that the priest and nuns wouldn't even know what happened until morning—but it was annoying.

Nevertheless, Putu checked all of the offices just to make sure the priest and nuns weren't going to sneak up on them. Once he was satisfied, he opened the front door. Several of the younger girls darted forward, but the older girls were quick enough to catch them and bring them back. Akłaq felt her control slipping.

Then she felt a tiny portion of the burden being lifted. She looked back at Latseen who was managing a Band around herself and the last five or six girls around her.

"I can help," she said. "I know I can."

Akłaq didn't say anything, just nodded once in thanks, resituated herself in her own efforts, and slowly made her way through the door to the outside. Once through, everyone again crowded around Putu. Drawing them in close helped Akłaq to manage her Band, and they snaked their way down to the gate which was still open.

"Do you think you can open a Paa?" Akłaq inquired of Putu,

already knowing the answer.

"To the Wheel? Probably," he said. "Anywhere else? No."

"Just thought I'd ask."

The girls couldn't help but cheer when they finally set foot outside the wall of the school. They let them have their moment of freedom before calling for quiet again.

"All right," Putu said, bringing them in close once more, "now then, we know you are not all of the same people, or the same reserves. So we need to know where you all came from. Do you remember?"

Some did, and some didn't. Some were too young to really know, and others had been gone for so long they'd forgotten the way. The good news was that most of them at least knew their people. If they started with that, then, Akłaq figured, they could go to any of the reserves and their own people could help them.

She kept up the Band as long as she could so they could find a place closer to town to rest and hide for a while. In spite of their new freedom, it was still the middle of the night, and some of the younger children began to complain about being tired. Hunger also made itself known.

"We'll stop here," Putu announced suddenly.

Akłaq didn't even comprehend his full statement before she released the Band and fell to her knees. Latseen and Putu both lunged for her, but Latseen became distracted by the youngest girls suddenly becoming afraid and starting to cry.

"You did well," Putu told Akłaq, kneeling beside her. "I was preparing myself to have to take over, but you did well."

She closed her eyes and let her head drop. "Putu, I can't even see straight and I think I'm going to be sick. What was our plan for afterwards again?"

"Stay here. If Latseen can manage it—" He paused and looked up. Akłaq guessed Latseen agreed to whatever he said. "—then she can watch the girls for a bit. You and them can get some sleep. I'll go into town and see about getting a team and a wagon."

Akłaq didn't have the strength to protest. Putu took no further input, just stood, told the girls to be good and he would be back soon, then departed.

It didn't take two minutes for Akalq to lie down and fall asleep. She remembered having some stray thought that she needed to stay awake and be on guard for the girls, but that quickly slipped past her as her dreams began filtering through instead.

Part of her hoped that she might receive a visit from the white bear, just to let her know they were doing the right thing or give them some direction to make this as easy as possible. If she did get such a visit or a message, she didn't remember it.

When she woke, it was still dark, but there was some commotion about. Feeling rested and suddenly alert, Akłaq jumped to her feet.

"Relax, it's all right," Putu said.

Akłaq looked around, finally able to take in their surroundings. They'd laid down in a depression, just over a rise near the road. Latseen and Putu were waking everyone and herding them over the slope.

"How long has it been?" she asked, rubbing her eyes and helping to move the children.

"Not long at all," Putu replied. "I Banded to town and back, and then I Banded you so you could be fresh and alert, but I figured the girls would be better off sleeping in the wagon."

Akłaq rubbed her eyes again as the two of them crested the rise and slid down to the road where a team and wagon waited in the gloom. Latseen and another girl were busy hoisting the girls in one at a time. It was quite a crowded affair, and Akłaq knew that few of them would sleep comfortably. When the last girl was loaded, Putu climbed into the driver's seat, and Akłaq climbed up beside him.

"Is everyone ready?" Putu asked.

"More than ready," Latseen told him.

Putu clicked the reins and the wagon lurched forward. Looking back, most of the girls were fast falling asleep. She looked at Putu.

"Banding aside, I almost feel like that was too easy," she admitted.

"The Banding is what made it easy," he told her. "Can you imagine trying to sneak fifty girls out of that place with all those squeaky boards, sleeping nuns, and locked gate?" He glanced at her. "Akłaq, this is what our power was made for, to help people, to breeze past impossible barriers as minor inconveniences."

"Do you think Everett had as easy of a time?"

"I hope so."

"What do you think will happen when they find out?"

"A massive search of the grounds and the surrounding area most likely. But they won't believe that so many children would be able to get as far away as we'll be by morning."

She looked back again. "What's to stop them from just going back to the reserves and taking the children again?"

Putu sighed. "Honestly, nothing. If the people don't fight back, the white men can take whatever they want. All we're doing is giving them a chance. We're taking our children and going north. It's up to the other peoples to decide what they're going to do the next time."

"Do you think we should have killed the nuns, or burned the school?"

"Killing the nuns would have done nothing. Burning the school, maybe, except they'll only build more. They are building more. What really needs to happen is for people to realize that stealing children is not acceptable and to just leave us alone."

Akłaq frowned and she shifted uncomfortably. "In the old days, the old ways, many indigenous nations would kill and steal each other's children all the time. When did we decide it was suddenly unacceptable?"

Putu's expression was unreadable. "Maybe when we were suddenly barred from ever getting them back. I don't know."

"I regret nothing we've done tonight," Akłaq said, "and I would gladly do it a thousand times more. But sometimes I wonder if we don't inadvertently lay traps for ourselves when we try to reason or reconcile our actions."

"A lot has changed in the last hundred years, the last three hundred years," Putu stated. "The way of things has been uprooted, and I fear that we may never know the true history of all that has happened. Even this—" He jerked his head back toward the sleeping children. "—I expect will be ignored, denied, covered up, justified in its own way, maybe erased entirely. But what matters is now, getting these girls back to their mothers and their people, where they belong."

Akłaq nodded. "We will just have to stay alive, then, and make sure people know and remember what has happened here."

Putu grinned humorlessly. "Don't speak of everything as being the past yet. There are still plenty more schools out there, plenty more children who need rescuing."

After that they rode in silence except for the rumble of the wagon and an occasional hubbub from the back as sixty girls tried to get comfortable in a wagon only big enough for twenty. Neither Putu nor Akłaq Banded, both for their own sanity as well as to make it to daybreak when they would have a little better light.

When morning came and the girls started waking up, they stopped for breakfast. No one actually had anything, so Putu went out and hunted down a couple of deer with the assistance of a Band. Akłaq got a fire going, and they took a short time to cut and cook the meat. While the girls were eating, they took a brief census. All but the girls from the Tlingit reserve were Chilcotin, and those who remembered where they were from named half a dozen different reserves. Only one actually knew how to get to their particular reserve from their present location.

"Do you suppose Everett will attempt the same thing with the boys?" Akłaq wondered. "Do you think he will come looking for us when we don't show up back home in good time?"

"I think word will spread about the return of the girls," Putu said, gnawing on a small cut of meat. "I think he'll figure it out."

"As long as word does not spread too quickly to the white men. We don't need to go home only to find them waiting for us."

He did not say anything to that. Once he was done with his food, they rounded up the children once more and loaded them onto the wagon. It was now about midmorning. There would be more travelers on the road. No doubt the nuns had discovered the missing children and were already sending word near and far to be on the lookout.

No one came after them that day. Akłaq Banded as much as possible, whenever they were alone on the road and after it got dark. They made their way to a Chilcotin reserve, Banding their way past a couple of soldiers who would no doubt find it highly suspicious that there was a wagon load of children coming into the reserve rather than going out to a school.

It was a six year old who announced them to the village.

"Mama!" she cried.

The child had jumped off the wagon and begun running to a suddenly frantic woman before anyone could stop her. Mother and daughter embraced, and soon the wagon was surrounded by men and women, everyone shouting names and asking questions.

"How did you do it?"

Akłaq looked down at an old woman standing beside her on the ground.

"News has already spread about sixty girls gone missing from one of the schools," the old woman went on. "How did you do it?"

"A little determination and a lot of provision from the spirits," Akłaq told her.

The woman nodded slowly. "You know they'll come back for them."

"We went to rescue our children, and we brought them home for a second chance at life as well. It's up to you what you decide to do with that second chance, what you are willing to do to defend them."

Eleven girls returned to their families in the village, and Putu got directions to four more reserves as well as a warning that soldiers would no doubt be looking for them.

So it was for every reserve they visited. Tears, joy, gifts of thanks, promises to defend the children next time the soldiers came. If the Tlingit could do it, so could the Chilcotin.

The last reserve they stopped at, Akłaq saw that there were a number of boys running around, and the people confirmed that Everett had indeed been through not even a week prior, heading north with a small group of Tlingit boys. A few days later, when they finally returned to the Tlingit reserve, they found Everett and the boys already there.

Girls ran to their mothers, and Gáx, Tlaganis, and Nooskw ran to Akłaq and Putu.

Akłaq wept as she hugged her boys again. Even though she had done the same thing for her girls and other people's girls, Everett had done it for her.

"It wasn't easy, but we made it," Everett said, approaching.

"Now what?" Akłaq wondered, wiping her face.

"We'll rest here for a day or two," Putu stated. "Then we'll begin moving the children north."

"And that's it?"

Both men looked at her. Everett asked, "What do you mean, that's it? That's what we planned."

"Yes, but..." Akłaq shook her head. "Those soldiers are going to return. They're going to take the children again. And even if they somehow don't, there are still a lot of schools out there with stolen children."

"What are you saying?" Putu wondered. "Akłaq, we can't raid all of them. Even if we did go there, if Latseen is right, some children have already turned traitor. She knew which ones to avoid, but we won't have that same benefit."

"Gáx said something similar at their school," Everett agreed.

"So we risk taking a few children home who might say, what, that they were taken? That much is obvious. But if we do nothing, then we are guaranteed to lose all of them." Akłaq shook her head. "You move the children here north. I'm going to return south. If nothing else, it will act as a distraction, keep the soldiers busy in the south."

"I'll come with you," Latseen said, stepping up. At Akłaq's look, she added, "You're going to need the help." She looked at her brother. "Gáx?"

Gáx hesitated a moment, then nodded. "Yeah. I'll come, too."

Putu and Everett glanced at each other. Finally Everett said, "I can see you won't be dissuaded. But at least be careful."

Akłaq dipped her head once. "Of course. We are nothing if not careful." At Putu's look, she said, "We'll buy you some time and join you in the north in the fall."

Putu nodded. "Good luck."

Avgun Iñuiñaq Itchaksrat
Mother Bear

Akłaq, Latseen, and Gáx caused quite a circus for the schools that summer. The priests and nuns would wake up one morning to find that some, most, or even all of their students had vanished in the night. As the summer wore on, the alarming methods became increasingly creative. Bells were hung on doors and windows, keys were hidden in more personal spots, and even dogs were put on patrol. It became almost like a game.

It also got easier to tell who the traitorous students were. Apparently terrified of being spirited away in the middle of the night, they would tie themselves to their bed, a rope around their ankles and maybe one around a wrist, and clutch a Bible or a crucifix or a rosary to their chest. And, like angels, Akłaq and her children would pass them over. Of course, this gave the school wardens the idea that all children needed to be bound to their beds and holding these assorted icons. But where they could potentially force a child to be tied to their bed, they could not force a child to hold a Bible all night long, and those who had dropped or even thrown these things away from them were mercifully released from their bonds and taken away from the school.

Working with Everett again, Akłaq had begun to master Galo'ondiha ale Agi'a, or, as some called it, Gravity. And, through trial and error, she and her children discovered that sometimes, if there were only a few children that they were rescuing, it was easier to simply use Gravity to lift the children and take them out of the school, still asleep, rather than wake them, bring them into a Band, and then herd them along to safety.

It was quite an adventure, to say the least. As they made their way south to what was probably going to be their last rescue for the year before heading north to meet the others, Akłaq reflected that this was probably the first time she felt like she was making a real difference for her people. True, she wasn't Tlingit, but a difference nevertheless. It wasn't hoping and praying, it wasn't politics and negotiating. She was out here physically rescuing children from a future of ignorance and misery. She wished Aniqan could see her now. Doing all of this with her children, she wished Nika could see her, too.

She wondered if there were a way for her to speak to Aniqan or Nika, or speak to the white bear or Anagalisgi so they might pass on a message to them. But her prayers to that effect went unanswered, or else they were answered and she just didn't know it. Whatever the case, it had little bearing on the task at hand and she did her best to push it from her mind.

It was a small school, the building unfinished and not even having a name yet, simply called "the Methodist mission." Of all the various denominations and the schools they built, the Methodists always seemed to be the most humane in their treatment of the students overall. While they engaged in many of the same assimilation practices that the others did, like making students wear uniforms and learn everything that Canadian students might be taught in their schools and churches, they still maintained a certain level of respect. Christian hymns were translated into indigenous languages, traditional crafting was permitted provided that all themes were staunchly Christian, and the students were not forced to style their hair in a certain way—that is, the boys, were not forced to cut their hair—upon entry. It was highly encouraged, with many Biblical references and a lot of peer pressure, but the boys were not strapped to a chair and sheared like sheep.

But for as humane as their treatment might have been, they were still trafficking children. Their involvement validated the kidnapping of these boys and girls from their homes and families, and they needed to be punished for it.

They'd been directed to this school by a girl from their last rescue. She and her brother had been split up, but she had heard that he had been brought here. If they could rescue him, too, it would make their mother very happy. Akłaq knew very well what that felt like and readily agreed.

"What do you think?" Akłaq wondered.

She, Latseen, and Gáx circled the school twice. There was no wall, just a nice fence that could be easily jumped by an adult and a polite gate that wasn't even locked. There were no dogs, no obvious traps, and she doubted there would be any alarms that were too elaborate on account of the ongoing construction.

"I think it'll be a nice end to this year of liberation," Latseen said. "Nice and easy."

"Yeah," Gáx agreed. "I mean, we almost don't even have to sneak in. Just walk in through there, grab the children, and get out."

It sounded simple enough, and they'd had no trouble so far. All the same, Akłaq didn't want to make stupid mistakes that could be prevented with the smallest bit of thought.

She started forward, her children following. At a certain point, they split up. Latseen would go through the front door, Gáx through the back, and Akłaq would find a side door or window if there was one. Given the state of this school, there were plenty of options to choose from. From there, most schools, regardless of denomination, were pretty similar in layout, and they each had a search pattern to execute. Latseen would locate the children and get them ready, Gáx would determine the easiest route of escape, and Akłaq would find and assess any threats before actually attempting the evacuation.

There was no window in the hole yet, and this probably should have been their first clue as Akłaq climbed inside. While unfinished, this room was clearly destined to be a classroom. Desks were piled in one corner, cabinets and shelving in another. The blackboard leaned against the wall where it was to be hung.

Actually, it was rooms like this that were most likely to give them away. If Akłaq bumped something the wrong way on her way through, she could bring the whole pile of desks crashing to the ground. Granted, she might not be too badly affected if she was able to Band or use Sound in time, but Latseen and Gáx were not yet so talented. The noise would be great, and they would be caught. They'd had no failures so far this summer, and she had no intention of starting now.

The new door did not squeak, but she opened it carefully anyway, looking for bells or other clever mechanisms of making noise and alerting the priests to their antics. She did not find any and slipped into the hallway like a mouse.

She methodically checked every room, finding mostly unfinished classrooms. One room looked like a storage room for various religious icons that would no doubt decorate the walls once the larger furniture was arranged. There were also boxes of other small items they had found in all the rooms in all the schools, things like books, maps, paper, and various mathematical tools, including the dreaded ruler. Useful for marking out precise measurements and for tanning the knuckles or backsides of unruly students.

Otherwise, there was nothing of interest. Akłaq found the kitchen and the common dining room. Next to that she found another large room which might have been destined to become some indoor recreation area, but, for the moment, served as more storage, at least partially.

From there she made her way to another hallway in the part of the school that was finished. Here she found the offices and sleeping quarters of the priests. The Methodists only had their priests, with no nuns like the Catholics. Methodists did, however, have permission to marry, and so sometimes brought their wives and children with them to the schools. Quietly pushing open the doors and looking in, Akłaq found only a few priests, with no wives to speak of. Probably they would be sent for once the school was complete.

A creak of the floorboards caused her to freeze and Band and look around. No alarm had been raised, and she'd found no evidence of a bed being slept in but its occupant missing. When she peeked around a corner, she found Gáx and Latseen. Gáx was leading, and his expression was just beginning to contort into a grimace upon hearing the floorboard under his foot.

Breathing a sigh of relief, Akłaq returned to her previous position and released the Band. A moment later, her children appeared. Gáx still looked a bit guilty about the floorboard, but it was Latseen's expression that was most curious. Akłaq Banded the three of them so they could speak privately.

"I understand why they do it, and I know it's coming, but I still can't stop stepping on the creaky floorboards," Gáx blurted.

Akłaq grinned. "Don't worry about it—"

"We won't have to," Latseen said. "There's no one here."

Akłaq gave her a look. "What?"

"There are no children in this school. Gáx and I looked everywhere. It's completely empty."

"Show me."

This school had only three floors. Having already done a sweep of the first floor, Akłaq followed Latseen and Gáx to the second. There were more classrooms and partial classrooms and storage rooms, as well as some rooms whose purpose was, for the time being, unknown. But the more they looked, the more Akłaq realized that there was indeed something missing from all of this. The priests, no matter the denomination, valued order and cleanliness. There was a place for everything and everything had a place. True, the ongoing construction made this a difficult principle to keep, but even so, there was, she saw, a distinct lack of anything childlike. There were paper and pens, yes, but the pages were all blank, the pens untouched. Even the papers on the teachers' desks were blank, no lessons, no notes, no lists, not even an odd drawing. The blackboards were perfectly clean; they didn't have the dusty sheen from writing and erasing that day's lesson.

They made their way to the third floor. There was less clutter here which made it easier to get around. The doors to the dormitory were already open, and they walked inside. The strangeness of the place was starting to make Akłaq a little skittish, and she crept around like a cat. There were beds already set up, and a dozen more were in pieces at one end of the room, awaiting assembly. But, as Latseen and Gáx had said, there were no children anywhere.

"Did we get the wrong school?" Gáx wondered.

Akłaq jumped a little at the sound of his voice, and she turned to face her children who had stopped at the doors. "Let's go back downstairs. I want to see something."

They moved quickly. Only because Akłaq used Sound to muffle their steps did they move quietly. All the way to the first floor and to the sleeping quarters of the priests. Now, rather than just look from the door, she went up to one of the beds. There were lumps under the blanket, but as she neared, she saw they did not twitch nor breathe. She ripped the blanket back to find bunched up pillows, clothes, and blankets tied with twine to resemble a human shape. Tied horsehair provided a sort of wig at the head.

"We've been set up," Akłaq said, backing away. She turned to Latseen and Gáx. "Go! Run!"

They started to run, but they only got to the front entry before they stopped. Frederickson and two more were waiting for them. Looking down the hall to the back door, three more were entering the building. Akłaq was willing to bet that there were even more surrounding the place, waiting for them to make a break for the side doors or a window.

"Well, well," Frederickson said, with the same attitude he'd carried in the Upper Fort Garry jail. "Akłaq Balabinov. We meet again."

"Been a while," she acknowledged, trying to figure a way out. "At least since you murdered Aniqan at Upper Fort Garry."

"Has it been that long? My, how times flies. And look. Your children are all grown up, aren't they?"

"Leave them out of this," Akłaq warned. "Your fight is with me alone."

He shrugged lazily, moving his arms in such a way that it drew her gaze to the pistol at his hip. "Oh, well, yes, you see, it was with you alone. You and the others who escaped. And maybe I would have let things slide a little, let bygones be bygones, except then you just had to go and start meddling again. Look at the chaos you've caused this summer alone, taking all these children out of school."

"You're kidnapping them from their homes, their families, their people. You are turning them into something wholly unrecognizable, cutting them off from their history and heritage. You are erasing us!"

"On the contrary," he said, never raising his voice, "we are improving you. Helping you. We're opening your minds to the bigger world, to art and culture and literature. Tell me, what's so wrong about that?"

In her peripheral vision, Akłaq saw the three men from the back door block the other hallways leading to the front entry where they stood. "Learning is not wrong. But the denial of learning about oneself, punishing children for being who and what they are, beating them for speaking the tongue of their ancestors, that is what's wrong here. That is what we're here to stop."

Frederickson nodded slowly. "An interesting compromise. Unfortunately, history has proven that if you suffer one devil to remain in your home, that devil will always bring others."

"Then the eastern peoples should never have allowed your first ships to reach shore."

"Big words from someone who married a Russian invader and bore his children."

Akłaq did not initially have a plan for what she was going to do if she did end up attacking Frederickson, but one came to her fairly quickly, and for that, she was grateful. She lunged toward him as if to fight him physically, something she knew would not go well for her. With her heightened perception of time, as well as a bit of Banding on her part, she was able to see and calculate the reactions from the others.

Frederickson was the Regional Manager; this was known, and it was not surprising to see him reach for a Band. The two men with him also started building Bands around themselves. Maybe they were a couple of Captains, maybe not, but they were Timekeepers anyway.

Glancing behind her, where Latseen and Gáx were preparing to fend off the other three men, Akłaq saw that those three were also reaching for Bands. So everyone here was aware of Time and what was about to happen. Not that she wouldn't have Banded or done anything if they weren't aware—Upper Fort Garry proved that much—but it gave her an idea of what she was up against.

But whether they were average Timekeepers or the Regional Manager, they were Timekeepers only, Time Agents only. They had no Akari abilities to speak of.

Akłaq pulled up from her physical attack at the last second. Frederickson, using his Time Band, entered her plane of Time and drew his gun. She let him do this and waited for him to pull the trigger. When he did, she did two things. First, she used an Akari Band to avoid the Time Tendrils he thrust at her, trying to keep her in place in the plane and so unable to dodge the bullet. She dodged the bullet, then used Sound to not only reflect the soundwaves back at him and his two men, but amplify them.

All of the glass behind them, in the windows and the door, shattered, and the force knocked the three of them off balance. They all lost their Bands, and they put their hands to their ears, shrieking in pain. The two helpers lost their guns, which Akłaq scooped up. She turned around to see her children struggling to stay ahead of the other three men and their Bands and Tendrils. Akłaq Banded and fired off a round from each pistol. With her invisible Akari Band and their attention taken by Latseen and Gáx, two of the men were unable to see or dodge the shots and they went down in a heap. The third man, startled, leaped back a good ten feet, dropping his Band.

Akłaq shoved the two guns into her children's hands and pushed them toward the door, yelling at them to run before Frederickson and the others recovered. The two of them took off, and Akłaq bent down to grab the guns off the two men she'd just killed.

Latseen and Gáx made it out of the building. Akłaq could have, too, but she paused for half a moment. Frederickson was nearly recovered, but the concussion from the soundwave made it difficult for him to

Band and get his bearings.

"You will never harm another child," Akłaq hissed at him.

She put a gun under his chin and fired. He was dead before he hit the ground. With only so much room, Akłaq discarded the previous gun and took Frederickson's. She looked at the three remaining men. Two were still dazed from the soundwave and the third looked too afraid to try anything. Probably he was still trying to comprehend everything that had just happened. Runners weren't supposed to be this powerful. Runners weren't supposed to be able to escape Time Tendrils, and they definitely weren't supposed to be able to do whatever it was she'd done with the guns and the soundwaves.

She decided to let them live. As she herself had said, the fight was between her and Frederickson, and now Frederickson was dead. The others might come after her, true, but she would deal with it then. In the moment, she had no quarrel with these men.

Once outside the school, Akłaq discovered that there were indeed more men waiting for them. But these were common policing agents, with no awareness of Time whatsoever. She didn't see Latseen or Gáx, so she assumed they had simply Banded and run to their agreed meeting spot. Indeed, when she did the same, she discovered that was exactly the case.

"Are we safe now?" Latseen asked.

Both her children were sitting on the ground, shaking. Latseen had dropped her gun several feet away and was now crying. Gáx still held onto his gun with white knuckles, looking a bit listless.

"Well, we got away anyway," Akłaq said. She sat down between them and pulled them both to her, like a hen gathering chicks under her wings. "Frederickson is dead, but I let the other three live. I don't think they'll actively come after us again tonight, but we can't stay here anyway."

Latseen wiped her face. "How did they know we were coming?"

Akłaq sighed. "Because they sent us here intentionally. I'd be willing to bet that the girl who told us that her brother was here—"

"She was a traitor," Latseen finished. "A plant."

"A weed is more like it," Gáx mumbled.

"We need to tell her people what she's done. She could have gotten us killed. She could have gotten others killed."

"She's probably long gone by now," Akłaq told her. "I'll bet that she ran away from her village that very same night, made it to the nearest town and sent a message to Frederickson that their plan was in motion. She's probably already back in another school."

"But why would she do such a thing?" Latseen asked. "Why would anyone do that to their own people?"

There were any number of things Akłaq could tell her, but for the moment she just ran her fingers through her daughter's hair and said, "I don't know, child. I don't know." She stood. "Come on, we have to get moving. It's time to go north."

Latseen and Gáx were slow to move.

"We can't do one more school?" Gáx wondered. "One more actual school?"

"No," Akłaq told him. "This is one instance where I think running is a very wise course of action. We need to meet up with the others in the northern clans and rest over the winter. Then we'll decide what to do come spring."

Neither child argued.

Latseen surrendered her pack. It was one she used to carry small possessions that the children might want to bring, things like dolls or a small craft. Now Akłaq used it to hold the guns they'd taken. Gáx had to practically pry his fingers off of his, but he set it in the bag with the other three.

The wagon they had stolen and placed on the road in order to carry the children was now gone, confiscated by the local police. Instead, with Akłaq Banding them through any uncertain spots, they walked to the closest town, only about five miles away. There they stole a few horses and rode off north. Akłaq continued to Band them until they were well clear of the area, then dropped it. Mostly it was for the safety of the horses, both hazards in the road and the potential risk of exposing them to Time.

"We really are Runners, aren't we?" Gáx said after a while. The sky was finally beginning to lighten.

"We're running, aren't we?" Latseen retorted, still sounding sullen herself.

"What do you mean?" Akłaq asked calmly.

"Grandfather told us stories about Ujurak and the work you did in the village. He told us about the Time industry, the Wheel, the Hands. He told us about the Timekeepers and the ranks. He made it sound so official and so...good. And yet, here we are, running from them. I mean, you just killed the Regional Manager. From every story I've heard, and what Grandfather and even Everett have told us, we're Runners. Does that make us bad?"

She hesitated. "I don't think it's about Timekeepers and Runners. Maybe back in Ujurak's time, when the Harvesters would take the Time Capsules for themselves rather than selling them to the Merchants. But what we're doing here, it goes beyond that. We are trying to liberate children who have been stolen from their families. Now, we could do this even without Time, without the Akari. It's been tried before, just no one has succeeded on the scale that we have. We are simply using greater tools that are available to us." She went on before Latseen or Gáx could speak. "Everett once told me that you could kill a man with Time and the Hands wouldn't bat an eye. All they cared about were the Time Capsules and the money to be made from them. Frederickson probably could have made a case before the Hands about how I killed Gerald, and now him, too. A case could probably be made against us because we use the Akari over Time. But this business with the schools..." She shook her head. "That was purely Earth-side justice. Or lack thereof."

"I don't understand," Gáx admitted.

"Those in power make rules for others that they themselves don't have to follow. And those rules can be twisted and reinterpreted to mean anything they want them to mean in order to ensnare others."

"How do we stop them?" Latseen wondered.

"I don't know, but I think we gave them a good run for their money this summer," Akłaq said, trying to cheer them up a little. When it didn't appear to work, she added, "All our peoples have been trying to figure that out since before my time. And I don't think we're going to find an answer to that today."

It was not a heartening statement, and the journey north was mostly silent. By the time they made it back to the reserve, Akłaq expected everyone to know about what happened. To what degree she did not know, but they would hear something. She thought about making a few detours to some of the other reserves where they had already returned children, to see if they'd managed to keep the children. That idea was quickly dismissed; she didn't know if any of them could handle the thought of their work being in vain. So they bypassed side roads and trails to the reserves, instead plodding ever north.

Actually she thought about also skipping the Tlingit reserve entirely and just going north. Putu had promised to pack up their things and keep them safe, so there wasn't much reason to return other than to talk to K'alyaan and any who remained.

After some time, as they put the incident further and farther behind them, Akłaq felt her more rational thoughts returning. Yes, it was unfortunate that the last expedition had been a trap, but it wasn't as though they had actually lost any children. No one had died other than those who deserved it. Yes, it hurt to think that there had been a traitor in the previous group, the one who had pointed them to the trap, but was there any reason to think there hadn't been other traitors in other groups? Maybe there had been previous attempts at getting them to go here or there but they all failed for whatever reason. After all, once they freed a group of children, it wasn't uncommon for a dozen of them to come up and tell them about this or that school where this or that brother or sister was being kept. They couldn't get around to all of them at once. They just happened to pick the wrong one this time.

So it really wasn't that bad. Akłaq more suspected that Latseen and Gáx were out of sorts because of the violence and watching their mother kill two men right in front of them, plus the knowledge that she had killed a third after they ran away. It was an idea that had probably always been in the back of their minds, that they might have to face some physical opposition, but the Akari and their Bands had rendered that threat all but moot except against the Timekeepers. Now they'd had to face that threat.

She would have to talk to them about it, Akłaq decided. That would be a conversation to have once they left the reserve and headed north. It would give her time to consider what she wanted to say. She had no regrets; she knew why she'd done it. The first two had been threatening her children. Frederickson had been hunting her for years. But Latseen and Gáx would not see it that way. They had been sheltered for a lot of years, and many concepts had been but abstract ideas until just recently. Looking at them now, they seemed to be recovering, as she was, with time and distance, but the thoughts would remain in their minds. If they weren't addressed, those thoughts could become toxic, festering wounds. She couldn't let that happen; she had to help them deal with it.

By the time they reached the reserve and rode into the village, Akłaq thought they didn't look so depressed. The smiling faces of the villagers who remained helped to reinforce the point that they had still done a lot of good over the summer. Looking at her children, their spirits appeared refreshed as well.

K'alyaan met them at their house, now devoid of occupants.

"We heard much good news over the summer," he said, smiling. He'd aged quite a bit in the time that Akłaq had lived with the Tlingit, and now, being gone all summer, he appeared to have aged even more. "Many families are whole again, thanks to you."

"It was not as easy as the rumors would have you believe," Akłaq told him diplomatically. "Have all the children been able to stay with their families?"

"Many of them, yes. From the reports we heard, once you started making a real name for yourselves, the white men became less concerned with kidnapping more children, instead focusing on how to keep the children they had already taken. With any luck, your endeavors will keep them scrambling for a while longer yet and take us into winter when they will not be so keen about moving people here and there. And by then, something more might be done, something more widespread than just three people wreaking havoc in the middle of the night."

He looked too optimistic for Akłaq to want to burden him with the tale of their recent failure and the murder of three men. Instead, she just thanked him, cited fatigue, and walked in the house like normal, Latseen and Gáx following.

Basic furniture still remained, but all small possessions had been removed. This didn't bother them one bit as they all found somewhere to sleep.

They were back on their horses before the sun was up, this time heading north. Truthfully, Akłaq didn't know exactly where they were going; she'd never been to Tlingit land before, and even so, she was oriented to everything from north to south, not south to north. K'alyaan had given her a map and some verbal directions, but when every tree and rock and bend in the trail was brand new, those directions felt foolish and distant.

"How are you guys doing?" she asked of her children one afternoon.

"When does the needing less food start to manifest itself?" Latseen wondered. "I'm hungry."

"It'll be a few more years for you. Here." Akłaq tossed a small pack of jerky to her. "Gáx?"

He just waved a hand dismissively, not looking at her.

Akłaq frowned. "Gáx, there's something on your mind. I know there is on your mind, too, Latseen." She shifted on her horse. "I know this summer, this past year even, has been...eventful. Exciting, maybe, too. And we did a lot of good. But I think that last incident is still buzzing around your minds like an annoying fly. Am I wrong?"

Latseen made the excuse that she was eating.

"Gáx?" Akłaq prompted.

"The elders like to tell stories of old, great warriors and the things they did," he said, still not quite looking at her. "Fighting bears and spirit creatures, going on great adventures to far away places that can't be seen by normal men." He met her gaze for a brief moment. "I thought this would be like that. You had special spirit powers, and we were going on adventures to distant places and doing good for the people."

"That's right."

He shook his head. "I didn't...I didn't know it would be like that."

"Like what?"

"I guess it never occurred to me that when the old warriors fought the spirit creatures, that the spirit creatures fought back."

Akłaq shifted. "Yes, they do."

"But the Timekeepers...they have powers like we do, like the spirit creatures, except they're still men."

"That's right."

His expression turned puzzled, and Akłaq suspected they were getting to the heart of his anxiety. "You talk about the white bear, and following the white bear. We've all heard the stories of the spirits, of creation, and the old warriors. Does this mean that we have the power of the good spirits, and the Timekeepers have the power of the bad ones? Wouldn't that make Grandfather a servant of the bad spirits?"

She blinked. "I wouldn't believe that for a moment."

"Well, I don't mean so intentionally, like Frederickson, but casual compliance is just as bad, isn't it? Maybe the people in the various towns didn't kidnap the children themselves, but they agreed with everything that was going on."

"Grandfather risked his life to get everyone to safety."

"Yes, in the physical world. But what if his Timekeeping and keeping with the evil spirits is providing them an anchor to draw men like Frederickson to us, to thwart our plans?" He kept going, the words pouring from his mouth. "And if these powers of the good and bad spirits can be taught to anyone, and not just the chosen few, then what is the point of the spirits in the first place? And if we still need the spirits and work on their behalf, then how is it any different from the Christians and their angels and demons and gods and devils and the men who serve one side or another through will or compliance? Why is it that compliance is always an act of evil, while good must always be an act of will?"

Akłaq had been so convinced that his problems revolved around her that she was entirely unprepared to consider that maybe his thoughts actually went beyond her to a deeper, more meaningful line of thought. Her gaze darted to Latseen, but her daughter looked just as surprised by her brother's outburst and hurriedly shoved another piece of jerky in her mouth before she was made to voice her opinions as well.

After a long few minutes of listening to the wind in the trees, morning birdsong, and the occasional snort by one of their horses, Akłaq admitted, "I don't know how to answer your questions."

Gáx shrugged. "I didn't think you would."

"Why is that?"

"Because if you could, I don't think we'd be in the predicament we are."

She considered this for a moment. "I admit that we probably would have done some things differently, and maybe we wouldn't have walked into that trap, but if you're talking about having to move the children and flee north, I think we'd still be in this situation."

"Why is that?"

"Because, first of all, there is a lot of evil in the world. And there are a lot of men who serve evil willingly. And you're not wrong in your observation that good is almost always an act of will, whereas compliance usually leads to evil. It would take a lot more than three people to overcome the evil we face, because we are not fighting merely an animal that can be slain; we fight a mindset, an entire culture, ideas themselves. You can't force a man to change his mind or beliefs, and the mind can be the freest of lands or the worst of prisons."

He gave her a forlorn look. "Does evil always win?"

"Do you think we'd be here if it did? I know we've seen a lot of bad things, but there is good in the world, too. And even if good must be an act of will, it does not always have to be a grand effort. K'alyaan and Naakilaan and the others staying on the reserve and not fleeing north, for example."

Now Latseen spoke up. "The white men and the priests think they're doing good by taking children and forcing them to be a certain way. But you told Frederickson that the schools were good. Which good is real good?"

Akłaq put up a finger. "I said learning is good. You can learn anything from anyone if you've an open mind. But change should be voluntary, not forced through kidnapping under the cover of darkness and killing any who oppose."

"Considering that we lived in a white-style home, speak a white language, and do other white things, how voluntary is it, really?" Gáx asked. "And why don't they learn anything from us? Why don't they learn our way of hunting or fishing or beading or crafting? Why don't they learn our languages?"

Akłaq sighed. "As I said, change must be voluntary. We fight ideas and the evil of complacency."

For a long time, no one spoke. Then Gáx asked, "A lot of people don't really like or trust Everett. They think he's too white. But he's helped us a lot."

"Yes, he has," Akłaq said, nodding. "We should be grateful."

"He dresses white, talks white, but he has the power of the good spirits and helps the people. Does that mean that the others are wrong to dislike or mistrust him?"

"I would say so, but it's not up to me to prove that to them. Nothing I do can change their minds about him."

"But he's treated badly by the whites, isn't he?"

"Yes, he is."

Her son looked ready to say more, but at the last moment, he seemed to retreat, no doubt with a whole new line of thought and questions.

Akłaq knew it was going to be a long ride.

Avgun Iñuiñaq Tallimat Malġuk
In Hiding

Putu and Everett had taken the children to one of the Tlingit villages on an island nestled in a string of islands in some thick marshland that was difficult to get to except by canoe. It was a wise decision, but no less frustrating for Akłaq, Latseen, and Gáx who had to carefully navigate out to said island.

Even so, it was good to walk into the village and see the children playing freely, without fear of being snatched away by soldiers. Tlaganis, Nooskw, and Tula'aan came running to meet them, and any lingering frustrations about the trip melted from Akłaq's mind as she embraced her children who she hadn't seen for the better part of a year.

In her peripheral vision, she noticed Putu and Everett across the way, trying not to intrude on the moment but their expressions almost demanding a report. Akłaq straightened, sent Latseen and Gáx off with their siblings, then went to meet the men.

"You made it," she said, grinning.

"So did you," Everett observed.

"What news?" Putu inquired. "By the time we got out here, we were just starting to hear of some of your antics in the south, but I'm afraid we are also some of the last to hear."

Akłaq glanced at the children. Gáx had Tula'aan on his shoulders, and Latseen was playing with a couple other young girls. Tlaganis and Nooskw were off bothering a few girls their own age, trying to impress them in some fashion. She looked back at the men. "Is there a place we can speak privately?"

The northern Tlingit were more connected to the old ways than

K'alyaan, and they still lived in their traditional huts. Branches and bent sticks formed a shell which was then covered with bark, mud, leaves, animal skins, anything that would keep out the elements. The three of them ducked into Everett's hut, a sparse thing, as he liked to keep it.

Without being prompted, Akłaq told them everything as best she could remember. The summer had been wildly successful with hundreds of children returned to their families and frustrated police and soldiers trying to contain what they perceived to be utter chaos. This gave Everett a good laugh, and even Putu managed to smile.

Then came the hard part, where she had to admit to being lured into a trap, and she reluctantly relayed the events at the last school, where she'd had to kill three of the men, including Frederickson. She opened the pack she'd kept with her ever since and laid out the four pistols.

"Well, that changes things a little," Putu said, shifting uncomfortably. "You know this means you won't be able to go back next year."

"But—"

"He's right," Everett agreed. "Not only are they going to step it up against the people when they go back to stealing children, but they'll be looking for you specifically. They may even use the manhunt for you as an excuse to raid the reserves, if they think they're harboring a fugitive."

Akłaq blinked. "What did you expect me to do, let them kill us or take my children?"

"Absolutely not," Putu stated. "You did as you had to do, but I fear that the setup was more complex than you may have given it credit for. If they captured you, then they captured you. If you escaped, then it would have been an eternal game of cat and mouse until something drastic happened. In forcing the situation, no matter what, they come out on top. By murdering three of them, especially Frederickson, that door is shut and sealed."

"So everything we did this summer...was for nothing."

"Maybe not," Everett answered, cutting off Putu. "It could very well be that you inspired something in the people to actually defend their children when the white men come again. But I do think that your work specifically is finished."

She sighed and went back on her elbows. She shifted position and rubbed her eyes. "Well, it was all just extra anyway, right? A diversion, so you could bring the Tlingit children here. At least that was accomplished. And Frederickson is dead, so he won't be able to track us here; his menace is gone."

Everett nodded emphatically. "Both very good things."

"Do we have anything to fear from the Timekeepers?"

"Akłaq, you murdered the Regional Manager plus two more," Putu said bluntly. "You think the others are going to be happy about that?"

"I guess not."

"They're probably not going to do anything more than they already have been," Everett pointed out. "They've been after us for how many years now? Since you killed Goldsmith? Since Upper Fort Garry? It won't be anything out of the ordinary, and we're pretty safe out here on this remote island."

"What about the Yukon school?" Akłaq asked, feeling miserable.

"Still quiet," Putu said. "But you might have noticed that this island is hard to get to and easily defended. No one is coming after the children here."

As she leaned back, rubbing her face, she made a sort of groaning noise that ended in something resembling a sigh. "At least it's something. Like I said, the southern schools were a bonus, a distraction. This is what mattered, this was what we were called here to do."

"And now that it's over, is it still what you're called to do?" Everett questioned sagely.

"I don't know, but I'm too tired to think about that right this moment."

They gave her directions to a hut which had been set aside for her and her children once she returned, and she went straight there. It was empty, but the younger children had been staying with other relatives while she had been away. She knew she would have to bring them back over at some point, but for the moment, it afforded her some peace and quiet.

She'd said she was tired, and she certainly did feel this way to some extent, though when she lay down, she found she was wide awake. It was her first real chance to relax in months, and now her mind was intent on reviewing everything that had happened. Sometimes they were funny memories, minor antics that happened on the road or when they had a crop of children they were returning. Sometimes they were tense memories, all the fear that naturally enveloped the situations they found themselves in as they sneaked past bells, guard dogs, sleeping priests, and squeaky floorboards. Many times, however, her mind circled back to the standoff.

Was there any way it could have gone differently? Each time she ran the scenario, she concluded that killing Frederickson had been the only absolute, else, as Everett said, it would have been an eternal game of cat and mouse. And as he'd had no qualms about killing her, it was clearly a case of self-defense. The other two? Well, they had been attacking her children, making it an even more righteous case of defense of children. She'd let the others live, but did it count for anything, or was it just a matter of letting them plan their own revenge?

And what about Gerald? Granted, it may have been some sort of revenge for Ujurak and the others, but she didn't know that at the time. In the heat of the moment it had been sheer frustration and anger.

And why feel guilty about this now? Why question herself now? Frederickson, fine, that was more recent, but she thought she'd already dealt with her feelings about Gerald. She'd dealt with that over the winter before she and Aniqan moved to Red River.

"Because it's not natural for one soul to take another."

At some point, lying in the cool darkness of the hut, Akłaq had fallen asleep, and now she woke in an unfamiliar place. Sitting up, it appeared to be meadow of some form, with tall grass littered with white flowers, like sea foam. Looking around, she spotted Anagalisgi walking toward her.

"What is this place?" she asked, getting to her feet.

"Somewhere we can meet when we are still far apart," Anagalisgi told her. "A place for you to see and understand the stakes of our work."

He motioned for her to follow.

As they crossed the meadow, Akłaq noticed a number of white animals poking their heads up from the grass. A few deer, an elk, a moose, rabbits and hares. Then, in the distance, she saw dark clouds gathering. They crested a rise and about half a mile away, the meadow abruptly ended. She saw some white trees, but only because they were starkly contrasted by a thick, black forest beyond. The sky overhead was crisp and blue, but the sky over there was black and menacing. Still they approached, and she saw another man standing near the tree line, his posture suggesting that he was not in the best mood. Her gaze darted back to the dark forest where shadows seemed to flit from branch to branch or bush to bush.

"Akłaq, may I introduce to you my nephew, Sabelu," Anagalisgi began in a friendly manner.

The second man, Sabelu, turned. He was young in appearance, not more than twenty, but his expression and especially his eyes said that he was far older than that. He did bear some familial resemblance to Anagalisgi, and it was a minute before Akłaq recalled that he had indeed appeared at the end of the Krydik's second Book.

"You're the prophet," she stated dumbly.

"Prophet," he grumbled. "Dark seer. Harbinger of destruction. Take your pick." He looked at his uncle, technically great-uncle. "Why are we here?"

"Because you need to work together," Anagalisgi said. His words were kind, but his expression told a different story; he was both saddened and annoyed by Sabelu's apparent bad mood. He looked at Akłaq. "You have done well to rescue the children from the schools.

Not only your own, but others."

"But did it really make a difference?" Akłaq asked. "The soldiers only have to go and kidnap the children again. After what I've done, I won't be able to save them."

Sabelu looked like he had something to say, but his uncle cut in before he could open his mouth. "You have shown them that escape is possible."

Sabelu shifted his stance. "They'll need it, considering the next fifty, sixty, seventy years are going to be only—"

"Silence, pup!" Anagalisgi snapped, giving his nephew a look. He turned back to Akłaq. "Escape is possible. They know this now. Like you, they are beginning to understand that where they are is not where they will always be. You have known this as both good and bad, and such is the way of things in this life. But you must show it to them for the better."

Akłaq shook her head. "I don't understand."

"Most of the time, you won't," Sabelu muttered.

"You must give the people a place to escape to," Anagalisgi said.

Akłaq blinked. "What, like Aktiya Waya?"

"Preferably not," Sabelu interjected.

Anagalisgi huffed. "Sabelu—"

"You knew what would happen. If you were really that concerned, you would have had us meet in person."

"What do you mean?" Akłaq wondered. "What happens? What's going on?"

"Dream-walking does things to him," Anagalisgi sighed. "It is the weakest, but also the strongest, barrier between dimensions. Some don't consider it a barrier at all, but a nexus of Time and Space."

She just blinked.

"I can't stop the visions on a normal day when I'm awake. It's like I'm constantly flooded with them," Sabelu stated crassly. "Coming here is like drowning."

"Then why are we here?" she inquired. "Why not have us meet in person?"

"Do you really think it would go well between Sabelu, Putu, and Everett?" Anagalisgi countered.

She considered this for a moment, then said, "Probably not."

"And anyway, the reason we're here, the reason he's here, really, and could have already been gone by now—" Anagalisgi gave Sabelu another look. "—is because there should be some coordination between Earth and Hlohi, between the Krydik and District Nine."

"How so? For what?"

"For the preservation and restoration of the people. Those schools and other policies will seek to destroy us. And, in some cases, they will be successful. You must be the force that pushes back."

"How do we even begin something like that?"

Anagalisgi grinned. "You already have. You must build on what you have already done." His smiled faded and he turned to Sabelu. "Tell Galiliga and Netami to meet with Akłaq."

"In the fortress, I'm guessing," Sabelu said sourly.

"That's right."

"The Akarin fortress?" Akłaq wondered.

Anagalisgi nodded. "The very same."

"The Akarin will help our people then?"

Again Sabelu made to speak, but Anagalisgi cut in, saying, "They'll not be allies as in war, but the fortress is a good place to meet. Neutral territory as it were. And it affords the opportunity to practice your abilities." He looked at Sabelu. "Go now, to your brother and sister."

Sabelu looked ready to refuse or say something else, but finally he nodded and started walking away, through the meadow. Then he crested the rise and vanished. Anagalisgi and Akłaq watched him leave.

"You were a prophet, too," Akłaq stated. "But in the Books you seemed so...kind about it."

"Because I was and am a prophet only," Anagalisgi said. "I live in the present and occasionally see things about the future, things which should be known only at specific times and told to specific people."

"And Sabelu?"

"He is a fire keeper, a truth teller. Some might call him an oracle, albeit a bad-tempered one. He sees the things that have been and the things that will be. The problem is that he sees all of it all the time for all the peoples. He knows the full history of Aktiya Waya. He knows their future. He knows the triumphs of every man, but also the dark secrets he keeps hidden away. He knows every tradition your people ever kept, and he knows every detail about the day your village burned."

Akłaq didn't even try to stop her expression from turning astonished. "That's...amazing. But I can see how it might be a burden, too."

Anagalisgi nodded. "Well, it doesn't help that, for as much as men proclaim that they want to hear only the truth, few actually do and even fewer handle it well."

"Then why bring him here? Are only certain people permitted to come to this place?" She looked around, trying to stay focused on the meadow and the white forest, but unable to stop an occasional glance at the dark forest.

"I'm trying to help him get a handle on the dreams and visions, bring them under some semblance of control so he doesn't do something stupid. Believe it or not, this actually went very well."

"I'd hate to see him on a normal day."

"He's not so bad in the waking world. As I said, this place is a nexus of Time and Space, where the knowledge and the visions flow freely. In the waking world, he has a better handle on things. His personality remains pretty sour, but he can manage." Anagalisgi shifted his stance. "But his problems are not yours. It is Galiliga and Netami you will be speaking to."

Akłaq nodded uncertainly. "Everett will have to take me to the fortress; will he be part of this as well?"

"He will, yes. And Putu. And your children."

She breathed a sigh of relief.

Anagalisgi grinned. "Sometimes good things do happen."

"Sometimes bad things happen, too."

He turned to face the forest, the white trees almost blinding against the dark ones. "Tell me, Akłaq. Do you believe evil is powerless?"

She gave him a look. "No, or else it wouldn't be so difficult to overcome."

"Then why do people act surprised when they take a hit in a fight? Why do they act surprised that there is a war at all?"

"Maybe it's not about the force of evil, but the lack of force of good."

"And is not compliance, evil? And good, an act of will?" He looked at her and raised a brow.

She met his expression. "Were you listening to our conversation, or did you have a hand in it?"

He laughed. "Gáx is a curious lad. Troubled and wrestling with questions he does not understand, the same as everyone does when they realize there is more beyond themselves, but not unteachable. You did well with him."

Akłaq couldn't help but feel a bit of pride at that.

"Now go," Anagalisgi said, still smiling. "Your work is not yet finished."

She nodded. "Thank you."

Now he faltered, just a touch. "Don't thank me yet."

She wanted to ask him more, but he would say nothing other than to wake and continue her work. Unsure of just how to leave the meadow, she figured her best bet was to just start walking.

Akłaq turned and found herself rolling over. She was back in her hut. Well, back might have been a misnomer; she couldn't have actually gone anywhere, right? She decided not to think about the implications of that and instead moved to sit up and stretch. She felt remarkably well-rested, considering how real it had all felt. She remembered the feel of the grass, the smell of the flowers. It was like she had actually been there.

She decided not to think about it. She had work to do, after all.

Akłaq stood and stretched one more time before ducking out of the hut, quite unprepared for the sudden, marshy wind and damp air, the morning fog obscuring everything three feet in front of her. It brought her fully back to reality, and she felt like a blind person as she made her way around the village. Finally she made it to Everett's hut and called inside. She heard some movement, and then, "What is it? Who is it?"

"It's Akłaq."

A moment later, he exited his hut, looking like he'd just woken up. "Everything all right?"

"We have work to do," she told him. "We need to go to the Akarin fortress."

"Now? Is everything all right?"

"I'll explain when we get there. Or maybe they will."

"Who's they?"

"Galiliga and Netami."

Everett rubbed his eyes. "How do you know them?"

"Please, Everett?"

He sighed but agreed. "Fine. If only for my own curiosity."

Not five minutes later they were in the Akarin fortress. It was amazing to see it after so many years, and it hadn't changed a bit. Akłaq recovered quickly from the Paa, but Everett took a little longer.

"This place is huge," she said, looking up the center of the spiral staircase. "Is there a normal meeting place for this sort of thing?"

"If you didn't specify a place," Everett said, sounding a tad annoyed, "then you might wait in the cafeteria."

The cafeteria was located in the south corridor on the first floor. They didn't even make it that far before someone called out to them, or rather, to Everett. They stopped and turned.

Two more humans, a man and a woman, crossed the open atrium under the stairs, heading their way. There was definitely a family resemblance to Sabelu, and Akłaq surmised that they were Galiliga and Netami.

"Long time no see," Netami greeted, still speaking to Everett. Her words were friendly enough, but there was a certain wariness in her tone that Akłaq found strange. "How are things in the Old Land?"

"Bad, as usual," Everett replied, his tone also very formal.

"You must be Akłaq," Galiliga guessed, nodding to her.

"And you must be Galiliga and Netami," Akłaq said, trying to bring some friendliness to the conversation.

"That's right."

"Maybe we should get something to eat?" Everett suggested.

The four of them retreated to the cafeteria. Akłaq didn't know what to expect for food, but the cube that she was given was not high on the list of possibilities. It looked strange and tasted even stranger. Galiliga and Netami had similar expressions.

"It's made for nutrition, not taste," Everett said.

"Everett, if this is what you've been living on..." Netami began.

"Hardly," he interrupted. "I have the same capabilities you do. Maybe even better."

Akłaq shifted uncomfortably. "I'm sorry, I feel like I'm missing something. And I feel like whatever it is, it's only going to hinder our efforts."

Everett huffed in sudden annoyance, set down his fork, and leaned back. "You remember how I told you that I was rescued as a child, taken to Aktiya Waya, and then I left?"

"Yes?"

"All true, but not the whole truth. When I was a young man, not more than fourteen, my mother and father were part of a small uprising against Yvgidahi. My father was executed for his role, but my mother was permitted to take me and return to Earth."

Akłaq blinked. "But, in the Books, the people of the uprising hated the sorceries, the Akari."

Everett nodded. "Yes, and my mother still does. Or did. As for me, I was determined to learn them. I don't know if I wanted to try and return to Hlohi and become part of Krydik life again, or if I wanted to learn it so I could kill Yvgidahi with his own weapon. Thankfully, the Author rescued me and brought me to a good place among the Akarin. But relations with the Krydik have always been...awkward."

"They don't have to be," Netami said. "It has been many years, and you know Yvgidahi is dead."

"Maybe so, but it was your father that my father tried to kill."

"We still fought on the same side in the war," Galiliga told him. "And it sounds like we may not have the luxury of grudges, if Sabelu is to be believed."

"He's never been a liar," Netami defended. "He just has a difficult time articulating what he sees."

"Polite way of saying he has a shit personality."

"I know what happened with Anagalisgi," Akłaq said. "What did Sabelu tell you about it?"

It was Galiliga who answered, and Akłaq told herself that his apparent dismay had more to do with the messenger than the message or the work. "He said that we have to help coordinate efforts on Earth to establish villages and safe havens for the peoples of Earth—North America, to be specific. These havens are to not only provide protection and places for the people to run to, but also operating bases for District Nine. Essentially, recreating what we have on Hlohi."

"And how much of that geography do you understand?" Everett inquired.

"I understand some, if only from the war. I suspect you know a lot more in that department. But we know more about building these villages from scratch in foreign lands."

"And with Sabelu's help," Netami added, with an eyeroll from Galiliga, "we can bring back some of the traditions that have been lost."

"Where do we even begin?" Akłaq wondered. "North America is a big place, and that's just land. Then we have to consider the white men and their empires."

"Sabelu suggested that once you get yourselves situated with the Tlingit people, you start in a place called Hudson Bay." Netami's expression said she had no idea where that was.

"Hudson Bay?" Everett questioned. He exchanged a glance with Akłaq. "That's back east again. You're sure he said Hudson Bay? Not Yukon, not Alaska?"

Now Netami and Galiliga exchanged a glance. Galiliga replied, "He said something about Alaska, but he said to avoid it for the time being. Too much attention if you start there."

Akłaq looked at Everett. "It would make sense. We started with the Tlingit. If the Timekeepers figure out where we are, they're going to assume that our next—my next destination would be home. Going east would throw them off for a time."

He nodded. "Agreed."

She shifted position. "When Ujurak and the others were killed, that wiped out basically all of the District Nine Time Agents in the north, but Putu said a couple others escaped. We'll have to find them again."

"It wouldn't be a bad idea to bring in more," Galiliga told her. "From what we've seen and heard, the peoples of the Old Land are powerless, defenseless against their captors and any who would take advantage of them. Aktiya Waya has long been an open secret among the peoples. For a long time, we assumed it was foolish pride that stopped many from coming, but perhaps that was our own error, as we send our roots deeper into our own land. An ancient oak is not easily uprooted." Akłaq thought of K'alyaan and his refusal to leave his ancestral lands. "Rather than bring the tree to water, perhaps you should bring water to the tree."

"Teach everyone about the Akari?" Everett questioned.

"Exactly. Everyone who wants to learn and everyone who doesn't. They must have some way to protect themselves and their families, and running away is not always the best answer."

"It sounds like we have some work to do," Akłaq observed, suddenly feeling overwhelmed by the task. Rescuing children from a school was one thing. Now it sounded like she was expected to rescue entire nations out of their occupation. Her standoff with Frederickson suddenly felt very...petty.

"And what about the Timekeepers?" Everett was saying. "Eventually our operation will grow, and they will come for us."

Netami didn't look concerned as she replied, "If you are the side with the greater numbers and the greater power, what do you really have to fear from a couple of Time Agents?"

She intended it as a bit of courage. Akłaq couldn't speak for Everett, but she herself was not feeling especially encouraged. If she clung to anything, it was simply the knowledge that they had a starting point. Establish the Tlingit village first and make that the first hub of operation. Once that was running smoothly, go east to Hudson Bay. Maybe by then they would have more leads and a better idea of what they were doing.

The four of them stood from the table.

"If you need help," Netami said, "we have many resources. Food, shelter, supplies. We know the white men withhold much from your people and make life very difficult. And Sabelu can offer insight into the old ways, for those who wish to learn but have nowhere else to turn."

"Although it might be smarter to ask him yourself and then impart his words of wisdom in a more pleasant manner," Galiliga said, his expression flat.

"We'll start where we are with the Tlingit and go from there," Akłaq said, trying to stay neutral, if not positive. "We have to start small and see what happens, what exactly we're getting ourselves into."

"Of course," Netami acknowledged. "Let us know if there is any way we can help. We can meet here, or I'm sure Everett knows how to get to Aktiya Waya or Lehoyed."

Everett made a strangled sort of sound and simply said, "Well, yes. Thank you." He looked terribly uncertain.

"Thank you," Akłaq said, trying to smooth things over.

The four of them left the fortress, each to his own world. Akłaq and Everett had departed from a small glade not far from the village where they hopefully wouldn't be seen, and, after waiting a minute or two to recover from the ordeal of the Paa, they made their way back. It was now well into the morning back in the village, and people were going about their morning routine, getting food or doing other chores.

Was she going to have to teach all of them the Akari? The whole

Akari, or just parts of it? She didn't even know all of it. Maybe it would be the same principle as training her children, just enough to defend themselves. How did the Krydik do it? Would she be able to visit them, maybe live with them a while and find out? On the other hand, Everett had lived with them, so he probably knew how daily life worked in that regard, what abilities were helpful and necessary.

"So you didn't join your father in the uprising?" she blurted before Everett could get too far away.

Everett paused, and it was a moment before he looked back. "No. I believed everything he said at the time, but he didn't want me to join him, not physically. I was his only son, and he wanted me to carry on in the event he was struck down by the evil sorcerers."

"But your father was half-white you said."

"Yes, and he always hated himself for that half. He was constantly fighting some invisible monster in his mind, believed himself corrupted by the white men. He wanted to do everything as in the old ways of his mother's people, the Cree, and yet, he never felt that he could, not truly. He thought Hlohi, Aktiya Waya, would purge him of his half-demon, but as he studied the nature of the sorceries, he concluded that they, too, were white demon corruption that needed to be eradicated, exterminated like pestilence."

"And your mother? If she believed similarly, why would she marry a half-breed?"

Everett shrugged. "Pity, maybe. Some belief that she could rescue his blood by giving him more pure children. Then I would be expected to marry another full-blood and increase the purity through my children, and so on. We haven't spoken since the war." He went on before she could speak. "It's been a long time, and she's probably dead by now. Even if she's not, she doesn't want to speak to me. Now then, we have our issues, like how we're going to pull off this insane plan."

Akłaq got her legs moving again and caught up to him. "Probably the same way we pulled off the insane plan to rescue a bunch of children from those schools."

"And now we're going to rescue everyone on the continent. I'm sure Putu will be entirely receptive to this idea."

The thought of explaining all of this to Putu was a bit daunting, she had to admit. At the same time, he wasn't the same man he had been in Red River. Since coming west, deciding to stop running, and taking on the role of a grandfather, he'd become a little more willing to talk plans and change and even combat. He was still quite gruff in his demeanor, but not quite as pessimistic. He might just be open to the idea of this network and rescuing the people and training them in the Akari.

"You're both mad," he declared.

This was to be expected, Akłaq told herself.

"Rescuing children is one thing. You can't rescue an entire continent," he went on.

"Why not?" Akłaq wondered.

"It's not a matter of taking them out, it's a matter of where you are taking them to. Keeping them rescued. I may not like the Krydik, but at least they understood the concept of true removal and leaving their oppressors behind, putting a very real barrier between them. You say this place will be our base of operations and that's all well and good, but we are still, fundamentally, in enemy territory. Just because our oppressors are a few hundred miles away does not mean they could not close that gap."

"And what do you suggest?" Everett wondered. "We need to provide somewhere for the people to run. We've rescued their children, now where do they go to keep them safe? Your children are safe here, but what about everyone else? And how do they protect themselves when we're not around?"

Putu folded his arms. "You sound like you're talking about arming them for war."

Everett shook his head. "No. Just because you give a man a knife does not mean you intend for him to kill someone. It is a tool for his own use. And, if something were to happen, if some threat were to arise, that knife can be used as a weapon to defend himself."

Putu grunted, gave Everett a look, then looked at Akłaq. "And the white bear told you all of this?"

"Not the white bear," she said. "Anagalisgi. And Sabelu."

"You've mentioned Anagalisgi before. Who's Sabelu?"

"Anagalisgi's nephew, who is also a prophet. He knows all things about all peoples, their history and tradition. Anything we need or want to know about the old ways, he can provide."

That seemed to intrigue Putu. "What do you mean? How does he know these things? How would he know anything about our people?"

"Anagalisgi called him a fire keeper, a truth teller. I don't know how to explain it, but I guess he has visions, constantly, of all of the people and their ancient ways. Krydik, Cree, Cherokee, all of them. We can rescue the people from physical and cultural oppression."

Putu considered this for a long moment, then finally nodded. She wondered if he would have been so willing had the two actually met in person.

"All right," Putu sighed. "Where do you want to begin? You've seen the village, it's not much. We're not exactly fortified against any kind of attack."

"We should remain discreet," Everett said. "Teach the people the Akari first. That will be a defense they can use and take with them wherever they go, regardless of any weapons or tools the soldiers confiscate."

"And the children," Akłaq added. "Latseen and Gáx were taught when they started to become adults, and I see no reason to change this, but children should not be entirely ignorant. As Everett said, take the wonder out of it so they are more prepared to handle it when they come of age."

"We should also find Lusa, Ikiaq, and Suluk," Putu said slowly. "They can help train as well, get things moving a little faster, set up some kind of hierarchy among the people, those who wish to do more than basic studies."

Everett faltered. "We're teaching them the Akari, not Time."

"Is there a real difference?"

"As a matter of fact, there is. Even if your own faith is lacking, the

Akari still encompasses abilities in Matter and Energy. Time does not."

Putu shrugged. "Then for those who want to learn Matter and Energy, they can go to you. If someone just wants to Band and run away, regular Timekeeping will work just fine. Or, as we used to do under Ujurak, Harvest the dying and preserve them in future generations."

"Why don't we just start by finding the others?" Akłaq suggested before the disagreement could brew into an argument. "We don't even know if they're still alive or what problems they might be having. The three of us can handle this village just fine on our own."

"The two of you," Putu said. At her look, he clarified, "How do you expect to find the others if someone doesn't look for them? If you want to teach the Akari to these people, then I will be of little help in that regard. With winter setting in, Everett doesn't stand a chance of finding the others."

"Oh." She hadn't thought about that.

He relented just a little. "I'll start out tomorrow morning, that way I can still say goodbye to the kids."

"Their mother was gone all summer, now their grandfather is leaving for the winter," Everett commented.

Putu ignored him and faced Akłaq. "Don't worry about me. You know I'm a survivor, and you've helped put some courage back in these bones. Honestly, it's the reason I'm willing to do this at all." She nodded reluctantly and he added, "But when I get back, whether it's in the spring or sometime later, I want to see something being done and I want to have a plan going forward. No 'maybe' or 'what if' or 'try to.' Understand?"

Akłaq couldn't help but grin. "Yes, Papa."

He smiled and pulled her into an embrace. "I'll be back." He stroked her hair once then pulled back just enough to look at her face. "I can't let you go on all the adventures."

She laughed. "No, of course not."

Then he released her and ducked out of the hut, calling for Latseen and the rest of the children.

"He really does consider you a daughter, you know," Everett said behind her.

"I know." She glanced back at him. "And I really do consider him a father."

With that, she ducked out of the hut herself. As she crossed the open area toward her own hut, slowly making a mental list of what needed to be done first, she was momentarily distracted by Putu as he picked up Tula'aan and swung her around, a huge grin on his face.

Avgun Iñuiñaq Tallimat Piñasrut
Rite of Passage

By midsummer, Putu still hadn't returned, and Akłaq couldn't wait forever to leave for Hudson Bay. The west coast was a nice place and the snow was minimal, but that wasn't true for the mountains or anywhere east of the mountains. She didn't want to push her luck if she didn't have to, and this time she felt like she actually had a plan and knew what she might be doing.

She hoped she knew what she was doing. Kneeling in her hut, packing her bags, she was acutely aware that this was going to be her mission. Latseen would be going with her, true, but Gáx was staying behind. He said it was so he could learn more under Everett, who was somewhat overseeing things, but everyone could see that he had his eye on a girl.

Akłaq looked up as something blocked her light, but it was only Latseen looking in, grinning hugely.

"Grandfather's back!" she announced, and ran off.

Abandoning her packing, Akłaq slid out of the hut and straightened, squinting against the bright sunlight. Once her eyes adjusted, she immediately spotted Putu. She almost didn't recognize the people with him except they were the ones he had gone to find: Lusa, Ikiaq, and Suluk.

Akłaq let the children mob Putu first. Although her children were growing up—Tula'aan was now eleven—he'd become something of the village's default grandfather, and the rest of the village's children had to welcome him back, too. Behind him, Lusa, Ikiaq, and Suluk looked on with some amazement, as if they couldn't figure out who this man was whom they'd been traveling with. Once Putu had sent the children away, Akłaq approached and gave him a gentler hug.

"Welcome back."

He gave her a look. "I thought you would have been gone by now."

She gestured toward her hut. "Just finishing my packing, actually. I wanted to hold out as long as possible for you."

"It's good to see you again," Lusa said.

"And you," Akłaq told her. "You didn't have too much trouble?"

"Finding them wasn't the problem," Putu said. "But your friend Sabelu was right about not expanding in this area."

Akłaq shifted her stance. "What's happened? Is it the Yukon school?"

"No," Ikiaq answered, "or not yet. Some prospectors found gold, and now miners from California are flooding the place. Thousands of them, covering the land like flies."

"They didn't treat you poorly, did they?"

"Not at first," Suluk said. "A lot of times they tried to hire us as guides, show them to our 'secret spots,' as if we were hiding gold in every fox and rabbit hole. When we didn't do as they asked, then they had a tendency to get rough, but we got through."

Akłaq looked at Putu. "Any news of other places?"

"White men heading to Alaska. Engineers, businessmen, official types, in addition to all the prospectors and miners."

"What do these official men want? Are they government agents?"

"Yes, but they're not looking for us or the children. They're trying to assess the feasibility of the oil."

"The oil?"

He nodded gravely. "That damn ground oil. Seems they found a use for it."

Akłaq let out a breath and ran a hand through her hair. "Any news that directly threatens or affects us?"

"We didn't come across anything." Putu gestured to the village. "Now then, tell me about what we've got here. If you're leaving, I assume Everett will be in charge?"

"In charge of the training, yes," she answered. "He is going to be our District Captain."

Ikiaq raised a brow. "Putu told us what you did to Goldsmith and Frederickson. Has there been other news?"

"No, but we need someone to lead. It seemed a bit presumptuous to call him the Regional Manager."

"I assume that Hudson Bay is going to be another District," Putu stated. "Do you intend to stay there, then?"

"We talked about switching, actually, once we have our center established. I would return here and he would go there."

"Why not send him east, then?" Lusa wondered.

"Acceptance. The people around Hudson Bay are still Inuit. They may not be Iñupiatun, but they have more in common with me than with him."

"Where is Everett anyway?" Putu asked, looking around.

"Out fishing with Gáx and a few other boys. They'll be back tonight."

Ikiaq shifted his stance and folded his arms. "Putu told us as much as he knew about what you're trying to do. Not that I have a problem with allowing the people to defend themselves, but do you ever think that this might just be inviting trouble? If not for you, then the people? Believe it or not, there are some groups that have no idea what's going on; they have yet to even conceive of a white man, never mind meet one."

"And what do you think will happen when they do?" Akłaq countered. "If there is even a speck of gold dust or a drop of oil, what happens when the prospectors and the engineers start bulling through the land? How long will those people survive? It's already been well-proven that the government doesn't care; they're the ones who will lead the charge. And it may be that the white men will make their way here to this island, and we may need somewhere to run. I don't know. I can't see the future, but I trust the words of those who can. They tell me to go east, so I'm going east."

"Putu told us about the white bear and Anagalisgi, too," Suluk commented, nodding. "I remember hearing stories about the Krydik, when the messengers would make their way north. For a people who couldn't defend themselves with these great sorceries, what makes you think we're going to fare any better?"

"Because the Krydik didn't listen to the prophets. We are." She huffed. "It doesn't mean that it's going to be easy, but we'll make it. Think about this: Sabelu said not to go north. Don't go to Alaska. If I had left this spring, as early as I could, and gone north anyway because I wanted to, I would be running into all the gold and oil hunters. But he said to go east, to Hudson Bay. That's what I'm going to do."

"And what do you expect of us?" Lusa wondered. "Do you expect us to just learn this Akari and wait for you to tell us what to do next?"

"I would greatly encourage you to learn the Akari, yes. But if nothing else, we need to reach out to the different peoples, beyond this village. We need to train them as well, if only in the basics, so they have a means of defense, even against the prospectors. They need to know that they are not alone, that they have support. If necessary, they have a place to go, without leaving Earth for Hlohi and the Krydik."

Ikiaq looked at Putu. "And you're perfectly fine with this?"

Putu turned to face him. "In all the years that we lived in the village and served under Ujurak, what did we do, how many people did we help? A few here, a handful there, a dozen over there? Always picking up the pieces, sweeping up the mess. But in just a few short years—whether you think we're following the white bear or not, whatever you think about the Akari—we've helped hundreds of children, hundreds of families, and this village here. Akłaq is getting ready to go east to do the same for more people." He went on before Ikiaq could protest. "Sixty of us were put down by Frederickson and his men, and we ran like frightened hares. Akłaq killed both Goldsmith and Frederickson. She could have killed others, but she didn't, and that speaks just as much. So you tell me whether she's worth following."

After a long moment, it was Lusa who spoke. "I'll follow." She looked at Akłaq. "I'll even go with you to Hudson Bay. I know where some of the eastern villages are; they may not be as ignorant as you fear."

"Thank you," Akłaq told her.

Suluk sighed. "All right. You may have a point. I admit, Putu, I was one who often called you a coward, but when the time came to fight, I ran, too. At least you've been doing some good." He looked at Ikiaq. "Like we all wanted to do, in the beginning."

Ikiaq grunted, still giving Putu a look. Finally he relented. "All right, I'll stay and see what you've got going on here. If nothing else, you might need a hand in defending this place if any of those prospectors or engineers come sniffing around these islands."

"It's a start," Akłaq said. She looked at Lusa. "You can stay with me in my hut and take a day to rest. We'll leave tomorrow or the next day." She looked at Putu. "Are you coming east as well?"

"I don't expect so. My migration instinct has been run out. The only instinct I'm following right now is the one that says I need to keep an eye on Everett while you're gone."

With that, the group dispersed. After introducing themselves to the village elders, Ikiaq and Suluk grabbed their things and went about looking for a hut to call their own, while Lusa followed Akłaq to her hut.

"I don't think I've ever seen Putu so happy," Lusa observed, ducking inside after Akłaq. "I wasn't too surprised when he told us that you'd adopted a mess of children, and it wasn't unreasonable to think that you might be masquerading as father and daughter, but I just witnessed genuine joy from him. I've barely ever seen him crack a smile."

"I think he's learned how to move forward in his life," Akłaq said, returning to her packing.

Lusa sat down beside her. "I think he's finally helping people. I haven't seen everything around here, but I can already tell that you have done a lot of good. When we stayed with other Tlingit on our way here, they talked about the work you did in the south, rescuing the children." She sighed and nodded. "Putu is right; it's more than any of us ever did under Ujurak. And it's more than any of us have done on our own since."

Akłaq began packing up her mementos, the last thing she always packed so that they were right there when she opened her bag. "Whatever did or didn't happen back then, it was a long time ago. This is what we're doing now. You said you've been east before?"

"Yes, a few times."

"What can you tell me about the people?"

"The islanders are still very isolated; few of them are even aware of the existence of the white men. But there is so little up there that I don't believe they're in any real danger."

"What about this mad rush for ground oil?"

"I don't know if there is any oil up there. Besides, it's much easier to get to the stuff here on the mainland."

"True. What do you know about the mainland people?"

"More exposed, but still isolated. A lot of them were employed by Hudson Bay Company as guides, but it was hardly devastating for them when the company left, or so I understand. They've maintained themselves and their way of life far better than anyone I've seen."

Akłaq nodded. "What do they think of their western cousins?"

"Distant, foolish, and unfortunate were words I heard frequently."

"Did you tell them of Ujurak's work? Did you show them?"

In her peripheral vision, Akłaq saw Lusa shrug. "I tried to explain it. At the time, they weren't worried."

Akłaq looked at her. "So if they weren't having any problems, why did Ujurak send you there?"

"At the time, I didn't know. He said it was about learning the state of things in the east, looking for threats. I mean, it made sense, but it still seemed a bit far-fetched. But maybe it was all just so I could be of use to you now."

"Well, if that's the case, then I have no argument." She cut herself off and looked past Lusa to the doorway where Latseen was waiting. "Yes, love, what is it?"

Latseen ducked inside. "I just didn't want to interrupt."

Akłaq made a motion. "You're not interrupting. Come here. Latseen, this is Lusa."

"From Ujurak's village," Latseen stated.

"That's right," Lusa confirmed. "Your grandfather told us all about you and your brothers and sisters on the way here. He says you did a lot of good with the children."

If Akłaq had felt any apprehension at all over the trip east, it soon dissipated as they spent the afternoon together, talking and laughing and reminiscing and packing.

"Mama told me all about the Akarin, and she and Everett even showed me the fortress once," Latseen said. "But she never said much about the Time industry. It makes a little more sense now, about the Timekeepers and who they are." She looked at Akłaq. "Will you show me the Wheel? And Gáx and Tlaganis, too?"

Akłaq shook her head. "No, my dear. We have no reason to go there. We take no part in their treachery, in their theft of Time and lives. We are Akarin; we follow the Whites and the words of the Author."

She noted her daughter's disappointment. While Akłaq believed what she had just said, she also didn't want to go and risk being arrested on sight, whether for old charges of Time theft or for the murder of Frederickson and the others. Escaping the prison in the Wheel was probably a tad more difficult than escaping one on Earth.

Everett, Gáx, and the others returned from their fishing trip as it was growing dark, and Akłaq and the others went to meet them. More introductions were made and plans refined. Ikiaq and Suluk remained skeptical of the Akari, but they pledged their loyalty to whatever greater plan was being concocted.

"He's very white," Ikiaq said disapprovingly when Everett walked away, taking his part of the catch back to his hut. "Are you sure we can trust him?"

"His grandfather was white, and he lived in Red River for some time," Akłaq explained.

"He could have outed us at any time while we were rescuing the children," Putu said firmly. "He didn't. He has been nothing but an ally, and he is another link we have between us and the Krydik."

Ikiaq grunted but said nothing more to that.

Akłaq, Latseen, and Lusa returned to their hut. Gáx was nowhere to be seen, and it was Tlaganis, Nooskw, and Tula'aan who met them.

"Where's Gáx?" Akłaq wondered, taking the fish they had caught and sitting to prepare them.

"Still fawning after Nisa," Nooksw answered teasingly.

"This late at night, he's not fawning," Lusa commented.

Akłaq couldn't help but grin, and she glanced at Lusa. "It's been a long time since we were teenagers, hasn't it?"

Lusa met her grin. "It certainly has." She looked around. "I noticed that the Tlingit seem to have stopped tattooing their chin as well."

"They don't want to draw attention to themselves, in the event they have to go to the mainland or otherwise encounter white men."

Lusa shot a gaze at Tula'aan who was attentively watching Akłaq prepare the fish. "I don't think that matters too much to the white men."

Akłaq coughed a laugh. "From my own experience, I can tell you it really doesn't. But they make their own decisions on that."

Now Lusa looked at Latseen, and Akłaq knew immediately what she was going to ask. "And what about you? You're obviously of age. Did you make the decision to not tattoo your chin as well?"

"No one on the reserve would do it, for fear of punishment," Latseen answered meekly. "Then we were out rescuing children, so I didn't think about it much. Since we've been here, I guess I just haven't given it much thought."

"Would you like to? I know how to do it now." Lusa looked at Akłaq. "The village where I fled to after Ujurak, they still maintained the tradition, and they showed me."

"Yet here you are with a bare chin," Akłaq said, raising a brow.

Lusa shrugged. "We have long lives, Akłaq, and I am not going to have children. I see no reason to put myself out there like that." She gestured toward Latseen. "But she's a pretty girl, young, with a chance to still turn away and have a life. I just want to give her the opportunity."

Akłaq set the fish over the low fire. "Lusa, we can have children. Akari-bearers can have children just the same as normal people."

"How is that?"

But Akłaq looked at Latseen. "We can talk about that on our way east. Right now, you should probably make a decision. If you want it, I imagine she can do it tonight—" She glanced at Lusa who nodded once. "—you can sleep it off overnight, and then you'll be ready for the journey tomorrow."

Latseen looked as ecstatic as Akłaq had ever seen her, and all she could do was look at Lusa with a huge grin and nod. Akłaq turned to Tlaganis and Nooskw. "All right, you two. Out! This is a woman's rite. Shoo! Go find your brother!"

The boys, who had remained silent but wide-eyed, scrambled to get out of the hut.

"Can I stay?" Tula'aan asked meekly.

Akłaq pulled Tula'aan close. "Of course you can. One day this might be you." She nudged Latseen who looked at her. "Set a good example for your sister, won't you?"

"I will," Latseen promised eagerly. She was still smiling.

"It's going to hurt, but you're not allowed to cry out. Understand?"

That caused her shining facade to dim just a little, and her smile slowly faded as Lusa gathered up the supplies she needed, trying not to disturb her packed bag too much.

"Hold still, child," she ordered, taking Latseen's face in her hands.

By morning, Latseen was the first woman to be tattooed in sixty years in the village, and the only other woman who was, a seventy-five year old elder, awarded her with a pendant she claimed would bring a fine husband to her.

"I'm surprised you didn't do it, too," Putu commented to Akłaq afterwards.

Akłaq shook her head and bent to pick up her pack. "No. One day I may look for a husband again, but not yet."

"Speaking of your Russian husband or Aniqan?"

"Speaking of my work, and the peace I want to achieve first. Nika was murdered by his own people because of the war and the part he refused to play. Aniqan was killed by a Timekeeper who thought us thieves and inferior beings."

"So your decision to look for a husband is predicated on peace throughout the entire North American continent?"

She sighed. "I don't know, Putu. I really don't. And what about you? Have you thought to look for another wife?"

"I won't say the thought has never crossed my mind. But there are few female, human, indigenous Time Agents who are of apparent age. If I were to find one who appeared younger, well, then we would seem to be as you and I are now, father and daughter."

"I never knew you were so concerned about what other people thought."

He shifted position. "I'm not concerned about others. It's my own thought process I worry about. I know you are well old enough to be a wife and mother, but I would never be able to see you as my wife."

Akłaq nodded. "I suppose I understand."

The two of them managed to shift their demeanor as Lusa and Latseen approached. Latseen's lower lip and chin were swollen, but the tattoo was finished. A line of dots straight down from her lip to the end of her chin, and on either side was one solid line and one dashed line.

"Are we ready to go?" Akłaq asked.

"Ready," Latseen said, her word marred a bit from her attempts to speak without moving her bottom lip too much.

They'd already said their goodbyes to Gáx and the others, but Tula'aan still ran to meet them and give them all one last hug.

"Promise to come back?" Tula'aan said.

"Of course," Akłaq told her, kneeling down. "And Latseen, too."

The eleven year old made a face. "What if she finds a boy, like Gáx found a girl? And Tlaganis is looking at girls, too. I know Nooskw will be, soon. I'll have no one left!"

"By that time, you might be looking at boys," Latseen laughed.

Tula'aan considered this, then shrugged and said, "Maybe." She looked at her big sister. "But if you do find a boy, does that mean you won't come back?"

"I guess that depends on how I feel about the boy."

"But what about how I feel about you? I don't want you to leave forever!"

"I'm sure she could visit," Akłaq sighed. "Or you could visit her." She stood and adjusted her pack. "Now then, you be a good girl. You listen to Grandfather and Everett and everyone else. I don't want to hear anything bad when I get back. Got it?"

Tula'aan nodded, but still demanded one last hug before she would finally let them leave.

The marshes between islands had not gotten any easier to navigate. In fact, it may have become more difficult with the hot, dry summer. Akłaq told herself that it was all necessary, that this little bit of discomfort and inconvenience was worth it to make the trip through the mountains easier.

"We should avoid drifting too far north as much as possible," Lusa said once they finally reached the hard ground of the mainland, "at least until we cross the mountains."

"I wish Paa were easier to conjure," Latseen complained. "Then we could just jump from place to place. We wouldn't have to worry about marshes or mountains or how many people we might run into."

"I can't say I disagree," Akłaq said.

"The Akari doesn't make it easier?" Lusa wondered. Akłaq couldn't decide whether her question was genuinely curious or mildly accusing.

"No. Actually, Everett says it's harder. He says it has something to do with the Wheel, that conjuring Paa is like crossing a river. Going with the current to the Wheel is hard enough, but trying to fight it to go anywhere else is terrible."

"So they don't have ranks or testing, or how do they advance? How do they make use of the fortress if it is so difficult to get to?"

Akłaq searched for words to explain it. "Their ranks are more social than skill. Beginners are called Novice, yes, and there are Captains who are like the leaders. But everyone in the middle is either General or Whisper. The General are those who have some skill and are dedicated to improving themselves and the Akarin at large, and Whispers are those who have simply faded away."

"Oh." Lusa seemed perplexed by the idea. "And that's it?"

"Basically. Someone who wants to become a Captain is called a Core, and they have some testing that they have to do. And then the Captains choose a Council from among themselves. But among the general population, there is only Novice for the beginners, Whispers for those who are now gone, and the rest are General."

"So Everett is a Captain, then."

"Not necessarily. He was a core, but decided he wasn't suited for such leadership, so now he's just a General with more skill than me and is willing to teach. I'm only a General myself and yet I've trained or helped to train Latseen and the others."

"If I wasn't coming, I'd be helping Gáx to start training Nooskw," Latseen threw in. "I have a feeling that Tula'aan is going to refuse to learn unless it's under me."

"You never know," Akłaq told her. "She's still pretty partial to Tlaganis, I think."

"Maybe, but in two years he's going to be just like Gáx, looking at all the pretty girls and not paying attention to his sister, or anything else for that matter."

"She's got a point," Lusa said.

"Yes," Akłaq acknowledged, "but you—" She looked intentionally at Latseen. "—can't say that you haven't been looking at the boys yourself." When Latseen did not speak, just shied away a bit in embarrassment, she went on, "This village is bigger than the reserve, but that doesn't mean it's so big that I don't notice." She grinned. "So do you like Ooskaw or Lipanis more?"

"Ooskaw," Latseen admitted.

"Have you known him?" Lusa asked.

"Not yet."

"Is that why you jumped at the chance to tattoo your chin?" Akłaq guessed.

The teenage squirmed a bit. "That might be part of the reason."

"So then why are you here?" Lusa wondered. "Even Gáx stayed behind for a girl, whatever excuses he gave, I don't know."

"Yes, but we have a mission to complete."

Lusa laughed, but it had a sad sort of undertone to it. "Oh, child. There will always be another mission. Another problem, another errand, another task. Always. The world will always need saving. But don't let life pass you by. I don't know where I stand on this Author business, but someone clearly favors your mother, enough to give her a family in spite of everything. Myself, Matulik, we weren't so lucky."

"You can have both," Akłaq told her. "If you have the Akari."

But the woman shook her head. "I don't think you can. The Akari and children, maybe, but you can't have our life and children. Look at you, Akłaq, leaving Tula'aan behind so you can trek hundreds of miles to help people you've never met. Maybe it's the right thing to do, I don't know. But I do know that there is an eleven year old girl back there who already misses her mother and sister."

"When she's older, she'll have the option to come along."

"Maybe." Lusa looked at Latseen. "Saving the world is a fine goal. Just don't neglect your family. If you get the chance to marry and have children, I suggest you take it."

It was not the last time they had similar discussions on their way east. Lusa had questions about the Akari. Latseen had questions about boys. With little else to do on the road, the discussions could get quite in-depth, but at least it helped to pass the time. If there ever came a day when she was able to open Paa by herself, Akłaq resolved that she would use it as much as possible and become absolutely proficient in it. It wasn't that she didn't enjoy the journey, but it took up so much time. Even Banding felt futile some days as winter inched its way closer.

If there was any good news, it was that they had no real troubles.

They did not run into anyone on the road, when they'd followed roads, and they had no troubles with predators in the wilds. Other than the lingering environmental hazards of bad weather and treacherous ground, their trek was largely uneventful.

"Do you suppose we'll reach the eastern peoples soon?" Akłaq asked Lusa as they crossed a large swath of open, frosted ground, breaths puffing in icy air.

"Shouldn't be long now," Lusa promised. "I think I spotted smoke earlier. If nothing else, we might get directions."

There was little else to be done. By the following evening, all three of them were fixed on a thin wisp of smoke rising into the air. The morning after that, they stood on a hilltop and looked down on a small fishing village huddled between slope and shore. There looked to be about twenty huts and maybe eighty to a hundred people, many of them in or near the water.

Suddenly Akłaq was struck by the magnitude of her task. And the fact that it was her task. She had to be the one to go down there and somehow communicate not only the facts of what was going on, the oppression of other peoples, but also show them the Akari and convince them to become some hub of activity, a safe haven for potential refugees? What, exactly, had she been thinking?

Sabelu, are you sure? she wondered silently.

By now, several heads were looking their way. Taking a breath, Akłaq squared her shoulders and led the way down the slope, hoping to appear as nonthreatening as possible. A group of three broke off from the village and started walking toward them. Each of them had a whaling spear in hand which they used as something of a walking stick to get them up the slope.

"Hello!" she called once they were within comfortable distance.

"Greetings," the leader of the trio replied.

Everyone stopped once they were about ten feet from each other.

The eastern peoples looked very much like the western peoples, Akłaq thought, and if she didn't know better, she might have said there was some southern influence in their features as well. She knew that their linguistic dialect was different, almost to the point of being barely understood, if at all. She also knew, from her visits to the fortress, that the Akari would translate everything she said and everything that was said to her. Latseen would have this gift as well, but Lusa would have to rely on her own knowledge to guide her.

"You are unfamiliar to us," the eastern leader stated. He was an older man, even older than Putu's apparent age, his face lined with years of experience of harsh living. "Are you from the west?"

"We are," Akłaq confirmed. She gestured to each in turn. "Akłaq, Lusa, and Latseen. We are Iñupiatun."

The second man, being of perhaps thirty-five years, spoke up. "You two, maybe." He looked at Latseen. "Not her."

Akłaq met his gaze. "She is Tlingit by birth, but she is my daughter."

The man appeared unfazed as he dipped his head once, saying, "Of course. Iñupiatun."

"I am Tarqiq," the leader introduced. "This is Petuwaq—" The second man. "—and Katjuk." The third man, who looked hardly older than twenty and had yet to speak. Tarqiq shifted his stance, relaxing. "What brings three women so far from the setting sun? Have you lost your men perhaps?"

"Our men are busy with an important task, and we were the only ones who could be sent," Akłaq answered.

Tarqiq made a kind of disapproving sound. "Your people are in trouble, then?"

"Our people have been in trouble for a long time. And that trouble will come this way soon. We've come to warn you and help you prepare."

The men exchanged troubled glances. Finally Tarqiq turned to Katjuk. "Assemble the house and clan leaders."

Katjuk made a gesture of assent, then turned and half-ran, half-slid down the slope to the village where, by now, most of the people had completely ceased their activities and now waited for some word on what was going on.

"We will see what you have to say," Tarqiq said, nodding. He turned partway and made a gesture with his spear. "Come. Follow us. We are but a simple fishing village."

With the way the light snow settled on the land and reflected the sun, it hadn't appeared as though the hill was so big or difficult to traverse. Only once they got down into the village and Akłaq turned to look back did she see how steep it really was.

The villagers all gathered round. A few had goods in hand as if to trade, but most stayed back, waiting for the house and clan leaders to say that all was well.

In the summer, shelters appeared to be very similar to the Tlingit huts, furs, mud, and leaves spread over a wooden frame. With the onset of winter, these shelters were slowly being phased out in favor of a type of *iglu* dug into the hillside but built of snow on the outside. They approached one such *iglu* and ducked inside through the low entry.

It was much bigger than Akłaq might normally have given it credit for, able to house the six of them plus another dozen men and a couple women, and still leave room to breathe.

Introductions were formal but brief, a few of the men complaining about how strange it was for a woman to represent any sort of political affair.

"If there is danger," Tarqiq said, "we should at least listen to the warning. She is not here to tell us what we must do to prepare."

Actually, she sort of was.

"Fine," the biggest complainer huffed. "What is this warning you wish to impart?"

Evidently they were expecting something short and easily explained, some simple message that one might find acceptable to entrust to a woman. Another village was planning a raid. Something had happened to the fish or the caribou and their sources of meat were going to suddenly change. Trying to explain everything that had happened to her, everything she had experienced, was neither short nor simple. Just by looking at their faces, she could tell which ones were immediately interested—these seemed to be the younger boys in training to become a house leader one day—which ones were at least giving the tale some modest thought—these being the older men who were past their prime—and which ones were dismissing every word she said as either folly or blasphemy.

A quick demonstration of the Akari at least proved her truthfulness, but it did nothing to rescue the perception of her intent.

"A woman does not get chosen for such things unless she is a witch," the complainer declared, standing and seeming to fill in the extra space in the *iglu*. "What evil *tuugrak* follows you? What demons do you seek to infect us with?"

"Sit down," Tarqiq ordered.

The man did not sit, but he at least stopped talking.

All eyes were on the three women.

"It is one thing to impart a warning," the leader said, looking at Akłaq. "But what you are suggesting is no less than war."

"We are trying to prevent war," Akłaq told him. "Even if we cannot prevent it, we want to ensure that our people are not helpless."

One of the clan leaders raised his voice. "We are only a fishing village—"

"Exactly. You are only a fishing village. A dozen well-armed men would kill you, take your women and children, and burn this whole place to the ground. You can't tell me you've never had trouble with raiders from other peoples."

That, at least, got them thinking for half a second.

Akłaq continued, "I understand the threat seems far away. You've barely even heard of these men with pale skins, and none of you have ever seen one. But they move like ghosts, swiftly and silently, and once they find you, they take hold, like a bear sinking its teeth into your flesh, and they don't let go. The Aleut and the Yu'pik tried to warn my people. My people did not listen, and our villages were burned. Our men were made into slaves, and women and children starved to death by the hundreds. The children now are stolen from their beds and changed so that their souls, the souls of the people, are exchanged for the souls of these white men, as hollow and alien as the rest of them, cut off from their land and ancestors.

"The southern peoples have had it far worse. There, the white men have already won. They have taken the land. But with the Akari, with these sorceries, they cannot take the people." She looked around at the leaders and the women who were serving smoked fish. "They have already taken the Tlingit, the Haida, the Blackfeet, the Cree, the Anishinaabek, and countless others. My people, the western Iñupiatun, have some hold, but it won't last long. You eastern Inuit are surrounded on all sides.

"You look around and see trees and water and stone. The white men see timber and mills and fish and ore and gems. Spirits help you if they ever find gold or ground oil. They will take it all. And the twenty or thirty men here in the village won't be enough to stop them." She let that hang in the air for a moment. "I can't guarantee that the Akari will stop them from attacking, or that it will be enough to preserve everything as you see it today. We lost Red River, yes, and the white men continue to build their infernal schools. But the Akari has allowed us, at the very least, to preserve ourselves."

The leaders looked at each other, exchanging glances and whispers of conversation.

"I expect, then, that you would wish to bring in some of the other villages and clans," Tarqiq guessed.

"Anyone and everyone," Akłaq confirmed.

The leader of the small village of a hundred people nodded slowly, then made a motion. A woman stepped forward. "Yura will show you a place where you can rest from your journey. The rest of us will remain here to debate."

It was the best she could ask for at this point. The three women made gestures of submission and thanks, then followed Yura outside.

Avgun Iñuiñaq Quliŋŋuġutaiḷaq
District Nine

After so many years of having to deal with the constant, daily cycle of night and day, Akłaq was glad for the long day. There was something bright and hopeful and refreshing about it, the thought that everything would be all right. The century had turned over and all was well.

It hadn't been easy convincing the eastern peoples to go along with her plan. It was hard to take a threat seriously when you'd never seen it, barely even heard about it. As they moved farther north to people who were even more isolated out on frozen islands, it got even more difficult. A few people had even admitted to going along with it only out of fear of her, Latseen, and Lusa, at least at first. Once they got going and started to understand what the Akari could do, that it was really a tool, many of the accusations of evil sorcery died away.

Akłaq ducked into her hut and fastened the fur that covered the entry, plunging herself into near-darkness. Only the light peeping in through a small crack on one side and under the fur offered any light to see by. This was no problem for her as she simply invoked Light, just long enough to find her furs and lie down.

Not five minutes later, there was a rustling at the door. A hand reached under the fur and tugged on the fastening string. Akłaq was suddenly blinded by sunlight, and she rolled over. There were some disadvantages to the long day.

"I asked you ten minutes ago if you were tired and you said no," Akłaq mumbled into her furs.

"Sorry," Latseen said guiltily, replacing the entry fur and securing it, bringing blessed darkness back to the room. "I decided it probably would be a good idea to get some rest before we leave."

Akłaq said nothing to that, just listened to her daughter, now a fine young woman, get situated in her own bed.

"Do you really think things will last once we leave?" Latseen wondered. "The eastern people haven't been as eager to accept and learn the Akari."

"We're not trying to raise an army," Akłaq told her. "We're not trying to recruit for the Akarin. On the one hand, we're simply trying to warn them and give them some means of defending themselves. If they have this knowledge, then they know what's going on, so if the people have to flee and settle down somewhere for a time, then they can and the locals will understand why."

"Will they, though?"

"We're going to hope so. Besides, we might be leaving, but Everett will be back this way."

"Why not leave Lusa in charge? She's more familiar with the people."

Akłaq shook her head uselessly in the dark. "She's too new, and there needs to be a man as the speaker. I suspect that's also why the people have been so resistant. If Everett comes out here, he'll have an easier time addressing the house and clan leaders. He's also a better speaker than I am overall, which should help."

There was some rustling in the darkness.

"Does this place remind you of home?" Latseen asked. "I know you've talked about the long day and the long night a lot."

"In a lot of ways, yes, it reminds me of home," Akłaq answered. "But we've also come so far north that dirt hardly exists, and even the mountains have been replaced by mounds of jagged ice. It's definitely not home."

"Will you ever show us your home? Yours and Grandfather's?"

"Maybe someday. We'd have to grab your brothers and sister first."

She could hear Latseen's smile. "I'm excited to see them again."

Akłaq again made a useless gesture. "So am I. I really didn't intend to be gone this long. People are a little more resilient than I thought."

"That's a good thing, though, right?"

"I hope so."

It was soon after that, that the two of them fell asleep. Akłaq didn't even notice when Lusa returned, but by the time she woke up, all three of them were in the hut.

In the dim light of the sun that was still shining brilliantly outside, peeping through the small cracks in the entryway fur, Akłaq glanced at their bags, all packed and ready to go. She wanted to be home by now, but she was discovering that, even with the guidance of the white bear and the apparent blessing of the Author, it was still very difficult to make any meaningful progress. More than once she'd lain awake, envisioning terrible things happening back west that she would never know about until too late when they returned to a decimated village. She told herself it was silly, that they were training for that very thing, to stop it, but her imagination rarely listened to logic.

Latseen and Lusa were still sleeping. In an effort to not disturb them, Akłaq used Light to bend the light away from them when she opened the flap and allowed sunlight into the hut. The two women never stirred, and she slipped out easily enough. Since having to once again contend with the long day and the long night, she'd become more than proficient in Light. It was one of the things that helped her convince the northern islanders to accept the Akari. During the night, whether it was the long night or not, it wasn't uncommon to see tiny spotlights in the distance as the people illuminated their fishing quarry.

It wasn't long before Latseen and Lusa got themselves around and dragged all their bags outside. From there it was a short walk to the shore where Hanta, one of the clan leaders, waited for them.

"Thank you for receiving us, Hanta," Akłaq told him graciously.

"Thank you for visiting, and showing us these wondrous things," he replied, though his words were still a bit stiff. Akłaq bet that Everett would have a little easier time of things. "We will do what we can and keep watch for evil things."

She tried to appear optimistic, though she had her doubts. Hanta had been one of her biggest opponents in the beginning, still wasn't the most enthused, and in spite of everything else, the islands were still very far away from any other village, city, or abandoned shack. It would be very easy for the people to lapse back into unskilled apathy.

Nevertheless, they couldn't stay forever. The women tossed their bags into the qayaqs and pushed out into the water. Hanta guided them expertly across the wide channel to the mainland where they helped tie off their qayaqs to his, forming a small train. He again wished them well, then started paddling back, not looking even a little fatigued from the trip whereas Akłaq thought her arms and shoulders were going to fall off.

"Well," she huffed, fastening her pack to her back, "we might as well make as much progress as we can while we have the light of the long day. We have a long way to go."

Latseen grumbled a little bit but did not argue.

They got farther than Akłaq expected them to, actually, but then, they hadn't used their legs much in the qayaqs, nor did they use their arms a whole lot while walking. And, without the approach of darkness, they did not become visually exhausted until they became physically exhausted.

"Do you expect all the miners and oil men to still be in the area when we return?" Lusa wondered as they pitched the tent.

"I don't see why not," Akłaq said. "Once they find one gold deposit, they'll scour for hundreds of miles to find another, no matter how small."

"The oil, too?" Latseen asked.

Akłaq made a face. "I'm not sure about that. They seem to think they've found a great use for it, but I can't imagine what that would be. It may turn out to be nothing."

"We can hope," Lusa grumbled.

They used the long day to their advantage. Even as they moved south and were again confronted with something that resembled nighttime—though at first it was little more than the sun barely dipping below the horizon and then rising again—they kept walking. The migration instinct, as many jokingly called it. By the time they were again west of the mountains, night had become a more firmly established part of the daily cycle.

"If the miners and oil men have left the area," Akłaq said, "maybe then we can go north."

No one said anything to the affirmative or negative, and soon enough they were back in the wet marshes. The landscape looked more familiar, and then they were climbing into a canoe to navigate the waterways.

"Do you think much has changed?" Latseen wondered. "Tula'aan is going to be all grown up by now! Do you think she tattooed her chin as well?"

"We'll find out soon enough," Akłaq told her, though she privately wondered the same thing. They'd been gone for a lot longer than expected. She hoped things hadn't changed too much.

"Akłaq's back!"

Akłaq had barely registered the island or the village before they were spotted, someone jumping up from the shore and racing back to the people.

"We've been announced," Lusa commented.

By the time they actually reached the island and dragged their canoe ashore, more than half the village was there to greet them. Akłaq and Latseen immediately went on the hunt for the boys and Tula'aan, but could only find Nooskw and Tula'aan. The two still welcomed them back with open arms, as did Everett and Putu. Tula'aan, now almost a woman grown, had indeed tattooed her chin.

"Where are Gáx and Tlaganis?" Akłaq asked, looking around.

"They've gone," Putu answered bluntly before Everett could say anything more tactful.

"What do you mean, gone?"

Everett gave Putu a look, then glanced back at Akłaq. "They stop waiting for you. They decided to marry and make the Akari and everything else a secondary part of their lives. Gáx already has two children, Tlaganis and his wife are expecting their first."

Akłaq blinked. "They did this without me?"

"Or me?" Latseen wondered, sounding annoyed. "Who decided whether these women were suitable for them to marry?"

"The elder women in the village," Putu said. He shrugged. "Life happens, with or without us. They waited as long as they could stand, but we had no good way to know how long you were going to be, if you were going to return at all."

"And Nooskw and Tula'aan?" Akłaq demanded.

"Both have prospects in mind, Nooskw a little more seriously than Tula'aan, but neither proclaiming marriage yet. They were a little more willing to hold out for you."

Akłaq had trouble comprehending the idea as her mind was filled with memories of little Gáx, only five years old when she took him into her home. And Tlaganis, the wily little boy who loved to go off exploring, the brother Tula'aan admired the most. Married? Children? For goodness' sake, she was a grandmother now? She barely looked old enough to have children over five.

Suddenly she felt removed from the life she left, as though she were entering into the life of a stranger. Even Latseen looked different to her. She was a woman grown. By appearance, they could be sisters, or cousins, anyway. No longer was she the little six year old trying to help bring her toddler siblings under control, or the fifteen year old who was terrified of being kidnapped and taken to an alien school. In reality, she ought to be married herself and having children. Akłaq knew she had fancied some of the young men of the eastern people, even knew that she had known a few of them. In the space of just a few minutes, Latseen, Gáx, all of her children, had become their own people. And she was left out in the cold.

"Otherwise, all has been well since you've been gone," Everett said, perhaps sensing her growing distress. "Everyone in the village is well-versed in the basics of Banding, and some have also taken to Feel and using Matter to heal all the minor wounds that pop up in daily life. Many in the surrounding villages are also trained."

"What of the miners and oil men in the area?" Akłaq inquired, still feeling a bit absent.

"The miners have gone home," Putu reported. "They cleaned the hills of gold and left. Oh, the towns are still around, and a few people still live there, but it's not nearly as big as it was. As for the oil men, they came, they left, and they came back. Sounds like they're trying to start an operation, but they're not sure how to deal with the winter and heavy snows. So far, there has been little threat to the people from that front."

"Is there a threat on another front?" Did she want to know the answer right now?

"A message for you. From the new Manager of Region Four."

"Frederickson's replacement. How did you obtain this message?"

"General delivery from the Wheel."

"Means he doesn't know where we're located yet," Lusa mentioned.

Everett nodded reluctantly. "Not yet. He wants to meet in Vancouver."

"When was the message received?" Akłaq asked.

"About three years ago. We sent a reply saying that you were not currently in the area and so unable to meet with him, but if and when you returned, we would pass along his request. We haven't heard anything since."

"Has there been any news from the south? Anything about the schools?"

"A few still operating in British Columbia," Putu stated. "Most of them are back east, in Ontario. But there has been nothing unusual, no."

"Anything of interest in the Time industry that you're aware of?"

"Nothing," Everett said. "It's almost as if he forgot about the request entirely, or else is actually going to wait for a reply."

"What does he want?" Latseen wondered.

"He didn't say specifically, just that he wants to meet. Take that how you will."

Akłaq could feel Latseen and Lusa both look at her. It was Latseen who said, "It could be a trap, just like the school."

"Yes," Akłaq stated, "but it's so obvious, isn't it?"

"All traps are obvious to those who set them," Lusa said. "The white men expect us to be mindless animals who wander foolishly into them after some kind of rancid bait."

"But what's the bait?" Akłaq looked at Putu. "The message didn't say anything other than wanting to meet? There was no ransom, no offer, no bribe, no threat, nothing at all?"

"Nothing," he confirmed.

"Curiosity, then," Lusa went on. "Sheer curiosity as the bait."

Akłaq shook her head. "I'm not convinced. Besides, the Akari has proven to be more than adequate at taking on meager Time. If he does try anything, we will have means of escape."

Lusa grunted indignantly. "Speak for yourself then. I won't be part of it."

Akłaq looked at Latseen. "You?"

Latseen hesitated and shook her head. "I want to see my brothers again. If they've moved to other villages, I'll have to track them down."

"Fair enough. Putu? Everett?"

The men agreed, and it was Putu who made the arrangements, setting up the meeting for one month from her return to the village. Akłaq figured that would be plenty of time for her to relax a little after the journey and reconnect with some people, not the least being her own children. She felt wretched for leaving them and briefly wondered how much success she would have to attain in order to make up for losing her children. It was a silly question, of course, but then she started to question why she would be sent on such errands if it meant the loss of her home. But then, wasn't the whole goal of her work preserving other people's homes and families? But why did it seem to cause such strain on her own?

Over the course of that month, she was able to see Gáx and Tlaganis. First she marveled at what fine men they made. Then she congratulated them on their weddings and children. Finally she got to meet her grandchildren—the thought was still quite a shock to her—and hold them for a bit.

Why had she left? Why had she missed such important days? Did this meeting with the new Manager mean she was going to miss the birth of Tlaganis' first child? As much as she told herself it was so the eastern people would not suffer terrible fates, it felt hollow comfort. Everett should have gone to the eastern people, not her.

But there was nothing to be done about it now. Even just six months ago, the meeting with the Manager would have felt like part of her calling, part of her destiny. Now, it just felt like a chore. When the day finally came for them to leave to go to Vancouver, Akłaq found that she really, really didn't want to go.

Just because you are currently in a place does not mean you will be there forever, the white bear had said. This was true for a variety of situations both physical and philosophical, and Akłaq found herself hoping that maybe her time of constantly running here and there to help people was giving way to something a little more fixed, a little more relaxed. True, she hadn't exactly been running military drills every day with the eastern people, but it had still been stressful, being so far from home with a people who weren't hers, having to adapt to an environment that was infinitely harsher than the one she was used to, and that was saying something. She just wanted a little respite. Was that too much to ask for?

They made their way south to Vancouver without incident. There were, as told, still a few schools in operation, but things were nowhere near as chaotic as they had been. Maybe her campaign over the summer a few years ago had truly had a positive impact. She could only hope that it remained so positive and this meeting, whatever its outcome, didn't undo everything she had so painstakingly won.

Putu and Everett had cautioned about going to any meeting inside a building. It was too easy to get trapped, Akari or no Akari. Akłaq agreed, so instead they agreed to meet in a park just outside the city proper. No one knew what the Regional Manager looked like, but it was fairly easy to tell who they were. The Manager would just have to come to them.

"Well, well, District Nine has arrived."

The three of them turned to see a man walking toward them. It took Akłaq a moment, but then she realized that this was one of the men from the school. He seemed to catch on to her sudden recognition because he grinned and tipped his hat. "Harvey Billings, ma'am. And I know you three quite well, at least by name and reputation. Akłaq White Bear, Putu Canoe Maker, and Everett Thunder Caller."

The man was white, about five-eleven, with brown hair and a brown beard though he still had a youthful countenance, and a decent physique. His expression did not appear malicious, but neither did it register as being fully honest about his intentions.

"You were at the school," Akłaq stated, "with Frederickson."

"I was," Billings acknowledged. "I was standing right next to Martin and Eric when you shot them. Then I watched as you blasted the hell out of the others and killed Wallace."

"So you're here for some kind of revenge," Putu said.

"As a matter of fact, I'm not." Billings turned his full attention to Akłaq. "I might have been, except, after you killed Martin and Eric, you looked at me. I thought for sure I was a dead man. I didn't know how you did it, or even what 'it' was. I just knew that I didn't stand much of a chance. But then you spared me. And Michael and David as well, even though they were perfectly at your mercy."

"You're not here to thank her," Everett interrupted, his voice a question.

"I am not here for that either, no," Billings informed him firmly. "But I can appreciate a respectable and respectful opponent. You were only looking out for your children."

"Why are we here?" Putu asked.

Billings sighed. "The murder of Frederickson is too small for the Hands or Grandfathers to care about, seeing how it is but a minor inconvenience compared to the cardinal sin of theft, and even the charges of stealing Time are so old that they'd probably be thrown out.

Were I to bring you to an Earth-side court, even when you were jailed, it would be nothing for you to escape." He faltered. "And I cannot say I don't understand. Not all of us are heartless bastards; you have some sympathizers, both in Time and in white society in general."

"What are you saying?" Akłaq wondered. "We don't have to hide anymore?"

"That's not what I'm saying at all. The Akari is still very much illegal from a Time standpoint. And the Gatekeeper for Earth is far less understanding or sympathetic. I convinced her to let me try to handle this first."

"And what are you handling?"

"This crusade you've got going on, effectively arming all the tribes and telling them to make war on the whites using Time or the Akari or whatever." He went on before anyone could protest. "Whatever you want to call it, however you want to frame it, that is how it is perceived."

Akłaq folded her arms. "But it's not evil when you do it?"

"This has nothing to do with Earth-side politics."

"The hell it doesn't," Putu said. "If our people weren't disarmed, forced off our ancestral lands, having their children stolen and turned into unrecognizable automatons, and forced to live in poverty and squalor, there would be no need for this. Call it 'arming' if you must, but the fact is that we are simply trying to give them some tools for survival."

"Good Lord, are you people not listening?" Billings questioned. "I didn't have to send this meeting request at all. I didn't have to wait years for a reply—years, which, I assume were spent spreading this Akari gospel to others—and lie to the Gatekeeper about hunting you down. I didn't even have to honor any implied guarantees about this being a peaceful meeting; surely you must have at least considered that this was a trap of some form."

"We did," Everett confirmed. "We also figured that this was going to be more than a pleasant afternoon conversation. What are you trying to accomplish here?"

"I'm trying to offer you a way out."

"We're not going to stop our work, or abandon our people," Akłaq cut in.

"Dammit, woman, I'm not telling you to! I am trying to give you a way to build a front. A facade. Does the term 'money laundering' mean anything to you?"

"A way to make ourselves look honest while continuing our work in secret," Everett summarized.

Billings threw up his hands. "Finally, someone gets it!"

"You want to help us?" Akłaq asked.

Billings shook his head, let out a breath, walked away several steps, muttered something, then returned. His tone now was calm, though forced. "Maybe it's my fault for not understanding just how blunt I have to be with you, but yes. Looking back, I realize that a lot of this started with Gerald Goldsmith. I can't help that; I can't change the past. Wallace and the Rebellion certainly didn't help things. As Regional Manager, and even before, I've come to realize that District Nine requires a special kind of governance and goes beyond physical borders, much to the chagrin of the Gatekeeper."

"You're going to recognize District Nine?" Putu wondered.

"I don't have the power to make it official, and the Gatekeeper is not inclined to put it before the Hands. Speaking off the record, however, yes, I am." Billings shifted his stance. "Here is my offer. Akłaq, you've been waiting a long time to be made a Master Timekeeper. What I saw in the school left no doubt that you are certainly capable of incredible feats. Michael and David have signed off as two of the three Masters you need to advance, and I will be the third. I will also name you as the unofficial Captain of District Nine. This is not a public title and holds no real political weight, but it will allow you to govern your own affairs."

"And anything we do regarding the 'arming' of the people, it's all just 'training' them in Time," Everett concluded.

Billings nodded once. "Exactly. I can't control any Earth-side politics that arise from this, if and when the people do use Time against the government, but it will keep you clean in the eyes of the Time industry."

"You already said that the Akari was illegal in the Time industry; what's really going to change?" Putu asked suspiciously.

"Just say that it's Time. Lie. Believe me, no one is going to want to check up on this. It's just more time and hassle than anyone wants to give, as long as things remain peaceful. And as I've said before, the cardinal sin of the industry is theft; any other use of Time, even murder, is secondary. Anything you do with it Earth-side is on Earth-side justice to confront. Believe me, Ujurak's operation was no secret; it was just a matter of getting up the will to do anything about it. Gerald had that will, but now he's dead. Frederickson had the will, and he's dead, too."

"So you're just trying to save your own skin," Akłaq said.

"That is one of my goals, yes. Gatekeeper thought I was mad to propose this idea. Among the Time Agents of Region Four, you are considered a very dangerous woman, Akłaq. Now you're arming the indigenous peoples?" He sighed. "I implore you to take my offer. The only other place this can go is up to the Gatekeeper, and she is no friend of yours, let me assure you."

"All things considered, though, why are you helping us?" Everett wondered, his expression like that of a man who knows he knows something but cannot bring it to the forefront of his mind.

Billings gave him a look. "One drop laws are a bitch, aren't they?" He looked back at Akłaq and Putu. "I imagine you'll want to discuss this with whoever is waiting for you back home, and I understand that it is quickly going to become more difficult to travel. I will give you until spring to decide."

"You were willing to wait for years to have this meeting," Putu stated.

"Yes, but now that contact has been made, an answer will be necessary." He lowered his voice. "I'm trying to buy you some time. There are some who didn't want me to let you leave without accepting. Don't make enemies where you don't have to; accept help when it is given. Now then, I will see you in the spring with your answer. Have a nice day and a safe trip home."

The expectation was that the three of them would depart first, and they obliged. None of them spoke of the conversation until they were out of the city and well on their way home.

"It's not what I expected," Everett stated.

"I don't think any of us were expecting that," Akłaq agreed. "What was he talking about one drop laws?"

"They're more popular in the United States, though they exist here, too. If you have but one drop of non-white blood, you cannot be considered white and are legally treated as a second-class citizen or lesser human being, as we are."

"He looked white enough to me," Putu grumbled.

"Maybe so. My guess would be a grandparent or great-grandparent. Without knowing his true age, it's hard to tell. But it seems to be working for us."

"You think we should take his offer?"

Everett gave him a look. "It's not a bad offer, and it's the closest that District Nine has ever come to full recognition." He went on before Putu could argue. "Even if the titles are ceremonial only, they can still act as the hierarchy we need among the people, exactly what we have been trying to accomplish through all of this training."

Putu grunted. "I still don't like it. I smell a trap, but I can't find it."

"Maybe there is no trap," Akłaq offered. "Maybe he really does want to help us."

"One drop or not, he is still white, still Canadian. Trickery is in their blood."

"Then maybe that one drop is holding back that trickery and is instead allowing compassion to flourish." She continued, "I wouldn't be surprised if there were a trap being laid somewhere. I just don't think we should completely discount the possibility that maybe we do have sympathizers. If we cut off every helping hand, eventually there will be no more helping hands."

Putu blinked. "You really want to go along with this? Form an alliance with one of the men who would have killed you and your children?"

She couldn't deny that the thought gave her pause. Was she mad? While some of the details had faded, she still remembered well the fear and confusion as she, Latseen, and Gáx tried to escape the school. She remembered the moment of realization that it was a trap, and she remembered being trapped in the entryway, surrounded by six men. She remembered killing the two men who accosted her children. She remembered killing Frederickson and taking his gun.

And now one of those men wanted to help them? Unofficially recognize District Nine? Name her Captain? Let her continue to train the people and basically lie about—?

"If we do this," she said suddenly, "and we start training the people in the Akari as we have been doing, then the Timekeepers will have the authority to arrest and remove every single one of us from our land. We're not training the people to fight against trained Timekeepers, just average soldiers. And if we did it as District Nine and went through the processes in the Wheel, they'll have information on every single one of us, our names, locations, all of it."

The realization hit all of them like a boulder.

"We'd be doing all the heavy lifting for them," Everett said quietly.

"Not about Earth-side politics," Putu growled. "It's always about Earth-side politics. Can't force us to stay on our land so they'll figure out a way to get us to incriminate ourselves and remove us."

Everett sighed. "Well, we hid from them for this long. I can't imagine they'll have any easier time finding us come spring when we don't show up."

"What do you mean?" Akłaq asked. "Of course we're going to show up."

"And you're going to kill him just like you killed Gerald and Frederickson?"

She grinned and shook her head. "No. We're going to take him up on his offer. But with some terms of our own."

"How do you mean?" Putu wondered.

She looked at him. "You're going to be the Captain."

He blinked. "Me?"

"You are a Timekeeper. Other than association, you've never had any dealings with or interest in the Akari or Akarin. Even if you were questioned, there's nothing they'd be able to fault you for."

"You're suggesting taking the facade, and making it real," Everett said. "What about the Akari? It is far more powerful than Time. Rather than just mere escape tools, why not train up the people?"

"And start an international, transcontinental war?" Akłaq shook her head. "Not yet. Not today. We start with Putu as Captain, train the people in Time, do everything perfectly by the rules. Wait for the Timekeepers to try and spring their trap and fail. Once they've made fools of themselves and slunk away with their tails between their legs, then we can start training people in the Akari again. I can't imagine it's going to take long, especially if we try to run with things as fast as they want us to."

"Turn their trap against them."

"Exactly. And, since this is partly predicated on unofficial recognition of District Nine, we might be able to more freely bring in some help from the Krydik."

Even Putu was nodding thoughtfully. "The last thing they would expect us to do is exactly what they tell us to." He huffed. "It could work, but I still don't like it. It feels like surrender."

Everett slapped him on the back. "Well, once you're Captain, you can make all the decisions about what is and isn't surrender."

Putu just gave him a look.

"What will you do, then?" Everett wondered, looking at Akłaq. "Since you're not going to be Captain, and you won't be able to go out and train the people, at least for a short time?"

She nodded slowly. "I think I'm going to take some time off. I'm going to enjoy life, watch the rest of my children get married, play with my grandchildren, and miss as little as possible for the time being."

"They would like that very much," Putu said. "They'll never say it to your face, but Gáx and Tlaganis were very upset that you weren't home for their weddings, Gáx more so when you missed the birth of his first child. And his second."

"I hope they don't resent me for it."

"They are deep hurts, but nothing that can't be remedied by being in the here and now." His expression turned grave, just like a father imparting wisdom. "If you say that you are going to stand back from this business with Billings, that you are going to turn over control to me and live your own life, then that is what you must do. No sitting on the fence, no trying to ride two horses. Understand?"

She nodded. "I understand."

"Nooskw is most likely to be married next, and he's glad you're here to see it. Now be here to see it."

"I will."

"That also means you won't be able to be named Lieutenant Timekeeper," Everett told her. He looked at Putu. "You probably wouldn't be able to name me, either."

"Ikiaq and Suluk will be my Lieutenants. They've shown no real interest in the Akari either. Seems to be my safest choice for the time being."

Everett chuckled. "Do we want to turn around and tell Billings our answer then?"

Putu shook his head. "Let him sweat until spring. We also need to figure out how to make this work so we don't end up in a worse situation than we already are."

"Ikiaq and Suluk should also know what's coming," Akłaq added.

"Agreed," Everett said. "And I should probably talk to the Krydik and let them know what's going on."

"Do you think they would still help us?"

"Of course they will. Their allegiances lie less with the Akarin and more with overall indigenous well-being."

"And...the Author is perfectly fine with this?"

"What is more important? Words and rituals? Or compassion and kindness, looking out for your people in a practical way?"

She nodded silently.

"Looks like we have our work cut out for us," Putu observed. "I don't think anyone here is going to have a boring winter."

"Indeed," Everett said. "And for as much as we're planning ahead, you should be there in the spring, Akłaq."

"Why?" she asked.

"Because they're expecting it. They want you there. You have to be the one to tell them that you are turning over command to Putu. He can take it from there."

"He's right," Putu said.

Akłaq considered this, then nodded. "All right. It makes sense."

"Ikiaq and Suluk will be there, too."

"Is that wise?" Everett questioned. "To have all of you in one place? It could still be a trap."

Putu gave him a look, glanced at Akłaq, then back to Everett. "Akłaq has killed everyone who has tried to kill her, and against greater odds. I'm not worried about this meeting in the least."

Akłaq felt proud and embarrassed at the same time, and she elected to say nothing. With any luck, she wouldn't have to add to an already bad reputation.

Avgun Iñuiñaq Qulit
Alliances

It was anything but a boring winter. The three of them kept things to themselves for the first few days upon their return to the village, and discussed the situation amongst themselves. Then they brought in Ikiaq and Suluk, just to ensure they would accept the Lieutenant positions. The two were skeptical of the overall situation and resulting plan, but they agreed to be part of it. They then informed Lusa and the village leaders and elders, and from there information was disseminated to the rest of the people and carried to the other villages.

Opinions were instant and fiery. Was this not the whole point of the training they had been doing for the last five years? Did they no longer strive for independence from the white men and their institutions, including this "Time" industry? A few immediately ceased their usage of the Akari because of it, as if to spite Akłaq and Everett.

Akłaq left it to Putu to explain things to them, seeing how he was going to be Captain and would be the one they spoke to about such problems. It was actually kind of nice, she thought, not having to jump in for every little detail and grumbling. For once she could sit back, watch, and let others take the lead. This didn't mean that she didn't still go to Putu to offer advice or complain about how he handled something, but at the end of the day, she could leave, go home, and enjoy her family.

Of course, Latseen and Tula'aan were the only ones still living with her, and even that wouldn't last forever. Nooskw was going to be married in the spring, and it stood to reason that Latseen wouldn't be long after. All that remained, then, was Tula'aan, for a little while longer.

Why would the white bear have her step back now, though? She'd been called to work when she had a family, and now she was, presumably, being called to rest when that family was grown up and forming their own families. Yes, bonds were tight, but it seemed like it would have been smarter to make it the other way around for her. She should have been home for these last ten or more years and just now being called to action.

"If life were convenient, what would be the point?"

It was like waking up exhausted, except she knew she was dreaming. As everything came into focus, she found herself in the forest, the white bear about fifteen feet in front of her and to the left. There was a river about a hundred yards away, and the bear was tearing into a fish.

"Do spirits need to eat?" she asked dumbly.

The bear gave her a very human look. "That's your first question?"

"Sorry."

It ripped another large chunk of flesh from the fish. "You humans. Shying away from every minor criticism as though you've been beaten."

"You think I should have started an argument?"

"No, but a misunderstanding is not an offense."

Akłaq blinked and shifted her stance. "Are you trying to say something about this meeting with Billings, the incident at the school some years ago?"

The bear sniffed at the small remains of the fish, then discarded them in the dirt. "You know what happens when you listen to us, listen to the Author?"

"What?"

"You start to understand."

"Then you are trying to say something about it. Is it a trap, or are we making it bigger than it needs to be?"

The bear snorted.

"I'm afraid he's not much for detailed guidance," a familiar voice said behind her.

Akłaq turned to see Anagalisgi sliding down a slope toward them. She did not see Sabelu with him. Once he was within comfortable distance, the white bear stood and lumbered off back toward the river.

"The bear's place is in protection and more broad guidance," Anagalisgi told her. "Just as the wolf's place is in communication, the rabbit for reconnaissance, and the hawk for observation."

"You speak of these things like you're planning for war."

"Life here...in this dimension...it's not about relaxing and loafing about in a land of plenty. Whatever you think about your struggles in what you call 'the real world,' they are but shadowy echoes or manifestations of what goes on here. Sometimes, this is the reason we cannot get to you when you ask for specific guidance. But this does not mean that the Author does not see you or continue to dictate what goes on."

Akłaq searched his expression. "Something big is going to happen, isn't it?"

Anagalisgi nodded resignedly. "Yes."

"Did Sabelu tell you about it?"

"I was able to sift some warnings out of his typical menagerie of sarcasm, dry humor, and self-loathing, yes."

"Will it affect the people?"

He laughed humorlessly. "It will affect the world. The good news is that the people will be largely unaffected unless they choose to be. And the choice will be too big to ignore; you cannot accidentally stumble into it."

Akłaq blinked and felt her cheeks burn hot. "I feel like my problems are so small now."

His expression was impossible to read, but she didn't like it. "Oh no. What seems to you to be a minor decision now will have ripple effects into a catastrophic climax that will dwarf what is coming for the mere world."

She gave him a look and folded her arms. "Oh. Well. When you put it that way, I feel like that might warrant something resembling a straight answer. What should we do, then? We're supposed to return to Vancouver in a month, what are we supposed to tell Billings?"

Anagalisgi just chuckled. "You are not helpless, Akłaq. As the white bear said, when you start learning to listen, then you start understanding as well. All the same, we thank you for consulting us."

"Then we're doing the right thing, putting Putu in charge and all that, doing what they least expect us to do?"

He nodded.

"What then? Where do we go from there? We've spent so much time and energy trying to train people in the Akari...I thought you were all for the Akari and the Akarin and everything?"

"When we are infants, we drink milk. When we are toddlers, we play with dull blades and smooth toys. Once we have matured, then we eat meat that we have hunted ourselves with sharp knives." At her look, he added, "Time was never evil. It is but a fact of mortal existence. The worship of it, and the fear of death that drives it, is the corruption that is evil. But as good must build walls to keep out evil, so evil seeks to build walls to keep out good, and therein lies its greatest weakness."

"Teach them regular Time now, and wait to teach them the Akari until after Billings and the others have humiliated themselves. So we were right about their plans to trap us."

Anagalisgi nodded.

"What about the Krydik?" Akłaq wondered.

"What about them?"

"I mean, they were supposed to help us set up cities, help us with what daily life is supposed to be like with the Akari, help with traditions, all those things."

"Is there a reason they can't do so now?"

"Well..." She thought about it. "I guess they can still help with the traditions, and implementing Time in daily life. We'll just have to hold off on the Akari for a little while. And actually it might be better to take things a bit at a time..." She gave Anagalisgi a look. "How bad did I mess up with the eastern people?"

He laughed. "Not bad. Not bad at all. The impact to them will be quite minimal, I assure you. What is more important is that a foundation has been laid, one that will be needed in times to come."

She nodded. "All right. I guess there wasn't much point in bothering you with all of this, not if something much larger is coming that's going to affect the whole world."

His grin faded. "Well, as I said, what you have already done, and what you begin here in about a month will one day blossom into something much bigger than the world. Never underestimate the impact you have on the world, or the universe. A small decision today could mean everything tomorrow." He went on before she could speak. "And even if this were a minor decision with few or no repercussions, it's not wrong to ask for a little enlightenment anyway, because it means you recognize that you don't have all the answers, that you are not the Author who sees all and knows all and writes all."

"But if she writes all, what use are my decisions?"

"Pick up a book, Akłaq. Any book. I think you already know the answer to that question."

She didn't, but she didn't get a chance to ask anything more before the dream began to fade and the blurry colors and shapes rearranged themselves into something resembling home. Then she was home, waking up in her hut like any average day.

A month later, she, Putu, and Everett were back in Vancouver. Despite Anagalisgi's assurances, which she then passed on to the others, there was still a certain element of fear and suspicion, that even the meeting was a trap of some form. They kept an eye out for Billings as well as any other people who looked a little too interested in what they were doing. This was a difficult thing to do considering everyone was interested in what they were doing. They were in the only dark-skinned people in the park.

"What do you suppose they're afraid of?" Akłaq wondered aloud, meeting someone's gaze as they walked by. The man gave her a dirty look while the woman with him said something quietly and tugged on his arm to get him to move quickly away.

"I've never been quite sure," Putu mused.

"They're afraid of being attacked and scalped, I think," Everett said.

"We don't do that, though."

"No, but the only time they hear anything about us is during wartime, and many southern peoples do, or they used to. So that's all they know. That's why they're afraid of us."

"But by their own teachings, we're all made in God's image and we'll all be judged alike in death."

"You're assuming that their teachings are true," Putu told her, "or that they even know what they believe."

Everett shrugged. "Maybe God has favorites, and we're not it."

It wasn't the first time Akłaq had pondered such things, and it probably wouldn't be the last. Truthfully she kind of wanted Billings to show up so she could focus on something else.

The man arrived, looking every bit as formal as the last time.

"I admit, I didn't actually expect you to reply and set up this second meeting," he said. "Actually I expected to never see or hear from you again, not in a friendly way, at least."

"We may have considered such a thing," Putu told him bluntly.

"Oh, I would be offended if you hadn't. But now that we're here, I'm assuming that you agree to the terms?"

"No," Akłaq said. "Not your terms. Ours."

Billings looked momentarily confused, as if he hadn't considered any other options outside of the ones he had presented. He shifted his stance. "This should be interesting. I'll entertain the notion for the time being." He made a gesture for her to continue.

"I will not be the Captain of District Nine. Even if the District is unofficial, it may still present something you like to call a 'conflict of interest.' Therefore, Putu will be the Captain."

Billings raised a brow. "And I assume you two will be the Lieutenants."

"I have already picked my Lieutenants and discussed things with them," Putu said. "In the event that this proved to be a trap of some form, they are safe and sound and ready to take over."

Billings nodded slowly. "Smart."

"More than you expected from us?"

"Are these your only terms?"

Putu folded his arms casually and shrugged. "Given that District Nine is not actually being recognized, I don't expect you'll need any more details or terms about us."

"Well, no, but as you are agreeing to this, I must reiterate that the Akari is illegal."

"If we didn't agree to this, would it make a difference?"

"No." Billings went on before anyone could speak. "However, I do want to add one more thing. Although you may be Captain of District Nine, it is, as has been stated many times, unofficial. A chance to govern your own affairs within your own peoples. But you are, to my knowledge, still residents of District One. You will act as Time Agents of District One under the direction of the Captain and his Lieutenants." He looked at Putu. "You may report to me as Captain of District Nine, but you will also report to the Captain of District One." He again shifted his stance. "I am instating or reinstating all of you as Master Timekeepers. Whatever criminal history you once had has been erased. I expect you to keep it that way and instead fulfill your Timekeeping obligations."

"And what would those be?" Akłaq asked, trying not to sound bitter.

"Apprehending Runners and turning them over to the Grandfathers in the Judgment Wing in the Wheel of Time. I understand that Mr. Thunder Caller here is skilled in opening portals, so he can assist you in such endeavors." Akłaq did not miss his unspoken, "without needing to bother me." Looking at the others, they heard it, too.

"Of course," Putu said, "although I doubt we're going to be the first choice for such things."

"On the contrary," Billings said, "you may end up being the first choice. You know your lands better than anyone—"

"We did, before you herded us like cattle onto small plots you call reserves and kidnapped our children into schools to rip them away from their people and heritage."

"I'm not talking about them, I'm talking about you. You still know the land. You have already clearly demonstrated an ability to go wherever you want to, regardless of any physical barriers. Every place we discover, you have already tread."

"That much is true, at least."

"So anywhere that a Runner tries to hide, you can find."

Putu looked like he wanted to say more but elected not to.

"And what do we get out of this?" Everett inquired. "What sort of assurances do we get?"

"Assurances?" Billings echoed. "What do you mean, 'assurances'?"

"How do we know you're not going to turn around, accuse of us some crime, and take us before the Grandfathers?"

"What would have been the purpose of all this, then? I have no need to manufacture crimes for you when you are all perfectly capable of committing them in your own time and in your own way." He gave Akłaq a look. "Some more brazenly than others." Without breaking the stare, he added, "Be glad that I have chosen this route of mercy. As it is, I could still have you arrested for murder."

"You'd never be able to tie her to Goldsmith or Frederickson," Everett said.

"I didn't say their murders—although Wallace's murder is still recent enough that I might be able to." Billings looked at him, relieving Akłaq of the discomfort and unease of the stare. "As I said, be glad I'm choosing mercy."

While the man did not move, his next change in posture and tone was reminisce of taking a step back and relieving some of the tension building within the group. "Part of being reinstated as Time Agents, especially as Master Timekeepers, is taking on Apprentices."

"We will be training our own people," Putu told him. "You've no need to worry about that."

"Maybe so, but it also entails training Journeymen and giving your recommendations on passing them to Master status."

"So now you do want our opinion on such matters."

"Trying to contain you has proven both difficult and costly, in both lives and resources. Given that the Time industry expands beyond mere Terran bounds and encompasses an array of species possessing a variety of abilities, some far greater than my own, I cannot rightly deny you some representation in matters which exist purely within the realm of the Time industry."

"Can you say that again?" Everett asked snidely. "I don't think quite all of your pride was sufficiently crushed."

Billings gave him a murderous look, but Everett did not relent.

"Knowing all this, then," Putu went on, echoing Everett's smugness, "are there any assignments you do have for us right away while we're here? Any Journeymen who need to be trained, Apprentices taught?"

Now that he appeared to be on the defensive side of the conversation, Billings appeared more interested in just wrapping things up and going home. "Not right now. As I said before, I'm first surprised that you even showed up, and secondly surprised that we've even come to an agreement."

"We aim to surprise," Everett quipped.

"Shut up," Billings snapped. "Just shut the hell up. I'm trying to find some way to make this all work out so no one else has to die and the order of the Time industry is maintained."

"You just don't want to give up your Earth-side power over us to do it," Putu stated. "I think there's a lesson to be learned here."

Now Billings was just getting flustered. "When I have something for you, I will contact the Captain of District One who will get a hold of you. As things are and should be. Now I suggest you go back to whatever rock you're hiding under and tell your people what's going on, what's been decided."

"They already know. We told them before we left. Our return will let them know that all went well and everyone got what they were looking for."

As amusing as it was to get the better of Billings, Akłaq also saw some real potential for violence brewing. They really didn't need to be responsible for the death of yet another prominent Time Agent, especially another Regional Manager, not today.

"And who is the Captain of District One?" she asked, trying to sound neutral.

"One of the other men from the school, David White," Billings answered, taking the out. "I doubt you'll actually see him, but that's his name." He huffed a sigh. "I expect you'll hear from him eventually."

"It's always good for the Captains to get to know one another," Putu said, getting in a last jab before Billings walked away.

They waited a moment more before leaving the park themselves. In spite of the many dirty looks they got from the white residents, the three of them left Vancouver with their heads held high and a certain air of satisfaction.

"That went well, I think," Everett stated finally once they had left Vancouver and were on their way home.

Akłaq broke out into a giggle, and even Putu grinned. But it was Putu who sobered up first and said, "We should still keep an eye out for any traps, or any followers."

That got them all to swivel their heads around for a minute or two, but the road itself was still too busy to say for sure.

"How does the mail system work in the Wheel?" Akłaq wondered. "How does the mail know where to go when even the Regional Manager doesn't?"

"It works simple enough," Everett explained. "I go to the Wheel to what's called, creatively, the Mail House. I write out my message and indicate who I want to send it to."

"Yes, that sounds logical enough, but—"

"Then the secretaries take the message and put it through a machine whose inner workings I do not fully, or even minimally understand. Somehow, it picks up on where you are assigned, where you are supposed to be. Then it is put into another machine that turns the standard letters of the Wheel into something more appropriate for the local setting, the correct paper, the correct ink, and so on. That machine then sends the localized letter to you in some fashion that makes it inconspicuous."

Akłaq blinked. "That...doesn't make much sense, honestly."

"I don't know how it works exactly. The technology of the Wheel is beyond me. If you want my personal opinion, I think there is some remnant of the Akari at work—the same as being able to forge documents so precisely—the manipulation of Matter."

"Is there anything that doesn't involve the Akari in some way for you?" Putu asked, his tone impossible to determine.

Everett gave him a look. "The Wheel was originally made for the Akari-bearers. Why shouldn't there still be fragments of its power in there?"

"It was?" Akłaq questioned.

At the same time, Putu said, "Ah, the celestial Garden of Eden, is that it?"

"Why couldn't it be?" Everett asked.

"I'm not saying it couldn't, except the Wheel makes no sense. The Akarin fortress is orderly and makes sense. Doesn't that seem to be the more likely dwelling of a people created by a so-called Author? There is a right way and a wrong way to speak and write. The Wheel is chaos, the wrong way to do things. The fortress is order, the right way to do it. At least, that's how I would do things."

"I don't know the details—"

"Another story to explain right and wrong, good and evil," Putu went on. "As I've told Akłaq, it's not that I don't believe in the spirits, I just don't think they're overly concerned with us. And that goes for all the spirits, whoever or whatever they may be."

Everett looked like he wanted to say more on the subject but elected not to. Instead he wondered, "How do you think we should proceed, as far as teaching the people and preparing them for more attacks and infringement by the government?"

"We've taught the people a fair amount already," Putu said. "And we've already discussed that we're going to have to hold off or lay low until Billings and the others, maybe even the Gatekeeper herself, try to spring their trap and fail."

"How long do you suppose that will be?" Akłaq inquired.

"Not this year, that's for sure. They have to suspect that we're going to be cautious, at least for a little while. I would say maybe three to five years from now. They'll want us to get comfortable, get complacent, and begin training again. That, too, would be cautious at first. Then, when nothing happens, we'd get more bold about it until we had the same operation as before. Then they would swoop in and arrest all of us."

"You're saying we're going to have to wait five years?"

"Yes, I am. Maybe more, maybe less, I don't know what they have planned. But we should proceed cautiously until that time." He went on before she could speak. "And anyway, you're not part of this anymore, remember? You're stepping back, taking time off to spend with your family. Let the rest of us take care of things for a while."

She knew it was true, but it still felt like a slap in the face to hear it put in such a way. Stand back, step down, mind your place.

"What about the Krydik?" she asked evenly.

"I've been in contact with them," Everett said coolly. "They're still willing to help. It may be that, because of this ongoing problem with the schools, some of the families here on Earth will want to 'flee to Aktiya Waya for the safety of their children.' What they learn while in Aktiya Waya is of no concern to Billings or the others; it's out of their jurisdiction."

"And they do plan on coming back, right? Else we might as well just go to Aktiya Waya now and save everyone the trouble of a facade."

"They have every intention of returning, I'll say it that way. But peace and security are powerful motivators." He shrugged. "And besides that, since their previous tragedies stemming from uncontrolled migration, the Krydik have implemented certain requirements that must be met before they allow permanent residence or intermarrying."

"Their problems are their own," Putu stated. "Our concern is with the people here and all over District Nine. I know we've discussed it amongst ourselves and sent general word to other peoples, we should probably send out further messages, letting everyone know what's happened."

The conversation remained largely between Putu and Everett. Despite being free from such obligations, Akłaq couldn't help but feel a bit left out. She'd been part of these plans for years; she couldn't honestly be expected to just drop everything and retire to the life of a housewife. She didn't even have a husband, and her children were grown. What was she supposed to do with herself? Her grandchildren were far too young to begin learning either Time or the Akari, and even so, with exception of Latseen—and that exception appeared to be severely wavering—her children had given multiple indications that they did not want to make Time or the Akari such a big part of their lives. The cycle of life and death had been instituted for a reason, they said, and who were they to interfere in such order? They were grateful for the training, grateful for the help it had provided them, but it was only a tool, a means to an end. For the moment, it appeared as though they had reached that end and now had no further need for the tool.

Did that mean, then, that Akłaq had reached her end? Could this be the end of her Book? She'd raised her children, helped the people, and was now passing everything off to Putu and the others to continue the work. Was this the end?

No, it couldn't be. Anagalisgi had practically said as much. If this were the end, then she could hand things over to Putu and walk away. And yet, Anagalisgi had told her that this seemingly minor decision would lead to something that would dwarf whatever calamity was going to strike the world. How could he say such a thing if this was where she were meant to depart?

This wasn't the end, then, but a resting period. Give it a few years, long enough for the Timekeepers to spring a failed trap and leave the people alone for a time. Something would come of it, she was sure. Something would happen where she would again be needed and have to rise to the occasion.

But what about her children? Would they be needed as well, or would she have to watch them grow old and die? What about her grandchildren? Suddenly she didn't know which was worse, the sudden ripping away of her first children as they were murdered, or the slow decline of her family now, inching ever closer to death. Was there any hope for heaven for characters of the Author, or did they fall away into oblivion, forgotten by everyone including their creator? Was all of this just a symptom of her own fear, the fear which the Time industry had monetized into an intergalactic business empire?

These thoughts plagued her all the way back to the village, a symptom itself of suddenly having far fewer responsibilities.

Their arrival seemed to trigger a massive sigh of relief.

"We weren't sure you would be coming back," Ikiaq said, meeting them, Suluk by his side. "We half-expected Billings and his cronies to come looking for us." He searched Putu and Everett. "They're not coming, are they?"

"Not that we are aware of," Putu told him. "The meeting went about as expected; he wasn't sure what to do with us countering his offer. Otherwise, everything is just as we planned it."

"Well, that's a welcome change," Suluk said sourly. "You're the Captain, then, of this nonexistent District?"

"And you two are my Lieutenants." Putu gestured toward Akłaq and Everett. "They have been reinstated as Master Timekeepers but are not involved in any political goings-on. That Billings is aware of at the moment. But that is for further discussion."

Putu, Ikiaq, and Suluk started walking away. Akłaq took two steps with them, but Everett touched her arm and she stopped. When she looked at him, she found him smiling.

"That's not your job anymore," he told her.

She relented. "I know. Habit, I guess." She looked around. "Where are Latseen and Tula'aan?"

"Why don't you go find them?"

With a last glance in the direction where Putu and the others had already disappeared, Akłaq turned away and headed for home.

It was later in the day, so it was no surprise that everyone should be out and about, but was it too much to hope that her children would be around when she got home?

While not necessarily hungry, Akłaq still wanted something to taste, so she started rummaging for something to eat. Latseen had begun to really feel the effects of the slow-aging caused by the Akari, but Tula'aan was still relatively normal, so there was still food in the hut. Akłaq grabbed a dried fish fillet and added some freshly foraged greens to make a light dinner. She was on her second bite when her two daughters finally returned home, smiling and laughing.

"I see where I stand, then," Akłaq said.

"You're home!" Tula'aan exclaimed, running to embrace her and nearly knocking the food out of her hands.

"And you didn't even come see what all the commotion was about. You know Grandfather is going to be in meetings half the night and you won't get to see him until morning."

"We know," Latseen said, sitting down next to her, "but we were a little busy."

"Out with a couple of boys?" Akłaq wondered.

"Mother, please, I'm a woman now. And Geetwein is a perfectly capable, handsome man."

"Well, when you put it that way..." At her daughter's look, she laughed. "I've known you both since you were children, and I remember that Geetwein was one of those who tried to help you escape the soldiers when they tried to take you to the schools. He's a fine young man."

Just sitting next to her, Akłaq could feel the heat of embarrassment from Latseen. "We talked about it some, after you and I returned from the east."

"Have you been planning a wedding behind my back this whole time?" She tried to say it lightly, jokingly, but if the answer was yes, Akłaq wouldn't deny that she would feel deeply hurt.

"Not exactly. There was the issue about the message from Billings, and we weren't sure what was going to happen, if I would be needed.

I did train Geetwein, at least I tried. We talked about marriage some, but I didn't really know what I wanted."

"You weren't sure you were ready to give up the slowed aging. Geetwein wasn't sure he was ready to embrace it and all the responsibility that came with it."

"That's right. We wanted to wait and see if there was going to be more trouble."

Akłaq laughed. "Oh, child, there will always be more trouble. Always, always. If not here, then somewhere. I may not be part of things as much as I used to be, but I happen to know that Grandfather is going to stir a few political pots as well. Not in the Time industry, but in the American and Canadian governments."

"Going to try and bind them with their own rope?"

"Something like that." Akłaq looked at Tula'aan who had been silent so far. "And what about you? Have you been secretly planning your wedding, too? Who are you eyeing? I know you've looked at several boys over the last couple years."

Tula'aan smiled shyly. "I thought about one, but then I realized I don't fawn over him like Latseen fawns over Geetwein."

Latseen elbowed her sister, but Tula'aan just laughed.

For a long moment, Akłaq couldn't pinpoint exactly what she was feeling. Then she realized that she was still, in her mind, waiting. Waiting for the next piece of news or information, waiting for a plan of action, waiting to hear her part and assume her role. Waiting for the next thing. Waiting for anything.

But it was done now, at least for a little while. And actually, unlike the time when she'd first adopted her children, when she'd known that she had been somehow charged with their protection from greater threats, she didn't have any idea what might be coming, as far as the white bear was concerned. The struggle against the Time industry was a constant thing, but there was nothing to direct her one way or another to a specific threat or a specific charge. She knew that there would be something, but she didn't know what.

It was a little frightening, but she also didn't want to contemplate whatever it was that awaited her in the future. Whatever it was that this recent decision affected that was reportedly going to affect more than just the entire world, she didn't want to think about it. If she did, then it was only going to consume her in a way that was going to take her away from this, from watching her last two children and only two daughters talk about boys—ahem, perfectly capable, handsome men— and getting married. She'd missed too much already.

The evening was peaceful, and Latseen and Tula'aan asked her more about the trip. They inquired a bit about the meeting, but they also wondered about Vancouver itself, what the town was like.

"Not any more friendly than it was any other time we've been there," Akłaq told them. "I think the only reason something didn't happen to me was because Grandfather and Everett were with me, and I think Billings himself may have been the reason something didn't happen to the three of us."

"They knew you were coming," Latseen stated.

"That's right. I think he didn't want to provoke a fight if he didn't have to."

"At least he acknowledges that we're more powerful than him."

"Yes, but once again, we didn't need a fight."

Tula'aan shifted position. "Do you think we'll ever be able to visit any of these places, or just leave the reserves, without worrying about being attacked or anything else?"

"Maybe," Akłaq told her. "We have to keep pushing hard, but we have to do it the right way."

"What is the right way?" Latseen asked, her tone dubious. "Two hundred years ago, it was about killing the invaders. These days, doing anything else is either surrender or their way."

"Kindness and patience are not surrender. We just have to remember that we are not fighting men. We are fighting ideas. Evil ideas from evil spirits that manifest within men. We can kill a body by many means, but it does nothing to kill an evil spirit. In fact, that is what feeds the evil spirit, because we have allowed ourselves to become host to hatred."

"But if a bear were to attack us right now, you would kill the bear to save us."

"Yes. To save you. Not for any hatred of the bear. In the same way that I did not kill all of the men at the school, and now look where we are. We may have an avenue to peace and acceptance, if we navigate the path correctly. But we must be patient."

"We have the time for patience," Latseen said. "Not everyone else does. Most people don't."

"Everyone has time for patience; that's why it's called patience. But even so, no one is guaranteed tomorrow. We should learn to live in the present moment, regardless if we have three years or three hundred years left to live."

"Does that mean you're going to be home for a while?" Tula'aan asked, her expression making her look like a little girl again.

Akłaq grinned and nodded. "Yes. I expect I will be home for a while, at least long enough to see you two get married, assuming you ever admit to liking boys."

That started another round of protests and corrections and talking over each other. Akłaq could only sit back, laugh, and marvel at life.

Micaiah

Avgun Iñuiñaq Qulit Atausiq
Vancouver

Forty years and two wars later, little had changed. The schools were still open and the people were still oppressed. In Putu's opinion, the usage of Time was keeping everything neutral, just barely tipped in the people's favor as they gained political power. If that was the case, Akłaq reasoned, then if they had been using the Akari for at least the last twenty years, they might be independent by now. The Timekeepers had tried to spring a trap on them some thirty years ago, tried to claim they were using the Akari—something about interference in the first World War—but that had fallen through because of the plan Putu and the others had come up with even before that. Since then, there had been no Time-side troubles.

Akłaq took a bite of her food as she sat on the shore and watched the calm ocean waves tap at the sand. The horizon was completely open, an eternal distance away. She was tired, but they were in the waxing days leading up to the long day, and she used the near-constant light to keep herself awake.

If she wanted to be completely honest, the main reason the people didn't learn the Akari—or Time for that matter—beyond basic knowledge useful for escaping a fight or otherwise saving one's skin, was because they didn't want to. It wasn't part of them, they said. It wasn't who they were as a people and culture. That kind of power was reserved for medicine men, shamans, priests, and other special chosen, but not for the average person. Even those who observed some Christian practices were more reserved about it, wondering if it was circumventing the appointment of death or else attempting to usurp the power of God and Creation. The Krydik had built Time and the

Akari into their identity, but the Tlingit, the Haida, the Iñupiatun, the Chilcotin, they had not.

But the final straw was the difficulty with which people who were more inundated had in conceiving children. There did not appear to be any trouble on the part of the men, but the women had some difficulty. A few of the Krydik women offered to teach them how to go about it, but there was no interest. What good was it to save themselves within their culture but forfeit the future of their people?

It might not have bothered her so much, except even Latseen had given it up as well in order to marry Geetwein and have children. Her oldest daughter, who had helped her rescue children from the schools and traveled across the continent to help other peoples, had given up the Akari. Akłaq did not fault her one bit for wanting a family, but it was entirely possible to have both.

But now, forty years later, all of her children looked older than Putu. Lingering youthfulness had worn off from Latseen and now she might have been mistaken as being Akłaq's mother. Tula'aan could, too, for that matter. Gáx and Nooskw were elders as well. Tlaganis had died five years ago, though he'd also begun showing his advancing age.

Akłaq still loved her children. She loved her grandchildren and the great-grandchildren that were starting to run around. But there was also a quiet glacier moving through her heart and mind. All those dreams and visions, all the guidance from Anagalisgi and the white bear, all the adventures and the training, and somehow it all felt meaningless. The people wanted nothing to do with it. They wanted freedom, but they didn't want to seem to do anything other than muddle around in white politics, whine when things didn't go their way, and then count it as some great victory when they got scraps from a rich man's table. She hated to give them credit, but at least the white Americans had fought for their independence. Even the Confederates had been willing to fight and die for their way of life.

There had to be more than this. Anagalisgi had once told her that the alliance they made with Billings would blossom into something greater than just a war. He'd visited her twice more since then to reiterate the point. Well, there had been at least two wars since the initial promise. What more was there? Sure there was some hubbub going on in the Time industry, but she was already full up on Earth-side politics; she didn't want to consider any Time-side politics right now. What difference would it make, anyway?

"Frustrating, isn't it?"

She looked up from where she sat on the bank. At first she thought it was a slightly younger Anagalisgi. Then she recognized Sabelu. Any remaining babyish looks he'd had when she first met him years ago had melted away; here was a man, and a man only, with the gaze of an elder. A bad-tempered one at that.

"Am I dreaming?" she wondered. "Or are you really here?"

He sat down a couple feet from her and looked out at the horizon. "Does it matter?"

She shrugged. "I don't know. You're the one who has trouble controlling what he sees, and I thought that dreams only made it worse."

"Please, you think I don't try to make things easier on myself, or that I haven't had some margin of success in the last few decades?"

"Maybe, but that doesn't explain why you're here. You've never come across as the social type."

"Believe me, I'm not, but my uncle sent me."

"Trying to get you to develop your social skills?"

"He gave up on that a long time ago."

"Then why send you?"

"Because he's busy."

"What about the white bear?"

Sabelu grinned but did not look at her. "I'm starting to think you don't want to talk to me." He went on before she could speak. "That's all right. I don't like to talk to me either. So to save us both the hassle of having to listen to me more than we need to, I will simply impart my uncle's message. He wants you to know that very soon, you will be presented with a decision, and you should make the right one."

Akłaq gave him a look. "Really?"

He shifted position. "Well, it may have been something more along the lines of, 'The decision made will either end the world or save it.' "

She raised a brow.

"All right, fine," Sabelu conceded. "Those are my words, not his."

"Something you saw? Or are you making this up?"

Now he gave her a look. "I see too much to want to make anything up. My uncle saw the same thing, but as I said, he's busy, and the white animals don't like me very much, so he sent me on this errand."

"So what is this upcoming decision?"

Sabelu sighed. "I told my uncle I would be as polite as possible and try not to direct you in such a way that it would impede free will."

Akłaq shook her head. "I don't understand."

"He believes that the choices one makes should not be of fear, vanity, or even a promise of reward like training a dog with treats. Decisions should be made with knowledge, thoughtfulness, truth, and love." Sabelu shook his head. "The problem is, any of those on their own are usually in short supply."

"But doesn't telling someone the truth sometimes provoke them to fear or vanity or hope of a reward, or a treat, as you put it?"

He did not look at her as he said, "If I told you that the next man—in Time—that you meet, you have to marry in order to save the universe, would you do it?" He continued before she could answer, "And if I told you that he was white—as white as any of the men you've fought against so far, maybe even whiter—would you still do it? Would you do it if I told you that it would be decades before your union produced these universe-saving results? What if I said that you would have to risk your life multiple times? What if I said that he would risk life and limb and ignore all of your warnings to the contrary? What if I told you that he would risk your life without your knowledge, permission, or ability to refuse? What if I told you that it would be nearly a century before you would even be able to have children again? But what if I also told you that to not do any of this would be to sentence the universe to death? Do you really want to know all that truth? Or would you prefer to listen to my uncle's 'tact and diplomacy' as he calls it?"

Akłaq blinked. "Is that what's going to happen?"

He shrugged casually and looked at her. "I don't know. Is it? Could it be true only because I have effectively frightened you into fulfilling this potentially-bogus prophecy? Considering how long I've said it's going to take to fulfill, what if you went along with it but it never came to be? Or what if you ignored it and sentenced the universe to death?"

"What if I punched you in the face and then went and did the same thing to your uncle?"

He burst into laughter. "If I thought you could, I would let you punch me just so I could go with you and watch."

"So what am I supposed to do?! Is the next Timekeeper I meet going to be a white man who I have to marry in order to save the universe? And why wouldn't you warn me about something like that sooner?"

Sabelu shrugged yet again, then took a sweet-smelling roll from his bag, put it between his lips, and lit it. He puffed out some smoke. "You wanted the truth. As I said, I know too much to want to make stuff up."

"Well, I hate you for it. And you can tell your uncle when you see him that I hate him, too, for sending you to me."

"Hate me all you want, everyone else does."

Akłaq glared at him. "You're incredibly selfish, do you know that?"

"I've been called worse."

"You claim to see all this stuff, but you never once mention any of the good things that happen. Festivals, weddings, the joy of a child. No, it's all about the bad stuff in the world."

He took another drag and looked at her. "I did tell you some good things. You're going to marry again. One day, far in the future, you will have children again. You'll even have the opportunity to save the universe. Those don't sound like good things to you?"

"Yes, well, you're cynical enough that even good things sound like bad things. You just want everyone to be as miserable as you."

He grinned around another drag. "Believe me, I do not. I would be more than content to live alone in my cabin, but, interestingly enough, I don't have much say over my life." He gave her a severe look. "You, however, do."

She searched his face. "Do the things you see change? If I were to decide not to marry this man, do you see different things? Different futures?" She blinked. "Or are you just saying this in order to get me to do whatever it is you actually see me doing?"

Sabelu sighed, took another drag, and studied the remained of his roll, blowing smoke from his nostrils. "This is why prophets have a hard life and do not belong in the waking world, whatever my uncle thinks." He stood. "I've told you what I can."

"What you can, or what you will?"

He went on as though she hadn't spoken. "What you do now is up to you."

He turned and started walking away, still smoking. Akłaq shouted at his back, "Oh! Right! It's only the fate of the universe we're talking about! Who needs clear answers about that?!"

He did not appear to react, and vanished soon enough. Akłaq shifted position and glared angrily at the horizon.

When I asked for an answer, I would have liked an answer, she grumbled in her mind.

But you got an answer, something replied. *You got an answer, a course of action, and the risks and benefits of either doing or not doing that action.*

Well, maybe, but did it have to be so...dramatic?

You were warned of this years ago. You've heard of the devastation of the wars, and you were told that your decisions would surpass even those. Why should you be surprised that some upcoming event would carry such decisions and consequences?

Did he really have to carry it all the way to the end, though? A century?

Wouldn't you have wanted to know?

She couldn't argue the point, but she kind of wanted to anyway. Mostly she just didn't want to admit that she was a selfish, self-defeating, wishy-washy human.

There was also a part of her that resisted the idea of marriage, at least marriage as Sabelu had presented it. The next man she met in Time, she would marry. This might not bother her too much, except she kind of enjoyed the thrill of spontaneity that Nika had shown her, and she also appreciated the freedom of movement that a more informal relationship with Aniqan had given. Now, it sounded a bit like being chained by both destiny and marriage.

And to a white man, too. Make no mistake, she still held a place in her heart for Nika who had been white—and Russian, for that matter, while the rest of his countrymen were burning villages—but that had been the exception. He had been an exceptional man. Every white man since had been, at best passive and average, and at worst hostile and trying to kill her or her people.

Was it really possible that there was another exceptional white man?

She didn't want to think about that now. Sabelu had gotten her too flustered. Sighing, she stood and made her way away from the shore back toward home.

She had returned to Qikiqtaġruk about four years ago. It wasn't the same as when she'd left, but since the Russians had gone, things appeared to have gotten back to normal somewhat. Some homes were traditional, others were log cabins, and a few were of a new style developed by the southern whites just now making its way to the frozen north.

Akłaq lived in a log cabin style house. It had been built as for one or two hunters, which made it the perfect size for her. As much as she had wanted to stay with her children and the Tlingit, she couldn't bear watching her children and grandchildren grow old, and differing opinions over the use of Time only made her feel more rotten and cast out. Being an elder by age but young adult by appearance wasn't helping her standing either. Despite Latseen and Nooskw and Tula'aan telling her not to go, she left and returned to her real home, her real people.

And now she was faced with the idea of marrying a white man. She hadn't even met him yet and already she was dreading it.

What if she said no? What if she didn't do it? Would the universe really end?

What if this man had a similar prophecy told to him, though? What if, even now, he was in the area, his head filled with words or images of having to find a particular woman and marry her in order to save the universe?

No, that was foolish. Sabelu and Anagalisgi wouldn't appear to white men, would they? Well, Sabelu might not, but Anagalisgi... He claimed allegiance to the Author before any people, even his own. Thinking about the Authored Books, there was a series called The Chivalrous Welshman. The Welsh were pretty white. Maybe Sabelu had been sent to her while Anagalisgi went to the man she was apparently supposed to marry.

But why should she be subjected to this celestial arranged marriage? It sounded so...rigid. Like stone.

Was the universe really worth it? There was no justice, no mercy, no righting of wrongs, full of suffering and misery and death. Why shouldn't she let it go to ruin? Every religion and spiritual belief she knew of acknowledged such pain, and many even stated that it would all one day come to head in a massive upheaval of death and rage. Some believed things would start over as perfect peace, and others said things would just end. Either way, it sounded like a win-win, better than trying to salvage whatever hell they were currently living in.

Then again, hadn't she just chastised Sabelu for his cynical views, for focusing only on the evils and never giving a thought to the good? There was plenty of good in the world, too. Marriage was a good thing. Her children were good, her grandchildren and great-grandchildren were good.

Sometimes, good was not a raging river, but a quiet stream. And a quiet stream of fresh water was worth a hundred times the salt of the ocean.

She didn't have to like it, and her minor epiphany only served to calm her racing thoughts enough that she could get in bed and have a hope of sleep. When she'd first moved in, she'd had heart-wrenching flashbacks to her life with Nika. Those had faded after a few weeks, but now, with the looming prospect of marriage, her thoughts again wandered in that direction. Many of the small details had long since gone, but the emotion was still there, in peripheral hallucinations and phantom sensation.

Maybe it really wouldn't be so bad. She had gone so long without anyone in her life, at least, not in that way. Aniqan had been her best friend and lover, Putu had been her father, and her children had been, well, her children. But she had never known a man the same way that she had known Nika. Maybe that was what really frightened her. Not that she wouldn't, but that she would. And this time, with Time and the Akari, the relationship had the potential to last a lot longer, at least a century if Sabelu was to be believed.

She lay in bed, staring into a darkness achieved only by the hanging of thick furs over windows and doors. The white men always had a harder time dealing with the long night and the long day. Could she convince this man to stay with her here, or would she again have to leave home?

She was able to get some sleep, though the constant light made any telling of time dubious at best. Regardless, she felt somewhat rested, and she rose to go about her day.

It was two weeks before anyone really sought her out. The Captain and Lieutenants for District One were all white, as expected, and the appearance of one of the Lieutenants caused quite a stir in town. Once the village leaders had given him their customary cold welcome, Akłaq went to meet him about the Time business he was clearly there for. She was the only Master Timekeeper in Qikiqtaġruk. Indeed, she was perhaps the only Timekeeper of any significant rank north of the Arctic Circle right now, and almost certainly the only Akari-bearer of any standing.

"Something wrong?" she inquired levelly. "Didn't think any of you would want to come north of Anchorage."

"I'm leaving just as soon as I can, believe me. But it's still very difficult to get messages through up here." He gave her an accusatory look.

"What can I say? Maybe the squirrels ran off with them." Or the fact that any messages she had received that were not reports of imminent danger were discarded, their receipt never acknowledged.

She could see he didn't believe her, but she didn't care. "At any rate, you're being relocated to Vancouver."

She raised a brow. "Oh I am?"

"Yes, you are. A couple of Journeymen are coming in, and Captain wants you to train one of them."

"But I'm way up here. Why not ask someone else?"

"If you took more care of your messages and didn't feed them to the squirrels—" He gave her another look. "—you might know that everyone else is either busy with their own Apprentices, or else out of the area for a while, or in the middle of a transfer. That leaves you. And if you don't, I'll have to arrest you for dereliction."

Akłaq rolled her eyes. "Yes, yes. The great evil of dereliction." She sighed. "When are these Apprentices supposed to arrive?"

"June 24."

So she had a little time to get down there. "How are they getting here? Or there?"

"They're flying in. The plan is for them to send me a message before they board, and I will relay their expected landing time to you." He turned as if to leave, then paused and gave her a final look. "And I expect you to actually read your mail instead of giving it to the squirrels as nesting material."

"What can I say? I care about nature."

Another reason she had returned home, it was a natural repellent to outsiders. The long day, the long night, the difficulty getting in and out, and the unfriendly locals.

The Lieutenant left just as quickly as he had arrived, if not faster. Like a ghost, he departed, leaving Akłaq alone in her home, her current life's trajectory irrevocably altered. If she did what was requested, she would be walking right into whatever fate Sabelu had envisioned. If she did nothing, she could be arrested. If she tried to flee the arrest, well, she didn't know what would happen, but it would change her path nonetheless. Maybe running was what caused her to enter into the prophecy. Who could know?

She found herself wondering whether it was really better to know the specifics of such things. Anagalisgi and the white bear were irritating in the way they espoused vague notions and riddles, but was Sabelu's candor really an improvement? Was there a way to get the straightforward answers of Sabelu but with the tact and kindness of Anagalisgi?

None of the three showed up to advise her on the matter, which was fine. She was annoyed with all of them anyway. All of their plans and promises and prophecies, and it felt as though no progress had truly been made for her people, or any peoples. All the power of Time, and, in the case of the Akari-bearers, Matter and Energy, and the best that the peoples had to show, in either Canada or the United States, were a few political movements. No liberation, no autonomy. Hell, they weren't even legal citizens. They were part of another people, they were told, but yet they weren't permitted to govern their own affairs and keep to their own ways or their own land. They were treated like cattle to be moved here and there at whim.

And the Time industry was no different, it seemed. She was being "relocated" to Vancouver. Just like that. Follow orders, or be arrested. She scoffed. Dereliction of duty. A prod upon blackmail, that's what this was. They were supposed to lie low for a while, train up the people in secret, so that when the Timekeepers or white soldiers came, it didn't matter what they did or said, because the people would be ready and able to fend for themselves.

Now her children were all past sixty years of age, and they all looked just so. Yes, they had families and were happy—and far be it from her to deny them the joy of a family—but what did they think would happen when the soldiers came again? Who would defend them? Who would even be able to appreciate what it was they were trying to defend and save?

The purpose of Sabelu's existence was becoming clearer with each passing year, but what was the point of offering such an astounding gift if no one cared enough to want to claim it? And what would happen if Sabelu were to perish, and all his knowledge with him? Would there ever be another like him, or was this perhaps their last chance at saving themselves?

Even she would admit that she didn't keep all the traditions. She did not tattoo her lip, and she found herself praying to God more often than the earthen spirits, on the occasions that she did pray, though she might still burn sacred incense. Her winter clothing was still made up of heavy furs, and she'd managed to keep hold of her mother's garments, the same ones she'd worn when fleeing the village now more than a century ago. Yet her summer clothing, like the garments she wore now, was very European. Granted, it was stuff she'd brought with her, as it was expensive to try and bring such things so far north for casual sale, but she still reached for the cotton over the leather.

Looking around, she couldn't deny that the log cabin was nice. She had lived in some very nice places, all things considering. Even life in Red River hadn't been terrible. So what was it that upset her so?

She didn't know, honestly, and she wasn't in much of a mood to dwell on it. Right now, she had to consider her options, what she was going to do about this new assignment she'd been handed. It wouldn't bother her too much except for Sabelu and his damn visions. If he'd been a little more like his uncle and could give her some encouragement about the situation going forward, instead of dumping the weight of the universe in her lap—maybe even literally—then maybe she wouldn't be so unsure. Maybe she would be happy to go to Vancouver, curious about what she might find. But no, she had to save the universe while she was at it. And all those other details...

If there was more than one Journeyman coming to Vancouver, and he'd said a couple, then it was a safe bet that it would be at least one man and one woman. Maybe two men and a woman. One man and woman might be posing as husband and wife—as some Time Agents were known to do—and the other man would likely be this fabled future mate for her.

It definitely made packing more interesting, thinking that she was packing for a wedding or a new marriage. Did he even know what was going on? Was he going to ask to marry her upon setting eyes on her? She hoped not. If he wasn't aware of these celestial marriage plans, did she want to bring it up? She had been a little more traditional, true, but at least she and Nika had Russian Orthodoxy in common. This new white man could be Catholic, Protestant, or something else entirely. Coming from another District, his background could be anything. How was she going to explain the white bear to him? Or the Akari? If they were supposed to save the universe together, they would at least have to get along, if not like each other.

Did she dare hope that this white man might be a half-breed? Maybe he was only white in appearance, an unfortunate inheritance from the wrong side of the family. Maybe that was the reason these Journeymen were being assigned to her, because no one else wanted to deal with them on account of their heritage. Yes, that seemed logical. Actually it made her feel a little better about the situation.

It was June 10 when she left Qikiqtaġruk, though not without a little spiritual temper tantrum. She wanted to go home and stay there for a while, damn it, without being disturbed.

Oh well, she figured. Nothing could last forever, bad or good.

She got passage on a small plane from Qikiqtaġruk to Fairbanks, then transferred to another small plane that got her to Anchorage. From there, a larger plane flew her to Vancouver.

Again she found herself questioning her anger. Yes, planes were a white invention. But were they really all that bad? She could have walked or taken a dog team from Qikiqtaġruk to Vancouver. It wouldn't have been especially easy, and it would have taken quite a bit of time, even with Banding, but she could have done it. And yet, airplanes made life that much simpler, that much easier. Was that a bad thing? If Paa could be fixed so they were not so strenuous and could be used more regularly by the average Time Agent or Akari-bearer, would she not use Paa to get from here to there? And would she not want to show others so they could experience such convenience? How great would it be if one did not have to wait so long for help? To be able to summon the best doctor to care for the sick, regardless of the physical distance between the two? To go home for a family emergency at just a thought and whim?

So why did she find herself glowering at a plane, an inanimate object which cared not for her feelings toward it? The same with the train on its tracks, or the cars lumbering along on the roads. She had crossed plains and mountains on horseback, and it had taken at least forever. Now, cars, trains, planes, she could go anywhere, and it was still slower than Paa, if Paa could be opened easily.

She had no answers, and this only served to frustrate her more. Certainly if Paa were easier to open blindly she might have actually stayed in Qikiqtaġruk and simply jumped back and forth as needed for the Journeymen.

Perhaps it was the difference between being swept away by a sudden, strong current, and going there intentionally. Or, as she'd also heard it said, the difference between trying to force a stubborn mule to move and letting it move on its own, going to its destination because it thinks it was its idea and not a forced one.

Anticipating her sloth in the matter overall, as well as any number of excuses which she might use to delay even further, the Captain had apparently already made living arrangements for her, a small apartment on the east side of town. Cheap, a bit dirty, exactly what she would expect to get if she had made the arrangements herself.

Her Timekeeping salary could sustain her for a while because she'd done nothing with it for the last forty years, but on its own, it could not hold her from month to month once the savings ran out. She would have to find a job at some point, but that wouldn't be for a couple years. By then, the Journeymen would have moved on, and she could return to Qikiqtaġruk. All the same, she might need to find some kind of work, just to occupy her time.

Once she had cleaned the apartment and tidied her things, she headed out to explore the city, acclimate herself to her surroundings.

Vancouver had changed dramatically in the last few decades. From a small town whose only significance and livelihood came from its position on the water and surrounding forest, it had grown to become a proper city with industry and development and hoards of people. It boasted ships and planes, trains and cars, transporting people and goods all over the country, to and from the United States and a multitude of other countries, taking advantage of the construction boom in the aftermath of the war.

Just locally, Akłaq saw dozens of new businesses being built, with more land being cleared and marked for various development projects. Power poles lay on the ground in precise intervals, the workers raising them one by one and connecting them using large wires, like stringing beads on a thread. There was no electricity in Qikiqtaġruk yet, though it was making its way there from Anchorage. For the people at home, it would be a novelty. For the people here in Vancouver, it was as much a part of daily life as the automobile, or the clothes they wore.

A strong current in an unfamiliar river, Akłaq thought. Or, maybe, an unexpectedly strong current in a once-peaceful river. A settlement, fine, where people could live and make and trade goods. That was how things had always been. But what was all this? What was its real purpose? What would happen if the electricity didn't work? What if the machines didn't function as intended? Would the people still be able to survive? For as much as the whites had stolen from her people, Akłaq couldn't help but wonder if they were also slowly destroying themselves, stealing from the future.

Eventually she returned to her apartment. From there she went to the Wheel and sent a message to the Captain and Lieutenants — as well as Putu — that she had arrived in Vancouver and would wait for the Journeymen. It wasn't even an hour after she returned to her apartment before she got a reply. It was basically just an acknowledgment, but from the Lieutenant who had visited her in

Qikiqtaġruk, there was also a sarcastic thank you for not feeding her mail to the squirrels.

Akłaq rolled her eyes and made another lap of the apartment. She didn't know what to do. She didn't like the city, didn't like the apartment. She felt confined, restricted. She wanted to do something, anything. She just didn't know what. Well, she wanted to go home, but that wasn't an option presently. If there was any good news, it was that she didn't have to figure it out right away. The Journeymen wouldn't be in town for at least a few more days. After that, she might be planning her wedding.

Avgun Iñuiñaq Qulit Malg̊uk
Double Trouble

After struggling with Sabelu's candor and too much information, Akłaq decided that she wanted as little detail as possible going forward. When she finally got the official date and time of the Journeymen's arrival, she asked only for the name to be looking for.

"Durvin" she was told.

She wrote the name on a piece of paper, folded up the paper and put it in her pocket, and walked to the airport. She didn't drive. Couldn't drive, in fact, not legally, because she was not a citizen and didn't feel like jumping through hoops like a monkey to get a license. That was fine, she figured. She could walk wherever she needed to go.

Like the rest of Vancouver, the airport was huge and still not done growing. Planes that weren't presently landing or taking off were lined up neatly on the tarmac, loading or unloading passengers while small baggage trains zipped around, full of suitcases and other luggage. Inside was just as busy, people buying tickets, inquiring about taxis, or standing around with signs as she was about to do.

She retrieved the folded piece of paper, opened and smoothed it as much as she could, and proceeded to wait and scan the crowd. She hadn't asked for any details on the Journeymen, though now she thought maybe she should have. Who were they? Where were they from? At the very least, maybe she should have asked how many were coming.

"Durvin" was not a common name, nor an English or French name that she recognized, and she couldn't match it to anything from any of the local indigenous languages. Maybe it was eastern indigenous. Or maybe it was a European name. She still found herself hoping that her charge—especially if he was also supposed to be her future husband—was, at minimum, a half-breed. Then at least they might have something in common.

Another flood of people signaled the arrival of another plane. The people in the crowd around her, all with signs, slowly began to depart, one or two at a time, going to meet a sister or son or parents or whomever. Akłaq watched as a man, fresh from the plane, scooped up a little girl who ran to him and swung her around. She squealed in delight, constantly repeating, "Daddy! Daddy!"

And still Akłaq remained, holding her "Durvin" sign. She looked around, searching for anyone who appeared quite lost. She even looked around for one of the other local Time Agents, in the event they had also been sent, in case she didn't show. She certainly wasn't the tallest person in the room, but she did have a fairly clear line of sight.

Well, maybe the plane was delayed; that wasn't unusual. Or maybe there was some delay in the passenger disembarking, some minor emergency that had to be tended to. She double-checked the notes she had written down; yes, this was the correct day and, according to the clock, slowly inching past the correct time.

Another group of people arrived, like the never-ending tide. Men, women, a few children. More hugs, more reunions, more taxis. Akłaq dug her nails into the paper, annoyed. She couldn't rightly blame the Journeymen for the faults of the plane or pilot, but she didn't like standing here like an idiot.

Then she noticed a couple of men walking toward her. For a moment, she thought she had double vision; then she realized they were identical twins, and identical was a bit misleading. One was large and fit, clearly worked out, maybe had fought in the war. The other was lean, and something about his posture denoted deference to the larger twin. Otherwise, they were as white as white could get with brown hair and clean chins.

"Durvin twins, at your service, ma'am," the bigger twin said as they walked up.

This was supposed to be her future husband? This big, lumbering oaf? This cocky, arrogant bastard? He had a heavy accent which she thought might be Scottish or Irish. There was no way they had any indigenous blood in them.

"Good, at least now I can put a face to a name." She crumpled up the paper and tossed it away. "Patrick told me you were coming."

"Here we are." The bigger twin looked confused.

She merely raised a brow, sighing internally. "Akłaq, Master Timekeeper, Region Four, District One. I'll be showing you around the city a bit so you get acquainted with how things are done here. Then I'll take you to meet the District Captain."

"And what about the Lieutenants?" the smaller twin wondered.

"They're posted in Alaska. I expect you might meet them, depending on how long you stay."

"Oh. Right."

She turned and started walking away, the twins trailing behind. She found herself praying silently. *Please, God, let them be mixed-bloods. Half, quarter, eighth, sixteenth, anything. I can take a lesson in humility, but don't make me marry it.* Maybe Everett would know more; he had a little more knowledge and sympathy with those affected by the one drop laws. Or Sabelu; he could tell whether there was any decent blood in them. She said, "And if you really impress me, I might take you to meet another friend of mine." She glanced back. "But don't tell the Captain I told you that. He doesn't like my friends."

She stopped and turned, interrupting an uncertain glance the twins exchanged between themselves. "One more thing. If either of you check me out again, I'll rip your eyeballs out by their nerves. Got it?"

The twins blinked, and it was the bigger one who said, "Aye, we get it, lass."

There was no way they had even one drop in them.

In an apparent attempt to salvage the situation, the bigger twin said, "Well, you told us your name, Aklak—"

"That's Akłaq," she interrupted, "but keep going."

"I'm Micaiah, and this is Micah. We're Journeymen, obviously, from Region Five, District Two, Ireland." They'd probably never even seen someone with indigenous blood before. "We studied a bit in Ontario already, but figured we'd come west, then go south to the United States, see what that's like." Like other Europeans, they seemed to think they could just waltz around anywhere they wanted to go and claim it as theirs.

Akłaq elected to say nothing. She didn't want to give this tour, she didn't want to train them, she barely wanted to look at them. Even Vancouver itself was starting to annoy her in ways she could not describe.

"So, we're not driving?" one of the twins asked. "Or taking a taxi?"

"I don't drive," she said simply. "And we can walk."

She could feel their eyes on her, almost tangibly feel the confusion, but they didn't say anything about it right away.

Was she being punished for something? Was she supposed to have continued with the Akari full steam ahead in spite of any opposition from Time? Should she have gone to Qikiqtaġruk sooner, later, maybe not at all? Was this one of those side effects of a decision she made years ago that was only just now manifesting? How was she to know? Was there anything she could do about it? Why did she have to put up with this? Hadn't she been punished enough in her life? Even pretending that she did eventually love this man—and twins were a cruel joke in this matter, in her opinion—any children they did have would be half-bloods. At best, they would be fifty-percent.

Could she really love another white man the same way she had once loved Nika?

That thought did absolutely nothing to boost her mood, and she figured she probably looked like a little walking thundercloud.

One of the twins spoke, she didn't bother to look to see which one. "So, Patrick gave us an address for an apartment that he arranged for us. Maybe we should stop there first, so we can drop off our suitcases?"

That would be the smart thing to do, Akłaq figured. After a long minute, she slowed her pace, finally stopped, then turned and held out her hand. "All right, what's the address?"

It was the smaller twin, Micah, who fished a piece of paper from his pocket and handed it to her. The one saving grace was that it wasn't the same apartment building as her, though it wasn't too far away. She actually felt a tiny bit relieved, that they weren't being given greater accommodations than she had been; they all had to deal with crummy living arrangements. At least she didn't have to share with anyone.

"All right," she sighed. "This way. Not more than a few blocks."

It helped to break the tension, anyway, jolt her mind away from the swirling storm of hateful thoughts brewing in her brain. She was still unhappy, but at least now there was a mission, a place to go. Maybe she could find a payphone, call Patrick, and just have him meet the twins at their apartment to give them whatever speech and tour he had planned.

Actually, while the twins were speaking to the manager of the apartment building, trying to get into their new apartment, she did just that. Standing in the lobby, she slipped a bit of change in the machine, talked to the operator, and waited.

"Patrick Lowry," came the voice on the other end.

"It's me," Akłaq said flatly.

"Hello, me, what can I do for us today?"

She rolled her eyes though he couldn't see. "Durvins are here; they're getting settled in their apartment now. Would you rather meet them here and—?"

"Akłaq, I work. I have meetings here to attend to. You can show them around just fine. Then we'll all meet for dinner as planned." He went on before she could speak. "We're not discussing this, and I have an appointment to keep. Goodbye."

She hung up before the last syllable was out of his mouth. Sighing, she turned just in time to see the twins heading for the elevator. On the one hand, she didn't care. On the other hand, it wouldn't be a bad idea to know where they lived so she could come and get them for training. Then again, they would probably want to know where she lived, too, and she didn't know how she felt about that.

Reluctantly, she followed them at least up to the correct floor, though she didn't go in the apartment they would apparently share. Their stay was brief, and then they were back in the hall, waiting for her.

"How did you get into the business?" she asked, a standard question for new Time Agents passing through an area.

"We've always been in it," one of them answered.

"Family business? That's unusual."

"No, not a family business. Just, Cai here has always had a talent for it. We figured that he must have been exposed at a young age somehow. When we got older, someone recognized it and picked us up before we could get into too much trouble."

"Time in the hands of a child?" Akłaq questioned, glancing at them. "Even we don't teach our children until they reach adolescence."

The bigger twin, Micaiah, shrugged. "I don't know. I just know that I've always been able to do things. It's how we survived on the streets after our parents died."

She nodded once but did not respond. Ah, yes, of course, the poor orphans on the streets. How original.

On the other hand, did they really have a reason to lie? And who was to say it wasn't true? And why would it be their fault?

"Where are you from then?" the other twin, Micah, asked. "Are you one of the native peoples from around here? You don't quite look like any of the Chinese running around the city."

She gave him a look. "Iñupiatun, originally from Qikiqtaġruk."

"Where's that?"

"Alaska, so far north that for part of the year the sun never stops shining, and for the other part of the year it never shows its face." She went on before either could speak. "But I've lived in Canada most of my life after the Russians burned my village."

The bigger twin said something to the other in their own language. Akłaq didn't need the Akari to know it was something along the lines of, "Well, that explains the hostility."

"Why come to this District?" she inquired evenly as they left the apartment building and started down the street. "I can understand coming to Canada to escape the war, but the war is over. And why come all the way west?"

"Why not?" Micaiah said, shrugging. "Europe is in ruins; even our little village was bombed though they said that it was a plane that 'got lost in poor weather and misjudged his location and target.' We're here, might as well look around a bit. After we're done here, we'll head south, probably to California, then head back east, leave out of New York."

The way he said it sounded almost innocent. And, if she wanted to admit it, fun. Just to go and do and see what was out there. Except everything she knew about "out there" said that the world was a violent, hostile place, especially toward her people. Why would she go looking for trouble when she could get enough of it right here at home?

"Truthfully, I've only been here a few weeks myself," she told them, pointing out this or that building as they walked. "The only reason they brought me down to train you is because everyone else is 'busy' with other things. Otherwise I'd still be in Qikiqtaġruk." She had seen nothing that would make her really consider the possibility of marriage, so she decided to omit that part entirely. "So the faster you impress me with your skills, the faster I can go home."

"Well," Micaiah said uncertainly, "we were told that today would just be moving in and looking around a bit, settling down as it were, and then tomorrow, it's up to you how you want to do it."

"Have you ever had an Apprentice before?" Micah dared inquire.

She stopped and turned to fully face them. "I have trained or overseen the training of every indigenous man and woman in western Canada and Alaska."

The twins glanced at each other. It was Micaiah who said, "You must not be very good at it, then, if you're the last choice to bring down for us, and considering your people are still pretty well subdued."

In that moment, she honestly considered killing him. Something on her face must have shown, because she could see him ready a Band around himself and his brother, and his posture shifted just enough to be ready if she did try something. As with Frederickson, in a straight physical fight, he'd have her broken in less than three seconds. With the Akari, she'd have a chance. A good chance.

In the end, she simply used the Akari to invisibly Band herself long enough to calm down enough that homicide was no longer the forefront possibility of the next two minutes. Then she released the Band and, through gritted teeth, said, "I did it to protect them, but most all of them consider it an affront to our way of life. They have the skill if they need it. They just don't think they need it."

"Too bad," Micaiah said, his posture relaxing moderately, though his level tone was forced and he still held a Band at the ready.

"The way I train you will probably be different from the way others have trained you," she continued. "If you don't like it, please, feel free to request someone else."

She deliberately turned away and started walking, pointing out buildings or other things of interest. She looked back only once to ensure the twins were following, mostly just so she wasn't out there by herself on a crowded sidewalk, giving a guided tour to no one.

After an hour or so, she called an end to the tour.

"I'm going to let you explore on your own," she told them. "I've shown you the major points of interest and given you a general feel for things, but I'm not your mother. I don't know what your needs or interests are. Take the time to look around and decide what you need to know for your time here. And see if you can't navigate your way to dinner tonight with the Captain."

"And when and where will that be?" Micaiah inquired.

She gave them the details. Then, without further ado, she cut them loose, turning and walking away, heading for home. Or the apartment, anyway.

She never could figure out how some people called this little block of space home. It wasn't necessarily the size of the apartment, for it by itself was larger than many Tlingit huts; it was the lack of freedom. You walked out of your block of space into a larger block of space.

And when you did finally reach what one might consider "outside" you were still trapped in a city which was comprised of many large blocks of space called buildings. Only once you got past all the stone and steel, sometimes a mile or more from where you lay your head at night, were you what she might consider to be "outside."

It seemed to her a miserable existence. She'd done what she could in her own apartment, trying to clean it up, liven it up, decorate it so it wasn't so...plain and industrial, but it never felt like enough.

She should probably get a job, she thought as she sat down at the small table. Maybe if she had something to occupy her time it would make things a little more bearable. She could not, nor did she want to, spend all her time training the twins—or even just one twin, depending on how things worked out—and having a job might give her some kind of escape from it, an excuse to not do something.

Well, that could wait until after dinner anyway.

When six o'clock rolled around and she made her way to the diner, Akłaq found herself hoping that the twins would already be there, or that they would show up in good time. Mostly she just hoped that they could follow directions so she didn't have to get an ear full from Patrick. Probably some accusation about killing them and dumping their bodies in the bay.

She spotted him through the window of the diner. When he looked up and saw her, without the twins, his expression turned into just that. *Where are they?* it said. *Did you scare them off already?*

Her only saving grace was that when she approached the door, she saw the twins, Micaiah and Micah if she remembered right, coming from the other direction. They were talking and laughing between themselves, but sobered up when they saw her. When they reached the door, Micaiah tentatively opened it and made an awkward gesture. Was he afraid she would yell, or did he think she didn't understand the concept of holding open a door for someone else?

Whatever the case, they entered the diner and joined Patrick at the table. Micaiah sat next to her, across from Patrick, and Micah sat opposite her.

"I see she didn't scare you off," Patrick said, evidently trying to make it a joke.

"Takes more than a scrap with a wet cat to do that," Micaiah told him, his words sounding annoyingly sincere.

The waitress appearing with a handful of waters and a few more menus helped to break the tension before it could develop into anything severe.

"Well, this wet cat—" Patrick said it with a certain amusement, as if he was glad Micaiah had coined the term and not him. "—is going to be your mentor while you're here."

Micah looked a bit wary at the thought, but it didn't phase Micaiah one bit, or not that he showed. Instead, the bigger twin inquired, "Is that to build our skills or hers?"

Now she gave him a look.

"Both," Patrick interjected. "And understand that while she may be only a Master Timekeeper, she has done extensive work with her own people of her own initiative. She knows what she's doing."

"I'm not arguing," Micaiah told him. He looked at her. "If you're not."

"I don't have much room to argue," Akłaq said evenly, "except that I can't imagine District Nine will be happy about it."

"I thought Region Four only had eight Districts?" Micah wondered.

"District Nine is unofficial," Patrick cut in before Akłaq could speak. "To an extent, it is intended to be a secret." He gave her a look, then glanced back at the twins. "It encompasses the various Indian tribes. The Inuit, First Nations, Native Americans, however you want to call them. Some years ago, Akłaq and some of her friends got in trouble for Running, teaching Time to the people without official oversight or authorization and with the intent of harming others, namely, us whites. Something like a treaty was negotiated, and now here we are. In District One." He gave her another look.

The waitress returned at that moment to take drink orders and inquire about food. No one had even looked at the menus yet. Drink orders were quick, and while everyone kept his menu in hand afterwards, no one really looked at it.

"And...you thought it was a good idea to assign a couple of pure white Irish to her?" Micah asked nervously, glancing at his brother.

"Of all of her friends, she's the nice one," Patrick said.

"Everett would be better," Akłaq commented, "but he's in District Five right now."

"So you're stuck with her. Unless you want to go to another District instead." Patrick's tone was resigned, as if hoping the twins might decide to move on in order to avoid future conflict, but not wanting them to move on because then it would reflect poorly on him.

"Oh, we'll give it a shot," Micaiah said before Micah could speak. "Besides, we haven't even had dinner yet." He looked down at the menu still in his hands. "Do you normally do this for visiting Time Agents?"

"Only for those assigned to her," Patrick said dryly. "And I try to be kind to those from the homeland."

"You don't have an accent," Micah observed.

"Well, my father and mother were from Ireland, and they raised me and my brothers to be proud Irish."

"Then what are you doing here?" Akłaq muttered, unsure and uncaring if anyone heard.

The waitress returned with their drinks and asked about food. The men wanted burgers, Akłaq ordered fish.

"How long have you been in Canada then?" Patrick asked the twins amiably once the waitress had gone.

"A couple years," Micaiah answered, again telling the story of their small town being bombed by a plane that had "gotten off course due to bad weather." His tone still said he didn't fully believe it. "The only reason we were spared was because we were taking our Journeyman test. But our parents and all our siblings but two, they're all gone."

"You're not very old then," Akłaq stated, "if you were still living with or in contact with your family."

"Born in 1923."

"How did only you come to be part of Time, then, and not your entire family?" Patrick inquired.

Micaiah shrugged. "It's something that I've always been able to do. Eventually, someone caught on. Sean first tried to arrest us for Running. When I tried to explain things to him, well, he explained it right back to me. He's been training us ever since."

Patrick's expression twisted into confused curiosity. "Really? I've never heard of someone being born with Time abilities. And neither of your parents were Time Agents?"

"No, or not that we were ever aware of."

"Fascinating. Well, whatever the case, we're glad to have you here with us." Akłaq raised a brow and Patrick met her gaze. "We are glad to have them here with us."

"Are you sure about this?" Micah wondered, noting her disposition. "We can come back later once another Timekeeper has some more free time."

"Oh, come on, a Mhicah, where's your sense of adventure?" Micaiah said. "You afraid of a little girl?" Akłaq kicked Micaiah under the table. He just laughed and put his hands up in mock surrender. "All right, all right. I yield."

"She doesn't have much of a sense of humor," Patrick said.

" 'She' is sitting right here," Akłaq informed them. "And 'she' would like to go home."

"If you don't want dinner, by all means. If you're talking about Kotzebue—"

"Qikiqtaġruk."

" —north of Anchorage, then no."

"Or what? You'll arrest me for 'dereliction of duty'?"

Patrick shifted in his seat. "No. That would be too easy, and, quite frankly, we both know you would win in a fight. No, I'll go after your people. Those you have trained and who, in all technically, use Time illegally. I think that fight would be significantly easier, don't you?" He went on before she could speak. "We have a truce. And I don't think you want to see your people suffer any more than they already have because you don't want to associate with a couple of white men for a couple of months. Train them. Pass them. Send them on their way. Then you can go home. But throwing a temper tantrum like a bratty toddler is not going to help anyone."

Akłaq glowered at him. "One day, Patrick. One day, District Nine will make itself known."

"With or without your cowardly Krydik friends who have already lost every war they've participated in?"

He was entirely correct that she would win in a fight. She'd never lost her skill in the Akari, only used Time when she absolutely had to. She could, without a doubt, kill him in any number of terrible ways. But it wouldn't solve anything. He was also correct in the implication that this was only a minor task. Train the twins for a couple months, pass their abilities, send them on to the next Master so they could advance to Master status themselves.

Was she still hung up on the marriage thing, then? Sabelu had said that the next man she met would be her future husband. By all rights, that would be Micaiah; he'd spoken first and introduced himself first. And yet, Micah seemed to be the twin with far more sense about him. On the other hand, that future husband bit might refer to ten years into the future, or twenty, or more. Maybe in five years Micaiah would have had a little more sense beaten into him.

"I think I'm going to agree with Micah on this," Micaiah said, interrupting her thoughts though she still glared at Patrick. "Should we come back later?"

Patrick broke the stare first, Banding for the blink of an eye and emerging bright and cheery. He held his hands out. "Well now, that does look delectable!"

Their food arrived at just the right time, Akłaq thought. She also Banded—deliberately using the Akari—and composed herself, bringing herself back to the present moment where they were in a diner and she was about to receive and eat fish and chips.

The first thirty seconds was little more than an awkward silence save for the clinking of cutlery. Then the joy of food started to kick in, and the people at the table who, a moment ago, had been ready to rip each other to pieces, started to relax.

There were definitely some advantages to not needing to eat constantly. In her homeland, Akłaq did not have to worry about being able to catch fish or trap game every single day, or even every other day. In the city, she was less concerned with the price of food at the market. But there was some advantage to eating, too, it seemed, beyond physical need for sustenance.

"Why don't we start over?" Patrick said, after the waitress had returned to inquire after them. "Micaiah, Micah, this is Akłaq. She is going to be your mentor while you are here as Journeymen."

"I thought I was only training one of them?" Akłaq questioned, most of her rage quelled by the fish.

"A slight miscommunication. Somewhere along the line, someone thought there was duplicate information being sent in regards to the twins, a misprint and a correction. Right hand, left hand, telephone game, point is, there was miscommunication. You'll be training both." He looked back and forth between the twins. "Besides, I imagine you can help each other, right? You can get along, I assume?"

"Of course," each twin affirmed.

"So there you go," Patrick told her. "It won't be too difficult, I imagine. We can already tell you're not going to go easy on them."

Akłaq decided to simply take the last bite of her fish rather than speak.

"And if she does get a little rough with you," he went on, looking again at the twins, "just let me know."

"What are you going to do?" Micah questioned. "If we're both having to train under her because everyone else is busy—and I can see why she's your last choice—what is going to change by us tattling on her like a couple of schoolboys?"

Patrick did not appear too prepared for the question. Akłaq seized on this as well, asking, "Yes, please, do enlighten me as to what I have to do to get out of this."

"This conversation just took an uncomfortable turn," the Captain said, sighing slowly.

"Oh please," Micaiah cut in. "Let's not shoot the horse before it's dead."

"Well it does no good to shoot it after it's dead," Akłaq told him.

He gave her a look. "All right, fine, don't shoot the horse before it's broken a leg." He glanced at Patrick. "We'll train together under Aklak —"

"Akłaq," she corrected.

Micaiah looked back at her. "Whatever. We'll train under you and see how it goes. You never know, we might just get along in the end."

He had to have known about the marriage prophecy, Akłaq concluded. Patrick and Micah looked uncertain at best. Only Micaiah seemed to have any kind of faith in what was going on, and he had no real reason for it.

So dinner didn't quite go as planned, but they all made it out alive in the end, everyone returning to his respective abode. On the one hand, Akłaq kind of wanted to see Sabelu or Anagalisgi and give them a piece of her mind. On the other hand, she really didn't want to talk about it at all.

She decided then that vagueness was probably the better option when considering destiny and prophecy. Seeing how Sabelu had given her a ton of specifics, it was affecting her in ways she didn't like. She probably wouldn't have such strong feelings about training Micaiah and Micah right now if she didn't know that she was somehow supposed to marry Micaiah and save the universe. If she didn't know those specifics, dinner probably could have gone a lot better. No, she wouldn't have been scrambling to get down to Vancouver just as soon as she was ordered, but she might have been able to meet the twins as neutral entities and not potential threats.

She didn't know what was so threatening about them, except it had been presented as an affront to her person, her ideas of love and marriage. Maybe she would have gotten along with Micaiah right away and things would be a lot better, a lot smoother. Could Sabelu have been writing the prophecy himself when he said that their whole mission would take a century or more? In telling her, knowing her resulting hatred, a five year prophecy would be stretched out to a hundred years?

Akłaq shook her head as if she might clear it or organize her thoughts better. She didn't understand the nature of the spirits or destiny or any of that; she was just a pawn in their game. A character in a Book.

She jumped as her phone rang. She really wasn't in a mood to talk to anyone, and she just knew it was going to be Patrick calling to chastise her about her behavior at dinner. After a few rings, she picked up.

"Oh, good, I wasn't sure I had the right number, or that you'd be home."

"Everett?" Akłaq wondered.

"The very same," the Cree half-breed confirmed.

"Are you in the area, or going to be?"

"Probably not for a while. But we do need to meet up, and not just because of the cost of a long-distance call. There's a big to-do in the fortress, and I think you might be interested."

"What kind of to-do?"

"Meet me there in an hour and I'll show you, or I'll try."

"Try" was an apt word, Akłaq thought, as she found herself in the Akarin fortress roughly an hour later. The crowds weren't bad, really, but there was an air of excitement, and even before Everett found her in the cafeteria, she knew what the fuss was about.

"A new Book," she stated, rising to meet Everett.

"That's right," he confirmed. As they left the cafeteria, heading for the staircase, he continued, "The first one to appear since *Alpha Wolf*, but not only is it not part of the same series, it looks as though it comes into existence ever farther into the future."

Akłaq shook her head. "I'm still trying to figure out how all of this works. Why do you think I would be interested? Have you read it?"

"I was able to get my hands on it, yes, before it was announced to the mob. First off, it confirms the release of your Book."

"*Chasing the White Bear*?"

"That's right. It also confirms the length of other series and the titles of those Books, though content is still largely speculative."

"As great as that is, that's not why you dragged me here."

"No. Better."

They reached the fifth floor and made their way to the Archives. The excitement over the appearance of the new Book seemed less intent on actually reading said Book and more intent on discussing the political, social, and religious implications of the Book, perhaps as they had done for the appearance of the very first Book, except this was a new Book in a new series.

The Akarin council was in the Archives, but they did not appear to possess the Book. Rather, it was in the hands of a small group of spectators who handled it as if inspecting an undetonated warhead. Even so, when Everett politely asked to see it, they handed it over to him, relinquishing what they evidently perceived as a problem. Then Everett handed it to Akłaq.

Bearer of Bad News, Book One of The Akari-Bearer. Scanning the first few pages, nothing seemed out of the ordinary. Yes, there were more promised Books, but that wasn't why she was here. She turned to the first few pages and started skimming.

Miach and MacEoghan. Twin boys from Ireland.

She flipped ahead some hundred pages. Micah and MacEoghan.

Another hundred or so pages. Micah and MacEoghan Dearbhfhine.

Toward the end, a plane to Canada, trying to get through customs, getting their names butchered by those who weren't too fond of the Irish. Micah and Micaiah Durvin.

Akłaq closed the Book and stared at it for a long minute. Then she looked at Everett.

"How did you know Micah and Micaiah were in Vancouver?" she asked. "They only just arrived today."

He shrugged. "Putu called me, laughing a little about your new assignment and how upset you were about it. I came here a little bit ago on some unrelated business, and that's when all this got started about a new Book."

"Do you know them? Do they come to the fortress at all?"

"Not that I've seen or heard. Maybe you can ask them since you'll be training them and all."

She shook her head. "Not yet. I want to see what they do first when they think it's all about Time and regular Timekeeping. Micaiah said that he's always had strange abilities that he can just 'do.' I want to see what they are."

Avgun Iñuiñaq Qulit Piñasrut
Mirror

Akłaq did not confront the twins immediately about being Akarin, or Akari-bearers at the very least. She wanted to see if she could tease it out of them, trick them into showing their true colors. She tried to devise trainings in which Matter or Energy was either the smarter option or, perhaps, the only option that wouldn't land them flat on their asses.

There was one time where she almost got Micaiah to tap into Gravity. Whether he caught himself or else was too inexperienced was unclear as he switched to Time at the last moment, but it was something to work with anyway.

She called up Everett to talk about it.

"It's been two months and I can't get either of them to fully admit to it," she complained. "Has there been any further news in the fortress?"

"Nothing," Everett admitted. "And the fact that they have a Book and are literally called out as Akari-bearers, yet no one knows who they are, is causing quite a stir."

"Could they be from one of the other groups? Maybe the Peaceful Akari-Bearers?"

"All inquiries to that effect have come up negative. Although there is some activity from the Cult of the Akari."

"The Cult of the Akari?" It took a moment for the name to register. "No one's heard from them in almost a hundred years, since they split off. What are they up to?"

"No one is quite sure, sounds like some shakeup in the leadership."

"You think the twins could be part of that in some way?"

Everett stifled a sigh. "I'm not entirely convinced they're part of anything unless it happened between the end of the Book and their flight out to Vancouver."

"You've read the Book then?" Akłaq questioned.

"I have, yes, and there is no mention whatsoever about the Akari, the Akarin, the Author, Books, any of it. There are indications of Micaiah having innate talent, as you said, but nothing that points directly to the Akari. If he is an Akari-bearer, he doesn't know it, and his Master is steering him along a path of straight Time."

"Well anyone can be an Akari-bearer; I've just never heard of someone being born with it."

"I don't know how to explain it either. I can only tell you what I've found. I guess the only thing left is to ask them directly. How are things going with their training?"

She shrugged though he couldn't see. "They're skilled, they're talented. They have a unique way of combining their abilities, making it easier on both of them. I'm inclined to pass them."

"And you haven't killed each other," Everett said. "That's an accomplishment."

"We haven't killed each other yet. There's a difference."

"Having problems?"

"I don't know. I'm bothered in ways I don't think I should be."

"Because they're white?"

"Maybe." She wasn't going to tell him about Sabelu's prophecy.

"Well, I won't spoil the Book for you, but I will tell you that they've seen some stuff. You might have more in common than you know."

Akłaq sighed. "Thanks, Everett."

She hung up before he could say more.

Because she really wanted to hear that. She was only slowly getting over her desire to hate the twins—she figured that if she was struggling to hate someone, and indeed wanted to hate them but couldn't, then her displeasure was probably better expressed by something other than raw hatred. But she didn't want to have to make the leap to being friendly and having things in common just yet.

She wasn't even sure what they would have in common. They were from two different peoples, two different cultures, two different continents. There was no possible way their experiences could have crossed paths until now.

The twins had gotten jobs in a shipping warehouse. Akłaq had found work as a housekeeper. When the three of them got together in the evening twice a week, the men were usually tired and she was usually grumpy. The day after Akłaq called Everett was also a training day, and Akłaq's disposition was no more cheerful for it.

The three of them met in the twins' apartment. The nice thing about Time was that, when done correctly, it was entirely silent. There might be some sound distortion caused by Banding, but it would not affect the volume of any sounds. As long as they didn't yell at each other, the neighbors wouldn't wonder.

"You look like you got some extra bad news today," Micaiah observed.

Akłaq almost asked him point-blank what he knew about the Akari. She refrained only because she figured she would read the Book first and see what in the hell Everett was talking about them having something in common. Instead she answered, "No, just some extra annoying work."

"At least you can work," Micah pointed out. "Most of the guys at the warehouse want to go on strike on account of the Chinese. They're not too thrilled about your people either, but the main focus right now is the Asians."

"Believe me, I know. It's not as if I haven't been accused of being Asian, either, or a half-breed." She rolled her eyes.

"Good news is, if anyone tried anything, you could sure give them a run for their money. Knock them on the head good."

"I've killed men because they were trying to kill me or my children. Getting knocked on the head will be the least of their worries."

The information was reflexive more than conscious, and Akłaq snapped her mouth shut. The men just stared at her, glanced at each other, then back at her.

"Patrick might have warned you," she stated awkwardly.

"Is that how you became part of Time, then?" Micaiah wondered.

"Part of it, yes. But it's not anything to discuss now."

The twins appeared grateful for the out, but the transition into training was still a bit stunted. She had just admitted to being a murderer, it was well known that she wasn't the most hospitable toward whites, and now they were supposed to continue their regular training in abilities that would give them a stunning advantage over ordinary people where she was still more skilled than them and held the advantage.

On the other hand, if they knew even the tiniest bit of Canadian history, they would know about the massacres and displacement that the British had inflicted on the native peoples—in the United States, too—so it wouldn't be too much of a stretch to think that she had simply gotten caught up in one of the many bloody battles or massacres. After all, it wouldn't look too good for Patrick to have told them, "By the way, the Master I'm assigning you to murdered the last Regional Manager plus half a dozen others and maybe more that we don't know about. Have fun at training!"

Yes, that seemed logical enough. Just another instance where she was getting ahead of herself because she knew too much about the situation; she was too involved. Of course she would be; it was her life after all. The twins only knew what she told them. Guaranteed Putu and the others wouldn't say anything, assuming they even met. Patrick couldn't risk the hit to his own reputation. So, yes, all was well.

"All right, over the last couple months, you've demonstrated that you know the basics," Akłaq said. "You can Band just fine, your residual abilities are reasonably polished, and you have a minimal understanding of Time Tendrils. All of these should be exercised and strengthened, but on your own time. Today we're going to talk more about Banding objects in motion."

While it was a necessary skill, true, she was still trying to get either of the twins to break out some Akari ability. Any ability. In the Time industry, Banding objects in motion was something learned through force and rote memorization, boxing everything up as just "Time."

With the Akari's ability to tap into Energy, it was easier to learn because the student already had a working understanding of all the forces involved and how they might be manipulated, all the kinetic forces adjacent to Time.

The only hangup she might have was that their previous Master back east, who had met them when they first arrived in Canada from Ireland and trained them some already, might have already shown them some of this. Demonstrating any talent in Time, therefore, was not necessarily indicative of Akari ability. She had to get them to demonstrate something concretely Akari.

She'd brought a tennis ball with her, and she now pulled it out of her bag. She bounced it on the floor a few times normally, then invoked Gravity a few times just to see if they would notice and say anything, then used an Akari Band a few times with the same intent, and finally used a regular Time Band. The twins did not react to any of her tricks, just watched her intently, waiting for some instruction.

Without Banding at all, Akłaq suddenly took the tennis ball and whipped it at Micaiah's head. A reflexive Band saved him, albeit just barely, and the ball sailed past without being touched, smacking against the wall behind him and bouncing back to Akłaq.

"What was that for?" Micaiah demanded.

"You were supposed to Band the ball, not yourself," she told him. "Stop the ball in motion."

"You think it might be more practical to have us try and stop it while you're just bouncing it?" Micah wondered.

"I bounced it a dozen times or more and neither one of you moved to touch it. I had to make sure you were awake."

"Fine, fair enough," Micaiah conceded, "but did you really have to aim for my head?"

Now she threw the ball at his chest. The elder twin—by two minutes, he bragged, much to Micah's chagrin—fumbled between a reflexive Band and trying to Band the ball. It hit hard on the left side of his chest toward the bottom of his rib cage. He gritted his teeth and grunted, and the ball went bouncing away, lightly hitting a wall and bouncing a few more times before rolling on the floor back toward Akłaq.

"Was that more to your liking?" she inquired, reaching to scoop up the ball.

"Damn it, woman," he coughed, not looking at her.

Micah was laughing hysterically, though he fared no better when she chucked the ball at him, hitting him in the shoulder.

"And this is just a tennis ball," Akłaq told them, retrieving the ball from the kitchen while the twins tried to discreetly Band their wounds to heal them. She returned to the couch. "Now imagine someone is trying to shoot you. Bullets move a lot faster than this ball. Or imagine if they were throwing rocks at you; that's going to leave a lot more than just a bruise."

"Can you maybe try tossing it at us first instead of trying to brain us?" Micaiah whined.

"Oh, come on, a Chai," Micah said. "You can't say you never Banded when you were a prize fighter."

"Prize fighter, huh?" Akłaq questioned, enjoying the look the elder twin got as she seized on the information. "Then why are you having trouble with this?"

Micaiah gave his brother a look. "Because I always Banded myself, not the other guy."

Akłaq shifted. "Always? Every single time? Without fail?"

"I didn't even know I could Band others—aside from Micah—until Sean found us."

She raised a brow. "What made Micah special that you thought you could only Band him and not others?"

Micaiah shrugged. "He's my twin. Why wouldn't I think that?"

She thought about this for a moment, then nodded. "All right, I'll give you that one. I still have a hard time believing that you could be born with it and yet not discover any of these things that I'm sure you're picking up at a fairly rapid pace." She looked at Micah. "And what about you? You never tried any of this or what?"

"I never had a natural talent, no," Micah said, shrugging helplessly.

"As kids, he always took the lead. On the occasion that I did try to do anything myself, I just...couldn't."

Akłaq nodded. "Interesting."

Maybe their Book would have a better explanation for this, both the reason that Micaiah had been born with innate Akari abilities and the reason Micah hadn't.

She shifted position again, fingering the ball. "Well, you have already demonstrated that you know how to use an External Band. You've done it on inanimate objects and people, and you've done it on slow-moving objects. This is simply a natural progression of skill."

Again she whipped the tennis ball, this time deciding to be nice and aim for the space on the couch between the twins. Again, there was some fumbling of Bands of all forms. One of the twins managed to Band the ball for half a second, but once it hit the couch and changed physics, the Band dropped.

"This is just simple stuff," Akłaq said casually, picking up the ball. "Wait until we go to the tennis courts and start Banding."

"Are we really going to do that?" Micah asked, looking paler than usual.

"Of course, why not? Unless you'd rather fight your brother, each of you trying to Band the other. Or I'm sure we could go out to some remote location and start shooting at each other; that would provide some motivation, wouldn't it?"

"I think we'll stick with the tennis courts," Micaiah told her, his expression unreadable, if confused.

Progress that day was limited, although by the end of the session, the twins were able to Band the tennis ball before it struck the back of the couch. They still lost control when the ball changed direction, but small progress was better than none.

Akłaq called up Patrick once she got home.

"I have a question," she said.

"Judging by your tone, it doesn't sound like a particularly serious one," he sighed.

"When Journeymen come through the District, are we supposed to assess their skills or teach them new ones?"

"Both." He paused. "Why?"

"Because I'm having to teach them things that I feel they should already know."

"We were all beginners once, Akłaq. There was a time when we did something for the first time."

"Banding an object in motion?"

She could hear him moving around and he let out a groan as he moved a chair and sat down. "You know, they called me just before you did. They told me about the tennis ball."

"I didn't break any of their bones."

"The object lesson was not in dispute, Akłaq, it's your malice towards them. You're not teaching them, you're punishing them. Whatever slights or offenses you think are being committed against you, it doesn't involve them."

"Are they going to leave the District?"

"I've convinced them not to for the time being, mostly because I don't want to give you that satisfaction. But if this disrespect keeps up, I will have you stripped of your rank—"

"Arrested, imprisoned, blah, blah, nothing I haven't been threatened with before. Tell me honestly, Patrick, what would honestly happen if I just went home right now? Back to Qikiqtaġruk?"

He sighed again. "You would be listed as a Runner, and it would be my duty to—"

"Arrest and imprison, yes, yes. Why? Because I want to be left alone? Don't you think that maybe that makes you the aggressor, not me?"

That, at least, gave him pause. After a minute, he said, "I'm not going to sit here and argue with you all night, Akłaq. I've indulged you a bit too much already, I think. But here is something to consider: I have to play politics. I have people above me breathing down my neck. I have people below me, like you, who are immensely unhappy. And I have to make it all work somehow. You don't have to do all that. And you're right, you could go home back to your frozen wasteland, and I don't think anyone in the near future would want to really expend the time and resources trying to bring you in, given your history. And I think you know that. I think you knew it before you came down here. But something brought you here. Boredom, curiosity, some guidance from your pagan gods, I don't know what. So either put your money where your mouth is and go home, or stop whining about the unfairness of it all. Good night."

Click.

Akłaq sat there for a minute in stunned silence. At some point she put the phone back on the receiver, but she did not move otherwise. She hated Patrick, but he was right. She had come down for a reason. She hated to admit it, but Sabelu had been the perfect one to deliver the message to her. If she'd been sent with some kind of vague notion from Anagalisgi about what she was supposed to accomplish, she probably would have left by now, maybe not even come in the first place. But with Sabelu's blunt prophecy and specific direction, the best she could do was whine about how unfair it was. Oh, she probably could pack up and leave right now, but she had a feeling that it wouldn't go over especially well.

Sleep was elusive that night, and she was in no mood to work the next day, as if she was ever excited about cleaning other people's houses. It wasn't that they were dirty, even, but because they were clean. A bit of dust, a pillowcase out of sorts, and people thought the world was going to end. If they were really so worried about it, why not do it themselves? Did they not believe in giving chores to their children, something to teach them a bit of responsibility? Or were such things too low for their precious little angels?

There were days when she considered living off her Timekeeping salary, just long enough to train the twins and get back home.

"You don't look happy," Micaiah observed as he opened the door for her at their next session a few days later.

"One of my clients had a sick kid, so I got to play nurse in addition to maid," Akłaq growled. "Then I got to be accused of pagan witchcraft because I suggested brewing tea with honey for the child instead of taking him straight to the hospital. But I guess that's just white culture for you. Attack the messenger even if the message is good and true, don't believe anything unless it comes from one of your own."

"What's that supposed to mean?"

But she was already moving past him toward the living room. "Are you ready?"

Micaiah didn't move. He folded his arms across his chest. "No. You're going to explain yourself."

Akłaq rolled her eyes and turned to face him. Micah, who had been silently waiting in the kitchen, echoed his brother's posture. She asked, "And what am I explaining?"

"For one, why you seem to think that your life as a feckless cunt gives you the right to drag us down into your misery." He went on before she could speak. "All right, so you had a bad day at work. I get it. I actually felt sorry for you until you started equating us with your cunt of a client. You don't like it here, feel free to leave. Believe me, we won't miss you."

"Why do I have to be the one to leave?!" The words exploded out of her. "I was here first! You are not from this place! You are not my people! You were not born and raised in this land! These are not your mountains, your trees, your skies and ancestors! I have watched for over a century as my people, and others, have sacrificed everything, even at the point of a gun, so you can create the exact thing you ran away from!" Tears were streaming down her face and she hated it.

"Is that what this is about?" Micaiah questioned. "Blame? Fine, let's start blaming people. I don't know if you know this, but the Irish were popular with slavers, too. Over three hundred thousand Irish slaves sold in North America and around the world. So if you want to talk about slavery and servitude, I agree. I imagine you're familiar with the boarding schools, but did you know that we have the same thing back in Ireland? Did you know that the same abuses that happen here also happen there? So if you want to talk about kidnapping and abuse by those we're supposed to trust, I agree. And did you also know that

Ireland isn't even a unified country? As a whole we still come under the jurisdiction of the English crown, and part of the country is under total ownership of England, all of this after centuries of fighting back and forth. So if you want to talk about conquest and occupation, I agree. And even today, there are places where a proud Irishman can't go. He has to dye his hair and speak with an unnatural accent—in a language not his own, mind you—and even then, he still might be turned away if he's outed. As it is, if our coworkers weren't so upset about the Chinese, they'd probably be upset about us. Because everyone is always looking for something to blame if they're not happy. And if it's not something they can fix, or fix easily, then blame turns to other people, whether it is warranted or not.

"I'm sorry that your home was destroyed. Ours was, too. And I don't buy the bullshit that it was a misguided plane. But I'm not going to make life miserable for one of the men in the warehouse just because he happens to have German relatives. And I don't want to be disrespected and equated with the IRA just because I'm a proud Irishman. Fine, so we make jokes about it, but there is a difference between good fun and cruel disrespect. Right now, you disrespect and insult us. We've put up with it for a while now, and not happily. Patrick asked us to stay, but I think you need to make a decision right now whether you're going to respect us during training and actually help us, or if you're just going to go home back to your miserable life in a frozen wasteland."

Discipline was uncomfortable enough. Such heady admonishment was utterly humiliating. Akłaq felt as though the whole of Vancouver stared at her in that moment, even though it was only the three of them in the apartment.

In the end, Akłaq quietly left the apartment, Banding so she could regain composure. She was already humiliated; she didn't need some well-meaning passerby to start prying into her business.

As befitting her mood, it was a rainy walk home. Or rather, back to her apartment. She really couldn't think of it as home, but it was where she laid her head anyway.

Micaiah's words circled round and round in her head. Could it be true? Was it possible that there were other people out there with similar experiences? No, couldn't be. But if it were true, why, then, did they run away? Why not fight for their own people? If they knew that the attack, the bombing, was deliberate, why not go after those responsible? Why did they have to come over here where she and her people had their own problems? Why did they surrender?

She didn't understand, then decided it was because they couldn't understand. They weren't like her people. They could walk into a room and still blend in as whites. They wouldn't be called out across the street. They were proving well that they had freedom of movement; they could go anywhere they wanted to in the English territories.

But then, she wasn't exactly destitute. She could go anywhere she wanted to in North America, thanks to the resources afforded to them as District Nine. She could return to Qikiqtaġruk and no one would stop her. It was highly unlikely anyone was going to burn it down again. No one was going to force her to go to church or convert to this or that denomination or orthodoxy. No one was going to cut her lip off for a tattoo.

At the same time, to live in this box within a box, to leave the building but still not really feel like she was "outside." What kind of life was that? What kind of culture stripped the land away from its people and hid the people from the land? What did it say about the people when their whole way of life depended on goods and other factors hundreds or thousands of miles away? Even her people, as isolated as they were, as much as they depended on trade, still found a way to live how they were where they were.

And somehow, she was supposed to marry this man.

Could Sabelu have been mistaken? Maybe he'd been leading her on, knowing that he had to say certain things a certain way in order to get her to do a certain thing to accomplish a certain end, even if that end had nothing to do with what he said.

No, she decided. That was too roundabout for Sabelu. She didn't know him well, but she knew that much. Anagalisgi was the one who offered up vague notions and complex riddles. Sabelu had given her an outline of the next century of her life and then told her to deal with it.

What was a husband? Traditionally, the husband was the one who provided meat and acted as the voice of the family in clan and tribal matters. When she'd married Nika, he'd proclaimed that it was the husband's duty to provide food, shelter, and comfort to his family, protect them from danger, and provide children to his wife. When she once asked him what separated a husband from any other man who may just be doing good deeds for a woman in need, Nika had said that a husband strives to bring out the best in his wife, to build her up in confidence and character, as two horses on a plow. And the same was true in reverse, he said. The wife should want to bring out the best in her husband, to build him up in strength and assurance.

"I don't know if I can do that," Akłaq said aloud to an empty room. "I hate him too much."

But what she hated about him, she didn't know. He'd never been mean to her, except for today. Although, with exception of the name-calling, admonishment was hardly an act of cruelty. She'd admonished her children countless times. She still admonished them and they were in their sixties. Maybe it was the fact that she had been challenged by someone she couldn't rightly oppose. He'd done nothing to her, but she'd done everything to him.

She wrestled with the idea for hours. If she thought of Micaiah as nothing more than a white man, it was easy to hate him, as easy as hating every other white man in the city. But when she thought of him as a person—possibly even someone who had traumatic experiences of his own—it was a lot harder.

What made it worse was when she considered that there was a way she could verify everything he just said, within reason. The Book was sitting in the Akarin Archives right now.

Was she afraid of it? Maybe. This new Book confirmed the existence of her own Book at some point in the future. The fact that hers hadn't yet appeared suggested that it was still being written, that her story wasn't over. Where did they intersect? What secrets would be revealed? Was she afraid of the truth? Honestly, a little.

It was somewhere around one o'clock when she finally got up the nerve to go to the fortress. Things had calmed down some and she had no trouble getting to the Archives or checking out the Book.

For a long time, she just stared at it, flipping around the first couple pages that weren't really part of the story, trying to figure out what it all meant. Books that were complete but not yet in existence because the stories contained within hadn't happened yet. What was she to make of it? What did it mean when she only got one Book, but Micah and Micaiah got a series? Was she just unimportant? If the twins' next Book picked up where this one left off, would she feature in some way? How did that all work? What did the Author have planned exactly? And for that matter, why was the Author white? Why was she dictating what happened to her, Akłaq? Or was the Author also affected in some way by the one drop laws?

Finally she flipped to the first page. Chapter one.

If she didn't believe that the Books were true, she never would have, reading the twins' Book now. In fact, if she hadn't read the Krydik Books first and gotten confirmation from multiple sources that they were true, she never would have believed in the Author or the Books or the Akari. She would have dismissed it all as the preposterous wishful thinking of those who wanted to pretend to understand the lives of those they crushed, justifying their persecution of others because they had also been persecuted.

And was she not doing the same? Was she not holding the twins accountable for the sins of men long dead? How would they ever be able to repay? It wasn't the twins she hated. It was the Russians who burned her village. It was the Russians who had turned on their own and murdered Nika and her children, tried to kill her. It was Goldsmith and Frederickson and those who killed Ujurak and the others.

But then, there had been many complacent bystanders, too, those who smiled as kidnapped children were paraded through their towns, on their way to forced assimilation. The smiling priests and nuns who promised the children that they would be greatly enlightened. All of those people were probably very nice among their own, but when addressing those outside their acceptable circles, the smiles always hid a vein of contempt and smug superiority, like entertaining a child or a dog that doesn't have the capacity to understand what's happening.

Reading about Micah and Micaiah—or Miach and MacEoghan—now, she found their words to be true. They did understand what the boarding schools were like. Unlike Latseen and all the children Akłaq had rescued over the summer, though, the twins had no one to fight for them, no one to come in the middle of the night to spirit them away to safety. And Micah had paid the price for it. Nothing changed until he finally told Micaiah and the two of them ran away, Micaiah's innate Akari talents the only reason they could.

It only made Akłaq all the more glad that she had fought so hard for her children. She couldn't even imagine her children in the hands of such monsters. The fact that they had spent even one night in those infernal places was like a punch in the gut. To think of Gáx and Tlaganis and Nooskw at the mercy of such vile people, such appalling excuses for men was...

She forced her grip to relax. The librarian was already protective of the regular works in the Archives; she didn't need to find out what he would do if any damage came to an Authored Book, especially a brand new one.

Even though everything played out exactly as expected, as the twins had described—though they had left out the part that they had been orphans up until they were about fifteen or sixteen—something about the story still startled her.

They were people. Even as she sat in the Archives reading a Book, Micah and Micaiah were in their apartment, sleeping, having dreams, waiting for the alarm clock to go off so they could go to work where, apparently, they would be hated except for the current greater hatred against the Chinese. There was something stunning about the revelation that even after she left their apartment, they had continued to exist. They'd had a conversation after she'd gone. Maybe they had called Patrick to tell him what happened. Then they had gone about their day.

They existed. In the same way that she existed. Different thoughts, different concerns, different physicalities, but the same existence.

Akłaq sat there for a long moment. She was a little over three-quarters of the way through the Book, but she wasn't sure that she was going to finish it right now. She was already sweating; she wasn't sure she wanted to risk any more revelations between here and the end of the Book. But then, if she didn't finish it now, she probably never would, the way things were going.

She owed them an apology. She didn't expect that they would want to go back to training under her again—and she kind of didn't want to anyway—but the apology she would do.

Then she owed Sabelu an apology, and a swift punch in the face. An apology, because of how she had disrespected his visions and the immense power and responsibility he held. A punch in the face, because of his shoddy attitude and interpersonal skills when it came to delivering messages and warnings to people. And after that, she might try to track down Anagalisgi somehow and ask him exactly what had gone wrong that he, Anagalisgi, was well and personable in his prophecies, where Sabelu was an insufferable jackass.

She had no further major revelations as she finished the Book, and for this, she was grateful. The twins went to the Wheel for their Journeyman test. They closed the portal, which meant that time at home would pass normally. When they returned, well, home no longer existed. They searched through the rubble, found their adoptive parents and most of their brothers and sisters. After the funeral they shared with dozens of other families, after the first round of grieving where everyone tried to figure out what to do next, the twins used the many resources found in the Wheel to forge the papers they needed to get into Canada. Not that it mattered since Canadian customs butchered their names anyway. But the twins just rolled with it and continued their training.

They roll with it and adapt because they've had to do so for most of their lives, Akłaq thought, closing the Book, *but they also still grieved for the loss of their family and home. Husbands and wives are supposed to build a home together, leaning on each other for support. And all I've done is mock and berate them. They have seen tragedy and they carry on, while I hang onto grudges over a century old.*

She thought of her children. She had often wondered why they had stopped fighting. The truth was, they hadn't. They had simply settled down and embraced a principle Putu had tried to explain to her once. She was a stormy ocean. He was a calm river. He did not rush, yet he always got where he needed to go. Her children had children and grandchildren and even great-grandchildren. They were fighting back through peace. A time for war and a time for peace. She couldn't remember where she'd heard that, but it seemed appropriate to the situation. The white bear had often chastised her for thinking and even wanting everything to be fixed and constant, when this was never the case. Maybe it was time for her to set aside her years of anger and hatred and go back to the peace and happiness felt when she was with Nika. Maybe it was time she learned to love again.

Taking a breath, Akłaq stood from the table and left the Archives.

Avgun Iñuiñaq Qulit Sisamat
Biography

It was over a week before she actually got up the nerve to go back to the twins' apartment. Some days she was too ashamed and she worried over what she might say, how she could best convey an apology. Other days she remained staunchly indignant and certain that they owed her an apology. Finally, realizing that she would never be "ready" for it, just as soon as her walk home from a client's house took her close enough to the twins' apartment building that she couldn't ignore it, she went inside. Up to the second floor, down the hall, and there it was.

She knocked.

Just when she was about to knock again, she heard some movement on the other side. A moment later, the door opened. It was Micaiah, not looking overly enthused by her appearance.

"Can I come in?" she asked meekly, her heart pounding.

He hesitated for half a second, then nodded and stepped aside. She only walked in far enough that he could shut the door behind her, though she did look around. "Where's Micah?"

"Offered to work some extra hours," Micaiah answered, his tone forcibly neutral.

Well that wasn't going to help things. Should she come back later? No, if she didn't do this now, she never would. If she had to, she could come back and apologize to Micah specially.

"I owe you an apology," Akłaq stated, turning to look at him. "It wasn't right what I said to you, or about you. And you were right to call me out on it. You're not my clients and you really haven't done anything offensive against me. But you are my students, and I've been treating you very poorly." She shook her head. "I spent years telling my children that we fought against ideas, not men, and yet here I am, punishing you for hurts inflicted by others."

For a long minute, Micaiah didn't say anything. His disposition wasn't entirely rigid, but he did appear to be searching for some kind of ulterior motive, some insult that he hadn't caught on to yet. At long last, he nodded. "Takes a lot for someone to admit to something like that, apologize for it. And I accept."

Akłaq let out a breath, though she tried not to make it too obvious.

He went on, "After you left, I called Patrick. Mostly I was curious as to what exactly you were blaming us for. He gave us Harvey Billings' number, and he told us about you, how you killed the Regional Manager, plus some others. He told us about your cavorting with heretical Akari-bearers and about the work you did in the schools and how you forced the unofficial recognition of District Nine. Granted, he told us to watch our backs around you, but at least it helped to make some sense about what you were crying about."

She nodded. "It doesn't make it right what I said to you."

"And I appreciate the apology."

"If it makes you feel any better, I did a little research on you, too. And if I didn't read it for myself, I never would have believed you about the schools in Ireland. And I'm sorry to hear what they did to Micah."

Now Micaiah's expression turned suspicious. "What do you mean? How do you know about that? It's only been a dozen years and the Catholic Church will kill you as soon as admit they hurt you. You ought to know that from the schools here."

"Have you received any strange books lately?" Akłaq asked.

His expression turned even more puzzled. "Books? Can't say that we're big readers. No one's given us anything."

"Nothing has randomly appeared, things you know you didn't pack but that you know weren't here before you moved in?"

Now he shrugged. "Truth be told, we stopped unpacking when we weren't sure we wanted to stay. I think Micah started repacking after last week, actually."

Akłaq hesitated. "I know I have no right to ask you for anything, but can you just check? You're looking for a book you don't recognize, called *Bearer of Bad News*."

He raised a brow. "Was your apology sincere, or are you trying for some ulterior motive?"

"I think if you find the book, you'll understand."

She could feel frost begin to form once more, but he agreed and headed down to one of the bedrooms. Half a dozen boxes were still stacked in a corner. Micaiah went to the first one, already popped open, and rummaged around briefly. Apparently finding nothing, he took it off the stack and opened up the next box.

For a moment, Akłaq was afraid he wouldn't find the Book. True, the Krydik had received a copy of their Books, but what if that was unique to the Krydik? What if there was something more than needed to be done before the Book appeared? There did seem to be a bit of a discrepancy between the end of the Book and when it appeared, so what if it just hadn't appeared here yet? But why would it show up in the Archives and not to the person it was about? Could it be among Micah's things?

"Is this it?" Micaiah asked suddenly, jerking her from her thoughts.

He straightened from where he bent over the second to last box. In his hands was a very familiar Book, the title clear as day on its spine. He held it out to her. "You're right, I don't recognize it. How did you know it would be here?"

She did not take the Book. "Because the other copy is sitting in the Akarin Archives."

"Other copy?"

"Open it up."

He did so. Initially he skimmed from back to front. Then something must have caught his eye because he slowed down and began to actually read. His expression twisted in a carousel of emotion. Finally he sat down on the edge of the bed and Banded. Not ten seconds later, he stood and faced her again.

"What kind of sick joke is this?"

She shook her head. "It's not a joke."

"There are things in here that no one should know even happened, never mind the details." He looked like he wanted to say more but didn't know how to put it all into words. "You said there's another copy...with the Akarin? The same Akarin Harvey said you've been running around with?"

"That's right."

He opened up to the list of Books. "And these Books are all there, too?"

"No," she told him. "Yours is only the third one to appear."

"Then what are all these others?"

"Already written, not yet come to pass. Mine is there, too, see." She crossed the floor and pointed to the one she believed was hers. "But I don't have it yet, and it's not in the Archives. It does seem that a little time does pass between the end of the Book and when it appears, but at this point, I can only assume that my story just isn't finished yet. Or I could go home and find it on my bookshelf."

"So you're saying that we're in a Book right now? That someone is reading our every word, could skip forward or back and...?" He flipped to the back cover. "And there's some author out there who's dictating our every word and action?"

She shrugged. "I'd say there's a chance we're in two Books simultaneously, mine and yours." She faltered. "As for the matter of free will, no one has quite figured out exactly where that comes into play, if at all."

Micaiah shook his head and made a few paces. He ran his hand through his hair. "This is fucked up—pardon my French. How do you expect me to react to this?"

"I don't know."

He stopped his pacing. "You said there are two more Books. Which ones are they?"

"*Wolf Pack* and *Alpha Wolf*. They're about the Krydik people."

"But *Lone Wolf* isn't available yet?"

"No."

"And there's apparently something big about this Chivalrous Welshman. The Hands of Time, well, we understand that as the Time industry. Your Book. What about this other single? *Of Saints and Sinners?*"

Akłaq shrugged. "Not a clue."

He shifted his stance several times. "But what I don't understand is why this Book calls me and Micah Akari-bearers."

"I suspect it's because whatever talent you were born with was the Akari, not Time. But because of how similar they might appear to outsiders, or because someone did recognize it as the Akari, your Master decided to train you up in Time instead." She felt her face flush with embarrassment. "Honestly, that's part of the reason I was so rough with you guys in training, because I was trying to force you to break out an Akari ability. But I guess if you didn't know about any of it, then I was just being cruel."

If Micaiah caught on to her shame and oblique apology, he did not react, still staring at the Book in his hands.

"The Krydik are a little touchy when it comes to their Books, and they're very strict about who they let near their settlements," Akłaq said. "But if you want to read their Books, I can take you to the Archives."

"The Akarin Archives," Micaiah stated.

"That's right."

"Am I going to be arrested for it? By Patrick or other Timekeepers, I mean?"

"Only if they find out. And even if they do, they'll try to arrest me first, so you should have time to get a good head start."

"That's not reassuring."

She ignored him and proceeded to open a portal to the fortress. There were some days when she wasn't sure that she would be able to do it. She didn't understand why it was so difficult. After how many centuries of operation, and the Time industry still couldn't work things out and make this easier? Sure, she wasn't going to the Wheel, but that was no picnic either.

Fortunately, Micaiah was smart enough that he didn't need to be told to go through just as soon as he could, and Akłaq followed him, the portal snapping shut behind her. Had it been a physical door, she might have felt the wind on her back as it slammed shut.

When her faculties started to return, she found herself sitting against one wall, Micaiah standing over her with a hand out. She drunkenly reached for it and got to her feet.

"Impressive place," he observed, looking around.

"This is nothing," she said, slowly coming around as if from a poor night's sleep. "Follow me."

She took him out of the small portal room to the southwest atrium and paused so he could gawk and gape. Of course, she couldn't say that she was immune to the splendor of the place, but there was something unique about the first time.

"Where are we exactly?" Micaiah wondered. "What are the coordinates?"

"Honestly, I don't know," Akłaq admitted. "Wherever we are, it's deep underground."

"What's outside?"

"There is no outside. This whole place is underground. There are no doors or windows that take you beyond this place." She went on before he could speak. "I've never had much of a reason to care. Once you can open portals on your own, you are free to explore as much as you wish. Until then, we're just here for the Archives."

"And where are those?"

"Upstairs."

She started for the massive spiral stone staircase in the middle of the atrium. Micaiah stopped at the base of the stairs and looked straight up.

"When you say upstairs...exactly how far are we talking?" he wondered.

Akłaq paused, about twenty steps ahead of him. "Mm...fifth floor."

"Is that human floors?"

She gestured to a larger alien meandering around the atrium. "Do you think he would be able to fit in a human building?"

Micaiah blanched at the thought but said nothing more as he followed her.

Akłaq wouldn't deny that she also dreaded the fortress stairs, but considering how little she normally visited the fortress, she figured that she could handle it without complaining. It would just make the stairs up to her apartment feel less daunting.

"So you have a Book," Micaiah said, his tone suggesting he was starting a longer line of thought.

"That's right," Akłaq confirmed.

"But it's not 'released' yet."

"Mhm."

"Because we're still in the Book."

"I believe so, yes."

"But my Book—or our Book, I guess, if Micah's in it, too—which comes out after your Book, but it already exists in your Book, because the events of my Book have already come to pass."

Akłaq nodded once. "Correct."

"And because my Book is only a 'book one' then it's entirely possible that we're in the end of your Book but the beginning of my second Book."

"What makes you think it's the end of my Book? What if there's a lot more to come?"

"Well, I mean, your Book is a single, isn't it? It's not like it's going to follow you over two centuries. Is it?"

She thought about that. "Well, your Book is, what, twenty years? The Krydik Books are roughly thirty and fifty years, respectively."

"I guess the question becomes," Micaiah said, "where does your Book start?"

The question lingered in her mind the whole way to the fifth floor. They were both winded and grateful for the end to the arduous trek. Still she pondered Micaiah's question, even as she showed him the Archives and got him set up with the Krydik Books.

Where would her Book start? Micaiah had a whole Book before the Akari was even mentioned. *Wolf Pack* didn't bring it up until about three-quarters of the way through. In her case, then, Red River was where she was introduced, so what events preceded that? Leaving Prince Albert after the murder of Gerald. Before that, the journey from Ujurak's village to Prince Albert. And before that, Matulik, Putu, and Aniqan finding and rescuing her and bringing her to the village, introducing her to Time. Maybe that would be the start.

Did that mean, then, that Nika would be erased completely? Would he appear at all? Would her thoughts of him appear? Or would he exist only in her memory? Would her memory of him even exist if it wasn't put into words? Well, she reasoned, it would have to in some sense; the Books did not follow people moment-by-moment, and they would have to retain some memory of day-to-day events in order to function in the in-between gaps.

All the same, she found it a little disquieting. If, within context of her Book, Nika existed only within her memory, did that hold any special meaning about her dubious marriage to Micaiah? And what if Nika did show up? Did anything change? She didn't know why it would, but the thought had already taken hold.

On the one hand, she kind of wanted to ask Anagalisgi and Sabelu about all of this, and on the other hand, she really kind of didn't. She wanted some kind of reassurance, but she also didn't want to get stuck with another century-long forecast of her destiny delivered to her by a cynical prophet.

Before Akłaq could get five paces from the table, Micaiah stood and stretched.

"Finish them both?" she wondered.

"The first one," he replied, leaning backwards and reaching behind him, looking up at the stone ceiling. "It's a lot to take in." He relaxed his posture and looked at her. "I'm guessing that Hlohi doesn't have much of a tourism department."

She shook her head. "No, not really."

"You're still the nicest one they can find."

"Well, I'm not Krydik, for one. And, actually, Everett is probably your better bet for friendliness."

"I don't know who that is, but I'll take your word."

He walked around the table a few times before sitting down to the second Book. Akłaq wandered off to browse through the collection. The Wheel of Time also boasted an extensive Archives—the largest in the universe, supposedly—but it was all digital and technological, information encoded in things called Glasses. More technology was required in order to show things in particular languages. Truthfully, she wasn't sure how it all worked.

The Akarin Archives, meanwhile, still used books and scrolls and codex manuscripts. However, just as someone within the Akari could speak their own language and understand and be understood in any other language, so the pages of any of these volumes would appear blank for just a second before rendering in the language of the reader.

She didn't bother actually looking for anything, since she knew it wouldn't take Micaiah long to read the next Book. Briefly she wondered what Micah would think if he got home and his brother wasn't there. Maybe nothing; she didn't know their daily habits. On the other hand, what if Micah was home when the two of them returned together? Would he have anything to say about that?

When she moseyed her way back to the main sitting area, she found Micaiah again standing and stretching and making laps of the table. She also saw that he had pulled the Archives copy of his Book and perhaps read it again. He did not notice her right away, and she took the moment to study him.

He still carried himself like an arrogant prick, she thought. For as impressive as his physique was, there was some subtle hint that spoke of purely selfish vanity. He had known women, she was sure of it. This did not surprise or offend, Akłaq told herself, but she had to wonder if there was any room for change. Marriage was different. There had been differences between her life with Nika and her life with Aniqan and her life with Putu and her life with no one at all. She could tell that he was wrestling with many things in his mind, the sudden expansion of knowledge, trying to reconcile what he knew with what he'd experienced with any number of other factors she could not comprehend.

After a minute or two, once he'd stopped pacing and instead just stood there, leaning on the back of the chair, staring at the Books laid out before him on the tables, only then did she approach.

"And?" she questioned.

He shook his head, mouth open but silent. Finally, "I don't know. I really don't. I feel like my whole world has been turned upside down in just the last few hours. So much makes sense now, but at the same time, I have so many questions."

"I'm sure you can talk it over with Micah first."

Surprisingly, he shook his head again. "No. I can't tell Micah."

"What? Why? The Book—"

"Reveals his shame for all the world to see. For all the universe to see." His words were firm and his gaze left no room for argument. "Believe it or not, he is still haunted by it. He still questions why God allowed the priests to do what they did. I can't just go home and tell him that, somehow, someway, some Author out there wrote it all down, and now everyone in the universe knows about it." He shook his head a third time. "I can't do that to him. Not yet."

Akłaq nodded. "All right. I guess I can understand that."

"And actually, I have a mind to track her down and find out how she knows about all of this."

"Track down the Author?"

He nodded. "She would have to be an Akari-bearer, or maybe a former one, to know about the Akari, the Akarin, all of this. My guess is that..." He hesitated. "On the one hand, she would have to be old school Native American in order to have such inside knowledge about the Krydik. I would say that maybe she is one of the Krydik. But then, how would she get to Ireland and record everything there?"

"Micaiah, look at the photo. She's white and blond. There's no way she's old school Native American."

"What about Harvesting? That changes your appearance, doesn't it? Is there something in the Akari that can do something similar? You've said it yourself, it's a lot safer to be white."

Akłaq raised a brow. "We're standing in the Akarin fortress which is populated by a multitude of species." She gestured discreetly to a handful of aliens scattered around the library within sight. "They don't know the difference, they don't care. We're just a singular species with varying physical features and skills, abilities, and intellect of varying proficiency within set parameters."

Micaiah blinked. "That sounds...oddly cold."

She shrugged. "I'm from the arctic, what can I say? But, really, it's true. Humans have upper and lower limits to everything. We know these limits, we know our differences. The average alien observer has no clue. Given that these Books appear one to the subject and one to the fortress, before any regular human has access to it—and won't for at least seventy years, judging by these copyrights—I think it's a safe bet that this is who she is, what she looks like."

"Then how would she know about the Krydik?" He gestured to Wolf Pack. "This predates the Krydik, even."

"I don't know. I really don't."

Micaiah let out a breath and studied the three Books laid out before him. "I don't know how I'm going to do this."

Akłaq shifted her stance. "Do what?"

"I want to track her down. I want to find her."

"Why?"

"I have to know how she knows all of this. Whether she be mortal or supernatural, I want to know how and why she watched my little brother be abused and tormented, and she did nothing about it."

Something in Akłaq's mind clicked, then, something she had never quite grasped, yet it had lurked in the shadows and recesses of her mind, a question perpetually lingering in the peripheral. The question why, and the ability to get an answer. The deep hurt of the soul and the ability to seek out and find an answer.

"Where will you start?" she asked.

Micaiah huffed a sigh, still leaning over the Books, one of them opene to the back cover. "Well, this little blurb here says Michigan. Seems as good a place as any to start. But I am curious about this...I don't know, code, here."

He pointed and she nodded. "I couldn't figure out that either."

"What's 'www'?" he wondered aloud. "And what does '.com' mean?"

" 'Com' could be community," Akłaq suggested. "Communication? Maybe those are places near where she lives. Clues for Akari-bearers to follow."

"And the first part?"

"I don't know. But it sounds like you've got your work cut out for you."

He straightened and turned to face her. "You sound disappointed. I would have thought you would be happy to ship me off to some other land and get me out of your hair." He relaxed his posture. "Or are you jealous?"

"Of what? The fact that you can go anywhere and do anything while I have to observe segregation?"

"To be fair, I don't think the colored folks would like it if I took their seats at the theater either," Micaiah pointed out. "Besides, a lot of that is changing now. What was it, last year or so that Saskatchewan passed equal rights? The rest of the provinces are slowly following."

She gave him a look. "You can speak and write as many words as you please, but you'll never legislate what's in a man's heart."

He reluctantly conceded the point. "That much is true."

"At the same time," she went on, "if I had never read the stories of the Krydik and knew them to be true, I never would have believed the words in your Book, and I probably never would have apologized. So there is still some value to words."

"Of course there is. And just because things are improving here doesn't mean it's the same everywhere. The United States is still pretty observant of their segregation, and theirs is codified."

Akłaq grinned humorlessly. "At least in the arctic, no one wants our frozen wasteland, so we can do what we please."

"I think you would do that anyway."

"You'll just have to wait for my Book to be released so you can find out."

They returned the Authored Books to the librarian and left the Archives, grateful to be going down the stairs this time.

"And what if you got home and found your Book on your shelf?" Micaiah wondered. "Would you let me read it?"

"Even if I said no, there's still a copy here."

"Yes, but I can't get here."

"Even so. Like your brother, everyone else would be able to read it, so one more set of eyes would matter little."

He did not respond to that right away, and Akłaq wondered if she'd just undone her entire apology from earlier. Finally he said, "I'm still not going to tell him. If nothing else, I'm going to find this Brooke Shaffer person and find out what she knows, how she can watch all this stuff happen and not try to help."

"There are plenty of historians out there who merely record events," Akłaq offered lamely.

"I wouldn't expect her to stop the Krydik's wars, although I would question her abilities if she didn't at least try, depending on her role. But to see a priest abusing a small boy and to simply sit there and scribble away in a notebook..." He shook his head. "Micah doesn't not believe in God; he just doesn't like Him very much, say it that way."

"Believe me, I understand."

They reached the main floor and headed to the portal room. With the knowledge that they were at least heading for Earth, Micaiah was able to lend a bit of strength to keep the portal stable enough for them both to pass through. Akłaq had chosen her apartment as the landing point, just so they didn't land in the twins' apartment only for Micah to be home and have a bunch of questions for them. This way, Micaiah could go somewhere, fabricate whatever he wanted about his evening's exploits, and keep Micah in the dark about the little Book of secrets.

They each made their way to a chair. She didn't know about him, but she had a splitting headache. She would probably just crawl into bed once he'd gone.

"I still don't know what to make of all of this," Micaiah said, not looking too great himself, "but thank you for showing me. And thank you for the apology; like I said before, it takes a lot for anyone to admit fault."

"I couldn't face my children and tell them I hated someone, especially after all the times I told them not to."

"How many children do you have? Are they Time Agents or...?"

She sighed and squeezed her eyes closed. There were no lights on in the apartment, but the ambient light from outside may as well have been the surface of the sun. "Maybe another time."

"Once your Book comes out?" he teased, though it was weak. "I understand. And I still have to get home."

"You won't have to fake having gone to a pub," Akłaq offered, still not looking at anything.

She heard him stand up. "Hey now. That's an Irish stereotype." He paused for a long moment, but when she finally got her eyes to open and focus on him, she found him grinning. "And it's one we proudly live up to. All right, I'll see you at the next training session."

"You still want to train with me?"

Akłaq rubbed her eyes, using Feel to locate the inflamed nerves in her eyes and brain and gently bring them back to normal so she could function.

"We have to get passed as Masters somehow," he told her, slowly livening up. "Then we'll be on our way south. Or maybe east again. To Michigan."

"How are you going to explain your quest to Micah?"

Micaiah waved a hand. "Leave that to me. For now, we'll just focus on surviving your training methods."

Groaning, she stood and faced him as he went to the door. "I know you said you're not going to tell Micah, but do you want to learn more about the Akari, too, while you're here?"

He thought about it for a second, then answered, "Not yet. Let me think about it for a bit."

She nodded. "It's a lot to take in."

"You just showed me my own biography, and I don't like it."

"If it makes you feel any better, I'm not too enthusiastic about receiving mine either."

He did not say anything to that, nor did he offer much of a farewell as he departed. Akłaq didn't mind, really, mostly because she was still too tired to care much. Maybe later she would be annoyed about it, but for now, she was just grateful that her apology had been accepted. Everything after that was a bonus.

She didn't know how much time had passed before she realized that she basically felt normal again and was accomplishing nothing sitting there at the table like an idiot. She also wasn't sure what she expected to do. All the adventures and the revelations had come and gone, and her motivation had left her as well.

So, Micaiah truly had been clueless about the Akari, and it sounded like Micah was, too. Micaiah wanted to keep Micah in the dark because of the secrets revealed in the Book, and it sounded like he was going to track down the Author and start asking some questions.

Akłaq leaned back in her chair and thought about that. Had anyone done such a thing before? Certainly she'd never heard of it if they had. Most aliens would have a difficult time of it, but what about other humans? The Krydik would have the largest grievance to bear, seeing how they had two Books and seemed to have suffered the most so far.

Had Michigan existed at the time of the first Book? Akłaq didn't know much, or really anything, about the regional history, but she didn't think so. And the binding the Book would have also been very foreign at the time. Even now, while the binding itself was becoming more common, the printing of the Books, the clarity of the cover images was stunning. However it was done...it probably didn't exist yet.

What if the Author didn't exist yet? Was that possible? No, couldn't be. That was preposterous. How could something write its own history? It would be like Akłaq composing the history of her village and the way it burned.

There was some missing piece, she was sure.

For a few minutes, she contemplated whether she couldn't somehow go with Micaiah on his quest to seek out the Author. She might have a few questions of her own she'd like answered. Why did her village have to burn? Why did her children have to die? Why did Aniqan have to die? Why did these schools have to exist? So many indigenous children kidnapped, orphan boys like Micah abused, what was it all for? Sure, Anagalisgi and Sabelu and the Whites were nice and all, a good intermediary for some of the more mundane aspects of existence, but what about the more philosophical and existential questions and crises that arose? Maybe Micah would like to ask the Author himself about why she didn't save him.

Akłaq remembered something one of the Orthodox priests had said a long time ago, that those who did not question God were not ready to serve Him. Not because he thought God was wrong and needed to change His mind, but because it might be the servant who had to answer the same questions from the regular public. The servant who did not know why he served was ultimately useless if his whole job was to bring others in to serve as well. This did not mean that the public would accept the answers, but a hard truth was better than bumbling incoherence.

Maybe she should go with him. Maybe all human Akari-bearers should make this attempt, a pilgrimage, if it could be called that. If they all got their answers and understood what was going on, both in their own lives and overall with the appearance of these Books, then they could take it to the rest of the Akari-bearers who could not freely traverse Earth. It seemed logical enough. Why speculate? Just the appearance of the first Book had caused terrible division, a dozen small splinter groups breaking away for seemingly petty reasons. Maybe if they actually went to the source, they could sort things out a little better, bring some of those groups back into the larger community.

It was late enough that she could justify going to bed, and she did so, if for no other reason than she actually hoped to speak to Anagalisgi or the white bear. Maybe they would have a lead on the Author, where in Michigan to start looking. Maybe they had a home address, just cut to the end. Mentally she shook her head. Even she knew it would never be that easy.

She did not see Anagalisgi, the white bear, or even Sabelu, and she would admit to being a little frustrated about it when she woke up and headed to work. Exactly what were the criteria for their visits? Why was it only that they visited her? Why couldn't she visit them?

But it was neither here nor there. Akłaq went to work, another day of cleaning other people's houses. What would she ask the Author, if she did find her in person? Would she bring up Sabelu's marriage prophecy? Should she bring it up to Micaiah before he left the area? They'd only just made up—well, she had only just made up. It wasn't as though they were planning on getting married tomorrow. She still wasn't sure how she felt about him. He was protective of his brother, which was a good thing, but how would that carry over? Would the twins be able to separate, or were they spiritually conjoined? And there was still that shadow of arrogance she saw in him. Sure, all men had their pride, but arrogance could be quite annoying.

Or maybe she would wait. Maybe she would let him go on this quest alone. If he found the Author, the resulting conversations—or confrontations—could be quite revealing. If he didn't find her, Akłaq figured that would be the bigger test of his character. There is little in the world so frustrating as the silence of a god.

Avgun Iñuiñaq Qulit Tallimat
Honest Work

The three of them had agreed to not train on weekends. The twins wanted to enjoy their weekends. Akłaq had them off most of the time, but every so often, a client wanted a Saturday morning clean so they could host a party that evening. Akłaq silently wondered why they bothered; the real clean up would be needed after the party. But that wasn't her problem.

So it was Tuesday the next time they got together for training.

Akłaq approached the twins' apartment building with some anxiety. She hadn't heard from Micaiah since he'd left her apartment, and she worried whether his forgiveness would really stand. What if he'd thought about it on his way home and decided that maybe she hadn't been sincere? What if he'd thought that she had only used the apology as a trap of some form, something to do with the Books and the Akari and all that? What if Micah had rejected the apology? What if he was suspicious? What if he'd managed to get his brother to tell him about the Book?

Well, that last part would be between them. If Micaiah couldn't keep a secret, that wasn't her fault. But the rest of it, she couldn't help but wonder and worry.

She paused for half a second before knocking on their door, then lowered her hand and used Sound to amplify any interior noises. What kind of conversation were they having without her there?

The only thing she really got out of her eavesdropping was a flushing toilet. Could be worse, she figured. At least she hadn't come in the middle of an argument.

She knocked.

A moment later, the door opened and Micaiah let her inside.

The first thing she noticed was Micah in the living room. He didn't look openly hostile, more like moderately annoyed. Like a teenager who doesn't want to do something or go somewhere but is being forced by his family.

"Micah, I—" she began.

"Cai told me what you said," he cut in. "He told me all about your apology."

"Well, he said he accepted it. Do you?"

He hesitated for half a second. "As he probably told you, it takes a lot for someone to admit they're wrong. But that doesn't mean that a bad habit is fully broken because of it. Now I'm not saying that I won't train under you, but I think if you want to be taken seriously, there are a few more people you need to apologize to."

Akłaq took an even breath and nodded. "I know." And she did know; she just hated being called out on it. "For tonight, though, at least, you're good to train?"

"As long as you're good to teach."

If she hadn't read his Book and known his history, she might have wondered why he was so tough on forgiveness. Between the priests and some apparent discrimination by society—the latter of which she still wasn't fully convinced of—he probably didn't hear too many apologies, and even fewer sincere ones.

She nodded and motioned for them all to head into the living room and get comfortable in their usual spots. The twins took the couch and she sat in a wingback chair.

"All right, why don't we start over?" she suggested meekly. "Show me what you know and what you've been working on, and we'll go from there."

If any of them were comfortable with this, it was Micaiah. His posture was thoughtful and he displayed his talents without gripe or comment. If she asked him to demonstrate a particular Band, he did so. Well, Micah did, too—he wasn't being obstinate about anything— but Micaiah just seemed to have the better attitude. Maybe he was thinking about how these abilities would be different in the Akari. Maybe he was thinking about how he used to do them before Sean taught him Time.

For goodness' sake, was she actually checking him out? No, she couldn't be. What was there to look at? Sure, he might look strong, but did he have any real skills? Could he hunt or fish? Did he know how to survive in the wilderness in harsh weather? How was he with children? Time Agents rarely had children, either because the women physically couldn't or because the men didn't want to watch a spouse and children grow old and die. But if he knew that it was possible, would he still be interested?

Was she still interested? She'd raised nine children already. Four had been murdered, one died in an accident, and the other four were slowly growing old. Could she really handle that again? So soon?

What did she want out of life then? What was her goal? What was her crusade? Did it have something to do with the Books? Was Sabelu's hundred year prophecy related to them somehow? Was it something entirely different? Damn it, she hated prophets. She also hated not being able to talk to them and ask questions at convenient times. She should be focusing on the training going on.

She turned her attention to Micah for a bit. He was still a bit suspicious, a bit rigid, but he didn't refuse to do anything she asked. What was he thinking about all of this? Did he think her insincere? Did he wonder if she had ulterior motives? What would they be, assuming she had any? If her only goal had been to just go home, why would she suddenly have a change of heart? Was she coerced in some way?

In a way, she supposed. Coerced by fate, the spirits, the Author, God, she didn't know. And she still questioned whether having such detailed knowledge of a prophecy—and, really, it wasn't all that detailed, just slightly more so than vague notations and riddles—had been a good idea. Maybe Sabelu was the one with ulterior motives. And he had the foresight to back it up.

Akłaq mentally shook her head. She had to stay focused. She'd gotten her second chance; she didn't need to waste this one on distraction and existential crises.

"All right, have you been working on your Time Tendrils?" she asked, addressing both brothers.

Both confirmed they had. As expected, Akłaq challenged them to prove it. She put up a Fast Band, just a simple one. If she really wanted, she could reinforce her Band—or just use an Akari Band—and keep them out with the equivalent of a steel wall. But for the purposes of the lesson, she just used what she might have termed a lazy Band. Easy to see, easy to match.

Micah was the first to try. He put up a Band of his own to buy himself more time to get situated, then used Time Tendrils like grappling hooks to bring his Band and her Band together, fusing them into a single Band and keeping them locked into the final ratio of one second: ten second. For every one second that passed inside the Band, ten passed outside.

Akłaq could have broken his Tendrils easily enough, but she made him hold them for ten seconds in the Band before having him release them. When he did that, she dropped the Band. Micah did not appear physically strained, as though he had done strenuous exercise, but he had the look of a man who has been stumped by the crossword puzzle in the Sunday paper and it was causing him some distress.

"Stable," she said, "but not especially strong." She looked at Micaiah. "Your turn."

Again she put up a Band. Micaiah did not start off with a Band of his own, but instead threw Time Tendrils into her Band just as it was forming. This allowed him to get into the Band must faster, and she wouldn't deny he had a decent grip, but he was operating with nothing to fall back on and, to prove a point, she threw him out of the Band, snapping the Tendrils.

"Strong," she told him, "but no stability. You're throwing yourself at a moving object, but if that object is stronger than you, you have no way to recuperate without taking up more time."

"I was kind of going for the element of surprise," he confessed.

"And for someone of equal or lesser rank or skill, you probably would have gotten the upper hand."

"Isn't that all that matters?" Micah asked. "Most Runners don't have abilities worth peanuts."

"Most, but not all. You forget that I was a Runner for a very long time. Some in upper management still consider me a Runner. And there have been other Runners who have attained great skill, if not rank. Cassius Hand was a very famous human Runner."

"Never heard of him."

Akłaq shrugged. "He disappeared a long time ago, around the time of the Missing Zero Hour. Maybe he was killed in the fallout, or maybe he just used the chaos to make his escape to some other world. No one knows. There were some rumors that he'd reappeared in Africa during the war, but in such chaos, men will see all sorts of things."

"Point is, we should keep training," Micaiah said.

"Exactly," Akłaq confirmed. "Anyway, you need to have a good grasp of Time Tendrils in order to learn a Time Web."

"Time Web?" Micah wondered. "Have you ever used one of those, beyond just being able to do it for a test?"

"Once, yes. Unfortunately, it didn't save the man I was trying to help, but it bought me enough time to get away." She went on before either twin could speak. "Now then, try again."

They stuck to the easy stuff that evening. Micah had a good grasp of keeping himself stable, and he was fairly quick, but lacking in strength. Micaiah had the opposite problem, where he had the strength, and even the speed, but virtually none of the stability. Telling him to work on it evoked a reaction that she might have likened to a policeman pulling over a man in his sportscar and telling him to stop speeding.

After each twin got in a few more practice tries, they lowered their heads and went into some private conference. Akłaq was curious, but decided to let them have their secrecy for the moment. It was Micaiah who spoke.

"Put up a Band, however you want," he said. "We're going to try this together."

Intrigued, Akłaq just nodded, leaned back in the chair, and reached for the same lazy Band she'd been using all evening. What she was not expecting was for Micah to whip out a Band—speed and stability in tact—followed by Micaiah coming through the metaphorical smoke to throw Time Tendrils at her and wrench her out of her Band into the new one that had fused between hers and theirs.

Only from past experience did Akłaq know that she could grab the Tendrils, half a second before Micaiah let them dissolve, and reverse them. The fused Band ruptured and threw them back into their original Bands. Thankfully, they all seemed to recognize what happened and let everything dissipate and cool down, including themselves. Though they had done no real physical work, they were still breathing heavily and sweating.

"Very good," she said, nodding. "Very good." She sat up and got herself resituated. "Do it again, if you can."

She didn't overexert herself in the next Band she created, but it was still high strength. She wouldn't say that she didn't feel the twins' attempts to latch onto it with Tendrils, but it was more like how a toddler might pretend to fight or wrestle with his father. The toddler gives it everything he has, his father goes along with it, but there is no real danger of harm from the toddler.

She eased back slowly on her Band, letting it loosen just to the point where the twins could get a grip when they put everything they had behind it. From there Micah was able to build up their Band and bring them up to the same level with her where Micaiah secured everything together. Neither one was in much shape to do anything more, and Akłaq took over everything and let it dissolve. The brothers had the appearance of having just climbed a mountain without any real practice beforehand.

"You've both got a long way to go," she told them, "but I admire your ability to combine your talents."

"Are you suggesting that we have to be able to do that individually before you pass us?" Micah asked, leaning back, his head on the arm of the couch, staring at the ceiling.

"If you do, I will most certainly be impressed." When he sighed, she grinned. "Not quite to that level, no. At the same time, you do need to hone your skills independently. You might travel together now, but I can't imagine you'll want to do so forever. Eventually, you will have to live your own lives."

"Maybe," Micaiah said, stretching, "but not today."

After a few minutes, Akłaq shifted position again and made a motion. "I want to see each of you try it on the other."

"That could be interpreted in multiple ways," Micah said, still staring at the ceiling.

"A Mhicah, be polite," Micaiah rebuked, swatting him.

"Hey, once a woman has proven herself to be a cunt, I say what I want. I don't give a feck."

"She apologized. And you'll notice that we've had a decent training session that is far less traumatic than before."

"Even so, a door has been opened."

Before Micaiah could say more, Akłaq cut in with, "I've been called worse, and I've had worse done to me. There is nothing you could say or do to offend me."

"Except exist, apparently," Micah quipped.

"I'm sorry," Akłaq said before Micaiah could speak. "You didn't deserve what I said. If you don't believe my apology is sincere, then I'm wasting my breath. If you do believe it's sincere, then why continue to punish me?"

The younger twin did not reply, though he did not give any indication that he cared much about what she said.

Micaiah swatted his brother again. "Come on, a Mhicah. One last demonstration."

Micah sighed again, but sat up, rubbed his eyes, and faced his brother. "All right, fine."

Micah Banded first, and it was nothing for Micaiah to throw Tendrils at it and lock them in place, without needing to build something more stable to back him. Akłaq called him out on this and had him do it again. He complained about it a little, but did as he was told. Micah aided this effort by strengthening the Band, making it more difficult to latch onto. Once Micaiah succeeded, with some more grumbling about how he felt very much slower, Micah dissolved the Band, and they switched roles.

Micaiah did not go easy on his brother, instead building a Band that he might have thought would be impenetrable, at least by Micah. But Micah had the sense, if not the speed, to build a stable Band for himself before attempting to grab hold of Micaiah's Band and lock them together with Tendrils. Micaiah figuratively danced away several times as he varied his Band, but Micah was successful before long and had the two of them held fast. Then everything was released, and everyone was back in Base Time.

"Micaiah, you need to work on your foundation," Akłaq told him. "All of this here is easy stuff and you can get away with just bulling your way through. It won't always be this way."

He said nothing to that, though his posture reminded her of her boys when they were young teenagers, just trying to prove themselves in the world.

"Micah, you have the form, but not the speed. Everything you're doing is technically perfect, now you just need to work on speed and improvisation. You look like you're doing everything from rote memorization. You need to make it part of you. Adapt to your brother's bullishness and make him work for it."

That statement alone seemed to finally break, or at least crack, the ice that still stood between the two of them. She was giving him permission, no, an order, to beat up on his brother a little, to make him sweat, to make him work. She didn't doubt that he did this anyway, but at least now if Micaiah complained, Micah would be able to point to this conversation and remind him that their Master for this part of their training had explicitly told him to do it.

Looked like brothers were pretty much the same no matter the culture.

"All right, I think that's enough for today," she said at last, noting the sighs of relief. "Practice as much as you can, and I'll be back on Friday."

"Can't do Friday," Micaiah said. "Starting inventory tomorrow at the warehouse, and it's not going to be pretty."

They worked out another day instead. As Akłaq prepared to leave, placing her hand on the door handle, Micaiah said, "And another thing." She turned. "Thanks for not being a pain."

She didn't know how to respond to that, so she elected to say nothing. What did he expect her to say? Sorry about all that, even though I've already apologized? You're welcome? Thanks for accepting my previous apology? Thanks for not being a total jackass yourself? Thanks for being a good student? How was anyone supposed to respond to something like that?

It was later in the evening, but still light enough that she wasn't worried. Of course, with her abilities, she wasn't worried about anything anyway. What was potentially a devastating encounter for an ordinary woman was only a minor annoyance to her, but an annoyance still. She wouldn't be treated fairly in a court of law, and she was tired of trying to hide bodies. She wasn't out looking for trouble, true, but that didn't mean that trouble didn't know how to find her when it wanted to.

But other than a few raunchy expressions and lewd comments from some obvious drunks, she made it back to her apartment without incident.

Things had gone smoother than expected, actually, even with Micah's cynicism, and if that was the worst that happened, well, she could handle it. She didn't really think she deserved it after an apology, but she remembered hearing once that forgiveness was a process, not a switch. For some, that process was as easy as the rising or setting of the sun and moon. For others, it was more like childbirth.

Whatever the case, things were back on track. Whatever was going on with Sabelu's marriage prophecy, assuming he hadn't had other ends in mind, it could take a back seat to the present moment. Right now, she was to train and assess the twins in their Time abilities and pass them to Master status.

She jumped at a knock on her door.

This late at night? Who could it possibly be? She'd just come from the twins' apartment, so unless they just filed a massive complaint against her that somehow warranted a massive, in-person response, it wouldn't be them. Few people even knew where she lived in the first place, and most of those were her neighbors.

She opened the door to find Micaiah.

"Did I forget something?" It was the only thing she could think of. Then, dumbly, "Did you follow me? How did you know where I lived?"

"Uh, this is where we landed after the Akarin fortress," Micaiah told her.

"Oh. Right." Akłaq could have kicked herself. "What are you doing here? Everything all right?"

"Mind if I come in so I don't sound like a lunatic?"

She nodded and stepped aside so he could enter, then closed the door behind him.

"I thought about waiting," he was saying, "but then Micah said he was going to head to the pub, and I thought maybe I would try to catch you before you went to bed."

"He wouldn't find it strange that you didn't join him at the pub?" Akłaq questioned, intending it as a joke.

"I told him I'd catch up with him in a bit."

"So why are you here?"

"As I recall, according to your Books or whatever, I'm supposed to be an Akari-bearer. I still don't even know what that is, even though I can apparently do it, have been doing it for most all of my life."

"So are you here for a philosophy lesson or physical training?"

Micaiah shrugged. "I don't know. Either. Both. Why are they different at all? Considering we're talking about bending the physics of the universe...how are there multiple ways to do that?"

"Isn't flying bending the physics of the universe, too, to overcome that which keeps us on the ground?" Akłaq postulated. "And yet there are the birds who are born with such power and it is no mystery to them. Then humans came along with their mechanics and built airplanes, and parachutes allow for a more controlled fall and greater likelihood of surviving long drops. For the rest of us—" She invoked Gravity then, just enough to get her feet noticeably off the ground. "—we have Gravity." She held it for a few seconds, long enough to watch Micaiah's eyes get huge and his expression dumbfounded, then slowly released it and returned to the ground. "All different ways to overcome a natural force of the universe."

After a moment, Micaiah rubbed his eyes and tried to compose himself. "Aye, but a Band is a Band, isn't it?"

"In principle, yes. Just like an airplane is an airplane. But there are different kinds of airplanes, aren't there? Different kinds of birds?" She grinned and laughed once to herself. "Everett once told me that the difference between Time Bands and Akari Bands is like the difference between male and female cardinals. The male is bright and flashy, but all he really wants to do is screw something. The female is less flashy, but her desire is to raise and nurture chicks."

Micaiah blinked. "I don't get it."

"Time Bands are very bright and flashy. The stronger you are, the more powerful your Bands, the brighter they are in their colors. But the Time industry has really only served to screw people over, be it directly in the buying and selling of Time, or indirectly as those like Goldsmith and Frederickson have used it to advance their own non-Time agendas. But Akari Bands are invisible and call no attention to themselves. The only ones who know they're there are other Akari-bearers—"

"You can't tell me the Akari is only used for good. I've heard of some of the shit that's happened. Never put much stock in it other than fringe fanaticism, but I have heard."

"I understand," Akłaq said, "but I know you can appreciate that many horrors have been committed in the name fo God by those who claim to serve Him."

He grunted, which she took as some form of grudging agreement.

Instead he asked, "And you still don't know anything about someone who was apparently born with such abilities?"

"No." Truthfully she hadn't given it much thought and even less pursuit. "But I'd be willing to bet that the last few years of formal Time training hasn't caused you to forget how to use Akari Bands."

As if to prove the point, he did so, bringing both of them into an Akari Fast Band. He did this with no more thought than brushing a bit of dust from his eyes. "You're right, but now that I know that there is a difference, that there's more to this than what I could have imagined...I don't know what to do with it. And considering all of this, and the Author...I don't know whether it's too fantastic to be believed, or too amazing to be disbelieved."

"Do you have any leads on where to find the Author?" Akłaq inquired.

He shook his head and dropped the Band. "No, but I haven't had much time to really look. Earth-side information is too limited, but the Wheel Archives aren't exactly a bastion of information on the subject either. And I can't even get to the Akarin fortress."

"How did you get to the Wheel, then?"

"Micah and I split the difference, as we usually do."

"And what was your excuse there?"

He gave her a cheeky look. "Looking up your record." When she raised a brow, he nodded. "Seriously. I wanted to know just what kind of psychopath we were studying under."

"I see. Well, it couldn't have been too bad if you're still here."

"Micah was more hesitant than I was. I just told him that we're not Masters or Managers, so we should be fine."

Akłaq sighed and rolled her eyes. "My legacy."

He laughed. "All right, so we've established that Bands are nothing. Easy enough to learn across disciplines. What about Time Tendrils? What about this Gravity stuff? Why didn't we use that in the fortress instead of climbing all those stairs?"

Now she laughed. "It's not a good idea to use Gravity in the fortress. Bad things happen when two Gravity tracks cross."

"Like what?"

"I'll show you when we get that far. Right now we'll focus on Time Tendrils and anything else you've already learned in Time."

There wasn't much to focus on seeing how he seemed to have greater mastery of the Akari version of his abilities than Time, even when he hadn't used the Akari version very much, if at all, the last few years. Fast Bands, Slow Bands, Double, Pinpoint, varying Bands, sliding Bands, he did all of it as though he'd simply been born with it, as a bird is born with the capacity to fly.

"Now that I know there's a difference, Time—from the Time industry, that is—feels so much more difficult," Micaiah lamented.

Akłaq nodded. "I know. That's because it's flashy and vain. When you do something to call attention to yourself, it does take a lot more work than just doing whatever the deed is."

"But why is philosophy translating into physicality? We're only dealing with physics here."

"Are we? Can we somehow separate physics from nature? Can we separate nature from spirit? Do not the spirits interact with what we call physics?"

He did not say anything, but she could see him mentally wrestling with it. She went on, "A lot of people, once they have seen Time, come to reject religion, whoever or whatever shape that comes in for them, spirits, God, something else. Have you?"

Micaiah let out a breath. "I can't say that I've never questioned it, and I admit that after the school, for as good as our family was to us, Micah and I aren't what you would call good Catholics. But I can't believe that these abilities, this Akari that I have, is just an accident or some next stage of chance evolution. What creature can reach into creation and change it? There's got to be more to it, whether it's God, this Author person, or something else, I haven't figured out yet."

Akłaq nodded. "Well, at least there's something in your heart to work with."

"And what do you believe, then?"

She chuckled nervously. "I think I'm going to reserve judgment until I read my own Book, whenever it appears. The fact that it hasn't, and it's been a century since Everett showed it to me, I'm beginning to wonder."

"What if it's not your Book, though? Then what?"

Akłaq shrugged. "I don't know. On the one hand, I guess I'm not as special as I thought I was and Sabelu is full of shit. On the other hand, I suppose it releases me from a few other obligations."

Micaiah raised a brow but did not press.

Instead they went back to the Akari, Akłaq trying to get Micaiah to transfer all of his Time abilities. As with the Bands, it wasn't difficult, for the Akari was far lighter and more flexible. Even his Tendrils had improved and he was almost able to conjure up some kind of stable platform as she'd been on him to do.

"Just don't forget to use Time when we all get together for Time training," she reminded him, "especially if you're not going to bring Micah in on this."

"But if I did decide to bring him in, then we'd all be using the Akari?" he questioned. "Is this the real reason you don't get assigned Apprentices?"

She shrugged. "They try to keep me as far away as possible without losing track of me, yes. And they do think I'm guilty of corrupting the youth."

"Are you?"

"Depends on how you define corruption."

"I don't know that I like where this is going."

"Rescuing children from being kidnapped is not corruption. Telling them that they are beautiful the way they are is not a call to arms. Telling them that they are not 'less than' is hardly violence."

"Well, telling me that I'm shit for something that happened a hundred years ago a hundred miles away isn't the best way to inspire sympathy for your cause."

"So what are you going to tell the Author if you find her?"

That gave him some pause, although he just looked a bit confused. Then, "What do you mean?"

Akłaq shifted her stance. "If the Author is just recording events as they happen, then there's no use being angry with her about the priests or your brother. If she's somehow causing events to happen, then you're in the same conundrum as people who blame God for war or any of the other bad things in the world." She made a gesture. "So which is it? Pretending you found her home address, knock on the door, and she opens it, what are you going to do or say?"

Micaiah opened his mouth several times, but the only thing he could come up with was, "I don't know. I mean, lots of people say they're going to have words with God when they get to heaven, but you'd have to be an idiot to actually think you're going to tell Him what to do." He folded his arms. "But the Author is a person. She lives in Michigan. She's married. Those are all indications that she is just a human being."

"So was Jesus, but we all know what happened to Him."

"I'm not going to kill her. At least, I don't intend to, but I make no promises if she comes after me."

"You're afraid of a woman?"

He gave her a look. "I don't know what's going on here, but just with this conversation alone, I feel like I have to know. God is God, and no 'Author' is going to change that. If anything, this is heresy at its finest. But I still want to know how she knows the shit she does and why she doesn't do anything about it."

Akłaq raised a brow. "What were you saying to Micah about being polite?"

"If you can murder a man, you can handle a few profane words of frustration." He shifted his stance. "I don't know where to start. I mean, this all has to do with the Books and the Akarin, something you only just introduced me to in the last week. I don't know the first thing about teachings or doctrine. If the Books are real and true and everything else, we're talking about a very powerful force at the very least. If this is some kind of impostor, something of this magnitude isn't going to just go away quietly, and it won't like being found out."

"And it's going to protect itself against greater foes than a brand new inductee," Akłaq pointed out.

"That, too." Micaiah frowned. "I don't know. I feel bad, you know? Like I've just joined a group and now I want to rip it apart without knowing what I'm really destroying. What if this is all a good thing that's happening?"

Akłaq nodded thoughtfully. "I heard it said once that the truth doesn't mind being questioned, but a lie doesn't like being challenged. If it is a good thing, then the Author, or whoever, is going to want everyone to see it. And if it is the Author, then she's going to keep doing, regardless of what we have to say about it."

"That's what I'm afraid of." He mused over this for a moment. "You've been part of the Akarin for a while. Would you be willing to help me? I don't know, maybe you think I don't have a right to ask, seeing how I'm white and all, but—"

"Why would I think that? My people have been guides for your people all throughout history, showing you the best places to loot and plunder." Even she didn't know how she intended to deliver those statements, so she moved on. "As for your observation that I've been part of the Akarin for a while, while that may be true, that doesn't mean I understand what's going on. I don't think too many people do."

"Then the blind can lead the blind. Does anyone in charge have any better ideas?"

She sighed. "I don't know. Honestly, I haven't worried about it too much. Like the Time industry, Earth is a nobody. Humans are no one."

"Obviously the Author doesn't think so."

While his ambition was admirable and his ideas intriguing, Akłaq was quickly growing weary of his enthusiasm. She had to be up early, and he probably did, too. "Listen, I'll see what I can do. Maybe someone has given this some thought and has an idea where to start. Maybe you can join them instead of trying to start an independent crusade."

He nodded, clearly not catching on to her growing annoyance.

"I think Micah might be missing you at the pub."

"Maybe," he said. He still didn't seem to understand that she really just wanted him gone at that point, but it got him moving toward the door, anyway.

"Just don't get so drunk that you start rambling on about the Akari — or Time, for that matter," she told him, slowly herding him out the door.

"Clearly you've never gotten drunk with an Irishman. We say weirder shit than that all the time."

"I'm sure you do."

With that, she closed the door.

There was that arrogance thing again, she thought. Get introduced to a group and then immediately want to rip into it. Was that a European thing, or a man thing?

At the same time, wasn't she even the tiniest bit interested in the Author, how and why she did things? Wouldn't it be helpful to know whether this person who was writing these Books was an impostor bent on destroying the Akarin through heresy and subjugation? Wouldn't it have been better to be rid of the evil priests before they had the chance to abuse vulnerable boys? Maybe the reason the Books were so slow in coming was because the impostor was just testing the waters to see what kind of reaction the Akarin would give, especially with the apparent promise of more Books in the future.

These were bigger questions than Akłaq was accustomed to encountering or addressing. Was she curious to know the answers? Sure. Did she really want to get involved? Again? If she did, guaranteed that Patrick and the others would come after her. Or worse, they would go after her children, now that they were too old and weak to really defend themselves. And even if others did come to their aid, they didn't have the skill to outlast even a Journeyman, never mind a Captain, the Lieutenants, plus the Regional Manager and maybe even the Gatekeeper herself.

Did she really want to abandon her children in their last days on account of yet another adventure? There was every chance that this was a dead end or else far bigger than anything they could have imagined. Either one didn't look particularly enticing in light of potentially losing her children. She knew they were going to die, but she didn't want to be the cause of it. Bad enough she was going to have to bury them.

Avgun Iñuiñaq Qulit Itchaksrat
Leads

It was a couple weeks before anything really materialized from that conversation. Akłaq still went over to the twins' apartment twice a week for training. Micaiah had been back to her apartment once for more Akari training. But as far as his pursuit of the Author's physical location, that did not happen right away.

That was fine, really. Akłaq still wasn't sure what she intended to do, but a letter from Gáx saying that Latseen was in poor health was slowly making the decision for her.

This was all that really consumed her thoughts as she opened her apartment to Micaiah, then opened a portal to the fortress. They were supposed to meet Everett, Netami, and Sabelu. Akłaq thought about Netami, how young and beautiful she was. Netami had once mentioned that her mother was just as youthful.

Akłaq couldn't help but think of how nice it must be to have that kind of mother-daughter relationship, where both could be youthful in body and yet possess the wisdom of experience as well. They could do things together without the daughter worrying about the mother's health, or the mother worrying about the daughter's inexperience. Of course, they would worry over these things, but there was a kind of relief about that worry being largely unfounded. How much worse, then, it was, for Akłaq to worry about her daughter's health as an old woman.

For as much fuss as the Books seemed to cause at their appearance, they seemed to have little lasting effect. It was as if the Akarin thought that by ignoring the Books, then maybe they wouldn't appear anymore and the people wouldn't have to deal with any consequences arising from either their mere existence or anything written inside. For the moment, that seemed to be the case. Everett was the only one even remotely tied to the Krydik who was active in any sense of the word, and Micaiah had only just been made aware of the existence of the Akari. And yet, Akłaq knew, deep down, that the time of ignorance and apathy would be coming to a rapid close.

They made their way up the stairs, Akłaq having to explain again that they could not "just use Gravity to get to the fifth floor." She wouldn't say that she didn't want to, but she understood why they couldn't. She might have to teach him that lesson next, just a quick one, to get him to understand. On a normal day, it was an acceptable question, but with everything going on in her head, it was annoying her more than usual. She kind of wanted him to shut up. She kind of wanted to ignore this meeting entirely and focus on her own problems, but knew that wasn't a viable option either. Her own curiosity demanded to be satisfied.

Then her mind went straight back to Latseen. Gáx hadn't been too specific about the exact illness, but that was to be expected, she supposed. One illness was as potentially lethal as any other. On the other hand, though, she did have the ability to stave off the illness, prevent it from becoming lethal, maybe drive it from her daughter completely. It had been a while since she'd done it, but when it came to her daughter, well, she would give it everything she had and not give up.

If it's not this illness, a small voice said, *it will be another.*

I can't just do nothing, Akłaq countered, staying a step ahead of Micaiah as they reached the fifth floor so that he wouldn't see whatever expressions were crawling over her face.

And will you stop death itself from taking her? Will you breathe Life back into her when she's gone?

I would rather she go peacefully in her sleep than gasping for air and in pain for days on end. I'm not asking to change her fate, just that it be a peaceful one.

The small voice did not say anything to that, although there was a certain feeling that Akłaq got, one she could not explain except that she was going to have to make a choice.

I'm tired of making choices. I'm tired of having to choose between two massive entities, two great adventures and paths in my life, two meaningful pieces of my destiny assuming I have one.

"You're no longer a child, Akłaq."

She jumped and whirled to see Sabelu approaching just as she put her hand on the door to the Archives. His expression was that of dead seriousness, as if he had been the small voice, or at least knew exactly what she had been thinking. He went on, "The easy choices are behind you, and there are yet harder ones to come. Either play the game or leave the match."

"Sorry, I'm not a psychopathic prophet like you; I actually care about my decisions."

In her peripheral vision, Akłaq saw Micaiah shift his stance and clear his throat. "I'm sorry, did I walk into the wrong meeting?"

Akłaq pointed at Sabelu and cut off his words. "Don't you dare."

She didn't like the look he got, but he kept his mouth shut and made a gesture for her to open the door. Once they were inside the Archives, Akłaq leading, followed by Sabelu and Micaiah, she tried to change the subject. "Where's Netami and Everett?"

"On their way," Sabelu answered simply.

Micaiah again cleared his throat. "Then am I to surmise this is Sabelu?"

"You are. And I know you're Micaiah Durvin. Or, in truth, Miach Meagher."

"You've read the Book, then."

"I don't need to. I know."

"You're the Author?" Micaiah's tone was disbelieving. "You don't look like a young white woman."

"I am not the Author, just the one she's chosen to carry the knowledge of almost all things."

"Except how to relate to other human beings," Akłaq grumbled, picking a table and sitting down. "Or how to express certain emotions like empathy, sympathy, or even the ability to fake it."

"I don't need to fake it; that's a woman's problem."

Micaiah sputtered a laugh, Sabelu got this infuriatingly smug expression, and Akłaq just glared at them both.

"But she is right," Sabelu said. "I don't get along with others, and it doesn't bother me one bit." He went on before Micaiah could speak. "And before you say that people like me are what won the war, just consider this: you didn't win the war."

Now Micaiah looked perplexed. "First of all, how do you know about the war if you don't even live on Earth? And two, we just won. We accepted the surrender—"

"Of one agent. A disposable one. Kingdoms rise and kingdoms fall. A void opens up and is filled again. Pieces are moved across the board, some taken in clever maneuvers, some surrendered in calculated decisions, some lost in stupid mistakes, a few miraculously retrieved. But the war is ongoing. And it will ever be going, whether you see it or not."

Micaiah looked at Akłaq. "You're right, he probably doesn't have many friends."

"As for your question of how I know about the war," Sabelu went on, "it is something that I know because the Author has decreed that I should know it. And so I do. I don't expect you to understand; it is not your burden to bear. Just know that when I say something, you better take it seriously."

Now Micaiah shifted in his seat, still facing her. "I admit, I've never really met a prophet, self-proclaimed or otherwise, but somehow I can't imagine folks like Isaiah or Jeremiah being so...rude."

"No, just suicidal," Sabelu quipped.

"But if they were, do you think that might be the reason they weren't heeded?"

"Well, next time you're trying to warn someone of their own stupid, self-inflicted destruction with potentially catastrophic consequences, make sure to do it with a smile and chocolate chip cookies."

"Where are Netami and Everett?" Akłaq cut in irritably. "You said they were on their way, but where are they?"

"They'll be here soon enough," Sabelu told her. "The only reason the Krydik really tolerate Everett and his sporadic comings and goings is because they currently hate me more, but that doesn't mean he isn't still under some scrutiny."

"How are the Krydik taking the new Book?"

"Everett is trying to keep them calm. He is trying to get them to see this meeting and Micaiah's quest as a good thing."

"The Books don't have anything to do with each other," Micaiah said, "other than they're written by the same person. Or are they mad that there's a Book about a white man?"

"You know how sometimes the oldest child in the family gets jealous when their parents show love and attention to the other children, their brothers and sisters?" Sabelu asked. "This is kind of like that."

"It's not as if they haven't known. In the front, it says something about the Chivalrous Welshman. Well, I'm Irish, and the Welsh are sort of like kinfolk. They're pretty white, too."

"As I said, it boils down to sibling rivalry. I don't control them, and they don't care to hear my thoughts on the matter."

"But you're their prophet," Akłaq stated. "They raised you and cared for you in a way that they never afforded Anagalisgi."

Sabelu opened his mouth, but closed it as a new voice that answered, "And they regret every moment of it, believe me."

The three of them looked up to see Everett and Netami approaching the table. It was Everett who had spoken.

"They don't regret it," Sabelu said. "They just wonder what sins they or their forebears committed that they got me as a prophet and not someone like my uncle."

"Does this have anything to do with trying to find the Author?" Micaiah wondered.

Everett and Netami moved to sit. Everett made the noise of half a syllable but was cut off by Sabelu who said bluntly, "You're not going to find her. I can tell you that right now."

Now Micaiah looked annoyed by the smug prophet, and Akłaq found herself oddly satisfied with it. "How do you know that? We haven't even begun to have a discussion on it."

"I know because I know. The Author does not yet exist."

"Have you seen those Books?" Micaiah gestured vaguely toward the case that held the three Books. "Two of them are about your own people. Your grandfather had one in his possession. I have one sitting at home. You're going to say that they were written by some kind of spirit?"

"You see things in three dimensions, the here and now, the physical world and present moment—" Sabelu deliberately put his hands on the table and made a motion back and forth. "—everything bound by physical dimension and a linear progression of time. But that's not how this works." He also made a vague gesture toward the Books. "If you leave right now and go in search of the Author, a physical house and location, you're not going to find anything. If you want to know anything about her, you're currently stuck with the Books."

"Well that's shit." Micaiah leaned back in his chair, though his disposition suggested that he didn't believe Sabelu in the slightest. "Because all I've gathered from the Books so far is that she's a sadistic cunt who sees suffering but does little or nothing about it, but if she really likes someone, she might send them a prophet who is either so vague as to be entirely unhelpful or so sarcastic and rude that you don't even want to ask for his help even if he does have all the information. Why send your people a prophet and a way out, and leave me and my brother to be abused by those we're supposed to trust?"

Sabelu grinned in a way that Akłaq had come to loathe, and she wouldn't have been surprised if Micaiah decided to demonstrate his prize fighting skills. "The story isn't over. Would you like to know what happens?"

"No!" Micaiah slapped the table, causing everyone to jump. In a nearby aisle of books, an alien grunted and made a gesture that might have been interpreted as "Sh!"

"Then what are you complaining about?" Sabelu wondered. "Go on your search, look for the Author. I'm simply trying to save you time."

"I think you've made your point," Netami said, her soft voice and calm demeanor immediately defusing the situation. She looked at her brother. "You should go now."

Sabelu looked like he had more to say, but at the last moment decided against it. He stood and left without so much as a "Have a nice day."

"How do you stand him?" Micaiah demanded of Netami once Sabelu had gone.

"Honestly, I'm the only one who does," she replied, sighing. "And I'm the only one he really listens to. He's good for information, not so much for diplomacy."

"I hope he doesn't hold any important positions within the tribe," Akłaq commented.

"Being a prophet is an honored and very important position," Netami informed her, though any pride in the fact was muted. "But the council prefers to keep him at arm's length."

"I'd rather not have him in the room at all," Micaiah said. "Is there any way to prove him wrong? Akłaq said you might have leads on where to find the Author."

Netami shifted position. "Sabelu is very rarely wrong. In the times that he is wrong, there is some speculation that it wasn't him intentionally misleading someone in order for them to gain something in a different way."

"That doesn't mean we won't help," Everett told him. "It's just something to keep in mind."

"So he might be saying that this mission is impossible because somewhere along the line, I'm going to have to draw on the need to spite him and prove him wrong in order to keep going and complete my mission," Micaiah concluded.

"Or it might actually be impossible. At this time. It's up to you whether you want to pursue this or not."

Micaiah looked conflicted, and Akłaq didn't blame him. Sabelu had done the same thing to her with his marriage prophecy. Was she truly destined to marry Micaiah, or had it perhaps been a way to get her to break through her simmering hatred of white people? And did that break open her up to the possibility of actually loving and marrying him, regardless of any prophecy or universe-ending doom that may or may not actually happen because of her decision to marry him or not?

Prophets were the worst people to meet, and it couldn't be much fun being related to one and having to live with them.

"Give me what information you have," Micaiah said at last. "Let's talk about it. I'll see if I can come up with anything to even get started."

"Everything is circumstantial, I'm afraid," Netami said, "and my knowledge of Earth is virtually nonexistent. Everett has filled in some of the gaps, but our interaction in white society is forcibly limited."

Akłaq Banded, just so she could catch any minute reactions to the comment, but Micaiah remained impassive.

"Michigan is a good start," Everett began, standing and retrieving one of the Krydik Books. "It's easier than scouring the entire universe, but it's still a lot of ground to cover. We couldn't find any information on this photography company; they might not exist yet either."

"How does that work, then?" Micaiah interrupted. "How can something that doesn't yet exist...dictate or record the past and essentially build the world up to the point where that thing exists? I mean, what if the Axis had won the war and invaded North America? Or the Soviets, for that matter, what if they invade? Michigan might not exist anymore."

"Apparently it does," Netami said. "Sabelu says we think too linearly. We are inside the maze while the Author looks over it. She knows where it begins and where it ends and the path to get through, but we see only the next choice, the next puzzle ahead of us."

Micaiah waved a hand. "Fine. What else? What about this code? What does 'www' or '.com' mean?"

"That we don't know, but we agree that it is important," Everett said. "Our initial thoughts are that 'www' has something to do with the world wars. Yes, it's three w's instead of two, but it's all we can come up with. And '.com' most likely refers to communications. Communications in the war."

"I remember reading something about code talkers in the war," Akłaq cut in. "The Navajo were the most used, but there were others, weren't there?"

Everett nodded. "A few, yes."

"What native peoples are in Michigan?"

"Primarily Ojibwa, Odawa, and Bodawatami. They're part of the larger Anishinaabek nation."

Akłaq shifted in her seat. "What if she's a mixed-blood? That would be a place to start."

Netami looked at Everett. "The Krydik did take in some Anishinaabek back in the early days. If she had relatives—grandparents, most likely—who came and stayed for a little while, it would explain how she knows so much about Aktiya Waya and Krydik goings-on."

"Or, if this hasn't happened yet, those grandparents could be among the Krydik now," Everett mused, his expression contorted as he tried to make it work in his mind.

"If that's the case, then nothing we're doing here is going to make a difference."

"I'm sorry, but I thought this was supposed to be my mission?" Micaiah cut in. "How did it get turned over to you?"

"Because if she is a mixed-blood, and if this 'small town' is actually a reserve, then there's no way you're getting within ten miles of her," Akłaq told him, "not once word of this gets out."

Micaiah made a flippant gesture. "Oh, aye, well, that's great and all, and I'm happy to help you in your quest, but let's not forget that I have a Book, too. And somehow this lady left the reserve and went all the way to Ireland to spy on me and my brother."

After a brief silence, Everett said, "Mixed Anishinaabek and Irish.

Not any different from the mixed Cree and Scottish in Red River."

"That's great and all, but what if she isn't mixed Anishinaabek?" Akłaq wondered. "It's one thing to focus on the Krydik, but given the detailed history of how the Cherokee became the Krydik, what if she's Cherokee-Irish? Or, maybe not her, but a grandparent or great-grandparent?"

Netami nodded. "Lot of Cherokee fled the hills after the war, those who didn't stay in Aktiya Waya. It's not impossible."

"There were some who left Aktiya Waya after the Civil War, too," Everett added. "They couldn't return to their old lands, and fleeing north to Ohio was common; Michigan isn't too far away."

Micaiah was rubbing his face in some exasperation. "So, just as a thought, are we to believe, then, that every character, or every Book, is somehow tied to the Author's ancestry? Are we supposed to believe that she's got Welsh in her, too? Not a stretch, considering Ireland and Wales are fairly close to each other. But what about Akłaq? Is the Author an Eskimo? And what about anyone else she writes about? We don't know who the Hands of Time is about, what if it's someone completely different? The note in the back of one of the Books even says that there's another Book that starts twenty years before *Wolf Pack*. What if that Book, given the apparent proximity to the Time industry, is about an alien race? Is the Author part alien, too? Aye, America might be a melting pot, but it takes more than a few generations to achieve that level of fuckery."

They really couldn't deny that he had a point. It was Everett who said, "It really is the best theory we have to go on. You're right, we could be completely off-track in our assessment. If that's the case, then let's hear your ideas."

Micaiah sighed. "I don't have any. A small town in Michigan still leaves a lot of possibilities. Honestly, I've only got the vaguest inclination of where Michigan even is."

"It borders Ontario in the south and west, surrounded by the Great Lakes."

"Everett, maybe you can send word ahead to the Anishinaabek,"

Akłaq suggested. "You don't have to tell them about all of this, the Books and whatnot, but just see if there are any women by her name and appearance somewhere in their lands. Even vague details would be better than going blind, and it might save a lot of time just by elimination."

Everett nodded. "I can do that." He looked at Micaiah. "How long do you intend to remain in Vancouver?"

Micaiah gave him a cheeky look and jerked his head toward Akłaq. "Until she passes us and lets us leave. Two months ago I thought we were going to be movin' on quick. Now I don't know."

"Another month or so," Akłaq told Everett.

"Should be enough time to get word out and see what comes back," Everett mused. "And it's not as though you have to leave once she's passed you. Unless she chases you out forcefully, but I doubt it."

Micaiah chuckled nervously "Two months ago, I thought she was going to. Some days, I'm still not sure."

"Some days you make me want to," Akłaq muttered.

The four of them sat in silence for a long moment. Each appeared to have his own thoughts, but no one appeared to want to voice them. Akłaq was still trying to make sense of everything. It was Netami who spoke first.

"I might have an idea," she said, chuckling nervously. "Spirits help us, but what if she's some descendant of Sabelu? Or Galiliga or Blaknik or myself for that matter? Prophecy appears to be entrenched in our family; what if it's not a matter of her traveling to all of these places, but that she simply sees all of these things and writes them down?"

"She does have Sabelu's questionable humor and dry sarcasm," Micaiah muttered.

"That's great, but it doesn't explain how the Books are appearing before she even allegedly exists," Everett pointed out.

"An ancestor, then, not a descendant," Akłaq offered. "What do you know of your family before Kiyuga and Anagalisgi? Do you have any white ancestors?"

Netami shook her head. "No, not that we're aware of, not before my father's father. My grandfather's parents died shortly after Anagalisgi was born. Before that...they were all of the people."

"Are you sure?"

Now Netami grinned. "Akłaq, if there is anything that Sabelu likes to complain about, it's his gift of sight and how no one ever pays attention to it, or that they don't pay attention the way they should. He frequently draws parallels between how he is ignored and how Anagalisgi was ignored. Given his gift of sight, if there was someone else who had the same thing—or maybe even greater, all things considered—then he would be complaining about them, too, whether they were also ignored or not."

"This is all well and good," Micaiah interrupted, "but it's not actually helping us find her. If she already exists, then either she's laying pretty low, or if she is one of you—Earth, Aktiya Waya, wherever—then you're holding out on me because I'm white. If she doesn't exist yet, as Sabelu seemed to imply, then all this is for nothing, and it won't be for something for an undetermined length of time."

"Well, you're partially correct on one thing," Everett told him. "If the Books remained within the realm of the Krydik or other native peoples, then we would most likely conceal her from you, if we knew who she was. Seeing how the Books have now broken racial barriers, your interest is understandable. However, you have my word that we are as in the dark as you."

Micaiah did not respond to that except to say, "Well then, all of this is turning into pure speculation and getting us nowhere."

The four of them stood from the table.

"I will send word to the Anishinaabek," Everett stated. "If they have any leads, I'll let you know."

"And I'll see if I can't get Sabelu to give us a little more information, too," Netami said. "He wants to help; really, he does. He just gets frustrated when others don't seem to listen."

She looked at Akłaq when she said it, and Akłaq wondered if Netami was aware of the marriage prophecy, or at least the conversation surrounding it. Then Akłaq wondered if Sabelu really was the only one of that generation who had the gift of sight. Maybe it did not manifest as strongly with Netami, but she did not appear to be entirely ignorant of the situation.

They began moving, leaving the Archives and heading down the stairs.

"Maybe if he was a little more personable, he might get better results," Micaiah said, still annoyed. "You can attract more flies with honey than vinegar."

"Nothing he hasn't already heard, I'm afraid."

"Anything you can get out of him would be appreciated," Akłaq told her before Micaiah could speak, "but don't abuse yourself for our sake."

Netami laughed. "I won't, believe me." She shook her head. "No, I can handle him."

"I'm going to guess that he isn't married," Micaiah cut in.

She shook her head no.

"Why haven't you pursued this before now?" he went on. "If there was so much controversy over Yvgidahi's Book, why didn't you, in some way, shape, or form, go after the Author yourselves?"

"You've read the second Book," Netami said. "We had other things to worry about. Just trying to hold the people together still feels like a never-ending, impossible task, or so says Galiliga. When your immediate concerns revolve around resolving disputes between clans who aren't entirely ready to give up their former tribal affiliations, words on pages written by someone a whole world away mean little. They already don't listen much to Sabelu; why would they pay mind to the Books?"

"So why are you?"

"I believe in my brother, even when no one else does. I believe him when he says you won't find the Author yet, but I also believe that even this futile pursuit is necessary for later things."

Micaiah sighed and rolled his eyes. "Are you a prophet, too, now?"

Netami grinned. "Well, I'm not Sabelu. I would never wish to be him or have his gift of sight. But as I said, prophecy is entrenched in our family. Sometimes I just know things."

"How convenient."

"Consider me the padding that dulls the prick of Sabelu's thorns."

"Aye, he's a prick all right. What about your uncle? He seems to be the more personable one. Is he still around?"

She nodded. "He is, but his never-ending, impossible task is trying to guide Sabelu."

"Oh, Lord."

"This on top of his other duties to the spirits and the Author."

"And he doesn't have time to pop in and help us even a little bit? Give us a little guidance on this, whether it's worth it?"

"Do you ask God what to have for breakfast every morning? Do you ask for a wondrous miracle to confirm something someone has told you? Sabelu has already given us the answer to the question we've asked. All you're doing now is deciding whether to pursue more questions."

In that moment, Akłaq knew a bout of wild jealousy toward Netami. Not for her gift of sight or overall gentle demeanor, but for her almost perfect disposition toward Micaiah, and, from that, the safety and security that she enjoyed on Hlohi. She would return to Aktiya Waya to be among friends and family and her own people. Everything that surrounded them was theirs. Every triumph and failure was theirs to own or improve. They had no reason to fear others because they always had somewhere to retreat. She could afford to be friendly with Micaiah. In spite of any past wrongs or hurts, whatever traumas or evils, Netami could forgive and move on because she had a manner of inherent safety.

It wasn't Micaiah's fault, Akłaq reminded herself. Perhaps worse than being conquered and oppressed by foreigners and strangers was being captured and abused by familiars, those you were raised to believe pure and trustworthy.

At the same time, she did have the ability to retreat into her old land, her own people. There were still villages out there, those in the east and the islanders who remained basically the same as they had since the beginning of time. Maybe they weren't Iñupiatun, but they were still cousins, in the same way the Krydik were no longer wholly Cherokee. She could adapt, she was sure.

She hated being so uncertain. Oddly enough, she found herself wishing for her father. She could no longer remember his face or his voice, but she did remember feeling safe with him. He always knew what to do, even when things were uncertain or frightening. She might have wished for Putu, but she knew the lecture she would get from him.

The four of them reached the main floor and headed to the portal room. After some standard farewells and promises to keep in touch with any information, they departed. Everett and Netami went to Hlohi, and Akłaq and Micaiah returned to her apartment.

"That wasn't so bad," Micaiah slurred, drunkenly crawling from the floor onto the couch.

Akłaq just grunted from her place at the kitchen table.

It was a few minutes before the nausea passed and they could function almost normally again.

"So what do you think about all of this?" Micaiah asked, sitting up on the couch and turning to look at her.

"About what?" she wondered, still resting her head on her hand at the table, eyes closed.

"This mission to find the Author, Sabelu saying there won't be anything yet, all of it. What do you make of it, speaking as someone who doesn't have a Book or a jackass for a brother?"

"I don't have a Book yet. There's a difference." She shifted and sat up, opening her eyes. The nausea had mostly passed, leaving only a lingering ache behind her eyes. "As for my opinion, I think I'd like to find the Author and ask her just what she's playing at. As you said, how does she know all of this? But also, why write about it and put it out there for all the universe to see? What's the goal here? What is it about my life that people need to know about or learn from? Or your life, or the Krydik?"

"And Sabelu saying there won't be anything to find yet?"

Akłaq sighed. "I don't know. I don't understand how you could write a universe into existence if you don't exist yet. But if you do exist, then why wouldn't you be able to be found?"

Micaiah shifted in his spot on the couch. "Well, I suppose if I wrote a book, I could write about the past and build the world I wanted, and then insert myself at the end."

"Yes, but that's a regular book. This is real life. You and the Krydik have Books based on real life."

"But what if they weren't? What if they're only true, only 'real life' because the Author wrote them that way?"

Akłaq stared at him for a long moment. Finally, "That makes no sense. And even if it did, I think your Catholic priests would burn you for a heretic if you said that outside these walls."

Micaiah shrugged. "Just a thought. And to take it a step further, what if it's not even about us, then, but something greater? What if she's not writing about us for us, but for others in her own universe to help them understand something far greater than themselves?"

"Now you really are making it up as you go along. You think maybe the priests hit you one too many times?"

She regretted the words as soon as she said them, but Micaiah did not appear fazed. He just stood and stretched and yawned. Then, "Well, that's possible, too, I suppose. As for your previous comment, I've already said that we're not exactly good Catholics anyway."

She waved a hand. "So go to confession, you'll be fine."

He laughed. "Aye, no kidding." He paused and gave her a look. "Wait, so was it the Methodists who came to your people? I know they're popular around here."

"Russian Orthodox, actually, at least when I was a child. These days, well, it's whoever wants to venture out from Fairbanks or Anchorage."

He nodded. "And I'm guessing you haven't consulted the Russians lately to ask their thoughts."

"I have not."

"Guess we'll have to go it alone, then."

Akłaq stood and stretched. "Guess so."

They went to the door and she opened it. Micaiah turned and looked at her as if to say something, but the only thing that came out was a simple goodbye. Then he left, walking hurriedly and, if she was any judge, deliberately not looking back. Even after he disappeared, it was a long moment before she ducked back inside her apartment and closed the door.

She returned to the kitchen table, sat down, and picked up the letter from Gáx. If there was any good news, it was that she didn't have to worry about others reading it, for it was written in Tlingit. Latseen in poor health. The situation was not severe yet, but it would be a good idea to come visit in the near future, emphasis on near.

"Sabelu, I hope you're right," Akłaq sighed.

No one answered her, and she wasn't sure whether or not she was relieved. On the one hand, how often had she longed or prayed for answers, only to be frustrated when the spirits were silent? Now Sabelu appears, dispensing answers almost at the drop of a hat and still she was unhappy. True, he was a bit of an ass and had no "padding" as Netami put it, but he was willing to give answers to those who asked. Considering her fickleness about that alone, and considering she would not be the only one to feel this way—likely most or all of the Krydik did, too—was it any wonder he had the personality of a rabid wolf?

What, then, did that say about her fabled marriage to Micaiah? If all went well, she would pass him to Master in about six weeks. Should she bring up the prospect in that time? If he had gotten some kind of similar guidance, then it would be on him to initiate, wouldn't it? What if he hadn't gotten such guidance? How would he react to the thought? Before, she imagined he would be a little skeptical. Now, having met Sabelu and argued with him, the idea that he had predicted or commanded their marriage might not go over so well.

She had questions, but she wasn't sure she really wanted the answers. Having answers only seemed to make things harder. Maybe because those answers interrupted any plans already made.

But then, staring at the letter in her hand, staring at the words written by her elderly son concerning her elderly daughter, death had a way of interrupting plans, too, and she didn't know of anyone with any answers to that.

Six weeks to pass the twins. Could she convince them to accelerate their training, do three days a week instead of two? Could she cut it down to four weeks, maybe even three? With Micaiah getting extra training in the Akari, and their talent of combining abilities, they could progress just fine in their own time. And it wasn't as though they were in any hurry to leave; there was no real timetable, no deadlines they absolutely had to meet.

Except Akłaq knew that she would never forgive herself if she wasn't there when Latseen passed. And when she did, Akłaq wasn't going to leave her other children. Regardless of their apparent age or lack of blood relation, they were still her children; she wasn't going to abandon them now.

"Sabelu, I hope you're right," she repeated softly.

She folded the letter and placed it in a special rack on the wall but couldn't quite let it go for a long minute. Six weeks was far too long. Even four felt like she was pushing it, still prioritizing herself and her work over her children.

The easy choices were long behind her. It was time to start making harder ones.

Avgun Iñuiñaq Qulit Tallimat Malġuk
Connections

Within two weeks, Everett started getting letters and calls back from his contacts among the Anishinaabek and even the Cree. While there were a few blond, white-looking women among them, that was where the similarities between them and the Author ended. Names didn't match, none of them had ever been to Ireland, none of them knew who the Durvins were, none of them had any Time or Akari talents to speak of, none of them were especially talented or interested in writing in general, and none appeared to possess any special gift of prophecy or other communication with God or the spirits. If any of them were the Author, they were not about to give themselves up.

"And without knowing a maiden name, we can't trace her that way either," Everett said.

He and Micaiah were over at Akłaq's apartment to discuss the situation.

"What about the Cherokee, since that was suggested?" Micaiah inquired a bit grudgingly.

Everett shook his head. "Netami asked along that avenue, but to no avail."

Micaiah sighed and studied his hands folded up in front of his face. He lowered his hands to the table. "This makes no sense. How does someone who doesn't exist yet write about the past in the past? That would be like me writing a book about Irish history and publishing it two hundred years ago. I don't get it."

"I guess Sabelu was right," Akłaq stated. "There isn't anything to find yet."

"We may learn more as more Books appear," Everett said. "There are plenty of them promised; one of them has to have something."

"In the back of one of them," Micaiah interrupted, "the author's note, it said that she made a video game out of it. What's a video game?"

"I have no idea. I think video has something to do with movie theaters. Perhaps it's a game related to a movie?"

"Oh, I'll bet the Krydik love that idea," Akłaq said.

"I haven't brought up the idea to them," Everett laughed nervously. "I claim to be just as clueless about it as they are, the same as the 'www' and '.com' code. And we could be completely wrong about any of it."

"Something tells me they don't care one way or another," Micaiah stated.

Everett gave him a look as he shook his head. "They don't. There are other matters to attend to of greater importance than words written by someone who doesn't even exist yet and would be a galaxy away anyway."

"And I'm guessing they're not listening to Sabelu much either, right?" Akłaq guessed.

"You guess correct." Everett leaned back in his chair. "So, I guess that means that either you strike out on your own investigation, knowing that no one knows anything, or they're not telling, or else you just wait and see if anything changes in five, ten, twenty years."

"Everett, the copyrights on these books aren't even until after 2020," Micaiah said. "That's more than sixty, maybe even seventy years from now."

"Fine, wait seventy years. Or don't. It's up to you."

"So you're giving up the investigation?"

"I have as much information as you do. I've read the same Books you have. Right now, there is nothing to find. If you hunt elusive prey, patience is more productive than force. You'll never catch a rabbit by chasing it."

Micaiah huffed a sigh and leaned back himself. "I don't know if I can be patient for seventy years, though."

Everett stood. "Seems as though you don't have much of a choice. If you do need help, though, getting into contact with any of the people, let me know and I'll see what I can do. Otherwise, I wish you luck."

"Thank you, Everett," Akłaq said.

She saw him to the door, then turned to look at Micaiah still sitting at the kitchen table. "I'm guessing that you're not quite ready to give up."

"I can't make it make sense, at least, not in any way that wouldn't be branded, as you said, heresy. There's something missing. But it's frustrating to think that the missing piece might not actually exist for another sixty or seventy years."

"Maybe. Maybe not. If the Books are already being released to us, the people or subjects or main characters if you will, then we may learn more in that time. The notes in the back all appear to be unique. Maybe that's how she will communicate between now and whenever it is that she actually comes into existence."

He sighed. "Maybe."

She sat down across from him. "Do you still intend to go to Michigan and look for her?"

He made a lazy, helpless motion. "I don't know. It's been, what, a month or so since you even introduced me to all of this? I hate to give up on it already."

"The seed in rocky ground?"

"Something like that, I suppose."

"Maybe what you really need to do is get something to eat, get some rest, and leave it for another day. You never know; you might come up with something."

She intended her words to be encouraging, but the result was less than stellar.

"Have you ever just sat down and thought about how insane this all sounds?" Micaiah wondered. "Even without the Books and the Author and all that, it sounds utterly mad. I mean, we can bend Time. Add in the Akari and you're talking Matter and Energy, too, the basic mechanisms of the universe. You see in movies that witches and wizards wear robes and hats and have magic wands and make all sorts of motions and gestures with evil words. But it's not like that at all. We just...do things. With our will, with our minds, because we can. Aye, some of it is more complex, but on the whole, it's just...doing. And you wonder how you never saw it before."

Akłaq nodded. "It does sound like something out of a myth."

"Maybe the real reason I want to find the Author and get answers and make this all make sense, is because I don't want everything to be in vain."

"What do you mean?"

"I understand why a lot of Time Agents leave God. I won't say I haven't been there, wrestling with my own questions and doubts. Then you come along and show me this Book filled with information only God should know. And, to be honest, it almost gives me hope that there might be answers out there and they can be found."

She nodded. "If there is no God, then you—and Micah, which I think is the bigger point—suffered for nothing and there is no punishment for the priests who break an empty vow. But if there is a God, or Author, or something out there, especially one that you can find in a physical place and talk to, then you can either find out what the bigger, better plan is, or else have a physical person you can hate, rather than yelling at an empty sky."

"Aye, something like that. But then there's the terrifying thought of approaching someone or something who has the power to see into our lives and write them however they will."

"That didn't stop you from arguing with Sabelu."

He grinned but it was hollow. "He might know a lot, but he's still an ass. And I doubt he has the power to back up his words, at least in a god-like sense. At least I hope he doesn't."

"So do I," Akłaq agreed.

Micaiah sighed, rubbed his face, and stood. "Well, I don't think I'm going to be much for company right now. I won't darken your home any more."

She stood as well, hoping she didn't appear too hasty. "You think an empty apartment and the noise from the neighbors is good company?" She gave him a look and made a motion. "Come on. You look like you need some cheering up."

They left her apartment and headed outside. Summer was waning, but the heat still lingered over the city, only the ocean breeze keeping the worst of it at bay. People were out and about, going to movies and restaurants and other casual evening events.

"I bet it doesn't get this hot up north of the Arctic Circle," Micaiah began awkwardly, putting his hands in his pockets.

"No, but that doesn't mean we don't see summer," Akłaq said. "What about Ireland?"

"Oh, it can get hot, but the ocean gives a nice breeze, like it does here."

"Do you think you'll ever go back, once Europe shakes off the war a little more?"

"I'd like to. But it would have to be pretty soon, if we wanted to maintain any kind of relationship with our brother and sister. Otherwise, we'd go back, they'd be old and we wouldn't have aged a day."

Akłaq let out a breath and nodded. "I know how that goes." She paused for half a second, then said, "I received a letter from my son—one of my sons. Latseen, my oldest daughter, she isn't doing well." She laughed humorlessly. "My children are in their sixties, yet I look like I could be their granddaughter."

She did not look at him, just wiped her eyes as he said, "I'm sorry to hear that."

"I want to get you and Micah trained and passed quickly so I can be with her, all of them. I think that once she dies, I'm just going to stay there until they're all gone."

He nodded. "That's understandable. And it makes sense now why you decided to increase the training nights."

"You thought I had gone back to hating you?"

"It crossed my mind."

Akłaq shook her head. "If I hate anything, it's the timing of all of this. Your training, your...quest, my daughter..." She huffed a sigh. "If it comes down to it, I'm choosing Latseen. Let the officers scream, but I choose her."

She could feel his eyes on her. "If the officers throw a fit because of it, I'll back you up."

Now she looked at him. "Why? It's my problem, not yours. You didn't know about any of this. You just knew that—" She paused and put up a Sound shield so others couldn't hear. "—I murdered half a dozen men and I hated you for no real good reason." She dropped the shield.

"Maybe so, but I wouldn't leave a woman to defend her children alone. And it's only worse because there's nothing to really be done."

She let out a breath. "Thank you."

"You don't talk about your children much," Micaiah observed.

Akłaq shrugged. "It was great at first. They thought I had spirit powers and that allowed me to save them from the schools. And they were happy that I was using those powers to help other children and other peoples. But then I started missing out on things. Two of my sons got married and had children, and I wasn't there. Then they—all of my children started getting married and shrugging off the Akari so that they could live normal lives. They tried to talk me into doing the same thing. At first it was just talk, a discussion for another day, another time.

"Then the days started adding up and the next thing I know, my grandchildren look as young as I do. Even Tula'aan, my youngest, looks like she could be my mother. True, I'm not gone as much as I used to be, but I still use the Akari in everyday life. Finally, the elders and clan leaders get together and tell me that I have to make a choice. I have the years of experience, but nothing to show for it. I do not have the wrinkles of time in my skin, the folds that hold our memories, triumphs, loves, failures, and regrets. If I wanted to remain part of the village, then I would have to give up the Akari.

"I tried to explain that it would still be some time before age took hold of me again. There was no good way to frame it, no way to save face in light of the elders and the spirits, so I did the only thing I could."

"You left," Micaiah stated.

"I stayed in Anchorage for a time, just in case something changed. Then my middle son died, and I returned to Qikiqtaġruk."

"And your children?"

She heaved a sigh. "They resent that I appeared to choose the Akari over them. I tried to explain it to them, too. Latseen had just begun to slow her aging when she ceased her usage, but no matter what I said...it just didn't get through. Honestly, I'm just grateful they haven't cut me out completely, that Gáx is at least giving me notice."

It wasn't the most pleasant notice, true, but it was better than leaving her to wonder.

"Listen," Micaiah said. "I know the Time industry can be cold and a little brutal at times, but I'm sure Patrick would understand if you had to go home for a family emergency. Not too many Time Agents can claim family emergencies, so I can't imagine he wouldn't honor it. So Micah and I have to suspend our training a little while, so what? Or maybe we get reassigned. Your kids are more important than that."

She nodded slowly. "It means a lot to hear someone say that." Now she looked up at the sky, a few clouds floating about. "Putu is probably already there."

"Who's Putu?"

"Well, we used to travel together as father and daughter, and I do consider him to be my father, in a sense."

"Oh, he's the District Nine Captain, isn't he?"

"That's right. He chastised me the most when I left the Tlingit. We haven't spoken much since."

"I'm sorry to hear that."

She looked at him. "Did you ever think about kids?"

He shook his head. "Not really, not after the school. We'd joke about it, after we were adopted, but it was more because it was expected of us."

"Your adopted family never knew what happened?"

"Any time we even approached the subject, we were treated to a lecture about strict discipline creating righteous disciples. Micah and I may not have been good Catholics, but the rest of them were. Micah had bigger issues with it than I did, but we both agreed that having a family again was worth any words they had to say. Words meant very little in light of the actions of the priests. But we were both afraid that if we started making accusations, that we might be punished somehow, or our new family might be punished, and we didn't want to bring any harm to them."

Akłaq nodded. "I can understand that."

"At the same time, if no one speaks up or does anything, nothing changes."

She did not say anything to that, and they continued their walk.

"Where are we going, anyway?" he asked after a minute or two.

She stopped and looked around as if suddenly broken from a trance. "Uh...honestly, I don't know. I kind of just wanted to get out and walk around instead of being cooped up all night. City life really isn't for me."

"It's not so bad, if you have someone to share it with," Micaiah said. "Would you be interested in going to dinner somewhere?"

Even as he said it, she felt her stomach turn over.

"It has been a while since I've eaten," she admitted. "It would be nice to taste something other than peppermint and butterscotch candies. Where were you thinking?"

There was an inclusive restaurant about three blocks from their current location. This didn't mean that they didn't gather some stares or glares—a white man with a non-white woman—but they were not turned away. Drink orders were taken, and the two of them studied their menus.

"What's it like, living up north?" Micaiah asked, not looking up from his menu. "Does the sun really not shine for months out of the year?"

She nodded, also focusing more on her menu. "It's true. And for other months of the year, we can't get rid of it."

"So what do you think of living down here, then?"

"The first time I lived in a place where day and night always existed —granted, the shortest days were sometimes no more than an hour long —I didn't know what to do or even think. The long day and the long night were part of me, part of the earth, part of the stories of my people. Regular day and night was as distant and mythological as anything else." She made a kind of shrugging motion. "But it's also kind of nice, to know that the sun is going to come up every morning."

Micaiah made an incredulous sound. "I can't even imagine."

"Would you believe that there are people who live even farther north than us, beyond the mainland on islands that are covered in ice almost the entire year?"

He gave her a look. "Why would you do that yourselves? The world is so big and you pick the most dangerous and inhospitable places to live. To try to live, to hope to live." He shook his head and went back to his menu.

"But for them, it's just life. It's the way things are. Why are you here and not somewhere else? Why don't you move somewhere warm and tropical?"

"The thought has crossed my mind."

"Yet you also talk about returning to Ireland. Because it's home."

Micaiah sighed but did not refute.

The waitress returned and took their orders. Both went with seafood of some form. The waitress took their menus and promised that their food would be ready in a jiffy.

"So then you've eaten whale, right?" Micaiah asked once the waitress had gone.

"Of course. And seal and walrus and caribou and polar bear and everything up there. If there was food, you ate it. That far north, especially more than a century ago, to question or deny food was to potentially risk death. Every day in the summer was simply preparing for the winter. For every meal you ate during the long day, you had to prepare two for the long night."

Micaiah let out a breath and shook his head. "I couldn't do it. I really don't think I could. I'd go insane."

Akłaq nodded. "A lot of Russians did. Most of them were somewhat accustomed to the extremes, but when you add the distance and isolation, bad things happen. If they didn't kill themselves, they usually killed someone else."

"At least you can go back now," Micaiah said, his change in tone and posture suggesting he was trying to lighten the mood a little. "Once you wash your hands of Micah and me, I mean."

"I suppose." She looked at her hands. "Can I tell you something, without it ruining dinner?"

Now his tone was more dubious. "Ah...you can try."

"You or Micah once asked me why I didn't just go home. Maybe you think it had something to do with retaliation against me through my children or my people—and I won't deny that those are very valid reasons that I am constantly reminded of—but it's not the only reason." When he did not say anything, she continued, "A couple weeks before I even got word of your transfer, Sabelu visited me at home."

"I'll bet that was a lovely visit," Micaiah commented.

She chuckled humorlessly. "Wait until I tell you what he said. You'll be amazed I let him live later."

"This sounds interesting."

Now she shifted uncomfortably. "He told me—first he told me that the next decision I made would either save the universe or end it."

Micaiah leaned back in his seat. "Oh, well, nothing subtle about that, is there?"

"He also told me..." She gave him a look that she hoped was somewhat apologetic. "He told me that in order to save the universe, then I was going to have to marry the next man I met in Time."

For a long moment, Micaiah just stared at her, his expression saying he was waiting for her to continue. Then it dawned on him. He opened his mouth and took in a breath, but then he stayed that way for another long moment. Finally his eyebrows went up and he said, "You are referring to me."

Akłaq nodded guiltily. "He didn't give me a specific name or anything, just that he would be white and the next man I met in Time. Couple weeks later, I get told that I am being reassigned to Vancouver and am taking on a Journeyman. And you were the first one to approach and speak to me."

He stared at her as if searching for the punchline to a joke. The best he could come up with was, "And you believe him?"

She grinned and managed a nervous laugh. "I have no idea. None whatsoever. He said that it would be almost a century before the consequences of my action or inaction would make themselves known. He could be perfectly correct or else trying to get me to say or do something that I wouldn't do any other way. But I don't know what that is or could be."

Micaiah shifted uncomfortably. "I think if he wanted to get you to do anything, your children would be a greater motivation than me."

"That's what I thought, too. But then that either makes him a liar or entirely correct. And I don't like those options either."

He shifted again. "Personally, I'd rather he be a liar, because then he might be wrong about being able to find the Author."

She thought about this, then gave a casual shrug and a nod. "You have a point in that."

"On that other hand, pretending that he is correct, what does he expect us to do, run off and get married tonight? And what does it matter if we're married or not, why can't we just work together in Time or the Akari or whatever to save the universe?"

"I don't know. He was too busy being a smirking asshole, and I was too busy yelling at him."

"Well, that explains what you didn't want him to tell me the other day in the Archives."

Akłaq shifted and sighed. "I didn't know what was going to happen with your endeavor, and I'd just gotten the letter from Gáx about Latseen. I didn't need to think about anything else at that meeting."

"Understandable."

Micaiah shifted in his seat. "Do you know where Sabelu lives? I get Hlohi and Aktiya Waya and all, but specifically?"

"He's mentioned something about living alone in a cabin," Akłaq said. "But I don't know if he does or if he wishes he does."

"I hope he does, because it will make it a lot easier to find him and kick his ass without anyone else interfering."

She grinned. "Why are you doing this and can I come with you?"

"You ever worked on something? A machine, a car, your kitchen sink? Generally, if someone helps you, and you ask for a tool, you want that person to hand that tool to you, not launch it at you out of a cannon. He seems to prefer the cannon method. Yes, he'll get you the right tool, but he might also kill you."

Before either one could say more, the waitress appeared with their food. They accepted the plates and spent a couple minutes enjoying the taste of food. For Akłaq, it was the taste of not-peppermint-or-butterscotch candy. Once the initial, ravenous bites had been satisfied and they slowed down to a more appropriate speed of consumption, conversation resumed.

"So marriage has never really crossed your mind?" Akłaq wondered. "I'm guessing since the school?"

Micaiah hesitated. "In a way, I almost wanted to get married more because of the abuse of the priests, to spite their supposed celibacy. When we got into Time and Sean explained the non-aging—and the implications of that on marriage and family and so on—I know it almost gave Micah some relief, that he wasn't going to be pressured into it."

"And you?"

"I don't know, but I guess my thoughts kind of flip-flopped. Like I said, our adopted family was very Catholic, very observant, and suddenly the idea of not getting married and having a family felt like a way to spite the priests."

"Because of their hypocrisy."

"Yes."

"Is that why you want to beat up Sabelu, because you don't want to be married?" She went on before he could answer. "I'm not suggesting we run off and get married tonight. Believe me, I have no such inclination. But considering the potential weight behind all of this, and the fact that a marriage in Time or the Akari would last far longer than a regular one..." She paused. "I want to marry a man I love and who loves me, not because we've been commanded to by some pedantic asshole."

Micaiah nodded. "That makes sense. I don't disagree. Unfortunately, I really can't say that I love you. And I don't think you love me. Right now, I just appreciate the fact that you don't hate me and that we can have dinner together and a civil conversation. We couldn't say that a few months ago."

"I know."

"But," he added, "if there is anything I do admire you for, it's your dedication to your children, even if they are old, even if you were rejected from your people. You still care for them. And, honestly, I think you are going to have to get through that part of your life before you move on to anything else."

She nodded sadly. "I think you're right."

Even if she didn't like to admit it, he was correct. There was no way she could marry anyone, Micaiah or anyone else, while her children began to struggle for life. Like every other part of her life, one chapter had to end before another could begin.

"Have you heard any more from your son?" Micaiah asked.

Akłaq shook her head and swallowed her bite of food. "Nothing. I need to get up there."

"Listen, tomorrow, I'll call Patrick and tell him what's going on—" He continued talking over her attempted protest. "I will make him understand. Or I'll kick his ass, too."

"You can't just go around beating people up."

"One man is being a pedantic asshole, and the other is using a woman's own children as blackmail against her. Tell me which one doesn't deserve it. And if I recall correctly, Goldsmith was also a smarmy asshole, and Frederickson was kidnapping children. Look what you did to them. I think I'm being nice."

Akłaq huffed a sigh. "Fine. But I had nothing to do with it. You are beating them up of your own volition. Don't call me if you go to jail."

"Who am I supposed to call? There's only a fifty-fifty chance Micah will bail me out."

"Then maybe don't go around beating people up until you have some contingency plans."

"Where's your sense of adventure?"

She just shook her head and took another bite of food.

"I suppose at the end of the day," he said, sounding thoughtful but also uncertain, "I'm not averse to marriage, I just never expected to have it now that I'm in Time and I never expected it to have been somehow prophesied."

Akłaq nodded. "I get it. I never expected to marry again after becoming part of Time."

"Again? You were—well, of course, you have children."

"This is my second time having children, and by technicality, they're adopted. No, I was married. A long time ago, to a Russian defector. And, really, technically, we weren't married. His people would have killed him if they found him. But we lived like it. We had children together. Then the Russian military found out and tried to kill us. They killed him, our children, and they tried to kill me but Putu, Matulik, and Aniqan managed to save me."

"I'm sorry to hear that. I guess you have seen some stuff. How old were you when you got 'married'? If you don't mind my asking, that is."

She felt her cheeks burn hot. "Fifteen."

"Oh." Micaiah blinked. "I see."

"My village had just burned and it was the long night. I survived on my own for a short time and the first cabin I came to..." She shrugged and sighed, not looking at him. "Nika was good to me. He was a good husband and father. I would have stayed with him forever. But God, the Author, someone had a different plan."

"Nice to know that God agrees with the assessment that the Irish are better than the Soviets," Micaiah said. He immediately cleared his throat and muttered, "Sorry. That was bad taste."

But she just grinned. "It's all right. It does no good to dwell on things over a century gone."

"Maybe, but he still means something to you; I can see that clear as day."

"I think it's the idea of losing my children. Again. I think it's being upset at Sabelu and this whole marriage business. On the one hand, I can't stand the thought of losing anyone else. On the other hand, I don't know what a centuries-long marriage would even look like."

"Well, I hate to say it, but I'm not experienced in marriage at all, so you have the advantage."

She waved a hand, but before she could speak, the waitress arrived to take their plates and deliver the check. Micaiah paid the bill and they stood to leave.

"Do you think the other patrons think we're insane?" Akłaq wondered as they headed for the door.

"I think there's a possibility," Micaiah said, looking around. "It will just give them something to talk about, something more interesting than just politics and weather and the latest church gossip."

"You saw the looks we got when we first walked in, right?"

"I did." He opened the door to the street and they exited the restaurant. "And I ignored them just like you did. I might almost think you enjoyed the looks. The glares, I should say."

She shrugged. "They amuse me."

The two of them stood on the street corner. Vehicle traffic was no less busy than it had been an hour ago, and sidewalk traffic had increased.

"Can I walk you home?" Micaiah asked.

Akłaq nodded. "I'd like that."

On the street, their conversation turned toward more common things. Weather, work, the latest political gossip, and local goings-on. Summer was waning into fall, work was full of drama and harassment, provinces were beginning to codify equality, and television had finally reached the west coast, the first channels broadcasting from Seattle.

"Do you suppose," Akłaq wondered as they entered her apartment building, "that some of these inventions are derived from the Wheel, and some human Time Agent is just taking credit for them?"

"It wouldn't surprise me," Micaiah answered, following her up to her floor. "I admit, I've thought about doing that a time or two. Nothing huge, not like television, but something small, something convenient, just to make a little money, maybe get my name in a history book, even as a footnote."

"You like to tinker, do you?"

"I do. I'd like to learn a little more about cars and such, maybe work as a mechanic in the future. Motorbikes are interesting, too, though I haven't actually ridden one yet."

"You mean motorcycles?"

He waved a hand dismissively. "Same thing. And what about you? You're not going to be a housekeeper forever."

Akłaq made a sort of scoffing sound. "I hope not." They reached her floor and started down the hall. "I don't know what I'd do. Typically, to stay among the people, at least at my apparent age, it's only proper to have a family. Otherwise, it's just existing."

"I'm sure you've got a lot to teach, though, things others have forgotten in the last hundred years?"

She fished for her keys and unlocked her door. "Yes, but that's where I started running into trouble with the Tlingit. I just don't look the part."

She opened the door and he followed her inside. His expression was puzzled. "I admit, I haven't spent a ton of time among any native peoples, but it seems to me that 'looking the part' is the least of the concerns."

Akłaq faltered and fished for words. "It's not about the color of your skin or hair. In my case, it's my relation to time. I have the years, I have the experience, but I don't look like an elder. It's...a defect. At best, I'm an odd novelty, regardless of how familiar someone is with Time or the Akari. At worst, I'm an evil sorceress."

"Maybe the Tlingit are a special case because of your children, but how does that stop you from teaching your traditions to your own people?"

"I could. And I have, to the best of my abilities. But there is also a kind of lack of desire to learn. In such a harsh climate, we have to be able to adapt and we have to take the strongest route to survival. Electricity, oil, kerosene, these provide means of survival. Cars, planes, ships, these bring supplies as a means of survival. Everything else has been rendered as little more than arts and crafts."

Micaiah nodded slowly. "I suppose I can relate a bit. Once upon a time there was a great difference between the Irish and the English. These days, that gap has shrunk. I know my ancestors probably wouldn't recognize me." He hesitated, then put his hands on her shoulders. "But that doesn't mean you give up. I see how you've decorated your apartment with your 'arts and crafts' as you say. And I'll bet that yours is the only apartment in this building, maybe this entire city, that has them."

She grinned and nodded shyly. "I would say so, yes. But then that leaves the problem of your apartment."

He raised a brow. "What's wrong with it?"

"There isn't anything uniquely Irish in it."

"Micah and I are uniquely Irish."

"And I am uniquely Iñupiatun, but I still decorate."

"Have we ever come across as decorators to you?"

Now she laughed. "No, I guess not."

"Well then, you might have to help us with it."

"I don't know enough about Ireland to tell you how to decorate."

He gave her a look. "Well, we'll just have to fix that, won't we?"

She matched his look and put her arms around him. "I guess we will. And I think there might be something uniquely Irish that you can put in me right now to start this cultural exchange."

He kissed her once. "Exchange? So what do I get out of this? I know what I'm giving; what are you giving?"

"Do you want to find out?"

He did, following her to the bedroom with no hesitation. Even afterwards, he did not rush to leave as if compelled by guilt or selfishness, but was happy to lie beside her.

"So you seemed surprised when I said I was married and having children at fifteen," Akłaq said, "but you are neither especially old nor are you a virgin. How old were you?"

Micaiah blushed. "Fourteen. I was finally starting to make a name for myself as a prize fighter. I won a match, went to a pub to celebrate, hooked up with a girl who had been watching me."

"Did the girls fight, too?"

"Oh, heavens, no. They'd come to watch their brothers or husbands, maybe try to use their eyes or other parts to fix a match. This particular girl, her brother was the one I'd just knocked out."

"And she still let you in?" Akłaq questioned.

Micaiah shrugged. "The man was a jerk, been beatin' her for months because she couldn't fix a match in his favor. She'd been betting that I could knock him out. And I delivered."

She smiled and kissed him. "Yes, you did." She sat up and put her leg over him again, though nothing came of it.

"Does this mean you're going to pass us to Master, then?" he asked, rubbing her body, his eyes not on hers.

She sighed dramatically. "Yes, yes. I was going to anyway." She put her hands over his as he groped her. "But maybe I'll just pass Micah, get him out of the area, and keep you here for more training."

"Is that what we're calling this?" He still didn't look at her.

"Well we can't call it sin if there's no guilt."

Now he looked up. "I think we can, actually."

"Do you regret it?"

"I didn't before you asked."

She sighed, grabbed his hips, and pressed hard against him. "Oh, please, what's the difference? I've known men, you've known women. We've already established that neither of us is especially religious.

And even so, when it comes to survival, my people have always been more open about it."

"Aye, but mine really haven't."

He removed her hands from his hips, then gently pushed her off him.

As he sat up and reached for his clothes, she asked, "Oh really? They haven't? You know how your ancestors were, when you just claimed that they probably wouldn't recognize you? Or is this the Catholic priests talking? You didn't seem to have a problem with it when you were fourteen, trying to do the opposite of everything they ever taught you."

"Shall I go out and murder someone, then? Because they say not to, and because if I don't feel guilty about it then it's not sin?"

She sat up in bed. "Earlier you were talking about beating people up."

"There's a difference between killing someone in cold blood, and coming to someone's defense—your defense, so you can be with your children." He shook his head. "And this marriage thing you told me about, from Sabelu...I admit, it's kind of getting to me. I don't know what to think about that, how it all plays in."

Akłaq sighed and rubbed her face. "I knew I shouldn't have brought that up."

"I think it's a good thing you did. I think it gives us a lot to think about. Even this here gives us a lot to think about."

She gave him an annoyed look. "How so?"

He spoke as he dressed. "You're right, I'm not a good Catholic. Obviously. And you know that my birth mum was a whore. But I still believe in sacred vows. Marriage is a sacred vow. You just admitted that it means less to you. So, pretending that Sabelu is correct and we should get married, either I have to deal with the fact that my wife could be whoring herself out with no guilt because it's just the way of her people, or else you have to deal with the idea of restraint and basically belonging only to me—and I to you. Because both ideas cannot exist together, and something would have to give eventually."

"And if Sabelu isn't correct?"

Micaiah paused for half a second before shaking his head. "Even if he isn't correct, the idea is already there. I know I was talking about kicking his ass before, but now I think I want to thank him."

Again he paused, then he approached. He bent as if to kiss her, but she looked away. He left without another word.

Avgun Iñuiñaq Qulit Tallimat Piñasrut
Master Pass

The following evening, Patrick paid Akłaq a visit at her apartment. She sat sullenly at her kitchen table while he sat across from her and tried to maintain a professional posture.

"What did he tell you?" Akłaq asked before he could speak. She did not look at him.

After a moment of hesitation, Patrick replied, "He told me about your children, that you had received a letter saying your daughter was in poor health. He also told me that you had plans of simply staying with them once...things started happening. And this was the reason why you bumped up their training."

"Did he tell you anything else?"

"Is there anything else I should know?"

Akłaq hadn't really decided how she would react if Micaiah had told Patrick that they'd slept together. On the one hand, it was inappropriate for teacher and student to sleep together, assuming there was no existing relationship. On the other hand, she kind of hated him for not telling. It was the honorable thing to do, and she almost couldn't stand the thought that he'd suddenly decided to be all noble about it.

Finally she answered, "No. That's basically what it all comes down to."

Patrick shifted in his seat. "Akłaq, I know that we've been pretty hard on you. I won't say that it's not warranted. But we're not heartless. You have something most human Time Agents could only dream of —"

"The opportunity to watch my children die and then bury them?"

She glared at him.

"The opportunity to have children and have them be aware of our lives," he said gently. "And we can only imagine your pain. I'm sorry if you thought me or any of the officers unapproachable, but know that we do have compassion. If you need to leave to see your children, then by all means. And I can understand wanting to be with all of them as they pass. I will assign Micah and Micaiah to other Masters—"

Akłaq shook her head. "Don't. They're ready."

"Are you sure?" Patrick looked skeptical.

"I'm sure. I've known that I would pass them for a while, even before the letter came. It was just a matter of formalities. I'm going to take them out this weekend for the final test, then officially pass them."

He nodded. "Have you told them?"

"I will tomorrow night."

He still looked a bit uncertain, but agreed. "All right. Once they're passed, you are free to return to your children for whatever arrangements you need to make. Don't worry about any of this Time business."

Akłaq barked a laugh and gave him a look. "I never have."

He did not say anything to that, just left quietly. Akłaq did not move.

After Micaiah left the previous evening, she'd lain in bed for a long time, confused and wondering what to do next. It wasn't the first time she'd been accused of being a harlot, just the first time it really got to her. Maybe because it had come from the man she was supposed to marry—according to Sabelu—and yet she still couldn't say that she loved him, not like she had Nika.

But then, why should she love them the same way? They weren't the same men, or even from the same people. Would she have reacted this way if Nika had accused her of such a thing? The Russian priests had always preached chastity and faithfulness, yet the soldiers had been well-known for taking advantage of the more open sexual practices of her people. Nika had never really said one way or the other, maybe because they had been so isolated that it hardly mattered.

Micaiah, however, had taken a stand. He'd set a standard. Whatever they wanted to do with themselves while they were single, that was their own business. If they did end up marrying, however, that was it. Either he was going to have a whore of a wife, or else she was going to restrain herself.

One part of her said to let him deal with her openness. She wasn't out on street corners at night, but if she happened to see a man she liked the looks of, then why not? White culture had been pushed on her since the very beginning, why not force a little of her culture on him? It wasn't as though she was telling him that he couldn't go after a pretty girl every once in a while.

But then, what was the point of being married? For her people, marriage was about having children and having political voice. The only real reason for the open sexuality was so that a woman could have more children even if her husband was away. It was about survival. In good years, women stayed with their husbands and men stayed with their wives. In bad years, the rules were loosened a little.

There was no survival here. Akłaq was already facing the deaths of her children; she had no desire to have more right now or at all in the foreseeable future. There was no reason for her to see other men. On top of that, life was prosperous and plentiful; she didn't need to worry about having children constantly, trying to ensure the continuation of the people as a whole. Seeing how children with Micaiah would be mixed anyway, whose people would they be advancing?

Akłaq arrived at the twins' apartment the next night feeling the same way she had when she'd come over to apologize for lashing out at them. And like last time, she'd been the one in the wrong. That didn't mean that she was going to propose getting married before she left to go north, but she was again faced with the reality that maybe she wasn't the end-all of morality.

She knocked on the door. It was Micah who answered and let her in. Micaiah appeared a moment later from down the hall.

"Here to say goodbye before you leave?" the older twin wondered. His tone and expression were impossible to guess. He didn't hate her in any fashion; that much she could tell. But neither was he dumbstruck with something awkward resembling love or lust.

"Patrick was over yesterday," she said instead. "He told me about the conversation you had."

"I told you I would call him, and I did."

"While I appreciate the intervention, I'm not going to leave before I pass you two."

"You expect to train us tonight, too, then?" Micah asked.

"No," she replied. "I'm just here to warn you that your test is going to be Saturday. Eight a.m. sharp. Meet me in the park outside of town. If all goes well, you should both be passed by nine."

"Why so early?" Micah whined.

"So that I can spend the rest of the day packing and not worrying about it."

Micaiah gave Micah and look and shrugged in some kind of nonverbal assent. Micah sighed. "All right, I guess we'll see you in the park on Saturday."

It really wasn't anything that couldn't have been said over the phone, Akłaq thought as she left the apartment. She didn't know why she had decided to deliver the news in person, except that maybe she thought Micaiah was somehow upset with her and she was going to have to deliver another apology. She briefly wondered if Micah knew what had transpired. She also found herself wondering how he compared, if he'd known a woman yet or if he was still too self-conscious on account of the priests.

It was an interesting line of thought that saw her home, one that intermingled with her other musings about open or restrained sexuality, as well as Micaiah's newly-proclaimed standards.

She kind of wanted to talk to Anagalisgi, ask if the Author had any insight. Seeing how she was the one writing the Books that they were in, what did she proclaim to be right and wrong? Were the sins of her characters a reflection on the morality of the Author, or was it simply a product of free will? Akłaq didn't think she'd come across any explicit commands from the Author about morality. What were they supposed to do, then? What had the people done in the time between Adam and Eve and Noah? Answer, become evil.

Thoughts and questions for another day, Akłaq figured, getting ready for bed. Maybe it would be something to ask the Author if anyone ever found her in real life. Maybe Micaiah could ask her such questions, try to settle the matter before they got married, assuming they ever did. But then, what if the Author didn't exist until after they got married?

Stupid questions, she told herself. Foolish, childish, fatigue-driven questions. She should be focusing on the test and passing the twins to Master status so she could go be with her children. Her daughter needed her more than she needed to get bogged down in morality crises. Then she was going to stick around so she could be with all of her children. One last time.

One last time.

Thankfully, it was only a few days to Saturday, though that didn't mean she didn't feel like he was really pushing it in her need to get to her children. Something deep down said that Latseen was only trying to hang on long enough to see her mother again, but if her mother didn't come in time, well, she could only hang on so long.

The forecast called for rain, but as Akłaq walked through the park at quarter to eight, there wasn't a cloud in the sky. The air was tinged with cold, and she knew that they were heading for the cliff that would see them straight into autumn and winter. Back home, the sun wouldn't be out for more than a few hours as they raced toward the long night.

The only people in the park besides her were some early morning joggers and a pair of bicyclists. That was another reason she wanted to do this early, less risk to any bystanders. They really didn't need to hurt anyone who just happened to be out for a picnic.

She turned a corner where the path diverged. Up ahead, she spotted a couple more joggers heading the opposite direction, though their trajectory suggested they were heading for a bench or the water fountain next to it. As they neared, she saw that the joggers were, in fact, the twins.

"Have you been awake longer than I have?" she asked, walking up to them where they stopped at the bench for water and rest.

"Probably," Micah answered as he sat down, looking more beat up than his brother.

"You do remember your test is today, right?"

"Of course, that's why we're here," Micaiah said, taking a drink of water but still not sitting.

"You do understand that it's going to be difficult, right?"

The elder twin just shrugged. "We're warming up." He took another drink.

"He's warming up," Micah said. "I'm just trying to keep up."

Micaiah finished his water and took a few steps back. "I did not force you to come. You could have stayed in bed."

"I'd never hear the end of it."

"Well, then, it's your own fault. Besides, it's good for you. I saw a few girls looking your way."

"Looking your way," Micah said, standing to get water.

"Don't sell yourself short, I'm sure at least one of them was looking at you."

"No, the girls were looking at you. The men they were with were looking at me because they knew I'd be the easier target."

"If you're both quite done?" Akłaq interrupted. "How about we get through this test, and then you can go back to arguing over who was looking at whom?"

"Sounds good to me," Micaiah said, still rather upbeat.

Micah just sighed and made a lazy motion of acquiescence.

"Is that what the frisbee is for?" Micaiah wondered, gesturing to the disc in Akłaq's hand.

"It is," she confirmed. "And maybe it is a good thing that you've been out jogging and 'warming up.' " She noted Micah's expression. "If it makes you feel better, Micaiah can go first."

"He can have it," Micah said, lazily waving a hand.

"Aye, let's do it," Micaiah said, bouncing on his toes. "What are we doing, what's the test?"

Akłaq gave him a look and glanced at Micah. "I'm only going to explain it once, so both of you listen carefully." She paused briefly. "The main thing that we've been working on has been Time Tendrils, but the test is going to encompass everything you should know by now. Unlike the training where I gave you some leeway to simply improve rather than be the best, there is a benchmark that must be met here. You'll have three chances to meet that standard."

"And if we don't?" Micah wondered.

"I doubt that will happen because you've met those standards already in training. But for your own knowledge, I will not be able to pass you. Normally you would have the option to continue training with me or go to someone else, but in this instance, you will not be able to stay with me if that happens."

"I don't remember this from our last Master," Micaiah said. "I feel like it would be something he would tell us about. Are these official requirements?"

"No, they're mine," Akłaq told him. "Because I didn't like having to train you in what I felt were basic things, and I don't want you going to your third Master as ignorant as you came to me."

"Was there anything we did right when we first came here?" Micah wondered, his tone annoyed.

"All right, what's the frisbee for?" Micaiah cut in.

"We're going to start with Bands and go from there," Akłaq said. "That part shouldn't take long. The frisbee is for the new stuff."

"Let's do it."

As expected, going through the basic Bands was not difficult. Fast Bands, Slow Bands, Double, Pinpoint, all of it acting as a kind of warm-up. Looking at his expression, however, Akłaq noted a kind of longing, or perhaps disappointment. He wanted to use the Akari. She didn't blame him. She almost wished he would. It was lighter, easier, more flexible. He'd been born with the talent, or exposed to it at an early age, and then it had been taken away from him, replaced with Time.

Had he told Micah about the Books yet? Had he even obliquely referenced the Akari, or the Akarin? Had he casually demonstrated the difference between the Bands he had done as a child and the ones they were using now? Or was Micah still in the dark? Was the younger twin going to have a harder time with the test, or was Micaiah at least trying to help him succeed? She couldn't imagine that Micaiah wouldn't help his younger brother—everything pointed to him being a good brother in that regard—but what was the disparity between the one with inborn power and the one who had only a pithy copy?

The first part of the test didn't take more than five minutes, and that only because of the Slow Banding. Micaiah did not appear affected in the least. On the bench, Micah appeared to have Banded himself so he could rest, and he looked refreshed and attentive.

"Do you want to do the first part, too, and get it over with?" Akłaq offered.

Micah shrugged. "Might as well. I didn't see anything that looked too difficult."

Had there been more people in the park, Akłaq could easily imagine them pointing and whispering. A squaw and two paddies, staring at each other in a park, babbling some nonsense and seemingly oblivious as to the proper usage of the flying disc in her hand. Maybe it was just her being self-conscious.

Micah stood, and she directed him through the first part of the test. The younger twin had no trouble, not even a minor slip-up. However, he also didn't have that same expression as if longing to do something different. He knew Time, he worked with Time, he used Time, with no inclination toward anything that might be lighter, easier, faster, or more flexible. Akłaq glanced at Micaiah only once while Micah was in a Slow Band, but the elder twin did not give any indication.

Then the test was done, another five minutes of them standing there basically just staring at each other, occasionally exchanging a few strange phrases that would mean nothing to anyone who was unable to discern the use of Time.

"That wasn't so bad, was it?" Micaiah asked.

"No, it wasn't," Micah confirmed. "Though I'm still skeptical about that overglorified pie tin in your hands."

Akłaq held up the disc. "Come on, it's all the rage these days. And you should be grateful that they're making them out of plastic now and not metal, or else this could hurt."

"Is this related to you hurling tennis balls at us in the apartment?"

"It could be."

Actually, it had been entirely spur of the moment as she walked by the toy shop the previous day. She'd never given a formal test before, and the only physical test she'd ever taken had been the awful Apprentice review in the Wheel. She'd just as soon assumed that all formal tests were like that, but when she'd been training her peoples, she'd had to improvise ways of teaching and testing. She didn't know what games the twins had played as boys, but when she walked by the toy store and saw the disc—and having seen plenty of them flying around the parks previously—she couldn't pass up the opportunity to integrate it into the lesson.

"Micaiah, are you still going first?" she asked, turning to the elder twin.

"Absolutely," he declared. "What's the game? You throw it to me, I throw it back? It can't be that easy."

"You are correct. It's not that easy at all. You see, I am at every disadvantage playing against you. I'm not so strong or so fast. But when I add in Time, I don't have to be."

She moved off the paved path into the grass. The clearing stretched a good hundred yards or so to the east and was about thirty yards wide with a duck pond in the southeast corner, a handful of trees dotting the area around it. There was another large maple in the northeast where the walking path curved along the fence line, making it so the area was more tapered than rectangular. At the far end was another entrance to the park with benches, shrubs, and another water fountain.

"Rules of the game," she began, stopping probably five yards from where Micah again sat on the bench, watching them. "The goal is to be the one holding the frisbee at the far end there, at the entrance." She pointed and Micaiah acknowledged the spot. "I throw the frisbee, we both try to catch it. Band, use Time Tendrils, whatever you have to do. As long as it is in the air or on the ground, it's fair game. Either of us catches the frisbee, the person with the frisbee stops, do not continue running, cease all Time activity, throw it again as hard or as soft as you want. Keep moving toward the goal. Band yourself, Band me, Band the disc, use Tendrils, weave a Web, whatever it takes to get it. The one holding the frisbee at the entrance, as I said, wins. You have to beat me to pass."

"So, I catch the frisbee...I stop running, stop Banding. You catch the frisbee...?"

"I stop running, and neither of us can use Time until the disc leaves my hand."

Micaiah nodded once and glanced back at Micah. "Looks like you're going to have the easier test if I get her all wore out."

"That's a lofty assumption," Micah shot back. "Because there she goes."

Halfway through the statement, Akłaq tossed the frisbee. As soon as the disc left her fingers, she was Banding. She started out by Banding herself and the frisbee in the same Band. Then she felt Micaiah pressing on her Band. Glancing at him, she saw that he was starting to realize the benefit of being able to have a stable base. The apartment did not allow for much movement, making it far more difficult to just throw Time Tendrils at her Band and hope they stuck, while simultaneously trying to have his Band keep up with hers. Already she was pulling away. Five yards. Ten.

The frisbee landed, skipping lightly over the grass once, twice, then settling. Akłaq reached for it, cutting off her Banding as she scooped it up. She did not stop long, did not try to get in any kind of perfect formation as she tossed it again. She was not the most coordinated, did not give the disc a perfectly smooth flight, but it was heading in the right direction anyway. Again, she Banded just as soon as the disc was in flight.

In the time it had taken for her to grab the frisbee—thereby ceasing all use of Time—and throw it, Micaiah had managed to get his act together and prepare a stable Band of his own. His mistake, however, was Banding himself and the frisbee separately. Akłaq used Tendrils to effectively grab the frisbee right out of the air. Micaiah went peeling away across the field while Akłaq stole the frisbee from his powerful Band and brought it into her own more casual Band. Then she did something a little mean, using a Time Web to not only lock him into his own Band, but prevent him from Banding anything outside. If she had really wanted to, she could have forced the issue and made the Web entirely impenetrable. For the purposes of the test, however, she did not make it so cruel. It would take a tremendous amount of effort on his part, but he could break out.

Of course, by the simple rules of the game, he did not have to expend the effort, and he did not. He simply waited for the frisbee to land and for her to scoop it up so she was forced to cease all Time activity. Then he simply started jogging back from wherever he'd ended up, waiting for her to throw the disc again.

Now the game started to intensify. The rules were better established, the players ready for the next trick. Akłaq threw the frisbee. Knowing Micaiah would reach for a Fast Band, she lashed out at the frisbee with a Slow Band. Unprepared for the tactic, his Time Tendrils failed. As soon as they came up short, Akłaq inverted the Band and brought it around herself, again forming a singular Band around herself and the disc.

She gained some decent ground, this time catching the frisbee in the air. However, when she threw the frisbee, she found herself unprepared for Micaiah to appear directly behind her. He Banded her and the frisbee simultaneously in different Bands. He put her in a Slow Band and the frisbee in a Fast Band. As he took off running— appearing to go much faster because of the Band—he also tried to weave Tendrils into a Web to keep her in place.

He was sloppy, however, and she broke free easily enough. She used a light Fast Band to get close to him, acutely aware that they were just one or two good tosses away from landing at the goal.

She reached for her previous trick, Slow Banding the disc and Fast Banding him. This time, however, he was prepared. Not only that, but he was able to use Tendrils to first drag her into his Band, then bring the frisbee in as well. Once they were all on the same plane, he took the Tendrils, wove them into a Web, and used it as a barricade between him and her. The Band around her began to dissipate and might have thrown her to the ground if she had been any less experienced.

She took control of the Band and used Time Tendrils of her own to bring her back into sync with his Band, though she did not attempt to combine them. From there she strengthened the Fast Band and outpaced him, beating him to the frisbee.

One more good throw, she thought, pausing for half a second before throwing. Micaiah, though he was not Banding, was still running ahead of her to the goal.

She threw the frisbee.

She'd fully expected him to reach for a Fast Band, so she went for a Slow Band. Instead, she found him going for a Slow Band, too. Their like-Bands met. As soon as they did, he speared hers with a Time Tendril, dragging them together and bringing the whole thing under his control. From there he inverted the Band, turning it into a Fast Band and bringing the frisbee right to him.

Akłaq told herself that she let him have it. He'd clearly demonstrated good use of his abilities, and that was what this was really about. This was a test of skill, not a game played for a prize. If she'd wanted to, she could have Banded and saved herself, inserted herself between his hand and the frisbee, and taken victory from him at the last possible moment. At least, this was what she told herself. Somewhere in the back of her mind, she was thinking more that she was going to have to do this all over again with Micah, and unless she wanted to hand him an easy victory because she was too tired, she should probably let Micaiah have his victory.

"Good game," she told Micaiah.

"Good test," he replied as they started back across the park clearing. "I'll take that over the Wheel any day."

"I'll take just about anything over the Wheel."

"Is that what you do for all Journeymen? Or, well, anyone else you've trained?"

She shrugged. "I change it up, depending on who it is, how many people I have. This is the first time I've tried this."

"Well, it only became popular in the last year or so," he pointed out. "So I understand."

She glanced at him. "What will you do, when you leave? Where will you go next?"

"We'll make our way south, maybe to California. I've wanted to see the Golden Gate Bridge since I heard it opened."

"You know it's not really gold, right?"

"I know, but I still want to see it. I hear San Francisco is beautiful."

Akłaq nodded. "Most of the world is. It's people who make it ugly."

"I don't know," Micaiah said. "I've met a few beautiful people."

"Do you think you'll ever be back this way, or are you going to hang around Michigan, waiting for the Author?"

"I haven't decided, about waiting for the Author, that is. As for coming back this way, I'd need to have a reason." She could feel him turn his eyes on her. "Do I have a reason?"

"I don't know, do you?"

He shrugged. "Well, I did meet a pretty girl while here, but I'm not sure she likes me. And even if she did, I don't know that she really likes me enough to want to really stay faithful to me."

She sighed. "Still on that?"

"If you can't keep a promise to your husband, why should anyone else expect any better treatment? And if I can't trust you with the foundation of my family, why shouldn't I keep looking for someone who I can trust? You're right that I'm not a good Catholic, and you're not a good Orthodox, but, as the Bible says, do not even tax collectors do the same?"

"I know."

"But first, your children need you. Once that's all wrapped up—whether it's one year or ten—then you can call on me when you're ready to make your decision."

She nodded. "All right. Fair enough."

"And it's not as though we'll never see each other between now and then. Author or not, I'm still going to be looking into this Akari business."

"Good to hear."

"I expect we'll run into each other."

"When you two are quite done flirting," Micah said loudly from the bench as they approached, "I was promised the ability to go back to bed."

"You can go to bed any time you want," Micaiah told him flippantly, tossing the frisbee his way. "Right now you got to outwit her."

"Do I need to explain the rules again or you think you understand?" Akłaq asked as the brothers traded spots.

"I figured it out just watching," Micah said. He nodded to a couple of men down the trail. "Although some of the other spectators might be wondering if there's something in the water."

"Let them wonder and let's get this over with." Akłaq jogged out into the clearing. "You've got the disc!"

Micah had apparently learned more than just the rules from watching them. He didn't just change up his Bands, but he changed up his play style, too. Akłaq, expecting him to whip it out far, as Micaiah had, found herself at a sore disadvantage when Micah only gently tossed the disc, not more than five yards at a time. He would Band himself, the disc, and her, use a Time Web to keep them separate, catch the disc, stop everything, and repeat. This method saw him using his physical advantage more than Time to gain a tactical advantage.

Once Akłaq saw what he was doing, she was far less kind about her counterattacks. She never made anything entirely impermeable, but she did make him work for it a little more. He was still a little dependent on routine and rote memorization, as he had a hard time getting the disc back from her once she changed things up, but he never seemed to lose control of the situation.

When they were within the last one or two throws to the goal, Akłaq decided to change it up one more time. She had the disc and was judging her throw. Micah was coming up quick, a Band at the ready although not in use so that he might be ready for anything. She threw the disc, Banded it, but did not move herself, not immediately.

Micah threw everything he had into Bands and Tendrils of his own, wildly overreaching and throwing himself off-balance. He even physically tripped over himself as he went from grass to asphalt. He could grab the frisbee or save his balance, but he couldn't do both. He chose the frisbee, hit the ground, rolled, and got into a sort of half-kneeling position, much to the astonishment and annoyance of a few onlookers just outside the park entrance.

Akłaq laughed and headed over to him. Micah self-consciously stood, dusted himself off, and handed her the frisbee.

"By all rights, I won," he began awkwardly.

"You did," she confirmed. "You got the frisbee at the goal. You won. You passed."

He let out a breath and relaxed.

"It didn't have to be graceful or coordinated," she told him, starting back across the clearing yet again. "That will come with time and practice."

"But are Time Webs really used?" he wondered. "They just feel so...cumbersome. Like if you're actually in a fight, I think more creative Banding, and maybe some regular Tendrils, would be more effective than a Web."

"What you practice, and the abilities you use, are the ones you will become proficient in. It sounds obvious, but think about it. There are a number of weapons out there. Guns, knives, bows, swords, things we probably can't even imagine. Our physical capabilities, our skill set, and even our mindset, will guide us to the one we need, the one we are good at. I'm not especially handy with a bow, but I know how to use guns. Maybe you're the opposite. Either one has advantages and disadvantages, but how we train, what we use, and what we're good at is what makes the difference. Same with Time. Maybe you're better at using clever Bands and Tendrils, but Micaiah is better with Webs and brute force. Each one is useful in its own right for the right situation."

"I suppose."

Micaiah met them halfway across the field.

"How'd it go?" he asked, looking as though he hadn't broken a sweat all morning.

"Your lack of faith in me is terrible," Micah told him.

"He passed," Akłaq said.

"Of course he did," Micaiah declared. "The question is, can you pass your own test?"

She barely got half a syllable out of her mouth before Micaiah snatched the disc out of her hands and tossed it across the field. Immediately, Bands were everywhere. Around her, around the twins, around the frisbee, everyone trying to outdo the other, though the twins were clearly teaming up against her. There did not appear to be any real goal other than to best her.

Akłaq let this go on for a few minutes, then finally decided to end the game. She put everything she had into her Bands, Tendrils, and Webs, making them impenetrable by the twins. Once she got the frisbee back, she broke through all the Bands and used Tendrils to tie everyone to Base Time.

"All right, you two, don't push your luck," she said, breathing hard but still grinning. "I seem to recall one of you whining about wanting to go back to bed."

Micah just shrugged.

She tossed the frisbee to Micaiah. "You can keep playing as much as you want. As far as I'm concerned, you passed. You can go on to your third Master."

"Oh, if you insist," Micaiah said. "But what if all this didn't count?"

"Why wouldn't it? Of course it will."

"I don't know. I mean, this right here was pretty fun, a better practical use of our abilities than just sitting in the apartment. We start talking about it, other Journeymen might want to train under you, which you certainly don't like the sounds of. If we don't tell anyone, then this might not count."

"Oh, for feck's sake, a Chai," Micah said, rolling his eyes. "Just tell her you like her."

Micaiah blushed, and Akłaq felt her face and ears burn hot.

"Even if I did, I don't think they'd let me on the reserve," Micaiah said.

A dozen different indignant replies sprang to Akłaq's mind in a flash of annoyance before she considered that maybe he was trying—and failing—to be nice and make some oblique comment about respecting boundaries and privacy. In the end, she settled for a simple, "No, they probably wouldn't."

Micaiah looked at his brother then and shrugged. Micah rolled his eyes again.

"Well, I'll probably stop by your apartment one last time before I go, just to say goodbye," she told them. "Right now I have to give my final report to Patrick."

"Oh, come on," Micaiah said. "You can't stay for one more game? We'll play fair this time, I promise."

She gave him a look. "I won't." She shook her head. "No, you keep playing if you want, or do whatever. I'll see you later."

With that, she left the park.

The air was warm when the wind was still, but as soon as a breeze picked up, she found herself wishing she'd brought a jacket. She'd been so focused on the exertion that the frisbee was going to cause that she forgot to consider the cool down afterwards. Oh well, what was a little chill? She was a veteran of the long night, a little autumn breeze wasn't going to kill her.

Unlike his less fortunate charges, Patrick lived in the suburbs, in a quaint little neighborhood northeast of the city. It was the poster child for the progress of modern Canada with trees lining the street, white picket fences surrounding every lawn, a car in every garage, children playing without fear of harm, the knife sharpener walking down one side of the street while the milkman walked down the other.

Akłaq was most assuredly not welcome here, as evidenced by the way children stopped playing or even ran away when she got within four houses, their mothers glaring as she herded her children inside. One man grabbed a phone and stood there in the doorway, phone in one hand, cord in the other, maybe talking to the cops to report a disturbance while his wife and children cowered behind him.

Your violence is no more righteous than mine, Akłaq thought, feeling old wells of hate bubble up inside of her. *Your hatred of me is no more justified than my hatred of you. Prisoner and guard, except I've done nothing wrong.*

She forced these thoughts to the back of her mind. She was literally here to make a final report before leaving the area entirely. She was going to see her children and be with them in their last days. Would these women even be able to comprehend that kind of pain?

Patrick lived alone, although that wasn't for lack of women who wanted to meet him and be part of his life. Had he been a normal man with a normal lifespan, he would probably be just another in the line of clones that populated the neighborhood. If there was any good news on Akłaq's part, it was that he was already awake and still home, so she didn't have to go looking around like a common burglar.

He opened the door after her second round of knocking.

"This is a surprise," he stated.

"Good morning to you, too," Akłaq said. "I'm just here to report that the twins passed their test. They're free to move on to their third Master whenever they want."

"Ah. I see. Good to know." He blinked and shifted his stance. "Was there anything else you needed?"

"No, but now that they're passed, I'm going to be leaving just as soon as possible to go see my children."

That seemed to bring him out of his stunned stupor, and he nodded vigorously. "Yes. Yes, of course. Absolutely. By all means, take all the time you need."

"Thank you."

With that, she turned and left, having never entered his house. This didn't mean that there wouldn't still be some gossip around the neighborhood, but it would be easier for him to say something about her being a housekeeper or some such thing. There were any number of ways she could have ruined his perfect reputation in this pretty little neighborhood, but as far as she was concerned, it would be like smearing mud on a corpse.

She left the graveyard of clones and headed back to her apartment. She needed to get out of here, out of her apartment, this city, away from these people. She needed to go back home and be with her children. She found herself irrationally wishing that her children would never die so she would never have to leave. Then she again picked up the letter Gáx had sent her, and she knew it would never happen. The best that she could do, then, was be there when they finally left her.

She looked around the apartment. She hadn't accumulated much stuff, so it wouldn't be difficult to pack. Maybe the real reason for her procrastination was a foolish hope that if she didn't do it, then she could put it off forever and nothing would happen.

Nika had thought the same thing once, and look where he was.

Avgun Iñuiñaq Qulit Quliŋŋuġutaiḷaq
The Long Goodbye

It hadn't taken but four hours to pack up her things and tidy the apartment. Even when she got her things packed up, she had to go back and reconsider some of the things she was taking. Modern housing and amenities were making its way into the reserves—Qikiqtaġruk was proof of that—and yet she didn't want to decorate like a white person. In Vancouver she might have been accused of bringing too much savagery into her apartment, but among the Tlingit, she might be accused of the opposite, bringing too much white. They already mistrusted her for other reasons; she didn't need to add any more.

At the same time, it wasn't as though the Tlingit were sheltered. They knew her, they knew about Time and the Akari, and as a people, they were quite bold in their desire for political power. They worked with Earth-side politicians and Time Agents. Why should they throw a fit over a bit of home decor?

Akłaq lay on the couch for a lot longer than she should have, contemplating such minor crises. It was Sunday morning. Thanks to Patrick and his good standing in Time and knowledge of the Wheel, he was able to procure a train ticket to the Yukon for her, slated for that evening. From there she would have to make her own way to the reserve, which didn't bother her.

She closed her eyes again, intending to just do a little more thinking, but she instead found herself in a forest. A river flowed nearby, bright and sparkling in the sunlight. She put her hand up to shield her eyes. A moment later, the great white grizzly came lumbering up the bank. Its fur was wet, claws and muzzle stained with blood as though it had just been out fishing.

"You're a relief," Akłaq said. "I hope Sabelu isn't nearby."

"He is not," the bear confirmed, and she imagined that there was some relief in its voice, too.

"Why are you here, then? Please, I can't take on any missions or responsibilities right now. You can't be ignorant of my children or what I'm doing."

"We are not." It was Anagalisgi who spoke, climbing up the bank and moving to stand beside the bear. He was wet up to the knees and smelled like fish. He went on, "We're not here to burden you further. In fact, we're here to tell you that it's all right."

"Latseen is well, then?" Akłaq wondered.

Anagalisgi frowned and sighed. "No. Such things have not changed, and they will not. But your fear that you are walking away from something important is unfounded. For the moment, all is well, and you've reached the end."

"The end? The end of what? Is this what Sabelu was talking about? Should I have pushed for marriage instead of just sleeping with Micaiah?"

The bear made a noise and put its paw over its face. "Honestly, he couldn't have made it any more clear." It snorted and lowered its paw. "Go to your cubs and be with them. All is well for now. You're at the end."

"The end..." She blinked. "You're talking about my Book."

Anagalisgi just nodded once.

"Why didn't you just say so?" Akłaq asked.

The bear snorted again and shook its massive head.

"But if this is the end...? What was this Book even about? What did I accomplish? What about everything Sabelu said, about the marriage and the universe and everything else?"

Anagalisgi shifted his stance, his expression thoughtful. "Everyone thinks of greatness as the things we do or wish to do that change the world. What is it that will be memorialized throughout time and history? What is it that will make our names known to people around the world or across the universe? But sometimes, our greatest achievements are actually made in the quiet moments that no one knows about, the times we have cried, the times we have doubted, the times we have cursed others or even ourselves, and the time we have simply spent with other people and being part of their lives. These are the times when we choose to carry on, to press forward, and it is then that we are able to do these things that others call greatness."

"If you haven't questioned God, you're not ready to serve Him," Akłaq recited.

"Exactly."

"But I'm not a good person. I'm not even sure I would call myself Orthodox, never mind a good one. And I've been a terrible mother, to all of my children. Even now, I've gambled with my daughter's life because of work."

"Are you going after her now?" Anagalisgi wondered. She nodded. "Then not all is lost. Jonah was late to Ninevah, but he still got there, and things still turned out well."

"And people remember who he was because of that," Akłaq said. "Otherwise, we might not know, just like we don't know about all the other thousands and millions of people who have had a change of heart."

"Do those thousands and millions of people matter to your children?"

Her breath caught in her throat, and for a long moment, she couldn't speak. Finally she found herself and said, "No."

"You will do great things," Anagalisgi told her. "One day."

"But if it's so far in the future, a century if Sabelu is right, why is there so much pain now? Plenty of people have learned and accomplished more in a shorter amount of time. Why couldn't I have a life with Nika? Why couldn't I stay with my children and the Tlingit? Micaiah admitted that he hadn't really considered marriage now that he's in Time, so it's not as though I had to compete against another woman." She paused. "Or would I have?"

"Speculation does no one any good; it produces only doubt. Know only that this is how things must be."

"Maybe," the bear said, "instead of wondering why the Author is taking these things away from you, be grateful that she gave them to you in the first place, to give you that comfort in a dark world."

"Things are changing," Anagalisgi went on, following the bear. "You will come to understand how this all fits together. But in order for any of it to happen, this must end first."

"So no matter what, I have to watch my children die," Akłaq stated, feeling tears spill from her eyes.

The man nodded. "Yes. And you should be proud and grateful for the lives they lived." He went on before she could speak. "But more than that, you should take comfort in the fact that many will know your pain."

"From the Book."

"Yes."

"Another vengeful god, taking children from their mothers."

Anagalisgi gave her a look. It was not unkind, but it was firm. "Do you trust the Author, Akłaq? Do you trust that she knows what she's doing, that she has things worked out in the end, if we let her guide the story?"

"She doesn't need us," Akłaq said weakly. "She can write anything she wants, raise and kill any characters she pleases."

"But do you think she wants to?"

A long silence stretched between them. Akłaq wiped away the tears as they came. Finally she took a breath and said, "I don't know. I know that death is natural, but I don't understand why I have to lose my children. They know about Time, they could have..."

She sniffed hard and wiped her eyes. Anagalisgi moved toward her and lifted her chin with a finger.

"Yes," he said. "But then they would not have known your joy, your life. They would not have understood the joy of children or being a parent, or being part of a people, growing old and gaining wisdom. You fought for them, to keep them out of the cage of kidnapping and forced assimilation; don't trap them in a cage of your own making.

They have their own lives to live and die. And you have your calling."

Wordlessly, Akłaq put her arms around Anagalisgi. He froze momentarily, then reciprocated the gesture. A few seconds later, she felt the soft fur of the bear brush against her. She did not cry, but it was the first time in a very long time that she'd been hugged and held.

"Thank you," she said, finally pulling away from Anagalisgi. If she was any judge of body language, it was the first time in an even longer span of time that he'd been hugged and held.

"For what?" he wondered, sounding genuinely confused.

She managed a small laugh as she wiped her eyes, the tears finally stopped. "For coming yourself and not sending Sabelu."

The bear made a grunting noise of displeasure. "You think he would have—?"

"It was nothing," Anagalisgi said, cutting off the bear. "Now, though, I think you need rest."

"How long?" Akłaq asked, before the pair could turn and leave. "How long until...?"

Anagalisgi hesitated for half a second. Then, "Latseen needs you now. The rest will go in their own time, over the coming years. As I said, take a rest."

"Will I still see you, either of you?"

"Oh yes," Anagalisgi promised. "That much is certain. After you've had your rest, when you call, you will be heard."

She nodded, then looked at the bear. "For all the years we've known each other, I've never learned your name. How will I call you?"

"The Author will hear you, and I will come," the bear said. Then it added, "And you already know my name. Atiq."

She couldn't help but laugh, though the amount of actual ironic humor did not match the laugh. Atiq. Of course.

"Be well, Akłaq White Bear," Anagalisgi said warmly. "We will see each other again. For now, take your rest."

She did not get a chance to say anything more even if she wanted to, as the man and the bear turned away and the dream began to fade. The next thing she knew, she was back on the couch in her apartment.

Her first thought, once her mind gathered itself, was not about her children or her trip north. It was not about Time or any of the training over the summer, or visiting the twins before she left. Rather, her first thought was actually, *I wonder if this thought is going to be in the Book? Was my dream the end, or is there something else that needs to happen? How is all of this going to appear? What really happens in the in-between moments of the Books?*

When she sat up and finally stood, Akłaq found that she was remarkably well-rested. More than just a day off from work or an especially good night's sleep, she found that she felt truly rested.

She left her apartment and headed out into Vancouver in something of a daze, as if removed from everything going on around her. This was not her city, this was not her home, these were not her people. And that was fine. She was going home to be with her children, taking her rest as Anagalisgi put it. And if he was to be believed, that rest would last for several years at least.

The only thing left to do, then, was say goodbye to the twins. As she got up and around, she marveled at how things had changed over the summer. She also wondered if they would last. It was easy to fall back into old habits with old friends, and the Tlingit were still at odds with the Canadian government. It seemed an odd and yet obvious thing to say that she didn't want to hate again. She was returning out of love for her children; she didn't want to lose the...respect she'd begun to cultivate for Micaiah.

But then, maybe everything would be all right. Anagalisgi said that things were changing. Seeing how things were always changing, the fact that he said it out loud probably meant that these changes were big and would affect most everyone. She could only hope that these were changes for the better.

It was a little after noon when she finally knocked on the twins' apartment door. There was some movement inside, and then it swung open to reveal Micah. Micaiah was inside, having lunch.

"You're late," Micaiah said. He gestured to his food. "I had to make my own damn sandwich."

"I'm late, you're early, what's really changed?" Akłaq shot back.

Micah laughed and even Micaiah grinned as he said, "Touche. I think we might get along."

"Too bad I'm leaving."

"Now?" Micaiah wondered.

She shrugged. "I've got a few hours, but I should be home by tomorrow morning."

"I'm guessing you're not referring to your apartment."

"No." She shifted awkwardly. "I wanted to say goodbye and to thank you. For as much as I was your teacher, you two also taught me a lot, too."

Micah did not say anything, but he nodded and his disposition was generally nonthreatening.

"I guess that cultural exchange thing worked out in the end," Micaiah said, finishing his sandwich. "Looks like it was a good thing that you were the only one available to train us."

"Looks like it," Akłaq agreed.

"How long do you expect you'll be gone?"

"Years. I'm not leaving my children until they've left me. Anyone who says otherwise can fight me for it."

"I'm not disagreeing. Like I told you before, I'll even help you." He stood and gestured to the door. "Do you mind if I walk you back to your apartment?"

Micah cleared his throat loudly and noisily slurped at a glass of water. Akłaq looked up at Micaiah. "That would be just fine with me."

The two of them left before Micah could protest.

"Did you tell him about us?" Akłaq wondered.

"He figured it out on his own," Micaiah answered.

"I take it he doesn't approve."

"Not as such."

"Is he a virgin?"

"To my knowledge, yes."

"The priests again?"

"That's right."

She frowned. "Is he ever going to let that go? I'm not suggesting he settle down with a wife and kids, but he shouldn't let it paralyze him like that."

Micaiah gave her a look that she might characterize as nervous humor. "Oh, sure, you want to tie me in marriage but let him go free."

Akłaq shrugged. "You tie yourself. You're the one who called me a whore."

He made a strangled kind of sound and cleared his throat, but he could not seem to find any words.

"It was always about the survival of the people," she said. "Women needed their children and they would take any man who could give it to them. But things are different for us, me and you. Without that press for survival, season after season..." She hesitated. "You're right that it really is just whoring around, with no real purpose or foundation." She went on before he could speak. "It doesn't mean that my mindset has completely changed, like flipping a light switch. I've lived like this for over a hundred years. There is a good chance that I will take other men to bed while I'm living with the Tlingit. Quite honestly, I would have no qualms about taking Micah, too, if only to break him of his fear and show him something beyond the evil the priests inflicted on him. I think both of you at the same time would be quite interesting. But, for all of that, I know what lies ahead, and I have to learn to accept that some things will probably have to change."

For a long moment, Micaiah did not speak. Then, "Well, I suppose I may have come off as a big, fat hypocrite, too, preaching about sacred vows after admitting to doing a girl after beating up her brother. I admit, my own words bothered me all that night, and I haven't felt right since. And since we're being honest—I don't know how much more honest you can get than telling a man you're supposed to marry that you'd screw his twin brother, or both at the same time—but every woman a man looks at, his first thought is whether or not he'd do her. It's a constant fight to stay loyal, assuming he wants to, but if a woman won't be loyal to her man, then he has no reason to be loyal to her. And I expect that goes both ways."

Their conversation ground to a halt and did not resume until they reached her apartment building.

"So then, what do we do?" Akłaq wondered aloud as they headed upstairs. "You can't come with me, and it may be years before I leave the reserve. I just admitted that I'm likely to take other men; it's not fair to demand you remain chaste."

He thought a moment. "Well, there's always portal travel."

She glanced back as they reached her door. "Stumbling through a Paa and being sick is not what I would consider an intimate posture."

He laughed. "Well, maybe you're right on that."

Akłaq unlocked her apartment. It really didn't look a whole lot different except for bare walls and the luggage sitting by the door.

"For what it's worth, I'm sorry you have to go," Micaiah said somberly, shutting the door behind him.

She nodded absently. "So am I. It was bound to happen, but I guess I had hoped it never would."

He came up behind her and put his arms around her. "I can't speak about your children. I don't know them. But I know that between us, I think everything will be fine. Because what I see is that once you set your loyalty to someone, you don't break it. Even though you say you were asked or told to leave, you are still fiercely loyal and protective of your children, willing to take on the whole of the Time industry to rescue them from whatever danger they may be in and be there for them, even in death when it hurts the most. That is what a mother bear is supposed to do for her cubs."

Akłaq willed herself not to get emotional. "But what does a mother bear do if she has no cubs?"

He kissed the top of her head. "Well, I can't speak for the bears, but for you, I think you'll find someone or something else to stick your loyalty to, and you'll fight just as ferociously if need be."

"And you're hoping that you're that someone?"

Gently he turned her around. "I'd like to be the man you come back to because you want to, because you love him. Not because some sarcastic jackass preordained a marriage. There are a lot of people who are married but are still dead inside. If that would be us, we might as well skip the formalities, not get married, and just sleep together every once in a while."

She nodded. "You're not wrong there."

"So then, what's it going to be? Should we just go our separate ways as familiar strangers? Or are we going to make something more of this, something to look forward to when the time comes?"

Akłaq managed a small smile. "Well, planning a wedding would give me something to do, something good to look forward to."

"As long as it's not the long night when we do it, and Sabelu isn't invited."

Now she laughed. "Absolutely not, never."

He kissed her, and she undid his belt.

An hour later they were still lying naked on the couch, talking about everything and nothing, things that wouldn't matter in five years, things that no longer mattered at that moment because she had left her job and didn't have to deal with pesky clients anymore.

"I'll be glad to get out of here, too, honestly," Micaiah was saying. "I don't think warehouse work is my real calling in life."

"Oh? And what is?" Akłaq wondered.

"I don't know. On the other hand, with such long lives, I think I'd be afraid of finding that kind of calling. Because then what do you do?"

She did not respond to that, just stretched and pressed herself back against him. Then she released the stretch and sighed. "Thank you."

He brushed some of her hair away. "For what? Giving you some, ah, cultural exchange?" He bumped her from behind and rubbed the inside of her thigh.

"For putting up with me and not leaving even when I was cruel to you."

He kissed her neck. "And see how you repay me? By leaving for years on end." She opened her mouth but he beat her to it. "I know. I'm kidding. I'm not going to fault you for being with your children." He kissed her on the lips. "All right?"

She sighed and looked away. "I guess I should get motivated and get to the train station."

Reluctantly, she got up and started picking up her clothes, tossing Micaiah's articles to him as she found them.

"Can I help you with your bags, ma'am?" he asked, pulling on his shirt.

"If you insist," she told him, mildly dramatic.

He took the two large suitcases and she took the small one. Only one neighbor wished her good fortune, and that because they happened to meet in the hall on the way out. Other than that, her departure went unremarked.

Micaiah flagged down a taxi and helped load the bags.

"Are you coming with me to the station, too?" she asked.

"Do I have anywhere else to be today?" he countered, ducking in the backseat after her.

She put up a Sound shield between them and the cabbie, after giving him their destination. "I don't know, you might have to go to confession after what we did."

"But would it matter, if we were just going to do it again?"

"With each other? Or others?"

He gave her a look that was part amused, part tender, and a little annoyed. "Each other. Or else I'll have the cabbie pull over and I'm getting out."

She tried to laugh it off. "All right. If you're holding me to it, then I'm holding you to it, too."

He leaned closer to her and lowered his voice though it was unnecessary. "Just remember, if you do get lonely, portal travel is still an option. The sickness might not be alluring, but it doesn't hang around long."

Akłaq found herself grinning as she replied, "And since time stops when in the Wheel, it'll be like we never even left home."

If the cabbie was watching them at all in the rearview mirror, he might have thought himself deaf, to see their lips moving but hearing no words or any sound at all from the backseat.

But for as fun as the banter was, it was distraction only, at least for Akłaq. Getting out of the taxi and facing the train station was instantly sobering, and Akłaq hesitated on the curb. She jumped at a hand on her shoulder, but it was only Micaiah.

"Help you with your bags, madam?" he asked.

"Do you intend to help me all the way to the reserve?" she inquired.

"If I thought I could, I might."

"Did you pack a ticket for yourself, to keep me company on the ride?"

He grinned but shook his head. "No. I think you need the next few hours to yourself."

When she did not reply, but frowned and looked away, he gently pulled her against his chest. "You are a good woman, a good teacher, and a good mother. I really don't know what else I can say."

"Say something that will make it so my children don't die," Akłaq said, bursting into tears.

He sighed. "I don't know any words like that. If I did, I would."

Her outburst didn't last long and she almost felt ashamed for it. She'd known about this for weeks now. She'd had time to process it. The problem was that she'd spent more time denying it, and now she was faced with a train and a one-way ticket to despair.

"It'll be all right," Micaiah said. Akłaq pressed her ear against his chest to listen to the deep rumble. "Not today, not tomorrow, but someday. It will be all right. Even just going home, that helps."

She took a breath and pulled away enough that she could wipe her eyes and try to regain some semblance of composure. She laid her hands on his chest. "You are far more than I deserve."

"Says who?" He looked down at her. "Listen, you go get on that train and go see your kids. They need you."

Akłaq forced a smile. "It's nice, you know. To be needed. Even though they're old, they still need me. Or they say they do." She looked him in the eye. "Will you need me? Afterwards? Five years, ten years?"

"Of course. You're the only person I know who plays Timekeeper frisbee."

That elicited a chuckle. She looked down at her luggage. "I really should get going, I suppose. Dragging this out isn't helping anyone, least of all myself."

"You'll be fine," Micaiah said, releasing her and bending to grab two of the suitcases. "You've done so much already. Maybe this is a chance to take a break for a while."

"Take a rest," Akłaq recited, grabbing the last bag.

"Exactly. Now then, which way?"

Finding the train wasn't difficult. Her bags were marked and loaded, and she reached in her jacket for her ticket. Before she could hand it off, Micaiah grabbed her arm, turned her around, and kissed her. Akłaq was stunned but did not push him away.

"For luck," he said when he released her.

"Is everything lucky in Ireland?" she asked, refinding her ticket and ignoring the looks from the train workers.

"Of course not. But love is luck wherever you go, and the Irish are the best lovers of all."

Akłaq's face was burning so hot she thought it might melt off. She didn't know how to respond to him, and she wasn't entirely sure she managed even a simple "Goodbye" as she handed over her ticket to be punched and ducked inside the train.

Once inside, she tried looking for him on the platform, but even now the smoke from the stack was too thick to say anything for certain, and she didn't dare open a window. She thought about going back out for a moment and saying a proper goodbye, but then the last call rang out. A few stragglers bustled onto the train and then everything was shut and locked down for the ride.

The front car, where negroes and other undesirables sat, had a perpetual haze to it owing from the engine. She was the only one in this car; few non-whites had any desire to go north, and apparently none but her wanted to go today. It was disheartening, but then, even if there had been more passengers here, conversation would be limited as no one wanted to eat the acrid smoke. Briefly she considered using Time to slip to one of the rear cars. She didn't need anything luxurious, just something with fresh air.

Even her sullen mood could not override this desire as the train lurched and then began chugging out of the station. Once they were well underway and the staff had ensured that their one undesirable passenger was safely tucked away in the smoky car, Akłaq Banded and made her way back, stowing away in the luggage car. It was quiet, smoke-free, and no one was around to disturb her.

The ride wasn't more than a few hours, or so it felt. The rhythm of the train lulled her to sleep, and she woke up just twenty minutes before their expected arrival. Akłaq yawned, stretched, and crawled out of the luggage pile she'd fallen asleep in. Then it was just a matter of Banding and returning to the smoky car for the last few minutes of the trip.

She hadn't told anyone she was coming, so no one was at the station to meet her. Most of the passengers were heading on to Anchorage, so her disembarking was a bit lonelier than she'd anticipated.

If she had any consolation, it was that most of the workers this far north were native peoples, and she approached a dark-skinned young man dressed as a porter.

"Take your bags?" he wondered.

"First I need directions," she said and gave him the name of the village.

"You don't look Tlingit," the young man observed.

"Iñupiatun," she told him, "but I have business with the Tlingit."

He rolled his eyes and shook his head. "Everyone has business with them these days." He seemed to remember himself, though he wasn't what one might call apologetic. "Not that it's any of my business." He lowered his voice as he stooped for her bags, and Akłaq suspected that although he muttered, he wanted to be heard. "What do I know, I'm just a Haida porter, a novelty in this shit town run down by alcohol and rich oil men and timber men."

He took her bags out to a taxi that was in far worse shape than the one in Vancouver.

"He'll get you to the coast," the porter said flatly.

Akłaq thanked him and got in the car, again explaining where she wanted to go. The driver, being white, didn't understand very well, and they spent some time looking over a map. Even when they finally got underway, Akłaq wasn't entirely sure that they were going to end up where she needed to be.

The next thing she knew, she was being shaken awake. Looking out the window, there wasn't much to see as it was dark, but she could hear the ocean waves and smell the fresh ocean breeze. They'd stopped outside a small inn, though it was a generous description. She paid the cabbie, took her bags, and watched him drive away.

She was still tired, and there was no way she was going anywhere in the dark. Reluctantly, she entered the inn. A little bell over the door jingled, but it was a minute or two before an old woman appeared.

"Welcome," she greeted. "How many to a room?"

"Just me," Akłaq told her.

The old woman nodded and turned to grab a key. "Where are you heading, dear?" When Akłaq told her the name of the village, the woman made a thoughtful sound. "I see. Do you know how to get there?"

"Usually it's by canoe. Unfortunately, I don't have a canoe with me."

That got a giggle out of the old lady. "No, it doesn't look like you have. Well, listen. In the morning, I'll have my grandson here. He'll take you out there."

"But you don't know me."

"I look at you and I know you well enough. Furthermore, if you know the name of a village, then there's a reason you know it and need to go there. I suspect you aren't a stranger."

"Thank you."

So Akłaq stayed the night in the inn. It was old, run-down, and the bed was terribly uncomfortable. In the morning, she found herself questioning her decisions, not only recent ones, but those as far back as Ujurak's village. What would she be doing now if she hadn't run off, if she hadn't provoked Gerald and the other Timekeepers? Would anything really be different? Had anything happened in the world only by her involvement?

Her children had happened, she decided. Otherwise they, too, would have been taken to a school with no one to rescue them, no one to defend their ancestral way of life.

True to her word, the old woman's grandson was waiting for her outside the inn. He was undoubtedly Tlingit; he might have been related to one of her children in some way, even, for as much as he looked like Tlaganis when he was young. He didn't say much as he loaded her bags and got them pushed off into the delta. Only when they were a fair distance from shore did he really speak.

"It's good you've come home."

"I thought you were a relation," Akłaq said.

"Distant, but yes. Tlaganis was my grandfather."

"How is Latseen, do you know?"

"Not well, and I am sorry I cannot be more specific. Most of my time is spent on the mainland."

She shifted position. "Did you know I was coming?"

"Not as such," he replied. "If you sent word, it was lost before it reached us. But Gáx was truly hoping that you would receive his letter and return in time."

"I had to wrap up a few things, but I could only condense things so much."

Akłaq sighed internally. She was making excuses. She should have dropped everything and come right away, not fiddled around with work and other meaningless trifles.

"Sounds like you spent a little too much time in the city. I think the person who will benefit the most from your return is you."

She gave him a curious look. "You couldn't have been more than ten when I left. I was asked to leave."

"And now you are being asked to return, so all is well."

It all sounded so simple, to hear him speak of it.

Akłaq said no more on the matter and simply reclined to listen to reports from the village. Marriages, births, deaths. The information was a couple weeks old, and she could only hope that Latseen was still hanging on.

When Akłaq and the others had first helped the Tlingit escape to the island, the village had been well disguised by vegetation and landscape. When she'd left, the dwellings could be basically made out from the shore. Now, it was obvious from a distance that there was a village on the island, and some of the old huts had been replaced by newer construction. Their arrival was announced, and several young men appeared to get the ferry up on the sand.

Akłaq stepped out of the canoe, feeling very much like a stranger.

"Akłaq."

She turned to see Putu approaching. He hadn't aged a day since she'd been gone, and although he'd opened himself up to his new family, he now wore the old, familiar look of brooding.

"You came," he observed.

"You sound surprised," Akłaq replied evenly.

"A little."

"They're my children. Of course I would come."

He had the look of a man who wanted to be upset but didn't have the strength for it. They were her children, but his grandchildren, and he had witnessed their decline as well. He nodded and motioned for her to follow.

"There's not much time left," he told her, his voice low. "She sleeps most of the time and is barely coherent even when she is awake. But she still asks for you."

Akłaq did not reply as they stopped outside a small house that must have been a quarter of the size of her apartment in Vancouver. Putu made a gesture, and she went inside.

There were only two rooms to the small house, so it was not difficult to find her daughter. Although she was near seventy years old and had aged even more on account of her condition, Akłaq couldn't help but see the little girl who had tried to emulate her mother so hard, who took care of her siblings in any way she could, who had revived the old custom of tattooing her lip, who did everything that had ever been expected of her. This old little girl lay abed, asleep, only a faint whistling sound giving any indication that she still breathed.

She was alone now, although there was plenty of evidence that this was a rare occurrence. Perhaps Putu had asked everyone else to leave once he realized who was in the canoe.

Akłaq sat down in the small chair beside the bed and took her daughter's hand. Latseen made several sounds with her mouth, and Akłaq thought she might have said something akin to "Mama" but she did not open her eyes or give any other indications of awareness.

"I'm here, love," Akłaq said, tears flowing from her eyes as readily as water from a faucet. "I'm here. And I'm not leaving you ever again."

Aullaġniiri Tuyuun
Author's Note

This book encompasses everything I hate about writing. I don't like writing single novels, and I don't like writing female leads, especially historical ones. There is so much more that could be written about Akłaq's life, her time in Ujurak's village, her time in Red River, her time with the Tlingit. And if I had chosen to center the plot around such events, this could have easily been a three or five book series.

Unfortunately, this approach saw me running full steam into my issue of writing female leads, especially historical female leads. Especially historical female leads of another culture. Akłaq comes from an isolated people who are under attack, and, in the events of this book, she never quite leaves that shadow. Her desire is to see her people restored, to see the legacy of her forebears carried on into a modern world, even as she struggles with the fact that things aren't going to return to the way they used to be.

Centering the story around her work in Time and the Akari would have been to draw too much attention to a mindset where she has to be the keeper, the provider, the doer, and essentially ignore what she was raised to believe about children being the future of a people, and to completely insult her almost perfect life with Nikita. Yes, Akłaq is very action-oriented; she doesn't like to sit around and wait. But it would shift the focus and the motivation more than I was comfortable with, more than I was hoping to convey, and it would end up as this sort of Mary Sue caricature.

On the other hand, by keeping the focus more on the culture and the children and the social and political changes that are going on, it gives a more reasonable explanation for her actions. She kills Goldsmith because she's tired of being kicked like a dog. She kills Frederickson because she is trying to save her children. She's causing all this chaos in the schools because she wants to save the people. It's not about proving that she's a warrior, but as she endures these trials, she is becoming one in her own way.

While not intended in the original plans, this book also functions as a very heavy philosophical nexus, both as a contained unit and the overall *Chronicles*. What would her life have been if she hadn't stayed with Nikita? What if she hadn't killed Goldsmith? Why is she hesitant about the possibility that her life may be recorded in a Book? Why are the Krydik so offended at the idea that the Author might write about others? Why does Akłaq resist Sabelu's prophecies? Is it because they don't line up with her ideas of the future?

As I said, Akłaq's Book is centered around her and her children, and protecting the people. However, veterans of the *Chronicles* know that her role is not over yet. Internal chronology will see her return from Tlingit land in *The Akari-Bearer* series to help Micaiah with his problems, some of which will prove to be quite large.

For as much as this book was a chore to write, it was also a bit refreshing. I hope you get something out of it and see Akłaq in a new way in the rest of the books.

www.ingramcontent.com/pod-product-compliance
Lightning Source LLC
Chambersburg PA
CBHW050944210726
48287CB00004B/1131